NOVELS BY DAVID A. KAUFELT

American Tropic

DAVID A. KAUFELT

Poseidon Press
New York

Copyright © 1986 by David A. Kaufelt

Published by Poseidon Press
A Division of Simon & Schuster, Inc.
Simon & Schuster Building
Rockefeller Center
1230 Avenue of the Americas
New York, New York 10020

POSEIDON PRESS is a registered trademark of Simon & Schuster, Inc.

Designed by Irving Perkins Associates
Manufactured in the United States of America
10 9 8 7 6 5 4 3 2 1

Library of Congress Cataloging-in-Publication Data
Kaufelt, David A.
   American Tropic.

    1. Florida—History—Fiction.   I. Title.
PS3561.A79A84 1986   813'.54   86-16859

ISBN: 0-671-52882-3

FOR MY SON, JACKSON SHIGERU KAUFELT,
WITH LOVE

Preface

THOUGH *AMERICAN TROPIC* IS VERY MUCH A work of fiction, I have tried, during its conception, to be true to history. I have not been so careful with historical figures, some of whom—notably Julia Tuttle—have taken on new, fictional lives in the pages of this book. (Though even with Mrs. Tuttle I managed to stay within the broad perimeters of the facts of her actual life.)

American Tropic had a long, difficult birth, and I'd like to thank—in no particular order—those who assisted: Pat Capon, editor extraordinaire; Bob Thixton, my best (and usually earliest) reader; Maryanne Lancaster, Monroe County Library director—Key West's pink library houses a historical gold mine; my literary adviser and friend, Rosemary Jones of the Council for Florida Libraries; Jean Trebbi and Lew Goldfarb of the Broward County Library, who always managed to locate the books I couldn't find elsewhere; the librarians in all the cities of Florida who provided me with the keys to their historical sections; Florida's historical museums—especially the Museum of Florida History in Tallahassee and the Historical Museum of Southern Florida in Miami—for bringing history to life in such innovative ways; such Florida historians and chroniclers as Charlton W. Tebeau, Arva Moore Parks, Helen Muir, and Thelma P. Peters; George Firestone, Florida's secretary of state; then-governor Bob Graham, who helped ignite my interest in Florida's history; the cities of St. Augustine and Pensacola for so conscientiously preserving Florida's heritage; and all those bookstores throughout Florida in which I found treasures both new and used, most notably Ray Nugent's Booktrader in Naples, Haslam's in St. Petersburg, Craig Pollack's Book Works and Mitch Kaplan's Books & Books in Coral Gables. And special thanks to my wife, Lynn, who provided moral and other support, and to Bill Grose, Ann Patty, and Dick Duane for putting it all together.

D.A.K.
Sugar Loaf Shores, Florida

The Cape of the End of April—1498

THE BOY SQUATTED IN THE CROW'S NEST, feeling both lonely and splendid, separated so totally from the men below. He had shimmied up the mainmast only a quarter of an hour before, but already he was a little hypnotized by the constant, unchanging view.

He studied the green land that lay to the west, beyond an endless line of bubbling white surf, searching for some irregularity that would indicate a place of entry, looking for smoke coming from a chimney, a horse at feed, some sign of humanity. Clouds filled the sky, diluting the light, making for another gray, chilling spring day.

From below, Roderick could just hear James singing out in his clear, sweet voice the hours of the fleet's progress as he turned the hourglass. The fleet consisted of three weathered, stubby ships, sea-worn caravels. One supply ship had been lost only a day out of port, and the other had been turned back a week later, leaking badly.

Roderick had gotten used to the sea, but he hadn't gotten used to his shipmates. Their rough talk and harsh humor, the strong stench of their bodies, their broad hints of needs that he might satisfy frightened him.

He felt free when he left home, shimmying up the mainmast to his position in the sky. From the crow's nest he could reach out and touch Henry VII's green and white flag. The admiral's—John Cabot's—far more flamboyant lion of Venetian St. Mark's flew just below it. Cabot was called "the Italian" by almost everyone. His name had been Giovanni Caboto until he had been taken up by England's king.

Roderick turned and looked behind him, to the north, seeing the two smaller ships bobbing up and down like toy boats in a pond. Below he could see James and Richard emptying the slop pails. In the beginning he too had had to perform that disgusting chore.

His stomach turned at the thought of the smell that permeated the lower decks. It had taken him a week to learn to keep his food down, and then only after Cook had forced him to eat a bit of salt beef and biscuit and told him that he could, if he wanted, sleep in the galley.

He had been promoted from deck-scrubbing and slop-pail-emptying to lookout page, thanks to his keen eyesight. The first mate had discovered Roderick's remarkable ability when the boy had picked out the green shores of Newfoundland a full half hour before the page in the crow's nest had seen the birds and the clouds indicating land.

Now he spent every other four hours aloft, studying the unending green of the coast of this New World, searching for river mouths and bay inlets and any other geographical landmark that would help John Cabot with his maps. Below, on the top deck, bent over a table set up for the purpose, Cabot and his navigator marked leagues, landmarks, and latitudes on the parchment spread out before them.

Map-making was the sole purpose of this illegal voyage. They had been supposed to turn back as soon as they reached Labrador, but the Italian had given his helmsman the order to sail south despite the fact that king and international law forbade it. Sail north and west, Giovanni, his sovereign had told him, but the king had smiled. The smile was all the encouragement Cabot had needed.

Henry VII had specifically charged his Italian admiral *not* to discover new worlds. Had Cabot done so, they would have been taken by the Spanish. But the king, known as the Navigator Prince, had an unquenchable thirst for maps, charts, knowledge of channels, currents, winds, and reefs. For "future" exploration, he said.

Roderick understood the implications of sailing south along this new coastline. An English ship had no right in these uncharted waters. Pope Alexander VI had set up the first line of demarcation in 1493, dividing the New World between Spain and Portugal. The lands Christopher Columbus had discovered six years before, in 1492, were to remain inviolate, undisputedly Spanish.

The crew aboard Cabot's flagship told hair-raising tales of Spanish torture, of the Spaniards' so-called religious conversions. Though the men were ignorant about most things and lied about others, when it came to Spanish torture, Roderick believed them. He kept as sharp an eye out for Spanish ships as he did for territorial landmarks.

At the moment, though, his eyes were centered on the land that lay to the immediate west, clearly in Spanish waters. The ocean had grown greener, the water and air warmer. He spotted a school of whales in the near distance, spouting water, their gray hides thick with hair and oil. Manatees—those gray-blue sea cows—swam closer to the shore, but the monk seals came right up to the ships, curious, their appealing faces resembling those of slightly tipsy clerics.

Overhead—sometimes so close he could have touched them if he reached up—flew birds Roderick had never seen before. Mocking birds, cardinals, woodpeckers, red-winged blackbirds, wrens, king birds, phoebes, towhees. Fascinated, he watched them ignoring him, feeling as if he and the others aboard Cabot's fleet had suddenly been catapulted into some strange but benevolent new universe.

The pine forests had given way to coastal plains and flat woods thick with saw palmettos, cypress, swamps, scrub trees, and bush. Purple-blossomed vines, sea lavender, and myrtle edged the outer sands.

From his crow's nest Roderick began to report on rivers and springs. He begged First Mate to allow him consecutive shifts aloft. He couldn't get enough of the wonder of discovery, of being the first to see what lay before him. Cabot, below, listened to what the page described from aloft, while he and his son, Sebastian, and his barber-surgeon, Juan Fernandez, and his constant companion, Diego of Castiglione, worked excitedly on their parchment charts and maps with the navigator.

Slowly in the beginning, but more rapidly now, they were filling in a portrait of an elegant flying foot of land, kicking out into the blue-green seas. It was a warm, green peninsula, the final southward sweep of the North Atlantic coast, pointing the way to the islands the Spanish had already begun to cultivate, deforest, and depopulate.

Cabot was as excited as if he were discovering the wealth of Hindustan, working on his maps for as long as Roderick managed to stay in the crow's nest reporting what his remarkable eyes were seeing. The air became increasingly balmy and sweet and the seas greener as the three caravels rounded the tip of the peninsula and sailed north until the land turned west again. At night the skies were filled with stars none of them had seen before.

The serenity of these new seas and the excitement of their discoveries touched all of the men, who stopped occasionally to stare at the land that now lay to the east. They marveled at the manatees and joked with the monk seals. They were amazed by the new, fearless birds, at the way their own spirits rose and their health improved in the constant sweet breezes that wrapped them in a comfort and an optimism none had experienced before.

Their fear of the unknown disappeared with the warmth of the sun and the change in the sea waters from a dense blue to an iridescent turquoise. Roderick's hunger—there was never enough food—had been replaced with a different sort of need. He lived for his hours in the crow's nest. He longed to put ashore, to touch this fantastic place. He thought that perhaps they had gone over the edge of the world after all but had landed in a paradise rather than in the oft-predicted hell.

When the Italian asked him if he had seen any sign of man, Roderick assured him he had not. He would have seen habitations, ships, animals if the land were inhabited. More disappointing, there didn't seem to be any natural harbor in which the caravels might lay anchor.

Finally, reluctantly, Cabot gave the order to turn back. The ships rounded the southern islands and sailed back up the east coast, slowly and closer to the shore. Suddenly Roderick gave a shout from the crow's nest that could be heard by all three ships' crews. He had sighted an opening to a large bay, a sandy cape, and a beach.

The Italian gave the orders to put ashore, and the ships sailed into the bay, the anchors were lowered into the shallows, the longboats were put down. Most of the men didn't wait for the longboats, jumping into the tepid, turquoise waters, swimming toward shore.

Roderick had slid down the mainmast and had already removed his boots when the order came. He was the first to jump into the bay, the first to reach the shore. He stood there, dripping water onto the snow-white sand, impatiently pushing his long, wet hair out of his eyes, looking across the wide beach, staring past the dunes and the saw palmettos into the pine forest as if he could see what mysteries, what riches, what fantasies lay within.

The captain entered in his log that night that Roderick Devon, Englishman, twelve years of age, was the first white man to reach the shores of this new place. They spent three days on that beach, washing themselves and their clothes in the clear bay waters, filling barrels with the exhilarating spring water First Mate discovered bubbling up through a pile of sun-bleached rocks. They ate turtle eggs and the figs and sea grapes they found growing wild and oysters dug up from the bottom of the bay.

At night the cooks broiled sweet, tender fish, easily caught in the bay, on open fires. Afterward the men sang in English, Italian, Portuguese. The first white men's voices to be heard on those shores.

During the days Roderick—"our eyes"—was attached to Cabot's party. He followed the Italian, his son, Sebastian, and Diego of Castiglione along the beach while the men cut down a copse of pine trees, the wood needed for ship repairs. Only Roderick seemed to mind the gap in the smooth line of trees. It looked as if a bully had smashed his fist into a young woman's mouth, ruining her smile.

Cabot was struck by the irony that he had discovered a new peninsula, rich with potential, which his sovereign could claim no knowledge of while the Spanish, who had a legal right to it, were unaware of its existence.

They made their last exploratory walk on the day of the Feast of San Diego, the first of May. When they came upon the wide fresh-water river emptying into the great bay, the Italian named it the Diego, after the day. Sebastian and Roderick wanted to investigate it, but the admiral said, "Investigation is not part of our mission." Given the fact that most of the voyage was illegal to start with, Roderick thought this an odd position to take. Then he realized that the admiral, the Italian, John Cabot, was frightened. He was as fearful of the jungle from which the river sprang as the crewmen were of their monsters. They were all scared of the forest, of the earth, of what lay inside this peninsula, and so they clung to the shoreline.

They spent that night on the ships, and at dawn the Italian gave the order to sail. Roderick received permission from First Mate to take his place in the crow's nest. As the flagship was leaving the bay, Roderick took a last look at the shore. Someone was standing there, watching the fleet leave. At first Roderick thought they had left a man behind, but this fellow was two feet taller than anyone in the crew. He was nearly nude, dressed only in a breechclout, with an ornamental medallion hanging about his neck. His skin was red and his hair was black, and he stood tall and straight, regal, a dark prince.

But he didn't appear threatening. Rather, he seemed curious, as if he wanted to know more. As he watched him, Roderick had the eerie feeling that that young giant could see Roderick as clearly as Roderick saw him. And somehow Roderick knew that there were others like him, that they had been watching, silently, all the time the crew were ashore. Then the lad on shore raised his hand in a universal sign of greeting. Roderick began to shout his discovery below but stopped himself for no clear reason and instead slowly waved back, with misgiving. He had the feeling that the red-skinned lad on the beach would someday know more about white men than he wanted to.

John Cabot kept his voyage a secret, but he had his maps and his charts, and he and his sovereign studied them for years. Henry VII was especially taken with the name Cabot had given his new discovery. He had named it for the day he found it: the Cape of the End of April. Later map-makers would call it by the common name for the peninsula John Cabot discovered: Cape Florida.

BOOK ONE

The
Black
Doves

When the Great Father first fashioned men out of clay, he baked them in an oven that would not heat properly. That first batch of men came out white and half-baked. The Great Father discarded these half-baked men, sending them to the unharmonious East, across the great Ocean Sea. Then the Great Father fashioned a new batch and cooked them in a proper oven. They came out evenly cooked and red all over. These men the Great Father sent to live with his other creatures in the World Below the Sky, where all was in harmony.

In time Three Black Doves will come from the East, from across the Great Water, to die and to be buried here in the Center of the Earth. Their seed will sink deep into our Sacred Soil, into our wellsprings, corrupting our waters, our forests, our creatures, our sons.

The Three Black Doves will pass on their fear of Mother Earth to the tribe that will spring up from their seeds. Lightning, Rainbow, Night will be lost. When, after much time and inglorious battle, all is out of harmony and the Great Spirit's work is destroyed, the Tequesta's World Below the Sky will end.

THE TEQUESTA LEGEND OF
CREATION AND THE END OF THE WORLD BELOW THE SKY

From a letter dated the Ides of April, the year of our Lord 1512, addressed to His Holiness, Pope Julius II, written by a papal emissary known only as Fray Sebastian.

. . . The recently elevated Bishop for the See of Segovia, Fray Gonzalvo de Pescara, in order to inspire new respect for the authority of the Inquisition, did declare an auto-da-fé. Great and elaborate preparations were made, but on the eve of the Holy event the Bishop was taken gravely ill and thought to be in the last extremities. At his request he was removed to a penitential cell in the depths of the monastery, midst the heretics who were to be burned on the morrow.

Evincing commendable modesty, he asked that the plainest, least important friar in the order hear his last confession. As the Dominicans began the March of the Green Cross, singing the Miserere *over the cries of the penitents, a mendicant named Las Mesas began to hear the Bishop's confession. The Bishop was dying as the* auto-da-fé *was commencing.*

As dawn broke, a blood-red sun rose in the heavens, and the Bishop—a whisper from death the moment before—was of a sudden recovered. He got himself onto his knees and took the young friar's hand and began to kiss it. Instead of seeing Las Mesas, he saw a Personage so beautiful, of so golden and warm and kind a visage, that tears came to his

14

eyes. *The Personage wore a crown of thorns and a golden robe. In His free hand He held three black doves.*

The Bishop inquired, Pray, Sire, why do You carry these dark birds about you?

I have brought them here, Gonzalvo, to set them free, He said. Whereupon he moved to the narrow window, magically devoid of bars, and sent the three black doves out into the clear dawn air. They will fly to the Land of the Flowers, Gonzalvo, He said. A new world. They will carry the seeds of My Word and plant them deep in the soil so they may grow and prosper.

Returning to the kneeling Bishop, He took his hand and held it. The Bishop felt his body and his soul recover under His touch. Follow my example, Gonzalvo, He did say. Demonstrate to all the tender mercies of the Holy Office in Christ.

Whereupon the Bishop, Fray Gonzalvo, closed his eyes in holy ecstasy and kissed His hands. When he opened his eyes he found the Lord Jesus Christ had left the penitent's cell and only the friar, Las Mesas, remained.

The Bishop decided that the Miracle be kept secret until further investigation, lest it undermine general belief in the Holy Office. The populace would feel cheated if, at that late date, three heretics escaped the fire. But the Bishop felt that the Lord clearly desired that he free three of the unrepentants to demonstrate His infinite Mercy.

Midst great secrecy this was accomplished. A Jew, an actress, and a hidalgo were spirited away and sent to the New World aboard a ship just then being prepared for departure. Las Mesas, the friar who was the vehicle for the Miracle, was sent to shepherd the three of them to the New World.

As the ship set sail, three black doves circled the quemadero, *the burning place, causing great unrest among the populace, who viewed them as symbols of misfortune. It was not until the doves flew toward the sea that calm was restored.*

1512

THE PRIEST, his thin, pockmarked face hidden under his cowl, knelt alone, sick in soul and body. His sickness didn't make him weak. Rather, it gave him a feverish energy that he could barely contain. He hadn't slept in weeks. It was as if he had been thrust into a nightmare of a maze that day, one month before, and was caught in it for eternity, every path leading to a dead end.

He kept his eyes closed as he waited for the sun to rise above the horizon. He imagined the sun as the eye of a monster, causing the blackness in his mind to turn a hot and bloody red.

Red. The color tortured him as if it had an unholy life of its own. He could smell it; it reeked of spilled blood. He could taste it in his dry mouth, stale and malevolent. And he could feel it on his fingertips, rough and corrosive.

The ship itself had been painted red to disguise its rotting age. He knew that when he stood up the front of his robe would have red marks on it where he had knelt and the paint had rubbed off, like some diabolical stigmata. Nonetheless Las Mesas continued to kneel on the top deck, between the rows of cannons, out of the way of the men. He had slept there from the beginning, even during the storms that had plagued the voyage since the brief stopover in the Canaries. He hadn't been able to stomach the lower decks or the stinking men with whom he was supposed to share a cabin. They had looked at him with fear, frightened of his priest's robes and powers.

Wrapped in those robes that offered him little protection against the sea winds, he was tired and hungry, his body reeking of stale and cold sweat, his mind filled with images of the lower decks, never cleaned, a breeding ground for huge cockroaches and rats bigger than the cats set after them. The rats ate their way through bulkheads, and the containers in the storerooms had tin coverings to keep them out of the food.

Closing his eyes, he tried to rid his mind of his own rats, eating away at his belief. Longingly, desperately, he tried to pray. Praying had been the one ecstasy, the one satisfaction vouchsafed him by the Lord during an otherwise unremarkable temporal life, and now it had been inexplicably taken from him. All he had ever desired, he had told his many confessors, was to serve his order and his Lord, to live a holy life. He had not wanted the miracle.

From the beginning he had had the blasphemous thought that it hadn't been the Lord who had appeared in the bishop's cell but Satan, impersonating our Lord Jesus Christ, orchestrating the liberation of the Three Black Doves. How else explain the fact that the doves were black and not white? His sudden, exhausting inability to pray? Or this malevolent ocean and godless, disease-laden ship christened the *Santa Cruz* but known even by its captain dismissingly as *La Nao, The Ship?*

It had been asea for nearly one month and still no sign of land. They were heading for the New World, for a city founded only recently on an island known as Boriquén, San Juan de Puerto Rico. Every league of the way a relentless interior voice tortured the friar with the knowledge that he was the vehicle not of Jesus Christ's miracle but of Satan's; that he was a dark escort leading the birds of evil to this New World. He felt that he would survive only long enough to ensure the arrival of the Black Doves and then he would be discarded into the yawning, gaping pits of hell.

Then Las Mesas heard her voice and knew he was already in hell. He opened his eyes and looked up and tried to cry out, but his throat was closed and parched with disuse, and no sound came.

"Poor *niño*," he heard her say, and for a moment he believed she was taking pity on him. Then he saw her profile illuminated by the half moon coming through a sudden break in the clouds. She was unaware of him as she held the Jew while he retched into the ocean.

Even in the dark of that godless night he could see the incandescent red of her hair. It was the reddest hair he had ever seen. Las Mesas had known few women in his life, but the moment he saw her—the Black Dove they called La Floridita—he had known she was evil. He knew his godly duty, and he had tried to pray for her soul.

Still, he had hoped that once they reached *La Nao,* she would be disposed of, thrown into the hold and left for the men to use. But during that overnight coach ride to the Guadalquivir River and *La Nao* she had worked her spell on the young hidalgo, Córdoba, and he had made certain she was provided for.

Now she stood but a yard away, cooing to the boy like a mother to a son as he threw up into the ocean the meal she had provided for him. The Jew—Antonio Levi—should have died early in the voyage, his body consigned to the sea and the monsters that lived in it. He was frail and weak from months of torture at the hands of the Holy Office, in permanent shock from witnessing his family burn at the stake. He couldn't even climb out onto the seats hung over the sides of *La Nao* to move his bowels but would have lain in his own filth if it hadn't been for her.

Las Mesas stood up, trying to quench the bile he felt rising within him. "Why do you not allow him to die and go to his reward?" he couldn't help himself from asking.

She turned, startled, her red hair glowing like the fires of hell. "Why did our Lord not let him die, Fray Las Mesas?" she asked, holding the Jew's hand in hers, one arm around his thin shoulders. "Why did out Lord not allow the three of us to die at the stake?"

She reached out, meaning to touch the rough wool sleeve of Las Mesas's habit, but he pulled back and she touched his hand instead. He put his hand in the sleeve of his robe, as if he had been branded. She was a decade younger than he, seventeen at most. Yet in that one electric touch she had transmitted the knowledge of all the infamous women that had ever been.

He knew it was his duty as a priest of the Lord Jesus Christ to attempt to save her soul. And the souls of the other two: that pale Jew, most of whose life had already been sucked out of him; the proud hidalgo, Ramón de Córdoba. But she, that steaming witch, held both their souls in her fine white hands. He was powerless in the presence of such consummate, tangible evil.

It was the three of them who should have been treated as witches. But instead it was the priest who was looked upon by the population of the ship as a pariah. The bad weather and the accidents, each meting out of the cat-o'-nine-tails, were blamed on his presence. None of them knew of the miracle, but they felt his alienation, his strangeness, and perhaps his madness.

La Floridita turned and left him, helping the Jew back to the cabin Córdoba—because of her—had secured for him. For a moment the wind stopped and there was a great silence. The Godforsaken friar could feel the ballast—huge gray stones—shifting below. During that silent moment he had a terrible need to follow her, to know her, to become, in truth, Satan's priest. But then the winds resumed their unholy noise, and Las Mesas wearily dropped to his knees, begging his Lord to give him the strength to battle this magnetic, awful power of the devil.

Yet when he closed his eyes against the yellow rays of the real dawn he saw La Floridita's red hair and he relived, yet again, that carriage ride that had brought them to *La Nao.*

The bishop's emissaries were too late to save the first of the condemned unrepentants: the elder Levi, his wife, and his daughter. But the next group of three—the younger Levi, La Floridita, Córdoba—were wrapped in friars' robes and rushed, in the bishop's coach, away from the confusion, the stink, and the noise of the *quemadero* without anyone knowing.

Las Mesas, gray and frightened, dislocated, sat with them in the coach. Antonio Levi, the blond Jewish boy, stared at nothing, his blue eyes unblinking. That morning he had seen his father, mother, and sister put to the stake, had breathed in air redolent of their burning flesh. He still heard their piteous cries. His boy's hands, with their bitten nails, clutched the hands of the red-headed actress as if he were drowning and she was his lifeline.

His father had been a rich merchant, a New Christian, whose partner had reported him to the Holy Office for observing a Saturday Sabbath. The elder Levi had provided a model of conduct to his wife and children, remaining silent throughout the long months of torture, refusing the reward offered repentants—garroting instead of burning.

But he had screamed—just once—when the Zarza soldiers lit the fire and he began to burn. Antonio's mother and sister gave the crowd—each of whom received a forty days' indulgence for attending—more pleasure, shouting hysterically until their bodies were black.

Inert as the boy's eyes were, the woman's were alive with excitement. She had been an actress, La Floridita—The Little Flower—accused of practicing the black arts, invoking a spell that caused a respectable theater producer and director to fall in love with her. His daughter, a Franciscan nun, had duly reported her to the Holy Office.

Don Ramón Luis de Córdoba sat next to her. Even in the humble friar's robe that covered the yellow *sambenito*—the sacklike dress painted with red flames all heretics wore to the stake—he was wonderfully handsome. His right leg, bare under the unaccustomed rough cloth, casually touched the woman's as the coach rumbled through the villages lining the road.

Córdoba's inquiring mind had caused him to be caught reading a Spanish translation of the New Testament, a great heresy. La Floridita looked at his muscular leg, touching her again, and then at him severely. He smiled innocently, showing the Córdobas' famous white teeth, and she broke into a girl's laugh that transformed her from a harridan with unkempt hair into a young innocent.

"We are alive," she shouted, unable to contain her joy, clapping her hands. She was the sort of person who couldn't help touching other people. As she put her arms around the young Jew's shoulders the friar's robe slipped off, revealing her shameful yellow *sambenito*. "We have that to be thankful for. We are alive!"

The Jew let his head with its blond curls rest on her shoulder. "We are alive, *niño*," she whispered, tears coming into her green eyes. "You must forget everything else save that: we are alive."

Las Mesas looked away, while the young hidalgo, Córdoba, was unable to look anywhere else. Las Mesas realized then that he was the only one of them who was frightened of what might come. The boy was in shock, but the other two were genuinely looking forward to the journey that lay ahead of them. He had expected repentance. He had thought they would be thankful to him for being the agency through which they were rescued. They barely acknowledged him.

He closed his eyes and attempted to pray, and it was then that he realized he had lost that power, that consolation. He opened his eyes to find Córdoba whispering to La Floridita of the riches he would find for her in the New World. Huge black pearls, he said. Golden crowns set with precious gems. Las Mesas could think only of the terrors that lay there, of the black miracle he had been a part of, of his holy duty to save these three heretics' souls.

Eventually, as the long night came, exhausted, numbed, Las Mesas, like

20

the Jew, fell asleep. He was awakened, startled by what he thought was an animal noise, and saw, on the opposite bench, illuminated by the devil's moon, Córdoba. His robe and *sambenito* had been discarded. His young body appeared blue in the moonlight, a pagan statue come to life. He was entering that hellhole of a woman. She lay on her back, her eyes closed, her *sambenito* up around her breasts.

The smells and sounds of their infamy filled the carriage. Finally, spent, they groaned like animals being killed, and the woman turned her face toward Las Mesas as Córdoba lay upon her. She opened her eyes, staring directly into Las Mesas's, and realized the priest had been watching them. "We are celebrating life," she whispered defiantly. "It is not a sin."

CHAPTER TWO

CÓRDOBA WAS AWAKENED by the sweet voice of the page singing the half-hour ritual chantey:

> *To our God let us pray*
> *To give us a good voyage,*
> *And through the Blessed Mother,*
> *Our advocate on high,*
> *Protect us from the waterspout*
> *And send no tempest nigh.*

There had been no waterspouts as yet, but high winds and rains engulfed the three ships making up the *flota*, Ponce de León's fleet. Since leaving the Canaries, nearly all the passengers had been ill. But Córdoba hadn't and neither had La Floridita. They were too vital, too pleased with themselves and their escape to allow rough seas to upset their stomachs. The others—including Ponce de León's wife and daughters—had kept to their cabins since *La Nao*, this rotting flagship, had set sail.

Just as well, Córdoba thought, turning, reaching for La Floridita. Ponce de León was aware that she shared his cabin every night, but it wouldn't do for the *adelantado's* family to have that knowledge. Córdoba was a Castilian, a proud hidalgo; he knew—in this instance at any rate—how far he might stretch his privileges.

Despite his months as a guest of the Holy Office, he had never been so happy, so excited. He was in love, it was true, but not just with La Floridita. The excitement of this journey—unthinkable, impossible only a short time before—to a new, mysterious world, the good fortune of it, made him want to sing and caper like a schoolboy. He was at a loss to know how to channel his energy . . . except during the night, when Floridita lay under or over or next to him, communicating her own electricity.

He felt like boiling water with the lid kept down, but none too securely. His imagination was caught and tempted and tortured by the New World. He wanted to know everything about it. He had always had a boy's insatiable curiosity to know more. He was a late child, and his family, provincial and inbred, an ancient line of nobles, despaired of him early, sending him to live with more sophisticated cousins in Castile.

As he lay in his bed aboard La Nao, in that cluttered cabin filled with the smells of food and lovemaking, Córdoba thought of his mother for the first time in months. She was a tiny, frightened woman, forever in mourning for some distant dead connection, hiding her faded, white-skinned black-eyed beauty under a ton of lace and thick, brocaded garments. His thin, aging father sipped *aguardiente* throughout the day, laughing his contagious laugh, concentrating on his pride and his pleasure, while the old pile of bricks called Castillo de Córdoba fell down around him.

Ramón had been home on a yearly visit when the Inquisitors had come for him, prompted by his younger brother, a neophyte Franciscan. He hadn't bothered to hide the new and blasphemous Bible when they burst into his room. Even though the Holy Office inspectors were willing to look away, his family honor had not let him disallow a crime he had so obviously been committing. Nor had he been studying the English Bible out of a need for a new religious experience. The Bible, smuggled into Spain by a Portuguese sailor, had had the undeniable appeal of being taboo.

His Córdoba pride and curiosity had given him strength to endure the racks and collars and screws of the Holy Office. He had remained unrepentant less because he had the strength of profound faith than because his pride would not let mere torture sway him. What's more, he was genuinely interested in each new device the Inquisitors brought round, engaging them—when he could—in conversation about its efficacy and the way in which it worked.

Córdoba smiled—revealing his father's legacy, those white and even teeth—thinking of his family. It could not have been a pleasant time for them this past half year. The family had had to make a public disavowal of him in order not to be gathered up themselves. Nor was he certain that his escape had made life any better for them. The miracle had been kept a secret, but still, some knowledge of it must have seeped out. There was something not quite aristocratic about taking part in a miracle. Miracles were a consolation for the poor.

Luckily, Córdoba's father—usually indolent—had roused himself the moment he heard of his son's last-minute escape. He had sent funds aboard the pilot boat. Ramón could imagine the elder Córdoba, furious at the inroads the Holy Office had made on the family name, working himself into what was for him a fever of activity, gathering the money from his affluent brothers, bribing officials and churchmen, putting himself in danger ... but he wouldn't think of that when his son, a Córdoba, was involved. Ramón was going to miss his father.

Floridita stirred beside him, and he opened his eyes. She was struggling into the elaborate gown he had bought from the most important merchant aboard, Quirinio. The cabin was nearly taken over by the foods he had also purchased from Quirinio: casks of the best wines from Jerez, tins of biscuits, jars of olive oil, dried fish, beans, salt pork, rice, sugar. Those unlucky enough not to have brought supplies and too poor to purchase them were already on half ration, bread and fresh water having become scarce.

"Come back to bed," he said, grabbing her thin wrist, pulling the red-haired girl down on top of him.

"No, Ramón," La Floridita said, trying to disengage herself. "I must go to Mass and then to Antonio—"

He kissed her neck and moved his hand under the fine fabric of the gown, and then he found her lips and he rolled on top of her, and for a few moments she forgot her Jew and was lost in the consummate pleasure they managed to give each other. He had known many women in his nineteen years, but he had never met another who managed to keep him so consistently aroused and interested. He had never met another woman who so readily admitted to enjoying lovemaking as much as he. Their bodies were rubbed raw, but often, during the day, after a long night of excitement, he would have the page call her, and, closing the porthole, they would start all over again.

That morning, afterward, she was angry, those extraordinary eyes half closed as she struggled back into the inappropriate gown. "I have to go to him now," she said, but, knowing he shouldn't, he reached out for her once more, putting his lips to her pale nipples as she laid her hands on his black hair and held him to her. "Ramón. Please. I must go."

"I love you," he said, releasing her, surprising himself. "I have never loved anyone before."

"A lie. You have always loved yourself." She placed the lace mantilla Quirinio—that one-man market—had supplied over her mass of burning hair, preparing to leave him. He liked the grand gestures, the ladylike way in which she spoke, when she remembered. The accent and mannerisms were nearly accurate. She had the actress's trick of overemphasis, which he found endearing. A girl from the slums of Seville playing at duchess.

23

She could imitate almost anyone after a short study. Her depiction of him walking across the cluttered cabin with his choreographed strut, that proud peacock pose, had angered him at first and then made him laugh. "Do you love me?" he asked, suddenly a child himself, catching her again, this time by the sleeve of her dress.

"Yes," she said, kissing his forehead, losing her momentary elegance. "I love you, Ramón. Too much."

She left him then, performing the maneuver she had learned from observing the sailors, crisscrossing the deck, holding onto the lines, seemingly oblivious of the winds and the rains. But although her hands and her feet were steady, she felt turned about inside. Ramón's tender infatuation had begun to take hold of her. He wanted to know all about her, but she had given him only the rose-colored version of her life. The truth was that her mother had died, worn out at twenty-four after giving birth to nine children in as many years, six of whom—five boys and Floridita—lived. Her father's second wife had taken her miseries out on Floridita while Floridita had become mother to her brothers. They owed her a great deal, but Floridita knew it was they—their need for her—that had given her the courage to survive the squalor and the anger that filled their household.

When they were all apprenticed to shoemakers and bakers and blacksmiths, when the youngest and sweetest—Roberto—was taken into a childless family of goldworkers, she too had left. She had got herself apprenticed to Señor Carlos Salvador Alvarosa's Teatro de Seville after letting him make love to her on a straw-filled pallet behind a stage set for a grand religious play. Alvarosa had worked on her, huffing and puffing, while she had stared up at a huge papier-mâché cross. She had been just twelve and had cried when she saw her blood on the mattress.

Señor Alvarosa asked if he had hurt her, and she had said no, she was crying from the pleasure he had given her, from the enormity and strength of his manhood. It was an effective lie. She had also been smart enough to appear dim and unattractive whenever the principal actress—Alvarosa's aging wife, Valencia—was in the vicinity. That was until Alvarosa was so deeply infatuated it didn't matter. Valencia was retired, relegated to a straw-roofed house in the country, and at fourteen Floridita inherited all of the important roles in the Teatro de Seville's ambitious repertory.

She hadn't loved Alvarosa, but she had liked him. And as he was more interested in being known to have a young, ravishing, red-haired mistress than in actually making love to her, La Floridita enjoyed the next three years. She liked being an actress.

It came to an end, abruptly, when Alvarosa's daughter, a nun in an order that had for its abbess a connection of the king's, reported La Floridita to the Holy Office for the practice of witchcraft. "If I had been a witch," La Floridita had told her Inquisitors, "would I not have destroyed Alvarosa's daughter, the nun?"

24

Alvarosa had died during one of the Holy Office interviews, confessing that he was bewitched by her, that she had smeared devil's blood over his private parts each night before he penetrated her. Poor Alvarosa.

La Floridita thought of him and her past as she made her way to the cabin Córdoba had secured for Antonio Levi. She had missed morning Mass, but that was, though a sin, a relief. Las Mesas was too incendiary, alienating the crew with his feverish eyes filled with a terrible madness, too often directed at La Floridita. When she entered Antonio's cabin she saw that he had fallen asleep sitting up, his curly head propped against the rough wood of the cabin walls. But at least he had slept. For the first few weeks of the voyage she had found him each morning standing in the center of the tiny cabin, rubbing his hands against the rough wool of the sailor's uniform Quirinio had supplied for him, his eyes glazed and unseeing. She was determined that Antonio was going to recover. He reminded her of her favorite younger brother, Roberto, also fair and shy. Antonio hadn't said a word, not one, since their escape.

Córdoba's page arrived with dried cod, black olives, which reminded her of Córdoba's eyes (well, she wouldn't think of Ramón's eyes or of his mouth just now), biscuits, and a flask filled with Jerez sherry. Antonio woke, slowly, disoriented, letting out a stifled gasp, as if he expected to find himself back at the *quemadero*, awaiting his turn at the stake.

"Good morning, *niño*," she said, taking his hand. It was still a boy's hand, but he no longer bit his nails. When she went to remove her hand to prepare his meal, he held onto it, and she looked at him. He was smiling. It was a sad smile. But he *was* smiling at her. He knew who she was. She found tears coming to her eyes.

"Do you want to talk to me this morning, *niño?*" she asked. Still wearing that sad smile, he shook his head, no. "Can you talk?" He didn't answer but looked at the food, for the first time with genuine interest. She held an olive up to his lips, but he took it from her and, using the trembling fingers of his free hand, began to feed himself. "I think, *niño*," the red-headed seventeen-year-old girl said to him, sitting back, "you are going to recover."

He continued to feed himself awkwardly with his left hand and to hold onto her hand with his right. She thought they were in some ways alike—to all intents orphans, dependent now upon themselves. She was in love with Ramón, and she knew he would care for her, but what would happen, she wondered, when they reached the New World? From the outset all he talked about was joining Ponce de León when he set out to discover the new, magically rich island the king had given him a patent for.

She would be left behind in some savage city, and what would she do then? It would be different if he would marry her, but she was under no illusions. He protested when she left his cabin each dawn, but she knew he preferred that she should. He was a hidalgo. He would marry a hidalgo's daughter. And she thought she knew whom. On the last day of sunshine, during the stopover in the Canaries, Floridita had come topside for fresh air after administering to Antonio. The scene she had come upon was reminiscent of one of Alvarosa's *tableaux vivants:* on the quarter deck the hero—handsome young Don Ramón de Córdoba, in finery purchased from Quirinio—was being presented by Don Juan Ponce de León to his wife and daughters, the youngest of whom was clearly the heroine. She had olive-black eyes similar to Ramón's, and she flirted with them decorously from behind her silk fan. When she dropped the fan, Ramón picked it up and held it for a moment before returning it to her.

Floridita shuddered now, remembering how she had felt, in Quirinio's silk gown, with her undressed red hair. She was coarse and unnecessary compared to the admiral's daughter. She had wanted to rip apart that carefully dressed hair, to slap that naïve, pretty face. She hated herself, reminding herself of her stepmother, but still, she felt empty and lost whenever she remembered that moment. That night Ramón asked her why she was sad, but she wouldn't tell him.

He knew. He hadn't missed her reaction, and she thought later that perhaps he had engineered the meeting to make her jealous. He held her to him, enjoying her tears, kissing them away, and then he reached into the trunk and took out a black silk fan purchased from Quirinio. "From now on I shall never pick up any woman's fan but yours, Floridita," he told her, and for that moment she believed him.

She was in love, for the first time, and though she knew she shouldn't, she thought about him—his dark-red selfish lips, his wonderfully inventive body—nearly all of the time. It was as if she had a worm, as if she were always hungry, no matter how much food she took. Her days were spent waiting for their nights.

She didn't know what she would have done without Antonio to care for. Sitting with him, she tried not to think of Ramón—impossible—nor of the future, though part of it seemed clear to her: Ramón would go off exploring with Ponce de León, and, on his return, he would marry the young daughter despite his protestations of love for La Floridita. In that particular melodrama there didn't seem to be any role for La Floridita.

But she had escaped a terrible death and a life that hadn't held much promise—Alvarosa and his rotten teeth—and who knew what excitement the New World would hold? Perhaps in that New World hidalgos did marry actresses and not admiral's daughters.

The admiral, Don Juan Ponce de León, looked in on his wife and daughters, saw that they were the same bilious green they had been for some time, and left their spacious cabins without disturbing them. He sent his page to find young Córdoba and invite him to his cabin.

Ponce de León knew Córdoba's family—his uncles were fine soldiers, having fought with Ponce de León against the Moors in Africa—and didn't care much about his sins. Nor was he interested in investigating the mysterious way in which he had arrived aboard *La Nao*. What mattered was that Córdoba was a true hidalgo, of the same background as himself, and a most attractive young fellow, full of enthusiasm. "The sort," Ponce de León confided to his wife, "the New World needs. If I had a son, I should like him to be like Córdoba. He is a man who never looks back."

Ponce de León's first voyage to the New World had been with Christopher Columbus's second expedition. He had helped to subdue Hispaniola's Indians, becoming governor of Hispaniola's Higuey province. He had had a formal, standard noble military education and, as a result, never had a doubt as to where his duty lay: to his sovereign. At the same time, he was a pragmatist who had married well and had amassed a solid fortune. He went about his life's work—that duty to his king—with a strong, unemotional dedication and an eye for self-enrichment. If he had no sense of humor, if he took himself too seriously, he did possess an imagination that allowed him to believe in both the mysteries of the Church and the myths of his time.

The most popular of these myths was the legend of the Fountain of Youth. Prester John wrote to the king of France and the pope that he had bathed in the Fountain of Youth six times and had only recently celebrated his five hundredth and sixty-second birthday. Sir John Mandeville claimed he had discovered the fountain in Asia. Peter Martyr said, with authority, that the fountain was in the New World, populated by Amazons, mermaids, singing fish, and perfumed alligators.

Ponce de León, after he had become governor of Boriquén (later known as Puerto Rico), was struck with the similarity of Indian and European myths. Fountains of youth were said to be located in an island to the north and west of Boriquén, and Ponce de León sent these supposedly eyewitness reports of life-giving waters to his king. On this return voyage to the New World, Ponce de León was a man approaching late middle age. He would have enjoyed a rejuvenation, but his primary goal, as always, was gold and glory. First for his sovereign and then for himself.

He was especially valued by his king because he understood, perhaps better than any other soldier of his time, how to combat enemies who refused to fight in the European tradition, those who eschewed the battlefield and attacked in small bands. He had served with valor in the Moorish campaigns, learning to use greyhounds with great effect. He said his own greyhound, Bezerillo, was worth a hundred soldiers, understood Spanish, and could distinguish between warlike and peaceful Indians. The Indians of Boriquén had seen Bezerillo snap a man's hand off, cut through his jugular vein, and feast on his eyes in the time it took a soldier to unsheathe his sword.

But in 1508, Ponce de León was replaced as *adelantado*—governor—of Boriquén, by Christopher Columbus's son, Diego. The younger Columbus claimed, successfully, that he had rightfully inherited that position by dint of the agreements the Crown had had with his father.

Hurt by his sovereign's decision, Ponce de León turned his energies to his

Boriquén cotton plantations, buying a number of slaves to work them. Among the slaves he purchased was an unusual Indian, a gentle giant of a fellow named Panthar. He said he came from an island to the north where the rivers gave eternal life, and riches were to be had for the asking. Ponce de León, having grown wily during the lost contest with Diego Columbus, returned to Spain to obtain a royal patent to secure the rights to Panthar's island and any others he might find. He took Panthar with him and was bringing him back to the New World aboard *La Nao.*

There was a knock on the door, and Ponce de León turned to find his page admitting young Córdoba, who was wearing that contagious smile of his. "Sit down, my friend," Ponce de León said, ordering his page to bring refreshments. Córdoba was just the sort of company he needed. He had kept Panthar's presence a secret lest the superstitious crew and passengers blame the long, difficult voyage on his magic. But he found himself telling young Córdoba about him as they drank *aguardiente.* Córdoba was as excited as Ponce de León knew he would be.

"I have longed to see an Indian, *Adelantado,* ever since my father met one at court, introduced by Columbus. Tell me, does he speak Spanish?"

"He speaks Spanish," Ponce de León said, laughing, delighted with Córdoba's excitement. "I taught him myself. Would you like to talk with him?"

"Is he liable to attack me?"

"He is perfectly docile, Ramón. He will answer all of your questions and more. As a matter of fact, he rattles on a good deal." Ponce de León hesitated a moment, trying to decide whether or not to give Córdoba more information and decided he would. "He says he is dead."

"Why?" Córdoba asked, his black eyes lighting up.

"He believes that when he was captured he died and was taken to a sort of purgatory where the half-cooked men—we—tortured him and then took him on a voyage where he was tortured again. This is his last voyage, and when we arrive in the World Below the Sky, protected by the Great Spirit, he will be allowed to join his dead kinsmen in the World Above the Sky."

"But why . . ."

"You must ask him for yourself," Ponce de León said, instructing his page to take Córdoba to Panthar's cabin. The seas had grown even rougher, and the admiral, truth to tell, was not feeling as well as he might. Córdoba went off willingly.

The page left Córdoba at the savage's cabin door, smiling, twirling his finger at his forehead to indicate the occupant's state of mind. Córdoba knocked, and hearing what sounded like an assent, let himself in. It was a small cabin, but it was cleaner than most, well furnished with a bunk, a desk, a chair. Sitting on the floor in the center of it was the tallest man Córdoba had ever seen. Ponce de León had presented Panthar to the king, Don Fernando, dressed in a dark cerise tunic, complete with a delicate cambric shirt, ruffles, slit sleeves, and hose. He had been taught to bow before Don Fernando, to tell his stories in his simple Spanish of the fountains that ran with gold on the island of ancient giants where he had been born. Now, his arms and chest bare, his crossed legs hoseless, he was dressed only in breeches.

The Indian stood up quickly and bowed when Córdoba entered, like a child who had learned a lesson well. Córdoba returned the bow, and the two men looked at each other. The Indian was emaciated—he couldn't eat his captor's food—but there were still signs of his once magnificent physique in the long, smooth muscles, in his posture.

"I am Don Ramón de Córdoba," Ramón said, somewhat discomfited by the mixture of pride, suffering, and humanity he faced in a man the same age as himself.

"I am Panthar." The Indian pointed to the chair, saying, "Will you not be seated, Don Ramón?"

Córdoba seated himself, and the Indian sank back down onto the floor in a movement that was as graceful as his bow was awkward. They stared at each other for what seemed, to Córdoba, like hours. He could feel La Nao shift from side to side. The sound of the sea suddenly was deafening. Despite all the questions in his mind, despite his usual poise, Córdoba could not think of a single thing to say. This was not the colorful, savage Indian of his imagination.

Panthar broke the silence, believing that it was up to him, as host, to be polite, by saying, "Panthar is dead, you know." He said it in a kind of mock Spanish social voice he had picked up somewhere, which Córdoba found particularly chilling.

But the Tequesta's matter-of-factness broke through Córdoba's misgivings, and he said, "How did you die?"

"Panthar began to die a long time ago. White birds came to the shores of my island when I was a boy, carrying the half-baked men. They ate fish and sang songs and lit great fires and went away. Panthar stood on the shores and watched them leave. Later, when the great cacique of my tribe decided it was time to join his spirits in the World Above the Sky, it was my duty to help him prepare. He was my father's father and an important cacique, with many magical powers. I was to take him on his last voyage."

Panthar was used to recitation, both as a tribal storyteller and later, at Ponce de León's urging, as an entertainment for those interested in the New World. He told Córdoba how he had escorted the great cacique into the big water, where they found a sea cow. Panthar lassoed the sea cow, and as the manatee sank under water, he drove a stake through its right nostril. Leaping from the canoe, he rode the sea cow until it died, and then he tied it to his canoe and brought it back to his village deep inside the pine forest.

The great cacique died at dawn, and Panthar described for Córdoba the funeral ceremony in which the flesh was cut away from the cacique's body, the remaining bones placed in the sacred box, lined with deerskins. Panthar then cut open the sea cow's head, removed the two large bones, and placed them in the sacred box. "This was done," Panthar said, "so that the cacique would have transportation to the World Above the Sky, where his spirit went to live, and he could look down and advise me and his other children."

Córdoba had been leaning forward, straining to hear every word. It was as if a traveler from the heavens had suddenly descended and was giving him an eyewitness account of fantastic journeys.

"Afterward I drank of the magical wine, casina, and went once more to the shores of the great water to pray. But I did not pray. I saw again a great white bird. I believed," Panthar said, looking intently at Córdoba, who in his enthusiasm had slipped down on the floor and sat cross-legged beside him, "that messengers sent by the Great Father were aboard the great white bird, coming to guide the spirit of the cacique to the World Above the Sky. It was my duty and fate to welcome them."

But the messengers were half-baked men, part of a slave-hunting group of mixed nationalities who had landed on the coast of what they assumed to be another island, farther north and west than any yet explored. The Spaniards, in the dozen years since Columbus had made his great discovery, had depopulated the islands—Hispaniola (later Haiti and the Dominican Republic), Cuba, and Boriquén—on which they had settled. Spain was becoming the richest country in the world, and slave labor was essential to the New World's plantation and mine economy. As the local Indian populations died out, slaves became a source of new wealth, and slave ships searched for new sources among islands farther and farther away from the Spanish colonial capital at Hispaniola.

A young giant—Panthar—paddled out across the shallow, glistening bay waters in his dugout canoe to greet the half-baked men.

As the slave ship captain smiled and bowed and welcomed the giant aboard, he calculated how large a purse he could ask for him and how much his pearl-encrusted belt might bring. Panthar was clubbed from behind and thus "killed." He was taken below to the slave quarters, where he was put in chains.

The slave captain starved Panthar for a week to make him docile and sold his belt to a jeweler in Hispaniola. Then he sold Panthar to a Boriquén slave merchant, who in turn sold him to Don Juan Ponce de León to work on his Boriquén cotton plantation.

The Indian recited these last details mechanically. He stared at Córdoba without seeing him. "So you see," he said as if to himself, "I am dead. I am in the fourth corner of the universe, the land of the west, being tortured by the half-baked men. You demons," he told Córdoba, conversationally, "have made the spirit of Panthar pure. Now you are taking Panthar's spirit back to the place where his bones were buried by his sons, and then Panthar's spirit will soar to the World Above the Sky, where it will hover and rest, advising and guiding Panthar's children. It will be so until the Black Doves arrive, destroying our harmony with Mother Earth, and the universe is ended."

Córdoba stared at the Indian, wondering if he weren't, after all, some instrument of Satan. "Who are the Black Doves?" he asked, but the Indian sat silently, his eyes staring into space, suddenly and totally closed to Córdoba.

That phrase, "until the Black Doves arrive," unnerved Córdoba. He waited to see if the Indian might not come out of whatever trance he was in, and when he didn't, Córdoba quietly left the cabin. An enormous wave, some fifteen feet high, nearly swept him overboard, but he managed to hold onto the lines and return to his cabin, where Floridita and fresh clothing awaited him. The page was lighting the lamps, preparing their food.

"Where have you been, Ramón?" Floridita asked, worried by his new and sober expression. He dismissed the page, took her in his arms, and told her of his meeting with Panthar. For the first time the miracle of their escape seemed genuinely to be the result of heavenly intervention. Their lovemaking that night took on a different, more tender meaning. Afterward, as they lay in the narrow bunk, Floridita, with that street logic of hers, said, "Perhaps the Indian heard of the black doves after we came aboard. Perhaps he is only trying to scare us with his magic."

"Perhaps," Córdoba said, but he knew that wasn't true. Panthar was not a person capable of deliberately scaring anyone.

Córdoba returned every day to listen to Panthar. He felt an inexplicable need to hear about the myths of Panthar's people, their history. He learned about the cacique named Datha who had become a giant by softening and stretching his own bones in childhood, using a magic preparation made from the skin of a bear; about the great age the Tequestas reached, drinking the magic liquor known as casina, which was made from tree bark and the pure waters of the secret silver spring.

During those days, as the seas grew rougher and the passengers and crew more worried, with food and water running out and the one priest aboard— Las Mesas—even more deranged, Panthar talked about his homeland, painting a glorious picture of a place rich in all possessions that make men happy. At night Córdoba related all he had said to La Floridita, whose imagination was as fired as his.

One day he told Córdoba about a race of red men who lived to the far north on land where the braves grew even taller than he was and had huge, inflexible tails. He spoke of another place where the men lived lives three times as long as his, thanks to their miraculous spring water. The name of that place was Apalachen; it was filled with riches, and it lay to the north and the west.

Córdoba, like Ponce de León, could hardly contain his excitement. "Apalachen" was then a Spanish word for gold. He tried to question Panthar about the place, but Panthar had suddenly grown feverish and had begun to lose his Spanish, praying to his spirits, to the Great Father, in his own tongue.

On the last day he spent with him, Córdoba understood only one word: storm.

CHAPTER THREE

LAS MESAS, his eyes rheumy, his hands trembling, managed to get through evening prayers, but only a handful of passengers were able to brave the winds to attend, and the crew was too busy battling the sea. La Floridita, wearing the cowled friar's robe in which she had arrived on board, knelt in front of him on the quarterdeck, but for once he didn't see her, lost in the hell he had given himself up to.

"If he is a priest," the captain said, "he is a priest of the devil." *La Nao* was weeks late in reaching her first port, and the captain had been forced to call upon the generosity of his more wealthy passengers to help the others get through. It hadn't been his favorite moment, and the grudging allowances he received had hardly made it worth while. The rumors among the passengers and crew were becoming increasingly incendiary. *La Nao* was hopelessly lost, it was said. A devil from the New World was performing magic rites in his cabin, assisting the evil priest, Las Mesas, who was leading them into hell.

After prayers Las Mesas remained alone on deck, kneeling, attempting to pray. Suddenly the wind stopped blowing from the southeast, as if someone had snapped a finger and given an instantly obeyed command. *La Nao* and the two ships that made up the *flota* were becalmed. The inexperienced travelers were pleased at this unexpected lull, but the more sophisticated looked at one another with a terrible fear.

There was a supremely serene moment when not a sound could be heard, when the wind and the ship stood perfectly still. And then the wind resumed with a hundredfold power and the sea began its work. Huge green and foaming waves tossed the three caravels from side to side as a child takes vengeance on no longer amusing toys.

The captain shouted against the roar of the wind, ordering everyone below who was not required for the operation of the ship. A cask of *aguardiente* was brought topside and distributed to the crew. They were going to need courage.

32

"I will get Antonio," Córdoba said, seeing the concern on La Floridita's face. "He will be safer with us."

"He will not come with you," she told him. "I must go to him."

"We will go together."

They were nearly blown overboard by the winds and were almost crushed when the longboat, being taken aboard to be tied to the deck, slipped out of a sailor's hands and crashed near them. The ubiquitous lines were being tightened by frightened young pages who had been pressed into duty. Floridita and Córdoba held onto the ropes as they crossed the deck, giant waves doing their best to loosen their grip. They had to wait for a moment while the regular sails, which had been taken down, were stored below and the storm sail was hoisted, placed as low on the forward mast as possible, to avoid strain, to keep La Nao running before the wind.

Córdoba went first, holding her hand tightly in his, fighting his way against the crew coming topside and the passengers being herded down into the hold. It felt to La Floridita as if they were being swept into Bedlam—the dark and the stink and the fear below worse than the raging storm above.

Antonio looked fearful as they entered his cabin, but La Floridita took him in her arms and comforted him. "We are going to Don Ramón's cabin," she told him. "We will be safe there."

"We are not going anywhere," Córdoba told her, moving the bunk against the door, barricading them against others who didn't want to go down into the hold. Beneath the sounds of the wind and the sea they could hear the hatches and passageways—even the ventilation ports—being battened down to keep the sea from washing below. There was no longer a way out. "We will be just as safe here," he said.

Someone tried to break down the door, to get into the cabin as La Nao was flipped on its side and back again by the largest wave yet. La Floridita let out a cry, and the two men reached for her hands. She held onto them both, tightly. "We are the Black Doves," La Floridita shouted, and she could just be heard above the sea and the wind. "We are not destined to die aboard a ship in a storm. Our lives and our deaths are waiting for us in the New World, in the Land of the Flowers." Those shouted words were not, both Córdoba and Antonio knew, said for theatrical effect. They gave Antonio a new reason for living. They made Córdoba, nearly always brave, suddenly fearful.

Las Mesas found himself herded down into the hold, surrounded by unlucky merchants whose top-deck cabins had been requisitioned by servants for a platoon of soldiers on their way to a garrison in Boriquén. There had been no water for washing since the Canaries. Several men vomited as the ship was tossed from side to side, and not a few lost control of their bowels. They fainted and fell where they stood in that airless, unlit place.

The stench was all-consuming, more insistent even than the noise. In the dark—no candle would stay lit—Las Mesas felt as if he were among the rotting dead. He dropped to his knees in that hellhole, in the accumulated filth of two months at sea, and prayed to the Holy Savior to take him now, to end his suffering. But the only answer to his prayers was the unholy sound of the wind and the sea, repeatedly tossing La Nao on its side, flipping it back over again.

Las Mesas was forced to stand. There were three feet of water in the hold, and those who had fainted drowned. The survivors screamed, prayed, begged their Lord for mercy. A hand suddenly grasped Las Mesas's robe. "The captain wants you," a young voice said.

Las Mesas followed the page through the hysterical crowd, topside, up into the gray morass of water and wind. The sound was deafening, as if the universe were breaking apart. Ropes had begun to twist and break. Lines and spars covered the deck.

The captain stood in the waist of the ship, allowing the seas to roll over him, bellowing orders. Four pumps were being continuously manned. "The admiral has requested that you pray for us," the captain shouted into Las Mesas's ear. "So pray."

Las Mesas tied himself to the deck not far from the captain, and for the next twelve hours he tried to pray—unsuccessfully. His mind refused to empty itself of the images Satan had put there. At the end of that half day, when the seas and winds suddenly subsided, he untied himself and, rising, said, "We have survived the storm. The miracle—whether it be the work of our Holy Savior or of Satan—is not finished. The Black Doves must reach the New World."

One of the pages had opened the passageway and called below that the storm had passed. Passengers attempted to come up, but the captain and the crew shouted at them to stay below. Córdoba managed to lead Floridita and Antonio out of the passageway before the door was banged shut, and he saw that Panthar had come out of his cabin as well. He tried to go to him but was stopped when Las Mesas screamed. "We have a sign. Look up into the heavens."

Three black birds, doves, flew above the ship in a small expanse of blue sky. Las Mesas turned, holding his arms out as the crew tried to keep passengers from coming up onto the main deck. "We have a sign," he shouted, pointing first at La Floridita, Antonio Levi, Don Ramón de Córdoba, then at the sky. "The Black Doves will survive this storm. You will die not on water but in the Land of the Flowers, and your seeds shall take root and grow. Satan is vanquished. The Lord, our Holy Savior, has battled the pagan forces and won. The miracle has not ended yet. Not for the Black Doves. Look above you."

The three of them stared at the wild-eyed Las Mesas and then upward as the birds disappeared in a hail of rain. The other wall of the hurricane was enveloping La Nao. Córdoba looked for Panthar, but he had already returned to his cabin. He flung Antonio and Floridita and finally himself back into the passageway, pulling the door after him.

As giant waves and new, stronger winds assailed the ship, two of the can-

34

nons Las Mesas had used as shelter broke loose, catching his robe, forcing him to roll with them across the deck. They broke through the far side of the ship, dragging Las Mesas, his arms and legs trapped in broken lines, screaming into the sea.

The hurricane raged for four more hours and then subsided, leaving Don Juan Ponce de León's *flota* battered but still afloat. The dead were gathered up and buried at sea and the sick were seen to. Córdoba had gone to Panthar's cabin to tell him that the storm was over and had found the Indian on the cabin floor, wearing only a breechclout he had fashioned from his court presentation clothes, his arms folded across his chest. Córdoba knew instinctively what had happened to Panthar. Panthar had seen the Three Black Doves in the sky during the storm and had believed that the old Tequesta legend was being fulfilled. His universe ended, Panthar had willed his own death. Córdoba insisted that Panthar's body be held and eventually, secretly, when they reached their destination, turned over to natives for an Indian burial. He also insisted that manatee bones be included in Panthar's sacred box. He wanted to be certain Panthar had transportation to the World Above the Sky.

Not many gave much thought to the dead Indian slave, and nearly everyone was relieved by the death of Las Mesas, blaming the hurricane on the evil priest. But the Three Black Doves mourned them both, wondering at their prophesies, at their conviction that the miracle had not yet come to an end. That night, after the hurricane had passed, La Floridita and Córdoba made love with a renewed passion, glorying in their twice-saved lives. Antonio Levi, though still mute, was more interested in the world about him. He realized, as the others did, that they had been singled out by some providence. "The miracle has not ended yet," Las Mesas had said. "Not for the Black Doves." Each of them wondered what he had meant and what the remainder of the miracle would signify to them.

La Floridita had never breathed such air. It was thick and enveloping and sweetly perfumed. It buoyed her up, made her feel suddenly healthy and even clean again. She dressed quickly—there was that dark-red haze in the east indicating the rising sun—and, kissing Ramón on the lips, she went to Antonio.

There was a new life aboard *La Nao,* an anticipation and excitement that hadn't existed before the storm. It had been three days since the hurricane and Las Mesas's and Panthar's deaths, but it seemed as if a century had passed. Land clouds and birds had begun to appear overhead, and that afternoon the page in the crow's nest shouted the long-awaited words. Land-ho. He had finally sighted their New World port, though he wasn't quite certain what it was being called. Once it had been known as Boriquén, but that was a year or two before. Names of newly discovered places were constantly being changed, and someday this island would be called Puerto Rico and its capital, now known as Puerto Rico, would be changed to San Juan.

Passengers and crew came topside to view what was considered an even greater miracle than lasting out the storm. Despite the miseries and the mysteries of the voyage, they had survived and had reached the New World, where riches and adventure waited for them. These were the chance takers, the ones not content to remain where they had been born, the merchants and soldiers and adventurers who were making Spain the richest, most powerful country in the world.

Don Ramón de Córdoba, standing on the quarterdeck in a position of honor with the admiral and his family, could barely contain his excitement. His pride and joy in who he was and the adventure he was about to embark upon gave him a radiance no one could resist. He studied San Juan—a dark jungle of an island except in those areas where the Spaniards had chopped out places for themselves and their new slaves. He thought Panthar's island would be a vastly superior place, filled with the gold and the adventures Panthar had told him about. He would have started for it at once had he been able to.

Leonora, Ponce de León's youngest daughter, divided her attention between the green island in front of her and the young hidalgo at her side. When Córdoba looked at her, she didn't see love in his eyes. But she saw affection and interest and the assurance that he would perform his hidalgo duty, that he would marry her and sire hidalgo children, continue the Córdoba line. Leonora believed she would be happy with that. She allowed herself one small triumphant glance at Córdoba's supposedly secret red-haired mistress, standing with a group of merchants and servants on the hastily repaired top deck, and then looked away, not toward the island but up at Córdoba's perfect profile.

La Floridita saw that look and was chilled by it. "Are you ill, Señorita?" Quirinio asked. The merchant stood too close to her, his perfume spoiling the warm breeze, the top of his polished dome reflective in the noon sunlight. "I have never been more well, Señor Quirinio," she answered, moving away from him. She refused to look at Ramón, standing with the admiral and his family, the girl with the olive-black eyes staring up at him as if he were a holy statue.

She realized then that her dream of Córdoba marrying her—that there would be a new and democratic social structure in the New World in which her past was forgotten—was just that, a dream. She knew, suddenly and unquestionably, that she couldn't depend on Córdoba for her welfare in this New World. He was a boy in love, but the excitement of exploration and pride in his family would eventually cool his ardor. Once again she was on her own. Quirinio was right. She did feel ill.

Then she felt a hand on her arm, and she looked up to find Antonio by her side. He seemed aware of La Floridita's pain, and though he still wouldn't talk, his mild embrace reassured her. She had a friend—a brother, after all, a Black Dove—who wouldn't leave her. Her excitement returned. "Our new home, Antonio. You will get well here, I promise you." She looked, in that battered blue gown and lace mantilla, in that unguarded moment when she had no one to please but herself, once again like a girl playing dress-up. She summoned her irrepressible spirit and forced herself to banish her fears. This was, after all, the New World.

On shore a cannon boomed, welcoming Don Juan Ponce de León, one of the most important and genuinely esteemed men in the New World. Córdoba, across the deck, over Leonora's dark head, gave La Floridita his brilliant smile. She turned away but in such a way as to let him know that she wasn't genuinely displeased.

She wondered as she stared at the island if there was a theater in its capital and if the Church would allow her to act in it if it existed. She tried to divine the mysteries of this New World island, at the same time wondering how soon she might wash her hair and acquire a new gown. La Floridita held Antonio's arm and wondered despite her fears, and as always with a scarcely controllable anticipation, what was going to happen next.

CHAPTER FOUR

DON RAMÓN DE CÓRDOBA REMOVED, gingerly, his white-hot metal helmet, singeing his fingers. He wished that he could take off his heavy mail breastplate as well. If it rained—and the cloudless, depthless blue of the sky made that unlikely—he thought the raindrops would boil. Almost hourly someone aboard fainted from the heat. Córdoba stared enviously at the Indian slaves, who wore nothing but breechcloths.

In was only April in the year of our Lord 1513, but the sun was relentless, reflecting off the sea and the sails and the brass and the breastplates the men wore, baking the newly painted decks of the *San Cristóbal de San Juan*. Ponce de León's new flagship was a neat caravel with broad bows, a high, narrow poop, and new, expensive lateen sails. He had assumed the title of *adelantado*—governor—as a right of his royal patent, though he had yet to discover a land to govern. This *flota* of two seaworthy but old caravels had been gotten up to remedy that situation.

Córdoba, bored, listened to the monotonous chorus of the cows and milch goats tethered below, giving off a pervasive odor. The sun bouncing off the sea hurt his eyes. There was nothing else to look at. Certainly not another ship. The *adelantado*'s patent gave him command of these seas; the slave-catchers were forewarned, and no other country would dare to cross the line of demarcation Alexander VI had defined in 1493, dividing the New World between Spain and Portugal. It would be another decade before Verrazano, sailing for France, explored the east coast of America; a half century before the English began expeditions to North America and Raleigh's expedition landed in Virginia.

Córdoba looked aft where Don Juan Ponce de León stood conferring with his navigator, Hector, both grim with disappointment. The royal patent had included a proviso that he explore the island of Bimini, where the Fountain of Youth was said to be located. There had been no fountain and no gold on Bimini and few, if any, potential slaves. Bimini's people had long been removed to Hispaniola, where they were given such brutal treatment in slave-labor gangs that even the bishop finally lodged a protest at court, which was largely ignored.

A new slave industry—importing Africans, who were hardier than the local people—was thriving, and Ponce de León was not, at any rate, interested in rounding up potential slaves. After the difficult voyage from Spain he had settled his family in San Juan and set out to accomplish three goals: serve his sovereign, discover gold, and acquire glory.

He had gone to Yuma, a port city in Santo Domingo, to outfit his two ships, sailing them across the boiling blue Mona Passage to San Juan and then upriver to San Germán. There Córdoba met him, and they loaded the ships with cows and goats, pickled pork, vegetables, fruits, oils, and wine vinegar, some little part of it purchased with the funds Córdoba's father had smuggled to him.

Córdoba was, he reminded himself, to share in the riches of Panthar's island, if and when Ponce de León discovered it. But more than gold, he longed to see Panthar's country and the giant men who lived for hundreds of years. He daydreamed about the Tequestan hermaphrodites with their male and female organs and their strange beauty and sexual powers. He wanted to see the huge collars of bubble-sized pearls worn by the caciques, who wed their own mothers and sisters. In his mind he saw himself bathing in the rivers filled with curious animals, inhaling the perfume of the magic forests.

In reality he was being boiled alive in his armor and heavy boots, sailing on a caravel that was going nowhere in uncharted seas, amidst a crew of unholy adventurers and godless savages.

He thought ruefully of La Floridita and felt a great longing for her. He had established her and Antonio in a small house, owned by Quirinio, on a little hill above Puerto Rico's central plaza and bought her a slave named Cabeza de Vaca—"Cow's Head"—to care for them. He himself had lived with the *adelantado*'s family in their stone house, which dominated the plaza. It faced the governor's mansion and was twice its size.

During the day, waiting for the *adelantado* to return from Yuma, escorting Doña León and her daughters to and from the church, he would catch sight of her. La Floridita would adjust her mantilla over her mass of red hair, unfold her fan, and place it in front of her face, her green eyes laughing as she so dramatically ignored him. Everyone couldn't help but be aware of their intimacy.

At night, Córdoba, furious at the inroads on his pride, would make his way to the two-room adobe house thinking that she genuinely deserved a beating. But once she touched him, he had no other thought but to immerse himself in the warmth she radiated. He was certain she was a witch. A red-headed witch. Standing aboard the *San Cristóbal,* Córdoba wished he had magic powers, that he could conjure her up at that moment, if only to caress her white body. They had spent the nights exploring each other's bodies, but each evening she seemed new to him, as rich and mystical as Panthar's island. By morning, when he returned to Ponce de León's polite, ordered house, overseen by the *adelantado*'s decorous wife and her charming daughters, Córdoba was bleary with exhaustion.

Only Panthar's island, with its ancient, tailed giants, its rivers flowing with gold and life-giving waters, could have taken him away from La Floridita at that moment. She hadn't said that he shouldn't go, but he could sense her fears.

"I will spend the rest of my life with you," he told her on that last night. "This may be my only chance to see Panthar's island."

"You must go," she told him. "If I were a man, nothing would stop me." He loved her all the more for holding back her tears, for giving him her last kiss with a smile.

But thus far the voyage had been disappointing. The weather, despite the heat, had been uniformly fine as the ships moved north and then east in familiar waters. The skies and the seas seemed as if they had been hand-painted an hour before by a master of dark and light blues, greens, pinks.

While the *adelantado* conferred with the navigator, the captain of the flagship, Juan Bone de Quejo, came up to Córdoba. He was a short, dark man, with curious black lips that he twisted in odd ways, one of the first Spaniards to be born in the New World. Quejo had last captained a profitable slaver and had the advantage of being one of the few men thoroughly familiar with the waters they had sailed in.

"We are about to sail into uncharted waters," Quejo said portentously, as if he were announcing the end of the world.

Córdoba was suddenly happy. "Uncharted waters are what I came for," he said, staring greedily as the caravel rounded the first of the Caicos, its white sand beach ringed with flashing ocean surf, looking less like an island than a star in a new, sun-lit galaxy set in a heaven of turquoise waters.

"Do not excite yourself, Don Ramón," the captain said, working a sliver of wood around his rotted teeth, spitting thoughtfully over the side. "These islands have neither riches nor slaves. Others arrived first. Out there"—he gestured to the north and the west—"there is nothing but water, and godless water at that. Excellency, perhaps you could use your influence to persuade the *adelantado* to turn back. We do not even have a priest aboard to guide us. Don Ramón," Quejo said, his guttural voice rising, "it is the will of our holy Lord that we proceed no farther."

Córdoba looked at him as if he were one of the insects that had got inside his armor on Bimini, in the scrub pines, burning welts all over his body. "Being cowardly and religious is a bad combination, Captain. You should try to keep your fears from the men."

They anchored at dusk among the reefs off Samaná. The cooking fires were lighted in the sandboxes on the open decks, and the Indian slaves were brought up and unchained so they could cook the meat. The ship's lanterns swayed back and forth on their sterns while the page continued to turn the sandglass, to sing out the hours. Younger boys sang the evensong to God and the Blessed Mother to continue their safe voyage.

"I wish it were less safe," Córdoba said to himself.

Restless, he sought out Ponce de León, and they sat on the quarterdeck playing a card game—*lunes y marti*—by the light of a lantern, drinking *aguardiente*, until late in the evening. The *adelantado* was a soldier and knew how to wait. Córdoba did not. Time was standing still for him.

Easter Sunday fell on the twenty-seventh of March. Captain Quejo was palpably unhappy, his hands working each other rather than the sliver of wood, which had been put aside for the holy day. "Mass cannot be said," he told the navigator, Hector, who had not attended a Mass since he was fourteen. "There is no priest aboard."

Prayers were said and hymns were sung, but Quejo was not appeased. He had argued long and hard for a priest during the early negotiations. But as the king's patent hadn't specified one and Ponce de León circumvented the colonial church when possible, Easter Sunday was spent in what Quejo repeatedly called "a state of sin." "There will be," he warned, "consequences."

The weather, as if in answer to the captain's prophesy, turned uncomfortably cold, the damp and the wet causing general misery. The winds grew unpredictable, the seas rough, the skies glowering. Quejo changed course to west by northwest, but he said the weather was now against them, and so it was. The waters—calm and turquoise the day before—became black, rolling and wind-beaten, taking the *San Cristóbal* and her sister ship where they wanted.

The *adelantado*'s expedition had crossed, unknowingly, into the until-then-unheard-of Gulf Stream. Quejo, certain it was a judgment from the Holy Savior for neglecting Easter Sunday, battled against the unexplained force, praying all the while, if only for his own salvation.

At nightfall he asked permission to address the *adelantado* and was granted an interview. "We must turn back, *Adelantado,*" Quejo said, his dark eyes burning and black lips twisting with the knowledge of God's might. "I cannot fight these waters. Were there a priest aboard, I would have him pray for guidance from the Lord our Savior. As there is not, we must turn back. We cannot weather Satan's winds and seas. Please, *Adelantado,* we have already fulfilled the royal patent. We have taken Bimini for the king. Now we must turn back."

Córdoba, who stood behind Ponce de León in the small cabin, said, "Taking Bimini for the king, Captain, is like giving him a whore for a bride. Bimini is not a prize."

Ponce de León put his hand up, indicating that Córdoba should keep his temper to himself. "Ironic, is it not, Ramón, that the tempest that nearly destroyed *La Nao* was blamed upon the presence of a priest, and now, aboard the *Cristóbal,* it is blamed upon his absence." Ponce de León, still not looking at Quejo, dismissed him, saying, "I and I alone will decide when and if we turn back, Captain."

"You and the Holy Savior, *Adelantado,*" Quejo said, bowing, grimmer and more sallow than ever.

The *Cristóbal* and her sister ship continued through the storm, sailing north by northwest for the next three days, fighting the winds and the rain and the mercurial waters that would one day be known as the Gulf Stream. The lookouts, miserably wet in the crow's nest, reported, over and over again, nothing but water.

Finally, on the morning of April 1, 1513, the northwesterly winds dispersed the gray clouds and the sun began to break through. Córdoba—bored and angry—said he was going up to the crow's nest himself. "The pages are nearly blind with lack of sleep and Quejo's fears. It is time for a fresh pair of eyes."

Ponce de León said it was a pointless exercise but let him go. In the meanwhile he ordered all men to assemble on the quarterdeck. They were a miserable group of men, defeated by the weather and their captain. Fear of the unknown seas hung over them like a shroud, and Ponce de León at that moment decided to give up. "There is no island to the north," he heard himself say. "We are going back."

Quejo and the men went about their tasks with more energy than they had shown during the entire voyage. The *adelantado* stood at the bow, looking old and defeated as a rejuvenated Quejo bellowed orders to turn back.

But before they could be carried out, there was an urgent shout from the crow's nest. They all stopped what they were doing and looked up to where Córdoba stood, his famous smile back in place. "Land," Córdoba shouted. "Land, *Adelantado.*" Ponce de León looked to the east, as did the crew. They saw nothing but dark waters. "No, *Adelantado,*" Córdoba shouted with impatience, "west. Look to the west. It is Panthar's island."

They all turned, and a great, spontaneous shout of joy rang out. Extending across the entire horizon, from north to south, bathed in the eerie after-storm sunlight, was a huge expanse of sandy beaches and groves watered by small rivers that flowed into the sea.

Córdoba joined Ponce de León, the navigator, Hector, and the master builder on the quarterdeck, all of them anxious to find a place to land, to touch this new place. "Too many shoals," Quejo reported. "Too many sandbars, *Adelantado*." They spent the better part of the day sailing north, impatiently searching for an entrance.

"She is like a desirable but respectable woman," Córdoba said. "Inaccessible and tantalizing."

At dusk, when he could stand it no longer, Ponce de León—as excited under his patient exterior as Córdoba—ordered Quejo to drop anchor. "We are three miles offshore," Quejo objected, "in a scant eight fathoms over a hard sandy floor. *Adelantado*, we cannot—" Ponce de León repeated the order. They were halfway between what is now St. Augustine and Jacksonville Beach.

At dawn, after hasty prayers, Ponce de León ordered the longboat put to sea. He chose Córdoba, Hector—the navigator—and the master builder to accompany him, deliberately omitting Quejo, filling the boat with half a dozen men and Bezerillo, his greyhound.

The longboat skimmed in easily with the tide, and it seemed to Córdoba that Panthar's island welcomed them with a rainbow of color. The sky was a clear, pure blue, the sun a hazy pink and red, the waters green and blue, filled with all manner of fish just below the surface. A yellow sand beach lay between the blue-white irregular line of surf, while rows of oversized sea grapes and coco plums grew just beyond a grassy dune.

No Christian has ever been here, Córdoba thought, receiving the honor of being first ashore, jumping out of the longboat, wading through the surf to the sand. "We are the virgin's first white lovers." Overcome, he knelt down and kissed the sand as his *adelantado* and the others joined him.

They tried to move up to the beach, their eyes stinging with blown sand. But their heavy red-leather boots made walking difficult, and the weight of their armor caused them to sink down into the wet sand. Córdoba looked at the others, halfway to their knees in sand. Laughing, he removed his armor, took off his boots, and raced up to the peak of the grass dunes, staring westward at the thick and dark woodlands that lay stretched in front of him as far and as wide as he could see.

The others, following his example, joined him on the dune. Even Bezerillo seemed to be holding his breath. The coastline and the forests went on endlessly, no other shore in sight.

Hector handed Ponce de León the stave he had been entrusted to carry. The *adelantado*, barefoot, armorless except for his helmet, and yet with great dignity, planted the stave with its scarlet banner in the sand of Panthar's island. While the others knelt and prayed he solemnly intoned the Latin words of possession. He nearly wept. This was the culmination of his life's work. Before him lay the discovery that would make him rich and renowned, that would fill his sovereign's and his own coffers with gold, that would cause his name to be written alongside Christopher Columbus's and Vasco da Gama's. This was the discovery that would make up for the pain and indignation he had suffered when he was removed as *adelantado* of San Juan.

Despite his disregard for the trappings and superstitions of the Church, Ponce de León knew without a doubt that the Lord had guided him to his island. He had made his discovery five days after that Mass-less Easter Sunday, during the Spanish holiday known as the Feast of Flowers, *Pascua Florida*.

And so the *adelantado* named his island. His low voice booming, speaking into the wind, he said, "I call this place, in the name of my sovereign, Don Fernando, and in the name of my Lord, our Holy Savior, Jesus Christ, Florida."

Córdoba, kneeling at the *adelantado*'s unshod feet, thought of his own Floridita—passionate, mysterious, full of joy—and felt it was an entirely appropriate name.

They spent five days on that beach, waiting for natives to appear, for some sign of life outside the dark woodlands that surrounded their camp. Córdoba wanted to explore the interior, but Ponce de León trusted his greyhound's instincts. Bezerillo and the others, brought to shore, acted oddly, whimpering, refusing to eat, refusing to set foot anywhere west of the dunes. "There will be time for further exploration," Ponce de León said. When pressed by Córdoba, he told him there were not enough men to warrant an inland excursion. He knew enough about San Juan's natives and, remembering Panthar's stories of wars and battles, was distrustful of those inviting pine forests. At the end of five days he decided to reboard the *Cristóbal*, to sail around his green island so Hector could draw a map and they could see if there were signs of inhabitants.

They sailed down the seemingly endless coast, around a low, sandy cape one day to be known as Canaveral. There were no signs of life on land, but the waters and the skies teemed with it. Schools of manatees and flocks of gulls followed the ships, living off their refuse. Finally the lookout spotted a lagoon in the shape of a cross, which Ponce de León thought a good omen.

The longboat again landed without incident. The master builder hewed a cross out of the hard coral they found on the shore and the men erected it. While the *adelantado* led his men, kneeling in front of the cross, in prayer, Córdoba wandered up the beach. The tallest sand dune he had yet seen—some forty feet in height—lay at the edge of the lagoon, and he wanted to know what was behind it.

Six Indians were waiting for him. Córdoba managed to shout, to alert his *adelantado* and the others before a huge Tequesta knocked him out with a wood-handled weapon shaped like a hammer. Córdoba regained consciousness a moment later, losing it again as the brave stabbed him with a fire-hardened reed arrow, penetrating Ramón's chain armor just above his heart.

While the others were racing to the longboat under a hail of arrows, Córdoba was dragged into the beach scrub. Half conscious, trussed, and tied to a spear like an animal, he was carried through the pine forest to the Tequesta village, three miles into the interior. It consisted of forty mud huts, built in a circle in a place in the forest considered magical because it had been cleared by fire from a thunderstorm. In the center of the village was a platform and behind it the huts belonging to the chief and the medicine man, painted with ancient signs and decorated with icons made of seashells.

The Tequestas believed they had captured a black dove, part of the legend forecasting the destruction of their world. They tortured him accordingly, hoping that if his spirit was properly weakened, his seed would die with him and the prophecy would be aborted.

It took a week. After a time the half-baked man would become used to the pain and they would have to devise different methods of torture. They kept him conscious by forcing him to eat herbs and magic grasses that held him in a constant narcotic state.

Córdoba believed—not unlike Panthar—that he had died and was in purgatory, being tortured by Lucifer's demons. He longed for the moment when his spirit would break free from his body and join those with Christ in heaven. He wondered, in those moments when he was allowed to recover so it could begin again, whether he was being punished for reading the New Bible or for some greater, collective crime. The medicine man's work was not so very different from that of the Holy Office's Inquisitors.

At the end, when his mutilated body was tied to the stake, he believed that he had never been saved, that his journey to the New World was a dream, that he was still in Spain at the *quemadero*. For perhaps the first time in his life he longed for a priest. He, who had lived life so fully, hoped for death. At the end he had become afraid of their tortures.

As the flames were lit Córdoba thought, finally, of La Floridita. He conjured her up in front of him, bending over him, her red hair providing a curtain for them to kiss behind. And then, as the flames grew higher, La Floridita's hair turned to fire. He found, as he burned, as the terrible sounds and smells of his frying flesh broke through his damaged senses, that he had one ability left to him. They had left him his tongue so he could cry out and release his evil spirit into the night. But he managed, with his last conscious effort, to remain silent until his body was consumed by the fire.

The Tequestas saw Córdoba's silence as an act of bravery and an ill omen. They had failed to destroy the spirit of the black dove. Two more were coming, the medicine man said. To destroy the World Below the Sky. To destroy our harmony with Mother Earth. To destroy us.

Ponce de León mourned his young friend, knowing that part of the delight of his discovery would always be tempered by Córdoba's death. He prayed that it had been a speedy one. He had seen, during his early colonizing days, the results of more than one Indian torture. Yet the fact remained that he had spent nearly four decades in the service of his sovereign battling Moors, Indians, and Caribs. He had lost many friends. It would be unthinkable not to go on.

But the Indians, now that they had made their existence known, dogged him up and down the coast, preventing his landing. They knew well of the half-baked man's treatment of their brothers. Some of them traveled fairly regularly to the Bahamas for seeds, and they had seen, firsthand, the results of the Spanish slave raids. Ships had been wrecked on their shores, and surviving slaves had told them of the Spanish methods of Christianization. At least one slaver had visited and had captured Panthar. They were prepared.

Ponce de León followed the coastline south, around the half-moon of islands someday to be known as the Florida Keys—tiny islands, formed by shifting coral and mangrove roots. Ponce de León laid claim to them, naming them Los Mártirs—The Martyrs—because of their tortured shapes. The two ships then sailed through the Dry Tortugas's boiling currents and north again along the dense west coast all the way to what would one day be called Pensacola Bay. Despairing of finding the northern perimeter of his island on this voyage, his men anxious to return to their home port, the *adelantado* gave a relieved Captain Quejo the order to turn back.

He had found and claimed Florida for Spain, and it would remain Spanish for nearly three hundred years. He vowed to return to settle her, to find her gold ("Apalachen," Panthar had said), to revenge Córdoba's death on her Indians. It would be another eight years before he was to see his island again, but there wasn't a waking moment when Florida was out of his consciousness.

CHAPTER FIVE

NO ONE HAD THOUGHT to tell her. Not that anyone had to. The *San Cristóbal* had been in port a day when she had known. Had he been aboard he would have come to her immediately; certainly, after two months apart, he would have come for just one embrace despite his obligations to the Ponce de Leóns.

Still, she waited for someone to come and give her some official, some definitive word. But Ponce de León arrived home to find Puerto Rico had been sacked by a tribe of rebellious Caribs; they had refused to go down into the tin mines to die of starvation and beatings. They hadn't done much damage to the town, but his fine stone house had been destroyed. The Caribs had believed it belonged to the governor, Diego Columbus, and some of the Puerto Ricans thought Ponce de León got what he deserved for building such a grand edifice. Luckily his wife and daughters had been at the cotton plantation during the raid, and now they were living, ironically, in the governor's house while Ponce de León went off to deal with the Caribs.

Two of the rebels had approached Floridita's little house on the hill, but Cabeza de Vaca, the Ciboney Indian from Cuba whom Córdoba had given to Floridita, talked to them in their own language, and they had gone away.

Leonora, Ponce de León's youngest daughter, felt that someone should visit La Floridita and tell her of Córdoba's capture. She had seen La Floridita, looking plump and disheveled, in the plaza, and she had felt a great sorrow for her. One afternoon, not able to stand the thought of Floridita's pain any longer, Leonora waited until her duenna had retired for the afternoon siesta and then made her way to the little house on the hill. The front door was open, allowing the sea breeze to cool the house, and when no one answered her knock, she walked in.

La Floridita was sitting on an oversized, oddly shaped chair, her small, white, beautiful hands in her lap, holding the black silk fan Córdoba had given her aboard *La Nao*. Cabeza de Vaca had gone to get Antonio, who had been loosely apprenticed to a baker. She was alone.

The two women looked at each other. They were the same age and of the same nationality, but their upbringing had made them as foreign to each other as if they had been born on different planets. Leonora's black eyes—reminiscent of Córdoba's—met La Floridita's glittering green ones and they held for a few moments.

Leonora hadn't prepared what she was going to say, and suddenly she found, in that little adobe room filled with sorrow, that she didn't know how to begin. La Floridita did it for her. She would not reveal her anguish. Her voice was clear and cool. She did not want consolation, only information. "Is he dead?"

"Yes," Leonora said, not quite knowing what to do with her gloved hands, her eyes still fixed on the other woman's. "He was captured by the Indians on the new island Papa discovered. It is called Florida."

"Land of the Flowers," Floridita said, pulling her mantilla around her, suddenly chilled despite the heat, thinking that one of the Black Doves had fulfilled the miracle. "But perhaps he is not dead. Perhaps they . . ."

"Papa says we must pray that he is dead, that he is in the keeping of our Holy Savior. Papa says we must not forget Don Ramón but that we must go on and live our lives." She stopped, realizing she sounded like her father's

46

parrot, seeing the tears in La Floridita's green eyes. "I thought you had better know."

"I thank you," La Floridita said, standing up, placing the mantilla Córdoba had given her on her mass of red hair. "But I will not take your father's advice. I will pray that he is still alive, that one day we shall be together in the Land of the Flowers."

Leonora tried to offer assistance, but she couldn't find the words, and finally, mutely, she took her leave. She could hear the red-haired woman's weeping through the door. It would be a long time before Leonora could forget the cool, distant countenance the woman had presented and the racking sobs she had allowed to escape the moment Leonora had left the rude house.

"I can cry now," La Floridita told herself. "I am allowed." She had refused to cry when he had left. She had put her arms around his broad shoulders and held him to her one last time, giving him her most cheerful smile. He had returned it, loving her for it. That happy attitude had cost her something, but his answering smile had made it worth while. Now she let all of the two months' pain and anguish and uncertainty wash out in those tears. She was able to stop only when Antonio arrived and put his thin arms around her.

Antonio Levi, long after his physical recovery, continued to wake several times each night, the stench of burned flesh, the piteous cries of his mother and sister—and that one terrible shout of his father's—as real to him as if they were being burned alive just outside the door. He had become able, however, to care for his own needs, to clean and feed himself, to accompany Floridita, shaded by Cabeza de Vaca with a huge parasol, on her strolls about the plaza. The baker had taken a liking to him, and when it was suggested that he work there, and Floridita had agreed, he began to feel better about himself.

He liked the smell and feel of the flour, and he didn't mind the heat of the ovens. He supplied La Floridita's household with bread and the occasional chicken the baker's wife gave him. He was able to make himself understood, though he hadn't spoken since the day of the auto-da-fé when he saw his mother, sister, and father burned at the stake.

That afternoon he returned to the little house on the hill from his work at the baker's and saw La Floridita sitting in the awkward chair, tears running down her face. He went to her, placing his long hands—still white with flour—on her shoulders. She covered his hands with her own and looked up at him, communicating her great sorrow and her need for comfort. Finally, in a hesitant, harsh whisper, Antonio Levi spoke his first words in nearly a year. "May I offer you some bread, Señora?"

Floridita held her breath for a moment and looked at him in amazement through her tears. "No," she said, forcing a smile. "Your voice is enough. You are getting well, niño. Soon you will be totally healed." She stood up. The top of her flaming red hair just reached under his chin. "Córdoba is gone," she said, thinking aloud. "For a long time and possibly forever. The money he left is nearly gone as well. Worse, we no longer have protection against the Church, much less anyone else—" She stopped and looked up at his concerned face and began to laugh. She laughed until she had to sit down.

"What shall we do, Señora?" Antonio asked in his rediscovered voice.

"Something will happen," La Floridita said, still amused by her recital of their troubles. That recital, that litany, sounded to her as if an untried actress were reading poorly written lines. La Floridita never could get herself to believe in trouble. She hadn't even quite believed in the inquisition. Yes, she believed in Christ, but her own Christ, a kind soul Who would not allow the Holy Office to torture in His name.

Antonio Levi took her hand in his once more. "I will care for you now, Señora. It is my turn." La Floridita laughed again, with new tears in her remarkable eyes. No one had ever made that promise before. Sitting on a dirt floor at the end of the world with a slave who resembled a cow, a sixteen-year-old New Christian invalid in her charge, a tarnished reputation and no husband in sight, Floridita realized she should not have been laughing. But she did, and finally Antonio joined in. Something was certain to turn up. It always had.

Something did. Inigio Roberto Quirinio was a master at biding his time. He had waited two weeks after Ponce de León's return and another week after he learned of Ponce de León's daughter's visit to the house he had leased to Córdoba. He wanted to make absolutely certain La Floridita knew her position.

And she did. She, Antonio, and Cabeza de Vaca lived on the bread Antonio brought home from the bakery, on the wine and vegetables Cabeza da Vaca managed to beg from the households where other Ciboneys were slaves. She was abandoned and destitute in a sanctimonious colonial town where there was hardly a tavern, not to speak of a theater in which she might find work. She could, she knew, throw herself on the mercy of the Church, or become a servant. Neither option seemed feasible, much less attractive. Quirinio had counted on that.

There was a pair of oddly shaped chairs in the little house on the hill now, both made by Cabeza de Vaca. The slave had clearly missed the point of European furniture, but Quirinio sat in one of the chairs nevertheless. He had timed his visit for that hour when Cabeza de Vaca had gone to fetch Antonio at the baker's. The sight of the oversized Ciboney carrying a dainty yellow and red parasol to protect the fair Jew, whose clothes were covered with flour, was one the Puerto Ricans had taken some time to get used to.

Cabeza de Vaca had once been sold to Quirinio for next to nothing by a Spanish explorer with the same name. Quirinio had sold him for a nice profit to Córdoba, who in turn had given him to La Floridita. She had improved his

Spanish and taught him to take care of the adobe house, to prepare meals in the Spanish rather than the Ciboney style. The first time he had served a broiled yellow and brown corn snake had been the last.

He was wildly protective of both La Floridita and Antonio, following them everywhere with great lurching steps, carrying that dainty yellow and red parasol to protect them from the sun, more awkward and outsized than ever in contrast to his mistress and her adopted brother.

Quirinio was tall too, but slender and sinuous. He reminded La Floridita of the snake Cabeza de Vaca had served. For his interview with her he had groomed himself carefully. His bald head seemed as polished, as beautifully cured as his dark boots. His arched eyebrows had been artificially darkened. He oozed amiability at La Floridita, who sat quietly, dressed in a long white cotton dress devoid of ornament and suited to the climate and her indeterminate station.

"I have merely come to make certain that the house Don Ramón leased is all it should be," he said, beginning with a lie. "That you are comfortable."

"Quite comfortable, Señor," Floridita said, wondering what he wanted. She had offered him a glass of the barely drinkable local wine, which he had accepted. He sat perched on the awkward chair sipping it as if it were the finest Andalusian sherry.

"You were an actress in Spain, were you not, Floridita?" he asked after he had crossed his long legs and looked at the wine through the light from the door. "I have a great love of the theater," he went on, not waiting for an answer. "I saw you perform once in Segovia. It seems so long ago. The play was *La Celestina*. You were brilliant. The toast of Segovia. Your name and praises were on everyone's lips." His own lips were thin and carmine colored, as if nature had had an assist. He passed his hand over his oiled pate, smiling, uncrossing his legs, seemingly at home in the impossible chair.

He finished the pale yellow wine, indicating it was time to get to the point. "I myself, Floridita, own a theater. It is situated on the beautiful island of Cuba in the glorious new port city of Havana. Oh, it is a small theater, but the appointments are superb. No expense has been spared, I assure you."

He hesitated, and so she asked, "And what company is playing in your theater, Señor Quirinio?"

"Alas, it is empty. I am looking for a special person, Floridita. A manager with taste and expertise. Someone who knows theater. Someone who can produce, direct, and star in the lavish productions I dream of for my Teatro de Havana. Cuba—and especially Havana, being such a new sort of place—is remarkably free of Holy Office interference. You would find it a most agreeable place, given your background, Floridita."

"But if Havana is such a new place, Señor Quirinio, who will come to see the plays?" Floridita asked, confused. She had assumed he had come for a simple seduction; he wouldn't have to tempt her with a theater in Cuba for that.

49

"Havana is destined to be one of the truly great cities of the modern world, Floridita. It possesses a great natural harbor. It is situated on the most central of the trade routes between the New and Old Worlds. Already Havana plays host to sailors and merchants and soldiers, many of whom are superior personages, longing for the cultural delights of our mother country."

He crossed his legs again and set the empty glass on the dirt floor. "Shall I come to the point?" he asked, characteristically not waiting for her assent. "You and I might make our fortunes with the Teatro de Havana. You have the skill and the artistic knowledge. I have the capital and, of course, the theater. I will pay your passage and a salary and give you a percentage of the profits. Do not answer me just yet. We must have further conversations, you must have time to—"

"What is the percentage?"

"Ten percent of the net profit."

Floridita gave him her youngest, sweetest smile. "Seventy-five would seem more reasonable, Señor."

"Shall we agree on fifty?" he asked, leaning in her direction, a wave of his perfume enveloping her.

"I will be ready to leave a week from today." She moved a little farther back in Cabeza de Vaca's chair.

"You are a woman who knows her own mind, Floridita," he said, standing up. He would have kissed her hand had she not been holding, so obdurately, her black silk fan. He contented himself with smiling, revealing stained, broken teeth, and saying, "A week from today."

La Floridita remained in that odd chair long after Quirinio had left. She opened the fan Córdoba had given her and began to work it, stirring the breeze that drifted in from the ocean. If Córdoba were alive (and somehow she still believed he was), and if he came back, he would marry Leonora Ponce de León. By then her poverty and her troubles would not be so amusing. She remembered her mother's face, lined and dry, when she had died at twenty-four. Puerto Rico was not a city to offer her opportunities in any direction. She would not be a servant. She had longed for something to turn up, and so it had. One part of her demanded that she stay and wait, insisted that Córdoba was coming back for her. The other—that part of her that was the street child of Seville—knew better.

She had another interview with Quirinio, attempting, not too successfully, to get more information about his theater, convincing him to pay Antonio's and Cabeza de Vaca's passage. "To Havana," Quirinio had said, holding up the glass of thin yellow wine.

"To Havana," La Floridita agreed.

CHAPTER SIX

LA FLORIDITA STOOD ON THE QUARTERDECK of the brig, feeling faint and frightened. Antonio stood at her side, solemn but no longer mute, and Cabeza de Vaca solicitously held the red and yellow parasol over her head, protecting her from the sun.

It was early morning, but already the heat and humidity were making the day uncomfortable. Quirinio had been on the brig, disappearing below, like a bad omen, when she boarded. Clearly he did not want a public association with La Floridita, a red-headed eighteen-year-old woman with a suspicious past, little present, and no future. He had his wife, his family, his good name to think of. Their business association was to remain secret.

The redolent smells of Puerto Rico's harbor—accumulated detritus from the ocean and the stench of human waste from the town—increased her discomfort. She reached out and grasped one of the lines that crisscrossed the deck, reminding her of that voyage aboard *La Nao*.

She wondered at how young she had been then, just a year before, how full of life and spirit. Already most of *La Nao*'s passengers—even Las Mesas—were faded images in her memory; only Córdoba remained insistently alive, his smile and his touch coming back to her at odd moments, making her shiver.

She refused to think of Córdoba. Instead she concentrated on the details of leaving Puerto Rico. Licenses to sail and certificates of confession had been obtained by Quirinio. An Indian slave had come with mule and cart to carry away her possessions. The cart hadn't been necessary, but she had been aware that the more demands she made upon Quirinio the more he would respect her.

They had been driven through the plaza, crowded with soldiers and merchants seeking licenses from the governor and the Church. She felt oddly sentimental about that exuberant plaza, so full of theater and life. Antonio had stopped to say goodbye to his baker, and while they were waiting, La Floridita saw Ponce de León's youngest daughter, Leonora, accompanied by servants, leaving the church, having attended early Mass.

The two women looked at each other for a long moment. And then Leonora, nudged by her duenna, was made to go into the governor's house, where she stood at a window, watching the red-haired beauty who had been Córdoba's mistress leave Puerto Rico for who knew what adventure. Leonora de León, whose life was clearly set out for her like the predictable chapters of a religious book, had never envied anyone more.

Floridita took one last look at the plaza, at the governor's mansion, and wondered what it would be like to stay in that house, where comfort, affection, and protection were to be had effortlessly. And then Antonio, dusted with flour like a rich man's roll, got back onto the cart, and she told the driver to move on. That sort of comfort, affection, and protection weren't for her, and she wouldn't waste her time longing for them.

As the brig with its filthy decks and cutthroat crew moved out of Puerto Rico's port, Floridita stayed topside, watching the island of San Juan recede, thinking again, despite a resolve not to, of Córdoba and their nights of passion in that little house on the hill. She wondered how she was going to live without that consolation. She wondered how he would feel, what he would do if he were indeed alive and returned to Puerto Rico to find her gone. He would follow me, she decided. He would take me back with him to his new land.

She shook her head impatiently. That is not how the world works, she told herself. But still, she couldn't stop herself from believing that one day all the Black Doves would reach the Land of the Flowers, fulfilling the miracle.

La Floridita felt a bit nauseated as the sails filled out with the ocean breeze and the brig picked up speed. She was an eighteen-year-old woman. She had beauty and intelligence and was not oblivious to the desire she instilled in men or the power that desire gave her over them. Ignoring her queasiness, she turned her remarkable green eyes away from Puerto Rico, looking instead toward Havana.

Quirinio disappeared ashore the moment the brig reached Havana. He had, however, arranged for a small open carriage to meet La Floridita. Cabeza de Vaca—ecstatic to be home—and the driver, a native Ciboney, chattered away up front while La Floridita and Antonio sat in the back, looking at their new home.

"It would appear," La Floridita said, struck by the beauty of the natural port and the lack of development, "that there is only one properly finished road." It was called Los Oficios and ran east-west across the plaza. La Floridita played with the fan Córdoba had given her, pretending to ignore the sailors and merchants' clerks who stood staring at the carriage as it passed.

She wished that Quirinio had provided a closed conveyance but supposed that he wanted to display his new actress-manager for publicity purposes. Despite her nausea and the plain provincial gown she wore, she tried to play the part. The air was sweet and clean, and the sky seemed even bluer than it had in Puerto Rico. As she attempted to look sophisticated and worldly, she felt an excitement she couldn't repress. They were in a new place. Another new start. Antonio felt it too. When he turned to her and gave her a genuine boyish smile, he seemed more like fourteen years old than seventeen.

"We have arrived, Antonio," she told him, squeezing his arm.

"It is a very new place, is it not, Floridita?" he said, looking about him at the primitive colonists' houses, not much better than the crude, thatched adobe huts of the Ciboneys.

"It reminds me of Seville," La Floridita said, suddenly not quite so happy. The poor adobe buildings with their troughs and pumps evoked a picture of the slums she had been raised in. The houses stood cheek by jowl on rough streets that the planners had purposely made narrow and thus easier to defend against attackers than wide boulevards.

They were easier to cool as well. La Floridita looked up at another memory from Spain: shade awnings stretched across the narrow streets from house to house, protecting those passing below from the sun. "Did you have to attach the awnings each morning?" she asked Antonio, thinking how she had liked to do that as a girl, rising before anyone else, running up to the roof, alone for just that moment.

"We didn't have close neighbors," Antonio said, and she remembered that he had grown up in a rich house with servants who performed such tasks. She felt alone again as they passed into the Plaza de Armas. She was depressed by the church, constructed of wattle and mud, with only a poor thatched roof. "They should at least get a tiled roof for the church," she said, shocked at that particular sign of the city's poverty.

But Havana was a provincial city, only recently founded. Cuba's capital, Santiago de Cuba, was a thriving city, but Havana was an afterthought. It had been established because a port was needed on the Caribbean, and, after several false starts, it had finally been located between a natural deep-water harbor and the open ocean.

Havana exceeded all expectations. Fortuitously situated on what had developed into the major trade route between Spain and her New World colonies, it became in a short time the New World's most important port. In plan Havana differed little from Puerto Rico and was built according to the pattern set by the Council of the Indies: a central plaza around which the church and other official buildings faced one another. The streets, such as they were, radiated from the plaza.

La Floridita noted the new merchants' and colonial administrators' houses boasting tiled roofs and made not from adobe but from *mamposteria*—broken stone and sand mixed with plaster. She was rapidly losing her enthusiasm. "I would like to know," she said, assuming her duchess airs as the carriage rumbled away from the plaza and back along the waterfront, "where the rich and titled audiences Quirinio spoke of are hiding their houses and their personages. I would like to know—or perhaps I would not—where the most magnificent theater in the New World is located—this perfect jewel, this flawless gem." She closed her fan. "I have a terrible feeling, *niño*, that we would have been better off had we stayed in Puerto Rico. What is that disgusting smell?"

A pervasive odor of rotting meat, spoiling the air, came from an open market, Havana's principal slaughterhouse. The mules had decided, mercurially, to stop in front of it. Bloody beef, fly-encrusted, hung from hooks. Hides were the principal export from Cuba to Spain, the Spanish having an insatiable need for leather. La Floridita looked at the raw beef and the stretched hides, inhaling that unforgettable odor of death and chemicals and began to shiver despite the late afternoon sun. "I am going to be sick."

"You are never sick," Antonio said.

"I must get out."

Cabeza de Vaca lumbered down to assist his mistress. He and Antonio held her as La Floridita was indeed sick. She stopped retching finally and, holding onto Antonio as Cabeza de Vaca went to find water, unexpectedly laughed. "A glorious entrance for the Teatro de Havana's new actress manager." Cabeza de Vaca returned with a cup of water and an invitation from the proprietor of the Rojas Ships' Store and Chandlery, Señora Amelia Rojas, to rest for a moment in a cool place.

Amelia Rojas had watched—as had most citizens of Havana—La Floridita's progress in her open carriage from the port, through the plaza, and back to the waterfront. It wasn't only the red hair and green eyes and that extraordinary white skin that attracted notice and instantaneous gossip. She was riding in the carriage belonging to La Casa de las Niñas, driven by one of the Casa's Indian slaves. She must be, it was thought, one of the new *niñas*, one of Quirinio's new girls.

Amelia Rojas, widow, aged twenty, standing in her chandlery, was even more interested in the red-headed woman's companion. She stared at him with her big and plaintive brown eyes and thought she had never seen a more beautiful man. The sea voyage had completed Antonio Levi's physical recovery. His hair was bleached nearly white and his skin was as brown as his fair complexion allowed. He had an appealing, confused look about him, as if he were continually finding himself in places he didn't expect to be.

Amelia Rojas told herself not to be a fool and opened the doors of her chandlery to the woman who was the object of all Havana's curiosity. She did admit that she opened them a bit more readily because of the blond young man, and then she told herself again not to be such a fool and dutifully tried to fill her mind with the fast-receding image of her dead husband.

She watched the slow progress of the red-headed woman and the pale blond man, assisted by the odd-looking Ciboney. She welcomed them, introduced herself, got the ailing woman into a chair, and had a slave bring a dampened cloth for her forehead. After supplying her with a glass of *aguardiente*, a biscuit, and a great deal of motherly comfort, Amelia sat back, at-

54

tempting to suppress her curiosity. These two were so young and so obviously new to colonial Spain. They reminded her of Roberto and herself when they had first arrived. Amelia Rojas wished that she could give them her knowledge, so hard earned, along with the hardtack and the sherry. Her heart ached for what she knew they would have to learn.

"The señora, is she going to die?" Cabeza de Vaca, frightened, asked in his odd Spanish.

Amelia laughed. "The señora, she is going to live. The señora is full of life. Her own. And someone else's." She looked, with those big brown eyes, at the beautiful young man and realized he had no idea what she was talking about. Amelia Rojas took pity on his ignorance. "Your wife," she said, "is going to have a child. A certain amount of illness is to be expected."

Antonio looked at Floridita. He was pale and surprised but happy. "She is not my wife."

"I am his sister," La Floridita said, holding onto the side of the chair she was sitting in, afraid she might faint. Of course, she told herself, I'm with child. I should have known, but the grief hid it from me. Attempting recovery, hoping to erase the shocked look from Señora Rojas's plump, pretty face, she tried a smile. "My husband," she improvised, "is exploring the north islands with Don Juan Ponce de León." She looked at Antonio and touched his cheek. "I have not made my condition known to my brother in order not to unnecessarily worry him. We have come to Havana to await my husband and to take over the directorship of Señor Quirinio's Teatro de Havana."

"Teatro de Havana? There is no theater in Havana, Señora." Amelia Rojas spoke with such finality, there didn't seem to be any reason to doubt her. "There is a place," she went on hesitantly, "sometimes associated with Señor Quirinio. Men go there to gamble and drink and have other pleasures. It is known as La Casa de las Niñas. It would not be an appropriate house for a woman with child, though there are many women there."

La Floridita took this in and understood it all in a moment. She knew why Quirinio didn't want to be publicly associated with her and why, after that dissociation, he had paraded her through the streets of Havana in La Casa de las Niñas' open carriage. She was to be the new attraction at his "theater."

"Is there an inn, Señora?" she asked after a moment.

"You could not stay there. Please, you must remain with me. At least until you make your plans. My house is large and empty, and I should so much like to have you here."

Floridita accepted Amelia Rojas's offer and allowed herself to be persuaded by the woman to retire, to forget her troubles, to rest, if only for the sake of her unborn child. As she drifted to sleep under the other woman's ministrations, Floridita thought of Córdoba. She saw, in her mind's eye, his smile; she felt his touch. He would never be dead now. She was carrying his child, and for that child she would do whatever she had to.

* * *

Amelia looked down at the sleeping woman, recognizing the grief and pain of lost love on the lovely, pale face. Like Roberto, she sensed that La Floridita's husband would not be returning. She felt an overwhelming compassion for this woman, a kinship based on her own experiences.

Amelia and her husband, Roberto, had been in love since they had been children, New Christians, growing up in Segovia. Their fathers had been wealthy merchants, Jews converted to Christianity for safety's and commerce's sake rather than out of genuine conviction.

But Roberto Rojas had been a secret practitioner of the Hebrew faith, constantly chafing against the constraints of Inquisitional Spain. He had, at the first opportunity, married Amelia, persuading her to accompany him to the New World, where they could, he hoped, shed their New Christianity and live a finer, freer life according to the tenets of Judaism.

But Roberto Rojas had been bitten by a rat on the ship crossing the Atlantic and had contracted the plague. He had seemed to recover in Havana's temperate weather, was taken unexpectedly ill again, and died a year after his arrival in Cuba.

Amelia had grieved deeply, but she was, after all, a shrewd businessman's daughter. She had risen to the occasion. The chandlery was already a success, Havana's port becoming more popular each day. The complications and hardships of managing a business she knew little about, of living in a place where she had neither acquaintances nor family to fall back upon, took all the energy she might have spent mourning Roberto. When she thought of him, it was with an affection tinged with impatience. "It was so like Roberto," she said to herself, "to take me from my comfortable home to this savage place and then die."

She turned away from the sleeping woman, hoping that she would prove resilient and strong enough to survive the situation she had been manipulated into. She didn't have much hope. Amelia Rojas knew Quirinio's reputation.

Three days later, after a deliberately leisurely breakfast, La Floridita set out with Cabeza de Vaca protectively holding the parasol over her in Quirinio's open carriage. Quirinio had located her quickly enough, but she had had Antonio answer all his messages with the announcement that "La Floridita is weary from her journey." She let him stew those three days. She told Antonio—who had been helping Amelia Rojas in the chandlery, making candles, storing rope—that she didn't want Quirinio to think that she had no other choice but to do what he wished. "I want him to believe that we have possibilities. That we have friends in Havana."

"We do," Antonio said, looking at Amelia Rojas.

The house was impressive from a distance, one of Havana's largest. It was built in the shape of an E without the middle bar. A high adobe wall surrounded it and a tiled roof gave it the feeling of Spain. But the wall needed repair, and as La Floridita and Cabeza de Vaca drew near, they could see that tiles were missing from the roof, and the elaborate gate was swinging open, one of its hinges missing.

La Floridita and Cabeza de Vaca—the latter holding the parasol high—got out of the carriage and stepped through the gate into a courtyard strewn with garbage. Half a dozen bleary-eyed Spanish seamen were just leaving. "New merchandise," one of the sailors said, eyeing her. She covered her hair and part of her face with her mantilla, as if she could protect herself from his eyes, from the house she was about to enter. A servant had opened a door, and behind it Quirinio was smiling, his bald head shining as if it had been given a last-moment polish.

He was all affability as he escorted her through a narrow passage into a room that accommodated his height. It had a high beamed ceiling, tiled floors, and windows opening onto a small but luxuriant garden. The scent of jasmine and orange blossoms fought with Quirinio's perfume, and La Floridita forced herself, by an effort of will, not to be sick again. She concentrated on the religious paintings Quirinio had hung on the walls and studied the furniture: leather chairs, a beautifully crafted desk, a daybed she didn't like the look of.

"*Aguardiente?* Biscuits?" Quirinio asked, indicating a leather chair, seating himself on the daybed.

"I have not come here for refreshment, Señor Quirinio," she said, trying to set a tone, attempting to mask her fear. If this wouldn't work out, Floridita had no idea what she would do. She was alone, with child, and moneyless in a city two steps away from the jungle. Still, she knew she had to appear strong.

Quirinio lay on the daybed, his head propped up by a pillow, his long legs crossed, sipping at a glass of *aguardiente*. When she was a child, a man with a caged monkey would come through her neighborhood, forcing the monkey to do tricks. Quirinio, oiled and perfumed, reminded her of the monkey's master, a thin smile always in place. He inquired about her health. He spoke about the furniture that he had made, the paintings he had brought from Spain, the garden he had designed and that flourished despite the Ciboneys' inability to comprehend ornamental growth.

He indicated that he could spend the day talking about her health, his possessions. That he had nothing else on his mind. La Floridita knew she too could not be in a hurry. She opened her fan and busied herself with it as he spoke, disturbing the warm, too sweet air. At last Quirinio touched the top of his bald head with the tips of his splayed fingers gently, as if his skull were made from some especially fragile material, and said, "Perhaps we should talk about the theater."

"There is no theater," La Floridita said after a long moment. "There is no theater in Havana."

"Of course not. I thought you understood." He sat up. "I assumed you were more worldly, Señora. Most people understand that the word 'theater' is a euphemism, another way of saying . . ." He held his hands out in a gesture meant to convey sympathy, despair, leavened with humor.

La Floridita stood up. "And that offer you made to me in Puerto Rico, Señor Quirinio? To manage this 'theater.' Was that some other subtlety I did not understand, or did you simply want me to 'act' in it?"

"My dear Floridita, I meant every word I said." He too stood up, and even that oversized room seemed too small for him. "I have interests throughout the New World. I am leaving in the morning to attend to them. I made a bargain with you, and I assume we will both keep to it. The last manager, a Portuguese harlot I was taken in by, ran off with a slaver a month ago, nearly destroying my business." He moved a step closer. "You will be wonderfully adept at managing this house. After all, what greater theater is there in the world than the one in which men attempt to buy—and women to sell—their passion?"

She moved away, out of range of his perfume, allowing him to give her a glass of *aguardiente* as a delaying tactic. She accepted a biscuit. The room, the house itself, was the most luxurious she had ever been in. She had no compunctions about becoming the manager of a bordello. It was better than working in one, but she wanted to make that point clear.

"I will not sell *my* passion. You understand that, Quirinio?"

"There will be certain royal personages, *adelantados*, members of the Church . . ."

"I will not sell my passion."

Before she could stop him, he had wrapped his arms around her and kisssed her, moving his odd, wide-tipped fingers under her bodice, touching her full breasts. She pushed him away. "I am with child."

"Good. Then I shall not have another bastard to support." He pushed her down onto the daybed and fell on top of her, lifting her gown. The smell of his perfume was overpowering now, his moonlike face with the painted eyebrows like an image in a dream. "I have wanted you more than I have ever wanted anyone in my life." He had removed his codpiece, and she could feel his flesh pressing against her. But La Floridita hadn't survived the slums of Seville—protecting her virginity for that moment when she needed it—without learning something. She brought her knee up quickly, with just enough force to render him helpless for the moment.

"I mean what I say, Quirinio." He had fallen back onto the tiled floor, having screamed once. "You will find in our future dealings that that is always true. I will say this just once: I make love only to men *I* want to make love to."

He lay still for some moments and then, painfully, got himself up. Not looking at her, he retrieved his codpiece and limped out of the room, shouting for a servant. La Floridita rearranged her garments, ate another biscuit, poured herself another drop of the *aguardiente*. She looked around her. It was the most beautiful room.

He returned a quarter of an hour later looking grim. "If I did not have to leave on the morrow, Floridita . . ."

"And if you did not need someone to take over immediately, Quirinio . . ."

"I have underestimated you, Floridita. For the last time. My offer, however, still stands."

"Then I accept your offer. Sixty percent of all net profits—"

"Fifty, and I shall be very careful, my dear, when going over the accounts."

"—and I shall need separate apartments for myself, my servant, and Señor Levi. That is, separate from the rest of the 'theater.' Is that possible?" He nodded yes. "And a free and total hand in the theater's operation. I will make you a fortune, Quirinio. That is what I promise you."

"You must begin tomorrow. There is no one—"

"Provided I receive a signed letter of agreement from you tonight and you vacate your apartments in the morning. I shall move in and take over tomorrow at noon. In the future, anything you wish to convey to me may be done through my adviser, Señor Levi."

"There is one thing I am going to convey to you in person, Floridita," Quirinio said, standing up, unable to hide his anger, knowing he was trapped for the time being. "Next time I am in Havana. I promise you and myself that." He stood up, with some pain, and opened the door. "You shall have your agreement tonight."

The agreement, written on parchment, was delivered that evening. Antonio and Amelia—the only woman Floridita had ever known who could read—studied it carefully and pronounced it sound. Floridita signed it with her mark, Antonio and Amelia witnessing it.

In the morning La Floridita said goodbye to her hostess. "You won't want to know me after today," Floridita said, holding out her hand to the wise, pretty woman who had been so sympathetic.

Amelia Rojas refused her hand and instead opened her arms. For a moment Floridita allowed herself a comfort she had never known before. She let her head rest against the well-upholstered shoulder, feeling warm and protected, her eyes closed. For that moment she didn't have to be an astute business woman, pretending to everyone around her that she knew what she was doing, that she was in full control. For that moment she was a girl, vulnerable and frightened.

Long after she had renounced all women as potential allies, Floridita knew she had found one. The warmth and good wishes emanating from the embrace of the Jewish widow, only two years older than herself, gave her strength and comfort.

"We may not be acquainted during the day," Amelia Rojas said, releasing her. Amelia was, after all, a businesswoman herself, eminently practical. "My business and respectability thrive on each other and keep the priests at bay. But there is nothing to deter us from being friends under cover of night. When you are ready," Amelia said, glancing at Floridita's slightly thickening waist, "I will come to help, day or night, Señora."

"Señora Córdoba," Floridita said, naming herself forever after the man who had been her natural husband. "But you must call me Floridita." She kissed Amelia on the cheek and was gone.

The weather had changed. Gray clouds hung low over Havana and a northwesterly was beginning to blow. Quirinio had left the Casa de las Niñas that morning and had set sail for Peru.

La Floridita arrived in the open carriage in the early afternoon, Antonio beside her, Cabeza de Vaca urging the two white mules on. The courtyard was filthy but empty except for a shy, slight servant, a baptized Ciboney named Simone, who had been sitting, cross-legged, waiting for her.

They stood in the courtyard under the dark sky while La Floridita gave instructions. Simone was to take Antonio to the counting room, where he could study the ledgers. Cabeza de Vaca was to see to the cleaning of their private apartments. She herself wanted to look at the public rooms and then at the salons where the clients received their services.

"Would you not like to rest first, Floridita?" Antonio asked, putting one of his beautiful hands on her shoulder.

"I would," she said, "but we have business to attend to, *niño.*" She made a tentative move toward the house but stopped and looked around the courtyard, as if she were buying time, as if she were unwilling to commit herself by entering the Casa.

"Señora does not wish to see the women first?" Simone asked, waiting under the portico, surprised. "Señor Quirinio said you would want to see the women first, Señora."

"If I am going to create a theater of passion, I had better begin with the set, then go on to the props, and interview the actresses last."

"What about the play?" Antonio asked. He was intrigued, as always, by the businesslike manner Floridita assumed whenever she set out to accomplish a task of which she wasn't quite certain. She might have had her doubts, but no one watching her would realize it.

"We all know the play," Floridita said. "It is how it is produced that is important." Antonio, for one, did not know the play but decided not to admit that for the time being. He looked at her as they stood in that courtyard under the nearly black sky, recognizing that haughty expression as a mask for her fear, and he too suddenly felt frightened.

Finally the heavens opened up and it began to rain, a thick tropical rain, the water coming down in what seemed like solid sheets. For a moment they stood in the downpour, allowing it to soak them through, as if they were being purified in some New World baptismal rite. And then Cabeza de Vaca opened the door, Antonio Levi stepped aside, and La Floridita entered La Casa de Las Niñas.

CHAPTER SEVEN

IN 1519 Hernando Cortes conquered Mexico with four hundred men and six horses. In less than a year—with the treasures of the Aztecs sent to Castile via Havana—Spain replaced France as the most powerful nation in the world.

Two years later, in 1521, Ponce de León decided to return to his island and colonize it. His wife had died. He had remarried a young and charming woman. He was rich and renowned. He could have retired gracefully to his cotton plantations and lived out his years as an esteemed elder statesman. But his dream of gold and glory had been stolen by Cortes, his name eclipsed. While Cortes was becoming the hero of Spain, Ponce de León was fighting a devastating and obscure bush war in the Lesser Antilles against the Caribs. Though he had cowed them, he hadn't received many rewards for his efforts. He felt used, tired, old. But not too old to forget his Florida, to give himself one last chance to fulfill his dream, to have his name set alongside that of his old commander, Christopher Columbus, and his rival, Hernando Cortes.

He squeezed every penny he could out of his San Juan cotton plantations, finding enough money to equip two ships—a caravel and a brig—and set out to find gold in the Land of the Flowers.

Being a practical man, he meant to colonize his island as he stripped it of its riches, bringing with him two hundred colonists, fifty horses, six priests, and assorted livestock and farm implements. In early February 1521, after an uneventful voyage, the two ships arrived at the beautiful oblong inlet on Florida's southwest coast, which would one day be called Charlotte Harbor, near the future Fort Meyers. Charlotte Harbor, teeming with fish, reminded Ponce de León of that other harbor, on the east coast, where his young friend Ramón de Córdoba had been taken seven years before.

At dawn on the following day Ponce de León was in the first boat ashore. Appropriate prayers were said, and soon the sound of the men's axes could be heard, metallic and relentless, frightening away birds and other animal life. By the time the sun went down, a series of crude buildings had been erected and the men prepared to retire.

When the first fires were lit, the Indians, making that reverberating, unholy war cry, attacked. The men fought in the firelight with swords and daggers. But the Indians, who crouched low and jumped high, routed them easily with fire-hardened, shell-tipped arrows. Over a hundred Spaniards—colonists, soldiers, priests—were killed. The others—including a wounded Ponce de León—ignominiously escaped in the longboats to the ships waiting in Charlotte Harbor.

Ponce de León, despite his wound, insisted on staying topside, watching. The Indians, whose village lay just south, at Eastero Bay, built huge fires, burning the remains of the crude shelters the colonists had erected, illuminating the terrible scene on the beach.

Squaws undressed the white men—some still alive—cutting off their genitalia, skinning their legs and stripping them of muscle to secure the long bones needed for the victory ritual. The braves, ignoring this woman's work, were fascinated by the horses that had been brought ashore. They had never seen such animals and approached them warily, believing them to be related to the treacherous greyhounds Spanish slavers used to capture their people.

In the morning Ponce de León's flagship, the *San Telmo*, sailed for the closest port, Havana. The city had changed a great deal in the years since Cortes's lieutenant, Pedro de Alvarado, had sailed into Havana Bay after his master's victory, on his way from Veracruz to Spain, heading a treasure fleet carrying gold, jewels, and feathered Aztec cloaks. Alvarado's fleet was later attacked by French privateers, who cut out two of the galleons off the Azores. The Spanish, afraid of more attacks, began to form convoys to protect themselves from the dangerous run across the Atlantic. The convoys invariably met and departed from Havana, bringing a steady prosperity to that port.

When the *San Telmo* docked in Havana, the city's surgeon found that the ship's surgeon had removed the arrow from Ponce de León's thigh too quickly. Part of it lay embedded in the bone, close to the femoral artery. There was nothing to be done. It was said that a beautiful woman with flaming red hair visited Ponce de León on his deathbed. She came to ask him about a lost love, a hidalgo who had been taken by Florida's Indians on Ponce de León's first voyage of discovery. But in his fever Ponce de León believed she was asking about his island, his Florida. "Lost forever," he said just before he died.

Ponce de León's body was taken to San Juan, where he was buried. He left his title and his plantations to his family and his dream of conquering his island, Florida, the Land of the Flowers, to others.

In that same year, 1521, Francisco de Gordillo sailed up the Atlantic coast from Florida to South Carolina, proving Florida was a peninsula, not an island. But for a time Ponce de León's failure discouraged serious colonization attempts. *Cabalgadas*—slave-hunting parties—did not, however, apply to the Crown for patents, and often during the fifteen years after Ponce de León's death they hunted the Florida coast.

Ponce de León's sovereign, Don Fernando, had died, and Cardinal Cisneros, the regent, remained unconvinced of Florida's potential. However, the new emperor—Charles I, founder of the Hapsburg dynasty—allowed a patent to be issued. It was given to Pánfilo de Narváez, more to rid Spain of him than from any genuine belief in Florida's riches. In 1527 Narváez traveled to Havana from Spain with four ships and a small brigantine, eighty horses, and four hundred men, who had been promised enough gold to make their fortunes. The gold was to come from Florida's Indians and from the land Narváez swore to conquer.

CHAPTER EIGHT

1527

AFTER NEARLY FIFTEEN YEARS La Casa de Las Niñas seemed at first little changed. The handsome desk had been placed in front of the open windows overlooking the tropical garden, now more lush and less manicured. The daybed had been removed, but the religious paintings remained. A small pale pink rug had been introduced, warming the dark tiled floor. Red and pink flowers—hibiscus and bougainvillea—were arranged in natural clay Ciboney pots and bowls and replaced each day. It remained an elegant, formal, high-ceilinged room, but it had become inviting as well as beautiful. More than one disarmed purveyor of goods—victuals, wine, reputed virgins—had to remind himself he was in the reception room of a Cuban bordello and not in a grandee's sitting room in Seville.

Pánfilo de Narváez's steward, a captain named Balbontine—a man not usually concerned with fine settings—was impressed nonetheless as he stood in the center of that high-ceilinged reception room. The woman behind the exquisite desk returned his inquisitive stare with the greenest eyes he had ever seen. What's more, she was actually saying no to his request.

La Floridita had changed in much the way the room had. At thirty-three—when most women of her time were considered middle-aged—La Floridita was more beautiful than she had ever been. An old customer and longtime suitor called her the ripest rose in La Casa's bouquet, though she warned him and others that she was not ready to be plucked.

Her skin, protected by Cabeza de Vaca and his parasol, was as fine and white as it had been when she was eighteen, her hair as thick and as startlingly red as it was that day when she arrived and paraded across Los Oficios in Quirinio's open carriage. If her breasts and her hips were fuller, she still gave the impression of being slender and, when she chose, vulnerable.

Quirinio had not lived long enough either to pursue his threatened enjoyment of La Floridita or benefit by the success of her efforts. He had been killed by French pirates who had taken his brig off the coast of Peru. The ownership of La Casa had gone by default to La Floridita. Concerned for his afterlife reputation, Quirinio had left no record of La Casa, not wanting his executors or his confessor to discover that a portion of his wealth came from a brothel.

"Señora," the steward repeated carefully, attempting diplomacy, "perhaps I have not made myself clear. The great soldier and *adelantado* Pánfilo de Narváez has arrived just this day in your port. He intends to reserve the entire facilities of La Casa for his men while he and they are here."

"You mean, Captain, that Pánfilo de Narváez's reputation for disaster is confirming itself once again. Half of his men are threatening to desert, his treatment of them having been not far better than the notorious way he has dealt with the Indians during previous sojourns in the New World. Now the great Narváez wants to turn his men loose on my actresses. He thinks the promise of many nights in La Casa will go a long way to appease them." She put her fine hands together and stared down at them but not before Balbontine had seen the anger in those green eyes.

"But my actresses, Captain, are not cows," she went on after a moment, looking at him again, the anger replaced by determination. "La Casa is not a cattle ranch. If Don Pánfilo would like to make separate appointments for his men, if he would like to discuss individual rather than wholesale prices, I suggest that he talk to *my* steward, Cabeza de Vaca."

Balbontine thought he should be the one to be furious, but all that he felt was amazement, as if a dog had spoken. It was difficult to believe that the fragile-looking woman sitting behind that desk had such knowledge—How on earth had she learned about the men's threatened desertion?—and spoke with such authority. La Floridita was, he had been told, one of the more important women in the New World. But even in Spain important women were rare and usually turned out to be puppets of powerful men. He had been disdainful when told that a woman who ran a colonial whorehouse was both intelligent and influential, but to his surprise, Balbontine now rather believed that she was both.

"Narváez," he ended up saying, "never forgets, Señora. And he never forgives."

"You should embroider that on a sampler for him, Captain. And now I have other—"

But before she could dismiss Balbontine, a thick door on the far side of the room leading to her private apartments crashed open, and the most handsome youth the captain had ever seen raced into the room. He had blue-

64

black hair, an infectious smile revealing remarkably white, even teeth, and an air of such liveliness, such infectious curiosity, that it was difficult not to return his smile. It was clear that he was the woman's son if only because of his eyes, emerald green, electric with the excitement of being alive.

"Mama," he said, "I have just come from the harbor. Pánfilo de Narváez's ships are in, and everyone says he will be sailing to Florida to find—"

"Ramón," La Floridita said, standing up, "you know you are not to interrupt me here."

"But, Mama, Pánfilo de Narváez has come to Havana. He—"

"That is enough, Ramón. Please leave at once. I shall talk to you presently."

Ramón de Córdoba—La Floridita had given her son as well as herself the benefit of his father's name—said, "Yes, Mama," and cast down his eyes as if he were properly chastened. But as the boy left he smiled at his mother. It was an unforgettable smile, filled with rueful exuberance and naughty charm. Pánfilo de Narváez's dour steward found himself smiling too. He wondered if he—or if anyone—had ever been that young or that happy.

After the boy had left, his mother—La Floridita—pulled on a brocaded cord, summoning Cabeza de Vaca to escort Balbontine out of La Casa. She too had trouble suppressing a smile, evincing the first positive emotion Balbontine had seen in her: maternal love. He thought, as he made his way back to the harbor and Pánfilo de Narváez, that La Floridita had been more than a match for him, but that her son would never lose in any real contest with her.

It was going to be a different sort of battle when Pánfilo de Narváez took to the field. That he would, Captain Balbontine had no doubt. The captain was not looking forward to conveying La Floridita's answer.

Alone in her office, Floridita remained at her desk, contemplating those fine white hands, thinking she had worked too hard and too long to allow herself to be ordered around by another arrogant Spanish conquistador.

It had taken her years. In the beginning every penny she had earned had been put back into La Casa, refurnishing and refinishing each and every apartment, public and private. La Casa had become the richest, most important building in Havana. It provided all sorts of entertainment: fine foods and wines, refined company, and less refined amusements. It was the most democratic institution in Havana, a theater—La Floridita maintained—in which class lines were, if not ignored, at least not a barrier to enjoyment. Sea captains and colonial administrators, ships' crews and plantation owners could assemble and feel comfortable. It was a house that catered with great imagination to the needs of men away from home and, increasingly, to the needs of men at home, as Havana grew into the New World's most important port and women were at a premium.

The single gate had been replaced by four: one for soldiers, seamen, crew; another for officers and gentlemen; a discreet one for those who didn't want their patronage known; and a fourth for La Floridita and the members of her personal household.

The wine and the food were the best, it was agreed, in the New World. The actresses were Spanish, Portuguese, French, Ciboney, and one memorable lady who claimed she was an English lord's daughter, captured and resold by a succession of pirates. When Floridita overheard the pale girl curse in fluent street Spanish she had had her doubts, but she kept them to herself. She was not trading in reality.

There were few brawls. In the public rooms, tiled and columned, with a full moon, clouds, and stars painted on the ceilings creating permanent night, the atmosphere demanded decorum. What went on in the private apartments was rarely discussed outside of them.

La Floridita made one appearance each evening, establishing the tone of the night's performance, ascertaining that all was as it should be. She always wore long gowns of white woven with golden threads, made of San Juan's finest cotton. She carried the fan Córdoba had given her but had replaced his black mantilla with a white one. It was said she was in mourning, but few had the temerity to ask for whom or for what.

She had told Quirinio that she would never sell her passion, and she hadn't. But there had been occasions over the years when, for political reasons, she had given her favors away. There had been a nephew of the king who presented her with a huge ruby. This she had sold, using the proceeds to give the church a tiled roof. Later there had been a bishop and after him a governor who had secured for La Casa licenses of trade in perpetuity, and two or three members of the colonial Holy Office, which regularly issued certificates of confession to all the inhabitants of La Casa. When a French pirate sacked the town, he spared La Casa after an episode with La Floridita.

She had thus built up her protection until La Casa was a monument that could withstand virtually any attack—certainly one from such an adventurer as Pánfilo de Narváez.

"You turned Pánfilo de Narváez down without even a counteroffer?" Antonio asked, having passed Balbontine in the courtyard. He seemed even paler than usual, pacing back and forth across the reception room. "Do you want hundreds of men descending on La Casa, paying nothing and leaving nothing, Floridita?"

She looked up at him and smiled. A somewhat chastened Ramón sat beside his mother. "Do you know who Pánfilo de Narváez is?" Antonio stood for a moment behind Ramón's chair, resting his hands on the boy's shoulders, not letting her answer him. "He was a shipmate of Ponce de León's on Columbus's second voyage. He has scavenged around the Indies since he was a boy. He is a giant, ugly as sin, with hair as red as yours, carrying around masses of scars from his battles with Moors, Indians, Frenchmen, our own countrymen. He has been captured and lovingly tortured by the Hispaniola Indians. As a consequence he has perfected the art of torture himself. The fiercest Indians turn white when they hear his name, Floridita."

"Antonio," she began, "I beg you—"

But he wouldn't stop. "He was sent by the Crown's Indies representative, Velásquez, seven years ago to Mexico to arrest Cortes. No one else would take on the job. But Cortes arrested him first, Narváez losing an eye in the process. Next thing anyone knew, he was Cortes's most trusted lieutenant, both of them agreeing that torture and slavery were the only road that would lead the Aztecs to Christianity. The sole reason the emperor gave him—"

"Antonio, I know—"

"—a patent was to get him out of the way so he could get on with his war with the French. Pánfilo de Narváez is—"

"Niño, stop! Please!" Floridita stood up, laughing, putting her arms around the man she thought of as her brother. He had filled out in the last fifteen years but he was still slim, and his hair had remained so fair, it was nearly white. "I remember," she said, pulling him down into one of the leather chairs, keeping one of her fine hands over his mouth, "when you would not say a word, and now you will not shut up. Antonio," she said, "I know all about Pánfilo de Narváez, and when his steward returns—as he most certainly will—I shall offer him a reasonable alternative to closing La Casa to everyone but Narváez's ruffians."

"What if he sets them lose, Floridita, on La Casa?"

"He will not. He has many enemies here as it is, and the uproar would be too much even for the Crown. His patent would be revoked—"

"Have you seen the ships, Antonio?" Ramón couldn't help asking. "He is going to Florida to find gold and precious stones, to have great adventures and perhaps, even, to find my father. If I could only go with him . . ."

"That is enough, Ramón," Floridita said in a voice he knew enough to obey. "Why don't you go to your quarters and study?" she asked, looking up, giving in to a smile, receiving the boy's kiss, kissing him in return. "He sounds like his father," she said to Antonio after Ramón had gone. "Much too much like his father."

"He is a man, Floridita," Antonio said, sipping the *aguardiente* Cabeza de Vaca had brought him.

"He is a boy," she insisted, standing up, turning to the windows and the garden, trying not to reveal her anguish. "He is apprenticed to you. He is going to be a rich merchant. He is going to stay with me. . . ."

"No, Floridita," Antonio said, going to her. "He is too curious. He does not want to live in dull Havana. He wants—just like his father—to explore new lands."

"He will change." She couldn't bear the thought of Ramón's leaving her. "People change," she said, turning to him. "Look at you, *niño*."

"You changed me," he said, taking her hands, looking at Floridita with the warmth he reserved for her. "You and Amelia."

When Ramón was a month old and Floridita was beginning to rebuild La Casa, the widow Rojas, Amelia, had asked Antonio Levi to marry her.

"I need help with the chandlery, she had said, which was true; the two clerks she had hired and the three Ciboneys she had bought needed more supervision than she could provide. Sea traffic was growing at an extraordinary rate, attracted by Havana's location and perfect harbor.

"I also need affection," she had added boldly. "So do you. What is more, we are both unconvinced New Christians." She had let that sink in for a moment, and then she added the final and, for her, the most authoritative argument: "La Floridita agrees that a marriage between us would be a most advantageous union."

Ideas, not necessarily of marriage but of some sort of union with Amelia Rojas had been upsetting Antonio. Living and working in Floridita's theater had given him, finally, a very good idea of what the play was. He had found himself increasingly aware of the plump and pretty widow Rojas and never more so than at that moment when she had proposed.

It was late in the day. They were standing in the closed chandlery, surrounded by ships' stores, barrels of aromatic pickled meats, coils of hand-woven ropes. The Ciboneys had put out the lamps, and the only illumination came from the flame of a single candle. "I would have to continue looking after Floridita's books and accounts," he said, not knowing where to put his hands or his eyes, his cheeks going red, betraying his need for her.

"Of course," Amelia said, coming from behind a counter.

"And I would want to instruct her child when he reaches a certain age, to teach him his letters, his numbers, his history."

"I would not have it any other way," the indefatigably good-natured Amelia said, a soft smile on her pretty, plump face. She longed to put her healthy arms around him, to hold his thin body close to hers, to caress his white-blond hair, his girl's skin.

"But you are a widow," Antonio said almost accusingly, retreating. "Sophisticated in the ways of marriage." His back was up against one of the rough-hewn beams that supported the low ceiling. "I am not well versed in matrimony."

"I shall teach you the ways of marriage, Antonio," Amelia said, cornering him, taking him in her arms, putting her soft, giving lips against his.

He shed his first, damaged youth in the next few years, finding himself suddenly whole and—he couldn't quite believe it—happy. If occasionally he woke in the night, choking, the smell of his mother's flesh burning in his nostrils, and had to get up and stand on the balcony and look out at the harbor to keep from screaming . . . well, that was not a great price to pay for the life Amelia and La Floridita had given him. "The Holy Savior has given it to you," Floridita said, correcting him. "Even if you are not a convinced Christian, He believes you are worthy. He gave you the miracle."

"Being a Black Dove was only my first miracle, Floridita. Amelia is the second."

"There will be a third," Floridita said. "When we fly to the Land of the Flowers and are reunited with Córdoba." As the years went on, she believed more and more in Córdoba's survival and their ultimate reunion. It was a dream that allowed her to keep other men from pursuing her too seriously, but it also sprang from a great loyalty to the miracle. "Our journey, our miracle," she liked to say to Antonio as they sat drinking *aguardiente* in her reception room at the end of each day, "is not over."

"I am," Antonio liked to whisper to his wife late at night as Amelia held him in her arms, "a man of many miracles."

Pánfilo de Narváez did not send his steward a second time to bargain with La Floridita. He came himself, and he came that night. When he had learned about the loss of two of his ships and the desertion of two hundred men, he had gone berserk. And now a madam of a provincial bordello was telling him, Pánfilo de Narváez, that his custom was not welcome. He stormed ashore and strode into La Casa, pushing aside Cabeza de Vaca and the other stewards—stalwart men—as if they were so many wisps of straw.

Narváez crashed into the reception room and suddenly stopped short. He was surprised, not only at the appointments of the room but mainly at the woman who sat fully composed, looking as if she had been waiting for him—and not with fear. Balbontine had offered him the barest information, and he had expected an old woman, a crone who wanted to haggle. He stood in front of the desk, towering over it, for once in a room where the ceiling was high enough for him. And for once he found himself at a loss for words.

Floridita sat perfectly still, patient, looking up at the red-headed giant. He stared down at her with his one good eye, a patch over the other, thinking she would break if he touched her and tempted to do just that. But she seemed so fine, so very fragile, he refrained.

"Will you leave, Don Pánfilo?" she asked. She received no response. The giant continued to stand over her, staring down at her with that one astonished eye. Still, she wasn't discomposed. When Cabeza de Vaca returned with a musket, she indicated that he should retire. Reluctantly Cabeza de Vaca closed the reception-room door, standing guard in the corridor.

The airy wave of the hand she had used to dismiss her Indian steward galvanized Pánfilo de Narváez. She seemed to be saying she was in full control, she could handle the situation. Well, Pánfilo de Narváez could also handle the situation. He grabbed Floridita's shoulders with his hamlike fists, lifted her over the desk, and held her to him as he ran his hands over her body.

Floridita remained perfectly still, inert, looking at him with unshakable poise. He kissed her as hard as he could, bruising her mouth. She remained impassive. Finally he pushed her away from him and watched as she adjusted her gown and her mantilla and resumed her seat behind the desk. It was as if he hadn't touched her, as if he didn't exist.

"How much?" he asked.

"If you would like to talk to my steward," La Floridita said, "he can give you a complete list of services and prices, Don Pánfilo."

"How much for you?"

"I am not for sale, Don Pánfilo." She pulled the bell cord, and Cabeza de Vaca opened the door instantly, musket in hand.

Narváez took a last look at her with his one eye. "You have won this skirmish, Señora. But on my soul, you are not going to win the next one."

He slammed out of the room. Floridita let out a long breath, but she hadn't been so frightened as she had been curious about whether or not he would have raped her had she shown the least bit of interest in him.

Cabeza de Vaca brought her a glass of *aguardiente*. He thought it was the white man's magic drink, a panacea for all ills. He waited for his mistress to drink it. She held the glass in her hand, but she didn't raise it to her mouth. Instead she sat staring into space. After a long moment she put her fingers to her lips where Pánfilo de Narváez had bruised them, and then she sent for her secretary, an astute Spaniard named Mira. She thought she had better make Narváez an offer before he attacked again. She wasn't at all certain, for the first time in a long time, that she was going to win.

The letter La Floridita instructed Mira to write proposed that each night while Pánfilo de Narváez's fleet was in port, ten situations would be reserved for officers, twenty for crew. Those availing themselves of her actresses' favors would comport themselves in a gentlemanly manner. If there was one transgression—one brawl, one injured actress—the agreement would end for everyone. The rates for these services were discounted by 20 percent as a patriotic gesture, but five hundred pieces of gold were to be placed as an insurance against damage and returned when the *flota* sailed.

La Floridita decided not to entrust Cabeza de Vaca with the delivery of the letter, being aware of Narváez's nearly insane prejudice against Indians. Instead, early in the morning she sent Ramón, who had been longing for a closer look at the huge ships. Balbontine showed Ramón into Narváez's cabin. Ramón had never been aboard a ship before. He stood perfectly still, inhaling the briny aroma, the atmosphere of adventure, hypnotized by the maps that lay discarded on a shelf.

Meanwhile, in a neutral voice, Balbontine read La Floridita's proposal to Narváez, who reacted by slamming his huge fist on the table in front of him so that nearly every object in the cabin, including Ramón, jumped.

"You are that woman's son?" Narváez asked, his voice so loud and so deep it sounded as if it came from the grave.

"Yes, Don Pánfilo."

"Tell your mother Narváez agrees. This is her second victory. There won't be a third."

Ramón hesitated for a moment and then gave Narváez the benefit of the Córdoba smile. "Mama says that I am to ask you to sign the agreement and . . . to bring back the gold if you do."

Narváez took a quill pen and scratched his name across the bottom of the parchment, tossing it to Ramón. "Tell your mother that I will bring the gold myself tonight."

La Floridita found herself spending the day waiting for Narváez. She could not rid her mind of that ugly giant. On several occasions she found herself touching her bruised lips. Her few sexual encounters over the years had been based on necessity, not romance. If she could have, she would have avoided them. Whenever she felt a physical or emotional need, she summoned up Córdoba in her mind and then busied herself with La Casa, with Antonio and Amelia, with her son. But now La Casa was running itself, and Antonio and Amelia were increasingly involved with their own children. As for her son, though she denied it, Ramón was indeed becoming a man, finding his own amusements.

She felt, suddenly, alone. Her fantasy that Córdoba was alive and king of Florida, awaiting a ship to rescue him and bring him back to her, seemed just that, a fantasy. Although Narváez was far from the idealized romantic image of male good looks, she had to admit that she found in his ugliness a kind of masculinity that appealed to her.

I'm being a fool, Floridita decided. I'm too old to think of romance, and Narváez is the worst sort of brute, the last man I would ever consider. He's signed the agreement, he's bringing the gold, and after that I won't have to see him again.

She spent the afternoon with her actresses, advising them on skin care, on new ways to wear their hair or the possibility of changing their styles of performance. She usually liked this sort of afternoon. She felt like the abbess of an important nunnery, organizing solace for its members. But not today.

First of all, Nani, the young French virgin she had bought from a Portuguese pirate, was nowhere to be found. She had gold-colored hair and deep blue eyes and such a shy smile that La Floridita had decided not to make her an actress just yet but to keep her behind the scenes. Cabeza de Vaca reported that Nani had gone for a walk, an activity not exactly forbidden but not encouraged either. Especially not today, with Pánfilo de Narváez's men in the town.

Pánfilo de Narváez. Everything that day seemed to focus on him, including her imagination. She went back to the reception room and sat at her desk, looking out at the garden, at the red and pink and purple hibiscus in riotous and full bloom. She took up Córdoba's faded black fan and put it down again. She asked for Ramón and was told he too was not to be found.

She and Cabeza de Vaca went to supervise a much delayed cleaning of the storerooms. There she discovered Quirinio's old daybed and decided to have it moved back into the reception room. Immediately. She told herself it would be a convenient place for an afternoon nap, an activity she had never indulged in.

She barely ate the early supper she habitually took with Ramón, who had come back oddly silent from wherever he had been. For days he had been full of Narváez's ships and the expedition to Florida, and now, after he had been aboard the ship he had been so excited about, he barely spoke. He left her soon after and she went to the reception room. The desk had been moved back into the center of the room, and the daybed was now under the windows.

She lay on it, inhaling the potent jasmine from the garden, her eyes closed, thinking, against her will, of the red-headed giant who had smelled nothing like jasmine when he had picked her up as if she were a feather and crushed her against him. La Floridita wasn't a woman who was successful at lying to herself. She admitted, as she lay on Quirinio's old daybed, that the sensuality she had repressed for the past fifteen years seemed to be reasserting itself and that the object of this new, absurd, unwanted, unnecessary passion was the ugly, one-eyed, red-headed giant named Pánfilo de Narváez.

Normally she would have laughed at the irony, but now she nearly sobbed when his steward, Balbontine, arrived with the gold retainer and the announcement that Don Pánfilo had decided not to keep his appointment since other affairs needed his attention. His crew and officers were already being accommodated, and Pánfilo de Narváez, through his steward, trusted La Floridita would keep to her part of the bargain as he would to his.

She drank more *aguardiente* than usual that night, and still she didn't sleep. Pánfilo de Narváez, she thought to herself, had been right after all. He had won the third battle of their war by simply not appearing for combat.

In the morning she surrendered, sending him a note asking him to come to an interview in which they might discuss certain matters not covered in the first agreement. Pánfilo de Narváez answered, through his steward, that he would do everything he could to be present, but Señora Córdoba had to understand the exigencies of his position, the demands on his time.

CHAPTER NINE

PÁNFILO DE NARVÁEZ'S losses were never with women.

He kept his second appointment with La Floridita. He arrived late, bathed and perfumed. At La Floridita's insistence he sat in one of the leather chairs, dwarfing it, drinking *aguardiente*, explaining he had been unable to appear the previous night. He had had pressing personal business. "I was finding suitable quarters for my wife. Out of the city, for reasons of her temperament and health."

The insistent scent of jasmine filled the room. La Floridita could hardly breathe. If the fact that he had a wife, out of the city or otherwise, was supposed to be a thrust, it hardly penetrated. She felt sick with desire. She had acknowledged her reawakened sexuality, but she didn't like it. The fantasies that had played in her mind throughout the day, like an endless demonic pageant, had left her weak and feverish. She wanted Narváez to get on with it, and he seemed to know that. He was paying her back in kind for her initial arrogance.

He made small talk. He said, in his booming voice, that the first men who had sampled her theater had been wonderfully complimentary. He spoke of the sweet Havana air, of the way the Cuban moon seemed to hang low and heavy in the sky. Finally he looked at her with his one eye and said, "Since we have come to a satisfactory business arrangement, Señora, I am curious as to why you have asked for this interview. Is it not something my steward can manage?"

She would have liked to be able to dismiss him. To say that it was something his steward could probably manage a great deal better than he. She wished that her need wasn't betraying her so baldly. She felt like one of her clients who had just reached port, desperate for relief after a long voyage of female deprivation. She stood up and put down the faded black fan Córdoba had given her fifteen years before. She was going to bring this bit of refined torture to an end, one way or another.

"I want you to make love to me," she said, opening her gown, revealing her body, which had never been more beautiful. She surprised him. In an age when artifice and convention were the goals of women everywhere, Pánfilo de Narváez had never before met a woman who was so direct. It was as if their roles had been reversed. He stood up. She came to him, put her arms around him, kissed him, and led him to the daybed. He lost his pose of nonchalance and distance. He couldn't remember ever having been so excited. He pushed aside his codpiece and entered her in one long movement, filling her body and her need.

"You are so ugly," she told him later, after he had removed his clothes and they had made love again, this time with a slow, deliberate, and seemingly unquenchable passion. She traced with her index finger the scars that ran up and down his body, souvenirs of a lifetime of soldiering.

"This is from Mexico, and this long gouge is from Haiti . . ." It was as if he were a map of New World adventures. Surprisingly, he was gentle with her, holding her as if he were afraid she would break. "I wish," he said, in that booming voice he tried to keep down to a whisper, "that I was more lovely for you, Floridita."

He returned the following night and the night after that. La Floridita was giving in to fifteen years of suppressed passion. But Narváez, who had, when he could, sexual intercourse several times a day with as many women, was experiencing something else. He was, for the first time in a long, eventful life, in love.

* * *

Some years before, La Floridita had built a huge stone mansion, similar to Ponce de León's grand house on the plaza in San Juan, on Monserrate, a street at the top of a hill facing the harbor, not far from where Antonio and Amelia lived. She had decided after it was built that it was too large for her and had rented it to the governor's Havana emissary. He had died, his widow had returned to Spain, and now it was empty.

Floridita now felt it was time to leave La Casa to live in her fine house. Pánfilo de Narváez openly took up residence, becoming part of the household. "He would be content to sit and hold my hand," Floridita admitted to Amelia. "But I am in a sort of heat. Like some greyhound bitch. I cannot get enough of him. It is a sickness—the dengue. It will kill me or it will pass. But in the meanwhile I think of little else. My body longs for him throughout the day. I count the minutes until nightfall."

She had taken to smoking the Ciboneys' black cigars, Cabeza de Vaca believing tobacco a cure for impatience. He lit one for her. Antonio had stayed on after his wife had gone to supervise their children's supper. They sat on the balcony of the house that faced the harbor, Cabeza de Vaca pouring *aguardiente*, watching over them.

"You have worked all these years, Floridita, building a reputation for purity," Antonio began. "And now . . ." He was not angry but bewildered. Don Pánfilo's residence in her house was the talk of Havana.

"I cannot help myself, Antonio." She put the cigar aside and took up the new, white lace fan Narváez had given her. She had never been more beautiful, peering at him with those eyes from behind the new fan, which fluttered in her hand like a white bird. "Is Amelia unhappy with me?"

"No. With me. She says I must leave you alone while he is here, that you are entitled to a grand passion every fifteen years or so. I asked her if she were and she said no."

"Why not?"

A blushing Antonio Levi confessed, "Amelia says she has a grand passion every night."

When she wasn't thinking of Pánfilo de Narváez, La Floridita worried about Ramón. He had understood her position since he was twelve, but not his own. He was not, despite his name and looks, a hidalgo like his father. He would need a career, and La Floridita was determined it would not be owning and managing La Casa. Ramón made no secret of the fact that he desperately wanted to take orders, to sail, but Floridita refused to consider that.

"I will not lose you too," she told him. After much discussion he agreed to be apprenticed to Antonio, a man whom he loved as a father. He would be taught the chandlery business. "You will be a rich man," Floridita told him, relieved.

"I do not want to be a rich man, Mama. I want to be an explorer. I want to

74

see Mexico and Peru and Hindustan. I want to see Florida. I want to find gold and rubies and tame the lions that fly and the fish that walk on the land. I want to look upon the serpents with two heads and the women with fishtails. I want to bathe in the silver fountains . . ."

Ramón had picked up and swallowed whole every legend that had touched the port of Havana. He had been listening to that old gossip Cabeza de Vaca—and worse, to Pánfilo de Narváez, who always had a fantastic story to amuse the boy.

Disgust and shame, she knew, might come, but in the meanwhile she lived for those moments when Pánfilo shared her bed. Ramón waited for him with nearly as much anticipation as his mother. He hung on every word, believing all of Narváez's stories of the Indies twenty years before, stories of horrible wrecks and terrible battles on strange islands' shores; of the heat and the gold of Mexico; of the cruelties of the Indians and the bravery of the Spanish. When Narváez spoke of the treasures he would find in Florida, Ramón's eyes grew large. He often reminded Narváez of a promise he had made to search for his father.

Like Floridita, Ramón believed that Córdoba was alive, that he had become a king in Florida, with thousands of subjects and untold riches. "You should search for your father yourself," Narváez told him despite La Floridita's warning looks. "Florida is not so far away."

On an overcast morning in mid-March, Floridita found Ramón in La Casa's reception room, pretending to be there as if by accident. But he was too transparent to scheme and she knew immediately he had been waiting for her for a reason. He tried his smile, but he was uncharacteristically nervous. She suspected he wanted to tell her he was going to break his apprenticeship with Antonio, an action she would not under any circumstances allow.

For once he was less than exuberant. "Mama," he said, "I have something I must tell you." She wasn't going to help him. She waited. "Mama," he began, "I am a man, you know, and no longer a boy." He tried his smile again, and for a moment she was transplanted back in time, fifteen years earlier, to that little adobe house on the hill in Puerto Rico, with Córdoba breaking the news that he was leaving, joining Ponce de León on his expedition to Florida.

"Mama," Ramón said, bringing her back to La Casa, "I have fallen in love."

This was the last confession La Floridita expected, and she nearly laughed, which would have been a terrible mistake. Love, she knew, could be managed. Floridita breathed a sigh of enormous relief. "With whom?"

The boy hesitated before saying "Nani." Well, at least he had good taste, Floridita thought. Nani was the pale French virgin bought from a Portuguese slaver. Floridita had been saving her for a spectacular introduction, perhaps when a representative of the Crown appeared. No longer living at La Casa, caught up in her love for Narváez, she hadn't seen—or thought of—Nani in months. Ramón looked at his mother and, realizing she was not as displeased as he had feared, gave her a more assured smile and went on. "Nani gave birth, a week ago, to a boy. She insisted I tell you. I am a father, Mama."

La Floridita thought that for the first time in her life she might possibly faint. "How could you have kept this from me? For all these months?" Floridita stared at him, realizing her Ramón had not only become a man but one she didn't know.

And then another idea forced itself into her consciousness: If Ramón was a father, she was a grandmother. "Where are they?" she asked, for once totally discomposed. "Bring them to me immediately." "They" were waiting on the other side of the corridor door. Cabeza de Vaca, his moon-shaped face looking to La Floridita more absurdly doting and cowlike than ever, carried the baby as if he were the mother. The child had black hair and green eyes, and when Floridita took him in her arms and held him to her, she decided she wasn't going to faint after all.

Floridita fell in love with the child in the time it took to transfer him from Cabeza de Vaca's arms to hers. She wanted them all—immediately, right this moment—to move into the stone house on Monserrate, but Nani insisted they stay where they were, in La Floridita's old private apartments in La Casa. Nani was intelligent as well as beautiful. "In this way, Señora," Nani said in her charming French-accented Spanish, "I can keep an eye on the business." Well, that was what she wanted, and it seemed to Floridita a perfectly reasonable arrangement. Nani could manage La Casa. She could continue to be Ramón's mistress. Ramón would in time marry elsewhere and well, after he prospered as a chandler.

She kissed her grandson and then Nani and finally Ramón and made her way back to her mansion feeling happy and complete for the first time since Pánfilo de Narváez had come into her life. Of course she had to break off the affair at once. A grandmother could not continue to behave in the way she had been. She resolved to tell Narváez that he had to move out of her house.

But he kissed her before she could speak and took her to their bed, and she forgot all of her resolution as he made slow, passionate love to her. It was a relief when, two weeks later, he told her that his *flota* was leaving for Florida. It couldn't have come at a better time. Her need for him was over. She had a new preoccupation: her grandson, Fernando.

La Floridita was surprised, as she stood on the balcony overlooking the port, watching the ships sail out of Havana, when she burst into tears. Both Amelia and Nani, who had come to watch Narváez's departure, comforted her. "I am a foolish old woman," she said, going to her room, putting away the white fan Narváez had given her, retrieving the faded, black one Córdoba had presented her with so long ago. "But I think I am at last over my madness."

The house on Monserrate seemed empty without that lumbering red-headed giant. La Floridita sat on the balcony long after nightfall. The slaves had lit the lamps, but the night was especially dark. It was moonless, clouds obscuring the stars. She asked Cabeza de Vaca to find Ramón and, taking her seat on the balcony, faced north where Florida—the Land of the Flowers—lay.

She felt unaccountably lonely. She thought she might insist that her grandson be brought to live in her house and not in La Casa. She remembered his green eyes, perhaps a shade lighter than hers, and his blue-black hair and the dimple in his chin, which certainly came from his mother. Yes, she would definitely talk to Ramón about having Fernando brought to the house.

But Cabeza de Vaca, a worried look on his round, kind face, did not return with Ramón. Instead he handed her a letter. She knew, suddenly and unquestionably, what it said, but she sent for Antonio anyway. Antonio read the letter to himself and then looked at her with sorrow.

"Do not protect me, niño." Floridita said. "You taught him to write, Antonio. Now you must read his words."

" 'Dear Mama,' " Antonio read aloud slowly and sadly by the light of the lamp Cabeza held. " 'I go with Don Pánfilo to Florida to find my father and bring him back to you. When we return we shall cover you with gold and precious jewels. When we return we will make you laugh with tales of our fantastic travels. You must not be angry. And you must not be disappointed. I love Antonio very much, but I was never meant to be a chandler. I am going to be an explorer, like my father, like Cortes, famous and rich. I leave you my son and my love, dearest Mama. Your faithful Ramón.' "

She didn't bother to wipe away the tears. Cabeza de Vaca had told her of a Ciboney legend that said tears washed away one's sorrows and kept one youthful. Tears, according to that legend, were the fountain of youth. La Floridita had never felt so old or so vulnerable.

In the morning she went to the church in the Plaza de Armas and prayed, but without conviction. Afterward she directed Cabeza de Vaca to take the carriage across Los Oficios to the chandlery, where she found Amelia. And Amelia held her in her warm arms, just as she had fifteen years before, offering her maternal comfort.

"Amelia," La Floridita said, looking into her friend's plaintive brown eyes, "I have another, terrible confession to make. I tried but could not tell the priest."

Amelia looked her friend up and down and smiled. "I know, Floridita. You are, once again, with child. After all these months with Don Pánfilo, it is not, you know, unusual."

"But at my age. And a grandmother as well. I am being punished for my sin by the Holy Savior."

"You are not being punished, La Floridita," Amelia said, taking her friend in her arms once more. "You are being rewarded. You may have lost one son to the world, but is it not miraculous how the Lord provides? Now you will have another."

She didn't expect to live through the delivery. Not at her age. But six months later, on September 8, 1528, La Floridita brought into the world—with the help of a midwife, Amelia, and Nani—not a son but a daughter, with flaming red hair and extraordinary green eyes.

CHAPTER TEN

MOST OF THE CAVALIERS wore chain mail, it having been finally determined that full armor was unsuited to the New World sun. But Narváez had found Ramón an old cuirass, which the boy had polished until it reflected like a mirror. He wore a helmet that should have made his head ache with heat and weight; it could have weighed twice as much and he would gladly have sworn never to take it off.

At first the other officers and the men had avoided him, this son of Narváez's whore. But his enthusiasm, that infectious Córdoba smile, his willingness to take on any task aboard the flagship, won them over. Indeed, his presence helped to give the men a new optimism despite their fear and distrust of Narváez.

Ramón chafed and sweltered under his cuirass while Narváez kept them waiting aboard the ships anchored in Tampa Bay. The voyage to Florida had been uneventful, and it would have been possible to land upon arrival. But like Floridita, Narváez had a sure sense of theater and waited for the dramatic moment. Nude and curious Timucuas—less warlike than the Tequestas Ponce de León had found—watched the ships openly from the beach while Ramón and the others studied them. The Timucuas were proud and tall in their natural state in contrast to the converted Ciboneys, who wore ill-fitting European clothes and seemed eternally cowed.

After a sleepless night Ramón finally heard, at dawn, Good Friday, April 3, 1528, the order he had been waiting for. Narváez, who had seemed to forget his existence from the moment the *flota* set sail, singled Ramón out to accompany him in the first longboat to head for shore.

Pánfilo de Narváez's landing on the shores of Tampa Bay was everything

Ramón could have asked for in pomp and pageant. He stood sweating under his cuirass as his boots sank into the sand on the beach and the sun blazed overhead, repeatedly reflected in the men's helmets as they held a crucifix and Narváez's banner aloft.

His booming voice directed at the retreating Timucuas, Pánfilo de Narváez—like Ponce de León before him—took possession of Florida. Unlike his predecessor, Narváez felt obligated to explain to the natives—in Spanish, in that sepulchral voice—his personal theories of occupation, the creation of the world, and the holy Catholic Church.

Several men fainted from the heat, but Ramón stood at attention as Narváez, hypnotized by his own visions of the temporal and religious worlds, continued to educate the Timucuas, who couldn't understand a word he said. He told them that if, when "informed of the Truth," they did not convert, he would "take the persons of yourselves, your wives, and your children to make slaves, to sell and dispose of you, as Their Majesties shall think fit. And I will take your goods, and declare to you that the deaths and damages that arise therefrom will be your fault and not that of His Majesty, or mine, or of these cavaliers who accompany me."

Narváez went on to describe the glories of conversion as Ramón struggled to remain upright. But the animals weren't so patient, the Andalusian horses neighing uncomfortably, the greyhounds growling softly, held in check by the men trained in the use of dogs in war.

Behind the palm thickets that lined the beach Ramón could see the Timucuan braves, crouching down, staring at the palefaces, sweating in their mail and armor, surrounding the ranting red-haired giant. After a time, as Don Pánfilo continued to broadcast what was gibberish to them, the Timucuas gathered around their leaders and began to confer.

The most important leader, their cacique, was as tall as Narváez but half as broad. Like Narváez in his armor, the Timucuan chief ignored the heat, wearing a fur-lined cape, drawn together at the neck and extending below his knees. The collar of the cape was made of hundreds of enormous freshwater pearls. His skin was decorated from head to toe with an intricate pattern of blue tattoos. Next to him stood a shaman, their medicine man. His thick white hair was fixed in a knot, he wore ear spools of purple stones, a beaded belt, and a chamois sash over a fringed chamois apron. Around his neck, covering his chest, was a much hammered silver medallion. He carried in his hand a pouch made of marten containing the medicines and sacred objects of the tribe.

When Narváez finally ran out of words, after speaking for nearly two hours, he knelt down and kissed the sand. Then he kissed the crucifix. Finally he stood up and faced the Timucuas. It was as clear a challenge as if he had made it in their language, and they stepped forward, emerging from the palm thickets, following their leaders to the place on their shore where the red-headed giant and his men waited.

The cacique indicated that most of his men should wait while he, a dozen braves carrying fire-hardened reed spears, and a woman approached the trespassers. The woman, over six feet tall, had a lined face but a slim, youthful body covered by a skirt made from Spanish moss, treated in such a way that Ramón thought it was made of silk. She wore bracelets and necklaces made of iridescent seashells. Her hair, long and black, had bright beads woven into it.

Though they were as different as they could be, she reminded Ramón of his mother. There was that impenetrable poise, that emotionless mask Floridita too could assume when she was especially angry. There was no doubt that the woman accompanying the cacique was especially angry.

The cacique was called Hirrihigua, and she was his mother and his wife. They stopped a few feet from Narváez, and Hirrihigua pointed a long tattooed finger at him, saying in Timucuan, "I am the cacique of this land. You and the half-baked men are to leave these shores. At once. You are trespassing on sacred land."

Hirrihigua's message was perfectly communicated. Narváez didn't waste a moment on negotiations. He drew his finely honed sword and, with one stroke, slashed Hirrihigua's nose down the center. Blood gushed out, staining his pearls and his marten cape an orange-red. The only sound came from Ramón, who shouted, "No, *Adelantado*. No." He had lived all of his life in a law-abiding world. He had imagined torture and bloodshed, knowing it was part of being a cavalier, but he had never seen it before. He hated what he was seeing.

Narváez didn't hear him, his hatred of Indians concentrated on the Timucua still standing in front of him, creating puddles of blood in the sand. The greyhounds, starved for days, began to salivate and growl at the smell of the blood. For a moment that was the only sound heard on that beach.

Hirrihigua's mother-wife broke the silence, emitting an unholy Timucuan cry, clawing Narváez's face, leaving tracks of blood where her nails had dug into his skin. Narváez smiled. It was all the incentive he needed to establish his Florida Indian policy. He gave the signal, and his men unsheathed their swords, surrounding the Timucuas. Ramón stood among them, the Toledan sword Narváez had given him held slackly in his hand, still staring at Hirrihigua, at whose throat a captain was holding a knife.

Ramón's attention was diverted from the bleeding cacique when Narváez grabbed the Timucuan woman by her neck and dragged her along the beach as if she were a house pet needing discipline. He forced her to the edge of the shore where the greyhounds were tethered, the salt foam sticking to their thin legs, their mouths agape, revealing spittle against pink gums, long white teeth sharpened and refined by their caretakers.

Ramón knew what Narváez was going to do to the woman, and he started to run toward them. But his friend Catos tripped him and held him back. "You don't want to get yourself killed, my boy, because of some Indian crone, do you? Be quiet and stay still and pray Narváez has been too preoccupied to notice you."

Narváez was preoccupied. The woman, fighting all the way, unable to break Narváez's grip, lay perfectly still when he threw her down upon the sand, a few feet away from the salivating greyhounds, straining at their leashes. He looked back, up the beach, to the place where his men held Hirrihigua and his braves captive, knives at their throats, making certain he had everyone's full attention.

Then he gave the signal. The starved greyhounds were released. Catos continued to restrain Ramón as dogs tore the cacique's mother and wife apart. She tried to scream, but the first dog had gone for her throat, tearing it out of her neck with his sharpened teeth. In fifteen minutes, as Hirrihigua was forced to watch, she was ripped apart and devoured. All that was left was the red sand and the bones the dogs continued to gnaw on long after the flesh was gone.

Narváez, deciding the Indians had understood where arrogance would lead them, ordered the braves chained together and commanded his men to search each of the huts in their village, just inside the palmetto thicket. Ramón, dazed, full of horror, was barely able to comprehend the order. Catos pushed him along, taking him with him as they searched the huts, finding little, until a cry was heard.

A small chamois bag filled with gold dust had been found in the largest hut, the cacique's. Narváez had Hirrihigua brought into the center of the village. The bleeding had stopped, but the cacique was in pain, his face badly disfigured, his hands and feet in chains, the pearl collar and the fur cape now part of Narváez's collection.

Through Ciboney slaves—whose language held certain similarities with the Timucuas'—Narváez demanded to know where the bag came from. The gold had driven all other thoughts from his mind. He pushed the interpreters out of the way, grabbing Hirrihigua by his hair. "Where is it?" he wanted to know. "Where is the gold?"

Hirrihigua, maintaining his dignity, took his time answering. One of his braves had found the gold on the beach two years before, lying among the bits and pieces of a wrecked Spanish galleon. Hirrihigua had kept it as much for the excellent quality of the chamois as for the gold. Narváez, his one eye blazing in his sunburned face, made him aware of the importance of the bag of yellow dust.

Hirrihigua waited until the tip of Narváez's dagger had pierced his neck, and then he said one word. "Apalachen." It was the same word Panthar had once excited Ponce de León with. Narváez withdrew the dagger. In that moment Narváez knew that he would find gold, that Cortes's fame would evaporate like the water on the beach, that he would become the most famous conquistador who ever lived. "Apalachen" meant gold.

He demanded to know where the gold was to be found, indicating that Hirrihigua was to draw a map in the sandy soil. The cacique did so, slowly, sending Pánfilo de Narváez on an inland march north and west, the cold route evil souls took on their journey after death. It was a march that would eventually lead to Narváez's death. Pánfilo de Narváez, in his obsessive hate for all Indians, in his arrogant belief in white supremacy, never for a moment believed a Timucua cacique capable of deliberately misleading him.

The Spaniards, gold fever keeping them awake with dreams of riches, glory, and power, spent the night in the Timucuan village. Hirrihigua and his braves, forgotten, had been chained together in the medicine man's hut. Ramón, looked after by Catos, was in shock over the violence and brutality his idol had perpetrated on the defenseless Timucuas. "I thought," Catos said, laughing at him, "you wanted to be a great Spanish cavalier and lead a life of high adventure. This, my boy, is it."

Ramón didn't answer, and Catos, seeing the revulsion in the youth's face, left off teasing him. "You will soon get used to it, Ramonito. Believe me."

In the morning Narváez ordered the brigantine back to Cuba for more supplies and sent half his men by ship up the coast. Hirrihigua and most of his men had managed to escape from Narváez's chains during the night. The conquistador was left with three young Timucuan braves to act as guides for the inland march.

Astride his white Andalusian horse, Pánfilo de Narváez led his mounted troops northward through the jungles and pineland, following the Timucuan braves and the map Hirrihigua had drawn in the sand. His ships and the other troops were to rendezvous with him in two months' time on the Gulf of Mexico.

Ramón had been chosen for the inland march. He was the last member of the convoy. Sick at heart, he stopped his horse a few miles into the interior to watch a stag with huge antlers crash through the forest undergrowth. He had never before looked upon such a creature. It was the kind of fabulous animal he had come to see. He realized he had been left behind only as the stag came crashing back through the forest, stopped, and stared, as if he wanted a second look at the boy in armor on horseback. Then he crashed away again, having had his fill.

Laughing at the stag's awkward humanlike behavior, Ramón momentarily forgot yesterday's horror. With the sun streaming through the pine trees, he spurred his horse to catch up with the others.

It was too late. When the last men in the convoy heard Ramón's startled shout they looked back and, horrified, raced to catch up with the others. Ramón was left to the Timucuas who had surrounded him.

CHAPTER ELEVEN

TRUSSED AND TIED BY HIS ANKLES and wrists to a spear, half conscious, Ramón was dragged through twenty miles of pine woods by Timucuan slaves.

The braves wailed piteously as they marched, mourning the woman who was their cacique's wife and mother. Their wails were intended to speed her spirit's ascendance to the World Above the Sky, where her forefathers' spirits lived. But the chants were filled with despair. Her spirit was doomed to wander through the netherworld for eternity since her bones could not be buried in sacred ground. They had been used as gristle for the Spaniards' greyhounds.

Ramón was ignored except by the hermaphrodite detailed to look after him. At first Ramón thought he was a child. He was four feet tall, with undeveloped features, tiny hands. But then Ramón saw the white in his hair and the spotty beard on his cheek and finally, with horror, his fully developed though hairless male genitals emerging from the rouged lips of a vagina.

The half-man, half-maiden dwarf took tiny nicks with his honed fingernails from Ramón's body as Ramón was dragged along, popping the bits of flesh into his little mouth. As they traveled he prodded Ramón with a sharp forklike instrument, drawing blood, so that Ramón's body was constantly covered with mosquitoes and other insects eating his blood.

The pain, after the first day, drifted to the back of Ramón's mind; the dwarf—except for occasional spurts of enthusiasm—began to lose interest. A young girl, no more than twelve or thirteen, who apparently enjoyed a freedom and respect denied to others, came to observe him the first night after camp was made. Ramón, still trussed to the spear, had been dropped on the ground far from the fire where the shaman was chanting, the braves dancing around him.

Hirrihigua, stripped of his cape and ear studs by Narváez, believing the evil spirits had come to the World Below the Sky, wore only a breechcloth and a necklace of shells. Except for his height and his ruined beauty he might have been any one of the other braves participating in the night-long dance mourning the tribe's dead queen.

Ramón, forgotten, dazed, lay watching the dance, hypnotized by the chants and the sinuous movements of the nearly naked men. It was as if an evil child's tale had come to life before him: devils dancing around Satan. He didn't notice the girl as she inched her way toward him. She wore a skirt of woven Spanish moss, indicating she was a member of the royal household. She was nearly as tall as he, her blue-black hair intricately dressed with multicolored beads, her eyes so dark they seemed unseeing. Her skin was a deep gold color, her features Oriental in their regularity. She was, by Timucuan and Spanish standards, beautiful.

Ramón noticed her only when she knelt directly in front of him, blocking his view of the dancing. Startled, expecting some new attack, he looked up at her with fear in his eyes, trying to pull back. She shook her head. "I do not wish to hurt you," she said, and he understood her intentions if not her words.

She bent over him, whispering comfort, shielding him from the others, soothing his body with an herbal plant leaf, driving the blood-sucking insects away, healing the tiny wounds with aloe salve. He gave himself up to her like an infant to a mother. But when he closed his eyes he saw the hermaphrodite and lived over again the thousand tortures of the day. She touched his eyes gently and he opened them to stare into hers. Then she touched his lips with her fingers. When he opened his mouth she fed him grasses that dulled his senses and blessedly set his mind free from his body. It was as if his consciousness had been released and he was observing himself from above.

Because of the grasses Ramón was able to get through the long days of little tortures. Hirrihigua was leading the way south, around the great Tampa Bay, to his tribe's most isolated, protected village, the tribe's sacred home. It was there they would attempt to purify themselves of the debasement and evil the half-baked men had visited upon them.

They marched through open woods of pine and oak, across shallow lakes with sandy bottoms, through stagnant swamps emitting pervasive odors that even penetrated the protective shield created by the grasses the girl had fed Ramón. Though his senses were dulled, his imagination was heightened, and he viewed the animals that lived in those woods as magical creatures: deer, rabbits, bear, mountain lions, geese, ducks, herons, partridge, and most especially the brown quiescent, ubiquitous opossum.

Each night the girl came to him while the men of the tribe mourned their queen. She was Hirrihigua's youngest and favorite daughter. She taught Ramón her name by saying it over and over again as she soothed him with the herbal leaves and fed him the pain-killing grasses. Ulele. It sounded like a song to Ramón the way she said it, and he found himself repeating "Ulele" over and over during the day, a chant to help him remain fixed in the somnolent state the grasses induced, even when the dwarf was at his worst.

84

Ulele for her part had been drawn to the half-baked man because of his strangeness. His helplessness evoked her sympathy. He was like the rabbits she had set free from her brothers' traps. She was fascinated by the deep green color of his eyes, by the softness of his skin. Once he managed to smile at her, dazed, thinking she was Nani. That first smile, so wonderfully dazzling, so strange and godlike—Timucuas did not smile—was to stay with Ulele for the rest of her life, a memory she would bring out and take joy in whenever she had a need.

When the hermaphrodite was at his worst, poking at Ramón's genitals, inserting the fork into the tender flesh under his arms, when the herbs could not mask the pain or the horror of what was going to happen to him, Ramón retreated in his mind to his childhood. He was in his bed in La Casa; Cabreza de Vaca was calling him to breakfast; Antonio was teaching him his letters; his mother was caressing and comforting him, making certain his hair was combed and his hands were clean. Eventually the features of his mother and the Indian girl became confused in his mind, and all day long, until night came, he would chant Ulele's name.

For thirty years the Indian tribes of Florida had shared rumors and then real information about the white man. They gathered their facts from Indians on the East Coast who had been to the Spanish-devastated Bahamas, from Indian slaves shipwrecked on their own shores, from the *cabalgadas*, the slave-raiding parties that occasionally descended upon them. No longer were the white men feared as gods; now they were dreaded as human symbols of evil.

Hirrihigua's winter village was situated on the Manatee River, not far from the southern tip of Tampa Bay. He had taken a long, circuitous route to reach it, wary of the Spaniards and their greyhounds and of his most powerful enemy, the rival Timucuan chief, Mocoso.

The village consisted of sixty thatch-roofed mud huts standing in a circle, surrounded by lakes, marshes, fallen trees, tangled underbrush, impossible for white men to locate, difficult even for Mocoso.

In the center of the circle was the starfire, always burning, on which a kettle constantly simmered; it was fed by sticks gathered by the lesser wives and slaves. There were no mealtimes, the braves eating when they were hungry, using the wooden spoon in the pot. Another cooking pot fed the women and the slaves.

Isolated outside the circle was the windowless hut in which the slaves who had been carrying Ramón deposited him. The dwarf, oddly nervous, taking care to remain as close as possible to the entrance of the hut, untied Ramón. He gave Ramón one last vicious jab and then, taking the spear, shut and fastened the leather door, leaving Ramón alone.

There didn't appear to be a guard. The late afternoon sun revealed a tiny flaw in the thatched roof. Ramón thought that if he were strong enough to stand up, he might be able to reach the roof. He felt a sudden excitement, a rush of elation that cut through the daze of the herbal grasses. He would break through the thatching, escape, and make his way to the coast to find the ships returning from Cuba, which were to rendezvous with Narváez. He began to test his legs when he heard a sound that filled his mind. It was an evocative sound, reminding him of a toy Antonio had given him when he was a child—beans in a gourd, meant to be shaken, to amuse.

This rattle was meant to warn. It explained why Ramón had been left alone in a hut with a broken roof, without a guard. As his eyes grew accustomed to the dark, he saw them. There were at least three and possibly more, as thick as a man's torso, painted gold and red and yellow, hopelessly entwined, coiled in the far corner like the huge heaps of ships' ropes in the chandlery, shimmering, moving constantly. They were the serpents Cabeza de Vaca had warned him about, New World snakes known as rattlers for the noise they made, able to swallow a man whole. Each time Ramón moved, they moved, as a mass, toward him. He willed himself to remain perfectly still. All through that eternal night he remained inert, his eyes staring into those of the serpents.

They took him out in the morning. He began to shake, to rant, insane with fear. Hirrihigua watched as they dragged the nude, crazed Spanish boy to the stack of wood that had been piled in the center of the village circle. When Ramón's eyes focused on the wood he was shocked into sudden sanity, knowing what was going to happen to him. "In the name of God," he pleaded, getting on his knees, facing Hirrihigua.

Hirrihigua had heard Narváez and his men invoke that word, "God," enough to know what it meant. But the half-baked men's god was evil. They came in his name to murder and enslave, to defile the Timucuas' gods and destroy the sacred earth. Hirrihigua, in a new fur cape with a more opulent collar of pearls, touched his deformed nose and thought of his mother, his wife, and the pain her spirit would always suffer. He gave the shaman the order to begin. Like his father, Ramón was to be burned to death in a religious ceremony called *barbecosa*, a word that would one day be translated into "barbecue." It was a slow process; the longer the burning took, the more thoroughly was the offending spirit destroyed. Ramón was tied to the grill as the shaman ignited the wood, lesser wives fanning the fire to make it burn.

Ulele and her mother, Hirrihigua's second wife, waited in the cacique's hut. When Hirrihigua entered, Ulele spoke first, though Timucuan protocol demanded she should remain still. "He has suffered enough torture at the hands of the dwarf and never once did he cry out, not even when he spent the night with the red serpents," she said, moving closer to Hirrihigua, touching his arm. "He is brave, Father, and good, and you will be as bad as the half-baked men if you burn him and scatter his bones so his spirit will have no resting place. Instead it will turn evil and will spend its time riding the winds, bringing yet more evil to our tribe." She took her hand from his arm and turned away.

But not before Hirrihigua had seen the tears in his favorite child's eyes. He looked at her mother, a woman of great insight. "Our daughter, Ulele, has wisdom, Hirrihigua," she said. "We must not burn the Spaniard. He is not our enemy. He has been sent by the Great Father to teach us the ways of the half-baked men so we may better defend ourselves."

Hirrihigua returned to the center of the sacred circle. The smell of burning flesh corrupted the air; the slow fire had begun to blacken Ramón's skin. Ramón was chanting the name "Ulele" over and over, softly, impressing the shaman dressed in his coat of snow-white heron plumes. "Set him free," Hirrihigua said, and the shaman, agreeing, ordered the fire banked, Ramón untied.

They placed him on a bed of leaves, and the shaman applied unguents to the burned flesh from his magic chamois bag. Ramón, lying on the ground, looked up and saw Ulele standing above the shaman, tears in her eyes. He gave her his smile, because he knew, intuitively, that the beautiful, golden-skinned girl had saved him.

Ulele had him sent to the hut where the ill were housed. She had begged from the shaman his most potent and magic unguents, those made from the sacred manatee's blubber. She visited Ramón several times each day, applying the soothing salve with her cool hands, staring into his green eyes, waiting for his smile. When it came, she attempted, hesitantly, to imitate it. It felt strange, but it made her feel joyous. She practiced her smile a good deal when she was by herself.

Two weeks after he was rescued from the *barbecosa* Ramón, if not totally recovered, began to feel the stirrings of his old curiosity. He was interested in the world around him again. He had begun to recognize certain words, to string sentences together. When Ulele came in to apply the unguents he took her hand, drew her down next to him, and smiled for her.

She touched his lips with her thin, graceful fingers. Ramón, copying her gesture, touched her lips, tracing them with his fingers. "Give me your smile," Ulele said in Timucuan, making hand gestures, "and I will give you mine." He understood. He brought her head down to his own, pressing his lips against hers, both of them smiling. Kissing was also unknown to the Timucuas, but Ulele found kissing, like smiling, made her joyous, and she continued to press her lips against his and then her body against his until they both were aroused, and they made sweet, slow love to each other.

For another week, while his wounds healed, Ulele came to him, but no longer with unguents. She was the medicine, and their lovemaking was the final cure. But at the end of that week she appeared several hours before dawn and woke him. He attempted to make her lie with him, but she wouldn't. The half moon illuminated the hut, and he could see that she was serious, and he guessed she was frightened. She began to whisper, and by an effort of will, Ramón was able to understand most of what she said.

"My father has been visited in his dreams by a black dove, a terrible symbol meaning destruction for our land and our tribe. This night he has told my mother that he was wrong to listen to a woman's advice. That the gods, his fathers, have warned him in dream and omen that you must be sacrificed for your cacique's crimes.

"To spare me, he would have you killed by a swift arrow, a noble way to die, unlike the *barbecosa*. My mother has told me all of this because she and the other women believe you are a god yourself. She and the other women are not aware that I fed you the magic grasses. They do not understand how you withstood the hermaphrodite's tortures and the red serpents and the *barbecosa* without crying out. My mother and the others believe that great misfortune will come to our tribe if you are sacrificed."

She stopped talking and looked at him, her depthless eyes troubled but her face composed in the traditional Timucuan nonemotional way. Only her hands, holding his, gave away her sense of urgency. "Do you understand?" she asked.

"Yes, Ulele, I understand. But what do you believe? That I am a god or a demon?"

"I believe you are a man," she said. "Touch me with your lips." He did so, again attempting to draw her down, but she resisted. "You must leave this place and me, now."

She had brought a breechcloth and a spear she had made for him. It was heavy, thick as a man's arm, and she had painted it with snake's teeth to give it the power of the red serpents. "I do not want to leave you, Ulele," Ramón said, fear coming back. "I want to stay with you."

"You cannot stay with me and live." She took his hand, leading him out of the hut with that certainty and bravery that characterized everything she did. Ramón knew he was in capable hands. He followed Ulele's sure lead out of the security of the village and into the dark wilderness, through the rattle-snake-infested saw palmetto scrubs, along narrow trails, until they reached the mouth of Tampa Bay.

Ulele made a high birdlike sound and suddenly a Timucua, one of Mo-coso's braves who had been standing guard, as still as a tree, revealed him-self, returning the sound. The call meant that neither was on a mission of war, that a momentary truce was called for communication. Ulele went to the guard and spoke quickly and earnestly. He listened. Ulele was only a woman, but she wore royal shells around her neck and magic beads in her hair. She was one to be respected even if she came from a rival tribe.

The guard retreated, appearing some time later, nodding assent. Mocoso would take Ramón into his village because he was Hirrihigua's enemy. But he would take Ramón only as a woman, because no half-baked man might be a Timucuan brave. In the Timucuan world there were occasional men who could not—either out of lack of interest or ability—act like a brave and so were treated and thought of as women. Some became lesser wives, and some lived out their lives in the women's hut, working at women's tasks. No great shame—other than that, of course, of being a woman—was attached to it.

"I am not going to be a woman," Ramón said, catching the word and the meaning from Mocoso's guards.

"Then you will be killed by my father. Or you will wander through the swamps until the snakes or the bears attack." She drew him away from Mocoso's guard and held him to her. "You will be a woman," Ulele told him. "To live. For me. To touch my lips once more." She kissed him. Ramón reached out for her, but she was gone.

For one year Ramón was to all intents and purposes a woman. He lived with the women, cut wood with the women, kept the kettle going with the women, and talked with the women, learning to speak the Timucuan language as if it were his own.

When a brave named Ligu, attracted by his smile, wanted to use him sexually as a woman, Ramón put up enough of a fight to ward him off and also other potential lovers. For the most part the braves ignored him, as did Mocoso.

But his sunny nature and innocent curiosity made him a favorite among the women, several of whom wouldn't have treated him as a female if the punishments for women's enjoying one another hadn't been so stringent. He fitted in easily with the cheerful, disorderly Timucuan village life. At night he longed for Ulele, for the touch of her lips, but he found himself thinking less and less of Havana. If he speculated about Narváez's fate, about what was happening to his mother, Antonio, Nani, his son, it was never for very long. Even to him as a woman, each day presented some new and fabulous experience he would never have had had he remained home in Cuba. Most of all, he longed to be a brave—the greatest adventure of all.

At the end of that first year an important brave—Mocoso's son, Opu—returned to the village from a hunting expedition carrying a small half-baked man on his shoulders. He had found him on the shore, and had believed him to be a sign from the gods. The only other half-baked man Opu had ever seen was the woman, Ramón, who did not count.

Opu's white man, evidently ill, was placed in the infirmary hut outside the village, and Ramón, as the lowest of the women, was ordered to care for him. "My name is Jean Valois," the sick man told Ramón in heavily accented Spanish, not surprised to find a nearly nude Spaniard nursing him. Jean Valois, feverish, was past surprise but not without guile. "I am a Frenchman from Marseille. I was aboard a rotten slaver, quarreled with the captain, and he set me adrift in a boat you would not put Satan in. I had enough water for a day, but I was asea for a week. Finally I hit a storm, and the next thing I knew that foul-smelling savage dumped me here. More water," he demanded. "And some of that mush."

Ramón, giving him water and a cereal made of ground meal and herbs, had so many questions, he put them all to the nearly delirious man at once. Valois looked at the Spanish Indian. "Is there any wine?"

Ramón shook his head no. "What happened to Don Pánfilo de Narváez? Did he find gold?"

"The ships supposed to meet him never found him. They think that he and his men just kept getting deeper and deeper into the jungles and that finally Narváez and what was left of his party reached the Gulf of Mexico. It is believed they set sail for Mexico on the rafts they made and were all drowned in a storm two days out. No one is too unhappy, Narváez being the beast he was."

"Do you know Havana?" Ramón asked. "A woman named La Floridita—"

"La Casa," Jean Valois said, and then he wouldn't or couldn't say any more, no matter how many questions Ramón put to him. Ramón tried to ease his discomfort with the herbs and grasses he had learned about from the women, but it was clear the Frenchman was going to die. As Ramón bathed his skin, burned by the sun, he dropped the poultice and stepped back. The sunburn had masked the red dots that covered Jean Valois's skin.

His captain hadn't set him adrift because of an argument. Jean Valois had measles, and the captain had been attempting to save his crew from an epidemic. Jean Valois died two days after being brought into the village, and his body, under the shaman's direction, was put back into the sea. But it was too late for Ramón. He awoke a week later feverish, his skin covered with the red dots. The women took him to the infirmary, where another victim lay: Mocoso's son, Opu.

Mocoso's first wife and the shaman moved into the hut as well, to help nurse Opu. The two sick men were covered with salves and bandages made from Spanish moss. The air was thick with smoking herbs as the shaman said prayers over Opu and the braves chanted outside the hut. Ramón, dazed, listened to the chanting voice of the shaman and allowed his fears of death to be lulled. He had been close to the black god so many times since he had arrived in Florida. He realized, as he lay in the infirmary, that he no longer feared death as much—though dying in a bed seemed preferable to being burned alive—as he disliked it. He had too great a need to know what was going to happen next to die now. He wanted to touch Ulele's lips, her golden face, once more. "No." he shouted in Spanish, "I will not die now."

And he didn't. Whether it was because, as a European, he had been exposed to measles before or whether it was a result of his willpower, Ramón recovered. Mocoso's son Opu, like countless Indians who would come after him, succumbed to the half-baked man's disease.

Mocoso's shaman had never been one of Ramón's champions, considering him an outsider and counseling the cacique, early on, not to take him in, even as a woman. Nevertheless, at a meeting of village elders he agreed that they had received a sign from the gods indicating Ramón was to be given the opportunity to become a man. Opu's body had died, but his spirit now shared the body of the half-baked man. If Ramón passed the tests of courage that entitled a Timucuan youth to become a brave, he would be given Opu's full honors and importance and take his place as Mocoso's son.

Ramón's first test, appropriately, was to guard Opu's body on its log bier deep in the pineland where the great snakes made their home. The old terror returned when he was left alone with Opu's corpse, remembering the night he had spent with the red serpents. The night grew darker, and weak from fear and his recent illness, Ramón slept. He woke at dawn to find that Opu's body was gone.

Ramón thought of what the tribe would do to him when they found he had allowed the body of the cacique's son to be stolen. After they were finished with him he would beg them for *barbecosa*. But the sun gave him renewed courage and the thief had left signs. In the soft, muddy soil Ramón saw tracks, and realizing he had no other choice, he followed them, overtaking a huge gray wolf two miles to the west, deep in a foul-smelling swamp. The wolf sat on top of Opu's body and gave out an unholy cry, baring his teeth, challenging Ramón to try to take his prize.

In that moment Ramón lost all of his fear, furious that after everything he had gone through, this rank beast could be the cause of his death. Without thinking, he charged the wolf, killing it with a single thrust of the spear Ulele had given him.

Exhausted but triumphant, feeling as if he were indeed a man, he returned to the village carrying Opu's body, the wolf's carcass around his neck. Both the shaman and Mocoso agreed that the signs were clear. Ramón had saved Opu's spirit from an eternity of pain. He was accepted as one of Mocoso's hunters, as a brave.

At the end of his second day as a Timucuan man Ramón made his way to Hirrihigua's village. He was careful, forcing himself to move slowly, reminding himself that he was a brave from an enemy tribe. When it grew dark he silently entered the circle of thatched huts, crawling into the one in which Ulele slept. He knelt over her, putting his lips to hers.

She woke instantly, saw him, and felt a great fear. "You would not escape the fire again," she said, holding him to her. "Please, you must go."

"Come with me, Ulele. I am a man now." He indicated the bead-and-shell belt Mocoso had given him, which symbolized his bravery and his manhood. "I am a Timucuan brave—the spirit of Mocoso's son resides within me. Come and be my wife."

Ulele put her hand in his and, smiling, without once looking back, rose and followed him.

Ramón's days were filled with ritual and routine, but he was never for a moment bored. He ran barefoot on hardened soles through the virgin forests, his sun-browned body smeared with fish oil, his face covered with ocher, his beard plucked between clam shells by his Ulele.

He learned to kill a running deer, to swim, and to jump on a manatee's back, killing it with sharp sticks plunged through its nostrils. He could paddle a canoe for miles and days at a time, dancing all night with chanting lines of Indian braves around the ceremonial fire. He ate whatever turned up in the cook pot: fish with bones, birds, turtle, rattlesnake, opossum.

He lived the hard, exciting life of a Timucuan Indian brave, and only his irrespressible smile and emerald-green eyes gave away the fact that he was not born one. He had one disappointment. He and Ulele had no children. "Your gods, your fathers, are elsewhere," the shaman told him. "You must take another wife whose beauty and goodness will draw your fathers' spirits to this place to plant the blessed seed"

Ramón would not take another wife, even though Ulele herself begged him to. He loved her. He loved his life. It was the adventure he had always known it would be.

CHAPTER TWELVE

1539

IT WAS A WARM DAY late in April when La Floridita surprised everyone by announcing she was going to walk to the Havana docks. "I want to see the celebration," she told Antonio.

"You have not left the house in weeks, and suddenly, today of all days . . . Floridita, you will be mobbed. Watch from the balcony."

"I would miss the smells and the noise and the excitement from the balcony." She had insisted and of course had gotten her way. The sky had been ominously dark early in the day but had slowly grown paler until it was suddenly, thoroughly, cloudlessly blue, the sun beating down on the parasol Cabeza de Vaca held over La Floridita's head. She held onto two slightly grubby hands. One belonged to Antonio and Amelia's youngest son—David, an adventurous nine-year-old. The other belonged to her eleven-year-old grandson, Fernando, the serious-eyed version of his father, Ramón.

As they walked toward the dock David occasionally broke free, running ahead, glorying in the harbor noise and excitement. The waters were filled with brigantines and galleons and the docks with sailors and soldiers ready to embark, bartering with the Ciboney women for the sweet, pulpy tropical fruit they had taken a liking to.

La Floridita warned Fernando of the sea, of the danger of adventure. "You must remain in Havana," she told him. "You must protect the Córdoba interests. You must not listen to the stories they tell. Adventure always ends in death."

David—more Amelia's son than Antonio's—said, "Everything ends in death, Auntie, and why not enjoy oneself until it comes?" But Fernando held onto her hand and vowed that he would not leave Havana, that he would stay and, though he wasn't certain what the phrase meant, protect the Córdoba interests. Like his grandmother and like his father, he had taken the honorary name of Córdoba. When he smiled, which was not often, he reminded Floridita of her first love and her only son, both lost to her.

Fernando was a consolation. Isabella was not. Her daughter by Pánfilo de Narváez, she was ten years old, with bright red hair and emerald-green eyes and already a willful beauty. She was at home in the house on Monserrate with her duenna, an unfortunate Spanish noblewoman whom Isabella tormented from early morning till late at night. She was much like Floridita, with a bit of Narváez thrown in, and resented, noisily, everyone's—but most especially her mother's—authority.

Floridita treated her summarily, distancing herself while demanding that Isabella excel at her lessons. She planned to marry her off to the most expensive husband she could find at the first possible moment, preferably a minor hidalgo who would remove her to Spain. Isabella was a constant reminder of Floridita's infatuation with that ill-fated, one-eyed, red-headed giant, Pánfilo de Narváez. La Floridita tortured herself with recriminations for that passion which resulted in the birth of her unsympathetic daughter and the loss of her beloved son.

La Floridita was forty-three years old. Her white skin—still protected by Cabeza de Vaca and his red and yellow parasol—was as delicate as it had been the day she had stepped aboard *La Nao* wearing a *sambenito* beneath a borrowed monk's robe. Her hair, under the white mantilla, was as flame-red as it had been on the morning when, pregnant with Ramón, she had landed in Havana. The faded black fan she held under her eyes emphasized their unforgettable color.

But her age revealed itself in her eyes, which reflected tragedy and disappointment. She had grown old, she felt, on that day when the ships that had gone weeks before to Florida to rendezvous with Pánfilo de Narváez had been sighted reentering the port of Havana. She had believed Ramón would be a member of the land party, and she awaited his return.

Cabeza de Vaca, whose eyesight was better than hers, saw the ships first and tried to stand in front of her, but she pushed him away. Below, on the street, merchants and clerks and their clients stopped to look at the harbor. Those who heard La Floridita's scream never forgot it. It was filled with all the anguish and heartbreak of a mother learning of her only son's death. Pánfilo de Narváez's personal flag was at half mast. He had, characteristically, been impatient. His ships arrived three days after he and his men had tried to sail to Mexico on their makeshift rafts.

La Floridita believed her son, her Ramón, had drowned in the Gulf of Mexico three days before he might have been rescued. If she had hated Pánfilo de Narváez for his physical power over her, now she became sick with grief and anger when his name was mentioned. "Three more days. If he only waited three more days." For months she had asked the duenna, Señora Marte, to keep Isabella out of her sight.

She withdrew into the stone walls of the house on Monserrate. She insisted firmly that Fernando live there with her and her unwanted daughter. Nani, Fernando's mother, knew enough not to object, and La Floridita rewarded her for giving up her son. She said she could no longer deal with the demands of La Casa. It was Nani's to manage as she saw fit. "I shall take only a percentage of the profits," La Floridita said, looking around her reception room for the last time.

"Fifty percent," Nani offered.

"Sixty," La Floridita countered, out of habit. Over the years La Floridita had acquired land and houses, and these holdings Nani began to manage as well. Behind her cool French beauty Nani turned out to be a brilliant businesswoman, a confidante of the most important members of the colonial government, an important supporter of the Church.

It was necessary. The Holy Office and the Inquisition had found its way to the New World, since it was expensive to send heretics to Spain for trial. The Cuban division was notably lax, however. The Inquisition's inspector general, Archbishop Duermo, spent one hour three times a week at La Casa, hearing, he said, the confessions of *las niñas*.

Antonio and Amelia and their children became, apart from Nani and her own household, the only people La Floridita saw. She spent most afternoons with them on her balcony facing the harbor, smoking her black cigars, drinking *aguardiente*, falling into long spells of silence. The Levis attended Mass at the church on the Plaza de Armas each Sunday, practicing the laws of Moses each Saturday at home. "You are braver than I would be," La Floridita told Antonio, pulling her shawl around her, suddenly chilled, thinking of the family of Jews that had just that week been walled up alive in the new cathedral the Church was building, as a warning to lapsed New Christians.

The Levis did not heed it. "My first husband and I left Spain so we could be Jews," Amelia said. "Antonio's family was burned at the stake because they were Jews. What would be the point, Floridita, of all our suffering if we did not remain Jews? If we did not teach our children to be Jews? Who would ever remember?"

"I was thinking of myself," La Floridita confessed. "I could not stand to lose you. I could not be so utterly alone."

She left the house on Monserrate only occasionally, to talk with lawyers and members of the House of Trade, to go to La Casa to pore over the ledgers with Nani and Mira. But that sunny September walk was the first voluntary, just-for-pleasure outing La Floridita had made in years. The arrival, some months before, of the latest *adelantado* of Florida, Hernando de Soto, had excited her, and now she wanted to get a firsthand look at his chain-mailed army as they departed.

At thirty-six Hernando de Soto was rich and famous. He and Pizarro had conquered Peru. And like Ponce de León and Pánfilo de Narváez, he was always searching for new worlds to claim and old names—Cortes, Pizarro—to eclipse. The emperor, after the expensive war with France and the drying up of Mexico, needed a new source of wealth. Hoping it would be Florida, he made De Soto *adelantado* of both Florida and Cuba and gave him a patent to colonize the former.

This new attempt at colonizing Florida excited La Floridita more than any event had in the past ten years. She stood on the Havana dock holding Fernando's hand in her pale, pliant palm, a new freedom and determination coming over her. David Levi was running up and down the wooden dock, and she felt herself wanting to join him. She laughed, thinking what a fool she would look, an old woman cavorting after a young boy. But she did walk after him, looking up at the gulls and the pelicans, feeling for the first time in years a joy she had forgotten, glorying in the briny smell and the coarse sounds of the harbor, in the cut and sway of the brigantines and the galleons, in the excitement of the sailors and the soldiers setting out to sea, in the flow and panoply of the emperor's and De Soto's scarlet banners.

She stood among the poor people of Havana and held her breath at the sheer beauty of the procession: chain-mailed knights, bemedaled gentlemen, gorgeously robed members of the Holy Office, all astride Andalusian horses, embarking aboard the brilliant new ships, the sun reflecting from their polished surfaces, making them look like so many pieces of gold. The romance of exploration lifted Floridita's spirit as drums and bugles resounded through the air and as that La Casa client, Archbishop Duermo, attired in all his Church regalia, holding a gold cross in the air, prayed resoundingly and movingly for the success of this holy mission.

She waited long after the parade of grandees and hidalgos had boarded, not wanting to leave. Cabeza de Vaca held his parasol over her while David and Fernando found her hands as the sailors made ready and the ships began to depart. It was already late afternoon. The blue of the sky was now mixed with a pale pink as the sun began to set.

"I feel," La Floridita said, "as if it is I who is setting out on a new adventure." And then Fernando, looking up as the last of De Soto's brigantines sailed out of port, read the words that had been painted on its prow: *"La Paloma de Negra."*

She made Fernando repeat them. "La Paloma de Negra." The Black Dove. After not having thought of the miracle for years, she knew without a doubt that the brigantine was a symbol, a reminder that the miracle of the Black Dove was still with her. That her destiny was not to die in Cuba. "I am going to the Land of the Flowers," she said aloud as the wind picked up and the fleet's sails filled and Hernando de Soto's fleet headed toward Florida.

"When, Grandmother?" Fernando asked, looking up at her with the Córdoba eyes and, for a moment, that extraordinary smile.

"I do not know, Fernandito. But I do know I am going. And so is your father," she said to David. "We are Black Doves. It is our fate."

CHAPTER THIRTEEN

LA FLORIDITA SAT ON HER BALCONY looking northwest, toward the Land of the Flowers. Cabeza de Vaca stood behind her like a comforting shadow, worrying over her, filling her glass with *aguardiente*. She held the thick, filthy parchment envelope in her hands, turning it over and over. The priest had brought it an hour before and she still hadn't sent for Antonio to read it to her.

The priest would have left it at the entryway, but Floridita had caught sight of him standing below and demanded that he present the letter to her. He was an undistinguished friar, with that same look of fear and obsession in his eyes that Las Mesas had had. He hadn't dared to look at her. All she could get out of him was that he had received the letter from a soldier named Gabrielo who had died that morning. Gabrielo had been one of the handful of sick and emaciated survivors of Hernando de Soto's expedition who had found their way to Mexico and then Cuba after two years of terrible hardship and native savagery in Florida.

There had been an unsettling story of another survivor. It was said that he was an Indian with green eyes, that he had been a captive of the Indians for years, rescued by Hernando de Soto. But he hadn't ever appeared, and Floridita hadn't let herself hope.

Now there was this letter. She made an effort of will to keep her hands from shaking as she held it. She wasn't at all certain she wanted to know what it contained. She thought of Hernando de Soto, of his bemedaled followers, those beautiful young cavaliers, and how nearly all of them had met the same fate as Ponce de León and Pánfilo de Narváez. "If Florida is ever colonized," she said, "it will not be by seekers after gold."

Antonio, on Floridita's behalf, had interviewed one of the survivors, a man still in his early twenties whose mind had been damaged by his experiences. He had not spoken of a green-eyed Indian, but he had confirmed the reports of Hernando de Soto's monumental failure. The expedition had landed on the shores of Tampa Bay and promptly set about slaughtering the Indians they found there. De Soto had moved slowly through the pine-tree jungles, capturing Indian chiefs when he could, using them as hostages, forcing them to provide Indian guides and slaves, increasingly losing men and horses to the ambushes he provoked.

He did not reach the place the Timucuas called Apalachen—far in the northwest—until October. The huts in the village were not made of gold, the men were not nine feet tall, and there were no emeralds, sapphires, or rubies. All he had found was grain, beans, and pumpkins, gathered by the Apalachee Indians for the winter.

De Soto confiscated the food, and the Apalachees attacked, wounding him, forcing him to retreat. But his arrogance would not let him give up. He could not face the prospect of returning to Havana empty-handed after such great expenditure, so much talk, all that panoply. "There is an Indian city of gold," he insisted. "But it lies farther north. We must march northward, to Apalachen, to gold."

He died two years later at the mouth of the Arkansas River, having discovered the Mississippi River, cursing the Indians, his own men, and most especially the peninsula known as Florida, which had been his greatest enemy.

La Floridita held that thick parchment letter in her nervous hands, refusing to let herself hope, but the thought crept into her mind anyway. "Just let him be alive, dear lord. Just let him be alive." She looked up at Cabeza de Vaca who, after all those years, was able to read her mind, and nodded. He went to bid Antonio to come and read the letter to La Floridita.

> Dearest Mama, I am writing this letter to you on a brig called the *San Carlos*. It is anchored in the Gulf of Mexico, a mile from the northwest-ernmost shore of the place the Spanish call Florida. In a short while the *San Carlos* will be sailing for Mexico City and later to Havana with the six survivors of Don Hernando's expedition. I have spent the last three days deciding whether or not to accompany them.
>
> Soon after I arrived in Florida with Don Pánfilo I was taken captive by a band of Timucua Indians. Through the intervention of the cacique's daughter I was saved, and in time, after many adventures, I became a brave in a rival tribe, eventually marrying Ulele, the woman who saved my life.
>
> When Don Hernando and his great ships arrived in Tampa Bay he pretended to approach peacefully, but upon landing immediately ordered an attack. His knights cold-bloodedly slaughtered my tribe's unarmed braves. As I was about to be run through with a Toledo sword I found my voice and said to my attacker, in Spanish, "Kill me, Cavalier, if you will. But know you are slaying a Spaniard."
>
> I was spared and taken aboard Don Hernando's flagship, where, after

the fish oil was scraped and bathed from my body and face and my beads and loincloth were removed and I was subjected to much examination, it was decided by the ship's physician and other officers that I was indeed a Spaniard. I was garbed in Spanish clothes and presented to Don Hernando himself, to whom I related my history.

I finished by saying, "You have killed brave and good men, Don Hernando. May the Almighty Savior have mercy on your soul." Don Hernando ignored this and began to ask about the land and the people and most of all about Apalachen, the same village Don Pánfilo had had as his goal. I answered as best I could and then asked permission to leave the ship, to return to my home. I did not want Ulele or my cacique, Mocoso, whom I have come to love as a father, to believe that I had led the braves to their death and then deserted my tribe.

But Don Hernando ordered me put in chains. He said I was a traitor to my sovereign and to the Holy Savior and that, whether I liked it or not, I was going to be of use to him in finding the secret village made of gold. Then, if I wanted, I could return to my village.

The caravel set sail in the morning, anchoring at the northwesterly end of Tampa Bay, where De Soto's guides—Indians from the island of San Juan—indicated that the long trail to the city of gold began. My wife's father, Hirrihigua, a great cacique badly used by Don Pánfilo, was waiting with his braves on the shore, ready to do combat, spending their fire-hardened spears and arrows, which penetrated the cavaliers' chain mail, killing and wounding many Spaniards.

But Don Hernando's five hundred men were too well armed. After that first round, with few weapons remaining in their possession, the Indians had to retreat. They resorted to surprise raids, harassing Don Hernando's men over and over again as we—I was in chains, under guard—marched northwest to Apalachen. Apalachen was a disappointment, and Don Hernando decided that the real Apalachen lay even farther north and west despite all evidence to the contrary.

By the time we reached the great river he was raving and sick, and I took charge of the small band of survivors. Don Hernando died, badly, in great pain. I managed to lead the six survivors south and east to the shores of the Gulf of Mexico, where, as the gods would have it, the *San Carlos* was anchored, its longboats replenishing its water supplies from nearby springs.

The captain has offered to take me to Mexico and then to Havana, and though I long to see you and Antonio and the son I hardly knew, I find that I cannot return. Though life is often difficult, I am happy in the Land of the Flowers among my tribe, with my wife, Ulele. It is a difficult decision for me, but I am no longer a youth, and I fear if I returned to Havana I should never have another opportunity to come back to Florida, where my heart and my spirit belong.

I thank you, Mama, for giving me the courage and the intelligence to have taken that chance Don Pánfilo offered me: to live a life of adventure. Though it grieves me greatly that we will most likely never see each other again, I beg you to give my son the same opportunity you gave me. Encourage him to live his life to its fullest. My words to Fernando are: Do not be afraid, my son. Explore the new lands and the new worlds, and your life will be, I hope, as full, as exciting as mine.

I am sorry to report, Mama, that the dream we had of my father's becoming a great king in Florida was just that—a dream. But though I am certain he is dead, I feel his spirit living on in the World Above the Sky, offering me guidance.

I send my love to Antonio and to Amelita and to Nani and to my son, Fernando. Perhaps one day he will come to Florida and my spirit will watch over him. This is most likely the last time you shall hear from me, dear Mama, but you may live easy in the belief that I remain your loving son,

Ramón de Córdoba.

Floridita never showed Fernando his father's letter. He was not to lead a life of adventure. He was to remain with her in Havana. La Floridita kept the letter near her, often taking it out and looking at it as if she could read. The tears she spilled on it over the years made the ink run and eventually obliterated most of Ramón's words but never his meaning. Despite their separation and her sadness, there lay within her heart the joy of knowing he was happy.

She also knew, with great certainty, that though she might never see Ramón again, her spirit too would one day soar to the Land of the Flowers, like a black dove flying across the Straits of Florida.

CHAPTER FOURTEEN

IN THE FIFTEEN YEARS following Hernando de Soto's failure, dozens of Spanish adventurers—refusing to believe the evidence of De Soto's followers and others—supported by a desperate Crown, attempted to occupy and tap the resources thought to be hidden in Florida.

But with each attack Florida's Indians became increasingly sophisticated in warfare. Thousands of Spanish lives were lost, along with more ships and property than Spain—with no new Mexico or Peru on the horizon—could afford. Finally, Charles V abdicated, to spend the remainder of his days in a monastery, and his son, King Philip II, decided that enough Spanish effort had been wasted. "Florida is uninhabitable," he said. "The Crown will not attempt to colonize it again."

He reversed himself when Spain's enemy, France, began investigating the possibilities of French colonization of Florida. Gaspard de Coligny, admiral of France and an ardent Huguenot, built a fort in the northeastern corner of Florida on the St. Johns River, not far from where it emptied into the Atlantic Ocean. He named it Fort Caroline for Charles IX.

When Philip learned of it he announced that "the colonization of Florida is essential to protect Spain's rights in North America" and immediately appointed yet another *adelantado* of Florida.

Pedro Menéndez de Avilés was a beetle-browed, short-tempered thirty-five-year-old admiral who had dedicated himself to a fierce, furious Catholicism. He was more interested in converts than in gold. It followed, then, that he was an ardent hater of the Huguenots, those French Protestants who, Menéndez said, thumbed their noses at the true and holy Church. Thus he lost no time in sailing to northeastern Florida and locating the St. Johns, whose waters began in small streams and springs deep in the heart of the peninsula and flowed northward to the sea.

Menéndez sailed down the St. Johns to Fort Caroline, where he found what he suspected: the worst sort of heretics, Huguenots all. "They play cards," he wrote to his wife, "with packs of pasteboards displaying the figures of the Host and Chalice, saints with crosses on their shoulders, burlesquing the rites and sacred beliefs of the only and Holy Catholic Faith." He massacred them all; Fort Caroline became San Mateo, and French plans for a Florida colony were ended.

In August of 1564 Menéndez returned to Florida commanding five ships carrying five hundred soldiers, two hundred sailors, and one hundred colonists he described in his records as "useless people." Among the "useless people" was an old woman. The colonial House of Trade license and the certificate of confession issued by the Church gave her name as La Floridita de Córdoba and her occupation as widow.

With each passing year La Floridita had become more vocal about her conviction that she was fated to die in the Land of the Flowers. She was sixty-nine when she learned of the Menéndez colonization voyage—a great age in that time and place. But she was more determined than ever to fulfill the miracle of the Black Doves. It cost her most of her fortune to secure passage, but secure it she did.

She implored her grandson, Fernando, thirty-six years old, blessed with the Córdoba masculine beauty though lacking its joy, to accompany her. But all those years she had spent instilling in him a sense of duty and a fear of adventure had had their effect.

100

Fernando de Córdoba watched his grandmother with a mixture of affection and distrust as she strode across the recently retiled La Casa courtyard. She still walked like a girl, without a cane, one step in front of Cabeza de Vaca and his parasol. She seemed decades younger than she should have as she came into the reception room, beginning her argument in the middle. "Are you not tired, Fernandito," she asked, "of accounts and ledgers, of merchants and scribes and small-minded House of Trade officials? Do you not long to begin a new life, a life of adventure?"

"Can you imagine Esmeralda, Grandmother," he asked, pulling up a chair for her, "living in a makeshift hut, drawing buckets of water, and cooking her own food?" Esmeralda was the daughter of an impoverished, stranded hidalgo who had come to Floridita for help. She had arranged for the hidalgo to return to Spain with a certain amount of gold in his trunk after his daughter was married, with great ceremony, to Fernando de Córdoba in the cathedral on the Plaza des Armas. "Can you see my sons in makeshift clothing, without their horses or their tutors or their music lessons? Can you imagine me, Grandmother, anywhere else but here?"

With Floridita's assistance, Nani, Fernando's mother, had married a rich merchant and had gone to live with him in Lima years before, leaving her son to sit behind the desk in La Casa's reception room and manage the Córdoba interests. La Casa's specialized business had long since been moved to another, less conspicuous house, closer to the port. But the reception room remained the same. The scent of jasmine still floated in through the open windows, evoking for Floridita the ghosts of Quirinio, Pánfilo de Narváez and, most real of all, her lost son and Fernando's father, Ramón. Half closing her eyes, she could almost see him slamming open the door, racing into the room, his entire being alive with all the possibilities life offered him.

Fernando had little of his father's magnetism except in those rare moments when he smiled. He did so now, reaching for her hand. "I know, Grandmother, there is no possibility of my talking you out of going. But when you are ready to return to Havana, there will always be a home for you in the house on Monserrate."

Fernando loved her, she knew, but sitting in the old reception room—he had taken away the daybed, she noticed—Floridita sensed his relief. His disreputable old grandmother, not quite, it was said, entitled to the name she had given herself, would be removed from the scene. Fernando had his highborn wife and two aristocratic sons, but as the bastard of a hidalgo's bastard, engaged in trade, he had a need to continually prove his respectability.

"My home," she said, rising, embracing Fernando, "has always been in the Land of the Flowers. Finally I am going to it." She took a last look around that reception room where so much of her life had been spent, and telling Fernando to put back the daybed, she left it forever without a qualm.

Isabella, her red-haired beauty of a daughter, had—after all—grown closer to her over the years. Isabella had left the house on Monserrate at fifteen, eloping with and eventually marrying an adventurer named Ricardo San Mercedes, who gave her half a dozen children in as many years and then disappeared on a voyage to Spain. Isabella had returned to the house on Monserrate with her children and, when she had remarried, brought her merchant husband to live there as well. When Floridita had proposed, tentatively, that Isabella and her family should join her in the colonization voyage to Florida, she had immediately said yes. "I am, after all, your daughter, Mama," she told a surprised Floridita. "And sick of boring old Havana."

Antonio Levi, Floridita's old friend, her fellow Black Dove, was not as enthusiastic. What little hair he had was no longer blond but a wispy white. He walked with a shambling step. Amelia had died the way she had wanted, nicely, in her big bed, surrounded by her family, breaking Holy Office law: a Portuguese rabbi, who managed to keep one step ahead of the authorities by masquerading as a priest, was at her side.

She had died with the rabbi's blessings, holding her husband's and La Floridita's hands, a rueful smile on her still plump, comely face. "I leave Antonio to you, my dear Floridita," she had said. He couldn't live alone, and his sons' families, while respectful and loving, were far too lively. Floridita had installed him in the house on Monserrate in a bedroom facing north, toward Florida. He spent his days sitting with his old friend on her balcony, drinking *aguardiente*, remembering. Usually they didn't have to speak to communicate; they knew each other so very well.

Cabeza de Vaca continued to fan them, to light Floridita's cigars, to keep the *aguardiente* glasses filled, moving the old couple into the tiled salon when the fall storms began to blow.

Floridita found Antonio on the balcony, sitting in the outsized chair Cabeza de Vaca had made in Puerto Rico, his hands folded resignedly, his eyes half closed. "I am not going," he said without looking up, knowing Floridita was behind him waving that black fan she had had repaired over and over again, staring at him impatiently. "I am too old. Menéndez would not want me. David and his wife can go. He is still young. Floridita, stop bothering me. I am not going."

"You will be free to be a Jew in Florida, Antonio."

He laughed a sour laugh. "No one is ever free to be a Jew. First Jews have to die to be Jews, and then Jews have to fight to be Jews, and then they have to pay to be Jews. Being a Jew is never free."

She put her hands on his thin shoulders, and he could feel her sweet breath on his cheek, and for just a moment they were young again, sailing to Havana aboard Quirinio's brig, starting a new life. "You would not let me go alone, Antonio."

"You would not be alone. There is Isabella and her family, and my David and his family, and the Lord knows who else . . ."

"I would be the only Black Dove, Antonio."

He pushed her hands from him and stood up, supporting himself on the

102

balcony railing, still not looking at her. "Will you never stay in one place?"

"If I had stayed in one place, niño, I would be washing actors' soiled linen in a theater in Seville. And where would you be if I had stayed in one place? A penitent in a monastery in Puerto Rico? Come with me, Antonio. You must. It is our destiny."

"I am ready to die, Floridita. Leave me here in peace."

"You are not going to die until I say so," she said, her cheeks red with anger. "You are not going to die, Antonio, until we reach the Land of the Flowers and fulfill the Lord's miracle. And even then I am going to keep you by my side for years and years and years. Say you will come with me."

"We shall see."

"We do not have time for contemplation. I have to secure your license from the House of Trade and a certificate from the archbishop, and who knows how much that will cost? I am going to have to bribe half the colonial office. They are not enthusiastically recruiting the ancient and the infirm for this voyage. Say yes, niño."

"Have I ever said no to you, Floridita?" Antonio asked, finally goaded into anger. "Yes. The answer is yes. Now leave me alone."

She kissed him. "It is a good thing, because everything is all arranged. I knew you would come. You are just as curious as I am to see the place where the miracle said we would go. Tell the truth."

He said yes, he was curious, but the truth was he would not be going anywhere if it weren't for La Floridita, and he never would have gone anywhere if it weren't for La Floridita. He shook his head and went off to talk to his other sons, those who were staying in Havana, leaving La Floridita alone with Cabeza de Vaca on the balcony.

She felt tired but not in an exhausted way. There had been so much activity. So many details to see to. In a week they would be on a ship, sailing out of Havana harbor, headed for the Land of the Flowers. There was a sudden warm breeze, and she put her white mantilla over her now white hair and closed those still remarkably green eyes. She thought of that early voyage out of Spain, of those nights of love, and she felt the tears coming for her lost Ramón. And then she thought of that voyage from Puerto Rico, of how frightened she had been, dependent upon Quirinio, responsible for Antonio, pregnant with that other, unforgettable Ramón.

She stood up, wiping the tears away. Cabeza de Vaca looked at her mournfully with his plaintive cow eyes. "I am not sad," she told him, putting her hand on his arm. "These are happy tears, Cabeza de Vaca. All my great loves are in the Land of the Flowers. Soon we shall be there, too, beginning yet another life. At my age is that not a miracle?"

Menéndez's colonizing *flota* reached the northeast coast of Florida early on June 28, 1565. "It is a morning for miracles," Floridita said, standing on the deck among the other colonists, celebrating sunrise Mass. For the most part they were young men and women, who found themselves borrowing courage from this old white-haired woman with the sparkling green eyes of a girl. She acted as if this were merely a day trip to a familiar place instead of a voyage to an unknown shore involving a profound change of life.

Floridita stared over the priest's shoulder at the sea. Its waters were dark blue except toward the beach, where they became turquoise and iridescent, as if their magic clung to the shore along with the bubbling foam. For once Antonio had not accompanied her, refusing to leave his cabin, saying he was too ill to attend Mass. Floridita worried about him. He seemed genuinely ill, dazed, not certain where he was. The voyage had not done him any good. She would see to him as soon as this long Mass was over.

Menéndez and his officers had already been ashore, making certain it was a suitable site for a colony. Satisfied, he had named the place St. Augustine, in honor of the day, the festival of San Augustín.

La Floridita, anxious as a young woman awaiting the first glimpse of her betrothed, had to wait twenty-four hours after that interminable Mass before the order came for the colonists to disembark. The soldiers and young men had gone first and had already cut down a small pine forest, providing shelter in the way of a wall and crude huts.

She ran to Antonio's cabin to tell him, but he seemed at first not to know her. "I am too ill," he said from his bed, refusing to be helped. Frightened that Menéndez would send him back to Cuba, La Floridita found Antonio's son, David, who returned with two young colonists, and between them and Cabeza de Vaca they managed to get Antonio topside and then into the longboat.

"There is too much light," Antonio said as he sat next to Floridita, his head on her shoulder, just as it had been all those years before when they had disembarked from *La Nao*. She held his hand, comforting him. Except for her belief in the miracle, she had never been a religious woman. But as the longboat neared shore La Floridita felt her heart overflow with joy, with an ecstasy that was surely inspired by the Holy Savior. She felt so full of life, a woman of nearly seventy, that she was afraid her bosom might burst out of her gown, that she might leave all of her clothes and earthly trappings below and fly across the few yards of salt water, a dove coming home to the Land of the Flowers, as Christ had intended.

She turned to look at her *niño*, her Antonio, to share her ecstasy, but he was staring past her at a vision of his own. "I am coming, Papa. Mama. Pepita. I am coming home to you, Amelita." He managed to get to his feet, to evade Floridita's and his son's arms, to climb out of the longboat and stagger through the shallow water to the beach, where he fell, kissing the sand. "I am home," he said as Floridita joined him, kneeling beside him, oblivious to the salt water ruining her boots and gown, taking him in her arms.

He looked up at her, not seeing the white hair or the wrinkled skin. She was once again the flame-haired, smooth-skinned Floridita of his youth. Her never-changing green eyes had filled with tears. She had taken the place of his mother and his sister, and she had found him the wife who had given him love and happiness for so many years. He reached up and touched her cheek. "A Dios, my Floridita," he whispered. The group of late arrivals stared helplessly down at the old woman holding the old man in her arms, sobbing uncontrollably, as the tide began to wash over them. Finally David reached over Floridita's shoulder and closed his father's eyes.

They buried him a half mile west of the new settlement, in a rough coffin built by the ship's carpenter from new-cut Florida pine. Antonio's was the first grave in what was to be St. Augustine's cemetery.

A Mass was duly said at the burial site and a cross was placed over the grave. The colonists crossed themselves and, after all, not overly concerned with the death of an old man, returned to the site on the Matanzas River where the pine copse had been chopped down and rude huts put up, the site of the first city in Florida.

Early in the hours before dawn, while Menéndez's men and the colonists were sleeping, Floridita and Cabeza de Vaca made their way along the beach, the sand aglow in the star-reflected light. The guard, a sleepy boy, tried to stop them, but Floridita said she was taking a stroll advised by her physician and that Cabeza de Vaca was all the protection anyone might need.

At Antonio's grave she knelt. "The Lord forgive me, but Antonio was never a true Catholic, and I do not believe, dear Lord, that there is only one way to worship You. I believe that You are welcoming Antonio into your garden of heaven as one day soon You shall welcome me."

She reached across the newly dug grave and pulled the wooden cross out of the ground, giving it to Cabeza de Vaca. He made another mound some yards away and put the cross there. He didn't like to think what Menéndez would do to him and his mistress if this desecration were discovered.

La Floridita, not concerned with that sort of fear, buried in the sand just over Antonio's coffin a wooden marker Cabeza de Vaca had spent the afternoon carving. Since neither he nor his mistress had the gift of writing, the marker bore only a carving, that of a single black dove, a tiny Star of David on its wing.

La Floridita stayed on her knees for some moments, remembering her Antonio, thinking of that long-ago miracle and how it had so changed their lives. Now her old friend and her husband were buried in the sandy soil, and someday soon she would join them. The Black Doves. They had all come, as the Holy Savior had willed, to the Land of the Flowers, and now their seeds would grow in the New World soil and multiply.

Cabeza de Vaca helped her up, her rheumatic knees not being what they had once been. Nothing was the same, she thought ruefully. She looked down at the grave and had no idea how on earth she was going to get on without her old friend, wondering if he had ever realized how much she had needed him. Suddenly the grave was illuminated, covered with light. La Floridita turned to the east and saw a huge yellow mass rising over the dark waters of the great ocean. It was her first Florida dawn.

She wiped away her tears with the edge of her white mantilla and put it over her head. Cabeza de Vaca unfolded the old parasol, holding it so it shaded his mistress from this new, early, and unknown sun. Then the outsized Indian and the aged Spanish woman made their way across the sand back to the hastily erected walls that contained the first settlement in Florida that would take hold, grow, and thrive: St. Augustine.

In a shorter time, perhaps, than was seemly, La Floridita became less melancholy. She would mourn her Antonio as she had mourned her Ramón, but she wasn't anxious to join them. She found herself wanting to know what was going to happen next and thought that perhaps, after all, she might have a few more years to enjoy this Land of the Flowers.

EPILOGUE

1585

TWENTY YEARS AFTER IT WAS FOUNDED, the Spanish colonial outpost called St. Augustine could boast a council house, a church, several stores, and housing for all of its three hundred men, women, and children.

The people in Menéndez's colony had planted corn, Indian beans, pumpkins, melons, and onions. They had set out groves of oranges, figs, peaches, and pomegranates. They had learned to fish and gather oysters, to kill deer and wild turkey. They had no expectations of finding gold and thus had learned to coexist with the Indians, who, when not robbed and pressed to become Catholics, remained peaceful.

On the last day of that year, 1585, on a particularly beautiful winter's day, an old woman who had reached the miraculous age of ninety, lay dying. She had been one of the original colonists, and her house, nearly touching the old gates, was made of the first pine that had been cut. It had a glassless window to allow for the clean sweep of the sweet summer breezes and the warming sun during the mild winters.

The sun was not needed on that December day, the little house made warm by the presence of the woman's grandchildren and great-grandchildren and the grandchildren and the great-grandchildren of her friends. The officials of the town were present as well. She was their matriach; they had come to think of her as the mother of their colony. She had outlived the daughter and the Ciboney slave she had brought with her as well as many of the original settlers.

She had, it was said, lived a tempestuous life. But she was dying serenely. She lay in her bed, holding an ancient, much mended black fan in her hand, her descendants looking on, waiting for her last words. She smiled at a boy with fair blond hair she had heard called Antonio. Next to him stood one of her grandsons, a man with black hair and that breathtaking Córdoba masculine beauty. She touched the smooth cheek of a girl—a great-grandchild—who had flame-red hair and dazzling green eyes.

At midnight on the first day of the New Year, looking at that little girl, so full of life, so reminiscent of herself at that age, the old woman's last words came. "The Black Doves," she said in a clear youthful voice, "are free at last." La Floridita closed her remarkable green eyes for the last time.

BOOK TWO

The Middle Years

Lobo Levi—1814

HE WAS COLD AND HUNGRY, every bone in his body aching, wrapped up in a six-foot-long Seminole blanket that smelled to high heaven. Lobo Levi was happy. He was a man—at age twenty—at war. He held onto his Kentucky rifle for dear life and kept his ears sharp, listening for rattlers and signs of Red Sticks. He didn't trust the Tennessee boys on guard duty. They wouldn't know a Red Stick from a red rose.

He lay on the hard ground looking up at the Alabama Territory sky with his yellow eyes, thinking it didn't look much different from the Florida sky a few hundred yards away. He was a soldier in General Andrew Jackson's Citizen Volunteers of Tennessee: eight hundred men in ragtag uniforms, some with horses, most without, armed with an array of weapons ranging from ancient blunderbusses to efficient new Kentucky rifles. They came from every part of Tennessee, Alabama, and Georgia, brought up on stories of Indian torture and savagery, filled with a passionate hatred for the red man and the righteous belief that they were entitled to his land and his possessions.

The Red Sticks, one thousand strong, the most murderous members of the Creek Nation, were holed up in their camp, across the Alabama/Florida border. Incited by the British, who were at war with the Americans, the Red Creeks had just come from murdering, scalping, and mutilating the men, women, and children in the quiet Fort Mims stockade. They had no plans to move their camp, believing that the Americanos were not allowed by their Great White Father in Washington City to cross into Spanish Florida.

But the Red Sticks hadn't reckoned on Andrew Jackson, who was only waiting for supplies from Washington, weeks overdue, before attacking. "My men can't eat the Injuns," he said. In the meanwhile he was sending his Captain MacCrimmons to the Spanish port city of Pensacola to see if there weren't some way to find food and get it back to Alabama Territory. Lobo Levi had been chosen to lead the way when it was found he came from Pensacola and knew the route.

"Take care of that boy," General Jackson told Mac. "We may want to talk to the Injuns some day. He speaks Hitchiti." Lobo had learned Hitchiti and some Muskogee from the disenchanted members of the Creek Federation who had been drifting south into Florida ever since Spain had ceded Florida to the British in 1763. Peaceable Indians, they were escaping the chronic intertribal Creek warfare. The British, who had given Florida back to Spain after twenty years, had called these Creeks Wandering Seeds—Seminoles— and the name had come to be applied to all of Florida's newly arrived Indians. They feared their cousins, the Creeks, who often raided their villages, killing and looting.

Lobo Levi, who had spent as much of his youth in the Seminole villages as he could, had come to fight the Creeks in the hope that they would be driven north and leave his Seminole friends alone.

Mac had assured General Jackson he would take care of "the boy," though they were the same age. They were both fair, but that was as far as the similarities went. Even their blondness was different: Lobo's hair was a mass of nearly white curls, while Mac's hair was corn yellow and straight.

MacCrimmons was a Georgia farm boy, his muscles bursting through his flannel shirt, his baby face a study in innocent good nature. He had been orphaned early and brought up by his mother's parents. His grandfather spoke from the church pulpit on Sundays and worked the cotton farm throughout the week, alongside his wife. Mac's granny had a wen the size of a button on the end of her nose and a stubborn chin, and her stringy hair was washed on odd Saturday nights. But it was Granny who had taught Mac to love and respect women. His grandfather had given him a stern affection and a rigid sense of right and wrong.

The grandparents had died of influenza within a week of each, and after he had buried them, Mac spent a long winter and spring working the land by himself. He suffered terribly from loneliness and would have married Judy Anderson despite her silliness but she had gone off with a cousin to live in Virginia. When her brothers announced they were going to Tennessee to fight the Injuns, he leased his land to their father and joined them.

And when Andrew Jackson, suffering from dyspepsia and neglect from Washington City, saw MacCrimmons in the recruiting line, he nearly hugged him. Jackson saw himself as the father of his people, and here was this big, blond, muscular boy whose freckled, pug-nosed face revealed every one of his emotions. He could be nothing but what he was, the essence of Jackson's volunteer army, the epitome of the South's farm boy. Jackson made him a lieutenant straight off, and when Washington City sent Jack Church, that lily-livered Military Academy officer to spy on him, Jackson made Mac a captain to outrank him.

Mac found Granny's self-respect and his grandfather's morality personified in the single person of General Andrew Jackson. After that long, lonesome period of mourning, when he had felt lost in his own house, Mac found himself at home under the general's command. He believed completely

112

Jackson's contention that the redskins were savages to be wiped out, that the Spanish had forfeited their territorial rights by being so cowardly. Mac had never known an Injun, nor for that matter anyone who wasn't white and Protestant, except for a few black slaves, who didn't count. Yet he found himself liking this Spanish Jew, this Private Lobo Levi, who spoke English like an American and who knew so much about the Indians.

"Lobo ain't your real name," Mac said, to say something. All he could hear were the insects, and he couldn't see a damned thing, Jackson having outlawed fires in case they attracted the Creeks.

"My real name is Antonio," Lobo said, but he didn't say anything else. He was taciturn by nature, but he knew the forest as well as he knew the Creeks, and he wanted to listen for them in the event they decided to surprise everyone and make a nighttime attack. No one had ever called him Antonio. It was clear almost immediately, even to his mother, that Antonio was an inappropriate name. The first Antonio, dead for more than two hundred years, had been a scholarly sort of man. Lobo received the name he was to be known by after running away from home when he was just four. He had returned late at night to the frantic Pensacola household, a gray wolf cub in his little arms. He had found the cub in the piney woods that surrounded the small water's-edge settlement of Pensacola and, against everyone's objections, had kept it, tamed it, and loved it. The cub was called Lobo—"wolf" in Spanish—and in time so was Antonio.

Ever since he could remember he had wanted to be a soldier. As a boy he had followed the Spanish officers in their blue and red coats and knee-high boots around the streets of Pensacola, envying them their freedom and their swagger. The Tennessee Regulars were a far cry from the black-booted elegance of the Spanish regiment garrisoned in Pensacola.

Nonetheless he was content. But the thick-skinned country boys who made up the Tennessee Volunteers weren't happy when they learned that a Jew—a Spanish Jew from Florida, at that—had been allowed to enlist. Lobo was aware there had to be trouble, and when they pretended a heavy-handed friendship that first night, he knew what was coming and decided to get it over with.

Most of them, he realized, were afraid of him, the Jew devil. It was an unseasonably late summer in 1814, cold, with mist settling in around the pine and oak trees of the forest where they were camped. They took him a little way from the camp into the forest. "We going to show you a two-headed bobcat," Grimes, a sergeant and the ringleader, said. "Bet you never saw no two-headed bobcat down in Florida. Damndest thing you ever saw." He looked around at the other boys, who snickered.

They gathered round him in a clearing a lightning fire had made. He was ready, so it took four of the biggest to pin him face down, and even then they had to sit on him to keep him there. The ground smelled reassuringly of pine needles and red clay. "Sure don't scrap like a Jew," Davy Crockett, having just seen Lobo nearly break a Tennessee boy's jaw, said. "Scraps more like an Injun."

"How you know how a Jew scraps, Crockett?" Grimes asked, bending over Lobo. "You ain't never seen one in your life."

"Your mammy told me." This deadly insult was ignored, Crockett being older and tougher than Grimes, and besides, there was other business at hand.

Grimes and a couple of the others took turns digging their filthy fingers into Lobo's blond curls, feeling his scalp, and when they couldn't find horns, they pulled down his buckskin trousers and looked for his tail. That search also proved disappointing, so they turned him over, and Grimes held a candle over Lobo's privates so they could all see what a circumcised Jew handle looked like.

"Maybe we should burn it off," Grimes said, grinning, moving the candle closer, igniting a few of Lobos's pale pubic hairs, watching them burn with a satisfying crinkly sound and give off a good, nasty smell. "Want us to burn off your handle, Jew boy?" Grimes asked. He was looking for some reaction from Lobo, ready to do some real damage to get one.

"If you hurt that man, Sergeant Grimes, you hurt the only man in this army who speaks the enemy's language." Jack Church's educated, northern voice cut through the night. The man President Madison had sent to keep an eye on General Jackson, resplendent in his tailored blue and white West Point uniform, was taking one of his solitary strolls. "I don't think," Lieutenant Jack Church went on in his precise accent, "that the general would be keen on losing Private Levi or any part of him."

"The general will decide, Lieutenant Church, whom he is keen on losing and whom he is not." Andy Jackson, not averse to solitary walks himself, especially when he was suffering from his dyspepsia, stood looking at Jack Church as if he would spit in his eye.

From Lobo's point of view, on the ground, with his buckskins down around his boots, the pine needles irritating his back seat, and everything he had in the world exposed for all who wanted to see, both men seemed twelve feet tall. The general, chronically thin, his large white hand massaging his stomach under his tunic, looked like a mangy, red-headed scarecrow. Jack Church was as tall as he but three times as broad, a mass of muscle and fat. His pale eyes, of no particular color, were just as outraged as the general's. President Madison had a pretty good idea of Jackson's intentions to chase after the Red Sticks right into Spanish territory if he had to. Jack Church had been sent to stop Jackson if he could. The thought of Spain, weak as she was, coming into the war on the side of Britain gave Jim Madison and his advisers goose bumps.

But Church had been in camp less than a day when he realized Old Hickory was not going to let an international border or Madison's giant of a Military Academy lieutenant stop him. This was to be the first battle of the Citizen Volunteers' general, and he meant to win in a big way.

114

"You men let that boy up and stop your foolishness," the general said, massaging his aching stomach. He spat, just to the right of Jack Church's mirrorlike boot, and sauntered off, worried about supplies. His boys had to eat.

A week later the supplies still hadn't arrived, and the food on hand wouldn't last another five days. Which was why Mac and Lobo Levi were on their way down to Pensacola.

The moon had come out as Mac and Lobo lay on the ground, alternately too anxious and too exhilarated to sleep, waiting for the moment just before dawn when they were scheduled to leave. Lobo rested easier with the moon's appearance. The Red Sticks would never attack in the bright moonlight. He reached into the pocket of his buckskin shirt and found the gold locket he always carried.

He opened it and smiled at how accurately the portraitist had captured Renata's prim expression. Mac, prowling about, knelt down next to Lobo Levi and caught his breath, staring incredulously at the portrait of the black-haired woman. He had never seen anyone as haughty, as pale, as fragile.

"It's my wife," Lobo explained.

Mac looked at him disbelievingly. "If I had a wife like that, I'd never leave her," he said, carefully taking the miniature from Lobo and studying it as if he meant to commit it to memory. "She really look like this?"

"She does," Lobo said. "She reads and writes Spanish and English and knows how to balance a set of books, and she can out-trade any damned trader in Florida with her eyes shut." He lost his smile. He looked up at MacCrimmons, deciding finally he might trust him. "I left her without saying goodbye. That's why I volunteered to go on this jackass errand. There isn't any food in Pensacola, and even if there was, how the hell would we get it back here? Sail it up across Florida?" He held his hand out for the locket. "She doesn't know where I am. That's nothing new; but this time I want her to know I didn't just take off with the Seminoles. This time I want her to know I got a cause."

Mac, shaking his freckled baby face in amazement, reluctantly handed back the locket. The pale face with the perfectly parted, pulled-back black hair, the solemn black eyes, the aquiline nose, and the too red lips stayed in his mind, and he couldn't shake the vision out. He didn't care if this was a jackass errand. He wouldn't mind getting a look at that lady in person to see if Levi was lying or not.

Lobo closed his eyes, thinking he might get an hour's sleep, but he too couldn't rid himself of the image of Renata's face. They were cousins, both able to trace their ancestry back to the man he was named for, Antonio Levi, who had died upon reaching the Florida coast over two hundred years before. But his son, David, had prospered in St. Augustine, becoming a chandler. His father had been a chandler, and he knew that candles and ships' stores would always be needed, no matter how poor the community.

David Levi's sons and their sons continued to practice the Jewish religion while pretending to be New Christians. At the same time they expanded the chandlery business, trading with the Indians and the ships that put into St. Augustine, establishing outposts in Pensacola, Mexico City, Lima. Levi and Company eventually became the most important trading organization in Spanish America, headquartered in Havana, protected by the Crown itself.

The British blockades destroyed all trading, and when the British occupied Florida in 1763 the various branches of the Levi family fled St. Augustine, settling in Havana with many other Spanish families. Fifty Timucuas, the last of Florida's aboriginal Indians, went with them, leaving much of northern Florida's rich land for the disenchanted former Creeks, the Seminoles. But Lobo's father, Adamo, was unhappy in Havana, where the colonial Church was far more meddlesome than it had been in St. Augustine. In 1783, when Spain regained Florida, he decided to return.

But the family's St. Augustine trading post and houses had been destroyed, and St. Augustine harbor was a constant invitation to British and French pirates. Adamo Levi finally settled in Pensacola, where the bay was secure and the family had an already established Levi and Company trading post, which had begun to trade with the Seminoles during the British occupation. And in Pensacola, where traders of every conceivable nationality and belief crowded the dusty, narrow streets, it was easier to be a Jew, to observe the Jewish Sabbath, while continuing to be known as New Christians.

Adamo and his wife, Sara, then childless, brought with them from Havana a young cousin, Marita. She was like a daughter to them but was at once naïve, worldly, and stubborn. She had fallen in love with a Cuban hidalgo named Córdoba, a member of a delegation visiting Florida on a mission for the colonial government. Believing he would marry her, she had allowed him to seduce her and found herself pregnant soon after. But the hidalgo had returned to Cuba, and Marita Levi died in September of 1795 while giving birth to her daughter, Renata, without identifying the father. Renata had grown up in Adamo's household, taking her mother's place as the daughter of the family. In the meanwhile, two years before Renata's birth, Sara and Adamo had had a son, Antonio. Antonio, or Lobo, had never regarded Renata as a relative.

As he lay on the cold, hard Alabama ground, the aroma from his old blanket diluted by the scent from the pine trees, he felt himself wanting her. He always wanted her, even after he had lain with his Indian wife, his sensuous Tatami. Tatami was like the blanket, ripe and soft and enveloping. Renata was like the pine trees, cool and majestic and worthy of adoration.

Lobo Levi sighed as Mac came to tell him that their horses were ready, that it was time to leave for Pensacola.

CHAPTER TWO

LOBO HAD DECIDED to take the easier but longer route, approaching Pensacola from the west, making a wide circle around the town through the piney woods, stopping on a bluff near Fort Barrancas. Mac, who had never before seen a body of water larger than a river, halted his horse just behind Lobo's with a shout. He tasted, for the first time, the sharp, salty air of the Gulf of Mexico. "I ain't never seen anything that color," he said, hypnotized by the green-blue Pensacola Bay and the bluer Gulf water beyond it.

They had been riding south through the pine forests of West Florida for three days, stopping once to make camp by themselves and once in a Seminole village, where the braves had treated Lobo as if he were one of them, jabbering away at him in their own language. Lobo talked to them with as much ease as if he were speaking English or Spanish, maybe more. Mac, hungry, ill at ease, a little frightened, had been left with the horses until Lobo remembered him and brought him into the center of the village, where the sofkee—the stewpot—sat cooking on a starfire.

"Help yourself," Lobo told him.

"Oughtn't we to wait for suppertime?"

"There's no suppertime. You eat when you're hungry, and any fool can see you're hungry, so eat."

Mac took the communal wooden spoon and fished out a piece of meat that looked and tasted like turtle and thought it was pretty good, and then he got something else on the spoon that turned out, on close inspection, to be a green, white, and yellow snake's head. He just made it into the woods before he threw up. "It wasn't only the snake," he told Lobo later. "It's that smell. What the hell do them Injuns rub on themselves to smell like that?"

"Bear grease. And you don't smell any better to the Seminoles, in case you think you do."

There had been another white man in the Indian village. Short, thin, he wore buckskins and an Indian headdress. With his Scottish burr, red, freckled skin, great ginger beard extending halfway down his chest, and shoulder-length red-brown hair neatly parted in the center, he should have been ridiculous, but instead he was a man who commanded instant respect. Mac immediately sensed that he and Lobo were friends, the other fellow treating Lobo as if he were an equal.

"Laird's the most important Indian trader in Florida," Lobo told Mac the next day as they rode hard toward Pensacola. "Half the time he thinks he's a Seminole, and the Seminoles think he's a great chief. He just about brought me up. All the good things I know I learned from Laird."

Laird had come when the British left and had traveled the Indian nation from the far Western territories to the tip of Florida, establishing relations with the Indians that made him Levi and Company's greatest trader. Thanks to him Levi and Company was the undisputed trading company of Spanish America, controlling dozens of traders and forty-five thousand Indians and the hides they produced. The Spanish market for leather, both in the home country and in the colonies, was continuous. And Levi and Company owned most of the market.

It was Laird who had introduced Adamo Levi's son, Lobo, to the Seminoles, and it was Laird who had convinced Lobo to join Jackson's volunteers, to fight the Red Sticks. "You're not doing any good here," Laird had said in Pensacola, and Lobo knew Laird was referring to Levi and Company, to Renata, to his golden-skinned Seminole squaw. "Go. I cannot say I approve of Andy Jackson, but he has the right idea. Break their backs, once and for all time. If someone doesn't, we're going to find the Red Sticks in Pensacola one of these fine days wearing our coats on their shoulders and our scalps on their belts."

Laird and Lobo's father, Adamo, had been more than business associates; they had been great friends. "I respected him," Laird told Lobo soon after Adamo's death. "He was bookish, that he was, but he ran his business and his life with honesty, and that is the most I can say of any man. But better than his intelligence was his imagination. He could always put himself in another man's place and understand what it was to be that man. It is a great facility, lad."

But Lobo had been a stranger to Adamo. Lobo had no interest in the complexities of trading, in the fine craft of bookkeeping. His enthusiasms lay elsewhere. Early on, Adamo had looked for understanding to Renata, his poor, dead cousin's love child, who seemed more like his own child than his son. He explained to her the importance of the Scottish traders in his empire, of the looming importance of wood, of the crucial need to keep a diversified trade so that if one aspect of the business failed, another would act as balance.

And Renata had listened while Lobo went off with Laird to trade with the Indians. Adamo felt that within the tiny child, product of a New World Jewish woman and a Cuban hidalgo, lay a new life for the Levi family. She had the same steady, quick intelligence as Adamo. She loved the trading post and

118

the house Adamo had built—a wooden mansion at the corner of Calle Zaragoza, in the heart of Pensacola—as much as Adamo had. She watched and copied his every move, listening and learning, hiding on the balcony while he entertained business associates on the veranda below. Lobo knew it was right for Renata to take over the family business.

Standing on the Fort Barrancas bluff, Lobo was again, as always, surprised at how perfect that crescent of dark-green water was, as if the coastline of the bay had been painted by a master artist. The town of Pensacola was a complementary crescent, bordered on the west by Fort Barrancas and on the east by the stockade the British had left to Spain.

In the center of the crescent, surrounded by austere Spanish government buildings, was the old Spanish parade ground, Plaza Ferdinand. The plaza was the literal and figurative center of Pensacola; even at that early hour in the morning it was filled with people trading, milling about, exchanging rumors, learning the latest news.

At the water's edge, west of the plaza, were Levi and Company's warehouses and stores, the workers' houses and the Levi mansion. From the bluff, Pensacola seemed to be teeming with life. MacCrimmons, who had never been in a large city before, didn't know where to look first.

"You keep rubbing away at your legs like that, you're not going to have any breeches left," Lobo told him, shaking his head at Mac's wide-eyed, incredulous stare. Mac found everything that was foreign and new fascinating. He wanted to try it all on to see if it fitted.

Looking down at the town he had been born into, Lobo felt as if two teams of strong farm horses were pulling him in different directions: Renata and white man's civilization toward Pensacola; his golden-skinned Indian squaw and the free Seminole life toward the piney woods.

Reluctantly he led the way down the bluffs and into the town. "You sure know a lot of people," Mac said as they rode down Calle Palafox, Lobo nodding at people every few seconds. He was aware that the gossips in the plaza were already at work spreading the word: Adamo's prodigal son—Renata's roving husband—is back. He parted from Mac at the Levi trading-post porch, a large wooden deck crowded with Seminole chiefs in town to do some trading.

"You're going to have enough trouble getting victuals, but before you buy anything, you'd better go down to the docks and see if there's a boat willing to take them across the Gulf and up the Apalachicola River to Alabama. It won't be easy. Spain's not supposed to be helping England's enemy." He looked at Mac, who stood rubbing his hands on his thighs. "What's the matter?"

"I don't know Spanish," Mac said, turning red, as if he should have known it. "I don't know where the docks are neither."

Lobo looked at him with affection and exasperation. This was a captain in the Tennessee Regulars. "You can see the docks from here, Mac. And the captains all talk some English." His yellow eyes looked around and fastened on Perito, a boy whose father worked for Levi and Company. He sent Perito to show Mac the way. Then he entered the trading post, feeling like an animal being returned to his cage.

The trading post was long, low-ceilinged, and dark, redolent with the sharp smell of tanned hides, the principal merchandise. Just for a moment Lobo thought he felt his father's hand on his shoulder. Adamo had always put his hand on Lobo's shoulder when they were in the trading post, as if he could transmit his enthusiasm to his son, as if he could guide him in the right direction. Serious business was always conducted on the first floor of the brick and stone building in a wide, comfortable office known as the Talking Room.

A new employee, a fastidious little fellow with a bald head and shiny britches, asked him what his business was. "I came to see Señora Renata," Lobo said, not liking the way the clerk was looking at his none-too-fresh buckskins. The clerk said Señora Renata was busy, and Lobo wanted to hit him, but at the same time he liked any excuse that would put off the meeting. He sat down in a high-backed chair and said, "I'll wait."

The clerk looked at him suspiciously but moved off, and Lobo half closed his eyes, inhaling the smells of tanned hides and newly cured tobacco and the cooking coming from the cookhouse behind his father's mansion. Behind the cookhouse was the schoolhouse, where Monsieur Chevillot used to teach him and Renata what he called "the rudiments of culture and civilization."

Renata had enjoyed learning from Monsieur Chevillot, and when she wasn't learning from him, she was learning from Lobo's father, her Uncle Adamo. The tutor taught her French and English, while Adamo instructed her in the nuances of various trading styles (Seminole, British, Scottish, American, French).

Lobo hated the musty schoolroom nearly as much as he hated the trading post, regarding them both as prisons. He had spent as little time as possible in either, getting his education in the dusty streets off Seville Square. From the traders he had learned to gamble, tossing a pair of dice made from human bone with all the skill of a Portuguese sailor. From the Spanish soldiers he had learned to strum love songs on his guitar, to make love to the half-breed girls in their one-room houses at the edge of town. From Laird he had learned not to fear the Seminoles, and later to emulate them, and finally to recognize them as brothers.

It was the Seminoles who taught him to ride, to hunt, to fish, arts that his father had never been interested in, much less mastered. He felt an affinity with Laird and the Seminoles he had never known at home. He had been born with that Indian ability to be solitary, to be self-dependent, unafraid of the forest or the creatures in it. As he grew older and more apart from his father and his home, he spent more and more time in the wilderness, in

120

Seminole villages, with the Seminole woman he called his squaw. Laird became the translator between father and son, the interpreter who spoke both their languages.

As he sat in the trading post waiting for Renata he remembered his mother, Sara, shaking her head when he would come home smelling like an Indian, a guilty smile on his face. "He must have been bitten by that wolf," she'd say, calling for the servants to prepare a bath, dragging him to it by his ear. "The Lord knows where you've been or what you've done, but I hope He and you manage to keep the secet."

Feeling walled in by the dark trading-post walls, as if he were invisible to the clerks and traders intent on sales and purchases, Lobo began to pace the thick wooden floor. There was a portrait of his father on the far wall, a fair likeness, painted by the same traveling French artist who had painted the miniature of Renata. Lobo studied it, thinking he didn't look like the richest man in Spanish America but more like a scholar. The artist had captured Adamo's sadness. The painting had been completed in the early fall of 1809, some weeks before it became clear that Adamo Levi was dying.

Adamo Levi had known long before his family that he was dying from a damaged heart. When he was certain, he set about dying as quietly, as honestly, as efficiently as he had lived. No one had to worry that his papers were not in order, that he hadn't made peace with enemies and friends. When he realized that his death would occur in a matter of hours, he had three private conversations. The first was with his wife, Sara, in which he comforted her and assured her that her life would go on as it had.

His second conversation was with Renata: he asked her to promise that no matter what happened to Lobo, she would keep Levi and Company a going concern. Renata promised, kissing him on his sunken cheek. She left the room and stood in the wide hallway, giving in to tears. Lobo watched her for a moment and then went in to see his father.

When the door had closed, Adamo held out his fine, unblemished hand, palm upward. Lobo hesitantly took it in his own square, rough hand. Standing at the side of his father's bed, he had to fight the compulsion to drop his father's cold hand, to fling open the heavy door, to get on his horse and ride as fast and as far as he could into the piney woods, away from death.

"I have few words left," Adamo said, smiling at his son, so characteristically discomfited. "I must be quick, Lobo. I want a promise of you. If the Lord had blessed me with other sons, I would ask nothing from you but your affection. You are, however, the last Levi, and you inherit, difficult as it is for you, the long Levi tradition that must not be broken.

"You cannot allow Levi and Company to simply stop, Lobo. Closing our doors would bring disaster to too many, Indian and Spaniard alike. I do not ask you to be a great businessman or even to get involved in the trading. All I ask of you is this: that you marry Renata as soon as it is seemly. Renata will,

121

if you allow her, make you an excellent wife. More important, she is the only person who has the knowledge to manage Levi and Company. When you marry her you will give her a legitimate claim to it."

Lobo, who had believed himself already married to his golden-skinned squaw, looked away, staring at the window with its new glass panes. It offered no escape. "Will you marry Renata, Lobo?" Adamo persisted, tightening his hold on his son's hand. "I have not asked you for so very much, Lobo, but I do ask you this. Look at me, Lobo. Promise me you will marry Renata."

Lobo stared into his father's evanescent eyes and saw goodness and pain and death. "Yes, Papa," Lobo said. "I will marry Renata."

Adamo held out his thin, weakened arms to him, and Lobo had found himself held in them, crying for the first time since he was a boy and his wolf cub had left to return to the forest. It was the finality of death that made him cry. Now, he and his father could never understand each other. Yet both men recognized the love they had for each other. For once Lobo lost all need to escape, remaining in his father's arms until Sara came in and he heard her terrible cry. Adamo was dead.

Renata, when Lobo proposed three months later, agreed to become his wife but with one proviso: Lobo was to be the active head of the trading post. Still grieving for Adamo, he had even agreed to that. He would become the man his father had wanted him to be. He vowed he would never visit the Seminole village where his squaw lived. He went to tell her, and he ended up staying the night.

When he had come to Renata's room on their first night of marriage, her door was shut, and he didn't have the courage to open it. Upon Adamo's death, she had assumed some of his majesty. The next night her door was shut again, and Lobo, in awe of his young wife, didn't approach it anymore. He was not, he thought, nearly good enough for her. He believed he would do her some terrible damage if he made love to her. She was above such things.

By the end of the first month, Lobo hated the trading post far more than he had ever hated the wattle and wood schoolhouse. He attempted to get the great Indian caciques and the wiley Scottish traders and the Spanish quartermaster to talk to him on the open front porch, where there was fresh air, a feeling of space, but they never would.

The traders—and most especially the Seminoles—insisted on the Talking Room, even if they were only trading a few deerskins. The Talking Room was the Levi cacique's throne room, his magic place, and he would lose face if he were to be received anywhere else.

Lobo sat through the important conferences with Spanish government agents—the government was Levi and Company's most important client—staring out the south window framing the bay, clenching his teeth, forcing himself to stay. The wooden walls, floor, and ceiling, the low horsehair sofa Renata had introduced to make his clients feel smaller and to lend him, in his high chair behind his father's desk, authority, all seemed to be closing in on him, burying him under their weight.

Nor was he any good at trading, understanding intellectually why he should be sticking to his price but emotionally wanting to give those men sitting low on the horsehair sofa what they seemed to want so badly. He didn't understand or have sympathy for the elaborate arabesques and subtle movements of the trading dance.

Renata, on the other hand, understood every step, every note. He had urged her to begin taking his place behind the desk. And she had acted with an astonishing grace, holding to her price, her dark-red lips in her pale face never once betraying lack of resolution. Lobo began to absent himself from the trading post, once again hunting in the piney woods, fishing in its streams, making love to his doe-eyed Indian squaw, shedding thoughts of Pensacola and even Renata the moment he was out of the city and into the wilderness. But there was always the moment when his memory and guilt caught up with him and he had to return.

When the shocking news came of the Fort Mims massacre, when Laird had suggested he go off to join the Tennessee Volunteers, Lobo saw it as a solution and left for Alabama immediately, directly from the Seminole village. Coward that he was, he had asked Laird to say goodbye to Renata for him.

Lobo Levi, suddenly impatient, turned away from the painting of his father and went out onto the porch, where the Seminole caciques sat wrapped in their blankets, smoking dark, coarse tobacco, mourning the passing of their peaceful way of life. Once self-sufficient and proud, they were becoming increasingly less so with repeated Creek and Yankee raids on their villages. Lobo couldn't stand to see them looking so defeated, and he went back into the trading post. Pushing the new clerk out of the way, he flung open the door of the Talking Room. The Talking Room furnishings were simple, but it had one remarkable feature—an oversized window Adamo had insisted upon in the face of all contrary advice. It would add, the French carpenters said, to the flooding potential of the first floor, and the winds would drive the mosquitoes in. The sun in the summer would make the room an oven. Adamo hadn't cared. He had gotten his window.

It faced south, so that during negotiations Adamo could watch the ships entering and leaving the harbor and at the same time keep an eye on the warehouses filled with tanned hides, casks of *aguardiente*, baskets of dried beans, boxes of the highly colored beads the Indians loved, cases of new Kentucky rifles for those who could afford them.

And now Renata sat behind the desk that faced Adamo's window, studying the account ledger, a huge black-leather-bound book. The clerk had been lying to protect his mistress from what he thought was a rough backwoodsman. Lobo was surprised that he was happy to see her. More than happy.

Yet she looked as she had always looked. Unassailable. Her gleaming black hair was pulled tightly to the back of her head and wrapped in a smooth bun. She wore, as always, a black bombazine dress. It rustled when she moved (like a rattler, one bested trader had said when she had stood up, indicating that she had no more time to listen to foolishness, that the meeting was at an end). Renata wore no jewelry to soften the effect of the black hair and dress. Her skin was as white as the fresh sheet of paper that lay on the desk next to the ledger. She disregarded her beauty, but many who sat low on that horsehair sofa while she sat high behind the desk wondered if there was any passion behind that small, perfectly shaped mouth, with the lips as red as the sweetmeats sold in the plaza. They called her the Duchess, the Queen of Hearts, the Iron Maiden. They said she needed taming, loving, a strong hand. The Scottish and British traders thought about her as they traveled through the forests, wondering at a husband who could so disregard her.

She looked up at him with that perfect composure that was so unsettling to him. "How are you, Lobo?" she asked, as if she had seen him the day before. She stood up, the bombazine rustling, and came around the desk, standing in front of it.

"I'm fine," he said, thinking that he wasn't fine at all, that he always felt stupid when he was anywhere near her. "How is the business?"

"Well, the Seminoles have increasingly less to trade, and the government has increasingly less money to spend, but we're managing."

"I know you are," Lobo said. "Father would be proud of you."

Her eyes, polished black gems, softened at the mention of Adamo. "I miss him more than I ever thought I would. Often I find myself saying, 'Well, I'll ask Uncle Adamo, and he'll know.' He taught me so much." She reached into a hidden pocket for a square of lace and put it to her eyes, surprising Lobo. She so rarely cried. He reached out for her hand.

"I'm sorry I left so abruptly, Renata. Not saying goodbye. But I knew you'd be better off without me."

"That's not true, Lobo." She allowed her soft white hand to remain in his. "You are my husband, Lobo."

"We don't have a marriage," he said, forgetting why he had come back to Pensacola and why he had left it; forgetting everything but his need for her. He put his arm around her waist, and he felt her move closer to him. "You are too good for me, Renata," he whispered even as he turned her to him and kissed those surprisingly soft, red lips.

Renata allowed him to kiss her, feeling his hard, thin body press urgently against her through his buckskins and her bombazine. His hands moved up and around the dress. He caressed her breasts, and she felt her nipples harden, his lips press down on hers, and her mouth open.

"I want you to be my wife, Renata," he said. "I want to make love to you."

"In the Talking Room?"

"In the Talking Room." Lobo locked the door and gently pulled her down to the floor, forcing himself not to be rough, to make his love a gift, which Renata, surprisingly, accepted.

124

Afterward they lay in each other's arms on the Talking Room floor, their heads resting on pillows pulled from the horsehair sofa. "I came back to tell you that I'm going away to fight the Red Sticks, Renata," he said. "I never expected this to happen. I never knew you . . . "

"There's a great deal you don't know about me, Lobo," she said, burying her face in his neck. "I was too busy keeping my promise to Adamo to let you know." Holding onto him, she told him of that promise, made to Adamo on the night he died. Lobo could feel her tears, sweet and hot, on his skin. He felt weak with tenderness. He knew she wanted to tell him not to leave but thought she was too proud to ask.

"You will come back to me, Lobo?" she asked finally, surprising him again.

He held her around her tiny waist, wondering at the softness of her skin. "If I can, Renata, I will come back to you."

Lobo found Mac waiting on the trading-porch steps, staring at the crowded plaza as if it were a play being put on for his benefit. No captain was willing to take his ship up the Apalachicola for the Americanos. "Trip's been a darned waste of time," Mac said, adjusting his saddle, mounting.

After a moment during which he stared at the Levi and Company trading post, Lobo also mounted and led the way up the King's Road east and north, toward Alabama. "See your wife?" Mac couldn't help but ask, thinking of that locket Lobo carried in his pocket.

Lobo admitted that he had, finally, seen his wife.

CHAPTER THREE

THE LATE SUMMER OF 1814 was the coldest anyone on either side of the international border dividing the United States Territory of Alabama from the Spanish colony of Florida could remember.

Despite his flannel shirt and Tennessee Regular tunic, MacCrimmons was cold in a way he never had been before. It wasn't natural—not in August it wasn't. The damp in the pine forest seemed to envelop him, to find its way right into his bones. The superstitious boys said it was the spirits of the old

Indians who had died in the forest coming to haunt them, and Mac had to admit he heard some pretty strange sounds in that forest they were camped in. Though he was worked like a house slave, he was happy to be adjutant to Old Hickory, spending most of his time in the shelter of his tent.

Mac had been back nearly three days from his fruitless trip to Pensacola, and food and supplies still hadn't arrived from Washington City. Old Hickory had grown angrier with his each passing hour, directing most of his scorn at the President's representative, Lieutenant Jack Church. Anger and inaction had brought on increasingly acute attacks of dyspepsia, so that the general's long white right hand was constantly under his shirt, massaging his bilious stomach.

Near midnight on the coldest night yet, Jackson suddenly stood up from the camp bed he was desolately sitting on. He threw down the bowl of boiled hominy (the only nourishment he could take during those dyspeptic bouts) he had been picking at on the red clay earth. "He looked like a fire that had just got a little pig fat on it," Mac told Lobo later. "I never seen anybody that het up. That's when we decided he was going to attack them Injuns, food or no food, border or no border."

"Get all the officers in here, Mac," Jackson ordered. "With the exception of Lieutenant Church. Let the lily-liver sleep peacefully." When the officers—young, ill dressed, hungry—assembled, Jackson told them, "We're advancing on the Red Creeks in one hour's time. Get your men ready."

"My men are too hungry to fight, sir," one intrepid Tennessee captain said.

"They'll forget about their stomachs when they're killing savages," the general told him.

And in just one hour Jackson sat mounted on his horse, Mac at his side, looking back at the ragtag army behind them. "The United States Regulars in their tailored white ponce's uniforms with their academy degrees might laugh, Mac. But dammit, these boys know how to fight Injuns, and I'll put my money on them anytime."

It was Andy Jackson's first battle, and despite his decision to break international law, to go against the express orders of the President of the United States, he seemed as calm, as sure of himself as if he were going to Sunday dinner. "He's done a lot for me, Lobo," Mac told his friend. "But sometimes I think he's plum crazy. Just mention an Injun and his eyes get all pale and his face all red and he starts feeling for his stomach. He says they're all animals with men's bodies and wolves' brains, and we got to get rid of every single one. You ever kill an Injun, Lobo?"

Mac had been sent to check on the mounted men and had found Lobo in the last ranks, assigned to Grimes's company. Mac gave Jackson the sign indicating everyone was ready and waiting for Jackson's signal to advance. "No, I never did kill an Indian," Lobo said. Then Jackson's yellow-gloved hand rose and fell, and the Tennessee Regulars moved into Florida.

The Red Sticks were asleep in their village just north of the beautiful, me-

126

andering Choctawhatchee River, a few miles into Spanish Florida. Like most Indians, the Red Creeks didn't post night guards, believing the white man incapable of scouting out their camps or wily enough to quiet their dogs. They had been told that the Americans wouldn't dare insult Spain by violating her borders lest she come into the war on the side of the British. But neither they nor their British advisers knew much about Andy Jackson.

Most of the Tennessee Volunteers didn't know when they crossed the border and wouldn't have cared if they did know. Those with horses were ordered to surround the village, while the foot soldiers were bribing the Red Sticks' guard dogs with horsemeat. Jackson, Mac at his side, watched with satisfaction. "We're going to pay the Creeks back for Fort Mims, Mac, in like currency. You didn't see the scalped, limbless bodies of white women and children, Mac. I mean to crush the Creek Nation once and for all, to free their land and their stolen slaves for God-fearing white folk. We're going to start right now."

He began to raise his yellow-gloved hand to give the signal to attack but paused at the sound of a horse riding hard. The next moment Jack Church, for once disheveled, astride a horse far too light for him, forced his way through the circle of aides around Jackson.

"Lieutenant Church, sir," he said, presenting himself in that Military Academy way that never failed to irritate Jackson. Even on that little black and white farm horse he was nearly as tall as the general.

"I thought you were sleeping, Lieutenant," Jackson said.

"An oversight, sir. No one aroused me." Mac suddenly realized that the lieutenant was as angry as Jackson. The horse must have felt it as well, for it did an absurd little dance until Church gave it a couple of vicious jabs with the spurred heels of his boots. "If you will allow me to point out the obvious, General," Church said, his voice rising, nearly choking on the last words, "you are on Spanish soil."

"You lower that damned lily-livered voice, Lieutenant, before I make you incapable of speech."

"You cannot attack, sir," Church said, forcing his voice lower, reining in, with effort, his anger. "Can't you see you're endangering our country's entire effort against the British?"

"One more word, Church, and I will have one of my boys take you into the woods and shoot you as a traitor. And next time you appear before me, Lieutenant, you get your damned Academy britches properly done up, and you damned well *ask* permission to speak." Jackson neatly turned his horse around so that he no longer faced Jack Church and raised his gloved hand.

"If you give that signal, General, I am going to report to the President that you deliberately, knowingly, launched an attack on Spanish soil, thereby endangering your country's safety during a time of war. *That* would seem to be the definition of a traitor, sir."

There was a tense silence as the Tennessee Volunteer officers gathered

127

around their general, his hand still raised, the yellow glove a beacon in the dark, cold night. He turned his horse around a little and, still not looking at Church, said, "You going to give that report in person, Lieutenant?"

"I am, General."

"Good. Then start riding now, you damned interfering, lily-livered scoundrel." He let the yellow-gloved hand fall, slapping Jack Church's nervous little horse on the rump, sending it on its way, at the same time giving the signal for the attack—"on Spanish soil, God damm it"—to begin.

Jack Church, his mind filled with black anger, knew only that he had to get away fast. He spurred the little horse toward Alabama Territory, intending to get his kit together and make for Washington City. When he arrived at the desolate Tennessee Volunteer camp and dismounted, he was appalled to see blood on the flanks of the little horse where he had dug in his spurs. Despite his bulk Jack Church had never knowingly hurt man or beast, and he counted those bloody flanks as one more mark against Andrew Jackson.

He's insane, Church said to himself as he headed north toward Washington City. He bought a new horse at the first stable he found, but all through that long ride to Washington City he thought of the little horse's wounds and of the blindly obedient Tennessee Volunteers. It's an infectious insanity, Jack Church thought, based on twin lies: white supremacy and Andrew Jackson's infallibility. He wondered how many redskins and white men would die from it.

Grimes's company was selected to be in the advance party led by MacCrimmons. Mac searched out Lobo and maneuvered his horse so he was next to him. Since they had returned from Pensacola their roles had been reversed. In Pensacola, Lobo had been the all-knowing big brother and Mac the ignorant child. Now he felt responsible for Lobo. "You scared?" Mac whispered in the last moment of silence that place was to know for the next several hours.

"No," Lobo said truthfully. He was numb. All he could think of was that he had never killed an Indian before, that the Seminole and Creek Indians were his brothers. But it was the Red Sticks who came screaming out of their thatch-roofed chikees, making the most ungodly noise he had ever heard, carrying smoothbore rifles supplied to them by the British.

In the light from the village fire Lobo, who believed in the Indians' spirits, saw the Red Sticks as demons popping up out of the earth, bringing forth death. Favored with highly developed night vision, the Red Sticks killed half a dozen men in that first encounter. "Shoot that Kentucky rifle, goddamn you," Grimes ordered Lobo, giving him a vicious jab with his own rifle butt. "Shoot."

Lobo, who was a perfect shot when aiming at a bear, shot too high and then too low. But as one whooping, mounted Red Stick descended on Mac, his ax held high, Lobo Levi shot his first Indian. The Red Stick clutched his chest, and Lobo, despite the babble around him, heard the solid thud of the Indian's body falling to the ground.

"You all right?" Mac asked, but Lobo just shook his head, and Mac gave the order to retreat. "We ain't even got started," Davy Crockett complained, but he followed when the rest of the Red Creeks jumped on their horses and began to charge, still uttering that shrill, bone-chilling scream.

The retreat had been Jackson's ploy to lure the Red Creeks out of their village and into the open, where many were killed. Lobo stood next to Mac as they watched the slaughter, the whooping and shrill screams eventually dying out as the warriors died. "You did good," Grimes said, slapping Lobo on the back, and Lobo felt as if he had been branded. He kept hearing, over and over again, echoing in his head, the sound of the man he had killed falling to the ground.

The whooping ceased as the Red Creek survivors were driven back into the village, which the rawest of the Tennessee recruits had infiltrated, ready to fight the braves hand to hand. But there was little such fighting, the Red Creeks taking shelter in their chikees, the Volunteers going in after them with their rifles. "Ain't got to kill 'em like that," Crockett, holding back, said. "They're helpless and they're trapped. They ain't rabid dogs."

"Guess what them animals would do to us if the tables were turned?" Grimes asked, leading the way to a chikee where half a dozen Red Sticks were trying to defend themselves with bows and arrows. They were slaughtered by Grimes and those members of his party who had the stomach for that sort of action. Knives were used to save ammunition.

Most of the chikees had been set on fire. The smell of the burning straw mixed with the stench from hundreds of badly butchered Indian bodies made more than one soldier sick. Lobo wasn't physically sick. He stood in the center of what was left of the village watching the massacre progress, the scene lit by the burning chikees. Now it seemed as if the white men were the demons, torturing Indian souls in hell.

Grimes saw him out of the corner of his eye and ordered him to rejoin his party. "This is one dance, Jew, you ain't sitting out. I got the perfect job for you." The last Red Stick warriors had sought refuge in their medicine man's chikee, hoping his magic would protect him and them. Grimes and his men were going to storm the shaman's chikee. "You open that leather door, Jew," he told Lobo. "You don't have to worry about getting your hands dirty. The rest can do whatever killing needs doing."

Mac, accompanying a triumphant Jackson into the village, saw Lobo grasp the loop on the leather door. He and Jackson headed toward the shaman's chikee. "What's going on?" he asked Grimes as Lobo pulled open the door and stood in front of it, staring in.

The medicine man's ancient squaw, a three-hundred-pound, eighty-year-old woman sat cross-legged in the doorway. Had she been a warrior she would have been shot immediately, but Grimes and the others were surprised to see a woman and held their fire, while Lobo, who might have shot her, didn't. She was holding a heavy ceremonial bow and had to use her hands and her feet to draw it. A thick arrow, dipped in silver, lodged itself deep in Lobo's chest.

Mac pulled the dying Lobo out of the way as Jackson, infuriated, ripped the bow from the old woman's hands and, cocking his pistol, shot her in the head, slamming the leather door shut on her. "Set fire to that damned hut," he commanded, and Grimes ordered his men to light torches. "And when that boy dies," Jackson said, looking at Lobo as he lay in Mac's arms, "give him a proper burial. That boy wants a military funeral." He said this as if Lobo still had needs and goals and desires, as if a military funeral would help.

The chikee roof had fallen in, and everything seemed to have stopped except for the hideous screams of the fifty warriors burning alive inside. Lobo Levi, the arrow still in his chest, reached for MacCrimmons's hand. He pressed it and, looking up with his yellow eyes into his friend's blue ones as if he could find the answer to some pressing question there, died. Though he desperately didn't want to in front of Grimes, MacCrimmons felt the tears come to his eyes. He had never known anyone like Lobo Levi. Lobo had been honest and strong and more of a man than anyone he had ever met. Mac-Crimmons knew that Lobo's life and death had touched him and changed him permanently.

The burial detail came and took Lobo's body away while Mac watched, rubbing his hands against his thighs in that old nervous gesture, his tears under control. He started for his horse and realized he was holding something in his left hand, something Lobo had given him as he died. Mac opened his big fist. In it was the gold locket that held the miniature of Renata.

There was no food with which to celebrate the victory. Jackson blamed Jack Church and all the other Washington City lily-livers for the continued nonappearance of the government suppliers with the promised rations. He had Grimes and his men dig around under the Red Creeks' roasted bodies until they found the cellar where the Red Creeks had kept their food.

"Enough potatoes to feed two armies," Grimes said, emerging from the cellar. There was one problem: the potatoes had been stewed in the fat melted from the burned Indians. Jackson didn't care. His men had to eat if they were to go on, and he was determined they were to go on. Jackson, his dyspepsia abated, ate the first potato as an example. He laughed as the others, not happily, followed his example. "I said I was going to get my men fed if they had to eat the damned Indians, and I reckon that's just what they're doing."

The Creeks retaliated with expected fury. But Jackson and his Tennessee Volunteers—miserable with dysentery, unfed, unsupported by the War Office—were still more than a match for them. Jackson proved over and over again he knew the secret of beating the Indians. He broke the military power of the Creek Nation at the Battle of Horseshoe Bend in Alabama once and for all. He took for his suddenly grateful government half of their ancestral lands: twenty-three million acres, which made up one-fifth of Georgia, three-fifths of Alabama.

Many Creeks joined the British in their war with the United States. Others drifted down into Florida to live with the Seminoles, who no longer had to fear the devastating Creek raids. The big danger now was the Americanos, hungry for their land, their slaves, their cattle.

Jackson returned to his home, the Hermitage, in Tennessee, to care for his wife, Rachel, and his stomach, only to be infuriated again a few months later when he learned the British were in Pensacola. "Those damned scoundrels," he shouted, storming out of the house, looking for his aide, Mac. "Those damned law-breaking infernal scoundrels. Spanish Florida is neutral," he said to Mac as if Mac had proposed it wasn't. "We've got to get the damned British out of there."

Mac, grown wise, refrained from reminding Jackson of his own illegal entry into Florida. The irony was not lost on Washington City either. The War Office cautioned Jackson, but he managed to find new supplies, to regroup his Citizen Volunteers of Tennessee. President Madison agreed, secretly, to support him. And Andy Jackson agreed to accept his support as long as he promised not to send any damned lily-livered Academy soldier advisers. "I'm not going to forget Lieutenant John R. Church," Andrew Jackson said.

Mac, who thought he had tasted all the war he wanted to, found himself looking forward to the incursion into Florida. He assumed Jackson would head for Pensacola. He opened the gold locket and looked at the portrait of his friend's widow for what he figured was the two millionth time, wondering if any woman could be as beautiful as the painting of Renata Levi.

CHAPTER FOUR

Renata—1814

MOVING QUICKLY ACROSS PLAZA FERDINAND in her black dress and shawl, a servant following carrying baskets of fresh fruit, Señora Sara Levi looked like any of the other elderly Spanish women of Pensacola: dark, small, wrinkled from years in the Florida sun.

131

She wasn't like them at all. The other Pensacola *viejas*—old women—believed in fate, in the mercy of the Church, in the superior intelligence of their menfolk. Life was out of their hands. Sara Levi believed that she and she alone was responsible for her life, that she had made her bed years before when she married Adamo, and that if she hadn't liked that bed (she had), she could have gone out and found another. She mourned her son each moment of the day, but she didn't curse her God or the Fates or the Indians for his death. Lobo had chosen to become a soldier, and soldiers got killed.

Sara prided herself on being unemotional, but her mottled skin turned a scorched red when she saw the British soldiers strolling about the dirt streets surrounding the plaza. Born in St. Augustine, she continued to think of Florida's other city as paradise and considered her early years there her happiest. When she was a young girl, Spain had suddenly, inexplicably given Florida to the British. She had lived under British rule for a year before her father was able to take her to Havana. The British had hated St. Augustine, disgusted by windows without glass, houses without chimneys. "They were too ignorant to know," Sara would say, "that windows need to be open so the sea winds can sweep away the mosquitoes, that chimneys turn houses into ovens." So they tore down her father's house and chopped down her mother's fruit trees for firewood to use in the coquina chimneys they had installed in the houses they commandeered. And she had never forgiven them.

Making disapproving noises, she stepped into Señor Gaspar's bakery on the edge of the Plaza Ferdinand, but only after a British soldier had vacated the tiny shop. "The British," she said to the one-legged baker, "bring trouble to friends and enemies alike." She pointed to some round corn breads, and her servant put them into his basket. "It is illegal to sell to them, Señor Gaspar," Sara said to that longtime adversary. "Spain is a neutral in the war between the British and the Americanos."

"And pray, Señora Levi," Señor Gaspar asked with exaggerated politeness, "can you tell me *who* is aiming to be the leading supplier of gunpowder, whiskey, and blankets to the British garrison? Do not tax yourself. I will answer for you. Levi and Company. If you have problems with merchants breaking Spain's neutrality laws, talk to your daughter-in-law, Señora Levi."

"You are a spiteful, constipated one-legged woman, Señor Gaspar," Sara said, leaving the premises. Señor Gaspar shot back but quietly (the Levis were rich and influential even though there were only two females left) that he wasn't as spiteful as a constipated *old* woman. Then he banged his wooden leg on the floor three times, summoning his apprentice, meaning to take out his anger on the boy.

Sara made straight for the Talking Room, where Renata sat behind Adamo's old desk talking to an elaborately turbaned Seminole chief about a bill he had no hope of paying. "You're dealing with the British," Sara said as soon as he had left. "You, a Spanish citizen, a Levi. After what the British did to us in St. Augustine. It was the British who bought the rifle that killed Lobo."

"Lobo was killed with a bow and arrow, Sara."

"It's the same kettle of fish." She felt betrayed. Not only by Renata and the Spanish government, which couldn't even keep the British out of Pensacola, but by history, by the fate she didn't believe in. Her husband was dead and her son was killed and the British were back in Florida. This was a moment when she couldn't change her bed so easily. Tears began to run down her dark, dry cheeks.

Sara was the only woman Renata allowed into her life. She had taken the place of Renata's mother, and later she had been her friend. Recently, since Adamo's and Lobo's deaths, she had become Renata's child. Renata came from behind the desk and put her arms about her mother-in-law's tough little knobby shoulders and turned her around so she could look through Adamo's window out at the bay.

"If it's any consolation, Sara, I have managed to sell the British very little. Which is not to say," Renata went on with that inexorable logic Adamo had bequeathed her, "that I am not doing everything I can to sell them more. Look!" Renata gave her mother-in-law a spyglass. "The flagship is carrying Sir Alexander Cochrane, who burned down Washington City, and the fleet that's joined his ships in our harbor have come from the European campaign. They've put Napoleon in his place, and now they're going to New Orleans to put the United States in hers."

"Levi and Company has to deal with the British, Sara. There's no one else. The Creeks are caught up in the war and so are the Seminoles: their pack-horse teams that used to bring us molasses and pitch and pine and hides are disappearing. I have managed to stock all our warehouses, but we have no customers. The Indians can't pay, and Spain is nearly bankrupt. The government owes us hundreds of thousands of dollars. The British are our last chance, Sara."

Sara put down the spyglass. She had been able to see the hated British officers' wives parading the decks of the fleet in their bright yellow- and rose-colored dresses, in elaborate bonnets, attended by civilian officials on their way to establish the new British colonial government of Louisiana. In the soft fall sunshine—so different from that odd, cold summer—the British were jubilant.

Sara turned from Adamo's window to look at her daughter-in-law. She was only eighteen years of age, but she didn't seem young. Sara couldn't remember a time when Renata had a real happiness. "What should I do, Sara? I promised Adamo I would never let Levi and Company die, and I won't. I must find a way to get to the British supply officers."

"Go to see Don Orlando," Sara said with that touching faith she had in the Spanish colonial system. "He is our governor. Don Orlando will know what to do."

133

"I have talked to our governor, Sara." Renata led her mother-in-law out of the Talking Room, a place in which the older woman never felt quite comfortable, toward the Levi mansion, where she could sew and smoke her clay pipe and order the servants about.

"What did Don Orlando say, Renata?"

"He said to talk to the British."

Renata had waited in the crowded anteroom of the governor's exquisite Calle Palafox house each morning for a week until Martino, the plump, blond, pretty equerry in the tight-fitting white uniform had finally said that Don Orlando could see her "but for a few moments only, Señora Levi."

When the Spanish colonial government had been Levi and Company's most important client, the governor had come to Adamo. Now, when the Spanish colonial government was Levi and Company's most important borrower, it was Renata who had to seek the government out.

Don Orlando Ramón de Córdoba made a perfunctory bow but did not sit down or offer Renata a seat when Martino showed her into his reception room. The plump equerry stood looking at the two of them for a moment before he absented himself. He thought they looked like subjects for a painting. A beautiful, aristocratic Spanish painting. Martino was a romantic.

He was wrong, however. Renata's beauty was painterly but Córdoba's was sculptural. He was lean, dark, and far taller than most Cubans, having to stoop when he entered low-ceilinged colonial houses. He was possessed of emerald-green eyes and white, perfect teeth. His cheeks were carved planes, and his long nose, broken in a boyhood game, gave him a deceptive brigand's air. His head looked as if it had been set by the sculptor at an angle just a little high, so that one always saw Orlando Córdoba's chin first.

His arrogance at a time when most Spanish officials were groveling was a topic of wide discussion in Pensacola. He was intensely proud of his heritage, tracing his lineage back centuries to the famous Castilian Córdoba family. If he was aware that the female founder of the Havana Córdobas was the first brothel keeper in that city or that both she and his paternal progenitor were once sentenced to be burned at the stake for heresy or that they had never married . . . he never mentioned those facts nor did anyone else in his presence.

He had always had a great interest in Florida and was aware that more than one Córdoba had died there. He also knew of and was fascinated by the legend of the Black Doves. He had bribed and politicked and threatened his way to the post of governor of West Florida when the previous man had said that he had had enough, "that Pensacola was a place without charm or comfort."

Córdoba, leaving his wife and children in his ancient house on Havana's Monserrate Street—on the grounds that the climate, moral and social, would not agree with them—had found Pensacola a place of great charm and had brought his own comfort. He received official callers sitting behind the

134

leather-topped desk that had once been the centerpiece of the reception room at the long defunct La Casa.

If he seemed remote to his constituents, it was because of the shame that faced him each morning: more Spanish than any Castilian-born grandee, he hated the fact that Spain could no longer offer her citizens the protection to which they had a legal right. He had made a formal complaint to the British when they had garrisoned Pensacola. But the British commander, Colonel Fenworth, had responded with the reality that there was not much the Spanish could do—unless, of course, the British lost the war with the Yankees.

He didn't want them to lose this war with the Yankees. He was aware, more acutely than many in Havana and Spain, that the Spanish days in Florida were finally coming to an end, that either the British or the Americans would soon be in charge of Ponce de León's "island." He hoped the British, a civilized if heretic race, would prevail. He thought that if they did, he might be able to stay on in Florida. It was the only place he had ever felt he belonged.

He had delayed this meeting with Señora Levi long enough. He didn't like dealing with this New Christian who looked not unlike the portraits of his own forebears. He was a man who didn't like women, especially out of their place, and here was a woman who was demanding action that he had no power to take. "Is there no possibility, Don Orlando," Renata asked, "of Levi and Company being paid by the Spanish government?"

"None," Córdoba didn't see why he should lie to her.

"And if the British decide simply to take what they want, will there be any security provided by the government?"

"It is apparent, is it not, Señora Levi, especially to a woman of your intelligence, that neither I nor the government can provide any sort of reassurance, fiscal or military, so why have you come to belabor the obvious? To torment me?" His voice had gone up a register, though his demeanor remained calm. But Renata heard that thin crack in his façade.

"I wanted to make certain that I could no longer rely on you or the government, Don Orlando," Renata said, as if he were a clerk in her trading post and she was giving him notice. "Spain may be again giving Florida to the British, but this time Levi and Company is going to stay."

She put her shawl over her gleaming black hair and left with that rustle of her bombazine dress that some men found tantalizing. Not Don Orlando. "I would break her and Levi and Company if I could," he said, and then he told Martino that he could see no one else that morning. The equerry, understanding as always, let down the pale silk shades, emptied the anteroom, and brought Don Orlando a glass of *aguardiente*, standing over him solicitously as he drank it.

Laird arrived in Pensacola the morning after Sara had accused Renata of dealing with the British. His ginger beard seemed longer than ever, but his buckskins were as fresh and clean as if they had been put on the moment before. He resembled a sort of backwoods Scots leprechaun, but his forthright dignity and the intelligence in those bleached blue eyes prevented anyone from laughing at him.

"Collect the Seminoles' debts, lassie?" He was repeating Renata's inquiry, his burr getting thicker as he grew more angry. "*I cannot collect from the Seminoles* . . . because they cannot pay. The Americans are robbing them blind, while bands of Creeks are burning their villages and their farms. This war between the British and the Americans is spilling over into Florida. The Seminoles are scattering. Look out the door, lassie. You see men who only a year ago were great, rich *micos*. Now they sit on your front porch dazed, not knowing what has happened to their lives."

"Wrapped in Levi and Company blankets they haven't paid for," Renata said wryly.

"Aye." Laird looked at her with sorrowful and chiding eyes. Many of the chiefs had settled their debts by ceding to Renata great tracts of land under title given them by the Spanish king and honored by the second Spanish occupation. They felt, as did she, that since she now owned their land, she had an obligation to provide them with a meeting place.

"While our warehouses are filled with goods no one can afford." She stared stubbornly at Laird, but for once he thought he detected some emotion in those black eyes. Though it certainly wasn't sympathy for the Seminoles. "Lobo," she said, as if it were Laird's fault, "should have stayed in Pensacola. He should have let the Indians and the Americanos kill each other off."

"Aye, lassie, then who would buy your goods?"

"The British of course," Renata said quickly. "If only I could get to Sir Alexander. His agents won't see me."

"They're living off their supply ships," Laird said. "Waiting to go to New Orleans before buying, or pillaging, new supplies." He stood up and looked at her. "You're as single-minded as your Uncle Adamo, lassie. He taught you well, but Adamo had one quality you don't have, not yet."

"What's that, Laird?"

"Compassion. But I will see what I can do about arranging an interview with Sir Alexander Cochrane."

"You?" she asked skeptically.

"Yes, lassie, me. The British think I'm working for them, helping them arm the Indians against the Americanos."

"And aren't you?"

"Eventually," he went on, avoiding the question, "the Americanos, whether or not they win their war, are going to move in on Florida. They are a plague of locusts. They have a terrible hunger for Seminole land and Seminole slaves."

Renata realized in that moment that Laird's exclusive loyalty was to his Seminoles. The little Scot executed a graceful bow and repeated that he would see what he could do for Renata. She understood he felt a responsibility for her, if only because of his devotion to Adamo and Lobo.

After Laird left, Renata sat behind Adamo's desk in the Talking Room feeling contrite. Laird's compassion bullet had hit home. Whatever Adamo had done, he had always cared for the Indians. She felt no triumph when a note from Laird arrived some hours later saying that Sir Alexander Cochrane would see her in the morning.

Renata lay in her bed that night in Adamo's old bedroom, unable to get Laird's accusation out of her mind. Perhaps, she wished she had said, eighteen-year-old women running a large trading post single-handedly don't have time for compassion. But that would have smacked of self-pity, and she wasn't going to indulge in that. Maybe she did lack compassion. Indians didn't pay their debts. Indians had killed Lobo.

She told herself she wouldn't think of Lobo. Not tonight. Unable to sleep, worried about her morning interview with the British commander, Renata got out of bed and opened the shutters on the window fronting the bay. She saw the fleet's colored lanterns and the movement of the women's gowns against the darker background of the men's dress uniforms. They were dancing. They did so nearly every night. If she stood perfectly still she could just hear the music of the army band drifting over the black bay waters.

Not wanting to face her bed, she stood at the window until the music had stopped and the lanterns had been taken down. Then she turned and saw the bed, illuminated by the half moon. For a moment she saw Lobo in it, undressed, his yellow eyes staring, waiting for her.

She lay on the bed, and though she didn't want to, she gave herself up to the temptation she avoided during her long days, the one that visited her each night. She allowed the memory of those last moments with Lobo, on the Talking Room floor, to invade her mind. She could smell the musky aroma of his blond skin; she could feel his caress through the thin nightdress; her entire body yearned for him. She had to open her eyes to drive away Lobo's ghost.

She found them wet with bitter, furious tears. She was, she thought, like Señor Gaspar, an amputee, feeling the pain of the discarded limb long after the operation. Lobo's death—what dreams she had based on that one episode on the Talking Room floor—hurt as much now as it did when Laird had brought the news. She sat up in bed, telling herself she had to stop crying. But she couldn't. She was crying for Lobo but mostly, she knew, she was crying for herself.

Eventually she lit a lamp and went to the trading post, to the Talking Room. There were some figures she meant to go over before her meeting with Sir Alexander. Compassionate or not, Lobo or not, Renata was going to keep her promise to Adamo. Levi and Company was not going to die.

LAIRD HIMSELF rowed Renata out to the flagship. The early morning sun was burning the last of the mist off the waters, and the British ships in the harbor suddenly loomed before them. Renata thought they seemed too large for Pensacola Bay. A dugout canoe filled with silent Creeks, coming from the flagship, passed within a few feet, startling Renata. "It's a common occurrence, lassie," Laird said. "You musn't be frightened. The British provide the Creeks with arms and ammunition to fight against the Yankees."

"And what do they provide you with, Laird, for your Seminoles?"

He laughed. "The same thing, lassie. The same thing."

As Renata stepped aboard, a group of British officers' wives in pastel dresses and fussy bonnets were on their way to mid-morning tea. Fair and pretty, like a flock of spring birds, they suddenly stopped their chattering, unable to ignore the exotic beauty of the woman who had just come on deck. Renata, in her black dress and lace shawl, her skin flawlessly white and her black eyes shining, barely saw them, intent on her forthcoming meeting.

"Who is that?" Lady Margaret, Sir Alexander's wife, asked the captain as Renata was led below deck.

"One of the women of the town, ma'am."

"Do all the women of the town look like that, Captain?"

"No, ma'am."

"A good thing, or we would have no man left on board to dance with."

Sir Alexander received Renata in the paneled stateroom that served as his ship's office. Laird, who had business with the officer in charge of Indian relations, had not accompanied her. Sir Alexander was a portly, garrulous Englishman who had never, in his recollection, dealt with a woman in business before.

"Laird, with his usual gift for understatement, told me," he said, taking Renata's hand, "that the head of Levi and Company was an attractive young Spanish woman, but my dear, I am at an age when I can safely say, without fear of offense, that you are far more than merely attractive."

138

His aide provided chairs, and Sir Alexander watched, with something like amazement, Renata seat herself and wait for him to join her. Sir Alexander was relieved that he wouldn't need a translator, that this remarkable young woman with the perfect figure and the deep-red lips spoke English like a Kent gentlewoman. "Really," he said to himself, "she might grace any drawing room in London."

Renata smiled, because the tall gray Englishman was smiling at her. "I expect you had a difficult voyage," she said, in the way Adamo had taught her to deal with an English trader. "As if," Adamo had said, "you were the queen and he was Walter Raleigh."

"No, it wasn't difficult at all." Sir Alexander sat across from her, folding his hands, waiting for more. It had been his belief until this moment that only the English—and only the English of a certain class—knew the art of drawing-room conversation. Laird had had to make all sorts of threats and pleas to get Sir Alexander to agree to the meeting, but really—he thought of those evil-smelling, dour Creeks—this was a delight.

"And what, may I ask, is your opinion of Pensacola, Sir Alexander?"

"It is a charming village, Señora Levi. Full of amazements."

"And what do you think of the American threat?"

"After New Orleans, Señora Levi, there will be no more threat, I promise you. And now you must join me in a glass of flip. William"—he indicated his aide—"makes a wonderful flip."

"I'm not at all certain," Renata said, looking up at him, "I know what a flip is, Sir Alexander."

"It is a most fitting and perfect combination: British port and Spanish brandy."

Renata sipped the concoction and forced herself to smile, wondering how she was going to get the rest down. Sir Alexander looked at her encouragingly. "You have a family, Señora Levi?" he asked, signaling for William to replenish both their glasses.

"My husband recently died," Renata said softly, putting the glass down firmly.

"How very dismaying."

Renata could see that he was genuinely concerned for her. And that it was time to turn the conversation before he had yet another flip. "Yes, it has been a difficult time, one in which, as you can understand, our business has suffered. I find that Levi and Company has on hand a great surplus of rations, weapons, ammunition, hides. I should like to discuss with your supply agents the possibility of selling them at greatly reduced prices."

"That would be against international law, Señora."

Renata carefully looked up at him and deliberately held his eyes with her own. "Your very presence here is against international law, Sir Alexander, but no one—except possibly the Americanos—complains."

He laughed, as she had hoped he would. He thought she was a remarkable

139

woman. To know about international law and to best him on it too. He reached for his glass of flip. Renata knew there was a time in all negotiations when one had to stop talking. She pretended to drink the flip, allowing Sir Alexander to reflect.

Unfortunately Sir Alexander was reflecting on how much younger Señora Levi was than his wife. And so beautiful. And in such a pitiable situation—widowed, having to divest herself of a trading business, a complicated and difficult task, especially in time of war. He gave in to the temptation to reach over and touch her pretty white hand.

The hand-holding might have turned into something else had not his aide at that moment handed him a note. Sir Alexander excused himself and read it. "I am sorry, Señora. I must attend to this immediately." He stood up, as did Renata. "You have the most lovely smile, my dear." He sighed, leading her out of the stateroom. "I will have my agents call upon you in the morning with a recommendation to buy whatever we might need. Permit me to say that you are far too attractive and cultivated to be involved in the sordid practice of business, Señora. But I know it is a necessity."

He escorted her to the deck, where Laird was waiting for her. "Do not return to Pensacola, Señora Levi, with this old Scot. Stay," Sir Alexander said impulsively. "There will be dancing tonight, and I should very much like it if you would grace our poor party by attending."

"And I would very much like to attend, Sir Alexander, but I have pressing affairs in Pensacola." She gave him her smile and her hand, and he held it a moment as another group of Englishwomen promenaded by in their finery, as complaisant and colorful as tamed parakeets. "You don't envy them a bit, do you?" Sir Alexander asked.

She hesitated for a moment before smiling up at him. "I would not be so presumptuous, Sir Alexander."

As Laird expertly rowed the boat across the green waters, the sun's lights dancing across the bay, Renata looked back and saw that Sir Alexander was just turning away, but the English ladies were caught, staring after her. For one moment it occurred to Renata that the British might lose the upcoming battle of New Orleans. English arrogance would be the Americans' most effective weapon.

"You should have accepted the invitation, lassie," Laird told her as the boat neared Levi and Company's docks. "You would do better with the purchasing agents at a ball than in the Talking Room."

"In my black dress among all those pinks and yellows? I should have been the corpse at the wedding."

"You would have been," Laird said, "a swan among robins." Renata leaned over to stare at her reflection in the rippling waters. It was the one gesture Laird had seen her make that was characteristic of an eighteen-year-old girl. She wanted to know if she was pretty.

"You're a kind man, Laird," she said, sitting up, giving Laird a genuine smile, "but I had far better face the British supply agents in the Talking Room."

The following morning was even mistier than the day before, and the sun didn't seem to be burning it off the bay waters nearly as quickly. Not long after dawn Renata was in the Talking Room, preparing for the British purchasing agents. She calculated what she might charge them for brandy, rum, shot, molasses, the bolts of silk that had come from France via Havana. She thought of the Englishwomen in their gowns and decided she would do rather well on the silk.

She warned herself not to get overly excited. Anticipation, Adamo had taught her, was the worst indulgence for a trader. But she couldn't resist the possibility that she might sell the British all the cotton, tobacco, and whiskey in her warehouses. "Then," she said, talking to herself, "I'll restock with goods from Havana and Mexico." She had written off the Seminoles as both suppliers and purchasers. Her fervent hope was that the British would become a permanent presence in Pensacola, that they would become Levi and Company's principal mainstay.

"The Spanish came to the New World to convert lost souls," Adamo had told her. "The British come to trade with them." She knew it was a mistake Adamo wouldn't have let her make—banking everything on one possibility, the British. But she didn't seem to have any other choice. However, after the British had won their war with the Americanos, they would secure Florida's boundaries again, reestablish the Seminoles in their villages, and open the way once more for Laird and the other traders to acquire their produce and hides. She wouldn't let herself think of what would happen to Levi and Company—let alone to the Seminoles and Florida—if the Americanos won the war. It just didn't seem possible.

"If I can only sell the British these goods," she told herself, "then I promise, Adamo, wherever you are, that I will be cautious, balance my trade, weigh all the possibilities." She felt like a schoolgirl promising God that she would be good forever as soon as she ate this one last forbidden sweetmeat.

But more than a sweetmeat was involved. If her plan worked, she would save Levi and Company from bankruptcy, and that accomplishment would mean more to her than anything else possibly could. What might be keeping Sir Alexander's agents? Impatiently she took Adamo's spyglass and went to his window. For a moment she thought the mist was obscuring the fleet. But then she realized the harbor was empty. There was no longer a fleet; even the great flagship was gone. Renata clasped her hands together and put them to her lips.

"They're gone," she said, not believing it. She trained the spyglass on the channel between Santa Rosa Island and the mainland and saw, with a start, that the battery on Santa Rosa was in flames, that smoke from the burning building was adding to the mist. She moved the glass to the right and caught a glimpse of the last British ship leaving the bay.

"Maneuvers," she said, knowing that couldn't be right. Sir Alexander would have known about maneuvers; he wouldn't have promised his agents for the following day. And he did promise. She moved the glass still farther to the right and saw that Fort Barrancas, high on its bluff, was also in flames. Why on earth would the British set fire to the Spanish fort? None of it made sense.

Feeling chilled, she put the glass down and left the Talking Room, stepping into the trading room, where at that hour Pensacola women were usually lined up three deep, buying thread and materials, carefully, with what little money they had. The clerks behind the oak counters looked up at Renata expectantly for an explanation. There were no customers, only Sara, dozing in her favorite straight-backed chair.

Renata went out onto the trading-post porch. It was empty. The *micos* were gone. The chill that had begun in the Talking Room grew until she had to use great control not to shiver. Where had the *micos* gone to? There hadn't been a day of the week when they hadn't gathered on her porch, sitting, according to rank, on the pine benches, wrapped in Levi and Company blankets.

She had complained about their taking up space, but now she would have given anything to have them back. She stepped off the porch so she could see into the plaza, and though she expected it, the shock of an empty plaza—on a Tuesday morning in Pensacola—nearly made her cry out. The streets were empty as well, and she found the silence terrible.

Where was everyone? The town should have been alive with soldiers and peddlers and housewives, with black boys selling oranges, Spanish women selling meat pies, the air filled with guitar music and salt-air breezes and the gossip—in half a dozen languages—that was the lifeblood of Pensacola. But now there were only that sinister silence and the acrid odor of burning buildings.

She gave a start when the sound of Laird approaching on his brown and white horse broke through the quiet. He was leaving, that was clear, his saddlebags and pack neatly in place. He pulled up in front of the trading post a few feet from where she stood. For once, instead of looking up at Renata from the horsehair sofa, he looked down at her, his faded eyes serious and unsmiling.

"Andy Jackson and thirty-five hundred fighting Tennessee Volunteers have taken Fort Barrancas, Renata. Your governor is about to hand the city over to them."

"The British. . . ," she tried to say, but she couldn't get the words out. Her knees were weak, and she found herself leaning against the trading-post columns. For the first time in her life Renata knew what it was to feel faint with fear. "The British . . . ," she tried again, and this time the words came out, but as a whisper.

". . . have gone. They've burned their forts and left, saving their guns and ammunition for New Orleans."

142

"But Sir Alexander's agents were supposed to—" Renata began.

"Lassie, there's fifteen million dollars' worth of goods in the warehouses of New Orleans," Laird interrupted. "There's no need to pay Levi and Company for what they can have for the taking."

"The British will come back," Renata said as if she could reassure herself. "After they win at New Orleans."

To Laird, Renata seemed for the first time truly vulnerable. She stood on the trading-post porch, her arms folded protectively across her chest, her dark eyes looking inward. Laird needed to be off, to see to his people, but he didn't want to leave her alone with the Americanos about to descend.

"I am worried about you," he said after a moment. "I am worried about what Jackson will do to you, lassie. He has no reputation for kindness, and he won't spare Spaniards who traded with the British."

"I only *wanted* to trade with the British. I never quite managed it." She said this with something of the old Renata's spirit, and Laird took heart. She was wounded but not defeated.

"I do not think, lassie, that Andy Jackson is up to fine distinctions. You had better lock up and take Señora Sara, along with some servants, to one of the small plantations Levi and Company owns. You'll be safe there."

"But what will happen to my warehouses filled with goods?"

"Better be alive with empty warehouses, lassie, than dead with empty ones. He's going to get them either way."

She looked up at Laird, and he saw her eyes were shining, but they weren't wet. "You're a kind man, Laird. I will think about your good advice. Thank you." She turned and went back into the trading post, the black bombazine creating the only sound in the plaza.

He rode off in the end, not happy but having his own problems to deal with. Jackson in Florida meant the Seminoles had better go to ground. He tried to concentrate on solutions to all the problems that entailed, but his thoughts kept going back to that lonely woman in that noisy dress. He realized, as he tried to banish her from his mind, that he had a new respect for Renata. It was mixed with pity and, he recognized with a start, affection.

When Renata stepped back into the trading post her eyes were dry, her lips and hands were pressed together primly. "She acts as if it was just another day," one of the clerks said. "Nothing moves that woman." She sent them home after they had helped to shutter and lock the trading post and all but one of the warehouses. After dark she asked her house servants—Juan and Carita—to accompany her to that last warehouse, and they worked until midnight, quietly moving goods to the old schoolhouse.

Afterward she had found a worried Sara sitting on the upstairs veranda, smoking her clay pipe. Renata put her arms around the old woman. "Laird thinks you should go to Casa del Norte until this is all sorted out. And I agree."

"But you must come too," Sara had insisted.

"Sara, I can't go. I can't leave everything. There'd be no Levi and Company when I returned."

Sara had looked at her and had shaken her head. She knew about Renata's promise to Adamo. It wasn't fair for such a young, lovely girl to have that burden. Adamo shouldn't have made her promise. "If you can't leave, Renata," she said after a moment, "then neither can I."

"But Sara . . ."

"I don't want to hear another word about it." The two Levi women looked at each other with exasperation and affection and then, arm in arm, went into their home to wait.

CHAPTER SIX

TWENTY-FOUR HOURS AFTER LEARNING that the British were in Pensacola, and with tacit but unofficial authorization from the War Office, Andrew Jackson was marching thirty-five hundred Tennessee Volunteers, their Kentucky rifles slung over their shoulders, across the border into Spanish territory toward Pensacola. By the time the Volunteers were halfway up the bluff that housed the burning Fort Barrancas, the British warships were leaving the harbor. The Spanish were left to resist, and one impeccably uniformed battery actually did so. When they saw the column of screaming coonskin-outfitted Tennessee recruits, led by MacCrimmons, rise toward them like a pack of starved wolves, they got off one round of grapeshot for honor's sake and surrendered.

"We scared the heck out of them, sir," Mac said, laughing, remembering the look on the Spanish lieutenant's face when he saw Grimes, a Kentucky rifle in each hand, a Red Stick scalp at his waist, barreling up the bluff.

Old Hickory managed a small smile despite the dyspepsia raging in his stomach. The Spanish governor, Don Orlando Ramón de Córdoba, had replied to an order from Jackson with a note from his equerry. It was written on thick, creamy paper engraved with the Córdoba seal and indicated that the governor might receive the general after lunch. It was signed by Martino in a fine, spidery hand, "Your most faithful and grateful servant, who kisses your hand."

144

"Damned scoundrel can kiss my arse," Jackson said in a cold fury. With Mac at his side he led his men into what looked like a deserted town. "The first thing I want is a list of all citizens who traded with the British. I am going to set an example for anyone who in the future is tempted to break international law."

MacCrimmons refrained from pointing out that the Tennessee Volunteers, by their very presence in Florida, were breaking international law. Jackson had his men secure the town and then, taking Mac with him, rode up Calle Palafox to the governor's mansion. "I want that list and I want it, dammit, before lunch."

Martino, Don Orlando's aide, was waiting for them on the slate steps of the governor's house. His white uniform was decorated with elaborate red and gold trim, and he smiled prettily. Jackson glowered down at him as he dismounted. "Get the damned governor out on this street," he said, and Martino, who understood Anglo English but not the American variety, put his hand to his throat. "I beg your pardon, General?" Jackson pushed him out of the way, striding into the mansion past several bewildered servants, Mac and Martino following. They found Córdoba in his reception room, blotting his lips with a cambric handkerchief as a servant took his luncheon tray away. He stood up, only the flat planes of his cheeks, unaccountably red, giving away his anger. "General Jackson?"

"You are to vacate these premises immediately, sir. I have taken possession of the forts, the garrison, and the town in the name of the United States of America."

"Are you asking permission, General?" Córdoba smiled, showing the famous white teeth.

Jackson ignored that. "And I want that list of British collaborators, sir. Now. Or I'll march you and your pretty boy straight off to jail."

Córdoba looked at Jackson for a moment, his cheeks dark red but his long broken nose pale, nearly blue with fury. He nodded, and Martino gingerly handed Jackson a thick sheet of paper on which were listed half a dozen names. Jackson didn't look at them but handed the paper to MacCrimmons.

"Now git," he told Córdoba.

When Córdoba had received word during the night that Jackson was on his way, he had had most of his valuable possessions packed and sent to the little house he owned in Pensacola's Seville Quarter. But there were many things he loved that he had had to leave behind.

"I only hope that the General will respect my possessions," he said, and Mac realized what an effort those words cost him. "Many have been in my family since the Córdobas first arrived in the New World."

For answer Jackson sat down in the chair Córdoba had vacated, tipped it backward, and let his mud-caked, spurred boots drop on the leather-embossed desk La Floridita had inherited from the merchant Quirinio two hundred years before. Slowly Jackson drew his boots toward him, gouging double ruts in the fine old leather. "Git."

Córdoba bowed and smiled, but his perfect teeth were not in evidence. "At your service, General," he said, and Mac knew without a doubt that Córdoba would have killed Jackson in that moment if he had had a weapon. As Córdoba left, Mac looked at the ruined desk, and for the first time since he had been taken under Jackson's wing, he disliked him.

Jackson had seen that look. "Don't be a damned fool, Mac. That coward and his fancy boy have been working against us with the British. He'd be in jail if the Washington City lily-livers hadn't expressly forbade it. He's getting off light with a scarred table."

Mac looked down at the list of collaborators he held in his hand so he wouldn't have to look at Jackson. When he got to the last name on the list he read it twice and then once again. His hand went to the pocket in his tunic where he kept the locket Lobo Levi had given him. The last name on the list was "Renata Levi."

"Washington City didn't say anything about how I should treat the common traitors," Jackson said. "You're in charge, Mac. I want you to burn out everyone on that list. You've got two weeks. Do it slowly, but do it thoroughly. I want to teach the damned Spaniards a lesson they'll learn by heart. That's an order, Mac."

Unlike his general, MacCrimmons had a cast-iron stomach. The only time he had ever felt nauseated was when he was with Lobo and had fished a snake's head out of an Indian stewpot. He thought of Lobo, and then he thought of Lobo's wife. He didn't need to look at the locket to remember those red lips and black eyes. He studied the list one more time, but her name hadn't gone away. He knew from the set of Old Hickory's long jaw that there was nothing he could do about it. For the second time in his life MacCrimmons, that Georgia farm boy bursting with health, was sick to his stomach.

Fifteen days had passed since Andrew Jackson had invaded Florida when President Madison, apprised of his action, said he was "appalled." The popular press predicted certain war with Spain. The Spanish ambassador lodged a serious protest. But Jackson's lightning strike and the ease with which he had managed the Spanish capitulation pleased James Madison and his advisers in Washington City nearly as much as it inspired men in Georgia and Alabama, their eyes focused on the rich Florida soil and the slaves they said had escaped there. Jackson, having completed his business in Pensacola, had already given his men orders to march to Mobile, where they could prepare for the battle of New Orleans.

On that blue and pink Pensacola morning when the Tennessee Volunteers were moving out and Jackson was vacating the Spanish governor's mansion, MacCrimmons was preparing to complete the American retaliation against the citizens of Pensacola. He had balked at it continually, even asking Jackson to relieve him. "I didn't join the Volunteers to burn down other people's property, General."

146

Jackson looked at his boy captain with a baleful expression that his wife, Rachel, and only Rachel, would have recognized as affection. "If we don't retaliate, the minute we're gone the Spanish will be kissing British backsides again. You want to be a soldier, young Mac, you have to learn to hand out justice to the damned civilians. Now go and teach them the consequences of disobeying the law." The law was Andy Jackson's, and Mac didn't find it any more palatable for that.

On that final morning, his American-flag-blue eyes cloudy, Mac told Grimes to meet him at the Levi and Company trading post with half a dozen men carrying kerosene and torches. "I'll have your horse saddled, Captain," Grimes said. He was happy. He liked burning down houses, and he made no secret of it. He had had a wonderful time over the past two weeks as Mac had worked his way down the list of British collaborators. They had burned out Gaspar, the baker, who at the last moment had run back into his burning shop to retrieve his spare wooden leg, a gesture that caused Grimes and his men a great deal of amusement.

They had burned down the stable where the British officers had rented horses, but they had kept the horses for the Volunteers. They had burned out the French dressmaker who had made dresses for the British wives, and they had burned out the wineshop where the British enlisted men had gathered, and they had burned out the house where the British sailors had sampled Pensacola women.

Grimes, not a dedicated bather, had begun to emit a stultifying odor of kerosene as if he himself were incendiary, and the joke among his men was "Forget the torches, we got Grimes."

Mac told Grimes that he didn't want his horse. He wanted to walk, and he did, down dusty Calle Palafox. The British had called it George Street, but the Spanish, when they reacquired Pensacola, had renamed it in honor of the general who defended Zaragoza, Spain, against Napoleon. MacCrimmons, striding down the center of a silent Calle Palafox, watched by dark little Spaniards from behind shuttered windows, said to himself that he was that tired of generals, French, Spanish, or otherwise, and you might throw in a sergeant he could name, and if this was war, he'd rather be farming.

He kept his eyes on the green-blue water washing up against the weathered pier at the southern end of Calle Palafox. Pensacola Bay was exhilaratingly alive and begging to be swum in. Mac looked at the water. He rubbed his big hands against his thighs in that nervous boy's gesture, then got out the list again. He had a sudden urge to shuck his coonskins, which smelled like the Lord knew what, give in to temptation and take a flying jump into the bay in his birthday suit. "You ain't a boy anymore," he told himself, stuffing the list back into the pocket of his tunic where he kept Lobo Levi's locket. He willed his feet to march in the direction of Levi and Company.

The trading post looked deserted. Grimes and his men stood in front of it, Grimes wearing that terrible churchgoing smile he always assumed for such work. Mac hoped that the trading post was deserted, that all he would have to do would be to give the order to set it and the warehouses on fire and not have to deal with some hot little Spanish manager who would give Grimes an excuse to shoot him.

"Should we start, Captain?" Grimes asked.

"Hold your horses, Sergeant." The last time he had seen that porch, it had been crowded with Indians in turbans and his friend, Lobo Levi, had been waiting to meet him. He walked across the plank floor and stepped inside the trading post. The rich smell of tanned hides and foreign spices permeated the place. The shutters on the windows were closed, and it took him a moment to adjust his eyes to the gloom. He realized he was breathing fast. His big hands rubbed his thighs. The quiet unnerved him. He could hear the tide coming in down at the bay.

He nearly shouted when the still figure in the straight-backed chair at the far end of the long room stood up and said something to him in Spanish. He had thought, irrationally, that Lobo Levi's wife might be waiting inside the trading post. But of course she wouldn't be. She would have been sent with the other Spanish women to the plantations in the north.

This elderly woman was clearly not Lobo Levi's wife. Señora Sara came up to him. He was nearly two feet taller than she was and thought for a minute that she was some magical being, an elf or a tiny witch. She asked him, in Spanish, what he wanted, and though Mac didn't understand the words, he knew the meaning.

"El jefe," he said in one of the few Spanish terms he had learned during the past two weeks.

The old woman smiled. It was a good smile despite the tobacco-stained teeth. "El jefe," she said, pointing to the Talking Room door. He knocked on it, but no one responded. It was so darned quiet. "All I want to do," Mac said to himself, "is set fire to the place, not make a social call on some bearded, perfumed little general manager." He turned to go, but the old woman pantomimed opening the door, so he turned back, lifted his big fist to knock again, and decided not to. He was, after all, a captain in the Tennessee Volunteers, under direct orders from General Andrew Jackson. He threw open the door and saw, sitting behind an old desk, not some bearded little general manager but the woman whose face had haunted him since he had first seen her likeness in Lobo Levi's palm.

Mac felt himself turning as red as a ripe tomato. One hand went to the pocket where he kept her likeness, as if to protect it. He cleared his voice and clasped his hands behind his back, forcing himself to breathe normally.

Finally she looked up at him from a ledger she had been writing in. He felt as if he had been shot by those black eyes he had been worrying over ever since Lobo gave him that locket. "May I help you, Sergeant?" she asked in perfect English.

"Captain, ma'am," Mac managed to get out. "Captain MacCrimmons of the United States Tennessee Volunteers."

148

"Yes?" She sat at the desk, even more beautiful than in the painting, looking up at him with controlled patience, a quill pen in one hand, the other keeping her place in the ledger.

His heart was in his mouth, and she had to say "Yes?" again before he blurted out, "I got orders to burn your buildings, ma'am." He felt maybe thirteen years old.

"Whose orders, Captain?"

"General Andrew Jackson's, ma'am."

She put the quill pen aside and closed the ledger. "Perhaps, Captain, I had better speak to this general myself."

"He doesn't grant personal interviews, ma'am." He could see Grimes looking in through the big window that faced south and motioned for him to go away. "There's nothing you can do now, ma'am. We've been burning out all Spanish citizens who traded with the British."

"But I did not trade with the British, Captain."

"That's not what we've been given to understand, ma'am. I think, ma'am, that you and the older lady in the trading post and anyone else you might know of in the warehouse buildings should quit the premises now, as my men are going to start."

"What would happen if I don't quit the premises, Captain?"

Mac could feel little beads of sweat along his hairline. "You would be fried like Cherokee eggs, ma'am."

Renata stood up. She was taller than he had supposed. And more shapely. She looked around the Talking Room. She had, of course, known they were coming and had had all the important ledgers and papers and the horsehair sofa and the portrait of Adamo moved to Levi House a week before. She would have liked to save Adamo's desk, but none of the clerks had turned up, and Juan and Carita hadn't been able to move it.

She looked out of Adamo's window. There were whitecaps on the bay waters, more turbulence than she could remember outside of a storm. The bay was as angry as she. Renata kept that anger in perfect control, but she was afraid the fear would give her away. For once Renata had no idea of what was going to happen next. She was not going to be able to keep her promise. Levi and Company was not only going to be closed, it was going to disappear under the ashes of a fire set by the Americanos. She was angry at the Americanos, but she was more angry at the British, at Lobo, at Adamo, at all of them for deserting her. She wanted more than anything to cry, but Renata knew that she wouldn't.

Through the open door she saw one of the Americanos escorting Sara out of the trading post. Sara had been surprisingly philosophical during those long days, waiting for the Americanos and their torches. Jews always had to leave, Sara said, sometime or another.

Renata turned suddenly and looked at the oversized Americano dressed like an animal, staring at her. "I have committed no crime, Captain. You and your general are the criminals, Captain. I order you to leave, now."

Renata sat down, opened the ledger, picked up the quill, and with barely trembling fingers began to write. "When I do, ma'am, I am going to order my men to fire your buildings. Starting with this one." Mac, feeling big and stupid and helpless, watched as Lobo Levi's wife busied herself with the ledger, ignoring him, ignoring the men outside Adamo's window dousing their torches in kerosene, waiting for Mac's order.

Mac had no choice. He gave the order. Grimes cheerfully stuck his boot through Adamo's window and threw a lit torch into the Talking Room. Apologetically Mac moved quickly around the desk and carefully, firmly, took Señora Levi in his arms. "I have no orders to burn *you*, ma'am." Too conscious of his rank coonskins, of his muscles bursting out of the hand-me-down officer's tunic, of the nervous sweat beading his forehead, Mac was aware of only one sound—the rustling noise Renata's black bombazine dress made as he held her against his chest.

She didn't fight. She lay against him like a wounded bird, allowing him to carry her out into the street. He wondered if she had heard his heart beating as he set her down some way from the trading post, next to Sara, where she would be safe. Renata took her mother-in-law's arm, and the two women watched as Grimes and his men effortlessly set fire to the trading post and then, one by one, the outer buildings.

The wind had died and the smoke from the fire went straight up into the sky. Mac stared at Renata as she watched. She closed her eyes when the powder warehouse went up with an explosion that could be heard for miles.

Jackson, leading an advance guard to Mobile, was attracted by the sound and came to look, with satisfaction, at the fire. "Good job, Mac," he said, ignoring the Levi ladies, leaning down from his white horse to slap his captain on the back. "Damned good job. That will teach the lily-livers not to trade with the enemy."

Jackson rode off, not realizing that Mac had barely noticed him. Mac, in a daze, his mind filled with conflicting thoughts and feelings, was startled when Grimes—his ferret's face black with soot—approached. "The pretty one wants to know if we're going to burn her house out?" Grimes asked, clearly wanting an affirmative. His men were beginning to bank the outer buildings so the fires wouldn't spread to nearby properties.

"No, we're not going to burn down her house."

"But, Mac, the orders say—"

"The orders say nothing about people's houses, Grimes. Leave it be."

Mac turned his attention back to Renata and the old woman. "They are not going to destroy our home, Sara," Renata explained, and when the old woman took that in, she burst into tears of gratitude. Mac, staring at the desolation he had brought about, wondered what the heck she had to be grateful for. Renata Levi was crying too, Mac noticed, but those weren't tears of gratitude falling out of those remarkable eyes. More like tears of rage. She held herself as straight as he imagined a queen would, her head high, as she

150

helped her mother-in-law up the steps of Levi House. Mac touched the locket, praying that Renata Levi would look back. But she didn't. Not once.

CHAPTER SEVEN

IN THE GRAY MORNING LIGHT of an overcast day Renata surveyed the charred remains of Levi and Company. The few passers by—those who had begun to creep out of their houses now that the Americanos were gone—averted their eyes as if in the presence of a shameful death. Levi and Company looked like a huge tortured skeleton, its charred bones giving off a pervasive putrefied stench that caused Sara to hold a piece of perfumed lace to her nose.

The clerks had assembled, but one of the more delicate said he felt faint. Renata seemed not to notice the smell. She sent the sick clerk to Levi House to be revived by Carita and worked alongside the others, grubbing through the charred wood and ashes to see what, if anything, could be retrieved.

At noon Renata sent the boy, Perito, on an errand, and he returned within a few moments, nodding his head. Renata put on her black bonnet and asked Juan—that Negro who insisted he was Spanish—to bring round the cart. "You can't go anywhere like that," Sara said, looking at Renata's ash-covered bombazine dress, her sooty hands.

"I am going to see Don Orlando de Córdoba," Renata said, getting into the cart.

"Renata, at least wash your hands. Brush off your dress. He is our governor."

"This is the respect he has earned, Sara," Renata said, driving off.

Perito had told Renata that the governor had reoccupied his house on Calle Palafox. Córdoba had expected a great deal of damage, but the American general had again surprised him. Except for the scarred desk, the governor's mansion was as Córdoba had left it.

Martino met Renata at the door, shocked at her appearance. He knew, of course, about the fire and decided to make allowances for it. "Don Orlando is occupied, Doña Levi," he said, elevating her social status. "We are so very sorry about your loss. As soon as he is able the governor will issue a formal statement of regret, but we have only just returned, the mansion is in disarray . . ."

"I will wait," Renata said. She would have pushed past him, but he stepped back, afraid the soot on her dress would dirty his uniform. She chose the best chair in the anteroom, and Martino rolled his heavily fringed eyes at the thought of what the upholstery would look like when the poor woman stood up. He was genuinely sympathetic, however, and offered Renata brandy and biscuits, which she refused.

"The governor may be some time."

She would wait, she thought, for as long as it took. She had something she wanted to say to Don Orlando, and since there was no longer a Talking Room, his anteroom was not a bad place to sit and think. After an hour's time the paneled door to Don Orlando's reception room opened. Laird came out and Martino sped in, closing the door behind him. "I am that sorry, lassie," Laird said, standing over her, his faded eyes looking down at her with compassion. "If I can do anything . . ."

"It's good just to see you, Laird," Renata said, standing up. She started to give him her sooty hand, realized how dirty it was, and tried to withdraw it, but Laird took the hand anyway, and held it. "I lay the entire blame at the feet of the Spanish government. It is the government that must do something."

"The Spaniards are in no condition to do anything for you, lassie."

"And what are they doing for you, Laird?" Renata asked, retrieving her hand. "You came back quickly enough once Jackson left."

"Lassie, think: Don Orlando is sympathetic to the plight of the Seminoles."

" 'Plight of the Seminoles.' " She looked up at him and shook her head angrily. "And what about the plight of his people?"

"You must not be bitter, lassie. You will prosper once more. You have the means to start again. But my people," he went on soberly, his Scottish accent growing more pronounced, "do not know where to begin. Andrew Jackson is going to win the Battle of New Orleans. The British have sadly underestimated him. We all have. Jackson is a man who hates with a pure white heat. Nothing can stop that hate. And, oh, how he hates the Indians! He wants to rid Florida of the Seminoles and give their rich land, their cattle, their slaves to the Americanos. He will, lassie. He says the Indians are animals with men's bodies—but he is the wolf, the leader of his pack, devouring everything that stands in his way." The little Scotsman stood there in his neat buckskins with his ginger beard halfway down his chest, his pale red hair parted dead center, his freckled face bone-white with anger.

But Renata was too frightened, too filled with her own disappointment, and too angry herself to sympathize. "And Don Orlando, that great leader, what can he do for your people?"

152

"Do not underestimate him either, Renata. He would have stopped Jackson if he could. Don Orlando is a man who loves his country. He is well aware that the Spanish have an obligation to protect the Seminoles and he is willing to help arm them in preparation for the time when Jackson turns his sights on them. His family owns a munitions factory, lassie, manufacturing the new small-bore rifles. He can help the Seminoles fight back." Laird stopped and looked at Renata as if he were asking her for something—for help or maybe only for understanding. "There is so little time, lassie."

Renata looked back at Laird, revealing the fury in her black eyes. "You are a good man, Laird, but you must forgive me if I do not share your fears or your hatred of Andrew Jackson."

"He turned Levi and Company into ashes, Renata."

"Don Orlando turned Levi and Company into ashes. Andrew Jackson is a man like you, Laird, who protects his people." In her ash-covered dress she went to the reception-room door and opened it, stepping in with the dignity even her anger couldn't rob her of. Despite her inability to understand what he had to face, Laird couldn't help admiring her. Adamo would have been proud.

Don Orlando dismissed Martino and stood up wearily, studying her sooty face. "Señora Levi," he said after a moment. "I am sorry."

"I did not come for apologies, Don Orlando. I came to remind you that you had a duty to protect my property. Instead you offered it as a sacrifice to the Americanos."

The flat planes of Córdoba's face colored, and he raised one of his beautifully cared-for hands to touch that one imperfection, his broken nose. "Señora, what would you like me to do? Or say? The Córdobas have been in Florida for over three centuries. We came with Don Juan Ponce de León, and we came with Don Hernando de Soto, and we came with Don Pedro Menéndez de Avilés. Florida is in our blood, but once again we are being turned out. Oh, we will be," he said, reading disbelief in Renata's expression. "It is only a matter of time. Spain is tired. Spain is humiliated. The Córdobas are humiliated. I repeat: I am sorry. I am abjectly, abundantly sorry."

He found he could not look at her, and his glance once again fell on the scars Andrew Jackson had inflicted on his ancient desk. "Do you think I enjoyed having that ignorant savage, that Americano, take over Pensacola with barely a shot fired? Do you think I took pleasure from his burning my people's houses, depriving them of their livelihoods? I gave him your name, yes, but there were many others who would have given it to him. I could not court the wanton destruction he was capable of if he discovered I had been withholding the information he wanted. I am sorry, Señora Levi. You are a Spanish subject. I should have found a way to protect you. I did not."

She clasped her hands in front of her, wondering if he genuinely believed this little speech might satisfy her. "My people, Don Orlando, have been here as long as yours. Your people governed and protected, and my people provided the trade that made it possible. You can no longer protect, and I can no longer trade. Not as a Spaniard. I have come here today to renounce my Spanish citizenship. I am no longer a Spaniard, Don Orlando, so you no longer have to concern yourself about your inability to protect me. I will protect myself."

She left him standing under the Spanish flag, staring down at the desk Andrew Jackson had drawn his spurs across. Don Orlando Ramón de Córdoba was going to help Laird and the Seminoles fight a doomed battle against Andrew Jackson. Renata was going to keep her promise to Adamo Levi.

CHAPTER EIGHT

Laird—1818

THE SLIT OF A WINDOW in the earthen wall was too high for Laird to see out of. Through it he could hear the raw, hungry boys playing cards, tossing dice, and singing in the courtyard of the dusty St. Marks Fort.

The singers had reached the twentieth verse of a three-year-old ballad sung in every bar and schoolroom in the United States, celebrating Old Hickory's victory over the British at New Orleans. "Andy Jackson beat the heck out of the army that beat the heck out of Napoleon," ran the refrain. "And he did it with a good old Kentucky rifle." The American shame over previous military losses had been purged with that one battle despite the fact that it had taken place two weeks after the War of 1812 was officially ended by negotiators in Brussels. Jackson's 1815 victory had restored pride and a new sense of nationalism to the young, defeated, nearly bankrupt country. It had given Americans their first national hero since Washington.

Three years later, in 1818, Andy Jackson, more than ever convinced of his destiny to protect his people, had again invaded Florida. Five thousand land-hungry recruits from Georgia and Alabama responded to his call. He had led the grumbling, swollen army through the pine and scrub forests of Florida's panhandle to this lonely Spanish fort at the mouth of the St. Marks River. Old Hickory had been looking for Seminoles and in particular for Billy Bass, whom he blamed for killing and scalping a group of American women and children. He had also been looking for Laird.

"Well, he found me," Laird said to himself and wondered if that was a bad sign, talking to himself. After dodging Jackson for months, it was nearly funny how easily he had been caught. He had thought he had a day's jump on Jackson. The Seminoles needed rifles and ammunition, and he had foolishly come into the fort to inspect the arms Don Orlando Ramón de Córdoba had shipped from Havana to St. Marks.

While Laird was talking with Ojos, the fort's commandant and a Córdoba connection, the Tennessee Volunteers had surrounded the place, taking it without a shot. Jackson had walked into Ojos's office and, nearly as surprised as Laird, caught him examining a light-bore Cuban rifle. "Red-handed," Jackson said, spitting on the floor in disgust. "Wearing Injun clothes! A white man!"

Laird had long ago exchanged his buckskins for the costume of a Seminole Indian chief: fringed skirt, leggings, a plumed turban, and silver armlets. His ginger beard was parted by a breast ornament of silver crescents intricately worked with figures of bears and panthers.

Laird had been hustled to the cell in the bottom of the fort and left there while Jackson and most of his men went south looking for Billy Bass. But they couldn't find him, even after marching a hundred miles in eight days. All they had found were recently deserted Seminole villages. And a sick British marine.

"How's the fever, lad?" Laird called to the next cell, but he didn't receive much of an answer, and he guessed the fever was out of control. On the eighth day of that fruitless march, Jackson's men had captured Armbrister, hiding in the salt-water swamps near Cedar Key. His clothes were in rags and his skin had been ravaged by the sun and mosquitoes. He had managed to stand up, throw his narrow shoulders back, and identify himself as Lieutenant Robert Allyn Armbrister of the Royal British Marines before he passed out.

Armbrister had become separated from Billy Bass's men during one of their lightning escapes and had been living in the swamps. He wore what was left of a marine jacket, and in its pocket were letters from Laird warning Billy Bass of Jackson's overwhelming and advancing army, alerting him to Jackson's probable route.

Jackson was infuriated, his dyspepsia raging. He returned to St. Marks and confronted the diminutive Laird in his foul-smelling cell. "How the hell did you know what route I was taking? Who is the traitor who told you?" But Laird kept silent despite Jackson's threats.

"I can guess what he's going to do next," Laird said to himself, not caring if he spoke aloud or not. "I've been studying the man for years." Two weeks in that earthen-walled cell listening to the Georgia and Alabama boys in the courtyard hoot and holler hadn't helped his mental state. He knew that.

He wondered which would give first in this hole, his mind or his body.

He heard the key in the lock and thought that perhaps Jackson was about to make good on his threats. He would have welcomed it. Laird, who had spent most of his life out of doors, had used every control he knew to keep himself from breaking down. He was tired. He had made his peace with this world. He would have welcomed an end.

But instead of the raw-boned, ill-dressed recruit he expected, he saw a man two feet taller and considerably broader than he was, wearing a beautifully tailored, impeccably white and pale blue uniform of a captain in the regular United States Army. In the darkness, relieved only by that band of light from the inaccessible window, Jack Church glowed like the north star on a moonless night.

Laird, whose own invariable neatness had suffered greatly during his imprisonment, said admiringly, "I like a man to look neat." Church, trying to ignore the stench of the cavelike cell, wondered if the Scottish trader in the filthy Injun dress had lost his reason.

Jack Church had been sent again to deflect Jackson from entering Spanish Florida. By the time Jack Church had arrived in Alabama it was too late, and he had followed Jackson to St. Marks. This time he had been sent by President Monroe, a consummate politician, who wanted a man he could trust in Florida, one who would make certain that when Jack went too far (and, of course, he would), Monroe would receive word first. "Old Hickory's my tiger," Monroe said, "but I don't necessarily know where he's going to turn when he's let out of the cage."

Jack Church hadn't had any choice but to accept the assignment, though he knew Jackson wouldn't have forgotten or forgiven him for the similar role he had played four years before. However, Church had been anxious to return to Florida. He remembered the pink and blue Florida sky and the blue haze trailing across the pines in the early morning air. Washington City had seemed like a sentence he had received for unknown crimes. He had passed his time sitting behind a desk, turning out in full kit for ceremonial occasions, and thwarting mothers intent on their daughters' imminent matrimony.

Jackson, on being informed of Church's arrival, refused to see him. He was holed up in the commander's office, where he had had a camp bed set up. He had ordered Laird and Armbrister to be executed on the following day and knew Church would object and write to Monroe and cause the devil of a stink. "I'll see the lily-liver," he agreed, when told of Church's arrival, "but only after the traitors are executed."

When he learned of the imminent executions Jack Church demanded to be allowed to talk to the prisoners. Armbrister, delirious with fever, wasn't in any condition to talk, but Laird welcomed him.

"You know he's charging you with treason," Jack Church said, standing

156

against the earthen wall, while Laird stood as close to the open door as he could. The stale air from the corridor smelled to him like the purest ocean breeze compared to that in his cell.

"Ridiculous, is it not, lad? I have been protecting my people. I'm the man's enemy, not a traitor."

That seemed remarkably obvious to Jack Church as well, but he persisted. "Jackson says you incited Billy Bass to attack Americans on American territory."

"I don't know if I can take credit for that, lad," Laird said, trying to be fair. "Billy Bass made a retaliatory raid after Jackson engineered the burning of the Negro fort—on Spanish territory, mind you. Three hundred and fifty Indian and Negro men, women, and children were killed. You must see, lad, that Jackson wants only to drive the Seminoles out so his people can take our land, our cattle, and our slaves. The Seminoles must fight back."

Jack Church studied the little man, who seemed in remarkable condition for having been in this foul place for two weeks. He had few false ideals about America's hero, Old Hickory, but he wondered how innocent the Seminoles had been. He had read about Billy Bass's retaliatory raid. The number of scalps taken and women raped had been, it was reported, monumental. He said as much.

Laird laughed. "Scalps were taken, it's true, lad. But none of the women were raped. Redskins cannot abide white women. Their smell is insufferable."

"And you, Laird? Have you taken part in these 'retaliatory' raids?"

"Never. I don't hold with retaliation. But I admit, lad, that I have done everything I could to thwart Andrew Jackson. And I will continue to do so with my dying breath."

"By arranging with the Córdoba family for arms?"

"By making certain my people were always one step ahead of Andrew Jackson," the Scotsman said firmly. Laird knew there was no hard proof against Córdoba, and he wasn't light-headed enough to provide it.

The two men were interrupted by the arrival of a newly elevated major; a faded captain's insignia could still be seen on his tunic.

"Mac," Jack Church said, recognizing the good-natured farm boy whom Jackson had taken under his wing. He looked at the new major's insignia and laughed. "I guess you'll always outrank me, Major."

"I heard you were here, Jack," Mac said, his color rising. He hadn't wanted to be promoted, but Old Hickory had insisted. "That damned lily-liver is not going to outrank you," Jackson had said, sending for the company tailor. He was only a brevet major anyway, still getting a captain's pay. He held out his hand and Jack Church took it. Mac realized he was happy to see Jack Church. He had been the only man Mac had ever seen talk back to Andy Jackson and not give in.

Church hadn't changed much, but Mac, still farm-boy healthy, was thinner than he had been. Since the Red Creek massacre he had killed more men —red and white—in battle than he could count. For the last month he had been living on a quart of corn and three rations of meat per day. And spending four years as General Jackson's aide wasn't a life guaranteed to keep a man young. Nevertheless he retained his innocent freckled baby face, and his American-flag-blue eyes were still a true mirror of his emotions.

At that moment he was embarrassed by his new elevation, aware of how Jack Church felt about his commander and how Jackson felt about Jack Church. "General Jackson says he will see you now."

"He's not serious about this execution is he, Mac?" Church asked.

"You'd better talk to him, Jack."

Mac thought he'd do well to make certain there was boiled hominy for Jackson's lunch. If his dyspepsia wasn't bothering him now, it would after he'd seen Jack Church. Grimes was detailed to show Church to the commandant's office, leaving Mac and Laird together. It was the first time Mac had seen the prisoner since he had been taken. "I don't reckon you remember me," Mac said, somewhat uneasy.

"Remember you?" the little man asked. "As if it were yesterday, lad. You and Lobo came riding into Metholda's summer camp, you looking as if you were half dead with hunger, and then you went to the sofkee and pulled out a snake head and were sick all night. I remember you, lad. I remember Lobo Levi. If ever there was a wrong spirit born into the wrong lad, there it was. He was a thin, hard flame, but his memory still burns."

"I've met a lot of soldiers since," Mac said, "but I never have met up with anyone like Lobo." He put his hand to his tunic pocket and wanted to ask about Lobo Levi's wife but couldn't.

As if he had read his mind, Laird said, "His widow is doing nicely, I hear. You Americanos burned her buildings, but nothing can keep that lassie down for long."

Mac would have liked to hear more, but Laird's loquacity had run its course and he suddenly went silent, retiring back into his cell. As Mac made his way up to Jackson's office he thought, as he too often did, of Renata Levi's red lips and black eyes and the way her bombazine dress had rustled against his chest when he carried her out of the Talking Room.

Jack Church had told himself that he was going to use the diplomacy he had mastered in Washington City to make Andrew Jackson understand the implications of what he was doing.

"General Jackson, sir," he said, standing at attention while Jackson, his tunic undone, his hand under it, sat looking up at him with his gimlet eyes registering extreme disapproval. "I am pleased to bring you regards from the President—"

"Those men are being executed tomorrow, Church. Final word."

The Spanish commandant's office had seemed spacious moments before, but now it was barely adequate, overwhelmed by Church and Jackson and their mutual hatred. For Jackson, Jack Church *was* Washington City, filled with New Englanders and parlor bastards looking down their noses at the real strength of the country, his farm workers of the southland. And Jack Church, looking at the sour, whey-colored face of the hero of New Orleans, saw only a righteous, bigoted, law-breaking martinet and thought to himself, diplomacy be damned. "You cannot kill those men, sir. By all that's right in this world, they must have a proper military court-martial. It is against all international as well as United States military law and tradition to summarily execute—"

"Where was international law, Captain Church, when Billy Bass and those savages scalped, alive, innocent American soldiers' wives on American territory? A month ago, Captain Church, I walked into a shaman's chikee in Alabama Territory, and you know what I found inside that damned chikee? I found fifty white victims' scalps, still fresh, Captain Church, each sitting on its own stake, dripping blood. You ever see or smell a nine-year-old blond girl's fresh scalp, Captain Church?"

Jack Church, having heard enough emotional rhetoric in Washington City, was immune to it. He forced himself to speak evenly. "If you execute those men without a trial, General, you will not only have made enemies of Spain and England again—quite possibly precipitating another war—but America will be seen as descending to what you suppose is the red man's level of savagery."

"You damned lily-livered Military Academy scoundrel. Git," Jackson shouted. He stood up as if he would throw Church out himself. "Git. I have had enough of your damned Washington City reasoning. Out of my sight."

Jack Church saluted and left Jackson massaging his stomach, calling for Mac. "You'd better convene a military court-martial," he said, scowling. "First thing in the morning, lest the lily-livers up in Washington City have apoplexy."

Jackson spent the following morning while the trial was progressing drinking sweetened barley water, avoiding Captain Church, pacing along St. Marks Fort's ramparts. He was aware that Billy Bass and the Seminoles had for the moment defeated him. He and his army could spend years looking for them in the damned scrub and piney woods and never find them. But he was after bigger game than Bass, and he decided that United States honor would be redeemed with Laird's execution.

He was staring at the Gulf waters planning his next move when Mac, looking guilty and apprehensive, approached with the result of the court-martial. No one else on Jackson's staff would bring it to him. "Hang 'em in an hour's time," Jackson said before Mac could speak. Then he stared at Mac, standing at attention with that funny look in his eyes. Jackson felt a spasm in his stomach. "What is it, Mac?"

159

"Laird's to be imprisoned for five years. Armbrister's to be given fifty lashes and a year in jail."

Andrew Jackson removed his hand from under his tunic. His skin had turned that dead white Mac had learned to respect. "Hang 'em both immediately, and put everyone on that court-martial on half rations for a week."

"But, sir, the law—"

"Hang the law. Dammit, man, *I* make the law. They're both guilty of inciting the Indians to kill innocent Americans and abetting the savages, and you know it. There's a punishment for their crimes, and I mean for them to suffer it if I have to hang the bastards myself. And where's that Washington City Academy scoundrel? Send him to my office."

Jack Church stood at attention while Jackson lay on his cot, his hand under his shirt like an animal in a bag. "I was a fool to listen to you, Church. Those two scoundrels are being hanged in an hour's time, and if you say one word to me against it, you're going to be up there with them, that thick neck of yours in a hangman's noose."

Church could not believe what he had heard. "This is Spanish territory, General Jackson. You cannot execute an Englishman and a Spanish citizen on foreign—"

Jackson jumped up, his face so close to Jack Church's that he could smell the hominy on the general's breath. "I can and I will. You are wrong, Captain Church. When you leave this fort in the next few moments and take your fat arse back to Washington City to report on me, you will notice the United States flag waving from the standard. This is not damned Spanish territory, Captain. I have just annexed East Florida. We are now standing in, you will be pleased to know, United States of America territory. Tell that to Jim Monroe and those pink-bottomed New Englanders waiting to hear what big, bad, forever-damned Andy Jackson is going to do next."

"Spain will go to war, General. England and France will join with her—"

"Spain can't go to war, dammit. She's overflowing with debts and cowards. Tomorrow, Captain, I march to Pensacola to annex West Florida. I'm going to wipe out as many Injun villages as I can along the way. And when I get to Pensacola I'm going to have a few words with the former governor. Córdoba is going to stop arming the savages if I have to hang him too. You are not invited on that march, Captain. Now get out, and damn your eyes. I have work to do."

The young British marine lieutenant, Armbrister, was hanged first. Feverish with malaria and believing he was in the middle of a nightmare, he babbled incoherently as he was pushed up the narrow ladder to the hangman's platform. In the end he seemed to realize what was happening and called out for his mother. The rough farm boys gathered below sniggered, but nervously. He had been close to them in years, and he was so obviously ill.

Laird was a better victim. He walked up to the makeshift gibbet in his filthy Seminole dress, his hair neatly parted, standing as tall as he could, looking like a boy in a masquerade costume. He felt better than he had since he had been captured. "There is no sweeter pleasure than inhaling the airs of the Gulf waters, lad," he told one of the men who accompanied him as he took in great gulps of air. "It is one of the rare pleasures unaccompanied by sin."

He stood with his back to the Gulf, facing the north, where the pine-tree forests protected his people from Andrew Jackson's army. "That beard's going to make someone a right nice blanket," a wit from Birmingham, Alabama, shouted.

"You want to cry for your mama?" the soldier executioner asked, and the boys below laughed.

"No," Laird answered seriously, and the boys stopped laughing. By all rights the little man should have been a figure of fun, but his dignity robbed their jokes of humor. Laird took the noose from the soldier's rough hands and himself placed it around his neck as if it were a military decoration, something to be proud of. "I am going to meet my Lord, the Great Father," he said, and his solemn voice reached out and echoed around the stockade, demanding the attention of the nearly five thousand men gathered there to watch his death.

In that moment of silence Laird turned to look at Andrew Jackson watching from the parapet of the fort, on the same level with him, high above the crowds, as if they had arranged for a final confrontation. "I am pleased to die on this land, on this earth, this Florida, for my people. I have reaped many rewards. You," he said, pointing at Jackson, "want Florida soil so you can denude and tame it and build cities on it, and then you will only want to tame and destroy more. You are of a frightened race, General Jackson, fearful of the land and the water and the animals that live here. I have no fear of life and death, and I thank my Lord that I have been so spared. I go willingly to the World Above the Sky. My spirit will hover there, guiding my people as long as they are here."

The executioner was not an expert. It took Laird a long, painful time to die as he swayed over the palmetto brush that grew in the dust of the stockade, staring up into the blinding April sun. Even before he was dead, the boy who had thought his beard would make a fine blanket had snipped it off for a souvenir.

CHAPTER NINE

Mac—1818

MacCRIMMONS TOOK A RARE BATH and put on, for the first time, his new major's tunic. It had been waiting for him when he reached Pensacola, sent via packet ship by Jack Church. The last time he had received a present from anyone was on his eighth birthday, and it was from his grandmother. He was more touched than he liked to admit. He treasured the tunic. It fitted tolerably well, though it was a bit tight in the shoulders.

"You going courting or arresting?" Grimes wanted to know. He was tickled at the precise way Mac—who barely needed to—had thoroughly shaved his handsome boy's face. Mac, who had come to regard Grimes as an obligation, as his personal devil, ignored him. He transferred Lobo Levi's locket into the pocket of the new major's tunic. A cool, pale, red-lipped face filled his thoughts.

They had been in Pensacola for a week. Jackson had left a two-hundred-man garrison at St. Marks and begun a two-week march north and then west, through the watery wilderness of the panhandle. Effortlessly they destroyed all the major Indian centers west of the Suwannee River in an action that would be called the First Seminole War.

Before he had left Pensacola, Jackson had sent two messages: one to his friend and colleague General Gaines telling him to take St. Augustine, the last Spanish stronghold in Florida; the other to the President and his Secretary of War, announcing that he was in the process of annexing Florida. "Cuba is ours when we want her," he wrote, thinking that taking Cuba would be the last nail in Spain's—and particularly, Córdoba's—coffin.

The Spanish in Pensacola "showed a little gumption," but they were no match for the coonskin-capped army that wouldn't adhere to any of the rules of war, mostly because they didn't know them. Jackson had looked forward to once again turning Córdoba out of his home, but Córdoba had already vacated the governor's mansion for the small house in the Seville Quarter by the time he arrived.

Martino, slightly less plump, had been left to hand over the royal archives and to hear Jackson declare the revenue laws of the United States to be in effect in the new territory of West Florida. It had taken Andrew Jackson a week to put his laws into effect. Then he called for Mac. All Spanish citizens who had continued to deal with the British after his last visit were to be arrested and tried in a military court of law. "We will do it the Washington City lily-livers' way," he said, thinking of Jack Church.

Mac was not surprised to find Señora Renata Levi's name heading the list. He was going to see Lobo Levi's widow in a few moments, something he had dreamed of for months. This time he was going to have to arrest her. He tried not to think of the cell Laird had had to live in during the last weeks of his life. The Fort Barrancas cell Renata Levi would be kept in until her trial would not be unlike it.

Mac had tried to talk Old Hickory out of jailing a woman, but Jackson's chivalry extended only to American farm women. "Don't be a fool, Mac, and get on with your job," Jackson had told him, and so he had.

The Levi and Company grounds, though diminished, seemed neat and prosperous as Mac stood before the mansion. The trading post was now housed in the mansion's first floor, and the warehouse had been rebuilt. The plaza was again deserted. The Pensacolans, remembering the fires of Jackson's last visit, were taking a cautious approach to this latest invasion. Mac ordered Grimes and his men to wait outside. Taking a deep breath, Major MacCrimmons strode through the trading post entrance. Inside he stopped and let a low whistle escape his lips, astonished at how similar it was—right down to the rich, potent smell of hides and tobacco and cured wood—to the trading post he had had burned down.

During that first American occupation, the night before Levi and Company was set on fire, Renata had hidden, in a cellar under the old schoolhouse at the edge of her property, a store of China tea, a cache of Kentucky rifles, fifty gallons of rum, and nearly a hundred blankets.

After Jackson's troops had left and the rubble was cleared, she had had the French carpenters rebuild the trading post on the first floor of the Levi mansion. She herself supervised the installation of a window in the south wall of the new Talking Room. And she hadn't hesitated for a moment to sell her hidden cache of goods at quadruple their value to the British agents, French adventurers, and American traders who had begun to creep back into Pensacola only days after Andrew Jackson had ordered her buildings burned for "trading with the enemy."

She had kept one of the Kentucky rifles for herself. Laird had turned up shortly after the Battle of New Orleans, and she had asked the Scotsman to teach her how to shoot. After the first practice day she had had to apply liniment to her shoulder every night for a week, but that hadn't stopped her. In the years that followed, Juan often drove her in the cart to her plantation, Casa del Norte, so she could shoot her Kentucky rifle.

With the money she received from her secret cache, she had had the warehouses reconstructed, closer to the harbor for easier loading. She had filled them with whatever Indian goods she managed to come by and with whiskey bought from the British traders, rifles from the Cubans, and cotton and sugar cane from the plantations on the St. Johns River near St. Augustine.

The two Levi and Company ships she had managed to salvage were constantly at sea, braving the Gulf Stream, sailing from Pensacola to St. Augustine to Havana and back again. Although Pensacola was forgotten by the world powers, Levi and Company had prospered in those years after the Battle of New Orleans. British, Scottish, and Irish traders were seen again on the trading company porch, as were the now destitute Seminole *micos*.

During those years Renata had received increasing amounts of land in payment for Seminole debts. She held title to thousands of acres halfway between Pensacola and St. Augustine. Beautiful land, Laird had told her, verdant and rich. But there was no easy way to get to it, no white settlements for hundreds of miles, and no men willing to clear and work it.

Renata reasoned that when the Spanish left Florida—and to her it was obvious that they would—and the trading fell off, there would be time to develop the land, to create huge cotton plantations, using Indians for labor. What Laird was never able to make her understand was that the Seminoles considered it a fatal loss of face to work for a white man.

Even before Jackson returned, the Americanos came, believing, like Renata, that the Spanish were getting ready to leave. They had arrived in Pensacola with letters from Jackson to Córdoba. He refused to acknowledge either the letters or the Americanos. They didn't care. They bought property in and around Pensacola and drove out along the bay to Fort Barrancas in large open carriages for picnics. It was as if they already owned the town.

And then, in 1818, Andrew Jackson annexed it for them.

Mac, acutely aware that he had done this before, stepped into the oddly familiar, long, dark, reassuringly orderly and empty trading post. He felt as if he were returning to a childhood home. Instinctively he looked for Señora Sara in the chair at the far end of the post. But only her clay pipe was there.

He told himself to stop being a damned fool, as the general would say, and without allowing himself further hesitation, opened the door that led to the new Talking Room and stepped in. The shutters had been opened on the south window, allowing the late May morning air to cool the room.

Renata, several degrees cooler than the breeze, sat behind a desk similar to the one that had burned, her back to him. She was staring out at the water, which, in the distance, met the horizon nearly seamlessly, only a thin, uneven line of whitecaps separating the blue sky from the green bay. She still wore a black bombazine dress, and Mac could almost hear the sound of its rustle against his chest.

164

Forcing himself not to rub his thighs, keeping his hands at his side, knowing his face had gone red, he coughed and then "ahemmed," and finally she turned, her oval face as flawless, as beautiful, as remote as he had remembered it. For the past four years he had lived almost exclusively in a man's world, and the force of Renata's womanliness made him feel as if he had been hit by a cannonball. He nearly fell backward over the black horsehair sofa, righting himself just in time.

"Yes?" she said in English in a clear, unemotional voice. He thought he had remembered everything about her, but he had forgotten that voice and the way it made him feel—like a field hand caught in the wrong part of the house. Her black eyes stared at a point just above his chest, waiting.

"Major MacCrimmons, ma'am. Of the United States Army, ma'am." Lord, he felt like a fool.

"The man who burns down buildings. I remember you, Major. Are you back to burn down Levi and Company again?"

He put his hands behind his back and clasped them together so they would stay there. "I regret to inform you, ma'am, that I am here to arrest you."

"For what crime?" she asked calmly.

"Same as last time, ma'am. Even though Florida is now annexed to the United States, you are being arrested for breaking a Spanish law, ma'am. That is, you traded with the enemy of a neutral country, that being the United States of America, ma'am. Had Florida been part of the U.S. then, General Jackson would probably have hanged you, ma'am." Lord, he wished he could stop talking. "If you would get your things, I have orders to take you to Fort Barrancas, where you will await a military trial—"

She pushed her chair away from the desk and showed him the Kentucky rifle she held in her hands, aimed at his heart. Mac didn't know whether or not she was capable of firing it. All he wanted to do was stride across the Talking Room and take her in his arms and hold her. Despite the Kentucky rifle and the firm, unwavering voice, she seemed vulnerable and alone.

He might have tried if Grimes hadn't stuck his ferret's head inside the door to see what was keeping him. It was nearly comic the way Grimes stared first at his major and then at the black-haired Spanish woman, who looked like some sort of angel, aiming a Kentucky rifle at Mac.

"Don't shoot, Señora," Grimes said, looking at Mac. "What do you want me to do, sir?"

Mac didn't answer. He just stood there, all pink in the face, his hands behind his back, staring at the woman sitting behind the desk, pointing a rifle at his chest and suddenly looking as if she knew how to use it. It was the woman who gave the orders. "I want you, Sergeant," she said, not even looking at Grimes, "to go to General Jackson and tell him that if he does not appear here within the hour, he may send someone to call for the major's corpse." She allowed her right hand to let go of the rifle while she turned over an hourglass on her desk. The red-colored sand began to flow. "I will shoot him as a trespasser."

"The general, he ain't going to like this," Grimes said, shaking his head.

"Deliver the message, Grimes," Mac said, unable to look anywhere but at his captor.

Jackson, paler than parchment, arrived a few moments before the red sand had run out of the glass. Mac, his cheeks as red as the sand, looked at his commander once and then away. Jackson stood inside the Talking Room door, his head nearly touching the beams. Renata sat in her chair behind the desk, the Kentucky rifle casually aimed at the pocket in which Mac kept Lobo Levi's locket. Mac wasn't a man of ironies, but he thought it would be strange if Lobo Levi's widow shot him and smashed her own portrait at the same time.

"What am I doing here, Señora Levi?" Jackson asked, realizing that if he didn't speak, neither would she.

Renata knew she looked as calm as a stone, but she was aware of how nearly out of control she was, just below the surface. The thought of being imprisoned in a Fort Barrancas cell made her skin crawl. What would happen, she wondered, to Levi and Company, to Sara, if she were put in jail and left there until the Americanos decided to bring her to trial? What if she were imprisoned for years?

"What am I doing here, Señora Levi?" the general repeated carefully. Renata forced herself to speak, slowly, calmly, with authority. She knew if she allowed Andrew Jackson to see that she was afraid, she hadn't a chance.

"Before you send me off to prison, General, I should like to plead my case."

Jackson snorted. "I have never seen a less pleading woman." He wanted to put his hand under his tunic and massage the place where the dyspepsia was flaring up. He wanted, suddenly, to go home. He was tired of Florida and Washington City and of the Spanish, who pretended they didn't understand what he made so clear. At least this woman spoke English. But Mac, standing in the middle of the room, looked as if he had been struck dumb. Had it been any other man, Jackson would have let him be shot.

"Go on," he said, wondering at her serenity, with a rifle between her and hanging. Now, of course, she would have to be hung. "Plead, Señora Levi."

His sarcasm, his pale fury, didn't seem to unnerve her. She reminded Jackson of Córdoba: unbendable. She put her Kentucky rifle on her desk, and Grimes made a move toward her which Jackson stopped by putting his hand up. He had made a bargain. She was to be allowed to talk. And she did so in a reasonable, even voice, without a hint of fear.

"From the legal point of view, General, you may not arrest me on the grounds your major put forth: a Spanish citizen abetting your enemy."

She paused and looked up and brought off a credible smile. Jackson waited, intrigued, and finally again had to speak first. "And pray, tell me, Señora, why not?" He had never before met a woman who spoke with such

166

authority. He had never met a woman who would even attempt a legal argument. The only educated women he had come up against were the salon ladies in Washington City, and they had spoken a language of artifice and flirtation he hadn't begun to understand.

"Because *A*: the British are no longer your enemy. Your country's war with them ended three years ago when the Treaty of Ghent was signed."

"Your knowledge is extensive, Señora, but I adhere to the spirit of the law, not the letter. The British remain my country's enemies, and the Spanish, in helping them, are breaking the law."

"Which brings me to my second point, General. *B*: I am not Spanish. I renounced my citizenship immediately after you burned the trading post down and the Spanish government did nothing but lodge a hopeless protest. I am now a citizen of West Florida, General. And quite prepared to become a citizen of the United States of America. She protects her people well."

Jackson stared at her, and a look of astonishment and then amusement mixed with respect crossed his long, pale face. He threw back his head and—for the first time either Mac or Grimes could remember—actually roared with laughter. "I agree with you," Andrew Jackson said, recovering quickly from that historic laugh, once again his usual sour self. "You would make an excellent citizen, Señora Levi. I am also in accord with your argument that I cannot arrest you as a Spaniard aiding the enemy. You are cleared of those charges."

There was a moment's silence during which no one in the room dared move.

"But I am afraid you have committed a far more serious offense," Jackson said, breaking it. "You have threatened the life of a member of my staff, and I cannot let you go unpunished."

There was another silence, filled with despair and disappointment. And then Mac spoke with grave formality. "Permission to speak, General."

"Granted, Major."

"Señora Levi was not threatening me with her Kentucky rifle, sir. She was merely demonstrating what a fine weapon it is and, at the same time, requesting an interview with you. Sergeant Grimes, not used to polite English, misunderstood."

Jackson harrumphed disbelievingly. Mac was a good man. He would be proud to have him as a son. But he didn't have the makings of a great soldier. He had a soft spot. Had Señora Levi been a man, Jackson would have made her his second-in-command. He stared at them both for a moment. She made him think of his Rachel when she was young and pretty and had all her teeth. Mac, of course, was Señora Levi's willing victim. Any fool could see the man was gone on her. He reminded Jackson of himself at that age, a country boy willing to do anything for the woman he loved. He himself had gone against the law at that time, marrying Rachel, knowing all along that she hadn't been properly divorced.

Well, it was often said he made his own law, and it was obvious Mac was besotted, and as long as she had renounced her Spanish citizenship . . . He was wasting time. "You win, Señora. Mrs. Levi. All charges against you are dismissed."

There was not even a sigh of relief. Nothing to indicate the pressures of the gamble she had just taken and only, by the skin of her teeth, won. Jackson admired her the more. Putting the rifle aside, she stood up and gave a polite, hostesslike smile. "Would you like a glass of port, General?" She would almost have gotten away with it, but her voice quivered on that last word. The fear that had filled her body like new, raw wine, giving her strength, had suddenly dissipated, leaving her weak but not uncertain.

She felt as if this were the first moment of recovery after a long, difficult illness. She wanted them all to leave so she could savor being alive and healthy again. The fear of a vermin-ridden cell in Fort Barrancas, of being hanged or shot, had been firmly locked out of her consciousness during that interview with Jackson. But it had been there, waiting to pounce, to give her away.

She herself poured Jackson and Major MacCrimmons a glass each of her second-best port. She saved the best for important traders. "British?" Jackson asked, sipping it suspiciously.

"Spanish," Renata answered, turning the bottle around ostensibly to read the label but also to hide what it said: John Bolton & Sons, No. 7 Porchester Street, London, England.

Jackson upended his glass and took his leave, ordering Mac to meet with the Spanish commander at Fort Barrancas to take possession of his keys and records. Grimes went with Jackson. For a moment Renata and Mac were alone in the Talking Room. "Thank you, Major," she said, coming around the desk, her bombazine dress making that rustling sound that made him feel as if a piece of ice had been dropped down his breeches.

He looked into those depthless black eyes and unknowingly moved a step closer. "Would you have shot me if the general hadn't come?"

"Undoubtedly."

He reached across the desk with his wide, square hand and turned over the red-sand-filled hourglass. "Then all I can say, Señora Levi, is that I'm mighty glad Old Hickory came round."

Renata looked up at his wide open face and gave him the first genuine smile she had allowed herself since Jackson had returned to Pensacola. It was a secret smile, filled with relief and optimism and the youth she usually denied herself. It was a smile that admitted she was a woman after all. It was a smile that contained, though Mac could hardly believe it, affection.

"I am too, Major," she said.

The moment Mac had left, Sara raced into the Talking Room and wrapped her arms around her daughter-in-law. Renata acknowledged the anxiety she

168

would have denied to anyone but Sara. Finally, while Sara held her, Renata cried tears of relief.

"You are a brave woman, Renata," Sara said as she patted Renata's shoulder. "Adamo would be proud of you. I am proud of you. You are a Levi and more. Whoever your father was, he bequeathed you an inheritance you make wonderful use of. You should be proud too, Renata." The leathery old hands smoothed her daughter-in-law's fine, glossy hair back from her face with great tenderness.

Renata gave herself up to the sympathy and love of those thin, aged arms for some moments, and then she dried her eyes, kissed Sara on her wrinkled forehead, stood up, and brushed dust from the hem of the black bombazine dress. "I wonder," she said, gazing out of the window at the American ship entering the bay, "who Jackson's supply agent is?"

CHAPTER TEN

Mac—1821

"I AIN'T GOING TO ANY BALL, Andy." Rachel said it again for emphasis. "I ain't going to any ball."

She was a small woman who looked even smaller sitting on Córdoba's satin-upholstered oversized sofa in Pensacola's governor's mansion. Like a poor girl's doll, Mac thought, in a rich girl's dollhouse.

"Tell her she's going, Mac. We're all going. It's a matter of honor." Old Hickory sat across from his wife and next to Mac on the matching sofa, holding the new civil laws Rachel had pestered him to put into effect. They had put an end to "desecrating the Lord's day." Gambling, fiddling, guitar playing, and dancing were prohibited on Sundays.

"That Córdoba is giving a ball in our honor, Andy, only to make fun of us. Ain't that right, Mac?"

"I don't rightly know, Miss Rachel," Mac said, trying to be fair. "I never do know why Córdoba does what he does."

"It's to make fun of us, that's why he's doing it." She reached for her glass of milk and a thick slab of oatmeal cake. The Jacksons were having their late-afternoon refreshment. "I hate fancy balls," Rachel said as she chewed

169

the cake with her good back teeth. "I hate 'em." Mac saw the tears well up in her dark eyes and knew just what she was thinking. He liked Rachel nearly as much as he liked Old Hickory and in some ways more. She always said what she thought, and if what she thought was predictable, it was at least reassuringly familiar. The tears had come into her eyes, Mac knew, at the humiliating memories of all the fancy balls she had been forced to attend on what the newspapers had dubbed "the triumphal tour."

Three years earlier, after Jackson had taken Pensacola and General Gaines had taken St. Augustine, Old Hickory had felt his job was done. He left a garrison in Pensacola of which Mac had asked to be left in charge. "I need you more than Pensacola does," Jackson had said, and so, on May 13, 1818, Mac, thinking of Lobo Levi's widow, had regretfully accompanied Andrew Jackson to his home in Tennessee.

Jackson had solved the problem of Florida in a little under three months, a problem that had occupied diplomats of several nations for three hundred years. Washington City hadn't known how to react. The Spanish complained, the British lodged protests, and there were dozens of House and Senate resolutions calling for Jackson's censure. Still, it seemed obvious to President Monroe and his advisers that when the smoke cleared, Florida would become a possession of the United States, thanks to the feared and ridiculed backwoods General Jackson.

In August the President returned Florida to Spain so that Spain could honorably "cede" Florida to the United States, an action that predictably infuriated Jackson. Taking Mac and Rachel with him, he had made a triumphant procession from Tennessee to Washington City, cheered by the people everywhere he went. "I am the farmer's hero," he told an elderly but lively Thomas Jefferson at one more presidential dinner party, where Rachel had found the women in their low-cut gowns "wickedly sinful." "I have come," Jackson, oblivious to décolletage, said, "to convince you of the rightness of my actions."

Later, over cigars and brandy, Mac had overheard Jefferson, amused at President Monroe's dilemma, ask, "What are you going to do with your tiger now, Jim?"

"We might send him as minister to Russia," James Monroe had said poignantly.

"We would be at war with Russia in a month."

It had taken Monroe's ministers three years, but Monroe finally announced in February of 1821 that a treaty had been signed with Spain transferring the territory of Florida to the United States.

Jackson, disgusted, about to leave the army, was offered the governorship of the new territory, and he reluctantly accepted. "No one else," he told Mac, "can do the job." Rachel, dismayed, wondered if the dresses they had made such fun of in Washington City would be as ill received in Pensacola. "You think Andy's going to let me bring my pipe?" she asked Mac plaintively.

170

"I don't think so, Miss Rachel."

"They don't even have a preacher down in those parts."

"Tell her to bring her own," Jackson said.

Rachel held the thick invitation in her small, tough hands. "I ain't going to that ball," she reiterated, looking at her husband defiantly. "I ain't got a ball gown," she said, waiting for Jackson to look up from the papers he seemed to be committing to memory.

"Get her a ball gown, Mac," Jackson said, not looking up.

"I need material and a pattern and a dressmaker. . . ," and finally the tears spilled over and Rachel began making the mewing sounds that signaled she was deeply distressed. Jackson put the papers down, crossed the room, and, in a rare display of sympathy, took her in his scarecrow arms and patted her back.

"Mac. . . ," Jackson said, looking over her shoulder helplessly.

"We could go to Levi and Company," Mac said, touching the locket in his tunic pocket. "Mrs. Levi speaks English and she employs the Frenchwoman who is the best dressmaker in the territory, and Levi and Company has bolts and bolts of fancy material. I'm sure she can fix you up, Miss Rachel."

Rachel removed herself from her husband's arms, dried her tears with her handkerchief, and looked at Mac suspiciously. "You sure know a lot about this Mrs. Levi." She waited, but Mac didn't say anything and Andy was looking longingly at his papers.

Rachel gave a deep sigh, one Mac was familiar with, filled with pathos and resignation. "All right. We'll go see whether Mrs. Levi can fix me up with a ball gown that won't make them all fall down on the dance floor holding their sides, laughing and pointing."

Mac had been to the trading post a dozen times since his return to Pensacola. He bought a coonskin cap and sent it to Jack Church with a note written in his schoolboy's hand saying, "This should take some of the lily-liver out of you." He bought a comb made from deer bone, which broke the first time he ran it through his thick yellow hair. He bought: a bottle of Seminole-brewed corn whiskey, which he gave to Grimes for his birthday; a soft hat he never wore; and a brown clay pipe, which he smuggled into the governor's mansion for Miss Rachel. She didn't smoke it because her husband didn't hold with women using tobacco out of the home, and he didn't consider Córdoba's mansion home, but she did like to sit with its stem in her mouth while she did her needlework.

In all those times Mac had been to the trading post he had not once seen Lobo Levi's widow. She was always in the Talking Room, behind its closed door, busy with Jackson's supply officers, with her ship captains, with empty-handed Indian traders. She was involved with the difficult negotiations necessary to receive legal claim to the lands the Indians had used to pay their debts.

Señora Sara had been more visible, and despite the language barrier, the old Spanish woman and the young Americano had developed an affection for each other. Sara was the first person he saw when he escorted an unenthusiastic Rachel Jackson into the trading post. "Oh," she said when Mac introduced the two women. Sara removed her clay pipe from her mouth and made a little curtsy.

"That's a right pretty pipe," Rachel said, forgetting herself in her effort to get close enough to inhale some of the smoke issuing from it.

"It's just like the one you have," Mac said as Sara sped into the Talking Room, leaving a trail of smoke behind her.

"Only it has tobaccy in it," Rachel said longingly. Renata came out of the Talking Room looking, Mac thought, not exactly younger than she had three years ago but softer and easier. She smiled at him with those red, red lips.

"Major MacCrimmons. How nice to see you," she said in her fancy English.

He knew his face was red, and before he could stop himself, his big, square hands were rubbing his thighs. "Nice to see you too, ma'am. Real nice."

Rachel looked at him as if he had suddenly gone mad, but he deflected her interest by saying, "Mrs. Jackson and I are here to get her a gown for the ball Don Orlando is giving in honor of the general and Mrs. Jackson. There ain't much time, but I, we, was wondering if you could fix her up with something nice."

"I'm certain we can," Renata said kindly, looking at the plump and frightened woman the Pensacola French called Madame le Général. Renata Levi seemed for the first time since he had known her, if not happy, at least unburdened.

She told Perito to run and get the French dressmaker and instructed a clerk to fetch a bolt of particular fabric. Then, putting her arm into Rachel's, she escorted her into the Talking Room, took a place next to her on the horsehair sofa, and gave Madame le Général the sort of attention she rarely received anywhere but at home in Tennessee.

"I fancy red best," Rachel said. Mac breathed easy: Rachel felt comfortable with Renata. There was something of the preacher's wife about Mrs. Levi, the black bombazine dress rustling each time she moved. And she knew just how to treat Rachel—Mac could see that. She didn't kowtow like some of them or make secret fun of her like others. She was treating Rachel as if she were a distinguished customer. But not so distinguished that she might not give advice.

"You must pardon me, Mrs. Jackson. Of course if red is your choice, you shall have it. But I have a fabric that I am certain will suit you." As if on cue, the clerk brought in a bolt of fabric and rolled it out so that Renata's desk was covered with yards and yards of soft cream-colored satin. "It will go so well with your distinctive complexion, Mrs. Jackson," Renata said. Rachel Jackson's complexion was, admittedly, on the dark side.

172

"I cannot abide satin, Mrs. Levi," Rachel said, but Mac could see she was longing to be convinced. Renata didn't say anything. She bent down and gathered up some of the precious stuff and put it in Rachel's rough hands. "Well," Rachel admitted, "it sure ain't slippery like most satin."

"The color is especially mellow and rich."

"I feel like I can look right down into it." Rachel glanced up at Mac for assurance. "Well, maybe I can abide satin, just this once. Providing it ain't too costly. The general has ideas about what fabric should cost and what it shouldn't."

"It is a gift, Mrs. Jackson. It suits you so well."

Rachel put the fabric to her face, and she finally smiled, first at Mac and then at Renata. "Then I guess I'm going to accept it. Thank you, Mrs. Levi."

The dressmaker arrived, made a face behind Madame le Général's bumpy figure, and then brought out a sketch of a complicated gown that Rachel declared "the most beautiful I have ever seen."

"It's very pretty," Renata said dismissively, "but it's far too fussy for your figure, Mrs. Jackson. The empire pattern, I think, Hélène." Renata was full of a wonderful authority, Mac thought. "The short bodice and the long skirt will give the illusion of height and a certain slimness."

"If the proper corset can be found," said the dressmaker, whose original shop had been burned down on orders from Rachel's husband.

"A proper corset will be found," Renata said, and Mac saw that Rachel was won over forever.

"She's just like Andy," Rachel said to Mac as they rode up Calle Palafox in the leather-and-silk-upholstered carriage Old Hickory had requisitioned from Don Orlando de Córdoba. "She's so right."

Mac, thinking of that pale skin and that thin waist and that new, happy smile, thought she wasn't very much like Andrew Jackson at all, but for the sake of peace, he kept that idea to himself.

A proper corset was found, and Rachel, who continued to fear the ball, nonetheless looked forward to the daily fittings on a carefully spread blanket in the Talking Room. It was during the last fitting that she sprang her surprise. "You look lovely," Renata said.

"Ain't Andy going to be shocked?" Rachel turned herself this way and that, the creamy satin moving with her, making her look, if not slim, at least not too plump. "I owe it all to you, Mrs. Levi."

She looked at Renata in the mirror and made her announcement. "You are coming to the ball with me, Mrs. Levi. The general has gotten you an invitation." She dropped a thick white envelope on Renata's desk. "And I accepted for you. I ain't being generous, so don't thank me. I need you there. I need you to be with me when they start snickering. Oh, they will. Fancy dress or not. Now, don't say no, Mrs. Levi," Rachel went on. "I need you."

"I am a tradesperson, Mrs. Jackson. It would be highly unsuitable. I have no escort, no ball gown . . ."

"You gave me a present, Mrs. Levi. And now I'm going to give you one." She looked at Hélène and nodded her head, and Hélène disappeared and returned a moment later holding against her own shapely person a dark-red-satin ball gown. "I had her copy the size from your black dresses, Mrs. Levi. And I told you that first day I like red. And lots of it. With that white skin and that black hair and that tiny waist . . . well, if red doesn't suit me, it certainly suits you."

Mac had never seen Lobo Levi's widow disconcerted before. She had gone through the destruction of Levi and Company and her near arrest (in which she nearly shot him, with barely a tremor, and suddenly, at the sight of a red dress she couldn't speak. She touched the dress Hélène was holding as if it would break. "It is time, Mrs. Levi," Rachel said with her own brand of authority—that of a Tennessee backwoods woman—"that you got out of that black dress and had a dance. The Lord sent me here, I'm convinced, to see that you do."

Renata took the dress, held it up to her, studying herself in the mirror. "Thank you, Mrs. Jackson," she said in that cool, musical voice. "I will be happy to attend the ball." But this time her self-possession didn't fool Mac. He could see, in the mirror's reflection, the tears in those black eyes.

"And I," he said, meeting her eyes in the mirror, "will be happy to escort you."

The ball was held in the Tivoli High House, which housed Pensacola's most elaborate ballroom on the second floor, Pensacola's most popular gambling rooms on the first. Rachel was unaware of the gambling, and Mac did not enlighten her.

At the last moment Renata had wavered, but Rachel herself (with Jackson and Mac) had come for her in the govenor's confiscated carriage. There were tears in old Señora Sara's eyes as she looked at Renata in her red dress. "Finally the swan comes out," Sara said, embracing her daughter-in-law. "Oh, that Lobo and Adamo were here to see you. You are dazzling, Renata."

Despite her new and elegant gown Rachel Jackson felt equal to this grand social occasion only with Renata at her side. The elegant Spanish and French men and women might have come to laugh at the gauche Americanos, at Madame le Général, but stepping into the ballroom together with Renata, the two blue-and-white-uniformed men behind them, Rachel Jackson felt that for the first time in her life she was making a brilliant entrance.

Against their will the French and Spanish guests at the ball thought so too. They were too busy staring at Renata Levi to make fun of Madame le Général. She stood between Mac and Rachel (who wouldn't let her out of her sight) in the receiving line, color in her usually pale cheeks, the diamond earrings Sara had given her reflecting the candlelight as she curtsied and smiled at the startled Pensacolans. Where had she come from? Renata Levi,

174

the Jewish tradeswoman? Old Adamo's daughter-in-law? Impossible. She was, at the least, a hidalgo's daughter, some Córdoba relative. Mac, in his new uniform, purchased for the occasion, looked like the incarnation of Young America, a blond giant. Unaware of the admiring glances of the French and Spanish women, he served Rachel and Renata from the buffet. The general wasn't eating.

After the buffet Andrew and Rachel Jackson grimly took their seats at the head of the dance floor as if they were to witness an execution. "You sit next to me," Rachel told Renata. Dancing was always the most difficult part of these evenings for her.

In an effort to involve the Americanos, Jackson's army military band had been asked to supply the music. Its members had spent weeks practicing the unfamiliar waltzes, that dance having been introduced into English ballrooms five years earlier. At the sound of the strains of the first waltz Don Orlando Ramón de Córdoba walked across the Tivoli's polished dance floor, and the guests grew quiet in anticipation. They were going to have their fun now. The male host traditionally danced the first dance with the wife of the guest of honor.

Don Orlando, in a black dress uniform trimmed with silver, seemed even more arrogant than usual. His green eyes were opaque. The idea of the elegant Don Orlando pushing the plebeian Madame le Général around the Tivoli House dance floor was, as the French consul's wife said, "nearly too delicious." The guests held their breath in anticipation.

"Mrs. Jackson," Córdoba said, bowing from the waist, "may I have this dance?"

Rachel shook her head. "I don't waltz," she said in a nervous too loud voice that was heard by the hundred assembled guests. She paused and into the silence said, "But Mrs. Levi does."

The French dressmaker had been giving them lessons all week, but at the last moment Rachel had lost her nerve. She turned toward Renata, as did Don Orlando. He bowed again. "Mrs. Levi," he said, holding out his hand. It looked as if she too were going to refuse. But Renata saw something in his green eyes that she hadn't believed existed in that man: vulnerability. It would be too shaming for him to walk back across that floor without a partner.

Renata stood up, handing her fan not to Rachel but to Mac. She gave Mac her new, sweet smile and placed her gloved hand in Don Orlando's, allowing him to lead her out onto the floor. She had danced only with the French dressmaker in the Talking Room while Sara kept time on the wooden floor with her cane. But she followed Hélène's advice, allowing Don Orlando to guide her in time to the music, and it seemed, if not pleasurable, at least not difficult. She was, of course, intensely aware of the fact that they were the only couple on the dance floor, that everyone was watching them, that the only sound was that of the military band's first public waltz.

She kept her eyes fixed on Don Orlando's shoulder, but still she was aware of the admiring, incredulous glances. The Spanish and the French were not making fun of her. "They are quite beautiful together," the French consul's wife said. "Quite beautiful."

Afterward he led her back toward her chair. "It has been a great pleasure, Señora Levi," Don Orlando said, stopping with her just before they reached the Jacksons and Mac. "You have renounced your Spanish citizenship—perhaps with good reason—but your fate, like mine, is Florida. I must leave with my people. You will stay and prosper. My tragedy is that I will not fulfill my destiny, and your fortune is that you will. I will not return to Florida in my lifetime. But I know that someday the sons of my sons will." He looked down at her with his mournful green eyes and suddenly gave her that contagious Córdoba smile. "I wish you luck, Señora Levi."

"And I wish you happiness, Don Orlando," Renata said, surprising herself. She returned to her seat and took her fan from Mac, thinking that perhaps Don Orlando Ramón de Córdoba's arrogance was only a thin mask for broken dreams.

Though several men asked her, she did not dance again, being content to sit between Rachel and Mac and watch. At midnight Córdoba's equerry approached Rachel. "Is there any particular air or dance you would enjoy, Doña Rachel?" he asked, and Jackson, having had enough, said, "Yes. She would enjoy 'Possum up de Gum Tree.' "

"Would the military band know that particular air, sir?"

"They know it."

The band was given its instructions, the floor was cleared, and the wild melody of "Possum up de Gum Tree" filled the ballroom, played with great gusto by the military men, who were extremely tired of waltzes.

Córdoba stood at polite attention, but his guests didn't bother to hide their amusement as the long, haggard general with limbs like a skeleton and Madame le Général—that short, dark, fat dumpling in the Empire gown—bobbed opposite each other and sashayed up and down the polished dance floor in their performance of the American frontier dance.

"Ridiculous," the French consul's wife said, loud enough for Renata and Mac to hear. Renata looked up at Mac standing behind her, watching his general and his general's wife dance, oblivious to the scorn of the Europeans.

"Do you think they're ridiculous, Major?" she asked.

"I think, ma'am, that they're beautiful." His right hand, big and square, rested on the back of her chair. For just a moment Renata put her own hand on top of his.

CHAPTER ELEVEN

Renata—1821

RENATA AND SARA HAD BEGUN a custom of taking morning coffee on the balcony of Levi House. It was Cuban coffee, black and aromatic, served by Juan in tiny cups. They drank it without saying much, watching as the plaza merchants readied their shops for the day's business.

Rachel Jackson had joined them the morning after the ball, ostensibly to say thank you. Renata had offered Rachel a cup of coffee, which she found to her liking, and Sara had offered her one of the tiny black cigars that started off her day.

"The general don't hold with pipe-smoking," Rachel said, looking longingly at the dark smoke coming out of Sara's dry little mouth.

"This isn't a pipe," Sara said in her faltering English. She held out the cigar, and Rachel, as keen a tobacco addict as Sara, said that she just might take a puff. She came every morning thereafter for Cuban coffee and stayed with Sara, when Renata had gone down to the Talking Room, to gossip and smoke black cigars. Sara reminded her of her granny, only Sara had teeth.

One late Wednesday morning, soon after the summer heat had settled in, Rachel appeared on the balcony just as Renata was preparing to remove herself to the Talking Room. "I have good news," she said. "The general received word last night that Congress has finally ratified the treaty. In two months the Territory of Florida will be formally annexed to the United States of America. Now we can get rid of Córdoba." She lit one of Sara's black cigars, inhaled, and sighed with pleasure. " 'Course this also means we can go home."

For once Renata stayed on the balcony, listening to Rachel and Sara talk about the upcoming annexation. It could only be good for Levi and Company. The long Florida coastline was overrun with French and Portuguese pirates, against whom Spain had been predictably helpless. Twice Levi and Company ships had been boarded and raided. The United States would not allow that, Renata was certain.

There would be a new influx of Americans, buying land, building houses and farms and factories. They'd need lumber, and she foresaw that the woodlands she owned would prove more profitable than the trading business. The Seminoles, she thought, would suffer even more under American rule, their slaves and cattle fair game for the pioneers. Not that the elusive Billy Bass would give in without a struggle. They had stopped buying rifles from Levi and Company, but Renata knew the Seminoles were well armed. She had heard from the traders that Córdoba was supplying Billy Bass with the efficient short-bore Cuban rifles manufactured in Havana by his family. Córdoba would be leaving with most of the Spanish families, but he wouldn't, she suspected, sever his ties with Florida. Arming the Seminoles would be his long-term connection.

Rachel, already thinking of packing, had left. Renata became aware that Sara was looking at her speculatively and laughed. "What plot are you hatching now, Sara?" she asked, allowing Juan to pour her another cup of the dark Cuban coffee.

"When the Jacksons leave, Major MacCrimmons will leave."

"Since he is the general's aide, that would follow, Sara." Renata stood up and looked down at the plaza, awash with the early summer morning's sun. "It's late. I must get to work. Captain Mercer is coming to talk about a shipment of—"

Sara took her daughter-in-law's hand and held it for a moment. "He is a good man. He cares for you greatly. And you, Renata, need a man. You need heirs. Remember your promise to Adamo. Who will run Levi and Company after you? Think about Major MacCrimmons, Renata."

"I can hardly ask *him* to marry me, Sara." Annoyed, Renata made her way down the stairs to the Talking Room. Once there, she found she could not put her mind to business. She stood at the window looking out at the sun flooding light on the waters of the bay, thinking, against her will, of MacCrimmons's ingenuous face, of the thick, square hands he never knew what to do with, of the honesty that radiated from his American-flag-blue eyes. She suddenly became aware of her body under the black bombazine dress. She thought of Lobo and their lovemaking on that other Talking Room floor, and without thinking, she touched her breast.

"I am a woman of business," she said to herself, but another voice told her she was a woman of desire as well, and in her fantasies MacCrimmons had replaced Lobo as her lover. She was only half relieved when a clerk knocked on the door to announce that Captain Wilfred Mercer had arrived.

On Saturday, when the fog was so thick one couldn't see the water in the bay, and when the news of the official annexation had spread throughout the town, MacCrimmons came to the Levi mansion to make Rachel's apologies. She would not be joining the ladies on the balcony that morning.

Renata was already in the Talking Room and only Señora Sara was on the balcony to greet him. The old Spanish woman and the young Georgia major sat next to each other companionably, not saying much, Juan filling their cups, Sara puffing away, her smoke adding to the fog that enveloped Pensacola. After a half hour had passed Mac said, "I reckon Mrs. Levi is all involved in her business this morning."

Sara looked at him with her tired, knowing eyes and smiled. "I wouldn't want to interrupt her if she had anything important going on." He stood up and rubbed his hands on his thighs. "We're leaving here immediately after the annexation ceremony," he said, without having meant to. "I sure am going to miss Pensacola, Señora Sara. I liked this town the minute I saw it, when Lobo and I stopped on the bluffs and I caught my first glimpse of the bay. I sure am going to miss Pensacola."

Sara put out her cigar and stood too, putting her hand on Mac's sleeve. "Go to her," she said. "Ask her now. This is the moment."

Mac went down the stairs to the trading post, never questioning how Señora Sara could possibly know what he was thinking. The clerks worked only half a day on Saturdays, so he was alone. He stood at the thick door leading to the Talking Room thinking of the other times he had stood there, telling himself to breathe. Goddammit, all she could do was say no. Or yes. He knocked, and that cool voice told him to come in.

As it wasn't a regular business day Renata was wearing a new dress the French dressmaker had made for her instead of her usual black bombazine. It was pale pink, the color the English ladies aboard Sir Alexander's fleet had favored, and though she was twenty-six years old, it made her seem very young and nearly carefree. She was using what little light penetrated the fog and the south window to study papers. As she had predicted, she was having difficulty getting Jackson to give her clear title to the land with which the Indians had settled their debts.

She looked up at Mac standing over her. He seemed so strong, his muscles straining against the fabric of his blue and white uniform, his cheeks red with embarrassment and health, his hair bleached yellow-white from the sun. He is an honest man, she thought.

"I have something that belongs to you, Mrs. Levi," he said, unbuttoning his tunic pocket. "I should have given it back to you a long time ago, but I couldn't part with it. Now that I'm leaving Pensacola, probably for good, I think you had better have it." He put the gold locket on the desk. Renata opened it. The miniature seemed to have been painted in another time. That girl that stared at her with such uncompromising eyes was someone else.

She was stunned. "But how did you come by this?" she asked, closing it, putting it on the desk as if it were too hot to touch.

Mac, seeing how pale she had become, finally told Renata of his friendship with Lobo and of those last moments when Lobo had given him the locket. When he had finished, Renata sat very still, tears in her black eyes. "I'm so sorry," Mac said. "Please take it."

But she shook her head no, and picking up the locket, came round the desk and placed it in Mac's open hand. "Lobo wanted you to have it. And so do I." He closed his big hand around her small white one and, without thinking, brought it to his lips. Renata put her free hand to his face as he bent down, and, with infinite care, he kissed her red lips, drawing her to him. She stayed in those secure, solid arms for some time, aware of his body and hers, not wanting to break the moment. He pressed his body closer. He smelled so fresh and new. She could feel his excitement. She put her lips against his neck and tasted salty hot skin and felt the shiver that went through his body as he moved even closer. Finally she moved away.

"I would marry you, Major MacCrimmons," she said, turning from him, facing the south window and looking out at the fog, "on certain conditions."

"Anything." He came up behind her and put his hands on her slim waist, and she nearly turned to allow him to embrace her again but she forced herself to move away. She had married Lobo without thinking, without spelling out the rules and the consequences. She was no longer a schoolgirl and she would control this passion. MacCrimmons had to understand.

"The conditions are these, Major: that you agree to take the Jewish faith; that you change your last name to Levi; that you resign your commission."

She knew the extent of the sacrifices she was asking him to make. Jackson was leaving Pensacola and there was talk of his running for President of the United States of America in the next election. He would want MacCrimmons to accompany him, to share in the work and the glory.

Mac looked down at the sleek black hair, the proud back, and the tiny waist of Renata Levi. "I'm amazed," he said.

She turned to look up at him. "At my conditions?"

"No, ma'am. At the fact that you had them all right and ready. That you knew I was going to ask you to marry me."

"I asked you, Major."

He laughed and reached for her. But she stepped back. "Do you agree to the conditions, Major?"

"I guess I do. I reckon it won't take much to be a Jew. My granpappy made sure I knew the Old Testament inside and out, and 'Levi' is a lot shorter than 'MacCrimmons.' Besides, I owe Lobo a debt or two. I don't mind taking his name as long as I get his wife." He reached for her again and took her in his arms and kissed her red lips until they both felt weak. "Marry me, Renata," he said, saying her name aloud for the first time. "Marry me just as fast as you can. I'm feeling all gooey inside like a Spanish sweet, like I'm going to burst with love. I'm going to be the best husband you ever had, but let's get married real quick. Is that all right with you, Renata? *Real* quick."

Renata put her thin arms around Mac's thick neck, pulling his face down to hers, kissing his lips with all the passion she had denied herself during all those years, indicating "real quick" was all right with her.

Mac Levi, as he came to be known, was to wear his blue and white major's uniform once more. It was a blazingly hot July Thursday, the seventeenth, and the final annexation ceremony was taking place that noon. Renata surprised herself by not feeling guilty, still abed at the sinful hour of nine in the morning. Levi and Company was closed—as was everything in Pensacola—for this day.

She watched her husband, standing nude, backlit by the morning sun coming through the window. He was vigorously brushing his tunic. He glanced at her, but she pretended to be asleep, following his movements through half-closed eyes. He's beautiful, she thought. A narrow, thick band of blond hair ran down his chest, ending in a thicker patch of hair where his manhood lay.

Mac looked at her again, caught her looking at him, dropped the tunic, and came and slowly pulled away the bed sheets. There was an unusual, high color in her face and a new, nearly imperceptible roundness to her figure. He kissed her from head to toe before making long, sensuous, careful love to her. Renata had announced the night before that she was going to have a child.

"It will be a boy," she said after their lovemaking as he held her in his arms.

"How do you know it's going to be a boy?"

"All of our children are going to be boys," she said with such assurance that he laughed.

They had been married just two months before by a rabbi imported from New Orleans in a ceremony witnessed and celebrated by an unlikely group: Sara Levi, the territorial governor, General Jackson and his wife, Rachel, Grimes in his new lieutenant's uniform, and the French dressmaker, Mademoiselle Hélène.

Jackson hadn't been happy when Mac resigned his commission, but Rachel was, and she prevailed, and Jackson gave his blessing. "Never thought I'd end up as a Jew shopkeeper," Mac said on that wedding night.

"You're not going to be a shopkeeper," Renata said, putting her hand on his arm, finding she couldn't stop touching him. She didn't want him in the business. He was Jackson's friend and a farmer's son. He could clear the title to her land and see that the land was worked. Florida was going to need a government. If Renata had her way, Mac was going to be a member of that government.

And what she admitted to herself, finally, was that most of all she needed Mac to make her feel alive; that he had rid her, forever, of the ghost of Lobo. Mac was as surprised as Renata at the passion she displayed each night when she let down her luminous black hair, snuffed the candle, and led him to Adamo's old bed.

But each morning, her hair in place, she put on her crisp black bombazine dress. Her expression, except for a certain new light in her black eyes, was the businesslike one of Mrs. Mac Levi, director of the great trading concern of Levi and Company, Pensacola, the United States Territory of Florida.

And on that sweltering day in July, Spain, in the person of Don Orlando

Ramón de Córdoba, was going to officially give Florida to the United States. Juan knocked, announcing it was eleven o'clock, and Mac reluctantly got out of bed, leaving his wife, and began once again to put on his major's uniform. Renata said she thought she'd wear the pink gown, and Mac, staring at her loveliness, at her round pink breasts, said he thought that was a beautiful idea.

An hour later Mac Levi joined his former comrades-in-arms and his commander in Pensacola's green and timeworn Plaza Ferdinand VII. "Mac," someone said, and even before he turned he recognized that Washington City accent. Jack Church, as big and as beautifully turned out as ever, though in civilian clothes, was striding across the plaza to meet him.

The two men clasped hands. "I don't know why, Jack Church, but I'm always that glad to see you," Mac said, genuinely pleased to see his friend. "Where's your uniform? They drum you out in Washington City because you forgot to say please and thank you?"

"I resigned, Mac," Jack Church said. "I was offered a better job. I'm going to be Florida's Indian agent, stationed in St. Augustine."

"Oh, ain't Old Hickory going to like that. He wants to send the Injuns out west somewhere to free their land, and you—I just know it—want to keep the Injuns right where they are. Put them on government rations, right?"

"It's going to be a difficult road," Jack Church said, not denying Mac Levi's supposition. Mac sighed and smiled at the same time, relieved to be out of it.

They approached the platform erected for the event and stood talking for a few moments, bringing each other up to date. Mac told Jack about his marriage to Lobo Levi's widow and about his own resignation from the army. Jack said he had been sent to Pensacola to represent the President at the changing of flags and to remind Jackson to keep to the property arrangements agreed upon by the Spanish and United States ministers. "He's going to love being reminded by you," Mac said. He invited Jack Church to the Levi mansion for dinner that night and then took his place on the platform, just behind Jackson. He could see Renata on the far side of the plaza, standing with Señora Sara and a handful of elderly Spanish townsfolk, all save Renata dressed in black. Córdoba and his equerry, officially representing Spain, stood at the right of the plaza.

No one would have known it from his expression, but the departing Spanish governor was acutely, painfully aware that nearly three hundred years of Spanish rule had come to an end as, exactly at noon, the Spanish flag, raised for the ceremony, was brought down. Immediately the American military band began to play "The Star-Spangled Banner." With barely a gun fired, Spain had given up Ponce de León's "island" to a new, raw people who wanted their chance at cultivating Florida.

To Córdoba it seemed an ignominious end. To Renata the fluttering flag and the raising of the Stars and Stripes signified a good and important new beginning. She looked across the old square and smiled at her husband.

182

As the U.S.S. *Hornet* gave a twenty-one-gun salute from the harbor, the Stars and Stripes reached the top of the standard and snapped out over the new American territory. Jackson's soldiers cheered. Don Orlando Ramón de Córdoba, grim-faced, bowed to Jackson, to Jack Church as the President's emissary, and finally, sincerely, to Renata Mac Levi. Then he turned and led the group of Spaniards who were leaving Pensacola to the ship that was to carry them to Havana.

He remained topside as the ship left port, watching the town recede on its crescent of water, knowing that the rest of his life would be a disappointment. He had thought that he would save Florida for Spain. He had realized how fatuous that goal was only when confronted with Spain's bankruptcy and the savagery and fanaticism of Andrew Jackson.

He took one last long look at the pink and yellow town with the green plaza at its center, sitting nearly astride the dark green-blue water, and went below to write his report of the annexaton of Florida for the Spanish Colonial Office. "Someday," he consoled himself, "the Córdobas will come back. Florida is our destiny."

Another Spaniard mourned Spain's loss of Florida. Señora Sara clasped a huge black lace handkerchief in her painfully arthritic hands, and as the Spanish flag was folded and carried away, she held the lace to her tired old eyes, sobbing uncontrollably. Renata put her arm around the sagging shoulders, holding Sara close, as if the new life within her could comfort that brave soul who had been Renata's only support throughout so much of her life. She kissed Sara's wrinkled brow and whispered to her, "Don't fret. The Levis— Jewish, Spanish, American—will go on. You wait and see."

The following morning two workmen delivered a piece of furniture to the trading post. "A gift from Don Orlando," one said. Córdoba had not been able to take with him to Havana the desk Floridita had inherited from the merchant Quirinio. Renata had it put in the Talking Room, where it was to remain, the gouges Andrew Jackson had carved with his spurs in its leather top fading but never quite disappearing.

The people of Pensacola were delirious when the puritanical Jacksons left Pensacola. The following day was a Sunday, but the town broke out in celebration, lighting festive candles, holding a ball, drinking and gambling, and most of all, playing the guitar in the plaza, all activities prohibited by the Jacksons.

Old Hickory had lasted a short time as governor but he had achieved all he had set out to do. He left a united 13,073,631-acre territory, extending from the Perdido River in the west to the Atlantic Ocean in the east; from just below Georgia's desolate Okefenokee Swamp to the thriving "southern-most" island city of Key West. He had divided the entire territory into two counties: St. Johns, taking up the peninsula, remained for the most part un-explored; Escambia covered the better-known panhandle.

He had set up and left a system of military government that would survive for two years until, in March 1823, Congress gave Florida a civil government with a legislative council, judges, tax collectors, a marshal, and the first offi-cial territorial governor, a Kentuckian named William Pope Duval.

Mac Levi was among the first elected legislators of the new territory, meeting in Pensacola with the others at the first legislative meeting. Jack Church had sent with one of them a fine white waistcoat for Mac, "now that you are a member of the gentlemanly class," he wrote. It had taken the nine representatives from St. Augustine fifty-nine days to sail around the coast, thirty-six to sail back. Mac sent with them a buckskin shirt for Jack Church, "now that you're a member of the Injun class," he wrote.

Eventually a new capital city was created, halfway between St. Augustine and Pensacola, just eighteen miles north of St. Marks. It was located in gentle red hills among the live oaks near the ruins of an old Spanish fort. The Tal-lahassee Indians lived there on land they no longer owned; they had paid their debts with it years before. Their Spanish titles to the land (and thus the legality of their using the land to pay debts) had been finally confirmed by Andrew Jackson himself. Most of it was held by Levi and Company, the trading concern owned by the wife of Representative Mac Levi.

CHAPTER TWELVE

Jack Church—1823

JACK CHURCH, retired captain of the United States Army and current In-dian agent for the Territory of Florida, seemed to take up most of the avail-able space in the commodious office he had been assigned in St. Augustine's St. Francis Barracks. He sighed heavily. His secretary, Perkins, hearing this through the open door and regarding it as a command, stepped in with alac-rity from his outer office. "Would you like me to finish those letters for you, sir?"

If Perkins seemed too thin and sallow to be a living member of the human race, Jack Church appeared too large and golden to be a mere man. "No, Perkins, I thank you, but I must finish these myself."

184

Jack Church had spent the uncomfortably hot August morning writing to everyone he could think of at all influential in Washington City. His handwriting was large, unembellished, and clearly the product of a superior education. In those letters he asked—begged—the recipients to use their influence to persuade the President and Secretary of War Calhoun—under whose aegis the Department of Indian Affairs existed—to amend their Indian Containment Policy.

He and Perkins had returned the day before from a month-long trip. The first two weeks had been spent in Seminole villages inviting the chiefs and important braves to a great powwow, the forthcoming council at Moultrie Creek, not far from St. Augustine. The latter part of the journey had taken them through the sandy ridge of south central Florida which was going to be offered as a home to the Seminoles at the powwow Jack Church had been ordered to arrange.

Jack Church's heart was heavy with what he had seen. The memories of that desolate, sparse, uninhabitable place turned his despondency to anger. He took up his pen again to finish his letter to Mac Levi, the recently named Florida territorial representative to Congress.

> . . . Mac, it begins nearly dead center in the peninsula and extends to— but does not include—Lake Istokpoga in the south. None of the reservation's eastern or western borders is within twenty miles of the coast. I suppose this is to prevent the Seminoles from having any of their alleged dealings with Córdoba and other Cuban suppliers of arms; to keep them from using Cuba as a market for the slaves and cattle they are accused of stealing from Georgia and Alabama farmers. But it also will keep them from one of their principal food sources, the sea.
>
> You say, let them grow and harvest food; let them hunt on their new land. Mac, the Seminoles cannot live on that land. It is scrub country, with little or no game, impossible to farm. Confinement there would make the Seminoles increasingly dependent on the white man for food and every other necessity. Mac, the reservation they are being offered would make the Seminoles into parasites.
>
> There is another possibility: a reservation (see the enclosed rough map) composed of land just to the west, bordering the Gulf of Mexico. It is more fertile, there is more game, it is farther from Cuba, and most important, the Seminoles would have access to the sea.
>
> I beg you to present this alternative to the President and to the Secretary of War. I am certain they are being influenced by Jackson. But you and they must see, Mac, that containment is only the first step in Jackson's Indian Removal Policy. Once the Seminoles are in one place, it would be an uncomplicated business to move them to territories in the west where they can die of malnutrition and estrangement and will be out of the range of our consciences.
>
> When I first met the Seminoles they were a rich, proud people. Now, thanks to Jackson's destruction of all Seminole villages west of the

185

Suwannee, thanks to American raids on the once prosperous eastern villages, they are starving to death. It is a terrible sight to see once noble chiefs begging for money on the streets of St. Augustine, addicted to liquor the unscrupulous sell them.

But I am convinced, Mac, that no matter how we try, we will never completely break the spirit of the Seminoles. And make no mistake, Mac, despite their debasement, there are still many brave men among the Seminoles. And they are growing increasingly desperate.

I see a terrible bloody war in the years ahead. The council at Moultrie Creek is an opportunity to avert it, to offer the Seminoles a fair and reasonable treaty. We *must* give the Seminoles a stretch of coastal land to allow them to maintain their self-sufficiency.

I am weary and sad after my travels. I will be at my plantation for two weeks to recover my equanimity and prepare for the powwow. I will await your answer there and, in the meanwhile, remain

Your friend and fellow Floridian,
John R. Church.

Jack Church read the letter over, signed it, and gave it to Perkins for immediate posting. Tired of sitting, he stood up, stretched, and went to the window to try to catch whatever breeze came in from Matanzas Bay. Off to the left he could just see the huge, threatening bulk of the Castillo de San Marcos dominating the bay and the town of St. Augustine.

When he had written of "brave men among the Seminoles," he had had in mind one Seminole man—in reality, more boy than man—who had been imprisoned for a short time in the Castillo. Jack Church had a brilliantly colored memory of the day, five years before, when they had not so much met as collided.

It was in 1818, when Major General Gaines had marched into St. Augustine on Andy Jackson's orders, and had taken it as easily as Jackson had taken Pensacola. It was an illegal action, but no one thought of that, and Gaines's most pressing problem was where to raise the American flag. At first he thought it should be over the Castillo de San Marcos, but Jack Church counseled otherwise.

Jack Church had made his report to Washington City on Jackson's execution of Laird and the British marine from St. Augustine and had been "advised" to stay there to await further developments. General Gaines and his men were the further developments. Gaines had as much use for him as Jackson had, but he did listen when Jack Church said the huge old Spanish fort was in reality a prison and an unsuitable place for the American flag.

Instead he suggested St. Francis Barracks, and General Gaines had acquiesced. The flag-raising ceremony—Gaines had ordered it to be as unpublicized an event as possible—was to take place at noon. Jack Church had risen early, feeling once again shamed by being an American. This taking of St. Augustine without provocation was for him a debasing act.

186

He walked the narrow streets, for once not taking delight in the coquina houses, with their tiled roofs, balconies, and walled gardens. The streets were empty, the Spanish landowners, Negro slaves, freemen, and northern visitors aware of Gaines's smokeless victory.

Jack Church was approaching the barracks an hour before the ceremony, walking south along the Avenida Menéndez, when he saw another solitary walker. He was a young Seminole brave with a face so handsome he would have been thought pretty if it were not for his dark eyes, broad shoulders, and the manly way in which he carried himself. Jack Church, who had been spending his time in St. Augustine learning Mikasuki, meant to greet him, but just then half a dozen United States soldiers led by General Gaines emerged from St. Francis Barracks. One of the soldiers was carrying the United States flag.

"Church," Gaines said, somewhat embarrassed. "We decided to get it over with and moved it up an hour. No sense courting trouble. Glad you happened to be here." Jack Church, certain the general was not glad that he happened to be there, walked up the steps that led to the platform where the Spanish flag was being lowered unceremoniously. "Just as happy there aren't witnesses," Gaines said, discomfited by Jack Church's silence. "Don't want any trouble."

The Stars and Stripes went up, the soldiers saluted, and Jack Church walked down the steps of St. Francis Barracks, his eyes on his beautifully made boots, thinking that if the President had really wanted him to prevent Andrew Jackson and his chum Gaines from annexing Florida, he had given him singularly little power to do so.

Thus preoccupied, he walked smack into the Seminole brave, who was staring with those remarkable, sorrowful eyes up at the Stars and Stripes, digesting the idea that the Territory of Florida no longer belonged to the protective Spanish but to the Seminoles' enemies, the Americanos. The brave staggered under the impact of Jack Church's mass, and Jack Church reached out to keep him from falling. But the brave avoided his arms, twisted away, and still somehow kept his balance. Seminoles did not like to be touched by white men.

"I am sorry," Jack Church said in Mikasuki.

"I am sorry too," the brave said in English, bowing his beautiful head as one of the American soldiers hit him from behind with the butt of his Kentucky rifle. He fell to one knee, bleeding from a deep cut in his forehead. But when another soldier came and put his hands roughly on the brave's bare arms, he managed to shrug him off. Despite blood flowing into his eyes, he got to his feet unaided and was marched off in the direction of the Castillo.

"General," Jack Church called after the retreating Gaines, catching up with him in the St. Francis entryway. "General Gaines. I should like to know why those men are arresting that Seminole."

"He attacked you, man. What else should we do with him?"

"He didn't attack me. He—"

"I know what I saw, Church. And I know what you are. A damned Injun-lover. That redskin is lucky my men didn't shoot him. The only good Injun, Church, is a dead one."

Five days later President Monroe repudiated Jackson's annexation. Pensacola and St. Augustine were to be given back to the Spanish until a diplomatic accord could be reached. Jack Church, ordered to return to Washington City, stopped at the Castillo de San Marcos first, accompanying a Spanish soldier to the earthen cell in which the brave had been kept.

The brave stepped out of the dark cell into the courtyard, shielding his eyes from the sun, breathing through his mouth so that the stench of the white men wouldn't overpower him. He saw the Spanish flag flying over the fort and was confused and relieved at the same time. The Americanos were gone, but he knew they would be back.

Jack Church said in Mikasuki, "I regret what has happened. You are free to go." He offered his hand in the white man's way, but the brave wouldn't touch it. Still, the Indian felt some gesture had to be paid to this benevolent paleface so he held up his hand, palm outward, to Jack Church. He would not honor this man by speaking Mikasuki with him and spoke in English. But he gave Jack Church a present. He gave him his name. "Osceola," he said and bowed.

"Jack Church," Jack said, imitating the Seminole's formality.

"I thank you, Jack Church." Then he ran through the tunnel leading out of the courtyard, across the moat, up the still deserted Avenida Menéndez, leaving Jack Church among the Spanish soldiers reoccupying their fort, the name "Osceola" obstinately echoing in his mind.

In the years that followed, during the formal annexation of Florida, when the Florida Seminoles and the Alabama and Georgia white men had engaged in a series of futile, bloody fights, Jack Church often heard the brave's name. Osceola had taken Billy Bass's place as head of the renegade Seminoles, leading those retaliatory raids against the whites, going from village to village, counseling his people to resist the paleface. He spoke Spanish as well as English and, when Billy Bass died, traveled by horse, and canoe and finally white man's ship to Havana to confer with Córdoba, to ensure the continuance of the secret network of Cuban arms supply. Though he was young and only a brave, the old chiefs feared and respected him.

Jack Church, standing in his office in St. Francis Barracks, looked down at the place where he had met Osceola five years before. Osceola would have to lead his people onto the reservation. No other Seminole, not even the great micos—Micanopy, Jumper, Charley Emathla—would be listened to. Jack Church had hoped the Seminoles would be allowed to remain in their villages, but the enmity between the neighboring whites and the Seminoles was too deep. And the Seminoles were too greatly outnumbered. Now he realized their only hope was a protected, distant reservation. He prayed that someone in Washington City—Mac, perhaps—would listen and provide the Seminoles with the piece of coastal land that would help keep them self-sufficient.

He gave the wholehearted sigh that caused Perkins to come running into his office again. "Sir, is there anything . . . ?"

"Not a thing, Perkins. Not a thing."

Perkins idolized his employer. Just months ago, when he first accepted the appointment, Jack Church had been full of enthusiasm for his job. The officer corps, garrisoned at St. Francis Barracks, had had a great deal of amusement at his expense. It was a treat just to see him stroll across Charlotte Street, all two hundred and fifty pounds and six feet four inches outfitted in the breeches and velvet-collared frock coat fashionable in Washington City but not in St. Augustine. He was pink and blond, like some northern girl—he never tanned—and he would invariably be in earnest conversation, in Mikasuki, with a group of slim braves dressed in buckskins and moccasins.

"Jack Church and his choir," one wag named them. Jack Church, Perkins had to admit, did look like some overmuscled, overupholstered cherub of a choirmaster. And the solemn Indians seemed like turbaned choir boys, listening to his voluble nonstop attempts to persuade them to be more industrious, to keep away from liquor, to attend to farming and hunting.

The Indian agent's enthusiasm had been dissipated by his journey through the deteriorating Seminole villages and the desert of a proposed reservation. Perkins watched as a depressed Jack Church prepared to ride out to the plantation he had named "Serenity." He hoped Jack Church would be able to forget the frustrations of his job in the routine of plantation life. But he wouldn't have bet on it.

CHAPTER THIRTEEN

Jack Church and Emily Narvaez Smyrna Smith—1823

JACK CHURCH HAD BOUGHT his sugar-cane plantation soon after he came to St. Augustine from a Georgia cracker family that wanted to go home. He paid too much for the three-hundred-and-forty-seven-acre spread, but he had an inheritance and an adequate private income, and it was exactly what he wanted. The plantation lay five miles south of St. Augustine, not far from the St. Johns River, half of it undeveloped, with a thriving live-oak forest and two one-room log cabins. One was for him and one was for his slaves.

He had thought the plantation—Serenity—would provide work for the Seminoles, but the Seminoles, he learned, would rather starve than work for a white man. He gave up his plan, allowing his mother to give him half a dozen Negro field hands who were adept at farming. "Sugar cane, she won't grow here, Mister Church, sir," the most experienced, Abel, had told him five minutes after he arrived. He was kneeling down, running the earth through his fingers, smelling it, shaking his big head. "Cane, she won't grow. Too dry. You'd best put in cotton, Mister Church, sir. Cotton, she'll grow." Jack Church had decided to put in cotton and to make Abel his overseer.

Cotton had grown and the plantation prospered. It was as hot on the plantation as in town on that August Friday in 1823, the kind of day when the clouds were low and oppressive but unpromising. "She ain't going to rain, Mr. Church, sir," Abel told him, taking his horse, ordering one of the men to see to it. "She's stubborn," he said, shaking his big head at the thick, low-lying clouds. "She's that stubborn."

The heavy weather mirrored Jack Church's mood. "The boys," Abel said, "they're planting over to the near spread. Doing some good. If only she'd rain." Abel wanted Jack Church to see the new plantings, and Jack wearily obliged, saying he didn't need his horse, he'd walk.

His fine linen shirt was sticking to his fine pink skin when he arrived at the southernmost boundary of Serenity, where half a dozen of "his boys" were working. A fence had been erected to separate Serenity from his unknown neighbor's property. He was examining the neat rows the men were planting, pretending an interest he didn't feel, when he saw a woman in an ugly yellow calico bonnet and four young boys with flaming red hair in patched overalls. They were industriously working on the far side of the fence, planting cotton. Neighbors, Jack Church thought with a sinking feeling.

Jack Church, as courteous in the Florida backwoods as in Washington City drawing rooms, stepped up to the makeshift fence, removing his tall white raffia hat. "I'm Jack Church, ma'am," he said to the yellow calico bonnet bending down in front of him. "Your neighbor, ma'am."

The woman stood up. "I know who you are, Captain Church," she said in an unexpected, melodious voice. "Everyone does. The Indian agent. I am Mrs. Emily Narváez Smyrna Smith, widow twice over, mother of them boys over there, owner of this spread we call Amen, and proud of it."

Her accent was unusual—a combination of Spanish cadence and cracker twang. Her face was a surprise as well. He had expected a dried, leathery cracker face to look out from the stiff frame of that unbecoming bonnet, but he was, if not disappointed, surprised. Not that she was what the officers in the St. Francis Barracks would call a "dewy job." Youthful innocence wasn't her strong point. Her face had flat planes and high cheekbones and was unfashionably tanned a warm golden color despite the oversized bonnet. Her bottom lip was too full and her nose too short for her to be a great beauty. But as she stared up at him, a foot and a half shorter than he was, he caught the full effect of her dazzling green eyes.

"But I expect you know who I am too," she said, filling in the silence as gracefully as any senator's wife at a voter's meeting. "Call me Miss Emily, and you'd best put your hat on your head before the sun gets to you."

He felt as if it already had, but Miss Emily's face had darkened and that lovely wide smile had disappeared as she stared past him at Abel directing the planting of the cotton on the Serenity side of the fence. "Them your slaves, Captain?"

"They are, Miss Emily."

"I don't hold with slavery." Her face and body had assumed such an upright, uncompromising posture, he was reminded for a moment of Andrew Jackson and his omniscient pronouncements.

"They are well looked after," he said, as coldly, looking pointedly past Miss Emily at her four boys in their ragged though clean clothes. "Far better than many freemen."

"I'd rather be a free boy in torn overalls that a slave in silk and satin, Captain Church." Miss Emily's green eyes glowed with conviction.

"What if I told you that those slaves behind me have been offered their freedom—any number of times—and have consistently refused it?" Captain Church asked. "They are afraid, Miss Emily. Afraid of white and Creek slave gangs that would carry them off to Georgia and Alabama and make them slaves all over again—and under much worse conditions—if they had their papers."

"Oh, that's neat, Captain Church." Miss Emily let out a short laugh. "You're keeping them in slavery for their own good. It's an educated argument, but I am an uneducated woman. I don't hold with slavery, Captain Church, and if people like you didn't lie to yourselves, then there wouldn't be any."

Jack Church decided he had had enough of being neighborly. "It has been a great pleasure making your acquaintance, Miss Emily," he said, putting on the white raffia hat, more angry and excited than he had been since the order had come through to arrange the Moultrie Creek powwow. "I expect we shall see each other again," he said, making it sound the opposite.

"I don't hold with taking the Injuns' land away from them neither," she went on, ignoring the snub. "I would tell you to pass that on to Washington City, but I understand you already have. I don't like your slavery, Captain Church. But I do like your Injun policy."

He felt like a galloping horse pulled to an abrupt stop. He thought how extraordinary it was for him to be standing at the edge of his three hundred and forty-seven acres in the wet, yellow heat of a Florida summer noon, being

191

lectured by a cracker woman in an ugly bonnet about what she liked and didn't like about the way he ran his plantation and went about his job. He hadn't felt so confused or stimulated since he had taken on what had become the futile, frustrating position of territorial Indian agent.

"Who fixes your suppers, Captain?" she asked abruptly, looking up, staring at him with those emerald-green eyes.

"One of the Negro boys I keep in despicable servitude."

"It don't look much like you're wasting away." She moved away from the fence, talking to him over her shoulder. "Still, you'd best come to supper tonight. Six o'clock, Captain," she said, and walked off through the neat rows she and her boys had planted. He could just make out a log cabin in the near distance. She's the most self-possessed woman I have ever met, Jack Church thought to himself. He found that he was looking forward to Miss Emily's supper in a way he hadn't looked forward to a social occasion in years.

Emily Narváez Smyrna Smith walked to her home annoyed with herself. Why on earth had she invited Captain Church—that slaveholder—to supper? He'll barely fit into the room much less sit at table, she thought, remembering his size. And hadn't she had enough of men after two husbands? Miss Evangeline Washington was going to have a fit when she learned she had another body to feed, and Emily expected they were going to need a lot to feed that body. Where had her mind been, inviting Captain John R. Church to supper when all the rich old ladies in St. Augustine were trying to get him for their young daughters?

Yet, he had accepted. She thought of how big and sad he was in those fancy clothes and of the delicious, fancy way he spoke. He came from Washington City and had all sorts of education and upbringing and ... She thought of her own history, shook her head, and went round to the cookhouse to tell Miss Evangeline Washington, free woman, that a guest was coming to dinner.

Emily Narváez Smyrna Smith traced her ancestry back through her emerald-green eyes to one of the first settlers of St. Augustine, Isabella Narváez, and through Isabella to her mother, La Floridita de Córdoba. Emily had been born in St. Augustine, as had all of her ancestors after Isabella. Her family was one of only three Spanish families to remain during the twenty-year British occupation.

Her heritage, however, had not brought her money or status. She was a woman of no education, orphaned young and used to hard work. She had married, when she was fifteen, a short, round, good-natured St. Augustinian named Carlos Smyrna. Carlos wore a perpetual grin that in time came to infuriate Emily. He would bring her news of the worst catastrophe with his face wreathed in smiles.

He was descended from the colonists who were brought to Florida as in-

192

dentured servants from the Spanish island of Minorca in 1768, during the British occupation. They began that ill-fated Minorcan farming community called New Smyrna. The Minorcans were eventually released from their articles of indenture and invited to St. Augustine, where many became fishermen.

The perennially happy Carlos was a fisherman who enjoyed his modest life and his complicated wife, Emily, until it was discovered that he suffered from tuberculosis. He sold his boat and bought fifty acres of land between St. Augustine and Moultrie Creek. He died, hemorrhaging, in Emily's arms two years after they were married. The land had not been made ready for planting, and the log cabin he and Emily and their son were to live in was not completed.

Carlos Smyrna left his wife the land, fifty dollars, and the loyalty of Miss Evangeline Washington, a freed Negro field hand promoted to cook because Emily had a propensity for overcooking everything.

Emily waited six months before she married a determined Georgia cracker, an illegal Florida immigrant named George Hardy Smith. Hardy, as he was called, was not going to wait for the United States to take Florida before he got his hands on some of that rich land. He couldn't buy it—he hadn't the money—but he could marry it, and he did.

Hardy Smith had been a soldier in Jackson's army and had marched with him across the panhandle, destroying Seminole villages. He believed, as did many others, that no greater man than Andrew Jackson had ever lived. Hardy didn't talk much, and later, when Emily asked herself why she had married him, she supposed it was because at the time she felt weak and needy and alone. Hardy was strong and tough, his mind filled with ideas about what it was to be a man and what it was to be a woman.

"I don't like him much," Emily confessed to Evangeline Washington. "But he sure gets the job done."

He finished the house and put up the cookhouse for Evangeline and planted the crops—mostly cotton but some corn—and gave Emily three boys in as many years. "Ma's come," Hardy said, not having forewarned Emily, leading his mother into the house on a wet April afternoon.

"Why?" was all Emily could think to ask, staring at the giant of a Georgia woman emerging from a migrant cracker's cart, carrying a black shawl filled with her few personal effects, looking like death on a holiday visit.

"To teach Vangie Washington how to cook and to teach you and those boys the proper ways of talking and doing things." Addie Smith taught Vangie how to cook grits and Emily and her four boys how to speak English, cracker style, and how to treat her husband. "When he punches you in the head, honey, you kick him in the testicles."

When Hardy Smith was carried home, the loser in a bull-whip fight over a glass of corn whiskey, his face ripped in narrow shreds, one eye half out, the other on the floor of a St. Augustine grog shop, Emily and Addie took turns nursing him. He died a bad, silent death. Addie wrapped up her possessions in the black shawl, found a farmer going back to Georgia for his wife, and arranged to ride with him in his cart. She kissed Emily and her grandsons and the little Smyrna boy goodbye.

Waving goodbye to her mother-in-law, Emily had decided she was through with men. She hired two freed Negroes to work the farm and tried not to worry about whether Hardy had made the right decision planting cotton instead of cane. The Lord will provide, her neighbor to the north, old Señora Valdez said, but Emily found herself wondering if she was going to have enough vegetables from the garden and eggs from the chicks and plain old money to feed her children.

"We're making a go of it," she said to the boys each morning, and then she'd cross herself, not because she believed in the Church—she was an adamantly lapsed Catholic—but because she believed in bad and good spirits. She knew good times and prosperity drew the bad spirits the way newly planted seed drew scavengers.

Her ideas and ethics were an odd, benign distillation of Spanish, British, Minorcan, and American beliefs. Superstition, religion, and traditional good sense gave her a clear, unbending idea of who and what she was. Emily Narváez Smyrna Smith was a genuine Floridian.

When she went round to the cookhouse to tell Vangie about the dinner guest, the fat black woman shook her head. "Oh, no, Miss Emily. Oh, no," she said a few more times, theatrically.

"Oh, no what, Vangie?"

"Oh, no, Miss Emily. Just when things are going along so nicely, you have to go and gets you another man." Evangeline was enjoying herself. "Oh, no, Miss Emily, you go and uninvite him."

"Hush up, Vangie. I haven't gotten anyone. He's our neighbor, and there's no one to cook for him except some boy. And make sure you serve us some of your corn cake."

"Oh, no, Lord, don't let it happen, I'm begging you." Vangie Washington rolled her eyes and prepared to make a corn cake. "Not another man, Lord. Oh, no."

Jack Church had taken a bath in the creek. His gold-blond hair, just beginning to recede, was plastered down in Napoleonic style. His frock coat, so white it was nearly blue, fascinated Emily's sons. They too had taken dips in the creek, and their red hair was plastered back in a fairly successful attempt to thwart the natural way it grew. They wore their overalls but no shirts. Their green eyes opened wide at the talcumed, barbered, beautifully tailored sight of Jack Church tentatively entering the log cabin room where the dining table was set up, away from the mosquitoes.

"Miss Emily," Vangie called out. "Your new man is here." His bath soap and talcum scent vied with the smell of cooking being brought from the cookhouse into the log cabin by a new strong wind from the southeast. Jack Church, who was shy when he wasn't angry, looked at the four clean boys sitting at the table and at the black woman, who was nearly as large as he was, setting it, and brought out his stock social subject: weather. "Perhaps it is going to rain after all," he said, and Vangie shouted for Miss Emily again.

Miss Emily was, Jack Church decided, indecently socially adept. She came out of the other room, where she and the boys slept, still wearing her bonnet, having just had time to wash her hands and her neck after finishing with the boys. "It does feel lowering," she said. "Welcome to our home, Captain." She stared at the boys meaningfully.

"Welcome to our home, Captain Church," they echoed.

She introduced them. Carlos, the eldest, was eight and had his father's smile. George, seven, already appeared lean and hard, like his father. Willie, six, was the image of his mother, and Charles, known as Jolly, just five, looked as happy as his name.

"And this is Miss Evangeline Washington," Emily said. Vangie curtsied with grace. "Freewoman."

"We're not going to start all that again, are we, Miss Emily?" Jack Church said, finding his composure with Emily's presence.

"More than likely, Captain Church. Now, if you will be seated . . ." She pointed to the end of the long pine table, where Carlos would be on his right, Willie on his left. Emily was to sit opposite him, George on her left, Jolly on her right. He thought of the hundreds of formal dinner parties he had attended in Washington City. There had never been any children, and certainly the servants had not been introduced.

"You kill any Injuns, Captain?" Willie asked, breaking the ice, reaching for the pitcher filled with lemonade. He looked so much like his mother it was startling.

"No, sir, I have not."

"Good. Mama don't hold with killing Injuns. May I pour you some lemonade, Captain?"

"Yes, sir, that would be a good idea." Jack Church, thinking of the artificial poise of his Washington City dinner partners, wondered if all of Miss Emily's children were going to be as self-possessed as Willie.

At the far end of the table Emily sat down but was whispered to, loudly, by Miss Evangeline. Emily put her work-hardened hands to her head, felt the bonnet, and Jack Church was happy to see that she could blush. "I am that sorry, Captain Church, but I forgot I still had my bonnet on." She removed it, and masses of fiery hair cascaded down around her as if she had been suddenly crowned with some fabled material spun from red gold.

"Mama's pretty hair," Jolly said, and Jack Church, had he not been too much of a gentleman to comment on a woman's hair or to contradict a fellow guest, would have denied it. Her hair was far more than pretty, and it made Emily beautiful.

195

Evangeline Washington appeared at that moment with a platter piled high with pork chops and collard greens and fresh corn, complaining of the wind—"It sure is blowing up out there"—and set it down in the middle of the table. Emily suggested the captain help himself, which he did, and then the boys, wonderfully restrained, helped themselves, and Emily took her share last.

"The most delicious food, Miss Emily," Jack Church said truthfully.

"Miss Evangeline has been a better cook since she became a freewoman," Emily replied, and then she caught her boys staring at her, full mouths open, and laughed. "All right. She has always been a mighty fine cook. I promise, Captain, I won't say another word against slavery."

"And I won't say another word for it."

"Fair enough."

They talked about their plantations and were amused at the coincidence that they both had been intending to plant cane and had ended up with cotton. Miss Emily decried the lack of a school where her boys could learn to read. Jack Church said he was going to spend some time at Serenity, and perhaps, if the boys were willing, he might take an hour or two toward the end of each day to instruct them in their letters.

"The boys are willing," Miss Emily said over Evangeline's corn cake and George's protestations. Just then the rear door opened and Evangeline fell into the log cabin, with the wind and the rain right behind her, blowing everything that could move across the room.

"A hurricane," Vangie shouted. "A hurricane's coming."

"No need to take on," Emily said with that invincible poise, standing up against the wind. "Did you put out the cookhouse fire?" she asked, while Jack Church managed to close the doors against the eighty-mile-an-hour wind and the boys scrambled to get the shutters down.

"I put out the fire and I shut the cookhouse down, Miss Emily," Vangie said, genuinely frightened. "Oh, Lord, I hate the storms," she said. "I hate the storms."

"The chickens!" seven-year-old George said, heading for the door.

"They'll take care of themselves," his mother said, grabbing him by the arm, restraining him.

"The roof is going to come off, Mama," Jolly said. "Then what we going to do?"

"The roof in the other room *is* better." Emily shepherded them all into the bedroom and bolted the door against the wind. She joined the boys on the huge bed, while Jack Church sat in the rocking chair. Vangie sat on the window seat, listening as the sudden storm winds tore at the logs and made ghastly human noises outside. Emily pushed her hair back over her shoulders. Her green eyes were like gems in a jeweler's exhibit. A draft extinguished the single lamp, and she put her arms around her boys. She's less frightened than I am, Jack Church thought.

196

Carlos was trying to be brave, but Jolly gave in to his fear and began to whimper, which set Vangie going. To quiet them Emily began to tell the boys their favorite story—one passed down to her by her mother—in that odd, melodious voice of hers.

Jack Church, sitting in the dark of that strange room, in the midst of his first Florida hurricane, couldn't have wished to be anywhere else. Washington City intransigence and the Indian Removal Policy were as far away as if the hurricane had transported him to Mars. He felt like a boy again, listening to his nanny tell him a bedtime story. Emily was a brilliant hostess. She made him feel both comfortable and comforted. He listened to her story as if he had no other care in the world.

> The old Indians—them that were here before the Seminoles came—believed three black doves were going to come to Florida and plant their seeds here. They said the seeds would grow and destroy their world, and I guess them old Injuns were right. They ain't here now. Maybe those seeds will destroy the Seminoles' world too. Seems more than likely.
>
> Anyway, more years ago than anyone could count, we had a grandmother named La Floridita. She was the most beautiful woman in the world. She had green eyes and red hair like we do, only her green eyes were emeralds and her red hair was the pure flame of a great fire. She had many magical powers.
>
> The Spanish were going to burn her at the stake, but the Lord was looking out for her, and he made her one of his black doves. A handsome young prince was also made a black dove, and together they left the old ways and the old country behind them and came to this new place, this new world.
>
> The prince married her and they had a child, but the prince died, and later she married a famous explorer named Narváez and had a daughter by him named Isabella. She was old when she reached Florida, but she lived a very long time, long enough to see her seeds planted in this place and start to grow.
>
> We—you boys and me—are the magic seeds La Floridita planted through her daughter, Isabella. We are descendants of the doves the Lord sent to this land so long ago, and we must work to be worthy of His trust. The Injuns came first. Then us. It's our job to cultivate this land, and this little storm may set us back some, but it ain't going to stop us.

The boys had fallen asleep, and the adults sat quietly, waiting for the storm to pass. It moved on quickly enough. The house had survived, with little more damage then a leaky roof. Miss Vangie Washington went to look out for George's chickens, and Jack Church prepared to say good night. "It's been one of the more exciting evenings of my life, Miss Emily."

"I didn't have much to do with the hurricane, Captain."

"The hurricane was only part of the excitement," Jack Church said softly.

She looked up into his pale eyes and saw that he was a lonely man. She wanted to reach out and touch him, but that gesture might have been misinterpreted. "You will come to teach the boys their letters tomorrow, Captain?"

"I will, ma'am."

"And maybe you'll stay on to supper? I can't promise no hurricane, but Miss Vangie is threatening to fix fried chicken, and we'd all be mighty pleased to have you." Jack Church thanked her and, feeling less defeated than he had in some time, made his way home.

Jack Church spent his days preparing for the Moultrie powwow and his afternoons teaching the boys and, often, as not, Miss Emily their letters. His evenings were passed at the long pine table in her log cabin.

It was a happy time, those last days of summer. Mac Levi had written that he felt certain Jack's persuasive letters had gotten the Secretary of War to include coastal land in the reservation that was to be offered to the Seminoles. The boys—though not Miss Emily—proved to be apt students, cautiously reading from the primers he had had sent from St. Augustine.

Most of all, Jack Church enjoyed his evenings. He had never known the comfort of family meals. He had grown up a solitary boy, sent off to Kentucky's Frankfort Academy at the first opportunity, to prepare him for West Point. He had gone from rigidly controlled all-male mess halls to equally controlled Washington City dining salons. At Miss Emily's table he was realizing what he had missed.

He found himself liking Miss Emily's boys, who, after the shared hurricane, had gotten over their amazement at his wardrobe and his size. They treated him as someone to be respected, but that didn't mean they couldn't rag him. He took their jokes with good spirit, handing out a few himself, making up doggerel rhymes that made them laugh. "You put red ants down my pants/Made me do a bogey dance," was one that Jolly repeated until they all wanted to gag him.

Finally Jack Church announced he had to leave. He and Mac Levi, in their official capacities as Indian agent and territorial representative, had agreed to lead the panhandle Mikasukis and Tallahassees the last one hundred miles to Moultrie Creek.

"It's irksome," he told Emily as they stood in front of the log cabin on that last night. "Moultrie Creek is only five miles from here, but the chiefs need to feel that they are being duly honored."

"I hope the powwow goes right, Captain. For you and the Injuns."

"I think Washington City has come around, Miss Emily."

She reached out with her weathered hand and touched Jack Church's gentleman's hand. "You will be coming back, Captain?"

"As soon as I can, Miss Emily."

"You put red ants down my pants/Made me do a bogey dance," Jolly shouted from behind her skirts, and Jack Church went off to meet Mac Levi and the Indians with more optimism than he would have thought possible three weeks before. He carried with him in his mind's eye the picture of a woman with emeralds for eyes and the pure red flame of fire for hair hidden under a yellow calico bonnet.

CHAPTER FOURTEEN

MAC LEVI HADN'T CHANGED MUCH in the nearly ten years since he and Jack Church had first met. He still had his baby face and his freckles and his American-flag-blue eyes, but he had grown thicker about the middle, redder in the face, and his clothes fitted him better. His tendency to rub his hands against his thighs when he was ill at ease had been replaced by a restrained clasping of hands behind back, as befitted a high government official and the husband of the richest woman in the Territory. Levi and Company was now the sole provider of milled lumber in Florida, and lumber was in constant demand for the new houses, plantations, farms, and ships accompanying the mass Florida immigrations.

"You look a lot less hungry than you used to, Mac," Jack Church said to him as they sat across from each other at the starfire after the ritual sofkee dinner with the chiefs. Jack had been amused to see Mac, still squeamish, poking about in the pot with the wooden spoon, knowing that if he came up with something he considered unpalatable, he'd have to eat it in order not to insult the chiefs. He was lucky and had come up with only what looked like bear meat.

All during that first day at the camp Jack had tried to get Mac alone to talk to him. But Mac had been busy with the Negro interpreter, with Governor Duval's emissary, and with Gadsden, Jackson's sour old engineer, who had been put in charge of the powwow. Old Hickory, retired for the moment, was still going to have a voice in the dispensation of the Seminoles.

It was only now, after the sofkee dinner and the braves' hypnotic snake dance, that Jack was able to corner Mac. Jack was aware, of course, long before he had accepted the ritual flask of brandy, that Mac Levi had been con-

199

sciously avoiding him all day. He had guessed from Mac's behavior that there were to be no concessions to the Seminoles. Yet he wanted to hear Mac say it, and so he persisted.

"There's no reason to give them coastal land, Jack," Mac Levi said, taking another swig from the flask, letting the brandy burn his mouth for a moment before swallowing it. "They're not going to be there that long to start with."

"You're offering them a reservation to get them into one place so you can send them, easily, to the west." Jack knew at that moment that his worst fears were being realized.

Mac had been avoiding his friend's pale eyes, but now he looked into them. "You don't understand the Seminoles, Jack. You speak their language, but you don't know what they're saying. You think they're heap big noble fellows. Nature's children. Let me tell you something, Jack: a redskin lies as readily as a white man. This land means nothing to them. The last of the native Florida Indians—them that the Spanish didn't kill off—left with the British fifty years ago. The Seminoles are just a bunch of Creeks from Georgia who meandered down here, thinking their stolen slaves would be safer in Florida. They only want the best ticket out."

The others around the starfire had grown silent. Most of the chiefs didn't understand the rapid English, but they felt the forest grow still as the hatred and ignorance freed by the liquor settled around them. "You couldn't mean that, Mac," Jack Church said. "You know as well as I do that generations of Seminoles have been born and died in these very woods on this very soil. Would you tear them away from everything they believe in, send them to Arkansas, where the living is hard and the land is already occupied by their Creek enemies? I cannot believe that of you, Mac."

"They *are* Creeks, for God's sake. Look at them, sitting in the moonlight, crouched over their fire, like prehistoric men. They haven't progressed one iota, Jack. Old Hickory's right. They're animals, and they have to go. And how in heck do you know Arkansas living is hard? You, who've never lived a hard moment in your life. You, who ran crying back to Washington City, your tail between your legs, when Old Hickory was about to repay the Red Sticks. And you called yourself a soldier." He got to his feet, his face like a beacon in the night, red from perspiration, brandy, and anger. "Oh," he said, tossing the flask to the ground, "what's the use of arguing with a lily-livered spy?"

Jack Church got to his feet as well, his usually pink face ash-white with fury, irrationally stung by the old Andy Jackson gibe. "And what's the use of arguing," he said, "with a man whose wife has a vested interest in ridding the forests of their rightful inhabitants? What's the use of arguing, Mac, with a man whose only morality is based on his own gain?"

Then, surprising himself and the chiefs, who knew him as a peaceable man, Jack Church suddenly flung all two hundred and fifty pounds of himself across the starfire, landing on top of Mac Levi and bringing him to the ground. He had knocked the wind out of him but not the will to fight.

Mac Levi had been taught to fight by rough country boys, and he thought he'd get Jack Church off him by giving him several walloping punches to the head. When that didn't work, he tried kneeing him in the groin. He could hear the seams tearing in his fine-fitting coat, but his powerful punches seemed to be hitting air. Jack Church's rage made him insensitive to all blows. He punched away at Mac with his large cared-for hands as if he were attacking all of the powerful interests that wanted to rob the Seminoles of their world. Finally, when Mac had lost consciousness and Jack Church's gentleman's hands were covered with his blood, Gadsden and two other men managed to pull him away.

In the morning it was a painfully guilty Jack Church who came to Mac Levi's tent to apologize. "My dear fellow," Jack said, taking cover in his Washington City accent, "I *never* fight."

"Just as well. You might kill somebody." Mac held out his red-knuckled hand and Jack Church clasped it. "It was a good fight," Mac said with characteristic generosity. "It didn't change a darn thing, but it sure enough helped clear the air."

Mac Levi and Jack Church rode on to Moultrie Creek together at the head of three hundred and fifty Seminoles and Tallahassees. Mac Levi, despite his beating, radiated his usual ebullience. He was a great favorite among the chiefs. Ironically, they listened to his words with an attention they didn't accord Jack Church. The territorial representative was an emissary from the Great White Father in Washington City and had a power the Indian agent did not.

On the first morning of the powwow, after the trinkets had been handed out, Gadsden dictated the terms of the treaty—instant removal from their lands to the reservation. At that moment Jack Church spotted Osceola among the braves. He wore only a loin cloth, but his muscular, lithe body was streaked with yellow and blue paint, signifying he was a brave capable of making war. It seemed a childlike, hopeless gesture. Listening to Gadsden's hard words and looking at Osceola's war paint, Jack Church gave in and finally accepted his defeat. He had lost his battle to save the Seminoles from Washington City's Indian Containment Policy.

He looked down at his muddy boots as Gadsden read the Secretary of War's ultimatum: "The hatchet is buried. The white men's arms are stacked in peace. Do you wish them to remain so? It is your choice: either go to the reservation or . . ." Here Gadsden threw up his hands, indicating the Seminoles would be wiped out. "Brave warriors," he went on in his voice that was a monotone, "though they despise death, do not madly contend with the strong."

There were five thousand Seminoles and hundreds of thousands of Americans. The chiefs felt they had no choice. They signed the treaty, giving up all their Florida territory except for the barren, coastless land to the south.

Jack Church rode home through the five miles or so of piney woods to Serenity a defeated man—defeated not only by the treaty designed by Jackson and the venal men in the nation's capital but also by the feeling that he was a man out of his time. On that lonely ride he found himself thinking of his father, who had fought beside Washington at the battles of Princeton, Brandywine, Germantown. He was a soldier and his father before him had been a soldier. Before he died, he had made certain his son would be a soldier, setting aside money for his boy's military education.

Had I been born earlier I would have fought with ease, Jack Church thought. He had graduated first in his class from the Military Academy and had been promoted quickly, thought to have a brilliant future. But he hadn't been able to be a soldier in the land-hungry contemporary world he had been born into. He would have fought easily against overwhelming odds, against political tyranny. But he doubted if even his father, that consummate warrior, would have fought against a poor, starved, enormously outmanned people in a war for geographical expansion.

"You call yourself a soldier?" Mac's jibe had hit home. Jack Church wearily turned up the road that led to Serenity, but he kept on, going past his house. I'm not the man my father was. I'm not even the man he wanted me to be. I'm a failed soldier and, in fact, a failed Indian agent. He couldn't remember a time when he had felt more useless, when his life had seemed so pointless. He felt as if he had no past, no present, no future.

Emily knew as soon as she looked at him. He stood at the door to the log cabin, his white raffia hat in his hand, his pale eyes filled with sadness.

"You put red ants in my pants—" Jolly began.

"Stop that, Jolly. You go see what Miss Vangie's got for you out back," Emily said.

"—Made me do a bogey dance." Jack picked up Jolly and held him for a moment and then set him free to go to look for a treat in Vangie's cookhouse. The other boys were with the hired men out in the fields. Jack stood on the doorstep, listening to the chickens contentedly complaining, to the sound of the creek flowing. He felt the light, hot September wind and the cool touch of Emily's rough hand on his cheek.

"The Seminoles are going to the reservation, Emily. They're going to try it. The government's going to protect them, and the government's going to feed them. What they don't realize is the government's going to make them so dependent, so weak, that when it comes time for the government to send them west, they won't be able to resist. When Gadsden and Mac Levi gave out the traditional presents, trinkets, they seemed like handouts.

"And it's *my* job to see that they get to the reservation, to ensure that the government suppliers don't cheat them, to protect them from the white raiders who are just waiting to take their cattle and their slaves. I don't like my job, Emily, but I'm afraid to let anyone else do it." His voice, filled with despair, became a whisper. "They're going to wipe the Seminoles out, Emily,

202

and I am, God save me, going to help. I can't turn my back on the Seminoles now."

She took his hand and led him into the coolness of the cabin, into the far room. It smelled of sleep and comfort. She took off her bonnet, undoing the knot of her fine red hair so that it fell to her waist, shimmering around her like a curtain of fire. Then she drew him down beside her and kissed his sad, pale eyes and held him to her. Without either of them thinking of consequences, they made passionate, bittersweet love, blotting out the world.

CHAPTER FIFTEEN

Renata—1836

DURING THE DOZEN YEARS the Seminoles remained on their reservation their deprivation grew steadily as the rest of Florida, particularly the area around Tallahassee, prospered. At the end of those reservation years Andrew Jackson, nearing the end of his second presidential term, had a great need to leave office with one of his earliest goals accomplished: the removal of the Indians from Florida.

Thus the Seminoles, at a March powwow at Fort King, were told that the Moultrie Creek Treaty, which was to have been in effect for twenty years, was negated. They would have to be ready to leave their reservation for the West by the fall. Osceola signed the Fort King Treaty by running the sharp blade of his knife across his wrist and letting his blood drip onto the parchment. He was put in the stockade by General Wiley Thompson and then released with a reprimand after a few days.

In the fall the Seminoles did not turn up at the established embarkation stations for their removal to the West. Soldiers sent to round them up reported that the Seminoles had disappeared. General Wiley Thompson, who had headed the Fort King powwow, had been decapitated. Charley Emathla, a Seminole chief, had been killed after selling his cattle and land to the government. His body had been mutilated and left under a pile of the money he had received.

Three days after Christmas 1835, while Major Francis Dade was leading a relief column to Fort Brooke from Fort King, a Seminole band of braves and Negro slaves attacked and massacred one hundred and thirteen United States soldiers. Their naked bodies, without scalps or genitals, picked over by buzzards, were found in the palmetto swamp fifty miles south of Fort King. For the first time in the history of the United States Army an entire command had been wiped out by Indians.

The Second Seminole War had begun in earnest, led by Osceola. His strategy was one of terror. He hoped that after enough bloodshed the white men would sit down to a genuine powwow that would leave the Seminoles their Negroes and some land that would remain inviolate, perhaps in the far south of the Territory.

To this end Seminole bands struck at lonely farmhouses, killing, scalping, burning, and disappearing. Few whites dared to live outside a fort or a stockade, and both proliferated, seeds for later Florida towns and cities. Andrew Jackson, dyspeptic in Washington City, orchestrating his successor's election campaign, sent a variety of generals to battle the Seminoles, all of whom refused to learn from Jackson's lessons. They fought in the approved Military Academy method, based on European battlefield traditions. The Seminoles knew nothing of battlefields; they attacked in small bands, sometimes concentrating for weeks on one section of Florida, only to appear somewhere else when army troops arrived.

In those early days the Seminole attacks took place mostly east of the Suwannee, while residents of the panhandle, especially those in the new and huge plantation houses around Tallahassee, touched wood and prayed that the Seminoles would stay away, that the army would find Osceola and annihilate him and his men so they could all breathe easily again.

"I don't want to leave you," Mac said to Renata as they lay in the huge bed in the bedroom on the second floor. Renata was continually surprised that the strength of their love, after so many years, had never been diluted. She touched his still boyish face, kissed his lips, and got out of the bed.

"You're packed?"

"Grimes," Mac said in that short-cut language close-knit couples develop. He followed her to the French doors leading out to the veranda, which overlooked an avenue of live oaks that led to the house.

"If Grimes packed, everything will have to be aired the minute you reach Washington City."

"I wish I didn't have to go." Mac put his still muscular arms around her, turned her to him, and drawing her back to the bed, they made love one last time.

It was late when they reached the breakfast room. Their sons—Jackson and Adamo—looking like Renata but with Mac's American-flag-blue eyes— were sorry to see their father leave. He was going to Washington City at the President's request. Martin van Buren, Old Hickory had written, needed "all the help he can get to defeat those damned lily-livered Whigs. People here respect you, Mac. I want you."

"I'm leaving Grimes here," Mac said as he got into the carriage that would take him north. "He's fat, but he can still handle a Kentucky rifle."

"So can I, Mac Levi." Renata drew the elaborate housecoat around her, reached up, kissed him once more, and stepped back as the carriage pulled away and rode down the long avenue, Mac looking back until the gates disappeared.

A mile away Mac nearly told the driver to turn back. I just don't feel right, he thought, and then he put his right hand to his left breast pocket and took out Lobo Levi's locket. He opened it and stared at the picture for a moment and then shut it decisively and let the carriage go on. Renata's eyes had reassured him. He thought of her confrontation with Old Hickory as she pointed her Kentucky rifle at him and said, aloud, "Renata's always been a woman who can take care of herself."

It was a bright late fall afternoon. Renata sat on the first-floor veranda, dwarfed by two-story-high Corinthian columns, staring down the mile-long avenue, which led to the rural road, which in turn led to Tallahassee. She could hear the boys upstairs playing a complicated word game their tutor—still away on his vacation—had sent from New York.

The slaves who acted as house servants had their own quarters, as did Grimes, who was not welcome in the main house. She liked the feeling of having her home to herself. She loved her husband, but the house held a peace it didn't have when Mac was about.

Renata still wore her hair in the old-fashioned, tightly pulled-back style of the locket portrait. She was forty years old, but her waist measured exactly eighteen inches, just as it had when she was a young girl, learning from Adamo that intricate science of mercantilism. She thought of Adamo and felt that he would be pleased. She had kept her promise. Levi and Company was sounder, more profitable than ever. Her son Jackson wanted to be a soldier, but Adamo's namesake was keen on learning and moneymaking. She wondered briefly what her life would have been like if Lobo Levi had not been killed by a Red Stick squaw and if MacCrimmons hadn't marched in and filled a void.

She understood now, as a woman, why she had loved Lobo as a girl. She had been a child confined to home, needing Lobo to instruct her in how to be free. His father, Adamo, had taught her practical matters. She had seen Lobo as a romantic figure, skilled in the mysteries of the world. She had wanted Lobo to teach her about emotions. He had loved her, she felt. But his yellow eyes had been blind to her needs. Lobo had been a boy, not really understanding the first thing about her. Or himself. But Mac's love and need . . . ah, they had been as great as her own.

Renata took a deep breath, chasing away her ghosts. The air was clean and cool, unlike the thick, salty stuff of Pensacola. The gently rolling red hills surrounding the plantation were pretty to look at without stirring up all the emotions Pensacola Bay habitually did. She found herself of late sitting on the veranda thinking of the Levi and Company trading post, of sunlight falling on Pensacola Bay on a windless day, splintering the mirrorlike waters into shards of reflective glass.

I don't have enough to do, she decided, impatient with her memories, with her peace. The mill ran itself, making more money than one would have thought possible. The new railroad made delivery faster, and goods manufactured in New York factories were being imported and sold in Pensacola, obviating the need for the Seminole handcrafts and the elaborate system of traders. She thought of Laird, smoothed back her black hair, and wished that every memory she was having this afternoon wasn't associated with someone dead.

She already missed Mac. She could have accompanied him to Washington City, but the truth was he no longer needed her on these political trips and the thought of the journey made her weary.

I'd best get myself something to do, she decided, rocking slowly in the painted wicker chair, feeling old in spirit if not in body. All I need is a pipe and I can take Sara's place—another person in her life whom she had loved and who had died. Of old age the doctor had said, but Renata thought it had been discouragement. The Americanos were too much like the British for Sara. If Sara were still alive, she might have needed Renata. No one else did. Her sons had their tutor. And Mac, who took them hunting and fishing and riding.

She started to rise, to get out of the white-painted wicker rocker, to see if the boys needed anything, to look into the servants' quarters, to do *something*. But she heard a cry and remained where she was. Somehow she knew it was Grimes who had made that quick, unholy, and final sound. She saw a movement at the end of the avenue that did not fit in with the calm, pretty picture of the moment before. She sat still and watched. The field slaves were leaving, silently, one by one, their possessions wrapped in blankets. They were being directed by an Indian wearing war paint and a breechcloth. Casually, insolently, he carried a Cuban-bore rifle in his arms like an unheeded child.

Renata knew then, instantly and thoroughly, what was going to happen.

She raced into the house and up the broad main stairs and then up a narrower set to the house servants' room, where she found Juan, the Negro houseman who still claimed he was Spanish. He had come to them in Tallahassee after his wife had died. He was packing a wicker basket as nonchalantly as if he were going on a river-boat day trip.

"Take us with you, Juan." Renata wondered at how calm she sounded, as if she were asking Juan to take them on that pleasure excursion with him. But her mind was working steadily, furiously, at a terrible pace, like the new railroad cars, trying to find a solution for Adamo and Jackson.

Juan provided it. "Can't take you, Miss Renata. They won't let me. Would if I could, but I cannot. I can," he said, after a long moment, while Renata held her breath, her mind racing so fast it was out of control, "take the boys. If you help. Ain't much time, Miss Renata."

"I'll do anything you say, Juan." He had already thought it out, having gathered some field hand's clothes. It was a simple matter to get the boys into them, to blacken their faces and hands, to sit black hats on their heads and wrap colored cloths around their necks so they looked, as Juan said, like darkies going to church. Their dark hair helped as much as their sense of adventure. Renata kissed and hugged them until she thought her arms would break. Then they left with Juan in the covered kitchen cart, drawn by a pair of mules, pleased with themselves, believing their mother would follow soon after.

Juan was to take them to Pensacola, where they would wait for Mac. Reluctantly he had taken the money Renata forced on him. "How else would you all get to Pensacola?" Renata asked, impatient, her mind back on track, working fine now that she thought her boys would be safe, forcing Juan's old hand to make a fist around the dollars.

She went back to the veranda and stood behind a column, not breathing again, her heart out of control now as the cart moved slowly down the live-oak-lined avenue. The Indian brave stopped it at the gate, and Renata thought that for the first time in her life she might faint. She willed herself not to as the brave looked in the cart and stepped back, allowing Juan to drive on. The brave stood there at the end of the avenue, quite openly, like an usher at a theatrical event. Well, it was a theatrical event. She could see braves in their yellow and blue war paint all around the plantation now—Grimes, the only resistance, taken care of.

She heard the crackling sound and then smelled the fire long before she saw it. It reminded her of that day, long ago, in Pensacola. Only now there was no Mac in a tight-fitting tunic to reach over the desk and carry her out. She supposed they had started with the slave quarters, some distance away from the main house. She went upstairs and got the Kentucky rifle from her bedroom, loaded it, and brought it out on the landing with her.

They were already there, on the stairs, silently moving toward her. There were two of them. Renata thought they looked like men who had never known compassion. She shot the first through his heart, and he went tumbling down the steps like one of the mechanical toys Mac was always bringing back from Washington City.

The other kicked the rifle out of her hand as he brought his tomahawk down on her sleek black head, striking her with such force, it seemed to split her body in two, freeing her heart. Shouting one word, whispering another, Renata fell forward and died.

The Tallahassee Seminole who killed Renata Levi proudly wore her shining black hair from his belt until he was killed in the spring offensive. As a boy he had had dealings with the Spanish in St. Marks and knew a few words of their language. Until his death he took great pleasure in looking at Renata's scalp, remembering she had called him a wolf in Spanish. But Renata's last words had had nothing to do with her killer. She had looked into the sharp, remote face of the red man and seen someone else. She had said, quite loudly, in that next to last moment of her life, "Lobo." But the name on those dark-red lips when she died was a long, needful whisper. It was "Mac."

CHAPTER SIXTEEN

Emily Church—1837

"I'M AWAY SO OFTEN," Jack Church said as Emily helped him into his pale yellow coat, the silver buttons bearing the crest of his old brigade.

"Captain, we've had this discussion before."

"And we'll have it again, Emily." It was another round in Jack's campaign to get Emily to move into St. Augustine with the rest of the white settlers in the area. Neither of them mentioned Renata Levi in these skirmishes, but her death was often in Jack's thoughts. He had seen Mac Levi soon after and the man had seemed sadly diminished.

But Emily was as intransigent as Andrew Jackson. And as argumentative. "The Seminoles respect you, Captain."

"But there's no guarantee that every Seminole brave on the warpath knows this is my home, that you're my wife." He took her small chin in his large hand and studied those gemlike eyes, that fiery red hair, the full bottom lip, and he kissed her long and hard. "I couldn't live without you, Emily." They both knew that was no mere romantic sentiment. It was Emily who gave shape and direction to his life. It had been Emily who had insisted he stay on as Indian agent each time he threatened to resign.

"It's neither the war nor the side you would have picked if you had your druthers, Captain. But you don't. You won't be able to forgive yourself if you don't see it through."

They had been married fourteen years, but it felt for both of them as if they had been together forever. Their plantations had become one—Serenity—and he had freed his slaves. Emily wouldn't have married him otherwise. Abel was the foreman, paying consistent and futile court to Miss Evangeline. Emily's sons were all gone. Carlos Smyrna had his own cotton plantation and a pretty dark-haired wife and a red-haired son up near Cowford. George and Willy had a sugar-cane plantation and a guesthouse over on the St. Johns River for recuperating (and some nonrecuperating) northerners who braved the war and the Indians for Florida's healthful climate. Jolly had been taken up totally by Jack's mother and was in a fancy boys' school in Washington City, preparing for entry into Harvard College.

But Jack and Emily Church were not alone. They had been blessed in 1830 by the birth of Florida Mae (known as Flora), a strawberry blond child, with emerald-green eyes and her mother's determined, straight-lined, stubborn insistence on letting nothing get in the way of what she wanted. "I wish I could've given you a boy, Captain," Emily said as she lay in bed while Miss Vangie crooned to the child.

"You gave me four boys when I married you, Emily. I've been praying for a daughter."

Jack loved Flora nearly as much as he loved her mother, and she returned the sentiment. "I'm Papa's girl," she would say when Emily attempted to punish her for high-handedness.

"You're your mama's girl too, miss, and you'll listen to her," Vangie, outraged, remonstrated.

But she didn't. Flora listened, it seemed, only to her own strong, fully developed inner voice. When she was just two, Jack Church began devoting his mornings at Serenity to teaching her from the primers he had used in schooling Emily's boys. Emily, who had never quite learned to read, refused to be intimidated by her daughter's erudition. "When I grow up," Flora said, "I'm going to be a teacher. I'm going to teach the Indians. Papa says they don't know how to read and write, and I think that is a great waste."

Flora had her own little garden where she grew flowers. Emily didn't hold with *growing* flowers when they grew in the fields for the asking. "You're my wild flower," Jack Church told her. "Florida Mae's our cultivated rose."

"Pshaw, Captain," Emily replied. "We could use the extra vegetables."

Emily often wondered where she had gotten such a daughter—Miss Prim, she called her—but of course she knew. Florida Mae Church was right, as usual. She was her papa's girl, with an extra helping of Floridita, that original dove, thrown in.

On a Saturday fall morning in 1837, while the summer heat was lingering and the captain was getting into his yellow coat with the silver buttons, Flora Mae presented herself in her blue going-to-town dress. "Take that dress off this instant, miss," Emily said, brushing some almost invisible lint from her husband's huge shoulders. She herself wore a calico dress, colorless from washing and age, and was about to put on the yellow bonnet the captain hated. She had plenty of help, but she was going to work, as usual, in the fields. She wouldn't feel right if she didn't.

"Papa said that as long as we had to give up the lessons, he would take me to St. Augustine as a special treat." She wasn't a pretty child, but she was appealing, like a little adult. Emily thought for a few moments while the captain and little Miss Prim waited for Emily to make up her mind. Finally she conceded that "it couldn't hurt. Providing she gets her sleep and you don't fill her up with sweetmeats."

The Captain had been called to St. Augustine by Brevet Major General Thomas Sidney Jesup to brief him on the situation that could only be described as "steadily deteriorating." "You keep Miss Vangie in the house with you," Jack Church said, kissing his wife goodbye one more time.

Emily kissed him and then she kissed her daughter and, with a certain relief, saw them both off. Miss Vangie would remain out back in the kitchen house where she belonged.

Emily loved Miss Vangie, not to mention the captain and their daughter, but wasn't it nice, she thought, removing her bonnet, to be alone in the house for once. She would not go to the fields, she decided, where she wasn't needed in the first place. She spent a satisfactory morning working in her own vegetable patch, serenaded by the snores emanating from the cookhouse. Emily washed her hands, using water from the creek, and went into the house.

The house had been greatly expanded. There were a center hall, three bedrooms, and separate rooms for dining and talking. Jack and Emily's bedroom was privately considered by Emily to be the captain's room. She stepped into it, and was struck, as always, by what a handsome room it was.

She had made the white curtains from soft Sea Island cotton the captain had, as usual, paid far too much for. His pale-pink Oriental carpet lay on the painted pine-board floor. Emily worked her feet out of her old black working boots and—feeling naughty—stepped onto the carpet, rubbing her toes in it, marveling again at how a rug could make a body feel so rich and sinful.

The carpet, with its ripe flowers and queer, arching birds, also made her sensual. She looked at the oversized trundle bed. No little bed, the captain had said, shortly after they were married, could make him happy. Not like a little woman, Emily said to herself, smiling that lovely wide smile, continuing to rub her toes in the luxurious pile. Suddenly she realized something was wrong in the handsome room.

She knew it was the cabinet. It was a big rosewood coffinlike closet in which she and the captain kept their clothes. Most people hung their dresses and coats on pegs driven between the logs, but the captain had certain northern ideas he was never going to put behind him, and keeping his clothes in that closet—mildew or not—was one of them.

She had never liked that dark closet, and she liked it even less now. The good feelings about being alone were gone, and she was scared and angry, determined to find out who was hiding among the captain's fine coats. She approached it, realizing it was the rancid smell that had alarmed her. She recognized it. It was a combination of bear grease and blood. She knew it

210

wouldn't do her any good to try to run or scream. "All my life I've faced what the Lord put in front of me," she said to herself. "If death is lurking in the captain's fancy closet, well, I'm going to let death out."

She opened the doors, and the Indian inside looked at her with his flat black eyes, his tomahawk hung loosely at his side. Blood was coming rapidly from a wound in his chest, which was streaked with blue and yellow paint. He placed his free hand over the wound as if he were ashamed of it.

"Mrs. Church!" The soldiers had opened the front door and were already in the house, alarmed. "Mrs. Church!"

Emily closed the cabinet's rosewood doors, locking them, even then thinking how silly it was to have a lock on the doors of a closet one good kick of a boot could demolish.

"Mrs. Church!"

She found Vaughan Gibson, a nice blond lieutenant from Atlanta, standing in the new central hall. Through the open front door she could see his men. Even their horses looked apprehensive. The Churches, despite being redskin lovers, were popular. No one wanted to find Emily's badly butchered corpse.

Vaughan Gibson took a deep, relieved breath. "You all right, ma'am?"

"I am perfectly all right, Vaughan." She found herself taking on the captain's high-on-the-hog voice. She thought of all the accents—Spanish, English, cracker, Washington City—she had used in her life as the boy examined her, finally deciding to believe that the normally dark-skinned Mrs. Church was always that pale.

"We were chasing a band of Injuns, and one wounded brave looked as if he had ducked in here, and we didn't see the captain's horse and the house looked empty—"

"I am perfectly all right, Vaughan," she said again. She wasn't lying. She wasn't saying there was no red man on her place. She was saying only, in Jack's lah-de-dah way, that she was perfectly all right.

The lieutenant looked at her carefully. Mrs. Church did not seem herself. "Ma'am, you—"

"I am perfectly all right, Vaughan," she said for the last time, wondering where those words were coming from. "Now, if you get out of here, I will go back to my nap."

He smiled, dimpling, evincing that specifc southern male charm that works best in youth and old age. Then he was gone. Emily ran, in her bare feet, to the bedroom, unlocked the ridiculous cabinet door, and helped the wounded Seminole out of it.

She tried to get him to the bed, but he lay down on the floor, on the captain's Oriental carpet with the peculiar, elegant birds. He still held his hand to his chest, but the bleeding had slowed. Emily ran out to the kitchen house, where Miss Vangie still slept—she would sleep, Emily thought, through Judgment Day—and found the bandages.

He lay still, his eyes half closed, as Emily bandaged him. She was not particularly put off by the smell of the bear grease. She had overcome a great many unpleasant odors in her life, and this was not the worst.

He tried to get up when she had finished, but she put her hand on his round, smooth shoulder. "Lie still," she commanded, wondering if he understood English. Apparently he did, because he allowed his head to drop down while she went out to the kitchen house and fixed him a bowl of the corn soup Vangie had on the fire.

He was sitting cross-legged when she returned, visibly summoning up his strength. He opened his black eyes as she handed him the bowl and suddenly smiled at her. It's a smile the angels wear, so sweet and innocent, she thought. As if butter wouldn't melt in his mouth.

He drank the soup down without pausing and then, amazingly, stood up. He had been badly wounded, but he didn't sway or totter. He even executed a bow. "I thank you, Mrs. Church," he said in perfect English, "for your soup and your kindness."

Emily realized then who the beautiful Indian brave was, standing in her bedroom on the captain's carpet, nearly nude, with blood and paint smeared all over his body, reeking of bear grease, bowing to her. "Your husband, Mrs. Church," he went on, "is a true friend of the red man."

"Is that why you ain't scalping me?" she asked, resisting the need to touch her incandescent red hair, expressing the fear she had repressed since she first had smelled the bear grease in the captain's bedroom.

He didn't answer. Instead, standing very still, he asked his own question. "Why, Mrs. Church, did you not give me away to the soldiers?"

"The killing must stop, Osceola," Emily said, using his name for the first time, wanting him to know she knew who he was, wanting him to know she realized the magnitude of the crime *she* had committed. She didn't care. All she cared about at that moment was telling Osceola how she felt.

"The killing isn't helping anyone—white, red, or black—Osceola. You know that, don't you?" He didn't move but continued to stand as still as a deer, listening. "Had I turned you over to the soldiers, I would have been a killer too. I did not want to face that for the rest of my days, Osceola. I would rather be put in prison." She waited for some reaction, and the unwanted thought came to her that he still might hurt her. She put it out of her mind. "White men will not stop the killing. Not until there is no one left to kill. *You* must stop the killing, Osceola."

He bowed his beautiful head, and then he was out the window. Emily stood and watched as he melted into the pine forests that surrounded Serenity.

She didn't want to think about what had just happened. Not then. Instead she went to the kitchen house and got some of Evangeline's fresh goat's milk and returned to the bedroom to work on the single blood spot Osceola had left on the carpet.

When she realized it never would come out, she turned to the closet, re-

212

moved all of the captain's fine clothes and her not so fine homespuns. She aired them thoroughly, putting a sprig of jasmine from Flora's garden into the closet to fight the odor of bear grease.

Vangie found her there. "You all right, Miss Emily?" she asked.

"I am perfectly fine," Emily said and then, for the first time since Hardy Smith had died, she allowed herself to cry, giving in to the fears she had set aside, finding comfort in Evangeline Washington's enveloping embrace.

Emily Church never told her husband of the incident. And when Osceola was finally taken a year later, she felt—as did much of the nation—ashamed. He hadn't been captured in battle but by a ruse.

General Jesup had offered Osceola a powwow at Fort Peyton, where he would present a new treaty: the Seminoles could remain in Florida on a new reservation in the South; they could keep their Negroes and their cattle. If Osceola would come to the powwow, Jesup would personally guarantee his safety.

The treaty didn't exist. Osceola was arrested when he arrived at Fort Peyton, eventually sent to Fort Moultrie in Charleston, South Carolina, where he sickened and died. There was a national outcry at the way in which Osceola had been captured, and Jesup was replaced by a series of generals: Alexander Macomb, Zachary Taylor, Walker Armistead.

The resistance of the Seminoles was finally broken in 1843, after three thousand Seminoles had been captured and sent west and the last important chief had been hunted down and killed on the Lochlockonee River. All of Florida was safe to be settled by white men.

When Andrew Jackson marched into Florida in 1822, there were five thousand Seminoles living in twenty-five villages. Twenty-one years later, Old Hickory—with but a year to live—had very nearly gotten his way. Just one hundred Seminoles remained in Florida. They were allowed to disappear, forgotten, into the network of streams, saw-grass prairies, mangrove swamps, and hammocks that make up the Everglades. They built chikees and compounds along what would eventually be known as the Tamiami Trail. They began to trade slowly and suspiciously with the white settlers who lived on Biscayne Bay. They never signed a peace treaty with the United States and remained officially at war.

By the end of the Seminole wars, the Spanish—with the total defeat of their Seminole allies—were seemingly gone from Florida forever, busy attempting to hold onto their few remaining possessions in the Americas.

The close of the war opened Florida's gates to an avalanche of settlers, hungry for land and prosperity. In March of 1845 Florida was admitted to the Union as a slave state. Its first elected senator was the respected former territorial representative, Mac Levi. His eldest son, Jackson Levi, was graduated high in his class at the United States Military Academy at West Point. His youngest son, Adamo, headed the prosperous family business, Levi and Company.

Jack Church had, with Emily's support, resigned as territorial Indian agent on the day Osceola had been so ignominiously taken. He gave himself up to his land holdings, to writing antiwar tracts, to educating his daughter. Florida (Flora) Mae Church became in time a teacher at the Indian School her father helped to found in Tallahassee. Later she married a Cleveland man named Tuttle.

Julia

BOOK THREE

CHAPTER ONE

1874

IT WAS A HUMID, early Monday morning in late May when the *Emily B.*, a three-masted, light-draft thirty-ton schooner out of St. Augustine, sailed into the shallow waters of Biscayne Bay. Julia de Forest Sturtevant Tuttle stood in the prow inhaling the moist, buoyant air, feeling remarkably alive. Her father, Ephraim Sturtevant, had written about the air. She felt as if she could reach out and hold it in her stubby, capable hands.

She saw, as minor figures in the vast painting in front of her, a family of Bahamian Negroes drifting north along the shore in a flat-bottomed boat. A pair of Seminoles in satin turbans and colorful blouses sailed south in a dugout. I might as well be on a different planet, Julia thought. She had never seen anything like those people in their strange craft or like the blue herons that waded on shore just inside a mangrove swamp. She had never seen anything like Biscayne Bay.

It was so unlike Cleveland, where every object seemed concrete and tough. Here everything appeared soft, pliable. It reminded Julia of the diorama of prehistoric times that she and Alice had made when they were girls in school. It is prehistoric, Julia thought. Untouched.

The captain, an annoyingly informative little man, interrupted Julia's reverie. "Biscayne Bay, Mrs. Sturtevant, is south Florida's highway. The few families that live down here travel along it in their small sailboats."

"It looks like a very unused highway to me," Julia said dismissively, thinking of Cleveland's bustling streets.

Though she had plain brown hair and a somewhat squarish face (the sort called handsome), Julia felt for the moment like the blond, round-cheeked Viking figurehead in the Cleveland Museum of Art, leading the way to unexplored places. She had come to this relatively unknown part of Florida for her son's sake, but she couldn't quite hide from herself the conviction that surely some adventure, some new turn of life awaited her here. Julia recognized in herself all the symptoms of anticipatory excitement—beating heart, throbbing head—with which she had greeted each important new stage in her life: finishing-school student, debutante, wife, mother. All had proved, in the end, disappointing. She had a feeling that Florida just might live up to her expectations. But of course, she reminded herself, I thought that *everything* would live up to my expectations.

It had been a nightmare of a journey for a twenty-four-year-old woman with a six-year-old difficult daughter and a five-year-old sickly son. They had spent exhausting weeks aboard mostly rackety trains, and after Jacksonville they had endured the somewhat limited comforts provided by the *Emily B.* Fanny had complained every mile of the way, while Harry appeared, not always convincingly, to be losing strength. Harry had had a mild case of polio, which had left him with a withered arm and a weakened constitution. South Florida's climate, as glowingly described in her father's letters, was to remedy the latter.

Julia, trying to temper her schoolgirl excitement—really, couldn't the *Emily B.* go any faster?—leaned over the white-painted side of the schooner thinking she would see sand through the clear water of the great bay's depths. Instead she saw that the water was only a few feet deep and the bay's bottom was covered with thick sea grass, for all the world like an unkempt Cleveland lawn. Through the sea grass darted rainbow-colored fish and an occasional larger, grayish, and more ominous shape.

"Baby sharks," Alice Brickell said, leaning over her friend's shoulder, exuding the sweet smell of vanilla, which she put behind her ears every morning in the mistaken belief that it warded off mosquitoes.

She was a big messy woman with an incipient mustache beneath a long, bony nose, acerbic yellow-brown eyes, and colorless hair. Alice looks, an unkind relative had once said, like a mare put out to pasture. But she was comfortable with herself and liked nothing more than to shock and boss people around. She was the same age as Julia, who was her weakness. They had grown up together in Cleveland. Alice, awed by Julia's good looks, comparative daintiness, and general air of command, had played the wounded soldier to Julia's Florence Nightingale in childhood games.

"I have met my match," Alice liked to say when she was told that Julia was even bossier than she was. Julia, pityingly yet affectionately, thought Alice wasn't in the same race. Their fathers were lifelong and often feuding friends who had made money during the Civil War: Willie Brickell in the wholesale food business; Ephraim Sturtevant through a variety of schemes and inventions. Julia's father, who liked to call himself an entrepreneur but was in reality a very good salesman, had helped to sell people on the idea of the sewing machine and the double-dasher butter churn.

Ephraim Sturtevant had a roving, romantic disposition that had brought him a great deal of happiness and some sorrow. He had remained deeply in love with his wife during all the years of their marriage, and it was for her he had stayed in Cleveland for such a long time. She had died of an unexpected heart attack on the day President Lincoln was shot, and it had seemed that Ephraim, like his country, would never recover.

He had met his wife during his early wanderings when she was teaching at

218

the Indian School in Tallahassee. He had looked into Flora Mae Church's eyes at a church picnic and had immediately fallen in love. They were married at her parents' plantation, just south of St. Augustine, and then he took her home to Cleveland. For sixteen years they were idyllically happy.

Two years after Flora Mae's death their only child, Julia, made what was considered an advantageous marriage at the age of seventeen to the Byronesque Frederick Tuttle, heir to the Cleveland Ironworks fortune. Ephraim, who was against advantageous marriages in general and this one in particular, had left Cleveland immediately after the marriage.

He went to Florida with no particular goal other than a vague desire to heal his grieving heart. Flora Mae had believed, Seminole-style, that one's spirit returned to the place where it had been born. Ephraim found himself wandering through Florida at an age (he told himself) when he should have known better, searching for Flora Mae's spirit.

His friend, Willie Brickell, bored with Cleveland's and his own new riches, joined him. Ephraim hadn't found Flora Mae's spirit in Tallahassee or on the extensive Church cotton plantation below St. Augustine. However, when he reached the sparsely populated (six families) Biscayne Bay, he felt a sense of well-being, a completeness, that he hadn't experienced since Flora Mae had died.

"We have discovered the Fountain of Youth in Florida's Dade County," Ephraim wrote to Julia, who was ensconced in an impressive four-storied, Mansard-roofed house, Gaydene, in Cleveland, already the mother of Fanny and Harry. "Paradise on the shores of the Miami River. The Injuns say Miami means 'sweet water,' and I don't doubt it. I have never felt younger or more healthy. Willie Brickell's going to settle here. So, by God, am I."

For the last five years he had written to Julia on the first of each month, describing his delight with Biscayne Bay, from its dark, impenetrable jungle to the iridescent blue and turquoise waters of the bay. He spent his days in a small skiff fishing the bay waters, living at an inn in the settlement called Coconut Grove. He began to buy land. Willie Brickell was so enamored with the bay area, he went back to Cleveland, sold his wholesale grocery business, and returned for good. He brought with him his family, a governess, and a concert grand piano.

Brickell had left a leased house in Cleveland that, at the end of five years, had to be sold, and he had sent his eldest daughter, Miss Alice, to attend to its sale. Alice became for Julia the "adult and female traveling companion" Frederick had insisted upon in allowing Julia to make the trip.

Julia moved away from the sides of the schooner, breaking the hypnotic state the bay waters had induced. "I can't say that I'll miss being on this boat," Alice said, studying her friend's flushed face. "I only hope father doesn't put up a fuss when he sees you."

"Alice," Julia said, impatiently, adjusting her straw boater, "how long can this go on? Two grown men acting like children—and not especially bright children at that."

They were referring to their fathers' current and most serious feud, now nearly half a decade old. It had begun when Willie Brickell returned from Cleveland to find that Ephraim Sturtevant had bought a good deal of land north of the Miami River, land Willie had had his eye on. Willie accused Ephraim of "waiting until my back was turned to snap up the best land at the best price."

Ephraim, who had been buying it to share with Willie, knocked Willie off the dock. Willie, standing knee-deep in the bay, shook his fist and called Ephraim a "thieving bastard." Ephraim immediately checked out of Charlie Peacock's Inn (where the Brickells were boarding) and moved himself to the old Fort Dallas. It had been built during the Indian wars and had come to him with the land, on the north shore of the Miami River. An unspoken rule evolved: Brickell would stay south of the river, Tuttle would stick to the north.

"I wonder if they've killed each other while I've been gone," Alice said, twisting her thin lips as if she were sucking lemons. "They're *capable* of killing each other."

Other peoples' arguments didn't interest Julia. "Alice, please, I beg you, allow me to contemplate the beauty of this wild place in silence." Julia had assumed what Alice privately thought of as her "improving" expression, which entailed a certain raising of that squarish chin. Alice propped herself up against the *Emily B.*'s railing, deciding she was happy to be nearly home but uncertain about the wisdom of Julia's coming with her.

Before the two young women lay an uneven crescent of flat rock and sand-covered land overgrown with Caribbean pines and palmetto scrubs. To the right the Miami River emptied into the bay. On its banks, extending both north and south along the shore, in the center of the pine forest, was a hammock—a thick, lush green tropical jungle of live oaks, ironwood trees, gumbo-limbos, and strangler figs. One would need a machete to penetrate it.

"It's so untouched," Julia said, dispensing with that habitual, knowing air, looking for once—despite her matronly brown dress and the bun of hair at the back of her head under her straw hat—like the twenty-four-year-old she was. In that moment, as the *Emily B.* sailed slowly toward the point where the tea-colored earth of the jungle met the blue and turquoise bay waters, where the sea grapes and coco plums lined the shore, Julia felt the magic of the place. "It's so alive, isn't it, Alice?"

"It is," Alice—immune to magic—said. "There are snakes, spiders, panthers, and crocs, and some things you don't want to know about crawling around that jungle."

"It looks like the Garden of Eden," Julia said in a fruity, theatrical voice. "Moments after the Fall."

"Nonsense," snorted Alice.

Julia Tuttle ignored Alice Brickell. She was having a vision. It was the second great vision of her life. She had had the first when she had looked across a suffocatingly hot Cleveland ballroom and had seen the beautifully disdainful Frederick Tuttle, of the Cleveland Ironworks Tuttles, in profile. She had known immediately, standing among the potted palms of that hotel conservatory, that one day she would be the rich, socially powerful Mrs. Frederick Tuttle. Then one of her megrims had come on and she had had to be taken home.

Now she stared at the edge of the slim coastal rim of limestone-based earth that lay between the ocean and the Everglades. There was dew on every surface, as if a magician had carelessly strewn diamonds about. But what she saw was her own private world layered over the real one, like an architect's tracings over a building site. It was a city filled with dazzling white towers, its shores lined with spacious houses, each with a luxuriant manicured lawn surrounded by meticulously cared-for fruit trees.

"One could create a perfect Christian city here. It would be the most beautiful city in the world. There would be nothing to stop one—"

Alice interrupted her reverie. "You would have to own the land, to start with. And to end with, the settlers wouldn't let you. Most of the people who live here do so, Julia, because they want to get away from cities. They're tired of Reconstruction, of corruption and thievery. We're here, Julia, because we like the jungle."

Julia ignored her, lost in her vision. Her city would replace the jungle. It would stand for all that was good and moral in man. It would be a living testimonial to the financial Protestantism the millionaires in Cleveland practiced. Her father and Frederick were never going to be millionaires. They would never rival those other Clevelanders—Flagler, Anderson, and Rockefeller—who had formed their petroleum partnership just seven years before—and look at them now!

She had met Flagler once at a dinner party and had come home struck with his ordinariness. "Why," she said to Frederick as her maid helped her to undress and he, in a silk dressing gown, attempted to read, "anyone can be a millionaire."

"I would have thought you already knew that, Julia." Frederick hadn't deigned to look up from his novel. He would rather, Julia thought, read or daub away at porcelains than engage in the great post–Civil War adventure: the creation—by dint of imagination and hard work—of a fortune. How did I make such a terrible, thorough mistake? she asked herself. How could I have failed to see that Frederick hates the ironworks, that he considers work of any kind beneath him? It was I who was blind. I thought anyone as beautiful as Frederick had to be a go-getter as well.

But for all of his gentlemanly artistic pretensions—the thought of the painted urns and fruit bowls made her click her tongue and shake her head with impatience—he hadn't any genuine creativity. Not for making money.

As she looked at the approaching shore Julia thought, If I had only been born a man. She would have taken those ironworks and made them into a national institution. All over the world builders would be clamoring for Cleveland Ironworks iron. Cleveland society wouldn't have allowed it. But here, in this untouched place, she could make something happen.

"Mama!" A piercing, hysterical scream shattered Julia Tuttle's daydream. "Mama!"

"What now?" Julia asked as six-year-old Fanny, in a spotless white sailor dress, her straw hat even now perfectly centered on her head, its band caught under her chin, came screaming across the deck, frightening the herons. Tears, reddening her eyes, collected at the tip of her nose.

The child was breathless with fear, but she managed to speak rapidly. "Mama, Harry's captured a horrid creature called a scorpion and he's keeping it in a little box and he's torturing me with it and First Mate says if it bites I'll die a horrid death and Harry says he's going to put it in my bed tonight . . ."

She's so like her father, Julia thought regretfully, looking at her daughter, who was indulging in what Julia called "Fanny's daily blubber." She even looked like Frederick. But what was attractive in the father—that long, languid, aristocratic face—was petulant in his daughter. Her red hair and green eyes diminish the classic features, Julia decided, handing Fanny a handkerchief. "If I saw a scorpion," Julia said tartly, "I'd examine it, not run from it." Julia watched disgustedly as Fanny mopped her face and those green Emily Church eyes. "When your great-grandmother was a girl, she once went to the outhouse—"

"Oh, not the outhouse story again, Mother. Please. I can't bear it." Julia, who had a penchant for repeating stories she liked, fixed her daughter with her stern brown eyes, and Fanny subsided onto a bench next to Alice Brickell. Julia loved her grandmother. It was an irony Julia never saw fit to examine: while she was ashamed of her mother's "Floriday" background, her occasional gauche backwoods mannerisms, she was inordinately proud of Emily Church's pioneer ways.

Julia had met her only once, a month or so after Jack Church's death. Jack Church had, characteristically, been on the wrong side of the war, in sympathy with the Union, living in the Confederacy. He had died of disappointment as much as of pneumonia.

It was the first and last time Emily was to leave Florida. She was making the rounds of her children, saying, it seemed, goodbye to them, since she died soon after returning to St. Augustine. She had visited her Smith sons, devastated by the war but beginning to rebuild their plantations on the banks of the St. Johns and their guesthouses in St. Augustine, once again a convalescent center. She had traveled to Key West, Florida's most populous and newest city, built by the wreckage industry, where the one Smyrna—himself a granddaddy—was prospering. Then she had taken the necessary boats and trains to Cincinnati, where she consoled her daughter, Flora Mae, grief-stricken over her father's death.

"She's so little and knobby" had been Julia's first thought. At fifteen, Julia, tall and slim, was the haughtiest student at Miss VailDeane's School for Young Ladies. But Emily made it a point to spend as much time with Julia as she could, and by the end of the month Julia had been won over by her grandmother's bravery and strength.

Julia particularly liked Emily's stories. The lazy Union soldier who took a nap on the banks of the St. Johns and got bitten in two by a croc. Old Señora Valdora, who had been scalped and set on fire but had put out the flames with her own blood and spent the next twenty years shocking people by removing her bonnet and showing her scars. The blue mist that hung over the piney woods early in the morning which some folks said was Injun spirits, and the white egrets that nested on the salt pond, and the purple orchids that grew wild in the keys. Most thrilling of all was her story about their ancestor, La Floridita, and the Legend of the Black Doves.

For months afterward, Julia's imagination soared. She told Alice and all the girls at Miss VailDeane's that she was descended from a fabulous and great lady, a Spanish aristocrat who had nearly been burned at the stake but had been saved by the Lord to bring goodness and mercy to the heathens of Florida. Great knights had thrown away fortunes for her. In Julia's adolescent daydreams she was a Florida pioneer, conquering weather, topography, and savages.

That, of course, was before her vision, across the potted palms, of Frederick Tuttle.

Now Julia found Emily's stories of pioneer life useful in instructing her children—particularly the haughty Miss Fanny—in the rigors and truths of everyday life. As they sat on the static *Emily B.*—waiting for the tide to deepen the waters so the ship could continue to port—Julia brought out, like a tired but serviceable churchgoing hat, Emily's outhouse story. Fanny, as she sniveled beside Alice Brickell, chilled despite the morning sunshine, almost would have preferred her brother and his scorpion.

"One day your great-grandmother, that proud pioneer woman of impeccable noble ancestry, went to one of the rudimentary conveniences behind her plantation home. There were three, mind you, as your great-grandfather—an aristocratic Washingtonian whose own father fought alongside the Father of Our Country—insisted on privacy. When your great-grandmother had seated herself comfortably, she suddenly felt something nudge her from below. She thought it was one of the dogs, and she stood up, prepared to give it a piece of her mind.

"It wasn't a dog, Fanny," Julia continued in her admonishing, giving-a-sermon voice. "It was a rattlesnake. Red and yellow. As thick as a man's neck, all coiled up but as long as this schooner when fully stretched out." She waited for a reaction, and Fanny obligingly grimaced.

223

"Did your great-grandmother cry out? Did she run? Did she faint? She did not. She took the shovel and gave that snake a great whack across its thick ugly head. She didn't kill it—she was a little bit of a woman, after all—but she stunned it, and then she got your great-grandfather to shoot it. She said she never went near that privy afterward without feeling 'a touch scared,' but the point is she did go back to that privy. She didn't let a lesser creature scare the wits out of her.

"Now I want you, Fanny, to be like your great-grandmother. Go to your brother's cabin and show him that you're not afraid. Ask to see the scorpion. Touch it. I bet you a penny it won't hurt you if you're brave. I'm told scorpions are wonderfully interesting creatures—"

"Mama, it will kill me. First Mate said—" Fanny began to sob. Alice folded the thin, shaken little girl in her warm vanilla-scented arms and held her.

"Julia, stop," Alice demanded. "I can feel poor Fanny's bones shaking. Some compassion for your daughter, please. She can't help feeling frightened."

Julia watched Alice lead Fanny off and turned back to the vista before her. Fanny's not *my* daughter, she thought bitterly. *My* daughter would step on the damned scorpion. But if ever there's a doubt as to Fanny's paternity, all they have to do is set her next to her father and dangle a mouse in front of them. They both shudder in exactly the same way. It felt wonderful to be away from Frederick, free of his strictures and sensitivities. She hadn't had a megrim since she'd left Cleveland.

She looked down at the rainbow-colored fish and the gray baby sharks and sighed. Perhaps she was hard on Fanny. She pushed her, and the girl was too weak to be pushed. She'd make it up to her. She'd force Harry to get rid of the scorpion and she'd buy her a new frock. But Fanny's sniveling drove her mad. It never failed to remind her of Frederick.

That memory of Frederick renewed her fury, and she put her chin up and clenched her fists. "Damn," she said aloud, using the strongest profanity she allowed herself, "I deserve more than a life holding Frederick's weak hand and mopping Fanny's red nose."

At that moment the *Emily B.* began to move toward shore. In the near distance, across the dazzling bay waters, Julia, by putting her hand to her broad forehead, could see the Brickell trading-post dock. Several people were standing on it waiting for the *Emily B.* One man—Was it Willie Brickell? No, he was too young and blond and tall—waved. Julia didn't return the greeting. She was looking beyond the dock, at the jungle she was going to conquer. I am a Dove, she thought suddenly. Like Floridita, I belong here.

CHAPTER TWO

THE NARROW INLET in front of Willie Brickell's trading post was the only place where boats larger than a skiff could dock on the mainland shore of Biscayne Bay. When the *Emily B.* was finally secured, her gangplank was let down, and a tiny Negro boy on the dock, who had a sense of occasion, began to play "Dixie" on his harmonica. A considerable group for the bay area— three women, four men, half a dozen children, one Seminole—had gathered to see who and what the *Emily B.* had brought to the isolated community.

Alice was the first one off, kissing her younger sisters, smaller versions of herself, allowing her father, just her height but a little broader, to hold her in his arms for a moment before he remembered to give her the somewhat bedraggled yellow flowers he had picked for her. "Alice," he said, and for a moment there was the possibility that he might weep. He had sorely missed her. He was a widower and a dedicated sport fisherman, and he depended upon Alice, with her natural managerial abilities, to run his home and sometimes his trading post.

The sentimental moment passed when Alice said tenuously, "Look whom I've brought with me, Papa." She was uncertain what her father's reaction would be to members of Ephraim Sturtevant's family.

"Hello, Julia," Willie Brickell said, touching Julia's now gloved hand. Alice was relieved.

"This is my daughter, Fanny, Mr. Brickell," Julia said, and Fanny, in her sailor dress and straw hat, looking as if she had come from a shop window, executed a neat curtsy. "And my son, Harry." Harry, pale but game, offered his small hand, which Willie Brickell shook. Julia, chin up, surveyed the small, interested crowd of homespun-clothed women, coatless men, and half-dressed children. They—especially the women—were fascinated: Ephraim Sturtevant's fancy daughter had arrived in the bay area. But Julia found the little group lacking in interest, and turning her back to them, employing her most distant and regal voice, she asked, "Is my father about, Mr. Brickell?"

Willie's pink cheeks went white. He turned to the tall, blond young man who had waved at Julia from the dock and whose gaze she had been studiously avoiding. He had actually kissed poor Alice on both her dry cheeks and Alice had, flirtatiously, said, "So you're still here, you lazy good-for-nothing."

"I was waiting for you, Miss Alice," the young man said, smiling.

"Go on," Alice said, laughing.

Julie had found this interchange extremely common, but Willie Brickell brought the young man forward. "The Duke knows about your father," Willie said, closing his mouth as if he might never open it again.

The Duke looked like an actor, Julia thought, in a play. He wore only trousers and a satin waistcoat. His exposed arms were muscular and tan. A thick line of glistening curly blond hair began at his chest, apparently ran down under the waistcoat, and appeared again at his exposed waist. One could actually see his belly button above his rope-belted trousers. Julia was shocked. Worse yet, he was barefoot. His feet, like his hands, were large and were lightly covered with blond hair. His head, with its closely cropped blond curls, wide-apart blue eyes, short patrician nose, and deeply dimpled chin, looked as if it belonged to a statue of Apollo.

The Duke had a startlingly deep and scratchy voice, as if he were chronically hoarse. Its educated tones were tainted—Julia decided—by the hint of a southern accent. He was scrupulously, almost annoyingly polite. She wondered if Ephraim had been talking about "Julia's grand ways" and if this Duke person was making fun of her.

"Mrs. Tuttle, ma'am," he said in that odd voice that made Julia want to put her hand to her own throat. "My name is J. W. Ewing." He made a half bow. "Your father has bade me accompany you and your children to his home on the north shore. First I will see to your belongings. Panthar will bring them along in his canoe." He waved to an extraordinarily tall Indian who had been standing behind the women of the community. His hair was so black it appeared blue, and his features seemed to have been chiseled out of bleached mahogany with a blunt instrument.

"Everyone calls him the Duke of Dade," Willie Brickell said as J. W. Ewing—the Duke—boarded the *Emily B.* to see to Julia's trunks.

"Why?" Julia asked, feeling somewhat disoriented. She glanced at Alice, surprised to see her growing increasingly red as her father explained the origin of J. W. Ewing's nickname.

"Three, maybe four years ago Alice was caught on the bay during a surprise squall. Her little boat capsized. She was just a few yards away from shore in water no deeper than her knees, but the wind was up and the rain was coming down pretty hard, and I guess Alice was confused and she started screaming. I said let her be, she'll come to herself in a minute, but Ewing went out after her, trying to pull her in. She fought him. Alice is a pretty good fighter at the best of times, but she's especially scrappy when

226

she's lost her nerve. Ewing had to give her a good one to the chin to knock her out. Then he had to *carry* her in—and Alice is no featherweight.

"We were all watching from the trading-post porch, and little Lucy Adams said, all gooey-like, 'Why, he's handsome and polite and chivalrous, he's just like a duke. And this being Dade County, and Ewing being such an educated gentleman . . . well, ever since he's been known as the Duke of Dade. And he is a duke despite the fact he spends all of his time over at the fort with that good-for-nothing, thieving—"

Alice gave her father a good sharp kick with the pointed toe of her brown boot, and he managed to stop himself as the Duke came off the *Emily B.* "We are ready, Mrs. Tuttle," he said, smiling. His two front teeth had a small space between them, which made him seem like the sort of bad boy everyone adores. Julia found it irritating that this Duke was so obviously, so thoroughly a happy person. Not a care in the world.

Julia said goodbye to the Brickells and rather primly gave Alice her hand. "I trust we shall see each other in the near future, Alice," she said, still regal for the onlookers.

"I lead a very busy life here, Julia," Alice returned, taking the parting shot, turning her back to Julia, opening her arms to Fanny. Fanny threw her thin, pale arms around Alice's neck fiercely, as if she were losing her only friend. She would have cried, but her mother gave her a look that meant it wouldn't have been worth the momentary solace.

Harry, who had been examining the Negro boy's harmonica, giving it an experimental toot, was first on the little boat. He carried his box with the scorpion in it and placed it on the bench between himself and his sister. Fanny, who did not like boats, and most especially small sailboats light enough to be rowed, sat as far from the box as possible.

The Duke sat with his back toward the prow, facing Julia, who was on the center bench, her children behind her. The Duke examined Julia with eyes of such an icy blue, they looked as if they had been frosted over. Julia couldn't remember the last time she had met someone who made her feel so uncomfortable. The Duke stuck out one muscular leg and casually pushed them away from the Brickell dock. The skiff moved a few yards and then abruptly stopped, becalmed.

He didn't say anything. He just sat still, smiling, not two feet away from her, so that Julia, feeling she had to make some conversation, said, "Not much wind today." At the same time she looked pointedly at the patched, makeshift sail without confidence.

"No." He turned his blue eyes up toward the sky, still grinning happily. "Not much help for it. I guess I have to assist *Bessie* along."

"*Bessie,* I gather," Julia said as disapprovingly as she could, "is the name of this boat?" What could her father have been thinking of, sending this man for her?

The Duke of Dade didn't answer. He simply indicated that they should switch places—not an easy moment for Julia—and began to row. In a moment the little boat—*Bessie*—was moving through the clear green waters at a good clip. Julia found herself watching as the Duke's tanned, muscled arms worked the oars with graceful, rhythmic movement. Already there were beads of sweat caught in the hair on his chest. Julia, who prided herself on poise, now was distinctly uncomfortable. This Mr. Ewing was more nude than any other man she had ever seen. During their increasingly rare moments of clinical lovemaking Frederick wore nightclothes and insisted on total darkness. Afterward, in his silk robe, he would silently adjourn to his bedroom, leaving Julia with her nightgown up around her breasts, a sticky feeling between her legs, and an awful sadness.

Suddenly the heavy salt air, the nearly nude man, and the fetid perfume of the coastal jungle seemed overwhelming. Julia felt the first stirrings of a megrim. "I am not," Julia said silently, taking herself in hand, "going to be ill." As was often the case when she felt insecure, Julia launched an attack. "Where are you from, Mr. Ewing?"

"Charleston, ma'am," he said politely.

"And do gentlemen dress as you do in Charleston, Mr. Ewing?"

"They do not, Mrs. Tuttle," he said, his hoarse voice filled with an amusement Julia didn't know whether to share or resent. "That is one of the reasons I have not returned to Charleston, ma'am." He was rowing the boat close to the shore, and Julia could see the fruit on the sea-grape trees and smell the strange flowers that grew among them.

"What are the other reasons, Mr. Ewing?" She turned and saw Harry looking at her with his angelic smile, and she smiled back. Fanny was sitting directly behind, so she couldn't see the determined look on her daughter's face that usually signaled rebellion or fear. Harry had begun to slowly slide open the drawer of the box in which he kept his scorpion.

The Duke, who had never met anyone quite so direct as Julia, looked at her upright chin and her forthright eyes and decided to be honest. "My family sent me here originally, just after the war, to recover from a love affair I was having with a woman whom they considered too old and too married." Julia stiffened, turning to her children, but they seemed, blessedly, for once not to be eavesdropping. "At the same time," the Duke went on, "my family—who invariably have a financial motive for their actions—wanted me to see what could be done with the South Florida land they had unwisely invested in years before. My uncles had formed something called the Biscayne Bay Trading Company, and they had elaborate plans for first draining and then developing the territory. When your father bought the adjoining land and Mr. Brickell opened up his trading post and reactivated the post office, my uncles got all excited."

"As well they should, Mr. Ewing. Even I can see the potential for the bay area, and I've only been here an hour."

The Duke looked up at her speculatively. "Perhaps when you've been here a day, Mrs. Tuttle, you'll see that it would take a great deal more money than my uncles have to develop this land. And perhaps when you've been here a week, Mrs. Tuttle, you'll see that the land is better left as it is, no matter how much money one has." For once he wasn't smiling, and Julia took a certain pleasure in that.

They had just reached the place where the Miami River emptied into the bay when the sun disappeared and the waters became gray and choppy, little whitecaps, like dollops of whipped cream, beginning to appear. "Summer squall," the Duke said, pointing to the south. He put up his oars and turned his attention to the sail, which had filled out and had begun to carry the boat along. "But we'll beat it. The wind is with us."

Julia could see a long, low stone building up on the bluff overlooking both the river and the bay. "Does everything happen so quickly in this part of the world, Mr. Ewing?"

"Only weather, ma'am."

Julia heard a little scream from Fanny but ignored it, putting it down to the increased swaying of the boat, the lowering skies. She looked up into the mouth of the Miami River and saw that the jungle grew thicker as it made its way west, inland. A crocodile was lying on each bank, the two appearing like ancient guardians of the gateway to a secret land. "I should very much like to explore that river," Julia said. She could see her father waiting at the edge of a makeshift dock, looking anxious, calling her name.

"I will help you explore it, Mrs. Tuttle," the Duke said evenly. "Providing you promise not to help us develop it."

"You are against progress, Mr. Ewing," said Julia as he threw a line to her father. She stood up, like a statue of progress rising from the bay, and not waiting for a reply, gave her father her hand. "Papa dear, I'm so glad to see you."

"I am against progress, Mrs. Tuttle," the Duke said to himself, jumping onto the dock, making the line fast. Julia heard but was embraced by her father before she was able to reply; she was enjoying the conversation.

Suddenly Fanny let out an ear-splitting scream and fell backward, catching Harry's withered arm to keep herself from falling into the bay. The Duke jumped into the boat and lifted Fanny out, laying her on the dock. She looked up and met her mother's eyes. "I was trying to be like Great-grandma Emily," Fanny said before she fainted.

Harry, not having gotten the fully desired response from his sister, had opened the box and had been pushing it so close to Fanny that it touched her thighs through the white sailor dress. The scorpion, dead black, with a horned head and a spear-shaped tail, was looking up at her as if it knew her. Fanny, controlling her hysteria, summoning up all her courage, trying to be the brave girl her mother wanted her to be, had finally raised her fist over her head and brought it down with all her six-year-old might on the scorpion. She had crushed it to death but not before it had stung her, injecting its venomous poison.

But Great-grandma Emily didn't get bitten, Julia thought, frightened yet touched by Fanny's bravery. She followed the Duke carrying the unconscious Fanny up to the old stone fort, an abashed Harry holding onto her hand. She knew that if Fanny were seriously hurt, it would be her fault.

"People don't die from a scorpion's sting, do they?" she asked Ephraim, whose normally jolly face had taken on a distinctly perturbed expression. He was worried about his granddaughter, but he was also wondering if he had made a mistake by insisting that Julia and her children should visit his paradise. Already it seemed disturbed and distorted.

"Do they?" Julia repeated a little hysterically, correctly interpreting her father's silence.

"I am afraid they do, my dear," he said. "Especially children."

"We must call the doctor."

"There is no doctor, Julia." He looked into her stricken face as raindrops as thick and round as pearls began to fall, and he took pity. "Duke knows more than any doctor. He'll pull her through, Julia. You mustn't worry."

The rain, cooling while it fell, left the air much steamier when it stopped. Julia sat in the long, low-ceilinged room that had once been an officers' mess and was now what her father called his lounge, watching the door of the room Fanny had been put in. The Duke had discarded his waistcoat. She could see him in the light from the kerosene lamp, working over Fanny, his torso covered with sweat. Occasionally he came to the door with hoarsely whispered requests for hot water and towels and more whiskey, which Ephraim's little housekeeper, Minnie McCord, ran to get for him. He was attempting to force Fanny to sweat out the poison.

Julia had been in the sickroom for a time, but she had felt she was in the way and joined her father in the sparsely furnished stone-floored lounge. Soldiers had once lived in the buildings, afraid of Indian attacks, bored with the heat and the malarial mosquitoes. It wasn't a happy place to make a home, and she fancied she could feel the soldiers' resentment.

Harry had been sent to bed, all the more frightened for not having been punished. Father and daughter sat silently, looking out at the bay until the dark erased it.

At midnight the Duke came into the lounge and put on his waistcoat. He looked at Julia with those wide-apart eyes. "She broke fever," Minnie McCord said, standing behind him like a magician's apprentice. "The Duke broke her fever. Praise the Lord."

Julia stood up and found her legs were unstable. She hadn't realized how tense she had been, how tightly she had been holding herself for the last half dozen hours, waiting. "Then she is going to be well?" she managed to ask. Her voice, pleading, conciliatory, didn't sound like her own.

"She's going to be a very sick girl for the next week or two, ma'am," the Duke said. "But she's going to be a live one. He smiled his gap-toothed smile and looked young again.

Julia felt weak with relief. "How can I thank you, Mr. Ewing?"

230

"You can stop calling me Mr. Ewing, ma'am. Now I'm going to take a swim in the bay, and then I'm going to sleep for twelve hours." He rubbed his eyes and shook his head. "I think I got drunk from smelling all that whiskey. You'd better order some alcohol from Key West, Ephraim. Whiskey's a pretty expensive way of curing scorpion bite."

"Isn't it dangerous?" Julia asked her father after the Duke had left, "swimming in the dark at night?" She was thinking of the crocodiles guarding the Miami River.

"The Duke doesn't think so."

Julia looked in at Fanny, who had the pallor of a new corpse but seemed to be breathing regularly and even dreaming. There was a little smile on her lips, the top one too thin, the bottom too full, just like Frederick's. Julia was a woman who rarely touched other people and kissed her children only on those special occasions—before long separations, on birthday mornings—that demanded it. In fact, she never actually kissed Harry and Fanny but just turned her cheek to be kissed. Now she leaned over and pressed her lips against Fanny's damp brow.

Julia returned to the lounge and sat across from her father on an uncomfortable woven reed sofa and closed her eyes. "I feel as if every bone in my body has just melted," she said. Then she had a new thought: "What a terrible way to descend upon you, Father."

Ephraim looked at Julia, who seemed for the moment very young. Difficult to believe she was the mother of those two—Lord forgive him—unattractive children. He remembered her as a child herself, dressing up in Flora's gowns, playing a queen or Florence Nightingale. Julia putting on airs. He reached over and patted her hand, realizing that there were tears in her eyes. Ephraim couldn't remember the last time he had seen Julia cry. She had been dry-eyed at her mother's funeral, nearly nine years before, when Ephraim felt he was drowning in his own tears. The thought of good, kind little Minnie McCord waiting for him in the kitchen house bedroom triggered a memory of good, kind, matter-of-fact Flora Mae. Lord, he thought, I still miss her.

"I should never have brought Fanny," Julia said, breaking in on his reverie. "Fanny likes pretty houses and hothouse flowers, beautifully starched frocks, pretty coats. On the most beautiful day in the spring she and Frederick would be up in his studio, painting asters on bits of porcelain. The garden at Gaydene was full of *live* asters."

Ephraim, who at fifty could spend days without sleep tramping through the Everglades, was more tired than he could remember ever being. He had done the wrong thing, he thought. Fanny was not the only one who liked her own way. Julia did as well. What's more, Julia liked to meddle and change things about, and all he wanted was to have things stay the same. Her marriage to that sickly and barely male member of the human race had gone sour, that was clear. He'd been so happy a few hours ago, anticipating Julia's visit. Now Ephraim felt somewhat less than happy.

"Julia," he said aloud, deciding it best to get this conversation over with while Julia was remorseful over Fanny and thus vulnerable, "you're not happy with Frederick. I could read between the lines of your letters, and it's even more evident now that I see you in person. You—"

"Papa—"

"No. Let me finish. I won't say this again. You married Frederick because he was rich and well connected and presumably because you loved him. You were only seventeen, and I said at the time you were too young. Perhaps I was wrong not to have said it louder. You are still too young to be trapped in a life that causes you unhappiness. You are, to my prejudiced eyes, beautiful. You have two fine children—"

"Father, Harry has a withered arm," she said, like a child about a favorite, broken doll.

"Julia, your life is what I'm concerned about. I offer you paradise. You do not *have* to return to Cleveland, to Gaydene. Biscayne Bay is the most exciting place in the world. Have you ever seen a more beautiful place? Each day I live here I am humbled by a new discovery, the extraordinary sense of life I have found here. Others are discovering it too—all over Florida. Men are making fortunes in Key West, Tampa, St. Augustine. Orange groves and railroads and cotton farms—"

"Are men making fortunes on Biscayne Bay?" Julia asked, her eyes now quite dry.

"Funny thing, Julia, when we first got here, Willie Brickell and I were going to develop Biscayne Bay, make it the winter convalescent and resort center of the East. Oh, we had all sorts of ideas. Drain this, drain that. Willie got Panthar and some of his Seminole pals to put up his house in four days and his trading post in three. Then he got them to come in from their camps at the edge of the Glades and bring him alligator, deer, and otter skins, egret plumes, skunk cabbage (which you call hearts of palm), and the Florida arrowroot they make from the coontie root.

"Willie started shipping the stuff down to Key West, selling it, and before he knew it, he was back in the wholesale grocery business he'd left in Cleveland. He's not making a fortune, but he's making a good living, and he's not developing his land. Willie Brickell and I don't see eye to eye on a lot of things," Ephraim said wistfully, regretting his lost friendship, "but we do agree on one thing. Biscayne Bay is going to stay the way it is."

"But it *could* be developed?" Julia persisted, her weariness gone, suddenly energized.

"If one had all the gumption in the world backed up by a hundred thousand dollars."

A door closed somewhere in one of the stone outbuildings, startling Julia. "What was that?"

"The Duke, I reckon, going to sleep. Which is what I aim to do." Ephraim stood up, happy to make an end of this conversation and the long day. "You don't have to decide what you're going to do just yet, Julia. I only want you to

232

know I love you—you're my daughter—and if you want to make your home here with me, you and your kids are welcome. It's a good place to live if you don't mind living on possum, skunk cabbage, and fish."

Julia gave her father her cheek to kiss good night. "I thought the Duke was taking his swim and going home."

"This is his home," Ephraim said, yawning, moving toward the little room on the far side of the kitchen house. "His family told him that he'd better come back to Charleston, that they wouldn't send any more money. But he wanted to stay, so I made the former stables over into a little house and invited him to live here. The Duke is the best man I ever met. Closest to a son I'll have ever. Thinks just like I do. 'Night, Julia."

"Good night, Father." She went to her bedroom and stood at the windows overlooking the bay, staring out, trying to see through the thick darkness. Well, I've got gumption, she thought to herself, giving up, moving off to bed. And someone, somewhere must have a hundred thousand dollars.

She was never going back to Cleveland, Julia decided in that moment. Frederick could paint porcelains and let his ironworks run itself into the ground. She was going to make her life in the bay area. She wasn't going to live on possum, skunk cabbage, and fish either—not for long, at any rate. "I," Julia said to herself, testing the bed and finding it wanting, "have a vision."

CHAPTER THREE

"SHE SAYS if she eats another coontie biscuit, she's going to vomit." Julia, bored, had sought and found little Minnie McCord in the narrow, detached stone kitchen built around a huge brick fireplace, which stood at the rear of the fort.

"That means she's nearly well," Minnie, busy with a pot of something suspect, said. "Gal's got her appetite back."

The two women had established a truce during the nursing of Fanny. Julia had started out by speaking to Minnie as if she were a slave girl. Minnie, in her own sassy, Cracker way, had given as good as she got. Now there was an uneasy alliance. "What else could we feed her?" Julia asked.

233

"Possum," Minnie said, indicating the pot on the wood stove, confirming Julia's new olfactory prowess. "I'm fixin' up a nice mess of possum and—"

"I don't think Fanny is going to want possum, Minnie. Not again."

"Turtle, then," the little woman said. "I got a nice turtle steak from that Injun of your daddy's—"

"Panthar is not my father's Indian, Minnie. Panthar would seem to be nobody's Indian but his own."

"Don't you believe it, girl. Panthar does anything your daddy tells him and he does it quick. For an Injun."

The fever was finally gone for good, but for days Julia had been confined to Fanny's sickroom without much to do but look out the window. Florence Nightingale, she thought, at least had romantic wounded soldiers to care for. They couldn't have complained as much as Fanny. For once the center of attention, Fanny, from under her mosquito netting, was wringing every ounce of satisfaction she could get from her illness.

The days were long and lonely for Julia at Fort Dallas. She felt deserted. In the mornings she would watch as Panthar came canoeing down the Miami River, so at one with his boat, he seemed to Julia like some new mythical being; half man, half dugout. He came to take Ephraim fishing and swamping in the secret places in the Everglades known only to his tribe. "He runs a risk," the Duke said one night at dinner, "taking us into the great swamp. If his shaman knew he brought white men there, Panthar would be punished."

"What would they do to him?" Julia asked sarcastically, annoyed at all this talk that excluded her. "Five lashes with a wet egg noodle?" When she asked what swamping entailed, Ephraim told her unedifyingly, "mucking through the swamp." Sometimes the Duke went with them, but more often he went off on his own with an easel and a box of paints.

Harry had begun to desert her as well. Barefoot, pink from the sun, he had started going off with Minnie's nephews—Jeff and Freddy—in their skiff, "wrecking." Occasional bits and pieces of ships wrecked along the coast washed up on the beach, and these could be sold to Brickell. Last fall, an excited Harry told his mother, Jeff McCord got ten dollars for a barrelful of intact china dishes he'd found over on the mangrove-covered island to the north. Jeff and Freddy, several years older than Harry, unschooled, were not ideal companions for him. But it was either they or no one, and Ephraim thought it good for Harry to know "real" boys, so Julia gave way.

Early in the second week of Fanny's recovery, Panthar returned from the south shore with a note from Miss Alice saying she was sorry about Fanny's accident and would have visited but she was "busy straightening up the various messes" created by her absence. Julia had the feeling that Willie Brickell, carrying on his war against Ephraim, had at least as much to do with Alice's absence as the "various messes." Alice's note was accompanied by a huge tin of coontie biscuits.

Julia sniffed unappreciatively. "Don't go putting your nose up at coontie, girl," Minnie McCord reprimanded her. "Willie Brickell buys the coontie

234

flour from the Injuns and poor white folk. He doesn't give the Injuns money, just sugar, alarm clocks, and those worthless beads their squaws like to deck themselves out in. It ain't no fun to make coontie, I can tell you. I done it myself when times were hard, before your daddy took me on as house-keeper. Them roots are ugly smelling, and it takes days to pound them down into the flour. But it's the stickum that holds the bay area together. Them biscuits like as not cured your little gal."

Julie found that she liked this little plain-speaking woman despite herself. Nonetheless, after seven monotonous days she was becoming bored with Minnie's folk wisdom, with the tales of her husband's hard life and death, with her relentless energy, with being addressed as "girl." Had Julia known of her father's nocturnal visits to Minnie McCord's bedroom, she would have left his home. But Ephraim and Minnie both possessed a natural discretion.

On the last day of her second week in the bay area, when Fanny said she might sit out on the veranda for an hour, Julia intercepted her father on his way to Panthar's waiting canoe. "I want to visit Miss Alice, Father. This morning. How do I do that?"

Ephraim, seeing Julia grow increasingly testy over their nightly fish dinners, decided to accommodate her. "I'll have Panthar canoe you over."

"Very kind, Papa. How will I return?" Julia knew her father was capable of forgetting to get her back.

"Panthar will come for you at midday."

"Make it late afternoon," she said decisively. "I'm going to get Alice to give me lunch."

"What should I feed Miss Fanny?" Minnie wanted to know, that question still undecided when Julia, hatted and gloved, prepared to walk down the steep stone steps to the dock, where Panthar was waiting.

"Turtle," Julia said without interest.

"She says she hates turtle."

"Tell her it's chicken."

Julia waved Panthar's outstretched hand away and got herself and her wide brown skirts into the narrow dugout, settling against a pillow she had brought from the fort. It was another perfect day. Blue, cloudless sky. Turquoise water. It was hot but no hotter than summertime in Cleveland, and the bay breeze was refreshing.

There was, however, a distinct smell in the canoe. Panthar dressed his hair, the Duke had informed her, with bear grease. Julia thought that sometime in the near future she would get Panthar to stop using bear grease. She studied him, wondering if she might even suggest it now. He's an extraordinary-looking person, Julia thought. The Noble Savage. He knelt in front of her, his paddle so smoothly working the waters, it seemed a natural part of him, like another appendage.

"Someday, Panthar," Julia said to the back of his blue-black head, deciding to leave the bear grease for the moment and begin his education with larger matters, "all this land will be taken up by a great white city." She waited for an answer, and when one didn't come, asked, "Doesn't that excite you, Panthar?"

"I do not like white cities, Miss Julia." He had a low, musical voice. "I do not like white men, Miss Julia."

Julia, surprised, began to object. "But my father and the Duke . . ."

"They have the souls of red men. White men have taken my land and my heritage. They have killed and tortured my people, forcing us to live in the swamps of the great forest. In the end they will take the swamps as well. White men are cowards, afraid of all that was before them. They slay the children of the Great Spirit—his people, his animals, his land—and then build their houses on sacred bones."

"But, Panthar, we cannot leave the land to the animals. Then *we* would be savages." Julia's voice rang out across the bay, resonant with the sure strength of a truth she knew to be inalienable. "The jungle has to be cleared, the alligators removed, houses and hospitals and schools built. People must have proper clothing and medicine and education. That is the future. You cannot fly in the face of progress, Panthar."

Panthar was silent for so long she thought he might be angry. Quite suddenly he brought the canoe to a halt at the mouth of the Miami and pointed with his forefinger to a huge pyramid of earth and shells on the north bank. "Before the Seminoles," he said, "other Indians lived in this place. When their spirits were called to the World Above the Sky, their bones were placed in the sacred burial mound. The burial mound is the past, Miss Julia. And the future. In time all our bones will be buried in the earth. All our spirits will fly to the World Above the Sky."

"That pyramid is an old, dead monument, Panthar. We must now create new monuments. Living monuments. Great cities in which we will have happier, more productive lives."

"You are a strong white woman," Panthar said admiringly, beginning to paddle again. "You have many words. You believe them all. If you were a red woman in my tribe, you would be queen."

"And if I were your queen, Panthar, I would lead you to my city."

"We would not follow, Miss Julia," the Seminole said, shaking his head. "Red man's home is the forest."

"You and your people must come out of the forest and join the march toward civilization." But Panthar did not answer, and Julia let the conversation lapse. The absurd idea of being a queen in an Indian tribe kept her busy until Panthar pulled up at the Brickell dock. This time Julia allowed him to help her, ignoring the bear-grease odor, taking his arm, and stepping up on the dock with a sense of adventure. Not many women in Cleveland had a six-foot-four Seminole for a chauffeur. Panthar made a half bow and was gone, leaving Julia alone on the Brickell dock, suddenly deflated, beset by misgivings.

Everyone seemed to have a niche in the bay life but her. Even Fanny, sitting under a mosquito net Ephraim had rigged up for her on the veranda, reading her books and chatting away with Minnie McCord, appeared to belong. The bay's Young Invalid. Julia felt unnecessary. She looked at the odd blue birds perched on their long yellow legs ignoring her from the shore and thought what a strange, even eerie place it was. Except for the dock, it was as if man had never stepped foot here.

She felt like an unwelcome intruder. Again a feeling of uselessness swept over her. She had been useful, for those long days, as Fanny's nurse. Just as she had been when for three years she had taken Harry from Philadelphia to Boston to New York, from doctor to clinic to hospital, vowing to cure his polio.

She had counted on Alice to introduce her to bay life, but Alice here was a great deal less tractable and available than Alice in Cleveland. She had a hectic, demanding life, it seemed. She was a respected bay woman. Perhaps Alice didn't want to have a long visit. Alice could be ungracious. The thought of her isolation, of how remote she was from everything she knew, nearly made her miss Frederick. It nearly made Julia cry.

I will not feel sorry for myself, Julia resolved, clenching her gloved fist. I never have before and I won't now. With that thought in mind, she marched herself to the end of the dock, past the low trading post, to the house Willie Brickell had had the Seminoles build.

It was a large two-story wooden cottage with a porch the width of the house fronting the bay. Already weathered a dark gray-brown, it looked as if it had occupied this spot for fifty years. Alice sat on the porch in a green-painted reed rocker, fanning herself, emanating the scent of vanilla.

"Really, Alice," Julia said, irritated, stepping up onto the shaded porch, taking the rocker next to her friend, and removing her straw hat, which had been giving her a headache. "I thought you were so busy straightening out—"

"Friday, Julia, is my day of rest, and I don't remember the contract I signed with you saying otherwise." Alice threw Julia a triumphant look, but her expression softened when she saw her friend's discomfiture. "Are you staying for lunch?"

"Yes," Julia admitted. Alice went away for a few minutes to tell whichever of her sisters was cook for the day that they were having a guest, Mrs. Tuttle. Relieved, Julia realized she and Alice were the sort of friends who could be reunited after a hundred years and take up exactly where they'd left off. Alice returned to find Julia fanning herself with her paper fan.

"How is Fanny?" she asked, taking the fan back. Julia could give herself all the airs she wanted but not on Alice's home ground.

"Complaining bitterly, which means she's fine," Julia said as if it were Alice's fault. "She jumps every time she sees a lizard, and her arms and legs are masses of red bumps from the mosquitoes."

"You should get Minnie McCord to keep a black snake in the lounge, Julia. They love mosquitoes, especially those large, juicy ones."

Julia laughed dryly. "Can you imagine Fanny and a snake in the same house?"

"You needn't tell her." Alice looked at her old friend and softened again. Julia had that pinched-mouth unhappy look Alice knew too well. "Come," Alice said, rising, "I've just made some lemonade and coontie cookies—"

"Anything but coontie cookies!"

"—and I'll give you a tour of the house and then we'll have lunch—turtle steak—and you can tell me all the things we're doing wrong and be as grand and as irritable as you like with the girls. You'll have the time of your life."

"You're too good to me, Alice," Julia said, only a little sarcastic. Then she made a rare gesture. She touched her friend's arm. There was some comfort, Julia decided, to be found in the familiar.

Julia, with nothing much else to do, took to visiting Alice nearly every day. Alice's work suffered, but now that she had Julia she found that the one element missing in her life had been a contemporary, a peer to talk to.

"Tell me about Mr. Ewing," Julia said two weeks later. She was wearing a new white summer dress that Minnie McCord had helped her sew. It was of such a thin material, yet required so few undergarments, that it made Julia feel oddly free and happy. "Each time I bring up his name you go off on some tangent. Why don't you want to talk about him? Are you secretly in love with the Duke of Dade, Alice?" She had the pleasure of seeing Alice turn pink. "Maybe if you had blushed more, you wouldn't have been so unpopular at Miss VailDeane's."

"If I was not popular at Miss VailDeane's, Julia, it was because you were my best friend. Anyway, I wasn't *un*popular. I was captain of the croquet team."

"You were athletic, Alice. Not beloved. But I want to hear about this great pash of yours, the Duke of Dade. The other night at supper he mentioned Boston," Julia said, to get Alice started. Both immune to mosquitoes, they usually sat on the open porch. But today was such a fine late-June day, they walked along the sandy bay front, Alice identifying the low-lying scrub plants and the white and blue birds. They were waiting for Panthar to come for Julia. "Father has said that Mr. Ewing has been in Paris."

"He's been everywhere. He grew up in Charleston and comes from a fine family. He went to school in New Haven," Alice said proudly.

"Yale?" Julia was incredulous.

"He didn't finish."

Julia laughed. "He doesn't seem to finish much."

"He was bored, Julia. He took the tuition money and traveled. He lived in Paris for a time."

"Hence those peculiar paintings."

238

"I'm not going to say another word about him, Julia, if you—"

"My lips are sealed," Julia said impatiently. "Go on, Alice."

"When his father died, he returned to Charleston—"

"—where he fell in love with an older woman, and his family sent him to the bay area to see if they had thrown good money away, and he stayed on because he thinks he's found paradise, and he doesn't want paradise lost."

"Julia, if you know all this, why . . ."

"Because I wanted to know if you knew anything I didn't, and you don't. We should start a library, Alice," Julia said abruptly, leading the way to the land behind the Brickell house, which she hadn't as yet seen.

"Julia, there are only half a dozen of us who can read."

"Then we must begin a school." Julia stopped for a moment to pick a painful nettle from her stocking.

"And a sewing circle and a ladies' club, I suppose."

"Well, why not?"

"You are not in Cleveland, Julia, though Fanny wishes she were." Alice sighed and folded her hands in front of her, indicating exasperation. "The bay women have a thousand things to do each day and they don't include reading and socializing, even if they had a mind to read and socialize. You always want to change nature, Julia. You grew orchids in Cleveland. You'll attempt roses here."

"What's this?" Julia asked, coming to a stop at a small fenced-off piece of land where beans and an odd purple plant were growing.

"My vegetable garden. I get sixteen dollars a barrel for eggplant and seven dollars and fifty cents a crate for beans," Alice said, fixing a stake that had been blown over.

"Why, that's wonderful, Alice. Wonderful." Julia leaned over the fence and touched an eggplant as if it were an icon.

"It's not exactly a religious experience, Julia."

"It proves," Julia said, standing erect, her chin going up, her entire being beaming, "that civilized fruits and vegetables can be grown in this soil. Alice, can't you see? Your garden is proof positive that, with culture and nurture, the light of civilization can flower in the midst of the darkest jungle."

"It's only a kitchen garden, Julia."

"You're blind, Alice. It's much more than that. It's a symbol of man's victory over base nature." Julia led the way back to the dock, hurrying. She couldn't wait to return to Fort Dallas, to start planting a garden. "Where on earth could Panthar be?" *Bessie*, the Duke's disreputable skiff, was tied to the dock, and the Duke himself emerged from the trading post.

"Panthar has had to return to his village," the Duke said, joining Alice and Julia, throwing his purchase—a length of rope—into the skiff. "So your father sent me to get you."

"Odd to think of Panthar with a village," Julia said after she had bade

Alice a hurried goodbye and the skiff was under way. She was a woman who didn't like change unless she initiated it, and she had become accustomed to Panthar's canoeing her home. Besides, she wanted to talk to Panthar about her garden.

"He has a village and a tribe and two squaws and a dozen children. What did you think?" There was just enough wind to propel the skiff without Duke's rowing. He stretched out across the seat, his hands behind his head, his bare feet crossed in front of him.

"I thought he was somehow attached to the fort," Julia said.

"Like the piano?"

"You always twist my words, Mr. Ewing."

He laughed, revealing the gap between his square white teeth. "I'm sorry, Mrs. Tuttle. I'm afraid I enjoy teasing you. You're so unlike any woman I have ever known."

"In what way, Mr. Ewing?"

"You're so very handsome and so very serious. The two usually don't go together."

Julia's chin went up. "And you're unlike any man I have ever known, Mr. Ewing." It was true. Frederick, who seemed like someone she had known in a very distant past, was old and dry behind his beautiful face. The Duke was alive with youth and intelligence. Not that she would tell him that. She wouldn't even think that.

"In what way, Mrs. Tuttle?" he asked, amused, as if reading her mind.

Julia straightened her back. "You have had so many advantages, Mr. Ewing. Family. Education. Travel. It is very sad to see you throwing them all away, living an idle life devoted only to pleasure. What, Mr. Ewing, do you intend to be when you grow up?"

"Oh, dear," he said, grimacing. "You are determined to be serious."

Julia ignored the grimace. "You have such a golden opportunity, Mr. Ewing. Florida, this bay area, is spilling over with opportunities. Why, you could transform the wilderness your family owns into a prosperous city. That tangled mass of jungle vine and brush could be block upon block of lovely homes with modern improvements, surrounded by shade trees. You could build a city with—"

"—factories and machines and filthy streets." He sat up and looked at her with his frosty blue eyes, and Julia felt just a little afraid. "Look around you, Mrs. Tuttle. Do you really wish to replace this natural beauty with the worst sort of manufactured ugliness? Don't be like my uncles. They want to turn the Garden of Eden into a neat little metropolis, with booster clubs on every corner and flower gardens behind every house. Would you actually want poodles instead of panthers, goldfish in place of crocodiles? Why not leave all that in Cleveland and allow us to stay as we are?"

"Mr. Ewing," Julia began, not quite knowing how to proceed. She had never seen the Duke anything less than good-natured, and now he was being quite passionate. But she was spared the necessity of finding words. The skies, blue a moment before, suddenly opened, as they did almost every summer afternoon, and the thick raindrops of another summer squall began to fall. They were both drenched in the few moments it took the Duke to maneuver the skiff into a little cove protected by huge mangrove trees.

A lightning bolt, the jagged sort, streaked across the sky, and the boom of its thunder followed. Julia's white summer dress felt pasted to her skin. Her hair had come down in the deluge and was hanging around her face. She was startled by the lightning but stimulated all the same. The Duke, with his hair flattened against his sculptured head, his waistcoat opened, his skin as wet as if he had been swimming in the bay, seemed more than ever to be a statue come to life.

"I'm frightened," Julia said, surprising herself and not at all certain what she was frightened of.

"No you're not," the Duke said, staring at her so intensely she nearly looked away. But she didn't. She returned his stare, having no idea how strong and proud and beautiful she looked in that moment. "You're not the sort of woman who can be frightened of anything." He moved toward her and took her in his blond arms, pressing his lips against hers. For one moment, as their wet bodies touched, she felt immersed in him, intoxicated by his clean, warm smell. For that moment, as the jagged lightning streaked in the nearly black sky, as his mouth pressed against hers, nothing else existed for Julia.

And then, as he began to caress her breasts, she felt the sun on her closed eyes and, furious, pushed him away from her. The squall, as mercurial as most Florida summer storms, had moved off. The sky was blue again and the waters turquoise. Only the water draining down the mangrove roots into the bay was proof that there had been a shower. Julia looked at a thick, curved mangrove root turning against itself into the water and thought she had never seen anything so ugly.

"Julia—" the Duke said in that voice now even more hoarse, but she stopped him as she attempted to pin up her sopping hair, to pull the thin material of her dress away from her body.

"Mr. Ewing, I would very much appreciate it if you would take me home. Now that the danger is over."

"Julia—"

"Mr. Ewing," she heard herself shouting. She put her hand to her brow. "Mr. Ewing," she said in a calmer voice, "I should deem it a great favor if we were never to discuss this incident again." Julia felt the relentless pounding of a megrim beginning as the Duke silently sailed her back to the fort.

CHAPTER FOUR

JULIA STOOD on the stone veranda Ephraim had added to Fort Dallas, leaning on the balustrade, watching as the Miami River idly emptied itself into Biscayne Bay. Again she was bored. It had been a long, hot, uneventful August day. Ephraim had gone off with Panthar just before dawn to some unknown and presumably sacred fishing spot deep in the Everglades.

Harry, as bored as Julia, had spent the day at the fort. His salvage buddies—Jeff and Fred—had deserted him, accompanying their Aunt Minnie to the trading post. It was a big day at Brickell's. The *Emily B.* had arrived from Key West with the first mail the bay community had seen in over a month. Harry had desperately wanted to go, but Ephraim had, as he said, "put his foot down."

"Why not, Grandfather?" Harry asked, cupping the elbow of his withered arm. This, Harry had learned, usually got him what he wanted. "Mama's always at Brickell's—"

"She has a friend there. You and I do not." The bay area's very own civil war—Ephraim on the north, Willie on the south—hadn't abated during the course of the summer. Harry was not to go to the trading post.

Fanny, a pale bird in her mosquito net cage, had been taught to crochet by Minnie McCord. She had spent the day finishing a sweater she hoped to wear in Cleveland. "When *are* we going home, Mama?" she asked over the cold lunch Minnie had left for them.

"I don't know, Fanny. Do stop pestering me." Julia herself longed to be at Brickell's. Alice had said "everyone" would be there. And though Julia did not approve of Miss Alice's "everyone," she didn't like missing an opportunity to witness their fatal flaws firsthand. She had remained at home because she knew her father didn't want the bay settlers to think Ephraim Sturtevant's daughter was on cordial terms with Willie Brickell. It was all right to visit Alice on ordinary days, but to appear at the trading post on such a public occasion would be construed by the bay gossips as a traitorous act.

The Duke had said, the night before, that he might take Julia and Harry

242

sailing, but she had seen him walking off early in the morning in the direction of the burial mound with a picnic basket, his easel, and his paints. "He forgot about us," Julia told Harry, who worshiped the Duke. She looked closely at her son, who had never appeared healthier. Together they walked down the rear steps to the garden she and Panthar had planted. Panthar had cleared the land and done the actual planting. Julia had directed from under a parasol.

The trouble was that everyone loved the Duke. Since that day on the boat, which Julia tried not to think about, their relations had been strained. For a time they saw each other only at dinner. Inevitably Julia would begin talking about progress, and the Duke couldn't help teasing her, so soon they were on good terms again. But the Duke made certain they were never again alone in the skiff—or anywhere else, for that matter. Julia found herself regretting that lost intimacy and, despite her intentions, often thought of the moment in the skiff, the Duke's lips pressing against hers, his hands touching her breasts through the thin, wet material of her dress. . . .

"Can you imagine, Harry," she said now to her son, pointing to a cluster of baby eggplants, "how rich this place is? Look about you. If everyone had a garden, the bay area could be self-sustaining. What we need are cows for milk and chickens for eggs. What we need is someone with vision and money, and we could have a city as big as Cleveland, white and pure, a symbol of progress . . ."

Harry had stopped listening as soon as Julia had said, "Can you imagine." Mama back on the old progress horse again. He poked at a long black snake with his big toe, wondering if he could get it into a box and smuggle it into the house. Better not, he decided, remembering the catastrophic scorpion incident.

The black snake coiled and then shot out between his feet, tickling his toes, losing itself in the thick weed grass. Harry wished the Duke would come and take him, alone, sailing, as he had done on two memorable occasions in the past, even though the Duke had made him throw back the two small fish he had managed to catch. He wished Jeff and Freddy would come back from the trading post. He wished his mama would leave him alone.

Julia saw the glaze of boredom in Harry's eyes, and leaving him to pursue his black snake, she made a sudden decision. She would walk down to the Indian mound and see what the Duke was painting. He had never once offered to show her a sample of his work. This would be a perfect opportunity to see it in progress. She might offer a critique with a fresh eye. I will help him, Julia thought, refusing to acknowledge that this would be the first time she would be alone with him since he had kissed her.

It was a twenty-minute walk on the path someone—the Duke or her father—had cut through the hammock. The herons, which made their nests in the trees, caused an awful racket. Julia wore the thin white dress. Its hem caught on a detested mangrove root, but the material, she was happy to see, didn't tear. She thought of the first day she had worn the dress and of how nearly transparent it had become in the rain. She didn't want to think of the Duke's lips, but somehow a vision of his torso, wet and golden, forced its way into her mind. She was suddenly aware of her own body. Her breasts felt firm and her legs uncertain.

To distract herself she looked up at the sky. The long summer days were growing shorter. The sun was behind the clouds now, making them look picture-book pink against the dark-blue sky. She emerged from the mangroves and saw that the bay had become as still as a lake, its waters reflecting the sky and the pink clouds as truly as a mirror. The Indian mound, old and dry and brown, seemed a natural phenomenon. It was difficult to imagine men creating it.

There was no sign of the Duke, but the sharp smell of oil paints cut through the sweet, salty air. Julia walked around the mound. The easel had been set up so it faced north in front of a row of royal palms Emmanuel Acosta, a deserter from the Spanish navy, had planted nearly thirty years before. Without hesitation Julia examined the painting on the easel. It was a portrait of the palms, the bay sketched in behind them.

Julia found it irritating. "Why, these aren't the right colors at all. They're not even the right shape," she said aloud.

"They're the colors and the shapes I see."

She didn't turn around, her artistic outrage keeping her stunned eyes on the canvas. "You've made the royal palms crooked. They're not. They're upright and regal, far above the corruption of the jungle. They're like the city I am planning. Beyond reproach. You have made them sinister, nearly. . ." Finally she turned in the direction of the Duke's voice and stopped. The Duke had propped himself up in one of the shallow indentations of the burial mound. He was nude.

"I didn't expect company," he said, smiling up at her apologetically, the gap between his small square teeth making him seem like a young boy. "I've just come from swimming."

Julia resolutely turned her back to him and stared at the bay. She refused to be scared away. "I am, after all," she told herself, "an adult and a married woman." But she had seen the drops of bay water that had been caught in the blond hairs that usually disappeared under his trousers. She had seen the Duke's manhood. Despite her resolve Julia felt faint and shocked. But she wouldn't retreat. She busied herself studying the odd painting, assuming the Duke was getting into his trousers.

A sudden breeze stirred the herons; the reflection of the pink clouds shimmered in the turquoise water. "It is on this spot," Julia said in a firm and nearly normal voice, "that I see my city." She did not hear any sounds indicating the Duke was getting himself dressed.

"You knew I was here, didn't you? This isn't a casual meeting."

Julia ignored him. "My city will be unlike any other. Shining and white,

244

without the curse of liquor"—she had seen an empty wine bottle among the remains of the Duke's picnic—"gambling or moneylenders."

"You paint such a passionless picture, Julia." She felt his hand encircle her ankle like a leg cuff being affixed to a convict. Her knees, with a will of their own, went weak.

"It will be a city that will abolish disease, ignorance, and want."

"You suffer from a terrible disease, Julia." The Duke reached up and took her hand. She allowed herself to be drawn down next to him. She seemed to have run out of words. The dead stillnss of the air, the pink clouds, the Duke's nearness, his smell, confused her. "I am going to cure you of what I call Julia's triple-P malady," he whispered in that hoarse voice, putting his arms around her, drawing her to him. "Progress, Protestantism, Prohibition."

"How are you going to cure me?" she asked as if in a daze, wondering if this was how one felt when drunk. His moist lips pressed against hers. She thought of Frederick's dry kisses and sealed mouth, and she found her mouth had opened involuntarily as the Duke's hands began to undo her bodice. "I am going to make love to you, Julia."

"No," she whispered, but even to Julia it sounded more like "yes."

"I love you, Julia."

She kept her eyes shut as he removed her clothes. She felt the sweet, revitalizing bay air bathe her skin while the Duke kissed her in places Frederick had never even touched. It was so natural, she didn't think of protesting. She didn't think. When he was about to enter her, she stopped him and opened her eyes, looking for a moment at his maleness. It seemed enormous, beautiful and ugly in the same moment, as timeless, as godlike as the burial mound behind them. She touched it with both her hands and then reached up, pulling his head down to hers as she received him. When they climaxed, Julia let out a shout of joy that rang across the bay. It was as if that cry had been caught inside her all her life.

He lay on top of her for some minutes. "I feel," Julia said, "as if you've injected me with some magical drug."

"I hope I have, Julia," the Duke said, kissing her, and then, incredibly, she could feel him growing hard again, filling her. He made love to her again.

Later, as they lay together, she asked him why he hoped he had injected her with his magic.

"Why?" He nuzzled her neck. It took him a moment to understand her question and he answered it carefully. "Because I have never met a woman like you, Julia, who is so immune to natural beauty. You want to change all this," he said, one hand sweeping the scene before them. "That is your challenge. My challenge is to change all this," he said, running his hands up and down the length of her body, letting them come to rest on her breasts. "I said before that I loved you, Julia. I love you even more now. Not only for what you are but for what you could be." He kneeled over her. "You have the most beautiful breasts I have ever seen, Julia. Pink and brown and ripe, like some heavenly fruit." He put his mouth on her nipples, and as she felt them grow hard, she closed her mind to everything but him.

It was dark by the time they reached the fort. "Julia," Ephraim said, concerned, "we were worried . . ."

"There was a sudden rainstorm," the Duke said, because Julia didn't seem capable of speech. Minnie McCord looked at Julia's white crumpled dress, at the new pink blush on her usually milky cheeks. Then she stared at the disheveled Duke. "Must have been quite a storm," Minnie said knowingly.

"The *Emily B.* brought a letter from Frederick," Ephraim, not seeing anything, said. "Addressed to me. Duke, will you excuse us? Julia, come into my office."

"What is it?" Julia asked, the literal fear of God cutting through her daze. She was going to be punished, and rightfully, for what had happened. She followed Ephraim into the room that had once served the fort as an arsenal and now was her father's office. Ephraim held out the thick, creamy paper covered with Frederick's handwriting. She didn't take it. "The letter was to you, Papa. You tell me what Frederick has to say."

"He collapsed at the ironworks several weeks ago. He had been spitting up blood for some time. The doctors say he has tuberculosis. He wants you home, Julia. Right away."

Concerned, Ephraim looked at his daughter. Moments before, she had seemed filled with life, joyous, as if she were celebrating some important victory. Now she was pale and appeared exhausted and absolutely defeated.

Still, he felt he had to go on. "Reading between the lines, Julia, I don't think Frederick wants you to come home to nurse him as much as he wants you to come home to nurse the ironworks. He says he wants to try to turn it around, and he knows your interest in it, and . . . well, here, he writes, 'Julia has a wonderful head for business, and I think between us we might just save Cleveland Ironworks.' I didn't realize it needed saving. You'd have to be deaf, dumb, and blind to kill an ironworks these days. Julia, you don't have to go. . . ."

But Julia had stopped listening. It was instantaneously clear that she had no choice but to do just that. A sudden vision of the Duke kneeling over her came to mind, and she shut her eyes and saw Frederick. Frederick didn't want to leave Julia destitute when he died, and he believed his death was imminent. Julia looked at the letter, at that fine, spidery handwriting, and sighed. As a Cleveland matron it would have been unthinkable for Julia to have a hand in the management of her husband's business. But as the wife of an invalid, it would be very nearly the thing to do.

She went to the windows and looked out at the moonlit bay. Already it seemed artificial, unreal, like the vista the Duke had attempted to paint. Another woman—a foolish, childish woman—had had that experience this afternoon. Nonetheless she had an urge to run down the stairs to the old

246

stables and burst in on the Duke. She needed to have him take her in his muscular arms and hold her against his blond-haired chest, to kiss her and tell her it would be all right to stay, that he would take care of everything.

Abruptly Julia turned away from the window, from her reflection in the glass. "I know my duty," Julia said aloud, her chin going up, her hands clenching into fists. "I am going home to Cleveland, Papa. Would you send Panthar first thing in the morning to Brickell's to make certain the *Emily B.* doesn't leave without us? I'll pack tonight." She went to the door and turned with a last thought. "And would you ask Minnie and the Duke and anyone else you might think of *not* to come and say goodbye? I'm not fond of good-byes."

The Duke came anyway. He stood with Panthar, apart from the crowd on the dock, his fingers hooked into his waistcoat. The rope he used for a belt had been tied too loosely and his trousers hung low on his narrow hips. The one glimpse she allowed herself nearly made Julia cry out with passion and longing.

She busied herself with Harry's unkempt hair and gave her attention to Fanny's pale cheeks. Ephraim, refusing to appear at Willie Brickell's dock, had said his goodbyes at the fort. Julia resolutely turned her back to the Duke and Panthar and took Alice's hand. "You will write, Alice?"

"I said I would, didn't I, Julia?" Alice was looking ineffably sad. She kissed Fanny and Harry and then she looked at Julia. "I'm going to embrace you, Julia," she warned. "And then I'm going to leave. I don't want this crowd to see me cry." Awkwardly Alice put her arms around her friend and Julia smelled the vanilla and nearly cried herself.

"I'm going to miss you, Alice," Julia said as Alice turned and made her way back to her father's house.

Julia felt a hand on her arm. She didn't turn, knowing who it was. "Will you write to me as well, Julia?"

"Yes, of course I will write, Mr. Ewing." She hurriedly followed Fanny and Harry aboard the *Emily B.* and didn't look back until the schooner was well under way. Across the blue and green bay waters she saw the Indian mound and then, to the left, the bluff on which Fort Dallas stood. Still farther to the left, just south of the Miami River, she made out Brickell's dock. It was empty now save for two men. One was Panthar. The other was the Duke. He waved once, but Julia found she couldn't wave back. She had a terrible and certain thought. I'm making a mistake. I love this place. I am turning my back on my vision. My city. My love.

CHAPTER FIVE

1891

SEVENTEEN YEARS LATER, on a November morning, a Friday, in 1891, the recently scraped and painted and refurbished *Emily B.* once again sailed into the shallow waters of Biscayne Bay. Aboard was Mrs. Julia de Forest Sturtevant Tuttle, her two children, and all their combined personal effects.

"Seventeen years have not passed," Julia said to herself. "I was here only yesterday." She stood in the bow of the *Emily B.* experiencing a rare melancholy. This time Ephraim wouldn't be waiting at Fort Dallas. I have, she thought, forgetting her children, no close relatives in this world. At that thought tears welled up in her brown eyes, and Julia, irritated, gave herself a mental kick. This is not like me, she thought, putting her self-pity down to the exhaustion of the month-long trip.

She leaned over the side of the *Emily B.* and was reassured when she saw the remembered rainbow-colored fish working their way in and out of the bay's sea grass. Then, feeling more like herself, she looked up. The cloudless sky was the same hand-painted cerulean blue. The birds—blue and white herons, American egrets, roseate spoonbills—made the same racket.

Another day, as Miss Alice had said and would continue to say, in paradise. As the *Emily B.* made its slow way across the shallow bay, Julia began to make out familiar landmarks. Her eye swept past the Indian mound (I will not think of that now, or later) and rested, just to the south, on the bluff above the place where the Miami River entered Biscayne Bay. Fort Dallas looked a great deal more commanding from the water than it did close up, on land. Well, I have plans for Fort Dallas, Julia thought. I have plans, for that matter, for the entire bay area.

At that distance she could just make out the Brickell dock but not who was on it. Across the water came the faint but certain strains of "Dixie" being played on a harmonica. "That annoying and inappropriate song," Julia said. But she smiled, thinking of the last time she had heard it. It had been played just that way—badly—on a harmonica.

She could hardly wait to see how Miss Alice had fared over the seventeen years since they had seen each other; to reveal how beautifully Julia had survived. If she had a hope that other old friends would be waiting on the dock, she didn't acknowledge it.

Impatiently—the *Emily B.* was stuck again and had to wait for the tide—Julia took in the entire panorama before her. Emmanuel Acosta's royal palm trees still stood over the jungle, tall and beautiful and beyond reproach. The rest of Florida was going through the most extraordinary changes, thanks largely to such men as Henry B. Plant and Henry Morrison Flagler and their railroads. But with the exception of a few new cottages in the Coconut Grove settlement, time in the bay area had stood still.

Waiting for me, Julia, uncharacteristically fanciful, thought. Luckily she had changed. She was forty-one years old, parentless and a widow. For the first time in her life she was completely free of male authority, real or imagined. Her megrims, in the years since Frederick died, had become less severe, and she was in excellent physical health. If anything, Julia thought, I am more energetic than ever.

Her waistline had thickened just a bit since she was a girl, it was true. But her handsome face had remained, despite her troubles, unlined. Her chin was held even higher than before, her brown dresses seemed unnecessarily sober, and her eyes no longer held the youth that had once made them sparkle. But no one would have had difficulty in recognizing in the widow Tuttle the girl who had visited the bay area seventeen years before.

"Mama," the young woman beside her said in a querulous voice, "when do you think—"

"Fanny, not now, please. I'm concentrating."

"You're always concentrating, Mama."

"Fanny, I can't be attending to you every moment of the day. Where's your brother?"

"He's where he's been every day since we left Jacksonville. In the hold, cheating the first and second mates at cards."

Julia gave her daughter a narrow-eyed, disdainful look. Whereas Julia was handsome, Fanny was beautiful in a long, well-bred sort of way. Everything was long: her green eyes, her thin nose, the shape of her head. She had Frederick's bony structure and a subdued version of Emily Church's hot red hair. That few recognized Fanny's beauty was put down by Julia to the shrinking, complaining way in which her daughter presented herself. She was her father's daughter.

"You would sacrifice your brother for a penny, Fanny."

Fanny sighed. She was not interested in money, though she would gladly have signed Harry's death warrant for a penny's worth of maternal affection. Julia's barb nonetheless achieved the desired effect of keeping Fanny quiet. Hurt, Fanny carefully, so as not to soil her frock, sat down on a bench, folded her long, aristocratic hands (so unlike her mother's short, clenched fists), and reviewed again in her mind the litany of events that had brought her back to this place she so hated and feared.

When Julia had announced—only two months before—that their home,

Gaydene, had been sold to a rich clergyman and the ironworks to his merchant brother, Fanny had collapsed in a genuine faint. Restoratives had been administered. "Where will we live?" Fanny had wanted to know when she had regained consciousness in the familiar pink and violet bedroom Frederick had had decorated for her.

"We are going to move to Florida. To the bay area. We shall live in Fort Dallas," Julia had told her, and Fanny, desperate, had grabbed her mother's hand. "Please, Mama, don't make me go to that terrible place."

"Fanny," Julia had said, removing her hand from Fanny's grasp, clenching it into a fist, "you are twenty-three years old, unmarried, unengaged, and without prospect. At your age I was married six years and had two children."

"But, Mama," Fanny objected. "I am not going to make a brilliant marriage in the wilds of the Florida jungles."

"I shan't mince words, Fanny." As if she ever did, Fanny thought. "Your chances of making a brilliant marriage anywhere are not great," Julia went on. "But the kind of men you'll meet in Florida are made of stronger and finer stuff than the cardboard cutouts you seem to attract here."

"The scorpions, Mama," Fanny said, retreating.

"And the snakes and the crocodiles and the lizards. They make life interesting."

Fanny had lost her temper, shouting, "You want to go only because you have a pash on the Duke. Now that papa's dead, you hope he'll marry you."

Julia gave her daughter a look of such freezing anger, of such terrible contempt, Fanny had had to turn away. "I am not going to Florida to marry anyone, Fanny. I am going to Florida to create a civilized place out of a jungle. I am going to Florida to make the family's fortune and name, an occupation at which your father, whom you so greatly resemble, was singularly inept." Her chin in the air, Julia marched out of the room, and Fanny, in despair, hugged her satin pillow.

Now Fanny, aboard the *Emily B.*, watched her mother place an ugly, wide-brimmed hat over her brown hair, tie it carefully under her firm chin, and continue to ignore her as she scanned the shore in the near distance. Father would have hated the hat, Fanny thought. "Your mother," Frederick had once said, "has an unerring sense of the ugly and the tasteless. She always heads directly for what flatters her least."

Fanny took some consolation in the fact that she had inherited her father's sure taste and delicacy. She adjusted her own narrow-brimmed and rather distinguished-looking hat and tried not to think of scorpions and other disgusting creatures. Instead she brought out the tattered memory of the one period when Julia had paid attention to her: those weeks after she had been stung by the scorpion and Julia had been by her side, holding her hand. Whenever Fanny doubted her mother's love, she tried to remember that time.

Mother hadn't been nearly so sympathetic with father's illness, Fanny thought. On the day the twenty-four-year-old Julia had returned to Gaydene from her summer in Florida, she had established a downstairs bedroom-studio for Frederick and relegated him to it forever. The following day she met with his doctors, called in new doctors, and set up a regimen of diet and occupation—that painting of porcelain—which was to keep Frederick alive for a decade longer than the most optimistic of the physicians predicted.

She had enrolled Fanny at Miss VailDeane's and arranged for Harry to attend the Curtis School for Boys at Brookfield Center, Connecticut. The following Monday morning at eight sharp Julia had appeared at the neglected Cleveland Ironworks and announced to the appalled staff that she was taking over its directorship. Cleveland Ironworks was out of the red within three years and in five was very much where it had been when Frederick had taken over from his father. By the time Frederick had quietly died, an unfinished porcelain fruit urn in one hand, a fine Japanese brush in the other, the Cleveland Ironworks was a thriving business.

Six months after Frederick had been buried Julia received word—from Alice Brickell—that Ephraim had died as well, leaving all his bay-area land to Julia. Almost immediately Julia began mentally packing.

Throughout those seventeen years, though she had devoted nearly every waking moment to the Cleveland Ironworks, Julia had managed to find time to write monthly letters to Miss Alice, and biannual letters to the Duke of Dade. If she ever gave any thought to that late-afternoon romance by the old Indian burial mound, there was no evidence of it in her letters. The Duke, taking his cue from her, responded with long conversational letters filled with descriptions of the bay, of the subtle changes of seasons, of the progress of her garden, which he and Panthar were maintaining. In this way he hoped to keep alive Julia's memories of the place and of him.

Ephraim's letters were more economical and newsworthy. A year or so after Julia's visit he wrote that he had been elected to serve as Dade County's representative in Tallahassee. Though he didn't say so, Julia decided that he was lonely, that his feud with Willie Brickell continued to dishearten him, that he welcomed the chance to go to Tallahassee, where he had met his Flora Mae.

He so missed the bay area, he had imported Miss Minnie McCord to act as his housekeeper in Tallahassee. Even so, Ephraim had barely lasted the two years of his term. Just before he (and Minnie) left Tallahassee he managed to find a way to mend the rift between him and his old friend. At his recommendation, Miss Alice Brickell was appointed official postmistress of the bay area and given a stipend of fifty dollars per annum. When Ephraim arrived at the Brickell dock, Willie was there to greet him.

For the next thirteen years, while Miss Alice's self-importance grew slowly but inexorably, like Florida herself, the two men had fished, smoked cigars, eaten Minnie's delectable possum stew, and in general enjoyed the casual bay life for which they had left the amenities of Cleveland.

251

It was nearly noon when the water was high enough for the *Emily B.* to begin a genuine approach to Willie Brickell's dock. The sunlight, reflected off the bay's waters, was blinding. Julia, wishing Fanny would go away, squinted from under her hat, attempting unsuccessfully to make out who was on the dock. She could see only the land at the water's edge. Through the sunlight her eyes rested on the impenetrable jungle of live oaks, ironwood, gumbo-limbo, and strangler fig that began just beyond the Indian burial mound and extended west right up to the steps of Fort Dallas. "The jungle is going to have to be cleared," she said after a moment, thinking aloud. "The bay itself must be dredged if we're going to have a harbor for decent-sized boats. The land Papa left me won't be nearly enough."

Julia stopped thinking of who would be on the dock to meet her. She stopped seeing the jungle across the mirrorlike waters of Biscayne Bay. Instead Julia saw her dazzling white city, a place of progress and civilization. It would be named for its founder of course: Julia, Florida. She clenched her fists and lifted her chin. That's why she had come.

She saw Panthar first. He looked the same except for two new and deep lines that ran down either side of his monumental nose. He raised his magnificent arms when he saw her, bowed his head, and made an attempt, only half successful, at a smile. "Welcome," Panthar shouted over the harmonica playing of "Dixie." "Welcome, Queen Julia."

Julia bowed her head in acknowledgment. When she brought her head up, she expected to pick out and regally acknowledge her other friends as the *Emily B.* docked. But the Duke was already jumping aboard as *Emily B.* crew members were jumping off to make the boat fast. The Duke wore ancient rope-belted trousers and a faded red-satin waistcoat that might have been the same one he had worn when he greeted her seventeen years before. His blond hair was sun-bleached nearly white, his eyes were still a frosty blue, his body was still alive with muscles and energy. In her imagination he had changed, matured. She had assumed that now he would be more like Atlas than Adonis. But he had remained as beautiful and youthful as he had been when she had first met him.

The Duke's youthfulness did not make her happy. She was immediately aware that if she had been a twenty-four-year-old Aphrodite then, she was now a forty-one-year-old Juno. Majesty, not youth, was her asset. The Duke was looking at her, holding a bouquet of far too red hibiscus in his hand, and she knew that he was disappointed. He was seeing a Cleveland matron in a thick brown dress and a plain hat, a woman who had grown used to control, to giving orders. Her chin, which he had once thought adorable, was now merely square.

Julia turned because she couldn't bear the disappointment in his eyes. She was angry. Had he thought the clock would have stood still for her as well as for him? She hadn't been leading a life of tea parties and lakeside holidays. She had been running a difficult and complicated business, while his most difficult challenge had been to decide which wrong color to use to paint the royal palms. She had been caring for a tubercular husband, a backward daughter, and an increasingly idle son while the Duke of Dade was living a boy's fantasy, exploring the Everglades with Panthar. She had been swimming in the deep and often murky waters of mercantilism. He had been sailing along Biscayne Bay.

She found her anger, increasingly difficult to control, getting the better of her, and had a nearly irresistible urge to push past the Duke and those pathetic flowers and get on land without further ado. But she caught a glimpse of Miss Alice on the dock, still big and messy and gratifyingly older, accompanied by her mirror-image sisters and a grizzled Willie Brickell. She wouldn't give Alice the satisfaction of a scene.

Julia swallowed her anger and bowed her head in Miss Alice's direction, twisting her lips into what she thought of as her Queen Victoria smile. Alice was going to get heat stroke, Julia observed, if she didn't put on a hat.

The Duke stood in front of her, smiling, holding that absurd bouquet, until the two harmonica-playing Negro boys came to the end of that irritating song. He took Julia's gloved hand and said in that husky voice of his, "It is very good to see you again, Julia. It's been far too long." Julia gave an obligatory, social smile. It was too hot, she had too many conflicting feelings, and she wished the Duke would drop her hand and step back a pace. The Duke sensed this and said, "On behalf of each and every member of the Biscayne Bay community, I welcome you home, Mrs. Tuttle. It is Friday, November the thirteenth, 1891. A historic day in Dade County history. Won't you please accept these flowers as a token of our esteem?"

He handed the flowers to Julia, who had been holding out her gloved hand to receive them. Without warning she turned, inadvertently knocking the flowers to the deck, looking at the captain, who had been about to give the order for the plank to be set down and all passengers to disembark.

"Is this really Friday the thirteenth?" she asked the captain, as if no one else would tell her the truth. She had lost, aboard the *Emily B.*, all idea of time.

"It is, Mrs. Tuttle."

"Then I have no intention of disembarking." Ignoring the Duke and everyone else on the dock, Julia retreated below to her cabin, a distraught Fanny and a grinning Harry in her wake. She asked for and received the captain, for whom she was more than a match. "Not one single item belonging to me—including my children and the cows—is to be removed from the *Emily B.* until dawn, Saturday, the fourteenth of November."

"Mother," Fanny said after the captain had left, "everyone is waiting for us on the dock. Panthar and the Duke and all the Brickells. You're not going to put them all out because of an absurd superstition?"

253

"I am not being superstitious, Fanny. I am being cautious. Now please hand me that fan and leave me alone. I feel a megrim coming on." She closed her eyes, heard the door shut, and tried to keep her mind blank. It wasn't only superstition that held her back. It had been the disappointment in the Duke's frosty eyes, the feeling of being appraised by everyone on that dock and found wanting. She kept her eyes closed, but the Duke and his blue eyes wouldn't go away. She found that she had a full-fledged megrim and rang for Fanny.

"Perhaps she'll reconsider," the Duke said, standing on the dock with Panthar and Miss Alice as the other bay-area residents, deflated, left what had promised to be a holiday scene and went back to their respective occupations and recreations.

"I, for one, don't have time for Julia and her airs," Alice said. Nevertheless she had waited a quarter of an hour in the hope that Julia wouldn't continue to be "a darned fool." "She's too rich and too important for us now. You'd both better go home."

The Duke went to his skiff and Panthar to his dugout. Neither pushed off from the dock immediately, both looking up at the *Emily B.*, waiting. "Do you think, Duke," Panthar said at last, "that Miss Julia has come back to take away our jungle and our land and give us a white man's city?"

"She has land and money, now," the Duke said, avoiding Panthar's earnest black eyes, thinking of Julia's twice yearly letters in which she had never failed—not once in seventeen years—to mention "progress."

"Maybe," Panthar said at last, not liking the sad look in the Duke's eyes, "she is not Miss Julia, after all. Maybe an evil god, jealous, has possessed her."

The Duke considered the new, distant Julia, her humorless eyes and that seemingly permanent tilt of her chin. Pushing off from the dock, he said, "That's a real possibility, Panthar." Later, as he lay in his skiff, waiting without any real desire for a fish to bite, he decided Julia was more of a challenge than ever.

CHAPTER SIX

"YOU COULD HAVE STAYED ON," Julia said, not meaning it. It had taken most of the day for the Duke, Panthar and his men, and the McCords to move Julia's possessions from the hold of the *Emily B.* to Fort Dallas. The piano had come on Brickell's barge, the cows in the Duke's skiff, furniture and trunks and crates of dishes in the Seminoles' dugouts.

"You wouldn't have thought it proper," the Duke said, knowing Julia's reasons for not wanting him to continue to live in the old stables were more complicated than that. He had taken himself and his paints to Charlie and Isabelle Peacock's inn in Coconut Grove. "I might have corrupted your children," the Duke said hoarsely, trying to make Julia smile. But Harry, who had a thin mouth and loose eyes, and Fanny, who complained consistently and constantly about her lot in life, were so obviously already corrupted in one way or another that the jest was too close to home.

They were standing on the coral-stone veranda. The Miami River lay just to their right on the south side of the fort, while the bay spread out in front of them to the east. A pair of crocodiles lay, one on each bank of the Miami, and Julia fancied they were the same she had seen soon after she had first come to Fort Dallas and the Duke had kissed her.

"Julia—" he began, reaching for her stubby hand, which lay for a moment exposed and vulnerable on the balustrade. Behind them, in the house, Minnie McCord was making a great deal of noise, giving unpacking orders to her nephews—Harry's former playmates—hired for the day.

"Mr. Ewing," Julia interrupted, her chin going up as she removed her hand and made it into a fist, "if we are to continue to know each other, if you are to be welcome in my home, if we are to have any sort of friendship, you must forget the untold incident that came between us in the past."

"I thought, Julia," he said with a sad smile, "that that particular 'untold incident' had brought us together." He looked at her with those widely spaced frosty eyes, and for a moment she wanted to let go, to unclench her fist, to allow him to wrap those blond arms around her. Just for a moment.

"Mr. Ewing, if you insist on continuing to bring up that incident, I am afraid I will not be able to know you. I have not thought of it since."

"I think of it every day, Julia."

"Well, I sincerely hope that you will not think of it henceforth. Do I have your word?"

He shook his head and smiled again. "You have my word, Julia." He put out his hand, and she had no choice but to take it. His touch, warm and giving and as electric as a summer thunderbolt, nearly broke through her determination. But the distinct sound of a dish smashing broke the spell. She left the Duke on the veranda and entered the fort.

Of course it was Fanny. "I should have known," Julia said, hands on hips. Fanny had begun, unbidden, "as a surprise for Mama," to hang Julia's collection of china plates on the dining room walls. "Don't bother about that one," Julia said, watching Fanny attempt to clean up the breakage. "You'll cut your hands. What you've done is all wrong anyway. The smaller, more precious ones should be at eye level," Julia explained, feeling herself again. She began removing the plates Fanny had hung. "The larger, less interesting ones go on top and at the bottom." Tears appeared in Fanny's green eyes and toppled over, staining her cheeks.

"Mama," Fanny said in real distress. But Julia was involved in rearranging the dishes. She found it an agreeably mindless, soothing occupation. Fanny, drying her tears, humiliated in front of the McCords, went to her room.

Minnie, meanwhile, disapproval written across her plain face, supervised the disposal of fussy sofas and straight-backed chairs. "My father maintained the fort as a sort of men's club," Julia said, to Minnie McCord who silently disagreed. "I mean to make it a home." She had brought nearly everything with her: books and paintings; Frederick's hand-painted ornamental urns; Gaydene's garden statuary, which included a pair of fawns, a Minerva, and a pink fountain in the shape of an oyster shell; Flora Mae's Italian fish set; Frederick's reading chair, an intricately caned affair; Harry's and Fanny's baptismal robes; the concert grand piano that Fanny occasionally picked at. She had purchased the cows in Jacksonville, and they were now housed in the Duke's former home, returned to use as a stable and barn.

"What shall we do with the Duke's present, Mrs. Tuttle?" Minnie asked, reminding her of the gift that was taking up valuable space in the corridor. She had been waiting for Julia to finish the plate hanging, which looked all wrong to Minnie's uneducated eye, before mentioning it again to "Mrs. Tuttle." Minnie had known at first sight that Julia was no longer to be called "girl."

"You might interrupt the Duke's reverie with nature and ask him to help hang it in the office. Over the desk." Julia was taking over her father's office, the former fort's gun room. She stood still while the Duke and Jeff McCord struggled to hang the heavy painting, its frame carved of mahogany. "I can almost smell the gunpowder," Julia said, not looking at the Duke's gift, thinking instead of the officers lining up their rifles.

256

"A fitting place from which to launch your battles, Julia," the Duke said, his muscles straining as he and Minnie's nephew lifted the painting.

"And to celebrate my victories." In full command, Julia stepped back to look at the Duke's gift. She wasn't at all displeased. It was a life-sized portrait, painted by the Duke in vivid and for once correct oil colors. Panthar was robed in all his Seminole finery, the Duke neatly capturing the strength that lay beneath the copper-colored skin stretched across taut muscles.

"If I were a man," Julia said as the Duke and Jeff moved away, "I would very much like to look like that. All that strength. All that control. Thank you, Duke," Julia said, using his sobriquet for the first time since she had arrived. "It is a beautiful present."

"Is it possible," Harry asked, poking his head into his mother's new office moments after the work had been done, "to get some lunch? I'm famished, Mama."

"Of course, Harry." She turned and looked at the Duke for some moments. Even now, after all this time and all her resolve, his near nakedness was unnerving. She had determined to make it a rule that he wear a shirt and coat and shoes in her presence. But that rule had been formulated in Cleveland. Here, in Florida, she knew that if she made such an ultimatum, she would not see him again. She didn't want that. "You will stay for lunch?"

"I'll stay for lunch, Julia."

Julia went off to see Minnie McCord about the menu. Chicken in aspic, she thought. Cream of mushroom soup to begin. A local fish. And for dessert a pudding, possibly chocolate. Just because, she said to herself as she made her way to the kitchen house, everyone here has given in to the jungle doesn't mean that I will.

They dined on the veranda—the Duke, Fanny, Harry, and Julia. Panthar, who would not eat with white men, had had a meal with the braves who had helped move the piano into the lounge. They had gone back to their village, but he stood at the edge of the veranda, looking out onto the bay, as silent and as potent as his portrait.

The mushrooms Minnie's sister-in-law, Annie, produced had a "smell," and no one had had time to cream the cows' milk. "Jewfish," Minnie announced as she set it down on the table. Fanny gasped. Minnie hadn't removed the skin, the tail, or the head. Julia, setting an example, ate an entire portion, pronouncing it "delicious."

"The chicken's been poached, I see," Julia said, taking a tentative bite. It swam in one of Minnie's yellowish sauces. "It has a slightly tough texture." She examined it. "The meat seems more pink than white. Freshly killed, no doubt. Quite delicious, Harry. Do eat."

"It was freshly killed, Mrs. Tuttle, but 'twasn't no chicken," Minnie McCord said as she took away Julia's mother's fish dishes. "We used local game."

"And what local game did 'we' use, Minnie?" Julia, at the head of the table, asked.

"Rattlesnake."

Fanny sped off to her room to be sick. Even Harry turned white and left the table. Julia remained with the Duke, who was clearly trying to control his amusement. "Rattlesnake is a staple of the bay area, Julia."

"In that case," Julia said, offering Minnie McCord her plate, "I wonder if I might have some more."

"You don't have to eat it, Julia," the Duke said admiringly.

"I want to eat it, Mr. Ewing." Minnie gave her a large portion. Julia, cutting the meat decisively, looked at the Duke. "Tell me, what's happening in the bay area in the way of land development?"

"I'm relieved to say, Julia, nothing. We're too far away from everywhere to be developed."

"That's not true." She ate a piece of meat, chewed it thoughtfully, and went on. "Phosphorus and oranges are making men fortunes all over Florida. Why not here? Key West is one of the richest cities in the country, thanks to her salvage industry. Henry Plant has taken sleepy Tampa and given her a good shaking. He's built a railroad terminus and a port for ships that sail between Key West and Havana. The Cuban cigar makers that used to go to Key West are going to Tampa now, at Mr. Plant's invitation."

"It's said Mr. Plant likes a good cigar," the Duke observed wryly.

"He's not the only one. Henry Flagler—who, by the way, got his start in Cleveland—is replacing those narrow-gauge railroads and turning St. Augustine from a village for sick people into a great resort."

"You've certainly done your homework, Julia," the Duke said evenly.

She put down her fork and stared at him. "I didn't spend the last seventeen years making the Cleveland Ironworks profitable without learning something about the business world, Mr. Ewing. Florida is booming, and there is no reason in this world why the bay area shouldn't boom as well."

"Except, Julia, that no one in the bay area wants a boom."

"I do. I want to talk to you about that land your family owns."

The Duke looked at her cautiously. "You'd be wasting your time. I no longer represent the Biscayne Bay Trading Company."

She refused to be put off. "Someone must."

"My Uncle Thomas is on an extended visit here, actually. He's with me at the Peacock. Talk to him, Julia."

"I will make it a point to do so," she said, picking up her fork, satisfied for the moment.

"Are you still looking for a man with a hundred thousand dollars?" the Duke asked, remembering that figure as Julia's estimate for the construction of her city.

"Oh, I've got the hundred thousand dollars, Mr. Ewing," Julia said, chin going up. It was a lie. She had seventy thousand dollars, but she was aware now that even if she had had a hundred thousand dollars, it wouldn't be nearly enough. To start with, Julia knew she needed to buy more land.

258

Julia finished the last piece of rattlesnake meat, said she didn't want dessert, and pushed her chair from the table. The Duke stood up and they faced each other like adversaries in a blood duel. "We don't want Progress, Protestantism, and Prohibition, Julia. Not here. If you're going to empire-build, go somewhere else, I beg you. Don't ruin paradise, Julia."

"If you're against progress, Mr. Ewing, I suggest *you* go somewhere else. It's coming, and I mean to pave the way. There's nothing you can do to stop either it or me."

She joined Panthar at the balustrade and, after a moment, so did the Duke. The two men followed Julia's gaze. She was staring down at the jungle that surrounded Fort Dallas. Only a small patch of land—just below the kitchen house—was cultivated. It was Julia's garden, tended over the years by Panthar and the Duke. "I want to thank you both for keeping up the garden," Julia said warmly, returning her gaze to the jungle. "But everything else is running wild."

"It has always run wild, Julia. It is wild."

"The first thing I'd like you to do, Panthar, tomorrow morning, is clear my land of everything. I want a proper lawn."

"Julia," the Duke protested, "you had a proper lawn in Cleveland."

She ignored him. "Every single tree. And whatever else you find down there."

"But nothing will be left, Mrs. Tuttle," Panthar said. "You will destroy everything."

"So that I may create a thing of beauty, Panthar." She looked at the Duke's angry face and at Panthar's perplexed expression and suddenly felt a sharp pain in each temple. "Excuse me," she said. "I must lie down." She went to the French doors, and despite the bombs exploding in her forehead, she managed to turn and say, "Tomorrow morning, Panthar. Hire as many men as you need."

"Mrs. Tuttle," Panthar said, "I cannot—"

But the Duke interrupted him. "Do it, Panthar. You might as well. If it's not you, it will be the McCords, and they'll destroy every animal as well as every tree."

Panthar shook his head sadly. "You have a will like an iron tree, Mrs. Tuttle. Tomorrow morning," Panthar said with grim resignation, "we will destroy your land."

Julia couldn't remember when she had felt such anger. I very nearly hate them, she realized. Her head felt as if it were splitting. "It will be a small step," Julia said. "But it will be a step forward."

Julia lay on her bed. The pain had begun to lessen, but it was still there, a sore reminder of the dreadful afternoon. The early evening sky was a red, pink, orange, and blue painting, but it hurt to look at it. If she had had the strength, she would have drawn the linen curtains she had brought from her

Gaydene bedroom. Two megrims in as many days. She almost wished she had never left.

Sitting up, she drew the mosquito netting aside. She didn't need it. The mosquitoes, which had already ravaged Fanny, never touched her. "They like only sweet meat," Ephraim had once joked, but Julia had believed him. "I'm not sweet," Julia said to herself. Florence Nightingale was not sweet. Grandmother Emily was not sweet. She'd bet five dollars that her Spanish ancestor, escaping from the Inquisition and the Catholics, was not sweet. But they were strong and good and right, as she was. Let the Duke scoff. Nothing but death would stop her.

The pain was acute, and she lay back against the pillows. She could hear Minnie McCord banging away in the outdoor kitchen. Fanny, miserable, was picking at the piano in the lounge. The cows were making a reassuring moo-ing noise, drowning out the strange and alien sounds coming from the jungle that surrounded her.

A long lizard, black, a miniature dinosaur, was making its way up the far wall. Julia watched it as she once again played out in her mind the afternoon scene on the veranda. "How dare he intercede?" she asked herself, humiliated. That Panthar would accept the Duke's orders and not hers! She closed her eyes. The megrim was in full control now, and she felt herself giving up to the pain as she realized Fanny was tiptoeing into the bedroom.

"One of your megrims, Mama?" Fanny whispered, and Julia managed a nod. "I'm going to take care of you, Mama. I'll make it go away." Mercifully, Fanny drew the curtains, making the room dark. This was brave of Fanny, Julia decided. Coming into Julia's room, unbidden, to care for her. She had a soothing voice when she wasn't ruing the day she was born. Fanny would like to hear that, but somehow she couldn't tell her. Through half-closed eyes she watched Fanny pour a few drops of eau de cologne onto a soft cotton cloth. She placed it carefully across her mother's broad forehead, pushing back the dense brown hair, wiping away the perspiration with her hand.

"I am glad you have come, Fanny," Julia wanted to say, surprised that despite the ruined day, she was able to enjoy this rare moment of intimacy with a daughter who, at best, was distant. We never share our thoughts, Julia realized, finding she had covered Fanny's long, elegant hand with her own.

Fanny looked down at their two hands and felt the tears come to her eyes. Oh, Mama, if you had any idea of the pain and loneliness of my wallflower's life, she thought. And she wished she could say, "I love you, Mama." She wished she could tell Julia how frail and useless she felt next to her. There were so many things Fanny wanted to say, but even now, in the most tender moment they had had since Fanny lay sick in this same place and Julia had tended her seventeen years ago, the two women remained silent. The moment was lost. Fanny turned to put a few more drops of eau de cologne on the cloth and saw, out of the corner of her eye, something on the pink coral rock wall. The black lizard, apparently aware of interest, had frozen. It

260

looked like a black scorpion. It looked as if it had been painted on the wall. It's red, forked tongue darted out, proving that it hadn't. Fanny screamed.

Julia sighed and stood up to comfort Fanny, who had given in to the hysteria she had suppressed since they had arrived. "It was only a lizard, Fanny. I hate to think what you'll do when a ten-foot-long crocodile nudges your toe." Ineffectually, Julia patted her daughter's quivering, bony shoulders. "Do stop, Fanny."

Fanny couldn't. Minnie McCord took her to her room, gave her a hot cup of herbal tea, and finally Fanny fell asleep in Minnie's arms.

"It was a mistake to bring Fanny," Harry said over supper that night, finishing Minnie McCord's corn-bread pudding dessert. He had already made contact, Harry said, with a "couple of fellows" who lived down in Coconut Grove and was thinking about going into the salvage business "in a big way." Harry, who was a young twenty-two, hadn't at all minded leaving Cleveland for the bay area. When he thought about his gambling debts and the men to whom he owed the money, Harry knew he would have left Cleveland for darkest Africa. "Fanny's always a mistake," he said, wondering if his mother were listening to him.

She was not. She had put Fanny and Harry and the Duke and Panthar out of her mind. She was trying to decide how long she should wait before she paid a visit to Mr. Thomas Ewing, the Duke's uncle and a principal in the Biscayne Bay Trading Company, to offer to buy his land.

CHAPTER SEVEN

ONE WEEK AND ONE DAY after Julia and her household had arrived in the bay area, she still had not met with Mr. Thomas Ewing to discuss with him her purchase of the Bay Company's land.

On Tuesday she and Alice (with whom she had resumed her daily visits as if there had never been a seventeen-year hiatus) had sailed in Alice's skiff to the Peacock Inn. But Mr. Ewing had been on a day trip, visiting the mangrove-covered island that protected the north part of the bay from the Atlantic.

"Someone," the genial Charley Peacock said, "told him it would be a good place for a coconut farm. Ask me, I think he was just bored and needed something to do. That fellow's not buying any more land in the bay area. Once bitten."

The Duke, reluctantly, had promised to bring his uncle to Fort Dallas for lunch. But on the day of that proposed event the elder Mr. Ewing woke to find he had broken out in an incapacitating rash, caused—it was said—by contact with malignant plants encountered on his trek through the jungle of the north island.

Now, her second cloudless Sunday in the bay area, Julia sat with chin up and hands clenched on an unyielding bench in the old Gordon house in Coconut Grove. She appeared to be listening to the Protestant services being conducted by the droning, bewhiskered Mr. Gordon for the spiritual edification of the bay area families. She was not.

Fanny, examining her hands, sat on one side. Alice, her hair looking like a heron's nest under a straw man's hat, was on the other. She reeks of vanilla, Julia thought. Like a poor man's cake. Alice had grown even more eccentric since she'd become the official postmistress. She'd always been stubborn; now she was impossible.

Two days after her arrival Julia had entered the Brickell cottage—the hall of which had become the bay area's post office—at the same time as Mary Jane Cherry. Mary Jane, a young eighty, was carrying a plate piled high with sweet boiled coontie candies. "Miss Alice won't give me my letter from my boy if I don't give her something sweet."

"Her son can barely write," Alice said in defense when an incredulous Julia asked how she could do such a thing. "And when he does write, he only asks for money. Besides that, Mary Jane Cherry can't read. I'm only the postmistress, not the town reader. I have to get something for my services."

"And what must I give you to ransom my correspondence?" Julia, her chin at its most outraged, wanted to know.

"Nothing," Alice said in her logical voice. "I won't have to read your letters."

"I sincerely hope not, Alice." It was said that Alice routinely read every letter that came into the bay area, often not bothering to reseal the envelopes. It was also said she discarded all correspondence she deemed irrelevant.

But Julia was not thinking of Miss Alice as she sat on the Gordons' hard pine bench, trying to keep her eyes open in the wake of Mr. Gordon's sermon and the heavy stillness of the air. She was thinking of land, the Bay Company's land to be exact, which—if added to the land Ephraim had left her—would comprise some six hundred and forty acres on the north shore of the Miami River, fronting Biscayne Bay.

Quite enough for a city, Julia thought. But even if she bought it at a rock-bottom price, she would be using up most of her money. She would then need someone else to help develop it. Was she, she asked herself, prepared

262

to take the gamble? Should she sink her entire capital into land that no one else seemed in the least interested in developing? Should she purchase the Bay Company's land and pray that a Mr. Flagler or a Mr. Plant would find his way to the bay area and realize its potential?

During those years in Cleveland when she had returned from the bay area, Julia had subscribed to the St. Augustine *Gazette* and later to the Key West *Citizen* and the Tampa *Tribune*. Those journals had been her main reading matter for seventeen years. Consequently she knew a great deal more about Florida's development than most Floridians. She had met Mr. Flagler once while he was still in Cleveland. She had yet to meet Mr. Plant. But she felt as if she knew them both intimately from the journalistic reports of their keen commercial investments. She could, she mused, always invite them here. But would they come?

Julia did not have the answer to any of these questions and as a result did not greatly regret her missed conversations with Mr. Thomas Ewing. Until she had more information upon which to base a decision, there really wasn't much point in talking with him about buying the land he was so anxious to sell. Yet after that long service she couldn't resist leading Alice and Fanny to the Peacock for lunch, where there was a good likelihood she would meet him. Julia wanted to be convinced to buy.

"We need refreshment," Julia said, ignoring the bonneted bay women who had attended the service, leading her perfectly turned-out daughter and her somewhat less than well-groomed friend to the oversized weathered cottage that served as Peacock Inn.

The Duke, who had been expecting them, led the three women to a table in the interior dining room, which was supposed to be more protected from flies than the porch overlooking the bay. "Uncle is still in bed," the Duke said, "but he promises to meet with you Tuesday morning no matter what."

"I'm not at all certain," Julia said, rejecting the turtle soup, which she suspected was heavily laced with sherry, "I still want to meet with him."

The Duke smiled as Julia busied herself with her napkin and her cutlery. He had tried to reason with her and had warned her that his Uncle Thomas had been looking for just such a person as Julia on whom to unload the family land. He was happy that Julia was now having second thoughts.

"Who is that?" Julia asked, noticing a stranger who had entered the dining room. He was tall, with black hair and eyes and a beautifully combed and oiled mustache. He saw Julia's inquiring look and smiled. He had the whitest teeth any of them had ever seen—and, Fanny thought, sitting up very straight, the sweetest smile.

At a sign from the Duke, he approached the table. "Señor Córdoba, may I introduce Mrs. Tuttle and her daughter, Miss Fanny, and Miss Alice Brickell, the bay area's postmistress. Señor Córdoba is here to investigate possible business opportunities for his family's Havana-based export company."

"I am very pleased to meet three such charming ladies," Señor Córdoba said in an educated English made interesting by a slight Spanish accent. He bowed and smiled, mostly at Fanny. She reminded him of the wife of a British lord he had spent some time with during a sojourn in London. So long and so pale. Señor Córdoba liked elegant women.

"So that's Señor Córdoba," Alice said after he had moved on to the outdoor dining room. "Papa's been talking about him. He's some sort of Cuban gentleman-businessman."

"He doesn't look much of a businessman," Julia said disdainfully. "Or much of a gentleman, for that matter."

"Women, wine, sport, and then business," Miss Alice said, implying she already knew everything one needed to know about Señor Córdoba. "His family is more interested in keeping him out of Havana than in having him set up a bay area outpost. He talks to Papa sometimes about selling him goods but more often about the availability of game. He receives a monthly stipend, just enough to cover expenses. It is said he supplements it by playing cards—"

"Alice." Julia was no longer interested. "I have heard quite enough. Now, who is that short fellow? The Peacocks seem to be doing an extraordinary business."

The Duke, amused as always by Julia's snobbisms (she referred to the czar of all the Russias as a foreigner), said, "That 'short fellow' is a man you will be interested in knowing more about, Julia. A real American." In fact, he looked exactly like Julia's idea of what a certain sort of American should look like. He was five feet four inches tall, stout but not obese, had hair the color of old hay and blue eyes, and he wore a pleasant but not intrusive expression; his dark clothes were of a certain quality.

The Duke introduced R. O. Watson, who said in a reassuringly educated but certainly American accent that he was pleased to meet the ladies and hoped to see them again.

"Perhaps you would like to dine at my house one evening, Mr. Watson?" Julia said, startling Fanny and leaving Alice open-mouthed. "Hotel cuisine, no matter how good the Peacocks provide, must grow tiresome."

"That would be very pleasant, Mrs. Tuttle." Julia had hit him where his heart lay. R. O. Watson liked his food.

"Shall we say tomorrow night? At nine, when it's grown tolerably cool? Mr. Ewing will be joining us and can run you over in his skiff."

"How very kind, Mrs. Tuttle. Until tomorrow night."

Her three luncheon guests watched in silence as Julia bit into her turtle steak. It too had been doused in sherry, but Julia decided to ignore her antipathy to spirits just this time. Alice was the first to speak. "Julia, you invited a perfect stranger . . ."

"It appears that Julia knows who R. O. Watson is," the Duke said, impressed and alarmed by Julia's knowledge, decisiveness, and speed.

"And who is he?" Alice, for once at a loss, had to ask.

"He's Henry B. Plant's principal scout," Julia said, trying and failing to keep the excitement out of her voice. "R. O. Watson's been traveling throughout Florida, looking for likely investment areas for Mr. Plant. He's constantly mentioned in the newspapers as Mr. Plant's right-hand man."

"But what is he doing here?" Alice wanted to know.

"He's not interested in developing the bay area, I'm happy to say," the Duke answered. "This is a stopover. He's come from Key West on his way to St. Augustine."

"I wonder if he's meeting with Mr. Flagler there? Mr. Plant wouldn't like that. They are great rivals," Julia said. All her reading was coming in handy.

"At any rate," the Duke said, "you can ask him tomorrow night."

"I have a great many questions to ask Mr. Watson tomorrow night," Julia said, tapping Fanny's arm with her forefinger. Fanny's attention was on the table in the outdoor dining room where Señor Córdoba was sitting, staring back at her.

"Shall I bring my uncle, Julia?" the Duke wanted to know.

"No," she said decisively. "I shan't want to see him until after Mr. Watson comes to dinner."

"How was church?" Harry asked. He was reclining in the string hammock he and the McCord boys had fixed up at the top of his mother's freshly seeded lawn. Orange trees—as well as rose bushes—were to be delivered the next time the *Emily B.* came to port.

"Put on your collar, Harry," his mother said automatically, heading for the cookhouse. She had a great deal to discuss with Minnie McCord. Neither turtle nor possum was to appear on tomorrow night's menu in any of their various guises.

"How was church?" Harry asked again, this time directing the query to his sister, who seemed especially "moony."

"Mama had her prayers answered," Fanny said.

"By the look of it, so did you." Harry suspected Fanny of some secret happiness and didn't like it. He watched as she dreamily moved up the stairs that led to the fort, her head filled with oiled mustaches and soft, sweet smiles.

It was to be a dinner party for six: Mr. Watson, the Duke, Miss Alice, Harry and Fanny, and Julia herself. By morning the menu had been settled, and Jeff, the least offensive McCord, had been engaged to help Minnie serve.

By noon Julia felt the party was under control. Throughout the midday meal she issued a series of directives to her children on how to conduct themselves that evening. No matter that Fanny was twenty-three and Harry was twenty-one. "Harry, do not attempt to be amusing. Jeff has been warned, but if he forgets and offers you the wine, I want you to decline."

265

"That's rather poetic, Mama."

Julia ignored him. "Fanny, I want you to wear the pale-blue silk." She wondered if Mr. Watson was married—none of the newspaper reports had mentioned a wife—and decided it didn't matter. Anyone who worked for Henry B. Plant had to have considerable strength, not to mention nerves and brains. Fanny was too weak a flower for such a vital man. What's more, Julia did not fancy a short son-in-law.

"We shall have libations on the veranda," Julia decided, thinking aloud. "The Duke will escort Miss Alice, Mr. Watson will escort me, and Harry will escort Fanny. Afterward we can all adjourn to the lounge where Fanny—"

"I don't understand," Fanny said, finding strength in her sulkiness, "why you couldn't have invited a proper dining partner for me."

"Your brother is a proper dining partner for you," Julia returned. "And besides, who else is there?"

"Señor Córdoba, the gentleman we met yesterday."

"Señor Córdoba is no gentleman, Fanny. He is merely a foreigner. I do not have foreigners at my dinner table."

"The pale-blue makes me look pale," Fanny said, retreating.

"You are pale. There's no use disguising the fact. Besides, the pale-blue makes you look like a proper young lady," Julia said in a firm voice that meant the subject was closed.

An hour before her guests were due to arrive Julia, in a dark-blue serge that was hot and stiff but serviceable, asked to see the menu. Minnie handed her a scrap of paper on which the single word "turtle" was scrawled.

"Surely," Julia said, praying for the Lord to give her strength, "we're not having turtle, Minnie."

"No, Mrs. Tuttle. We're having turtle soup, turtle steak, tomato surprise—the surprise is it's stuffed with minced turtle—and my corn-bread pudding. Brickell's was all out of baby lamb, hand-fed beef, and snow-white veal."

Sometimes Julia wondered if she shouldn't have brought a cook with her.

Alice and Mr. Watson were somewhat out of breath when they arrived. "That walk from the dock up the stone steps, Julia, nearly did for me," Alice said, waving her hand in front of her to create a breeze. "Duke had to wait for us at each landing." She stepped into the former officer's lounge. "You sure went to a lot of trouble, Julia." The long room had been lit with as many candles as Julia could find, and the pink coral walls and floor fairly shimmered in the resulting candlelight.

"What a beautiful home you have, Mrs. Tuttle," R. O. Watson said, looking at Julia's china plate collection admiringly. He was a man who liked what he considered home comforts, but because of his job he was rarely able to enjoy them.

"You were born and raised in Cleveland, I believe, Mr. Watson," Julia said as they sat down to dinner in the little-used formal dining room. It was a square, dark sort of place toward the back of the fort and therefore close to the cookhouse. "As was I." Out of the corner of her eye Julia saw Jeff McCord fill Harry's glass with white wine.

"You know a great deal about me, Mrs. Tuttle," R. O. Watson said, dipping into the fourth bowl of turtle soup he had had in as many days.

"Mrs. Tuttle," the Duke said, "is a great reader of newspapers."

"Sometimes they even report the truth," R. O. Watson said with such a funny, plaintive expression on his round face that everyone—even Jeff McCord, waiting to clear the soup dishes—laughed. Julia made a mental note to tell Fanny she mustn't simper behind her fan. If Fanny wanted to laugh, for the Lord's sake, she should laugh.

"It must be exciting," Julia said later, over the turtle steak, "to work for such a man as Henry Plant."

"It is. He's one of the two great men of Florida." R. O. Watson allowed Jeff McCord to pour him another glass of wine.

"The other also being a Clevelander, Henry Morrison Flagler, I assume," said Alice, who had her own patriotic ties to her mother city.

"Mr. Flagler was not born in Cleveland, Alice," Julia said, correcting her. "But he certainly got his start there, with Mr. Anderson and Mr. Rockefeller."

"And he hasn't stopped since," R. O. Watson said. "Have you ever been to Cleveland, Duke?"

"No." The Duke had been quiet during the meal. He had been silently watching Harry put away half a dozen glasses of wine and observing Julia, who looked as handsome in the candlelight as when she had first arrived. He too had had several glasses of wine and found himself thinking of Julia's pink and brown breasts, as ripe as— He shook his head and forced himself to comment. "But I'm certain I would like it since all of you—"

Julia interrupted, not about to let the conversation get away from Mr. Flagler. "I understand you are going to St. Augustine, Mr. Watson. Perhaps you will see Mr. Flagler when you are there."

R. O. Watson looked at Julia Tuttle with his round, surprised-looking eyes. "That is a possibility."

"If I were Mr. Flagler, I would offer you a position."

That was just what R. O. Watson was hoping Henry Flagler would do—he was tired of Tampa and Henry B. Plant—and he was visibly startled. It wouldn't do for this piece of information to get back to his current employer, who viewed Flagler as "the man I most want to out-train and out-hotel and out-millionaire." He had underestimated Mrs. Tuttle and, under the influence of her wine, let too much information slip.

"I have a contract with Mr. Plant, however," he said and then turned to Miss Tuttle, who was as pale as her brother was red-faced. "And what occupations do you find to while away your time in this beautiful place, Miss Fanny?"

"I crochet," Fanny said coldly, thoroughly bored by his conversation. She thought him vulgar. And short.

After the corn-bread pudding Julia invited her guests into the lounge. Fanny was to entertain at the grand piano, and Julia meant to sit next to Mr. Watson on the white-painted wicker settee and ask him "pertinent" questions. Mr. Watson, alert to this ploy, and thinking he had answered enough questions, made a counteroffer. "While Miss Fanny plays, young Mr. Tuttle, the Duke, and I will repair to the veranda, where we can enjoy the strains of her heavenly music as we smoke our vile Havana cigars."

"Of course," Julia, routed, said.

Harry, however, having had too much wine, was unable to get up from the dining room table. He was allowed to stay where he was while Julia and Alice seated themselves on the white-painted wicker settee in the lounge and Fanny began to play a laborious "Clair de Lune." The heady bouquet of Havana cigars drifted into the long room like "smoke from hell" (as Alice put it), cutting through her vanilla scent.

Julia sat with her chin up and her hands clenched in her lap, while Fanny's music only partially masked the sounds of Jeff McCord getting Harry to his bed. Fanny segued into Rimsky-Korsakov's "Scheherazade," which she played with romantic abandon. Julia could stand it no longer and moved to the French doors, where she stood, listening to the conversation between the Duke and R. O. Watson.

". . . it would be a great crime, Mr. Watson, to destroy this natural beauty."

"I'm not saying it's going to happen tomorrow, Duke. Or even the day after. You can't develop a place without a railroad. When Plant pulled his terminus out of Cedar Key, that was the end of Cedar Key. When he decided on Tampa, well, then Tampa started to become Tampa. Flagler's done the same for St. A. You have to be able to get people and goods to and from a place in order to make that place profitable. I don't care how rich the earth is or how pretty the bay or how nice the climate. Boats are the transportation of the past. Railroads are the future."

"Railroads bring nothing but destruction and misery in their wake."

"But the railroads are coming, Duke. Get your handsome head out of the sand. Either Plant or Flagler is going to bring them. Someday. You might as well make up your mind to it."

"Mrs. Tuttle has," the Duke said wistfully. "She's trying to decide whether to buy more land here on the north shore."

Watson laughed admiringly. "So that's why she's had me to dinner. Well, if I were Mrs. Tuttle, I'd take every extra penny I had and put them into—"

At that moment Fanny's recital came to an end with a final crescendo, and the only sounds to be heard were those of the bay, the river, the jungle, and of Alice and Minnie McCord clapping. Julia stepped out onto the veranda. "And you would put them into what, Mr. Watson?"

"The bank, Mrs. Tuttle," Watson said, reluctant to give a woman any real business advice. "You're best off leaving business to the businessmen."

Julia looked directly into round, short R. O. Watson's eyes. "I don't believe you, Mr. Watson, I am sorry to say. I think you would put every penny you had into land. Which is just what I am going to do. Duke, do make certain your uncle is here first thing in the morning. I am ready to talk to him."

That night as Julia lay in her bed attempting to sleep, she imagined she could hear, above the clatter of the frogs, the sound of wheels on a railroad track. If R. O. Watson believes the trains are coming, then they will come. Mr. Flagler or Mr. Plant will bring them. I have the vision and they have the capital. "The trains are coming to help me build my city," she said to herself, closing her eyes, seeing white towers on Biscayne Bay. Her city. Julia, Florida. It was going to happen.

CHAPTER EIGHT

MINNIE McCORD set the painted tin tray down on the table and used her forearm to wipe the sweat from her eyes. She looked at the gold Chinese men and women cavorting under the heavy silver tea service and shook her head. Tea! Tea was drunk when one was ill. "Tea!" she said aloud and with feeling and then moved crablike back up the lawn—"Lawn!"—toward the fort.

Alice tut-tutted over Minnie's behavior, but Julia hadn't noticed. She poured a yellowish brew into a thin china teacup and handed it to Alice. Despite the sweat on Minnie's brow, the day, toward the end of January, was cool, and Alice was glad of the tea even though it tasted brackish. She looked at her friend, who was clearly in one of her moods.

"The roses look pecky," Alice ventured and received no response. Actually, though she hated to say it, they were doing quite well. The orange trees, under which they sat, were absolutely thriving, as were the coconut palms Julia had had imported from Havana to form a little copse at the bay end of the garden. Even the weedlike grass had taken hold and presented a coarser carpet of green within the pine fence Panthar had erected around the property.

Under Julia's direction Panthar had set Minerva in the center of the lawn and the matched fawns at the place where two new pebbled paths met. Julia had not as yet found a use for the pink seashell-shaped fountain, but Alice had no doubt that she would. Julia's white wrought-iron lawn furniture had been arranged under the orange trees, and though the trees were not yet in bloom, echoes of their sweet scent perfumed the bay air.

Julia's garden was a pleasant place in which to spend an afternoon after a hard morning's work as postmistress. It had been the talk of the bay area for months and unaccountably tickled the Duke. He always had a wicked smile on his face when he spoke of Julia's garden.

Julia did not have a smile on her face. She was looking at the blue-black panther skin, complete with preserved and fierce head, that was artistically draped across the bentwood table upon which the tea service stood. It had been a present from Panthar. "He still thinks you're queen of the white men's tribe, Julia," Alice said, but Julia responded with only an offhand "yes."

"Julia, you seem especially distracted today. You haven't touched your tea."

"I've been waiting for months, Alice, for a reply from R. O. Watson's Mr. Plant. I have written twice. *Rien, rien, rien,* as evil Mademoiselle Prunier used to say to us in French class. I have sunk every penny I have into this land in the belief that Mr. Plant would bring his railroad here, and I can't even get him to return a letter. The *Emily B.* put in yesterday and still nothing."

"You take things too seriously, Julia. You always have. Nervous disposition." Alice reached into her reticule. "If it will make you happier, here is a letter for you from Mr. Plant."

"Alice Brickell," Julia said, jumping up, furious. "Why didn't you—"

"I wanted you to enjoy the tea," Alice said aggrievedly as the thin brown envelope was torn from her hands.

Julia, unable to remain still, paced around the lawn furniture as she ripped open the envelope. She read the brief letter over and over again. Finally Alice asked, "Are you committing it to memory, Julia?" But Julia continued to pace. After several more moments of intense concentration she stopped, allowing her hand with the letter to fall to her side. She placed her other hand on her chest as she turned to stare off in the distance at Emmanuel Acosta's royal palms.

"Julia," Alice said impatiently, "these theatrics of yours are entirely un—"

"He's interested. 'Decidedly' interested. He's sending R. O. Watson and a team of men to look at my land as 'a potential resort city site.' Oh, Alice."

"When do they arrive?" Alice wanted to know. This was one letter she hadn't dared to read.

Julia consulted the letter as if she were seeing it for the first time. "He says he can't be certain but either the twentieth or the twenty-first of February. Absolutely no later than February twenty-second. The birth date of the Founder of Our Country. Alice, we must plan a celebration. We must . . . Alice, they're coming across the Everglades. Mr. Plant wants to drain them

270

and run his railroad across them. How long should it take to cross the Ever-glades, Alice?"

"With an Indian guide? Under a week. Without one, nobody will ever see R. O. Watson and his men again. Trouble is, Julia, Seminoles are not allowed to guide white men through the Everglades. It's sacred land. If they do and they're caught, they're severely punished."

But Julia wasn't listening. She was reading the letter again. "What exactly *are* the Everglades, Alice?"

"A huge swamp of saw grass, quicksand, and mud that extends from here to the west coast, inhabited by gargantuan snakes."

"How odd," Julia said, but it was clear she hadn't heard. She was looking at the royal palms again, seeing Henry B. Plant's trains speeding across the Everglades, carrying thousands of prosperous white American teetotal Prot-estant passengers to that new, shining city on the banks of Biscayne Bay.

R. O. Watson did not arrive on either the twentieth or twenty-first of Feb-ruary. Julia, however, had decided that a February twenty-second arrival would be best anyway and went through with her plans. "We will have a dual celebration," she said. "The birth date of the Founder of Our Nation and the arrival of Henry B. Plant's forward guard."

"Not exactly events of equal significance," the Duke said, having a sudden and unpleasant presentiment. Surely no one would be mad enough to try to drain the Everglades, one of nature's great gardens. Surely, the Duke con-soled himself, no one—not even Henry B. Plant—would be rich enough. Unlike Julia, the Duke had some idea of the Everglades' extent.

Jeff and Fred McCord, under the direction of their partner, Harry Tuttle, spent the morning making lemonade. Four gallons were suspended in a par-ticularly dark cove of the Miami River for cooling.

Six of Julia's twelve chickens had been sacrificed for the salad that Minnie McCord had made along with coontie biscuits. Alice had unearthed red, white, and blue bunting from the trading-post storeroom, and she and Fanny had wrapped it around the garden fence. The American flag Julia had brought from Cleveland flew from the old fort's flagpole.

"It all looks very festive," Julia decided, liking the flag waving in the bay breeze. Three black boys had been coached in a harmonica rendition of "The Star-Spangled Banner," which they practiced until Julia begged them to stop.

By noon, when there was still no sign of R. O. Watson, Julia ordered the lemonade served to the bay families who had been invited to greet him. They got the chicken salad at one and the coontie biscuits at two. By four o'clock there were only three boats tied to the Tuttle dock: the Duke's and Miss Alice's skiff and Panthar's dugout.

Panthar sat in a wrought-iron chair. It was the first white man's chair he had sat in and, he admitted to the Duke, he was finding it nearly comfortable.

"You'd better be careful, Panthar. Next thing I know, you'll be wearing a top hat and carrying a walking stick."

Fanny, in the pale-blue silk, sulked and daydreamed while Harry dozed in the string hammock. "It's a pity we didn't know what time to expect them," Alice said from the relative comfort of a bentwood love seat. When she received no reply, she said, "Julia, if you don't stop pacing, you're going to wear a track in your new lawn. Julia, are you crying?"

"Don't be ridiculous, Alice," Julia, who did feel a bit teary, said. She had gone to such work for this party. Half the chickens! "You don't suppose they're lost, do you?" Julia, her brown hair firmly fixed on top of her handsome head, her milky complexion paler than usual, came to a stop in front of the Duke, who lay on his stomach on the lawn. He had put on a fresh waistcoat in honor of the day but had held the line when it came to a shirt, a cravat, and shoes.

"Of course they're lost," he said, turning over, propping one leg on the other, his hands behind his head. "No Indian guide would take them. They were fools to start out in the first place."

Julia stared down at him, wondering why he never seemed to age. She looked at that thick line of blond hair that started at his chest and reappeared at his exposed waist, and for a moment a graphic vision of their lovemaking filled her mind. Impatiently she shook it away. "Someday, Mr. Ewing, when you're all grown up and looking about for a suitable occupation, you might think about the mortician trade. You're a natural crepehanger." She turned away from him, raised her chin, and made a decision.

"Panthar, I want you to take your canoe and go to look for them," she said to him quietly. "If anyone can find them, you can."

The Duke jumped up. "Julia, he can't do that. It's sacred ground."

"We can't let those men die, Mr. Ewing. They're lost in that swamp. Panthar doesn't want R. O. Watson's death on his conscience," Julia went on, looking directly into the Indian's sad eyes, "and I can't believe you do either, Duke."

"R. O. Watson's death in the Everglades, Julia, won't be on Panthar's or my conscience. It will be on yours."

Ignoring the Duke, continuing to stare up at the Indian searchingly, Julia said, "Panthar, will you please go look for Mr. Watson and his group? Will you go now?"

Panthar slowly rose from the white man's chair. He looked at the Duke, who was angrier than he had ever seen him. And he looked at Julia, so certain of her truth, like a powerful goddess, and he bowed his head. "Yes, Mrs. Tuttle, I will go now."

"Panthar," the Duke called after him. "The laws of your tribe forbid—"

"The old laws are not always true laws," Panthar said, heading for the dock and his dugout.

"You've corrupted him, Julia."

"I have educated him, Mr. Ewing. I have opened the portals of progress and enlightenment, and he has taken the first step through. I only hope to God he finds those men."

"So you can bring progress and enlightenment, Tuttle style, to the bay area, Julia? Well, I'm not at all certain I care if he succeeds." Standing up, he looked at Julia for a moment and then left with no further words.

The following day the bunting seemed the worse for wear, but the flag—which Harry had neglected to take down—still flew high. Despite invitations, none of the other bay families had returned, but the Duke, feeling guilty, had arrived with Miss Alice. Harry and Fanny were under orders to remain in the garden. "Panthar will find them," Julia said with conviction as another long morning passed.

Just when Julia was about to order the new chicken salad served, when she was about to give up on Panthar, a great whoop was heard, coming down the Miami River, echoing into the bay. Even the Duke stood up and looked at the small procession coming down the river. Panthar, in his canoe led the way, followed by a boat captained by a muddy, noticeably slimmer R. O. Watson and filled with six men in various states of disrepair.

They trooped up the lawn to where Julia stood waiting to greet them. "I bid you welcome, Mr. Watson, to Mr. Henry B. Plant's next terminus," Julia said.

"Food," R. O. Watson said and fainted at her feet.

The celebration was put off yet one more day while R. O. Watson and his men recovered. Alice had agreed to supply more chickens, though Julia had had to bribe her: Fanny was to be allowed to spend three days of each week at the Brickells', teaching Alice's younger sisters the art of piano playing, assisting Alice with her postmistress duties, and being exposed to the society of the Coconut Grove settlement.

"She'll never meet any young people at Fort Dallas," Alice—concerned for Fanny—said.

Julia didn't much care. She wanted the chickens and gave in. And so, for the third consecutive day, Minnie McCord's chicken salad was served on the Fort Dallas lawn in celebration of George Washington's birthday and R. O. Watson's arrival.

"It was as if," R. O. Watson told the Duke, "I had turned a particularly nasty corner of the Amazon to find myself safely on Main Street. However did she get those kids to learn 'The Star-Spangled Banner'?"

"Mrs. Tuttle is an indefatigable instructor."

Julia came up to them at that moment and led R. O. Watson to a chair in the center of the lawn. "Now, we've waited long enough," she said, handing him a glass of lemonade. "You must tell us all about your adventure, and don't leave a word out."

R. O. Watson was fairly certain his savior in the blue serge dress, Mrs. Julia Tuttle, was not so much interested in his "adventure" as she was in the land appraisal he was to make to Henry B. Plant. But she showed admirable restraint, and Watson was eager to share his story.

"We didn't find an Indian guide willing to take us on a tour of the Everglades—and we looked high and low, believe me, Mrs. T. 'Heap big trouble for Injun to take paleface to sacred swamp' is all we got out of the redskins in Tampa. In the end we did find us a guide, a slightly inebriated old army codger named Pasko.

"Found him on the steps of Mr. Plant's Tampa Bay Hotel. He'd been in the last of the Seminole War battles and said he knew the country backward and forward. He said he could get us across the Everglades better than any darned Injun. Well, Pasko said a lot of things.

"So we set out to see if the Everglades could be drained. If Henry B. Plant could build a train track across the Everglades to the east coast. If your land, Mrs. T., might not be suitable for Mr. Plant's first East Coast city." R. O. Watson lit a Havana cigar and inhaled. He was enjoying the suspense.

"What did you find, Mr. Watson?" Julia was not.

"What we found," he said, exhaling smoke, "was saw grass so sharp it cut right through our boots and into our feet, leaving long, gaping, and eventually infected wounds.

"We found mud, Mrs. T. We lost two of our boats the second day to the mud. I've never seen anything like that mud. It has a life of its own. The smell was enough to make you permanently nauseated. Three days in, our food ran out. Our tents rotted, and we were sleeping in that mud. One man always had to be on guard for snakes—rattlers the width of your shoulders and the length of a good-sized railway car."

Watson shuddered. "I don't even want to think about them. Pasko had brought along his own supply of whiskey and managed to get himself hopelessly drunk by ten o'clock every morning. Whereupon he'd begin having long arguments with himself at the top of his voice about which way we should go. This did not improve morale, Mrs. T.

"What's more, we all came down with swamp fever. And there we were, lost for who knew how long, tormented by the humidity, the sun, and the mosquitoes. Tell you the truth, Mrs. T., I'm an optimistic sort of person, but even I thought we were all going to die in that brown water we were trapped in.

"Then one morning we woke up and Pasko was gone. We had put our faith in a drunk, and when we saw we had lost him—I expect he drowned in the mud—we all gave up and started to say our prayers.

"It turns out Pasko had gotten us within a day's trek from the bay, but we wouldn't have known that if your Indian hadn't come sailing along and taken us in hand. You saved our lives, Mrs. T. There's no getting around that."

And finally, as the Duke knew she would, Julia asked the question that had been in her mind since Watson's arrival. "And what conclusions have you come to, Mr. Watson? What sort of a report are you going to make to Mr. Plant?"

Watson took refuge in geography. "Well, Mrs. T., I found that the Everglades, along the entire one hundred and sixty miles of its eastern border, is rimmed by a rock ledge. That all of the lakes making up that portion of the Everglades are several feet above sea level. That there is nothing to prevent the waters of the lake from flowing into the ocean and leaving the land dry if draining vents are cut into the long ledge of rocks." He hesitated when he saw the look in Julia's eyes. He had seen it before but only in men's eyes, men who spoke of buried treasure and untold riches. It was a fanatical look.

"Mr. Watson," Julia asked, a new unconvincing smile on her lips, "is it going to be a positive report?"

"I am going to tell Mr. Plant," R. O. Watson said, measuring his words carefully, "that a railroad line could be built."

Julia let out her breath. "That's exactly what I needed to hear." She stood up and moved away from the group. "It's going to happen," she said to herself as she walked to the fence that separated the garden from the jungle and looked out on the bay. "It's going to happen. I know it."

"You should have told her the truth, Watson," the Duke said when Julia had moved away.

"I did," R. O. protested. "A railroad *could* be built across the Everglades."

"At such enormous expense, Plant would never consider it."

"I'll let him tell her that, Mr. Ewing, safely, via the United States mails."

The Duke left R. O. Watson to his cigar and went to Julia. He put his hand on hers, but she didn't notice. "Every building will be white," she said. "Even the railroad station. It's all going to be white and beautiful."

CHAPTER NINE

1894

THE BAY AREA READING CLUB (founder and chairwoman, Mrs. Julia Tuttle) met the third Monday afternoon of each month at two o'clock sharp, usually at Fort Dallas. Minnie McCord's coontie cookies were the lure. These sweet cakelike confections were dismissed by the Tuttles but were addictive to many bay women. There were six active members of the club but, depending on weather and housework and transportation (one had to somehow get across the Miami River to Fort Dallas), anywhere from three to ten women might be expected.

Though few could actually read, they liked to listen to Miss Fanny. Even Minnie McCord, who didn't hold with book learning, would slip into the lounge and sit on the edge of the white wicker sofa, timing her entry to coincide with the end of Julia's reading, usually an improving work of fiction.

Then Fanny, in the soft, educated voice she used at such times, would read recipes from the ancient copies of *Godey's Lady's Book*, which Alice had brought with her when she had first come to the bay area. The recipes often called for such exotica as boars' heads and truffles, foods that few bay women would ever taste, but the romance of those foreign-sounding dishes fascinated them. Pheasant under glass always drew sighs.

On this particular June Monday afternoon only Julia, Fanny, Alice, and the elderly Mary Jane Cherry had turned up. The morning sky had been filled with threatening gray clouds, and Julia had moved the meeting to the Brickells' in order to save attendees from traveling in the potential storm. But the turnout was still disappointing. The storm, which eventually blew over, was not the only reason the others had stayed away. Two Key West boats had put in with orders for turtle steaks to supply New York restaurants, and the bay women were busy slaughtering the turtles they kept in traps and preparing their meat for transportation.

Julia, irritated, had opened the meeting ten minutes late with a chapter from *A Tale of Two Cities*. Fanny followed with a half-hour description of the preparation of a trifle called the Queen Victoria Tart. Alice laughed over an unseemly association ("tart, indeed"), while Mary Jane Cherry, jaws slack, hung on every word.

Julia's attention wandered. She gazed at a miniature American flag Alice had stuck in a dusty old vase and thought of the celebration she had given the previous year for R. O. Watson. The promised letter from Mr. Plant had taken two months to arrive and had said in unequivocal terms that he was not going to build a railroad across the Everglades and bankrupt himself.

Julia had written back, but neither Mr. Plant nor Mr. Watson had answered. I should have left R. O. Watson to wander forever in the Everglades, Julia thought, not for the first time. She still experienced moments of guilt over Panthar's punishment.

When his tribe's chief and shaman had learned that Panthar had guided white men through sacred waters, they had cut off the lobe on his right ear and forced him to spend a solitary month on a lonely key. Panthar had accepted his punishment, but Julia had been livid. For some time after, one of Julia's favorite topics of conversation for enlivening the dinner table—especially when the Duke was present—was the backward barbarity of the Seminoles.

276

While Fanny read a description of the tart's elaborate crust, Julia thought, I've spent nearly two years in the bay area, and all I have to show for it is six hundred and forty undeveloped acres and a letter from Henry B. Plant. The rest of Florida was booming. She had started a reading club, a lending library, and a garden club, and meanwhile men were making fortunes, lining both coasts with cities and hotels. Willie Brickell's grandfather clock played counterpoint to Fanny's recipe reading. Time is passing, Julia thought. She *must* do something.

Her thoughts were interrupted by Alice, who had taken Fanny's place at the makeshift podium. It was Alice's duty to read from the most recent newspaper available. As Alice's reading voice was simultaneously harsh and sing-song, and as the newspapers invariably came from Fort Dallas, Julia usually didn't pay attention to this segment of the reading group's proceedings.

Today, however, Alice was reading from the New York *Herald*. It had found its way to the Brickells' dark living room from one of the boats that had put in from Key West. A familiar name caught Julia's attention.

> . . . it has been announced that R. O. Watson, formerly with Florida's West Coast entrepreneur Henry B. Plant, has assumed the duties of executive secretary for Florida's East Coast entrepreneur (and Standard Oil millionaire) Henry Morrison Flagler. Mr. Watson will help identify and locate potential resort sites along the new railway line Flagler is extending down the coast of Florida from St. Augustine to a little known place called West Palm Beach. West Palm Beach is not far from Palm Beach (originally Palm City), where the Florida developer is said to be building his most extravagant resort to date. When asked if he was going to extend his railroad farther south, Flagler, through a spokesman, said no. "I have found perfection in Palm Beach. This is the end of the line."

"It is not the end of the line," Julia said, standing up, waking Mary Jane Cherry out of a sound sleep. "I refuse to believe that. I am going to write to Mr. Watson today. Now that he's with such a far-thinking man as Henry Flagler, he must surely see—"

"Mama," Fanny said, standing up and carefully drawing on her gloves, "you have written to Mr. Watson dozens of times. I don't remember there being many replies." There was a new independence about Fanny that Julia didn't like. She seemed to have grown even longer and more elegant during the past year, and Julia put it down to her three days each week at the Brickells' and to her new companion, Señor Córdoba.

"Where are you going?" she asked as Fanny adjusted her straw hat and moved toward the door. Fanny was, as always, beautifully turned out. Julia felt for a moment dowdy. And it was in that moment she realized what had suddenly made Fanny so different. She no longer needed Julia's approval.

"For my walk, Mama." The door closed after her with a certain finality.

"I blame you for this, Alice," Julia said, disregarding Mary Jane Cherry, who was finding this interchange nearly as good as the recipe for Queen Victoria Tart, "and no one else."

Alice busied herself taking the podium—the hall table—away. "He's a perfectly respectable gentleman," she said, not looking at Julia. "In the import-export trade."

"He's a Cuban ne'er-do-well, Alice. The commodity he's been importing and exporting these past two years is nothing I would care to name. Does he still get those remittances from Havana?"

"I am not about to breach the sanctity of the United States mails, Julia, by telling you—"

"It's too late to get religion about the mails, Alice. He is, to use a word I'm not ordinarily fond of but which is perfectly apt in this case, a bounder."

"Julio Córdoba is not a bounder," Alice said. "He is a charming, handsome, beautifully mannered—"

"I suppose you receive him in this house?"

"On occasion. Julia, Fanny and Julio are only friends."

"I will never give my permission, Alice. I swear to you. I would rather see her an old maid than married to that unemployed foreigner."

Alice shook her head. "Julia, you really are the most—"

Mary Jane Cherry did not find out how Alice was going to finish that sentence because at that moment the Duke and young Harry Tuttle came into the Brickell living room, bringing light and life into the place. Behind them, through the open door, Mary Jane could see the new, blue sky.

"Too late for Dickens?" the Duke asked in his hoarse voice, smiling that gap-toothed smile that made him look quite as young as Harry.

"Far too late," Julia said, giving Mary Jane Cherry a perfunctory nod as she slipped out the door, half a dozen coontie cookies in her handkerchief. "Next time," Julia called, "Sir Walter Raleigh. Spread the word, Mary Jane." She turned her attention back to Harry.

Harry had borrowed three hundred dollars from her to buy his own skiff and a third of Jeff and Fred McCord's salvage business. So far the most noteworthy salvage he had found was a barrel of lard from a wrecked British freighter, for which Minnie McCord kissed him. Cooking oil was a great treasure to the bay women. Among Harry's lesser finds was the better part of a pianoforte and a bolt of water-stained linen, which he gave, magnanimously, to his sister, with whom he was now on something like civil terms.

Julia was well aware that Harry spent his time either fishing with the Duke in the Everglades or with the McCords, gambling and quite possibly drinking spirits on the scrubby island across the bay. The brothers and Harry would often sleep in the mangrove swamps (Harry had become as immune to mosquitoes as his mother), waiting for something of value to be swept ashore.

Like the Duke, Harry wore only a waistcoat and trousers held up by a

278

length of rope. He was tan and fit. His withered arm seemed miraculously re-covered. He was attempting a mustache, with little success. "You look," Julia said to him, "like the poor man's version of Mr. Ewing. I suppose it would be too much to ask you to wear shoes when you come visiting?"

"Mama, if you want polite society, you must go to St. Augustine."

"You would like St. Augustine, Julia," the Duke said. "Mr. Flagler has built all sorts of monuments to progress right over the pretty little Maria Sanchez Creek that use to run through St. Augustine. In fact, there is no more creek, just Mr. Flagler's monuments. And his railroads."

"And I have good reason to believe," Julia said, not caring for the "pretty little Maria Sanchez Creek" or what Alice had read about Mr. Flagler's plans, "that he has every intention of bringing his railroad here. He's hired Mr. Watson," she added triumphantly. "Then, Mr. Ewing, you will be able to witness progress in the making in the bay area. On my six hundred and forty acres."

"Mama," Harry interrupted, "Flagler's said a dozen times he's stopping at Palm Beach. He's not coming any farther south. He has no reason to. Give the old progress horse a rest, Mama, please." Harry, thinking of his lunch, fol-lowed Alice into the kitchen. Julia, usually successful at avoiding the situa-tion, found herself alone with the Duke.

She went to the window that faced the bay and drew aside the heavy red curtains Alice had brought from Cleveland twenty years before. "I should have approached Henry Morrison Flagler in the first place," Julia said, trying to ignore the Duke's presence. "He is a man of vision."

She sensed that he had moved closer to her, but his voice, so low and so close to her ear, still made her start. "Julia, Harry's right. Give it up. Put the old progress horse out to pasture." He took her short clenched fist and held it between his two hands. "Your dream is a nightmare, Julia. Marry me, Julia," he said impulsively. "You've wasted two of our years. Let's not waste any more."

She turned toward him, but before she could say anything, he had put his arms around her. The bare muscles of his blond arms made her think of that long-ago episode of lovemaking. She felt helpless as those arms surrounded her, encapsulated her, made her feel what she couldn't believe she was: fe-male and fragile. He kissed her neck, moving his body against hers. "Let's live here in the paradise that already is, Julia."

Julia fought for strength and found it, breaking out of his arms, moving away toward the windows and the bay. "I will not give it up," she said, as much to herself as to the Duke. "I will not give in. I will not be somebody's wife, Mr. Ewing. I was somebody's wife long enough, and a lot of good it did me. I will not be your wife, Mr. Ewing, mending your waistcoats and cooking your possum. I am going to build a city, a great white city. I am going to make a fortune, Mr. Ewing, and if this threatens you, well, I am—"

The Duke spun her around and held her again, taking her chin in his hand, grasping it so tightly it hurt, forcing her to look into his frosty eyes. "Listen to me, Julia," he said in that husky voice that seemed to go right through her. "For once in your life, damn it, listen. I want to make love to you as I did so long ago on the beach. I want to feel myself inside you, Julia. I want to feel you come alive again. I want to hear the world reverberate again with your shout of freedom. You care for me. I know that you do. We can be happy. Damn you, Julia. Be my lover. Be my wife. Say yes, Julia."

"No," she whispered, pushing him away, freeing herself. "I don't want to marry you. I don't want to be possessed by you. I don't want to be your lover. I will not be another animal in this jungle. I am going to make a name and a fortune for myself. I am going to build a Christian city," she said in a clear, strong voice, her eyes filling with tears. "It is going to be a city of white towers. I am going to keep the beasts and the jungle out." She went to the door. Her hand on the knob was shaking, but her voice was firm. "I am going to Fort Dallas to write Mr. Watson a letter."

"He won't answer, Julia," the Duke said, for once looking his age.

"My letter won't require an answer, Mr. Ewing. I am taking my son's advice. I am going to St. Augustine. My letter will merely notify Mr. Watson that I am on my way, coming to meet with Mr. Flagler. He is a man with vision. He will understand." She stepped out of the house and looked toward the newly emerged sun illuminating Biscayne Bay. "I am not going to marry anyone, Mr. Ewing. I am going to build my city."

When the boat known as *The City of Key West* docked in St. Augustine, Julia felt the little bump of fear in her chest expand and grow. "Of course I'm doing the right thing," she said to herself, preparing to disembark. It had occurred to her during the smooth sail up the coast of Florida that this was the first journey she had ever undertaken by herself. There was no Alice or Harry or Fanny to occupy her. Only that little bump of fear.

She had ignored it, spending her time at sea alternately building her dream city and rehearsing what she would say to Mr. Flagler. In her city no alcohol would be sold, she decided, thinking of Harry's pink face. And there would be no gambling, she added, remembering the money Harry had won from the wreckers and lost to the fishermen. Thinking of Fanny, she decided there would be no foreigners either. No wild growth, no wild animals, no jungles with snakes and spiders and crocodiles. It was to be a city of white churches, hospitals, hotels, gracious houses surrounded by green lawns and blue waters.

She was going to have to make that clear to Mr. Flagler. I mustn't let him think that I'm intimidated or frightened. I must convince him somehow to visit Fort Dallas.

She was not a woman given to agonizing over her wardrobe. But she did wonder about the dress she was wearing. She had had Alice and Alice's sisters up half the night, cutting and pinning according to the pattern they had found in *Godey's*. But the magazine was at least five years old, and the only suitable material in the trading post had been a rather horsey brown-and-red plaid. "You think it will do, Alice?" Julia had asked while Alice sewed it together on one of the hand-driven machines Ephraim had sold to Willie years before.

Alice had had her doubts as she looked at the full and very plaid skirt, the white sateen blouse that seemed just a bit yellow, and the ill-fitting plaid mid-waist jacket. It was topped off by Julia's old straw hat, which Alice in what might have been misguided inspiration had painted black and adorned with carved wood cherries. "Of course it will do, Julia."

Reassured, Julia hadn't given the costume another thought until she walked down the dock to where R. O. Watson was waiting with a horse-drawn buggy. It was painted a shiny black and had thin gold lines around the door. It looked as if it should have belonged to a younger man. The buggy and Mr. Watson in a gray silk cravat were excruciatingly fashionable. Julia, her mind filled with misgivings, that little bump pulsating inside her breast, hoped she looked at least businesslike.

"It's a pleasure to see you, Mrs. T.," R. O. Watson said, helping her into the buggy, which was driven by a black man in a green coat. "I have often thought of you in the past two years, wondering how you and the delightful bay-area pioneers were getting on." He had thought of Julia, it was true. He had liked her particular brand of madness. "I have a very soft spot in my heart for you, Mrs. T.," he said, and Julia was nearly afraid the short man with the round eyes and the thin hay-colored hair was about to make a declaration of affection.

"I should hope so, Mr. Watson," she said in her driest voice. "After all, I saved your life." She declined a tour of St. Augustine, saying she had visited once, twenty years before during her first visit to Florida, when Harry and Fanny were children. "The *Emily B.* is returning south tonight. I want to be on it. More to the point, Mr. Watson, I have made a long, uncomfortable journey to talk to your employer, and I should like that opportunity as soon as possible."

R. O. Watson, amused by Julia's forthrightness, told the driver to take them to the Ponce de León "at once." Julia found herself being sped through a St. Augustine vastly different from the village she and her children had visited. The dusty streets she remembered had given way to cobblestones, along which ladies in gray fashionable clothing strolled.

"I thought the season was over," Julia said, noticing unhappily that the horses all wore brown-and-red-plaid blankets.

"You should see it in season."

The smart women were accompanied by stout mustachioed gentlemen. In their frock coats and high-collared shirts they looked as different from the bay-area men as if they had come from a different country. There were numerous grand hotels and less grand boardinghouses, but the old Spanish buildings that lined the square remained, giving the center of town a European air.

The Ponce de León, innovatively constructed of poured concrete and coquina, sat squatly on a huge piece of land where the Duke's Maria Sanchez Creek had once run, a short way from the square and the bay front. All of the strollers seemed to be either headed toward or coming from the hotel, which looked to Julia like a child's sand castle built on a mammoth scale.

The Ponce de León's main architectural feature was a huge red-tiled dome. But there were so many elaborate concrete towers and so much terra cotta ornamentation and such an abundance of Louis Comfort Tiffany stained-glass windows that it took Julia a moment to see the dome.

"Not bad, is it?" R. O. Watson asked as if he owned it.

"It's magnificent." Julia, her hands to her plaid chest, couldn't take her eyes away from the exotic architectural combination of the mysteries of the Near East, the grandeurs of Middle Europe, and the romance of Moorish Spain. "A work of great art." Under the weight of all that detail, of all those windows and towers and terraces and balconies and piers and arches and loggias and steeples, the Ponce de León managed to be graceful. "It is so much what I want for my city," said Julia, breathless.

She felt as if she were in a dream as Watson led her up the tiled stairs, through the arched entrance, and into the high-ceilinged lobby, where boys in green and gold livery and fashionable men and women seemed to be engaged in a stylized dance, a formal and grand pavane.

R. O. Watson, leading Julia up more tiled Moorish steps, wondered what she was thinking. At a tiny baroque balcony that served as a landing she turned to him and let him know. "Will he do this for me?" she asked. "Will he bring his railroad to the bay area, Mr. Watson?"

"He's a difficult man to read," Watson said noncommittally. "And hard to convince. If anyone can turn the trick it will be you, Mrs. T."

Julia didn't like his answer. She suddenly lost whatever confidence she had had in her brown-and-red-plaid dress and her painted straw hat with its little red cherries that threatened to come undone. All those women in their gray silks and all those millionaires had so totally ignored her. Nevertheless Julia lifted her square chin, clenched her hands, and plowed up the steps ready to do battle.

Henry Morrison Flagler received Julia Tuttle in his office, a paneled octagonal room with a soberly tiled floor and an anonymous male-club atmosphere. He wore a dark suit, a dotted cravat, and gold-rimmed spectacles. His hair and mustache were white. He was older, stiffer, and less forthcoming than Julia had thought he would be. He did not look like her idea of an empire builder.

But he took her hand politely, and when she reminded him of the dinner party they had both attended in Cleveland, he pretended to remember the occasion. His restraint and the sepulchral air in that dark office suite—so much at odds with the magnificent mysteries and kinetic elegance of the rest of the hotel—daunted her. There didn't seem to be a sound or a smell in the place.

Flagler, unnaturally still, had stopped being polite and was waiting. Watson had warned her she had but a quarter of an hour. He stood behind Flagler and pointedly tapped the face of his pocket watch. Julia, with an effort, shook off the gloom and her nervousness and began talking. She spoke of the beauties of Biscayne Bay, of its remarkably even and warm climate, of the extraordinary mix of flora and fauna, unlike any in the world. She spoke of the Miami River, of the obliging bay people, of the endless opportunities for relaxation and sport, for lively amusement, for quiet, healing meditation.

Carried away by her own rhetoric, Julia took off her hat and, opening both her arms, said, "It is the Garden of Eden, Mr. Flagler. The next great city on this magical peninsula and, in time, the most important metropolis on this coast. In the world. I invite you to come to us and sample our life, our natural luxuries. Mr. Flagler, I offer you half my acreage if you will come. All that's needed to turn the bay area into the city of tomorrow is your genius, Mr. Flagler. Your presence. Your—"

"—railroad." Flagler looked at the gilded clock on his desk. Julia suddenly felt ridiculous, holding her hat, her arms out, her mouth still open.

Flagler put a practiced hand under Julia's bent elbow and escorted her to the door. "It's been a most educational quarter of an hour, Mrs. Tuttle. Thank you for your valuable time."

"I have so much more to say," she protested. "You *will* think over what I'm proposing, Mr. Flagler?"

"I will give your scheme every consideration, Mrs. Tuttle," the great man said, and Julia knew she was being humored.

During the buggy ride back to the dock it had begun to rain. An empathetic R. O. Watson bade Julia goodbye, affecting not to notice the black drops descending on Julia's cheeks as the paint ran off the straw hat.

A week later Julia arrived, unscheduled, at the Brickell dock aboard the old *Emily B.* It had rained since she had left St. Augustine and it was raining in the bay area as well. The dock was deserted. Julia put the now half-black, half-natural straw hat on her head and made her way down the gangplank. No one in the bay area would care about the hat or the plaid or the fact that she had failed so miserably.

The Duke, watching her from the end of the dock, saw defeat in her lowered chin and in the limp, open hands at her side. He came to her and put his arms around her and held her to him while the rain soaked them both through. Julia was too weary, too much in need of comfort to stop him. "He didn't even give me time to invite him to the fort," she said, her tears mixing with the rain and the black paint.

She saw the paint running down the Duke's chest, ruining his good waistcoat, and freed herself. She took the hat off her head and sent it skimming into Biscayne Bay. "Julia," the Duke said, reaching for her again. A growing familiar lump in her chest nearly made her return to his arms.

But she saw the hat, refusing to sink, being swept north, its little wooden cherries afloat, and her hands clenched and her chin went up. "He didn't say no," she said, turning and heading for the Brickells' cottage. "Not unequivocally. There's still a chance. I'm not going to give up now." Halfway up the dock she stopped and looked at the Duke, who wore the irritating, sad smile he reserved for Julia when he was pitying her.

"Or ever, Mr. Ewing," she shouted defiantly. Taking a breath, feeling better, she resumed walking toward Alice's house. One can never tell with a man like Flagler, she thought. He didn't wear his emotions on his face like some she could name. At this very moment he might be giving orders to his teams of engineers to head for the bay, to start laying tracks, to get ready to build her city. She stopped on the Brickell porch for just a moment before entering. "I only need a miracle," she whispered to herself. "I only need a miracle to convince him."

Julia was never to know that Flagler had written her off as yet another land salesman with yet another undevelopable location. Six months later, during the Christmas of 1894, while still stubbornly waiting for Flagler's final word, Julia received her miracle. But even Julia had to admit it was a costly one.

CHAPTER TEN

ON CHRISTMAS EVE, 1894, the thermometer fell to fourteen degrees in Jacksonville, eighteen in Titusville, and twenty-four as far south as Jupiter. It was the first frost in recorded Florida history.

Overnight Florida's thriving citrus industry appeared to be out of business. Not that the orange growers didn't fight back. Every member of every citrus-growing family was out in the fields, keeping the smudge pots burning, working through the freezing-cold night. The men and boys drank the hot coffee the women brewed and the girls delivered in huge tin urns. In those rare moments when the winds weren't extinguishing the smudge-pot fires, they all got down on their knees and prayed.

Their prayers were answered. On Christmas morning, when the winds had died down and the temperature had risen, many of the orange growers believed they were going to make it. They set about nursing their surviving stock back to health and replanting.

By February sixth there was cause for cautious celebration. It was premature. The following day an even more devastating freeze hit Florida, killing not only what was left of the year's citrus crop but also vegetables and coconut palms as far south as Henry Flagler's Palm Beach.

More than one orange-growing family left dinner on the table and caught the next train back north, abandoning what they felt was a dead-end situation. Smudge pots couldn't combat this frost. Property damage was in the millions. Thousands of families were devastated, without income or the prospect of it.

It was Henry Flagler who came to their rescue. He could not allow fellow Christians to suffer, especially—as he said—when their calamity was a result of fate and not from lack of industry.

He also had an economic interest in putting the region back on its financial feet. His railroad's welfare was tied to the continued prosperity of the citrus farmers: everything they grew was shipped north on his trains, providing the bulk of his railroad's income.

His response was immediate. He had free seed given to every family who requested it so replanting could begin. To help impoverished farmers get through the worst of the recovery, he authorized hundreds of personal interest-free loans. Fertilizer was distributed without charge. He sent agricultural experts to all the farms with advice and supplies and, often as not, money. Everything Flagler and his organization could do to stabilize and reactivate the fallen industry was done.

In his heart Flagler believed that the people and the crops and his railroad would recover. Hard work always won its reward in the end. But he had learned a lesson: northern and central Florida were not immune to frost. There was always the possibility of another during the next winter.

He sent R. O. Watson on an extensive inspection tour. Watson's usually indefatigable spirit sank as he worked his way south from Jacksonville, visiting one devastated citrus farm after another. The pine and cypress farmhouses, surrounded by dead citrus trees, were concentrated pockets of misery and defeat. It was said that R. O. Watson was a man who never cried, but he had tears in his eyes during that trip.

At the end of his reconnaissance tour R. O. Watson experienced a deep depression. He had planned, when he came to the new end of the railroad line in Palm Beach, to go directly to Flagler to make his report. Flagler was ensconced in his newest hotel, Palm Beach's Royal Poinciana, making plans

285

for a second, the Breakers, and for a private residence, White Hall. At the thought of all that new construction, of all the talk and decisions that would attend it, R. O. Watson lost heart.

At the Royal Poinciana, before he could notify Flagler that he had returned, the desk clerk handed him a letter. It came from his old friend Mrs. Tuttle, inviting him to her fortress home. Standing in the center of the glamorous lobby, looking out at the sailboats on Lake Worth, trying to shake off a deep weariness, R. O. Watson wondered why on earth Julia Tuttle had chosen this extremely inappropriate moment to issue an invitation to what sounded like a tea party. Surely even Mrs. T. didn't expect Flagler's right-hand man to travel all the way to Biscayne Bay for stale orange pekoe.

Yet he thought of his last visit to the bay area, after the nightmare of the Everglades journey. He had been similarly depressed and exhausted then, but Julia Tuttle—with that naïve single-mindedness he found fascinating—had magically lifted his spirits. She might do so now.

"Mr. Flagler wants a full report on Florida's post-frost condition," he said to himself. "He's going to get one." R. O. Watson borrowed his employer's yacht and set sail for Biscayne Bay, Fort Dallas, and Julia Tuttle.

Flagler's yacht had too deep a draft to make it across the shallow bay. Watson had the captain lay anchor, and a cabin boy rowed the dinghy across the still waters to the Fort Dallas dock. It seemed unnaturally warm. Even in Palm Beach a wintry chill—a leftover from the frost—had remained in the air. Here, Watson realized without thinking much about it, summer reigned once again.

He was tempted to remove his coat, but he saw that Mrs. Tuttle herself was on the dock waiting for him. He wondered what on earth she was wearing, remembering the unfortunate plaid dress and the painted straw hat she had worn during the St. Augustine visit. He squinted. She seemed to have wrapped herself in some orange and green concoction. The poor woman had a terrible sense of dress, R. O. Watson thought, his spirits beginning to rise. What had she gotten up to, now?

"My Lord," R. O. Watson—not a man much given to invoking dieties—said. The woman was covered from head to toe with white blossoms. They were pinned in her hair and entwined around her throat, her wrists, and her waist. As the boat neared the shore he realized with a start that they were orange blossoms. "Where the hell had Julia Tuttle gotten enough orange blossoms to take a bath in when every damned orange tree in the state had been killed by the frosts?" he asked himself. As the boy made the dinghy fast and R. O. Watson stepped onto the Fort Dallas dock he understood the oddly timed invitation and the reason that Julia Tuttle looked like an orange grove. The bay area had had no frost.

"You look lovely, Mrs. T.," he said, laughing delightedly and taking her stubby hand. "The Orange Blossom Queen come to life."

286

Julia permitted herself a smile. She had known Mr. Watson would understand. He was, like his employer, a man of vision. "I thought it best," she said, taking his arm, leading him up the lawn to the garden near where her fragrant orange trees bloomed, "to emphasize the obvious."

She had gathered together the Duke, Harry, Miss Alice, Fanny, and Panthar to greet him. Minnie McCord poured orange juice and offered slices of orange cake. Harry wore an orange blossom in the lapel of his waistcoat. And Fanny was bitterly attired in the pale-blue, orange blossoms in her hair and at her waist. Watson, beaming, took in the group with appreciation.

"Will you be staying long, Mr. Watson?" Julia asked, while he drank his juice and ate his cake.

"I think I had better get back to Mr. Flagler as soon as I can. I have a report to make."

"I am certain you do," Julia replied happily. "But first you must see the orchard."

"Some orchard," Alice said under her breath. "Four orange trees and a skunk-cabbage palm."

Julia ignored her—and everyone—save R. O. Watson as she took his arm once more and led him to the little copse. The trees seemed to R. O. Watson a miracle, covered as they were with white flowers. "Panthar," Julia ordered, "will you cut down that branch of orange blossoms for Mr. Watson? Yes, that's it. The barely opened ones. Thank you, Panthar." She wrapped the stem in damp cotton Fanny had brought—on cue—and handed the branch to R. O. Watson. "I have never given flowers to a gentleman before, but I thought that in this one instance I might brave society's opprobrium."

" 'Society's opprobrium,' " Alice said sotto voce, shaking her head.

"Will you take these flowers for me, Mr. Watson, and give them to Mr. Flagler as a token of my admiration and esteem?"

Watson looked at her with affection. "Such a present would be well received, ma'am, at this time."

"I do think," Julia said, leading R. O. Watson back down the lawn toward his boat, "that Mr. Flagler deserves these flowers for all he's done for Florida." She stopped, took a blossom from her waist and held it to her no-nonsense nose. "Not one single orange was killed by frost, Mr. Watson. For a very good reason, Mr. Watson. There was no frost. Not in the bay area.

"Now, when you give Mr. Flagler my flowers, will you be certain to remind him that my offer still stands—half my land when he brings his railroad here?"

"I shall do everything you ask, Mrs. T." He looked at her standing on the dock wrapped in orange blossoms as the boy rowed him toward Flagler's yacht. All those orange blossoms. All those directions. She was vulgar, obvious, greedy. But R. O. Watson was more charmed than ever by that single-mindedness. After all the defeated men and women he had met during his recent travels Julia Tuttle seemed to be the only flower in bloom in the entire peninsula.

"Godspeed," Julia called, her voice smiling, the pure sound of victory echoing across the bay.

Watson met with Flagler that evening. He made his report, described his journey, and ended with his hour-long visit to the bay area. Henry Flagler held a sprig of Julia's orange blossom branch to his nose. The buds had opened and were a mass of white petals. Their perfume was sweeter than any he had previously known. The bay area was indeed a paradise. A frost-free paradise. "How soon," Henry Flagler asked R. O. Watson, "can you arrange for me to meet your Mrs. Tuttle on her home ground?" Three days later Henry Flagler stepped onto the Fort Dallas dock. Julia Tuttle had finally convinced a man of vision to share hers. The railroad was to come to the bay area. A grand hotel would be built. A city would follow. Julia Tuttle was to have her dream.

Henry Flagler made a second excursion to the bay area in early September 1895, accompanied by R. O. Watson, a team of engineers, and his chief of construction, a giant named John Sewell. They had come to choose an appropriate site for his new hotel, which he was tentatively calling the Royal Miami. Like the Seminoles, the newspapers had long been referring to the bay area by the same name as its river, Miami, which meant "sweet water." And Flagler thought he might as well take advantage of the public's awareness of the name.

Plans for extending the railroad south from West Palm Beach had been finished, and on the morning he reached the bay he received word that the laying of the track through the undeveloped coastal area had begun. "We must have a celebration," he said, and R. O. Watson invited the Tuttles, Willie and Alice Brickell, and the Duke of Dade to a breakfast party at the Peacock Inn.

A round table on the Peacock's dining porch had been reserved for Mr. Flagler's party. Julia, with Fanny and Harry in tow, arrived early to make certain Mr. Flagler's chair had the best view, that of the bay. It was a clear, warm September Saturday morning, but there was a breeze—thank the Lord, Julia said to herself as she rearranged the place settings Isabelle Peacock had spent some time in setting up. The bay waters had a slight chop, and Julia found the invigorating air more to her liking than the usual summer placidity.

Concentrating on the table, Julia was startled to feel a tap on her shoulder. As if I were some shopgirl, Julia thought, turning to find herself staring into what she called "the crocodile smile and the licorice-whip mustaches" of Julio Córdoba. "Mrs. Tuttle," he said, bowing and smiling, his full lips appearing to Julia like a red-hot branding iron. "We have been introduced but once—"

288

"Mr. Córdoba—if that is your name—" Julia said, her chin sky-high but her cheeks going red despite herself, "once was quite enough. I do not include foreigners among my acquaintance. If you will excuse me . . ."

"Mrs. Tuttle, I have something of the utmost importance—"

"Important to you, perhaps. But not to me. If you do not remove your presence immediately, I shall call Mr. Peacock."

Julia turned back to the table, her milky complexion shot with red. As if he were opening a rare fan, Julio Córdoba spread his beautifully cared-for hands in a lovely gesture of finality. Fanny was standing in the doorway, and he had to pass by her to enter the lobby. Julia, watching, was certain that they didn't touch. But Julio Córdoba might have put his arms around her and kissed her with his steamy lips for all the electrical energy in the air. He hesitated for just a moment, Fanny's long, doelike emerald eyes looked up at him, and he moved on.

"*Vaya con Dios, Señor,*" Harry said, grinning from ear to ear so that Julia wanted to slap him. She looked at Fanny, who was staring into the Peacock's lobby. At that instant Julia knew without a doubt that "that foreigner" had been making love to her daughter.

"Fanny," she began, but just then the Duke, Alice, and Willie Brickell arrived. Alice's father was not looking well; his breathing was difficult, his gait unsteady.

"How's the millionairess?" he asked, sitting down heavily.

"Not a millionairess *yet*," Julia said, attempting to digest the information she had just gleaned. She saw Alice looking at her with that knowing Alice glint in her eyes and was relieved when R. O. Watson and Henry Flagler came up onto the dining porch. She swallowed and smiled. She would address herself to the Fanny problem later.

"Never thought I'd be sitting at the same table with two empire builders," Willie Brickell said over the soup, but Flagler, facing the bay, wasn't listening. "Where you going to build after you build this city, Julia?" Willie went on despite Alice's warning glances. "Maybe you and Mr. Flagler will get together and drain the Everglades. Now there's a project for you."

He had caught Flagler's interest for a moment. "Perhaps later," Henry Flagler said. "When we get more sophisticated equipment. Right now it's too expensive."

"And this isn't expensive, Mr. Flagler?" the Duke, who had been unnaturally quiet, asked. "There will be nothing left of this place after you and your railroad and your hotels come in. Think of how much it would cost to replace the alligators and the great blue herons and the ironwood trees you and your engineers are going to destroy. Now, that, Mr. Flagler, would be costly. Try building yourself an ironwood tree."

"Mr. Ewing and Mr. Brickell," Julia said, like a teacher explaining the awkward behavior of wayward children, "are antiprogress, Mr. Flagler."

"We're antidestruction, Julia," the Duke said, pushing his chair back, standing up, going pale under his tan. "You, Julia, and you, Mr. Flagler, will

289

leave nothing of natural coastal Florida when you're finished. All that we'll have will be your filth-spewing railroads and your vulgar hotels and the slummy cities they spawn. You, Julia, and you, Mr. Flagler, are murderers, killing the beauty that is Florida. Surely somewhere in your minds, somewhere in your hearts, you must recognize that you are undoing what God has wrought. Won't you stop? Won't you help us preserve this priceless gift of nature instead of destroying it?"

"Please sit down, Mr. Ewing," Henry Flagler, unmoved, said. "You don't know what you're talking about. We're going to bring education and medicine and, yes, Mrs. Tuttle's much wanted progress, to this place. We are going to improve upon your nature, Mr. Ewing."

"Horse manure, Mr. Flagler," Willie Brickell said, standing up, supporting himself with one hand on the Duke's shoulder. "The Duke's right. You and Julia are murderers. And I don't take my lunch with murderers." He looked up at the Duke. "Let's go to the trading post, my boy. Where the atmosphere is more conducive." Willie Brickell and the Duke of Dade walked off the porch.

Alice stood up as well. "I am sorry, Mr. Flagler. Julia. Papa's not been feeling himself lately. I had better see to him."

"Surely, Alice," Julia said, grabbing her friend's hand, "you don't—"

But Alice was moving as quickly as she could, following her father and the Duke down the Peacock's dock to the skiff.

There was an awkward silence as the departing guests' places were cleared and turtle steaks were brought to the Tuttles, R. O. Watson, and Henry Morrison Flagler. The table seemed much too large, the cloth far too white. Julia, for once at a loss, concentrated on her turtle steak. After a moment she allowed herself to look at Henry Flagler, to gauge his reaction.

He was chewing away with decision, totally at peace, staring at Emmanuel Acosta's royal palms to the north, their fronds waving gently in the bay breeze, seemingly miles above the surrounding jungle. "We must save those royal palms," he said, laying his knife and fork down for a moment. "They stand straight and tall."

Julia watched him looking at the royal palms and felt a great happiness. She nearly kissed that pale, stiff cheek. "By all means," she said. "We must save the royal palms."

After the meal, shaking hands with an enthusiastic Julia, a remote Fanny, and a sycophantic Harry ("anything I can do, Mr. Flagler"), Flagler let his eyes wander to the royal palms again. "You know, Mrs. Tuttle," he said before he went off to meet with his chief of construction, "I have a good mind to name my hotel after those trees. What do you think of The Royal Palm?"

"I think it's perfect, Mr. Flagler. A perfect name."

Harry remained at the Peacock for reasons that either had to do with alcohol or gambling, but Julia refused to be made unhappy. She wouldn't think

290

of Willie Brickell's profanity and the Duke's misplaced passion. Alice would of course come around. Instead Julia concentrated on thoughts of The Royal Palm Hotel as she waited for Panthar and his dugout to come to take her and Fanny back to Fort Dallas. Fanny!

She turned to Fanny, who stood on the dock staring at her with reproach and, yes, hatred. Fanny was wearing a new slim gray dress. The dress and Fanny's elegance reminded Julia of the fashionable women in St. Augustine, of Frederick.

"How dare you look at me like that, Fanny," Julia said in a cold, angry voice. "Don't think I wasn't aware of what that foreigner wanted. Though why he should want to marry you now when he's had the use of you—don't bother to deny it—is a question that bears some examination. Could it be that now it appears I will be very rich and your lover smells unearned money coming his way? Perhaps Señor Córdoba is thinking of *you* as a property to be developed."

Fanny stared at her as if she were seeing Julia for the first time. "You're a terrible woman, Mama," she said after some moments in a voice so low that Julia had to strain to hear. "All my life I've wanted your love. I worked so hard for it, Mama. I did everything I thought you wanted me to do, and yet it never was right, was it, Mama? It's not like money or property. One can't earn love." Fanny shook her head slowly. "Funny, it's only now I realize how inhuman you are. You don't have any love to give. You have no sense of love, no feeling or understanding of it. Papa found that out early on, but it's taken me all these wasted years. I should have realized you're not capable of love when you spurned the Duke."

"Fanny—" Julia tried to cut her off, now more shocked than angry. But Fanny had finally found her voice.

"You turned him down because you said you wanted to build a dream city, you wanted to bring progress to the bay area. Another of your lies, Mama. You just didn't know how to accept the gift he offered. You didn't know what to do with Papa's love, and you don't know what to do with the Duke's. What you've missed, Mama."

Julia stood perfectly still, stunned, tears in her eyes. But Fanny was not moved. "Whom are you crying for, Mama? You or me? Are your tears being shed for my wretched life or for your injured dignity? Of course you're crying for you. You should feel ashamed of yourself, Mama, but you don't have that dimension either. I hope that someday I won't hate you, Mama. I hope that someday I'll only pity you."

Fanny turned and ran up the dock and disappeared inside the Peacock Inn. Julia started to go after her, but Panthar had silently materialized, and she allowed him to help her into the canoe. "Harry will bring Fanny home later," she said to herself, her daughter's accusations already a jumble, her temples pounding. "I won't think about all those things she said to me. We must spend more time with each other," Julia decided. "Now that the railroad is coming, I will have more time. We'll be friends as well as mother and daughter. I'll have time now."

Even the sight of the royal palms—*The Royal Palm*—didn't help. Back at Fort Dallas, she wandered through the silent rooms. From the kitchen house she could hear Minnie McCord singing an old song about a girl with a pink ribbon. She looked in at Fanny's room, so neat and orderly, the mosquito netting gathered together with a bow, the ivory-backed dresser set left just so. She stepped into the room for the first time she could remember and sat on Fanny's fastidious bed. Why do I feel so lonely? Julia asked herself. So desolate.

Of course she's coming back. But even Julia couldn't make herself believe that.

CHAPTER ELEVEN

1896

THE LAYING OF THE TRACKS over the seventy miles between West Palm Beach and the new bay-area terminus was accomplished by Flagler's men in record time. As the rails were laid southward through the raw stretch of coastal county, several small towns—Delray, Deerfield, Fort Lauderdale, Dania, Hallandale—were established, their buildings financed by Flagler. His workmen and their families needed places to live. By April of 1896 the first train had made the trip from West Palm Beach to the bay area. However, the ancient hammock land around Biscayne Bay, on the north shore of the Miami River, was proving harder to displace than anticipated. Julia had made a checkerboard agreement with Mr. Flagler: once the land was cleared, each would own every other lot. Some of the lots had been cleared, and Flagler was already improving his. But clearing the last tract of hammock just to the north and east of Fort Dallas was a problem. It was exactly the site where Henry Flagler wanted his hotel, on the north shore of the Miami River, facing Biscayne Bay, framed by royal palms.

Julia rose each morning to the sound of John Sewell's piercing whistle. Work began at six-thirty, without regard to heat or rain or mosquitoes. The workmen started just a few hundred yards in front of Fort Dallas, where

Julia's garden ended and the difficult jungle began. Julia liked to sit on the veranda and watch. "It's like a theater," she said, ignoring the noise and the dirt and the dust.

"A theater of war," Harry, just as fascinated, amended. He was spending his days at Fort Dallas now, happy as could be that his mama and he were going to be rich and live in a city with all sorts of amusement possibilities.

Julia and Harry would drink their morning tea on the veranda as Sewell, a giant in a bush hat, ordered his corps of huge black workers into a V formation. He walked among them inspecting the bush hooks of the first group, the axes of the next group, and the grubbing shovels of the last group. The men came from the Bahamas, from Georgia and Alabama. They were determined to destroy this last bit of jungle.

As often as not Sewell would send a man to the hastily constructed shed to sharpen his tools. When satisfied, Sewell would blast that piercing whistle again—it could be heard as far away as Coconut Grove—and then lead his army into the mass of vines and trees, intent on his mission to create a suitable site for Mr. Flagler's Royal Palm Hotel.

Early on, Sewell had discovered that the manchineel tree could be killed only by setting it on fire and that the ironwood tree was stronger than any of his men's axes and would succumb only to dynamite. This last length of hammock was filled with manchineels and ironwoods. The dynamiting continued day after day.

"Do you enjoy the sound of explosives, Julia?" the Duke asked. She hadn't seen much of him since Mr. Flagler's breakfast. She had been too busy with Mr. Flagler's lawyers and engineers, and it had taken her a while to realize he had discontinued his casual visits. Finally she had had to send Panthar to the Peacock with a formal invitation to lunch. She had also invited Alice and Alice's father, who hadn't been able to attend.

"He's heartsick," Alice said, worried. "This blasting isn't helping." She sat her bulk down on one of the wrought-iron chairs Julia had had Panthar bring up from the lawn. "I've had the new doctor look at him, but he can't find anything."

"New doctor?" Julia asked.

"Maurice Levi. Wonderful man. So understanding. He's an army captain posted here. The army, it seems, is looking at the bay area as the possible site for a camp. Cuba's so volatile and so close."

"I don't want to hear about Cuba or Jewish army captains from New York, Alice, if you don't mind."

"Captain Levi is not from New York. He's from Pensacola, and his family has been in Florida since it was settled."

"So has mine."

"But not continuously, like the Levis, Julia," Alice said, winning a point. "Dr. Levi has a beautiful wife and an adorable daughter, and he's looking to buy land here. He's fallen in love with the bay."

"He's not going to buy my land," Julia said. "No Jew is." She had convinced Flagler to include a clause in all deeds that restricted the sale and use of the property to Caucasians. What's more, she had won the prohibition battle. The new city—in Flagler's eyes a village to serve his hotel—would be a dry one. The only exception would be The Royal Palm, and then liquor could be served only during the three-month season.

"I wish *somebody* would buy your land, Mama," Harry said. Sales were not what they should have been, and Julia was borrowing heavily—against Flagler's advice—to improve her land as he was improving his. The checkerboard agreement was not proving as beneficial as she had thought. Julia, with her borrowed money, couldn't improve her lots in the same way Flagler, with his unlimited funds, could improve his. Flagler's lots were selling. Julia's were not.

"We must be patient," Julia said to Harry. "We must—" But another explosion masked her words. "All this excitement." Julia suddenly felt things were not going her way. She wished the Duke would look at her. It was almost as if he were afraid of her. After the explosions she instructed Minnie to bring on the chicken salad. Julia was living high on expectations.

"The herons have found all this excitement so stimulating, they've left. Or haven't you noticed?" the Duke asked.

"They'll be back," Julia said with conviction. She found she was showing that lingering smile the Duke didn't like, and she changed her expression. The Duke's reply was lost in a series of explosions that went on unabated throughout lunch.

"I can't stick it," Alice said during a lull. "The noise and the smell, and I'm worried about father. Thank you, Julia, but I have neither the head nor the stomach for this 'excitement.' " She managed to get herself up. "By the way," she said, dropping her own bit of dynamite, "I've heard from Fanny, Julia. She and Julio are married—"

"I don't want to know, Alice. I've told you before." Julia's eyes turned away. "I do not have a daughter."

"They're living in Nassau." Alice looked down at her old friend. "Write to her, Julia. Ask her to forgive you."

"Forgive me, indeed! Mind your own business, Alice."

Alice sighed and asked, "Is Panthar going to take me home?"

"I will," Harry said, following Alice down the steps of the dock. "I have to see some people about an investment," Harry called back to his mother. "Those people from Cleveland."

Julia had never heard of those people from Cleveland, but she supposed Harry knew what he was doing. "Harry wants to build his own hotel," she said to the Duke. "He's looking for capital."

"Very enterprising." He stood up, crossed the stone veranda, and leaned against the balustrade, looking to the area where a tent city had sprung up, stretching from the end of this last stubborn hammock as far north as the eye could see. It was populated by men who had come to work on Mr. Flagler's hotel. If the site were ever cleared.

Julia joined him, but he continued to stare at the forest of brown and tan canvas. "I can no longer smell the orange blossoms in your garden, Julia." He still wouldn't look at her. There was a time when, if they were alone, he could look at nothing else. "Which do you prefer? The open sewage of the tent city or that lingering scent of cordite?"

"Duke . . ." She put her hand on his arm, but he moved away.

"The jungle put up a pretty good fight, don't you think, Julia? I had high hopes when the fumes from the manchineels forced Sewell's men to their knees, made their heads reel and their faces swell. But the dynamite takes care of the manchineel and the ironwood and the gulls and the gators. It takes care of most everything. On the whole I suppose I prefer the tent city's raw aroma. At least it's natural. It doesn't have that manufactured satanic odor."

He turned and looked at her finally, but she wished he hadn't. His eyes were no longer a frosty blue but nearly colorless, as if they had been bleached out. "I've been watching every day," he said. "I felt as if my presence were required. As if this crime needed a witness. Yet I am the one who is being punished. Watching this destruction has been the punishment, Julia."

She found that she couldn't stand next to him, that she couldn't bear that reproachful stare. She turned and sat herself among the leftover luncheon things, already a feast for the mosquitoes. When she looked up she looked past him at the tent city, the bay, the Indian burial mound in the background. "Why don't you leave the bay?" Julia, angry, finally asked. "Why don't you go and live somewhere else if this is so painful?"

"I've been waiting for a reprieve." He showed her that gap-toothed smile, and for a moment it was twenty years before, they were both young, and Julia loved the Duke as much as the Duke loved her.

Only for a moment. "There is to be no reprieve," Julia told the Duke on that last afternoon, the gray dynamite smoke masking the sunshine. "In one week construction begins on Mr. Flagler's hotel."

He turned away and looked at what was left of the bay's hammock. "This is the place I have loved best in the world, Julia. I have loved it with the same sort of passion with which I might have loved you. It's ironic that you've destroyed it, Julia. I overestimated my love and underestimated your ambition. My paradise and my love, Julia, have both gone up in Mr. Sewell's smoke. I am leaving, Julia."

"You won't leave," Julia said, joining him again at the balustrade. For some reason today she couldn't remain still. "You can't. You're too curious. I know you, Mr. Ewing. You're going to stay to see what happens next."

"You don't know me, Julia. I'm a stranger to you," he said. She felt an odd weakness, as if she had just been told she had a terminal disease. She didn't know just how to react, how to comport herself. In his waistcoat, with those bare blond arms, the Duke of Dade somehow seemed less naked than ever; as if this new sadness somehow clothed him. "You have won, Julia. I thought I could change you. I thought with my love I could make you see the beauty of this place. You've never changed, Julia." He looked at her with a sad smile. "I so wanted you to marry me, Julia."

"You wanted me to marry you and be a wife again," she found herself saying with an anger that surprised her. "I didn't want to be a wife again, Mr. Ewing. I have been a wife. I wanted to be a power in this world, I wanted to create something—a city. And if I had been a man, you would all have been cheering me on. No one, not even you, wants to make Mr. Flagler a mere husband. Why should I have to be a mere wife? You blame me for my ambition only because I am a woman."

"I blame you," the Duke said in that hoarse voice gone even deeper with emotion, "only because everything you've done, Julia, you have done only for yourself. Without love."

"Fanny's argument," she said, but softly, the anger gone out of her. She meant to touch his hand then, to reestablish some sort of contact, but her attention was caught by Sewell's whistle. She turned to watch as he directed a sweat-dripping black man in the placement of half a dozen charges of dynamite under the last ironwood tree. Julia waited, fascinated, for the dynamite to detonate, to send up into the blackened sky in an explosion of feathers and hysteria the few pelicans and white herons that had dared to return.

After it had happened, after that last ironwood tree had been blown into bits and the birds had fought with one another in their panic to escape, Julia turned. The Duke had left. She looked over the balustrade and saw him boarding his faded blue skiff. He'll be back tomorrow, she thought. She wanted him to look up so she could wave, but he never did.

A week later the hammock was totally cleared, nearly ready for construction. The tent city had grown even larger, and the bay was filled with boats, few of them looking seaworthy. Former orange growers lived in the tents and on the boats, bankrupts who had come to work on Flagler's hotel. Julia sat in her customary seat on the veranda feeling especially alone. "I have a good mind to walk down to the site," she said to herself, even though she had been told to stay away. Sewell didn't like strangers about, especially women, when he was breaking ground.

She was bored, and though she wouldn't admit it, lonesome. Two days before, she had sent Panthar to the Peacock with an invitation for the Duke to come to lunch. But Panthar had returned with the invitation. The thin white envelope seemed especially inconsequential in his big brown hands. "Mr. Peacock say the Duke has gone. He take all his things and his boat and he sail away. He say goodbye to Panthar, but Panthar not believe him. Now Panthar believe the Duke. He go for good."

296

Julia sent Harry to get the full story, and Harry came back saying, "The Duke did it, all right. Charlie says the Duke headed south down to the keys. Charlie said the Duke wanted to go where Flagler and his railroad and his hotels would never find him."

"He'll be back," Julia said, willing herself to believe it.

Nor had she had the consolation of Alice's company. Willie Brickell was ailing, and Alice was spending all of her time with her father. "Perhaps I *will* walk down to the site," Julia said aloud just as Panthar appeared at the top of the stairs. For the first time in all the years she had known him, Julia could read an emotion on his face. Panthar was shocked.

"Mr. Sewell going to destroy sacred burial mound," he said. "His men going to dig up old bones, disturb ancient spirits. He going to defile Ishtohollo's blessed earth. Stop him, Mrs. Tuttle. Come stop him, Mrs. Tuttle."

"But there's no need for him to do that," Julia said. "Mr. Flagler himself told me he wouldn't disturb it. Of course I'll come." She followed Panthar down the steps and got into the dugout, all the time thinking: An outrage; Sewell has gone too far. But under her own shock, her own outrage, lay a thought of which Julia was only half conscious: When the Duke hears that I've stopped this desecration, that I've helped Panthar, he will understand that my motives are good. When the Duke learns I've saved the Indian mound, that place where he made love to me, he will come back.

Julia, all in gray—à la Fanny and the smart St. Augustine ladies—approached the site, with Panthar a few steps behind. Sewell, wiping the sweat from his eyes with a huge red kerchief, was just then ordering his men to dig into the mound.

"Stop, Mr. Sewell!" Julia said, assuming that false smile the Duke hadn't liked, the one that stayed on her lips a few moments longer than was necessary. "Stop!" she said, coming between Sewell and his men. He looked down at her, not so much as if he didn't know who she was but as if he didn't know *what* she was.

After a moment, when he saw she wouldn't go away, Sewell decided to recognize her. "Mrs. Tuttle," he said in his booming voice, while Panthar and Sewell's workmen watched, "I take great pride in the fact that I have never finished a job even a day behind schedule. On this job, Mrs. Tuttle, I am one full month behind schedule. The last thing I need, Mrs. Tuttle, is you prancing around my site making unreasonable demands. I cannot stop, ma'am. I have my orders from Mr. Flagler, and I aim to carry them out. Now."

"Mr. Sewell. There must be some mistake. I personally spoke with Mr. Flagler, and we're both agreed. You cannot destroy the Indian mound. It is a sacred and hallowed place. The Tequestas," she went on despite Sewell's throwing up his hands and his eyes and looking as if he might strike her, "buried their dead here. You simply cannot—"

"Dig," Sewell said, stepping around her, blowing on his whistle. "Dig, damn you." One of the men dug his spade deep into the mound and in that first load of dirt and sand pulled out a skull. He laughed nervously and handed it to Sewell. Sewell threw the skull with all of his considerable strength at the little group of pioneer kids who had somehow gotten across the river to watch. They shrieked, and the other men began to dig and throw the skulls and bones they found at the fearless and filthy pioneer kids.

Panthar watched silently for a few minutes and then, without warning, he strode past Julia and, clasping his hands together, gave the back of Sewell's huge head a resounding blow, forcing him to his knees. The clout made a noise as if Sewell's head had been split apart. Sewell, still on his knees, swiveled round and butted his head with precision and force into Panthar's groin. Panthar fell on the ground and lay there, attempting not to show his pain.

"Get that Injun out of here, Mrs. Tuttle." Sewell had arisen and turned his back on them, giving orders to his men to stop gawking and start working. "And perhaps, Mrs. Tuttle," he said after a moment, his back still to her, "it would be best if you stayed away from the site for the next few days. It could be dangerous here."

Panthar managed to get to his feet and to his canoe. Silent, radiating a critically wounded pride, he rowed Julia back to Fort Dallas. It would have been easier for Julia to have walked, now that the jungle was cleared, but she didn't want to further shame Panthar.

"Panthar," she began after he had helped her onto the dock, "I . . ." For once Julia had no words. She looked into his face, but there was no emotion there now. Only that unrelenting Seminole blankness. He got back into his dugout, raised a hand to her in a final farewell, and disappeared up the Miami River.

"It's not even as if they were of the same tribe," Julia said to herself some days later when she was certain that he too wasn't coming back. Fanny, Duke. And now Panthar. She had just come from visiting Alice, Harry having sailed her over in his skiff. He had gone off again, to see "those people from Cleveland." Julia stepped onto her father's veranda and looked toward the north at what had so recently been jungle.

"If they had to clear the Indian mound, they had to clear the Indian mound," Julia had said to Alice, who thought otherwise. "That is progress." She didn't tell Alice that she and Panthar had attempted to arrest progress and had failed. But of course Alice had heard.

Now the bay was filled with those smelly boats and the flatland was filled with those tents. An army of black men and white men had occupied the bay area, bringing with them all kinds of filthy habits and forgetting even the bare rudiments of sanitation. She smelled the raw sewage and the dynamite, which the Duke said had poisoned the air, and put a perfumed handkerchief to her nose.

The dynamiting had stopped, but its boom seemed to reverberate in her head, and she knew with a fatal certainty that a monumental megrim was coming. "I refuse to have any regrets," she told herself, putting her stubby hand to her broad forehead, raising her chin. She didn't miss any of them. Not Fanny or Panthar or the Duke. Nor the birds or the crocodiles that used to guard the hammock. She didn't even miss the royal palms. They had had to go, after all, but Flagler had promised to plant more.

It seemed to Julia, feeling the pulse pound in her head, as if none of them—the vanished people, animals, places—had ever existed. She looked at the dismal tent city, but she didn't see it. Instead she saw her shining metropolis stretching out before her, alcohol-less for nine months of the year, free of Semites and foreigners. A controlled environment. Civilized. Populated by honest Protestant women and men. A progressive holy city: Julia, Florida.

It was a filthy-hot July day. The three hundred and forty-three voters in the bay area had met the night before and decided to incorporate the new city. Today—July 29, 1896—important people were to meet to choose a name. Julia felt it suited her dignity to stay away from what she considered a formality. Alice, whose father had begun to recover, had promised to come straight from the meeting and tell Julia the results.

She was hours late. "Where on earth have you been?" Julia asked, receiving her in the lounge. "I've been waiting—"

"Flagler was immediately suggested," Alice said, seating herself on the painted white wicker sofa, accepting orange pekoe and coontie cookies from Minnie McCord, moving her bulk around until she was comfortable. "And immediately rejected. It was felt, I think I can fairly say, that he is already too prominent a force, and we don't want the world to think he owns us. More than one person believes the 'FLA' on his railroad cars suggests his name and not their destination."

"Alice, please spare me the benefit of your observations. Get on with it." She knew from long experience Alice meant to take her time.

"Sweet Water, Seminole City, Biscayne City, Bay City were offered and rejected."

"Of course they were. Entirely inappropriate. Go on."

Alice put down her half-eaten coontie cookie and looked at Julia. "They decided finally to give it the name it has come to be known by: Miami, Florida."

"Miami? But that was only a temporary—"

"The businessmen thought it wise not to confuse the northern captains of commerce and potential tourists who already know us as Miami."

Julia stood up and put her hands to her chest. "But I thought they were going to call it Julia. How could they not? After I asked them to. I was responsible for . . ."

Alice, with some difficulty, got up from the sofa and went to her friend, putting her hefty arms around Julia's square shoulders. They stood for a moment facing the china collection, silent, July's mosquitoes buzzing around the two women, leaving them alone. "If it's any consolation, Julia, everyone is calling you 'The Mother of Miami.' "

Julia moved away from Alice's arms and looked out at the tent city; at the place where Flagler's Royal Palm was being built, blocking her view of the bay; at the new city of Miami, Florida. "Well, yes, it is a consolation, Alice," she said. "The Mother of Miami," she said to herself several times and then once more, aloud, "The Mother of Miami."

Alice decided not to tell her old friend how the citizens of Miami felt toward her. They were furious at the prohibition and Caucasian clauses in her deeds, at the high-chinned manner in which she carried herself. Alice left without telling Julia some of the other names the new citizens of Miami, Florida, had for Julia Tuttle.

CHAPTER TWELVE

1898

IT WAS THE STENCH she couldn't stand—the stench and the September humidity and the desperate, lonely noises the patients made. Julia stood in the small tent that served as the hospital's admittance office, her hands to her breast, feeling the faint rumblings of a megrim, staring into the larger tent, where women on iron hospital cots were bleeding, vomiting, and soiling themselves—victims of typhus.

"I have got to leave, Alice," Julia said, catching hold of her friend's thick arm as Alice Brickell, moving more quickly than Julia could remember, tried to push past her into the hospital's largest tent, known as the dying ward.

"We need you," Alice said sharply, "to help admit people, Julia."

"I have a megrim, Alice. I must go."

"Then go. I'll get Isabelle to replace you." Alice left her, but once inside the dying ward, turned back. "If we ever play nurse again, Julia, just remember that I'll be Florence Nightingale and you'll be the wounded patient."

Julia stayed on for a moment, watching Alice approach the young Jewish army doctor, Maurice Levi, ministering to his wife, a woman who had once been the loveliest in Miami. Alice handed the doctor a bedpan as Louisianne Levi gave a stifled shout and a great cascade of blood shot from her mouth.

Maurice Levi, with a sob, took his wife into his arms and buried his face in her neck. It was clear from the way her body sank back onto the cot that Louisianne Levi, aged twenty-three, was dead.

Let Alice be Florence Nightingale, Julia said to herself, turning away. She didn't notice Isabelle Peacock's goodbye; she was concentrating on the ominous drum roll beginning behind her broad forehead. She walked up the center of the dirt street, made muddy by a recent summer squall. The smell was as bad as it had been inside the tent hospital. The soldiers shouted terrible words after her. At me, she thought bitterly, Julia Tuttle, "The Mother of Miami."

The soldiers were everywhere—like a plague. At first they had been welcome, protectors against a potential Spanish invasion. After the Maine had blown up in Havana and the newspaper-incited war had broken out, Flagler had offered Miami to President McKinley as the port of embarkation. But Henry B. Plant and Tampa had won.

All we've gotten out of this war, Julia thought, trying not to hear or smell or see, were soldiers. Four doughboys to every civilian. By the time they had arrived, all transport to Cuba had been commandeered by Teddy Roosevelt and sent to Tampa. So the doughboys were stuck in Miami. My city, Julia thought, a city of soldiers. They have no one to fight except one another and nowhere to go except the street corners. They've brought gambling and drink and typhus. "I'm sick of you," she found herself screaming at a group of boys who couldn't have been more than eighteen, passing a flask among them.

"Crazy old bitch," one said, and Julia realized she was shaking with fear and anger. She moved faster, past her vacant, unsold lots. I gave Flagler a city and he gave me advice, Julia thought bitterly. She had expected an instant fortune once the railroad had arrived and the hotel was built. She had gone into debt to improve her land, against Flagler's repeated and rejected advice. Now, with the war, there was no chance of selling it.

Exhausted, the headache reaching a new stage of pain, she managed to get herself up the stairs to the veranda her father had added onto Fort Dallas. She looked out at Flagler's Royal Palm Hotel. It was a much too plain version of the Ponce de León, and it blocked her view of the bay. It had opened in January of 1896 and she had been an honored guest, her photograph in the newspapers, a special card issued, signed by Mr. Flagler, entitling her to free use of all facilities.

Harry made use of it, swimming in the pool, eating, and, she presumed, drinking in the restaurants, making, as he put it, "important connections." Connections to what Harry never did say. Julia turned her back on The Royal Palm Hotel and entered Fort Dallas. She called for Minnie but remembered Minnie was at her sister's, nursing her nephew, who had been shot in an argument with a soldier.

She stood just inside the lounge, feeling the megrim build to a frightening intensity. Her eyes clouded and then suddenly refocused on the mounted collection of china dishes. She remembered making Fanny cry on that first day of their permanent residency, rearranging her arrangement. "Fanny," she called aloud, forgetting for a moment that Fanny was married to a Cuban and living far away. And because that thought was even more painful than the headache, she dismissed the vision of the young woman in the elegant gray dress and moved into her office.

She lay down on the daybed she had installed there, thinking of the soldiers in blue kerseys who had once stacked their arms against the walls, of her father writing letters about the beauties of the bay area from that old desk. The pain subsided as a vision of the Duke of Dade came into the room. He put his beautiful nude, blond arms around her and held her close until she slept.

A few moments later she awoke suddenly, screaming with such pain, she didn't think she could bear it. But mercifully it subsided, leaving her exhausted and beaten. She closed her brown eyes in an effort to recapture the image of the Duke but couldn't. When she opened them she saw, hanging on the far wall, the portrait the Duke had painted of Panthar. Panthar looked down on her with reproachful sadness.

"I won't think of any of them," Julia said, forcing herself to stand up, to move out onto the veranda. The stench of the doughboys' raw sewage made her wince. She leaned against the balustrade, the pain on the rise again, making everything in front of her—the soldiers, the tent city, the impromptu hospital, the not very impressive hotel—seem especially vivid, as if she were looking at one of the Duke's highly colored, not quite realistic paintings. "He's got the colors all wrong again," she said and laughed and then nearly collapsed from a new wave of pain that ebbed and flowed like the bay's tide on a stormy day.

By an enormous effort of will Julia ignored it. She forced herself to stop seeing what was before her and instead had a vision. It was a vision of *her* city. It had broad boulevards and elaborate hotels and houses surrounded by manicured lawns. Nothing ran wild. Liquor was not served. Gambling did not exist. Jews and foreigners were not admitted. Everything was so pure, of such an intense white, it hurt her eyes and she had to shut them. The megrim suddenly vanished. Julia Tuttle lifted her chin sky-high, clenched her stubby fists, and holding tightly onto her precious vision, died.

The Duke of Dade, when he heard, cried. But he wouldn't travel to Miami to attend the funeral. He was living near a fishing camp on an isolated key, seventeen miles north of Key West. Flagler's railroad didn't reach him until 1912, and even after it came he managed to live a life away from cities and men, a life devoted to the natural beauties of Florida.

Years later Harry Tuttle leased his mother's house to a gambling syndicate, which opened it as the glamorous Seminole Club. Panthar's portrait looked down upon the green tables around which godless men and women

302

laughed and gambled and drank. Today old Fort Dallas, neglected, stands in Miami's Lummus Park, a storehouse for the Daughters of the American Revolution. It is believed that the downtown Miami Howard Johnson's is on the site of the long since torn down Royal Palm Hotel.

One of the highways linking Miami and Miami Beach, built on landfill across Biscayne Bay, is called the Julia Tuttle Causeway.

BOOK FOUR

Modern Times

CHAPTER ONE

1914

NICK PRINCE handed the man two nickels and led the way up the rear stairway to the roped-off section reserved for coloreds at the back of the ferry's top tier. He did it naturally, holding the rope for Selma as if this were the sort of thing they did every day. As if she were the Queen of Sheba and he were her royal escort. As if white boys in white linen suits made a habit of sitting with Negro ladies in bright-hued dresses in the Colored Section on Henry Morrison Flagler's ferry.

The Colored Section was crowded—workers going over to the Beach for the afternoon shift—but Nick found seats for them. He had brought two beautifully pressed handkerchiefs, and he placed them both on the cracked, peeling benches so their clothes wouldn't get soiled. He waited for her to sit down, smiled that reassuring smile of his—"Don't worry," it said, "I'm going to take care of everything"—and sat next to her, bolt upright. He was the only white person topside. A diamond, Selma thought, in the middle of a coal heap.

The sun was shining something fierce up there in the Colored Section on top of the *City of Miami* ferry, making Biscayne Bay look like a sheet of glass. The briny smell of the bay waters reminded Selma of home, of Pensacola's darktown. It made her homesick to think of that sweet, quiet place, especially in the summer when the rich families from New Orleans would come and take houses on the bay, and the town would become all festive and gay. Home.

Selma sighed. She had on her new hat, a blue straw wide-brimmed model Ida and Irving Prince had given her for her birthday. "Made for you, darling," Ida had said, stepping back, looking at Selma as if she were something to look at. Well, she supposed she was. A six-foot-tall yellow-skinned Nigra lady with little yellow eyes, little nose, narrow shoulders, wide hips, and large feet and hands, wearing a white lady's hat.

Now, Nick was something to look at. Sixteen and nearly as tall as Selma, he had the posture of a military man and the grace of a Florida panther. In profile he looked as if he were a model for the Arrow-collar advertisements, straight and sharp and clean, his gleaming black hair combed smoothly. But his face was saved from magazine-fashion blandness by his eyes. An undiluted violet, framed by the thick upturned lashes one found on dime-store dolls. His lower lip was full and sensuous, and when he was angry he had a trick of pushing it out, creating a sneer that had caused more than one bully to back off.

And if the bully didn't back off, Nick knew, surprisingly, how to use his dukes. You couldn't be the only Jewish boy in Miami's new Central High School, looking like a fashion plate, with impeccable manners, and survive without learning how to take care of yourself.

Nick had been dressed by Irving, that consummate haberdasher, since he could walk and had acquired a fastidiousness that Irving, that consummate slob, could only envy. For today's outing he wore a white linen suit, a cream-colored shirt, a yellow piqué tie. "You sure are something, child," Selma said, staring at him, shaking her long yellow head in the round blue hat in wonderment. "You sure *are* something." She was so proud. The other blacks wondered who the hell she was, sitting with this white prince, but no one said anything. They just gawked.

Selma didn't pay them any attention. She had eyes only for Nick. She'd been staring at him since the day he was born, and she wondered how she was going to stop now, how she was going to tell him what she *had* to tell him. But she wouldn't have her say till the end of the day. This was a celebration. Nick's birthday present. He was taking her to that sandbar known as Miami Beach for her fortieth birthday. It was the place he loved most in the world. Selma knew Nick felt about Miami Beach the way she felt about Pensacola.

The ferry began to move. She leaned over the rails and looked down as the boat left the dock, recognizing one of the boys who worked the Miami end of the ferry. Buddy McCord. Gap-toothed, yellow-haired white trash if ever she saw it. He looked up and caught sight of Nick. "Hey, Nick the Prick," Buddy shouted, a big fat smile on his piggy face. "They're putting Yids in the nigger section now? *That's* progress."

He saw Selma looking over Nick's shoulder. "Hey, my apologies, Nick. I didn't know you had your mammy with you. You taking her over to the Beach to sell her to some fat sheeny for fish bait?"

"Someday I'm going to get you, Buddy," Nick promised as the ferry began to leave port.

"No you won't, Nicky. I'm leaving for college tonight. You won't see me for years."

Nick leaned over the rail, not exactly shouting but making certain his voice, just changed and now a rough baritone, reached Buddy. "I'll wait, Buddy, and I'll get you when you come back."

Selma looked at him with pride. She knew she talked like an uppity darky and Ida and Irving messed up the language something fierce, but Nick had made it a point to listen to his teachers at the Central Grammar School. He spoke the way the best educated people he knew spoke, getting his language right.

Nick sat back as the boat moved out, and Selma touched his arm shyly. She had spent the last sixteen years living for him. She had diapered him, fed him, held him in her arms while he cried his heart out. "You forget about that Buddy McCord, Nick. You make the sun look pale, child."

He put his hand over hers and looked at her through those dime-store lashes, giving her the full effect of his violet eyes, his reassuring smile. "I've already forgotten about him."

Selma wanted to tell him Buddy McCord wasn't worth his little finger, but Carl Fisher's dredges were making an ungodly racket, digging up fill from Biscayne Bay's bottom, creating his County Causeway, connecting Miami to Miami Beach. Not far from it was the Collins family's wooden bridge, which Fisher had helped to complete. In between the wooden bridge that was and the County Causeway that was going to be, more dredges were digging up fill to create islands, channels, docks. The federal government and the city had cut an eighteen-foot channel through Fishers Island to the sea. They called it Government Cut and had designed it for the use of large ships. There sure were plenty of large ships. Not to mention little ones.

In the seventeen years Selma had lived in Miami, Biscayne Bay had grown from a haven for rickety sailboats to a full-fledged port. That little channel Mr. Flagler had cut across the bay so his guests could sail their yachts right up to The Royal Palm docks looked downright insignificant now.

In Pensacola you were aware of the water all the time. The bay was part of the town. But there was too much going on in Biscayne Bay to look at the water. Pretty soon, Selma thought, they're not going to have any water at all. One of these days they're going to wake up to see it all filled in with bridges and causeways and little islands. One of these days a body's going to be able to walk back and forth to Miami Beach, and they're going to forget there ever was a bay here. She turned and looked back at Miami, catching sight of the golden spire of the First Presbyterian Church over on East Flagler and South East Third. It looked like fools' gold to Selma.

She had hated the place from the first day she arrived. The noise drove her crazy—trolleys clanging along Avenue B and automobiles hooting and beeping and competing for space with bicycles over on Twelfth Avenue.

It would have been better, she decided, if they had let her live in Colored Town, among her own people. Miss Ida didn't understood how it felt to be black, living isolated in a white neighborhood. Miss Ida was just as good and innocent as her Nick. How was she ever going to leave those two to fend for themselves with only Irving to set them straight?

Nick smiled and said something to her, pointing at the bay, at an island they were making out of landfill. She couldn't hear him over the noise of the dredges, but she saw the excitement in those violet eyes, the thrill he got from seeing the machines dig up the bay and pile up the man-made land. I hate those dredges like nobody's business, Selma thought. But I sure do love my Nick. She looked at him again and shook her head in amazement, forcing herself not to get all weepy and sentimental. He's a man now. She had kept her promise to Dr. Maurice. Despite her resolve, she had to turn so Nick, halfway over the rail in his fascination with the dredges, wouldn't see her tears.

Maurice Levi had been the first Levi to become a doctor. Every other Levi in the exclusive, self-sufficient Pensacola Levi family circle was somehow involved in "The Business." Levi & Sons was a chain of department stores boasting a branch in every major city of northern and central Florida.

Levi & Sons had been founded by Jackson Levi, Renata and Mac Levi's youngest son. He had survived both the Civil War and Reconstruction with one goal: to put the Levi name back where it belonged in the Florida world of commerce. He had done so by opening a dry-goods store on the site of the old Levi & Sons trading post. Jackson Levi had early on recognized the importance of the railroads, concentrating his stores in those cities served by Henry B. Plant's Southern Express or Henry Morrison Flagler's Florida East Coast Railway. The cities on the railroads lines prospered, as did Levi & Sons stores.

The Levi & Sons trademark was a reproduction of the miniature portrait Mac Levi had kept in his vest pocket until the day he died. It had been passed on to Jackson. Jackson Levi's first two wives had died and his third survived him only by a week. He had, all told, a dozen children. Maurice was his youngest and his most venturesome. He had studied medicine in New Orleans, and when he came home to Pensacola, he brought with him as his wife a sophisticated beauty, a member of one of the South's richest and oldest Jewish families, Louisianne Blum.

The Levis had their own ways of doing things—they were a law unto themselves in Pensacola and always had been—but so had Louisianne. She had black hair, red lips, and fine white skin, much of it—according to her new female in-laws—due to artifice. She imported concert singers from New York to perform at her parties, to which, often enough, other Levis were not invited. She dressed in outlandish Parisian fashions. Snails were put before the strictly conservative Levis on the rare occasions when they were invited to lunch, not a meal any of them savored. She kept only one servant (when the poorest Levi household had six), the outlandish-looking Selma, with whom she laughed and cried and carried on as if they were sisters.

Louisianne's mother had made connections with distant cousins, a young married and recently emigrated Polish Jewish couple who were starving on New York's lower East Side. Louisianne agreed to support them in booming Florida and perhaps find a job for the husband in the Levis' department stores. Their names were Ida and Irving Prince. It had originally been Pinsk, that city being Irving's birthplace, but the Irish immigration official at Ellis Island hadn't liked Pinsk for a surname. The newly named Irving Prince was a haberdasher by trade.

"There is no power on heaven or earth that will move me to bring a Polish Jew, some farfetched cousin of Louisianne's, into Levi & Sons," Milton Levi had said. He was an abysmally tall, pale, stiff-backed Levi, Maurice's older brother, the keeper of Renata's portrait and the new chairman of Levi & Sons. "Ida and Irving Prince," he said, after being introduced at one of Louisianne's snail luncheons, "are not our kind of Jews."

"Then neither are we," Maurice said, bringing the luncheon to an end. A week later Maurice accepted a commission in the United States Army and removed himself, Louisianne, Selma, and Mr. and Mrs. Irving Prince to what would soon be the new city of Miami.

When Louisianne died, a month after giving birth to Nichlaus Adam Levi, Maurice did not notify Milton. Milton, hearing of Louisianne's death through a clandestine letter painfully written by Selma, blamed himself. Had she remained in Pensacola, she would not have contacted typhoid. Maurice, who might have absolved his older brother, didn't have time. Sick himself, he spent his last weeks arranging for his son's legal adoption by Ida and Irving Prince, two people he had grown to love.

Nichlaus Levi thus became Nichlaus Levi Prince. In those busy days before his death Maurice had wangled a long lease for Irving on a handsome building on South West Twelfth Avenue, just above busy Third Street. There was room for a shop on the first floor and two apartments above it. Jews were not allowed to rent space in Miami any more than they were allowed to buy, but money solved that problem. When Maurice had started to hint at Irving's ethnicity, the owner had said, "Don't tell me. I don't want to know. Prince is a nice Christian name." Thus Irving Prince had had a dream come true: The New York Gentleman's Haberdashery.

As his final gesture Maurice Levi had deposited ten thousand dollars in a bank he trusted in Miami, to be held for his son until his twenty-first birthday.

On his last day before he entered the hospital Maurice took a bereft Selma into one of the empty rooms of the apartment and made her promise she would stand by Nick until he became a man. "I don't want the Pensacola Levis to get their hands on him and make him a damned window dummy. Miami's a new place and he's a new person and he'll be better off here. You won't leave him until he can take care of himself, will you, Selma?"

She promised, and he kissed her on her yellow cheek and went off to the tent hospital, knowing he'd never come out. He had seen enough people, including his wife, die of typhus to recognize the signs in himself.

Ida cried bitterly for days after Maurice's body had been sent to Pensacola for burial, holding Nick in her arms. "You're my baby now," she said, kissing him.

"He's our baby now," Selma said, taking him from her.

Ida, through her tears, laughed. "You got two mothers," she said to Nick. "One Jewish *mamala*. One colored mammy. It's not going to be so bad, darling. You'll see. You're going to turn out just right."

"You turned out just right, child," Selma said as the ferry began to move again and the dredges were, for the moment, blessedly quiet while the workers took their lunch.

Nick looked at her fondly. "Like Ida's potato kugel?"

"Just like Ida's potato kugel." She wondered how he would have turned out if Mr. Milton had been allowed to take him back to Pensacola, to "give him all the benefits of being a real Levi." It seemed a shame, though, that Nick didn't much care about his family back in Pensacola. She took him there once a year, each October, and they stayed at Mr. Milton's fine Palafox Street house. Mr. Milton would take him down to the site of the old trading post and tell him all the old stories about Renata and Mac Levi, and he even showed him the famous miniature. Though Nick was polite—he was the politest child Selma had ever seen—it was clear even to Milton that Nick wasn't interested in being a Pensacola Levi.

"I'm a Miami Prince," he told Milton, and, looking at that fine profile, that pouty lip, who, Selma wanted to know, could doubt it?

Mr. Milton, so long and thin and bald, he looked like a Ticonderoga pencil, would always make the same speech on the last day of the visit: "Nichlaus, I just want to remind you that you have a standing offer. You can always come and live in Pensacola and take your place in the family business. I'll back you all the way."

"That's old history," Nick would say later on the train making its poky way across the panhandle. "I'm interested in the future."

If Pensacola's old history, Selma thought now, and Miami's the future, she'd take Pensacola every time. Well, she was going to take Pensacola now if her heart didn't break first. She looked at Nick's thick lashes lying against those tanned high-boned cheeks and wondered just what that boy's future was going to be. He honestly, totally believed that the world was good, and Selma didn't want to be around when he found out it wasn't. If only they had gone back to Pensacola, where he would have been Somebody, a Levi. Here he was Nick Prince, and who was that?

"What're you thinking about?" he asked her as the *City of Miami* approached Miami Beach and the black folks on top got themselves ready to disembark. White folks first of course.

"I was thinking about that Buddy McCord," she lied. "Lucky you grew bigger than Buddy or he'd still be beating up on you. Remember that time at The Royal Palm?"

"I remember," Nick said quickly. For a moment, just a second, she knew she had punctured his self-possession. For that second Nick Prince looked uncertain.

* * *

From the beginning she had known that it was one thing working for Jews named Levi in Pensacola and another working for Jews named Prince in Miami. In Pensacola the Levis were above and beyond the first families, a class and a clan unto themselves. In Miami the Princes were not allowed to swim in The Royal Palm pool. Not even in summer, when the worst white trash paid their nickels and jumped in.

Not that that had stopped Selma. Every day during the summer she put on the white dress Miss Louisianne had bought her. It was a little tight now, but that didn't matter, it still passed for a child nurse's white uniform. Then she'd stroll her baby down along the bay to Royal Palm Boulevard, past the hacks and the horses, their tongues hanging out from the heat, and under the gates of The Royal Palm Hotel, which looked like a huge white-iced yellow cake, sitting on its fifteen acres of green lawn.

She paid the nickel to the man at the booth, who nodded to this symbol of off-season wealth, this darky maid, and then she entered the white and yellow swimming casino. She sat in the shade of the arcade and watched baby Nick play—by himself, he was that sort of child—in the shallow end of the enormous pool. By the time he was three he was carefully watching the expert swimmers at the far end of the pool, studying their every move.

By the age of four he had taught himself to swim, and when he was five he was executing fairly creditable dives. "My child is a water baby," she would say when people around the pool commented. Nick never even noticed. "I don't think that baby knows how good-looking he is," she said to Ida. "Even with all those people cooing and oohing and aahing."

"Vain he's not," Ida agreed.

On the opening day of the summer season, when Nick was eight, the trouble came. It was the first time he had entered the men's dressing room. Before that he had come to the pool with his bathing suit on, but now that he was eight he had decided that was undignified. He found his assigned locker, removed his white linen shorts, his cotton Fruit of the Looms, and unfolded the striped bathing costume Irving had given him for his birthday.

Buddy McCord, working his pudgy way into the tight cut-off knickers he used as a bathing suit, eyed Nick and his grand togs from the far end of the yellow-and-white-tiled dressing pavilion. He took in his pale, thin torso and his circumcised penis and laughed. He had found his target for the day.

"Hey," Buddy McCord said to the boys he had come with, "we got a Hebee Jebee here. We got us a Yid. Don't you know, boy," Buddy shouted down the length of the pavilion, "Jew bastards ain't allowed in Mr. Flagler's pool?"

Nick moved so quickly, he surprised Buddy McCord, half in and half out of his cut-off bathing shorts. Nick jumped on him, brought him down, and managed to get in a couple of good whacks before Buddy's friends pulled him off and held him down while Buddy gave "the Jew bastard what for."

"Say 'uncle,' " Buddy said, sitting on Nick's back, holding his arm way up, afraid he was going to snap it. Nick remained resolutely still, his nose pressed against the tile, scaring Buddy into thinking he might have passed out or worse. Buddy got up and gave him a kick in the butt and was relieved to see Nick move. "Thought you was dead." Nick stood up and jumped him again and got in some more good whacks before he was pulled off. Buddy, a little daunted by his victim's perseverance, satisfied his honor by tearing Nick's new bathing costume to shreds while his friends held Nick.

Nick sat on one of the white marble benches for a moment, getting his breath, willing himself not to cry. He dressed himself, retrieved what remained of his bathing costume, and left the dressing pavilion, solemn but dry-eyed. His eyes were already beginning to blacken and there was blood on his arm where one of Buddy's kicks had broken the skin. He went to Selma and stood looking up at her for a minute. "Child, what did those boys do to you?" she asked, catching Buddy and his gang looking apprehensively at her and Nick from the far end of the pool.

"Nothing," Nick said. He did not cry until they had left the casino and she sat down on one of Mr. Flagler's wrought-iron park chairs and pulled him to her. "I'll kill 'em," Selma said, holding him close, feeling the sobs racking his thin body. "I'll kill 'em."

It was the end of the swimming casino for Nick.

"Child, the attendant will let you in," Selma had argued with him the next day when she wanted to go back. Swimming in The Royal Palm's pool was Nick's one great pleasure in the summer. "He's been letting you in for years. You don't have to get dressed there. I'll be there, and I ain't going to let them boys—"

Nick looked at her with his mother's violet and melancholy eyes. He turned his profile to her, but she could see that lower lip curling. "I'm not going where I'm not wanted, Selma." Then he suddenly smiled, showing his dimples, his eyes lighting up with the innocence that worried and enthralled her. "Someday we'll go some place where we can *both* go swimming."

At Irving's suggestion, Selma began to take Nick on the ferry across the bay to the sandbar known as Miami Beach. There the Jews had their own stretch of sand and their own café. There was no pool. On the first few visits Nick sat quietly on the white sand beach, carefully watching the early practitioners of the new sport of surf bathing. On the fourth visit he stood up. "I'm going in," he announced.

"You are not. You could drown yourself."

"No. I think I understand how to do it now." She watched nervously, and sure enough, the boy swam with the tide, coming in on the fat waves, going out on the thin ones, making the water work for him.

When he was eleven he saved a fat man named Rosi from drowning and got a dollar and his picture in the Miami *Metropolis*. Nick ignored the picture. Selma stuck it on her dresser mirror and sent a copy to Mr. Milton. Ida talked about the rescue for weeks (" . . . a big chubby fellow, and my Nick only a string bean . . .") until Nick begged her to stop.

Mr. Rosi owned the beach-chair concession, and from then on Nick got two free folding chairs with red and yellow canvas seats every time he appeared. Selma knew he still missed The Royal Palm's pool and casino. He was a fastidious child. He didn't much like noise, sand, the unpredictable surf, the smells of his fellow bathers. But he enjoyed the ferry ride, and after his swim he liked to walk along the shoreline to explore the still wild island.

When he was twelve he announced he no longer needed a companion, and Selma thankfully stayed home. She *hated* the beach. Sometimes, on a particularly torrid summer Sunday, Irving would accompany him. "What are you daydreaming about, *pisher*, when you're lying half in the water and half out like a drowned cat?" Irving wanted to know.

"I'm not daydreaming, Irving," Nick told him. "I'm making plans."

"For what? The Second Coming?"

"For my future."

"You got plenty of time for your future." Irving had it all plotted out. Nick, who worked in the store three afternoons a week and all day on Saturday, would "come in" to the business with him. They would expand. "Did you ever see a better salesman in your life?" Irving asked Selma on the average of twice a week. "He doesn't even have to open his mouth. They come in, they see him in a white suit and yellow tie, and right away they have to have a white suit and a yellow tie. You want to know why? 'Cause they think they're going to look like him in it. He's a wonderful boy, my Nick, but don't you tell him what I said. God forbid he should get himself a swelled head."

This was the first time Selma had been to Miami Beach in four years. She and Nick walked across a sand road cut through the mangrove jungle which led to the Atlantic side of the island. She couldn't believe her eyes when they got to the beach. There was a new casino with dressing rooms, and a café with a dance floor, and a wooden pier in front of which a sign advertised *The Incredible Diving Horse*. "Child, this place is certainly coming."

Nick got his free beach chairs and an umbrella and sat her down in the middle of the beach while he went to change. Mr. Rosi's concessions man had, as always, looked at Selma with a gimlet eye. "Anything wrong, Mark?" Nick had, as always, asked.

"Not a thing, Nick."

Nick changed into his bathing costume and had his swim, and though he wasn't quite sixteen years old, Selma saw that half the women on the beach had their eyes on him.

"I hate salt water," Nick said, adjusting the umbrella to keep the sun off her and sitting next to her in the folding beach chair. His black hair, wet from the ocean, was slicked back. I don't know why, she found herself thinking,

315

but I always do feel sorry for that boy. He's so handsome and he's so smart, but he never did have a real mama and daddy, and maybe that's why he always looks a little lonesome. She thought of her own children, grown now, waiting for her to come back to be a grandma to their kids.

"You okay, Selma?" Nick asked, sensing her sadness.

"Just closing my eyes for a moment, child."

She could feel the salt spray on her face. She had removed the round blue hat. It hadn't been too comfortable to begin with. It was cool under the yellow canvas umbrella. Nick had brought her a root beer in a big paper cup. He knew root beer was one of her weaknesses.

"You know why I like this place, Selma?" he asked her with that fervor of his, that enthusiasm, breaking into her reverie. "Because," he went on, not waiting for an answer, "it's brand-new. It's not like Pensacola, all old and settled. Or Miami, which is already used. Miami Beach is still in the borning stages. They don't hate Jews or coloreds here, or not so's you'd notice. Each time I come, there's something new. Mr. Fisher has his dredges working every day, making it all up.

"Want to know my dream, Selma? When I'm twenty-one and come into my money, I'm going to buy a piece of land on Miami Beach and I'm going to build a hotel with a swimming pool. It's going to be a hotel where anyone can stay. A pool anyone can swim in. In school the teachers are always talking about this free land we live in. It's only free to some. But my hotel is going to be for everyone, Selma."

"Child, how you talk," she said, not wanting to wipe the glow of belief and enthusiasm off that face she loved. "You'd better come home with me to Pensacola. Your Uncle Milton says he'll send you to college, and he'll give you a nice job in—"

"—a department store. Not me, Selma. I've got my own plans. Right here on Miami Beach. Do you know the history of Miami Beach?" he asked. Selma shook her head and closed her eyes against the sun reflecting from the sea and the white sand. She felt her body relax in the stiff canvas sling. She didn't have to listen. She had heard it all before.

Four years before Nick was born, a man named Lum had planted a coconut farm on what would soon be called Miami Beach. He managed to get a New Jersey horticulturist and Quaker, John Collins, interested enough to invest five thousand dollars in the project. But Miami Beach, Lum had found, was too far north for coconuts to produce anything but a low, noncommercial oil.

Miami Beach was not then an inviting island. Oceanside a ribbon of sand stretched some two hundred feet to the base of a long sandy ridge formed by storm tides. A low scrub of glasswort, sandspurs, saltweed, and beach grass acted as a barrier wall, keeping the sand on the beach. Sea oats and sea grapes grew on the crest of the ridge. Sea rocket, pickleweed, and Spanish

316

bayonet thrived on the sheltered bay side. Sandwiched between the two shorelines, taking up two-thirds of the island, was an ancient jungle of giant mangroves flourishing in a marsh of foul-smelling salt mud.

The mangroves had grown back as fast as Lum could chop them down. He finally abandoned his coconut trees to be choked to death by the mangroves and the strangler figs, to sink into the salt marsh, to be eaten by the deer, rabbits, raccoons, and rats that thrived on the palms. Relieved, he left the plantation to John Collins.

John Collins had journeyed to Florida in 1896 when he learned that Julia Tuttle and Henry Flagler were selling mainland city lots for three hundred to nine hundred dollars apiece. He was a short, shrewd fifty-nine-year-old farmer, who came to see if his land was worth anything. He hired a launch, sailed around the island, and then walked across it, spending days exploring its mangrove jungles and sand beaches. The coconuts were obviously a dead issue, but there was a piece of land a mile north of Lum's old plantation that John Collins had a good feeling about.

It had taken a farmer and a man of quick intelligence to see its potential. It lay west of a tidal salt creek, surrounded by mangroves. "Just another mangrove swamp," the guide said, impatient to move on, but John Collins knew it wasn't that. For in the center of the marshy swamp he saw a stretch of tall pines rising out of the water, towering over everything in sight, even the mangroves. "That piece of land," John Collins said, "must have its own freshwater tables. Pines won't grow in salty soil." The height and luxuriance of the small pine forest was a sign that the rich, sandy, and salt-free soil was unusually deep.

John Collins, a plain man, had developed a taste for the exotic fruit known to Miamians as alligator pears ("avocados" to any other Americans who might have heard of them). Collins had seen avocados growing, though not in profusion, on a Coconut Grove farm. So he bought as much Miami Beach land as he could, believing that what he didn't plant with avocados, he could eventually sell. People were going to want to get away from Miami. Eventually several members of the Collins family came down to Miami to help, and John Collins started to build a wooden bridge that would span the bay and, he hoped, spur land sales. He then traded the auto-industry millionaire Carl Fisher a good deal of acreage in exchange for the money to finish the bridge. When it was finished, John Collins found that avocado sales were thriving, land sales were not.

Two brothers who had come to the bay area with Flagler became two of Miami's first bank presidents and made some money out of Miami Beach real estate. J. E. and J. N. Lummus arranged for their banks to give them loans so they could buy up land on the island's South Beach. They built a casino and sold lots for vacation houses to Miamians who wanted to escape the mainland's summer heat. Unlike Julia Tuttle and Henry Morrison Flagler, their contracts had no clauses restricting ownership to Caucasians.

317

"That's why the Lummus brothers came out ahead," Nick said, finishing his narrative. He took a deep breath of the ocean air and turned toward Selma. "Miami Beach is where I'm going to have my hotel and my swimming pool, and you and I are going to swim in it. You believe me?"

"You can do anything you want to do, child," Selma said. He took her to the café for hot dogs, ice cream, and more root beer. A three-man ragtime band was playing "Oh, You Beautiful Doll," and nearly everyone in the restaurant had gotten up to dance the two-step. Nick stopped talking and watched. Selma knew from the way he half closed his eyes, so his lashes nearly met, that he was concentrating, teaching himself to dance just the way he had taught himself to swim. He ordered more root beers as the band played a medley composed of "Gee, Ain't I Glad I'm Single," "Her Name Was Mary Wood but Mary Wouldn't," and "When Mariola Does the Cubanola."

"Let's dance," Nick said when the band—three elderly men in boaters and striped jackets—segued into "You Made Me Love You."

He was standing over her, looking down at her with that smile, as if everything were right with the world. "Child, they ain't going to let me dance in here. They're barely letting me eat in here. Child, we're just going to get in a mess of—"

He grabbed her large hand and pulled her up. "It's your birthday. This is Miami Beach. No Caucasian clause. We can dance."

"I can't dance. All I know is the Pensacola darktown strutters' shimmy. And if I did that, child, they'd have me in jail."

"You just follow me."

Nick put a hand on her waist, and waiting as carefully for the beat as he had once waited for the tide, plunged in, guiding her around the dance floor. There wasn't a sound in the café except for the music of that lugubrious song. Everyone stopped to watch the extraordinarily handsome sixteen-year-old Jewish boy and the not so handsome colored woman perform the two-step with grace and dignity. They were both smiling, but there were tears in Selma's eyes.

When the song came to an end, and in the silence that preceded the babel that followed, Selma said, "I love you, child. Today I know I kept my promise to your daddy. You sure are a man, Nick. A nice man."

"Happy birthday, Selma."

"*Oy vey,*" a little lady said to her husband. "A *shvartzeh* dancing with a white boy in front of my eyes. And a Jewish boy, at that. I'm going to faint, Morris. I never seen nothing like it in my entire life. Morris, get me some seltzer water before I pass out."

The sentiment behind those words was being repeated at tables throughout the café, but neither Nick nor Selma heard what was said. Nick paid the bill, and they went to the door, where John Rosi was standing. "Nick, that was some performance, but do me a favor, huh? No more dances with colored ladies, okay?"

318

"That was our last dance, Mr. Rosi," Selma said, fixing the uncomfortable round blue hat onto her oblong head.

"It was our first," Nick said, leading the way to the ferry.

They were alone, sitting in the Colored Section on the top of Mr. Flagler's *City of Miami* ferry, the day workers not due to return homeward for some hours yet. Miami, with Mr. Flagler's Presbyterian Church spire signaling the way, looked pretty in the pink glow of the sunset. The dredges had quit for the day, and the only sounds came from the ferry making its way across crowded Biscayne Bay. I got to tell him now, Selma decided. We get back to that apartment and Ida brings out that cake she's been baking for me and Irving winds up that Victrola and starts singing along with Galli-Curci, and I won't get one word in. I got to tell him now.

She touched his hand. "Nick," she said, and he turned to look at her with those vulnerable violet eyes. "I'm leaving you tomorrow, child. I'm going back to Pensacola, where I belong. My own children need me to help 'em with their kids."

"You're not going to really leave?" he asked, incredulous, in his new man's voice.

"I got to, child. You don't need me anymore, and I can't stand that city one more day. I hate it here. I've always hated it here."

"Then why did you stay?" Nick asked, confused and upset.

"For you. For your daddy." She looked at him with sad eyes. "Nick, I don't want to die in Miami. I'm too old to live in this place, and you're too old to have a mammy."

He took her hand. "You're not my mammy, Selma. You never were. You're my friend. My best friend."

"Child," she said, pleading with him, "let me go home."

"Okay," he said after a long moment of searching her plain face. "You go home, Selma." She could feel his sweet breath on her face. "But I want you to promise me something. When I build my hotel on Miami Beach, you have to come right back and swim in the pool."

"You and your father and your promises." She gave him her great lopsided grin and wiped away the tears coursing down her yellow cheeks. "I promise, child. When you get that pool built I'm going to be first in."

CHAPTER TWO

1920

"PISHER? Where you been?" Irving's raspy voice boomed down the long, narrow hall that divided the apartment's three bedrooms and bath from the kitchen, dining and living rooms. The living room, where Irving sat in his favorite chair, had three windows fronting Twelfth Street. The other rooms had one narrow window apiece, all facing similar buildings inches away. The walls and ceilings, painted a creamy white when the Princes first took up residence, now appeared a faded yellow.

There was too much furniture, most of it heavy mahogony-stained oak. The plain pine floors were covered with "American Orientals," the new machine-made carpets Ida couldn't resist. When Nick was away in the army and homesick in gray New Jersey, he found himself thinking of those rugs, of their bold purples and reds and pinks and blues, their borders and birds and flowers, the way the pile tickled his feet when he walked across them barefoot. He enjoyed remembering the moment when Ida had unveiled, with fanfare, the new "Oriental" she had found for the kitchen. "An Oriental rug in the kitchen? Are you crazy, Ida Prince?" Irving had shouted, looking down at the intricate pattern of Persian and perhaps Egyptian design on the kitchen floor. It was only when he stepped onto it that he realized he had been fooled. It was what Ida called "a linoleum of genuine Oriental extraction."

When Nick was drafted in 1917, Ida's worst and most vocal fears were realized. He had to go to Camp Kilmer, in New Jersey. He had graduated first in his class from Central High School, turned down Uncle Milton's offer of a college education, and had been marking time, getting ready to spend the money that would come to him on his twenty-first birthday.

When he left on the troop train, holding the box of cake Ida had insisted he take, looking like a recruitment poster, only better, Ida had flung her dimpled arms around his neck and held onto him as if she'd never let him go. "You look like a hero, *tateleh*," she said, setting him free only when the final whistle blew. "But do me a favor, Nick. Don't be no hero. For me, be a coward."

Nick didn't know or care much about the war. His big worry was that

Miami Beach wouldn't wait for him, that it would be all built up by the time he got back. He never doubted that he would get back. Luckily the war put a stop to the dredging and the construction. Carl Fisher patriotically planted vegetables on all of his Miami Beach holdings and lent his polo field to the Signal Corps for aviation experiments.

Now, years later, the linoleum Oriental had worn through at the two thresholds of the kitchen and in front of the stove. "Nick, I'm asking you a question." Irving shouted from his club chair in the living room.

"Leave him alone already," Ida, coming out of the kitchen into the small foyer, shouted back. She reached up and kissed Nick on his cheek. She smelled of flour and tomato sauce and sweet, honest sweat. "Go talk to him," she whispered. "Calm him down. He's upset. That bastard Troxyl the land-lord was here today with that bastard the son-in-law Nablo. Snooping." The lease Nick's father had contrived to get on the building on Twelfth Street was nearly up. A clause had been included that would give Irving an option on another lease at a new rental. Ida believed Troxyl the landlord and Nablo the son-in-law were suddenly coming round on frequent "inspection tours" as a scare tactic, preparing Irving for an expensive new lease.

"And your Uncle Milton's coming for dinner, in case you forgot."

Milton, the proud Pensacola Levi, had made it a point never to set foot in Miami. He had viewed Miami as the killer of his brother, the seducer of a nephew whom he might have had as a son. Milton and his wife were child-less. He had come to covet Nick like a rich man desiring a poor man's be-loved watch. But he had realized during the annual visits Nick paid to Pensacola that bribes wouldn't work. When Nick was a boy he had come with Selma. Later, after Selma had returned to work for Milton in his fine Palafox Street house, Nick had come on his own—more, Milton suspected, to see Selma than to spend time with his uncle and his Levi cousins.

This year, in a carefully worded letter, Milton had announced his intention of breaking with tradition, of visiting Nick "on your home ground." There was no question of his staying with the Princes. He would book rooms in Miami's best hotel. On the day the letter was received and read and reread, there was a discussion around the Princes' dining table as to "why Milton is coming to Miami after all these years." "He's coming," Irving said, "because Nick is twenty-two years old, he's got the money Maurice left him, and Mil-ton is afraid we're going to get our Middle European hands on it and bleed him dry. Does he know we don't even accept rent from this nephew?"

"I'd like to help, Irving," Nick said, using one of the oversized spoons Ida had brought from Poland to drink her finely strained chicken soup.

"When I want help," that man said, slurping soup, spotting his tie, "I'll ask for it, *yonkle.*"

"Why do you always have to think bad about everyone?" Ida asked, re-turning to the subject at hand. "You know what I think? I think Milton is coming because he wants to make amends. After all these years."

"Don't hold your breath, Ida." Irving looked across the table at Nick. "Why do *you* think he's coming, big shot?"

"I *know* why he's coming, Irving. He's going to offer me a job."

"A job? Doesn't he know I've already offered you a job?"

"You," Ida said, clearing the table, "offered him a job as a clerk in a haberdashery store. Milton Levi's going to offer him an entire chain of department stores. Levi & Sons."

"Pardon me for breathing." Irving stuck the edge of his napkin in the water goblet and began dabbing ineffectually at his tie. "What a terrible thing I did, offering this *pisher* an opportunity to come in as a partner—a full partner—in the thriving Irving Prince's New York Gentleman's Haberdashery." Ida took the napkin from his fat fingers and worked at the soup spots. "And did I ask him for money?" He pushed Ida's hands away and began rummaging under his chair until he found the socialist paper that was sent him from New York. Rattling its thin inky pages, he went to the living room to read it. "I'm a terrible, terrible person."

"What're you cooking?" Nick asked, inhaling the fragrant, heavy aroma coming from Ida's kitchen.

"Spaghetti and meatballs." Irving had rented the third-floor apartment to a large, warm Italian family of several generations named the Dianas. Signora Diana, a little golden mass of wrinkles and jewelry that tinkled when she moved, had opened the door to southern Italian cooking for Ida. Brisket, chopped liver, *kreplach* soup, noodle pudding were dishes of the past. Gnocchi, veal parmigiana, lasagna, and rigatoni alla Diana had replaced them.

"And this time," Ida continued, moving into the narrow kitchen, "I think I got it right. The secret? 'She'sa in the basil,'" Ida said, imitating Signora Diana, shaking her head just as the older woman did, shredding a basil leaf, mixing the dried bits into the tomato sauce. She looked up at Nick. "Go talk to him already. Milton's coming. Troxyl the landlord's irritating him. He's a nervous wreck. He's not a man who knows how to talk about what he feels." She looked away. "He thinks he's losing you." Nick kissed her round cheek. Everything about Ida was round. Her head, her eyes, her nose, her already graying curls, her compact breasts, her massive bottom, her little butterball hands.

"He's never going to lose me."

"So tell him."

Nick still didn't move. He was leaning against the door jamb, watching Ida move around the kitchen. She was like some mythic dervish, risen from the linoleum Oriental carpet, whirling around that cave of a kitchen filled with white-enameled appliances. She couldn't remain still for a moment.

She caught Nick looking at her, smiled and shook her head. "Where, I should like to know, did he come from?" Ida asked no one in particular as she stirred her sauce, poked the meatballs, fanned the pasta with a frayed dish towel. "Did you ever see such a smile on a human being? He's a god." She opened the oven and looked at the bread. "An exquisite black-haired, violet-eyed *Yiddisheh* god. And where is the goddess—pray she should be Jewish—for this god? That's also what I should like to know."

Nick laughed. "You're the only woman in my life, Ida."

The truth—which he saw no reason to burden Ida with—was that while he was in the army he had met a nice woman whose husband was a general stationed in France. She had taught Nick to tango, a dance for which she had a passion. During one weekend leave she gave him a lesson in the living room of her Central Park West apartment. Then she made love to him in the huge bed in the bedroom overlooking the park. He spent every leave he could wangle with her. Sometimes they would tango nude across the tiled floor of the living room, making love when the record on the Victrola came to an end.

But Nick's fantasy love was America's Sweetheart, Mary Pickford. Irving had introduced him to her years before when he had taken him to see a Griffith film *The Lonely Villa*. Alice Gibson looked more like Theda Bara than Mary Pickford. She had black curly hair and a generous ivory-colored body. Nick liked dancing and sleeping with Alice Gibson, but he found he was relieved when the war was over, General Gibson was coming home, and Nick was going to be allowed to return to Florida. To Miami Beach.

Carefully, using two dish towels for potholders, Ida removed the bread, a golden braided loaf, and set it on the window sill to cool. She tested the crust of the apple pie with a fork and, satisfied, put it next to the bread. "Sometimes, Nick, I get up in the morning and I think I'm still in that hovel in the middle of nowhere, Poland—or worse, in that rat-infested den you shouldn't ever have to know from in New York City. And then I look out at the window at the palm trees and I realize where I am and who I am, and I thank God I've got you and I've got Irving. Nothing—not Milton, not Troxyl, not the President of the United States—can take this joy away from me." She closed the oven door and turned her attention back to the sauce. "Go talk to him."

Irving sat in his club chair, an overupholstered and dark-red-slip-covered throne with a gold P embroidered in the center of its back, smoking a short, smelly cigar, reading the *International Citizen*. He wore a fashionably pale-yellow suit from his haberdashery, but the jacket was too long and there was a faint but unmistakable gray stain on the trousers. His tie, selected with care from the five-dollar rack, had gone askew, and the collar of his Arrow shirt had come undone. Nick knew it galled him that as hard as he tried, Irving couldn't achieve the fashion-plate image his adopted son attained so effortlessly.

At that moment, in the hard Miami afternoon light, Nick was startled: Irving, who had always seemed frozen in middle age, suddenly looked old. He was in his late forties, but on that Sunday afternoon in September, he could have passed for sixty. He was a man who didn't like mysteries, and he was suddenly confronted with a series of them. "All right, *pisher*," he said, putting the thin sheets of newspaper on the ottoman that matched the club chair, resting the cigar in the thick glass ashtray Ida had bought him. "Sit down. I want to talk to you."

He looked at Nick, sitting in the dark-green-slip-covered chair with the indolent ease of a magazine model, and shook his head as if he couldn't believe what he saw. "Answer me, this, Nick. Have I been pretty good all summer or have I not?"

"You've been excellent, Irving."

"You and the fifty-cent words. Good or not good."

"Good."

"You came home from the army, you said you didn't want to work in the shop anymore, did I make a fuss? No. You didn't want to work in the shop, so you didn't have to work in the shop. What was I supposed to do, get down on my knees and beg you? You're a man now. I accepted your decision. Tell me, did I say one single, solitary word?"

"You have an expressive face, Irving," Nick said, smiling.

"I should have been Ethel Barrymore." He put the stump of a cigar in his mouth and lit it with a kitchen match. "Have I asked you once where you been going every day, all summer? Did I say a syllable when you bought that contraption for five hundred dollars?"

"I needed a good car," Nick said.

"A bad car would have been just as good and half the price." Irving looked at Nick and shook his head again, his face heavy with jowls and, Nick realized, fear. "So you don't want to be a haberdasher. That's okay by me. But do me a favor and tell me something. What have you been doing all summer? Golf? Polo? Nibbling whitefish and pike with the rich and famous?"

Nick uncrossed his legs and leaned forward, resting his elbows on his knees, speaking with a wonderment, a total conviction few—least of all Irving—could resist. "You know what I've been doing, Irving? I've been looking at property over on the Beach. I've been watching the houses go up on Collins Avenue, and it's a miracle. Three weeks, and, boom, they're up. Each morning I've been going to a different construction site. You should come with me, Irving. You should see the way Carl Fisher operates. He decides the electric company should go there, and sure enough, they break ground there. He wants the railway company here, and here it is. He's making up his own town, Irving. It's a miracle."

Nick's violet eyes were purple with excitement. He stood up and walked over to the living room's three windows and looked across the bay toward Miami Beach. "I've been following Carl Fisher and I've been studying the land. I've been trying to decide where to put my hotel."

"You're still crazy over that hotel idea?" Irving said, but without real rancor. The cigar had gone dead again. He relit it. "I'm paying forty bucks a month to that *chozzer* of a landlord, and you're taking a course in how to throw ten thousand bucks plus interest away on a hotel the Jews and the *goyim* are going to stand in line to keep away from and the *shvartzers* won't be able to afford."

"Nine thousand five hundred dollars, Irving. I bought the Olds."

"I stand corrected." Irving looked at his nephew leaning against the window, the setting sun illuminating his profile as if he were one of the motion picture heroes Irving secretly idolized every Tuesday and Thursday afternoon at the Odeon. Silently he asked himself the same questions Ida so often asked aloud. "Where the hell do we come from, two *shlemiels* from Poland, to be lucky enough to have this boy, this good, smart, beautiful lunatic, as our son? I don't believe in You, God, most of the time. But when I look at that boy, I do." He put his hands on the round arms of his club chair and, sighing, pushed himself up and joined Nick at the window.

They made an odd pair. The short, paunchy middle-aged man. The other long, elegant, and young. Irving, who rarely touched anyone save Ida, put his big butcher's hand on Nick's broad, thin shoulder, and Nick turned to him. Instead of telling Nick how much he cared for him, he found himself returning to the old argument. "Why a hotel, Nick? Of all businesses in the world, why a hotel?"

Nick looked at his uncle and tried to tell him. "When I was a kid, I thought The Royal Palm was somebody's house and they let me go swimming when I paid them. Then I found out that even when I paid them, I wasn't welcome. I want to change that, Irving. I want to build a big home, Irving, and invite everyone to come. No restrictions. Okay?"

"Okay," Irving said, still touching Nick. "Whatever you do, *pisher*, it's okay by me. I'll stand behind you a hundred and ten percent." He let his hand fall away. "But you know, when you were a kid and I was dressing you in those little white suits, and nobody would believe you were my boy because you were so gorgeous and *goyish*, you used to tell everyone who came in the shop, 'When I grow up, I'm going in with my dad.' " Nick saw the tears in Irving's eyes. "I guess what I've been trying to tell you is that I'm just a little disappointed that you're not. That's legal, ain't it?"

Nick stood still, inhaling Irving's comforting barbershop smell of cheap cigars and Lilac Vegetal. "So *you'll* come in with me. 'What,' " he said, imitating Irving, his hands going out and up, " 'could be so terrible?' You'll have the men's shop in my hotel. There. It's all settled." He looked down and smiled. "I love you, Irving. I couldn't have picked a better father. I'm lucky."

"I love you too, Nick," Irving said finally. "I love you too."

And then Ida swirled in, saying, "Let's have a little light on the subject." She began switching on lamps, wondering where Milton was, inspecting ashtrays. Irving retired to his club chair as Nick, moving with that odd military grace, helped Ida "make the house look nice for company." My son,

325

Irving thought, remembering how empty life had been the past few years without Nick around.

"Milton Levi," Ida exclaimed, greeting him at the door. "I never thought I'd see the day that you would deign to set your delicate foot in Miami, Florida. After all these years. Come in, make yourself homely. We're going to eat right away because, to tell you the truth, you're a little late, and Irving, bless him, has some appetite. Come in. Come in. Nicky. Look who's here. Your Uncle Milton."

She led Milton into the dining room. For years after, whenever Nick thought of Milton, he would remember him standing pressed between the dining table and the china cabinet, tall and bald and despairing, Ida's fat arm linked in his, the two of them looking like an unlikely bride and groom.

Milton, acutely uncomfortable, offered his narrow hand, shaking Nick's. Irving, already at the table, offered his hand, which Milton touched, but barely. He felt as if he had been thrust into some foreign place. All this terrible furniture. All those garish rugs. The smells.

"Sit down," Irving ordered, pushing a chair out for Milton with his foot. "We'll talk as we eat. Ida, darling, get the dinner on the table."

Milton squeezed himself into the chair Irving offered him and looked at Nick while Ida brought out plates piled high with coils of spaghetti and meatballs the size and shape of baseballs. Nick smiled at his uncle reassuringly.

"Seltzer, water, or iced tea?" Ida wanted to know.

"Iced tea would be nice," Milton said. As a rule he didn't perspire, but he thought he might here. A thin brownish red fringe of hair outlined his pointed ears and polished dome. His cheeks were turning red from heat and discomfort.

Irving attacked his spaghetti as if it were an enemy to be vanquished, the napkin around his neck turning tomato red as he shoveled it in. "How's Selma?" Nick asked his uncle, who didn't seem to know what to do with the spaghetti.

"Fine," Milton said, on safe ground. "She sends her love and wants to know when you plan to visit. She talks about you all the time, Nick." He put his fork down, addressing only Nick, as if the others weren't in the room. The light from the little chandelier, in the style of Venetian glass, hurt his eyes. He decided to get to the point. "I came to Miami to see if we might not open a branch of Levi & Sons here. I thought you might like to work with the family, Nick, and run the Miami store. But I've changed my mind. Not about you. About Miami."

"How's that?" Irving asked through a mouthful of spaghetti and meatball.

"I am not," Milton said, his voice becoming softer and more southern with anger, "going to open a Levi & Sons in a city that is so blatantly anti-Semitic as this one."

326

"What happened, Milton?" Ida asked, suddenly and profoundly serious, resting her fork on her plate. When she was nine years old she had come home from the school her mother had sent her to with great sacrifice carrying a note saying Jews were not welcome. Soon after, three cousins were killed in a pogrom near the Russian border. She liked to believe that she had escaped what she thought of as European persecution by coming to America. Each time she heard of an anti-Semitic incident, she felt vulnerable, reduced to that nine-year-old Polish girl.

"Could we please, I'm begging you, eat?" Irving wanted to know.

"What happened, Milton?" Ida, ignoring him, asked again.

"I still can't believe it. I had a reservation at The Royal Palm. I have stayed at Mr. Flagler's hotels before, though I am aware his management does not welcome most Jews. But the Levis have been in Florida for four hundred years. My grandfather was the first Florida-elected representative to the United States Congess. That policy never seemed to apply to me. However, when I got to the desk of The Royal Palm, the clerk looked at my name and my reservation and then, without saying a word, he went and got the manager. The manager looked straight at me and told me The Royal Palm does not accommodate members of the Hebrew persuasion.

"What did you say?" Nick wanted to know.

"I said, 'I am not of the Hebrew persuasion, you little strutting peacock, I am a Jew. And I wouldn't stay in this barn if you paid me.' I had to keep myself from punching him in the nose only because I didn't want to wind up in the Miami jail. If that had happened in Pensacola to a Levi, that boy would be run out of town."

"You'll stay with us," Ida said. "My spare room is cleaner than The Royal Palm, believe me."

"Thank you, Ida," Milton said, still outraged, picking up his fork, looking at the spaghetti. "I'm surprised you don't have the Klan in Miami."

"We do," Irving told him, wiping up the sauce with a hunk of Ida's golden braid bread. "They offered to help the city police the streets, but, thanks God, the bums were turned down."

"I have always felt Miami was the wrong city for the Levis," Milton said, looking at Nick. "Your father and his wife died here. I should never have come. But I wanted to offer you, Nick, another chance to draw on your heritage. To work for Levi & Sons. I think I can promise you a superior life if you return with me to Pensacola."

"What about Ida and Irving?" Nick wanted to know.

"Irving," Milton said, giving up on the spaghetti, swallowing his Levi pride along with Ida's iced tea, "would be a welcome addition to the haberdashery department in our flagship store. Ida, of course, would find friends and a great many social occupations among the Levi women. You belong in Pensacola, Nick. I made an error years ago." He stopped for a moment, his Adam's apple bobbing. "I drove your father and your mother away. I have paid for my sins. I was an arrogant fool. I apologize to you, Ida and Irving. You are good people.

"And now I want you to come back with me, Nick. I have no sons of my own. I look at you and see your father all over again. Come. Be my son, Nick. Be a Levi. I offer you heritage and money and power. I am a good judge of men. I see no reason why in the future you shouldn't take your place as the head of Levi & Sons."

There was a rare silence around the Princes' mahogany-stained oak dinner table. They could hear the streetcars on Third Street and the Dianas having dinner above them. Nick looked at Irving, who seemed suddenly defeated, and at Milton, who seemed bitter. He would have liked to make them both happy—to go with Milton to Pensacola and to go downstairs in the morning with Irving and sell Palm Beach suits to the businessmen of Miami. But he couldn't do either.

"I'm sorry," he said to Milton. "I appreciate all that you would like to do for me. But I have a father—and a mother—sitting right here at this dinner table. I'm as much a Prince as I am a Levi. No one blames you for what happened twenty-two years ago, Uncle Milton. But the truth is, my future is across the bay, in Miami Beach. I have plans."

"And they are?" Milton asked stiffly, trying to hide his disappointment.

"I'm going to buy land there and I'm going to build a hotel. It's going to be a hotel where anyone can come—black, Jewish, green, or Martian. It's going to be a grand hotel, Uncle Milton. And I promise you, you'll never have to worry about a reservation being honored again. Not in Miami Beach."

The appalled look on Milton's businessman's face nearly made Ida laugh. It was clear from the way his eyes had widened and he had sat up in his chair that Nick's plan seemed foolish to him. "Nothing I can say could convince you . . . ?" he asked, deciding not even to comment on Nick's idiotic plan.

"Nothing," Nick said, looking firmly into Irving and Ida's joyful eyes.

After Milton had gone to bed Nick and Irving sat in the living room, waiting for Ida to finish up in the kitchen. "I'm going to do it, Irving," Nick said quietly. "And I'm going to start tomorrow. So if you have anything else to say, now's the time to say it. This is your last chance."

Irving rested his butcher's hands on his paunch, too tired and too pleased to argue. "I only got one thing to say. Good luck, *yonkle*. Whatever you do is all right by me."

"Not to mention by me," Ida said, emerging from the kitchen. "If I can put my two cents in."

CHAPTER THREE

"WHERE YOU GOING so fast? Like a horse on fire. Eat your breakfast. Nichlaus Prince! You're not getting out of this house until you eat those eggs. I don't care if today's the day you're going to become the proud owner of the Taj Mahal. Eat. Irving, tell him to eat."

"Eat." Irving, thin back hairs standing up, paunch pushing against terry-cloth bathrobe, elbows resting comfortably on the dining room table, lowered his newspaper and looked at his adopted son. Milton had left Miami in the morning, disappointed. "He came for an heir," Irving said. "All he got was the air."

"He's a very lonesome man, Irving. Have a little *rachmones*," Ida said, pouring freshly squeezed orange juice into Irving's and Nick's glasses.

"The day that I have pity for that anti-Semite Semite is the day they'll crown me the pope."

"He's feeling good," Ida said to Nick, interpreting Irving's behavior for him, "because you told Milton you already had a father."

"And as for you, *pisher*," Irving went on, "first of all, I been thinking all night about what you said, and today, in the clear light of the morning, I want to tell you what I think of your famous plan for throwing away nine thousand five hundred dollars plus interest. In plain English, it stinks. First of all, Jews and *goyim* do not sleep in the same hotel together. Coloreds in the same pool, let alone in the same dining hall, would be against the law. They're not even allowed to be on Miami Beach after dark, much less floundering in hotel swimming pools.

"Second of all, Jews can't own land in the fair city of tomorrow, Miami, Florida, thanks to Mrs. Julia Tuttle, Mr. Henry Morrison Flagler, and their famous Caucasian clause. Unless I miss my guess, it's going to be the same story on Miami Beach. Except maybe on South Beach, where the Lummus boys don't care who buys their land. They're calling it the People's Playground. They got Hardie's Casino, dancing, a carousel, motordrome races, deep-sea exhibitions, a balloon ascent, and Bigley's Diving Belles. Such a plain bunch of women you never saw in your life, but they dive.

329

"Maybe you *should* talk to the Lummuses," Irving went on, reaching for the scrambled eggs Ida had put on the table before returning to the kitchen. "Get *them* to sell you a piece of land. And maybe then, if you open a nice kosher-style hotel, you got a chance."

Nick chewed his toast while Ida brought a pot of hot tea. "Does what you said to me last night still stand, Irving?" Irving shrugged and nodded reluctantly. "Good. Because today I'm going to Miami Beach and talk to Carl Fisher's real estate agent. I'm buying beach property, and I'm buying it uptown, not down."

"Nick," he whispered so Ida wouldn't hear, "you want me to come with you?"

"You can't go with him," Ida, who prided herself on her hearing, shouted from the kitchen. "That bastard, Troxyl the landlord is coming."

"You know what you can do with Troxyl the landlord." Irving pushed his coffee cup away and put the soggy end of his stogie in his mouth. "Nick, you want me to close the shop and come with you?"

Nick shook his head and smiled at the rumpled man across from him. The last time Irving had closed the shop was the day Nick had gone off to Camp Kilmer.

"I appreciate it, Irving. But I want to do this myself."

"Before you sign anything, read the fine print and read it again and then get yourself a lawyer to read it. All real estate men are *gonifs*, especially if their name is Carl Fisher."

Nick managed to get out of the apartment by eight and was rattling over the Collinses' wooden bridge in his Olds a few minutes later. He was only dimly aware of the rumbling of the bridge timbers and the roar of the dredges, already at work. He couldn't concentrate on anything. He was filled with an electric anticipation. In his mind he kept repeating the phrase, "Today is the day." When he drove off the bridge onto Miami Beach, it was eight-thirty, and he wondered how he had got there. He looked up. The weather was being agreeable. The sky was the crayon-colored Miami blue he had dreamed about when he was stationed at Camp Kilmer.

He couldn't remember ever having felt so exhilarated. And nervous. His fingertips tingled against the steering wheel. He avoided the rear-view mirror; he didn't want to see the silly smile he had on his face. I feel like an expectant father, he thought, an image of Buster Keaton in that role, pacing a hospital ward, coming to mind. Today is the day. I'm going to buy land. I'll own it. I'll build my hotel. I'll have a home. It never occurred to him that Irving and Ida wouldn't live with him. They were all going to come home to the hotel Nick would build.

He felt as if the Olds were driving itself, as if it knew the way. Nick had driven and walked past the new, glamorous Spanish Mediterranean real estate office Carl Fisher had opened on the corner of Fourteenth Street and Alton Road dozens of times. He had memorized the announcement that

330

appeared regularly on page three of the Miami *Herald* and was displayed, tastefully framed in tarnished gold, on the blue-tinted plate glass window of the real estate office:

> We invite the closest analysis and investigation of our property. There is no uncertainty about Miami Beach Ocean Front. It offers so complete a combination of natural and artificial beauties, climatic advantages, and modern improvements as to rival the placid majesty of the ocean itself. It even surpasses in loveliness the banks of the Venetian canals of Italy. Every lot is particularly choice and attractive for home and investment.

Nick liked the hyperbole. He had picked out three adjoining lots on the ocean at Fifteenth Street after deciding that the site would one day be part of the center of Miami Beach. The lots were three blocks south of Carl Fisher's house, Shadows, within walking distance of Fisher's Roman Pools spa and the proposed Lincoln Road shopping thoroughfare. Nick had spent the summer doing his homework.

He read the advertisement once more, and then, half wishing Irving and Ida had come with him, he went up to the impressive Spanish-style door. He was still trying to get it open when he saw, down in the lower left-hand corner, a discreetly gold-lettered announcement: *The Carl Fisher Alton Beach Real Estate Office. Hours: 10 A.M. to 6 P.M. each weekday.*

He had over an hour to wait. At first he paced in front of the office, and then he thought that if the manager found him there, he'd look like a *shlemiel*, so he sat in his car. Then he decided he was too nervous to just sit there, so he drove around Carl Fisher's Miami Beach for perhaps the two-hundredth time.

Nick marveled all over again at the fortune—nearly a million dollars—Fisher had spent in developing his two hundred acres below Twentieth Street and above Third. Nick could hardly remember what Miami Beach looked like when he had first come with Selma to swim. Fisher had cleared the island's mangrove jungle—crocodiles and alligators were shot on sight—and was dredging up a new shoreline, pumping in millions of cubic yards of sand from Biscayne Bay for a new, white sandy beach.

Nick stopped the car for a moment to watch the dredges working the bay. They were great yellow machines, roaring dinosaurs feeding on the bay bottom's sand, creating a new basin to accommodate deep-water yachts. Nick drove south on Alton Road, along the bay, looking at the new marinas, docks, and speedboat race grandstand Fisher had built. He shook his head. It was happening so fast. For a moment he was afraid he was too late.

Quickly, to make certain his land was still there, he drove away from the bay, east toward the ocean. The anticipation of what he was going to do added to the excitement of what Fisher had already done made him feel

331

drunk. Fisher, of course, was way ahead of him. He had already planted palm trees, laid out a golf course, installed sewers, electric lights, and city water, and built a three-hundred-foot oceanside pier and a boardwalk. Fisher was like a giant's child, building a city out of colored toy blocks. Carl Fisher was Nick Prince's hero. In his eyes he could do no wrong.

At the end of Lincoln Road, at the ocean, Nick stopped the car. He couldn't remember the sky ever being so cloudless, so vibrant a blue. It even made the sun seem pale. The ocean was seductively calm, with only an occasional swell of curled, silver-crested waves breaking against the white sand. Nick looked south at the two hundred level acres of house lots Fisher had plowed and planted with imported Bermuda grass and ornamental trees suggested by his imported Japanese gardeners. He let out a sigh of relief. Nothing had been built in the last twenty-four hours.

He got out of the Olds and walked across the beach. He came to the spot where he wanted to build his hotel, and suddenly he saw it, an architectural combination of the Ritz Carlton in New York and The Royal Palm in Miami. It boasted a huge pool, and in it he could see himself, Selma, Irving, Ida, and Mr. Carl Fisher bobbing around. He shook his head, making the mirage disappear, and looked at his watch for the twentieth time in as many minutes. It read nine forty-five.

Fifteen more minutes. I'll drive slowly, he told himself. I'll take my time. He went back to the Olds, stood on the running board for a moment, and took a last long look at the improved lots Carl Fisher was trying to sell. "Three of you," he shouted into the mild ocean wind, "belong to me."

The receptionist, a suspicious blond wearing a long black dress she thought elegant but that was suitable only for mourning, had been alerted. A brass bell attached to the door had rung, signifying that the Carl Fisher Real Estate Office finally might have a customer. Or he might be another bill collector or the man come to see about the toilet. Customers had not been lining up at the door.

She slipped the page of "Believe It or Not" cartoons she had torn from the newspaper into her desk drawer, folded her hands demurely, and looked up brightly. Involuntarily her mouth opened unbecomingly. The man of her dreams was standing in front of her finally. She couldn't help but run her tongue around her rouged lips as if she were looking at a mouth-watering candy. "May I help you?" she asked in the British accent with which she had been taught to say those words.

"I'd like to talk to someone about buying land," Nick said. He was so serious. And so handsome. He looked so rich. She could have stared at him all day, but she had a job to do. "Who may I say is calling?" she asked in the pear-shaped tones of her elocution teacher.

"Nick Prince."

She managed to escort him to the sales manager's pecan-wood-paneled office without her knees buckling. "Mr. Nick Prince," she said before going back to her desk to daydream of being kissed by those lips. "Mr. Buddy McCord."

"Nick the Yiddish Prick." Nick recognized the grating voice immediately. "How the hell are you?"

Despite the plaid knickers, the plastered-down blond hair, the pencil-thin mustache, Nick would have known Buddy McCord's sun-boiled face anywhere. McCord, sitting back in his chair, propping his thick legs on his impressive sales manager's desk, looked at Nick warily. He hadn't forgotten Nick's threat at the ferry docks years ago, just before McCord's aborted attempt at being a college boy.

He took in Nick's white linen suit, his Arrow-collared cream-colored shirt, his pale-yellow tie. Nick's violet eyes were narrowed, and his lower lip pushed out belligerently.

McCord took a swallow from the pint of Dixie Peach whiskey he kept in a brown paper bag. "Cough medicine," he said and smiled that evocative, gap-toothed smile. Still the bad boy. "Want a slug?" he asked, rising because he didn't like sitting down when the Yid was standing up, and he didn't want to offer him a chair.

"No thanks, Buddy." The day, the pleasure were fading, threatening to disappear. He wanted to hold onto them. He tried not to see McCord as the bully of his youth but as a salesman of Carl Fisher's land. "I've come to buy three lots on the ocean at Fifteenth Street," Nick said matter-of-factly. "That comes to thirty-six hundred dollars. You don't have to show them to me. I've seen them. Can you make out the papers or do I have to see someone else?"

McCord took another swallow from the Dixie Peach bottle, wiped his mouth with the back of his hand, and leaned on the desk. His damp face took on that half-scared, half-gleeful expression Nick remembered from The Royal Palm's dressing room. It was as vivid as if he had ripped up Nick's new bathing costume that morning.

"And then the curtain fell and Louise woke up and realized it was all a beautiful dream." Buddy McCord shook his head and laughed. "Listen, Prince, you dope, and listen carefully, because I ain't going to say this again. Carl Fisher has a policy. He doesn't sell to kikes. You know what a kike is, Prince? A nigger with a nose. You got a nice nose, Prince, but you're still a kike. I got eyewitness proof 'cause I saw your circumcised dick with my own eyes."

Nick, standing so straight and still he might have been one of Medusa's victims, said, "I don't believe you. Carl Fisher wouldn't have a Caucasian clause."

"Bullshit he wouldn't," McCord spat out. " 'Cause he does."

"I'd have read—-"

"You think he advertises something like that? He's got a lot of Yid friends he doesn't want to insult. Listen, Prince, you weren't wanted at The Royal

333

Palm pool then and you're not wanted in Mr. Fisher's Miami Beach now. Do us both a favor and scram, okay?" Buddy McCord, still standing, took another pull from the Dixie Peach bottle.

Nick studied Buddy McCord for a moment through his narrowed eyes and saw a tough twenty-six-year-old Miami pioneer's son going soft with bootleg booze. Easy pickings. But the perfect day was ruined anyway. Carefully he undid his white linen handkerchief and wrapped it around the knuckles of his right hand. Buddy followed all of this attentively, trying to figure out what the Yid was up to. Nick held up his wrapped hand, showed it to Buddy, and deliberately, carefully, with all the power his anger had generated, leaned across the impressive desk and smashed Buddy McCord's nose.

The only sound in the pecan-wood-paneled office was the sharp crack of Buddy McCord's nose breaking and the mouselike "Oh" of the receptionist who had come in to see what was going on. McCord sat down on the tiled floor, blood ruining his new plaid knicker suit, his bottle of Dixie Peach whiskey slowly emptying itself on the recently laid rug.

Nick made it to Carl Fisher's Roman Pools in record time. The Olds looked like a folded accordion parked between those concert grand pianos, a red Stutz Bearcat and Fisher's Duesenberg. Nick, his eyes narrowed to slits, sat in the Olds, his hands clutching the steering wheel. "It can't be," he said to himself, looking at the rococo towers of the Roman Pools. "Carl Fisher wouldn't have a Caucasian clause." He felt like a young officer he had seen in the Camp Kilmer hospital. Shell-shocked. His body was in one piece, but his mind was in smithereens.

Eventually he got himself out of the Olds and stood staring at the tourists lining up to get into the Roman Pools café. Originally the Roman Pools belonged to the Collins family. Early on, through their Miami Beach Improvement Company, the Collinses had put up a bathhouse on Twenty-Third Street and the ocean, building it, Collins style, out of driftwood washed up on the shore. A swimming pool had been installed, for use when the ocean was too cold or too rough. There were few other amenities.

Then Carl Fisher took over the "spa" and, Fisher style, put three hundred and fifty thousand dollars into it, building a second pool, with a Dutch windmill device that pumped in seawater. He surrounded both pools with a restaurant, a stage, a ballroom, and a shopping arcade, changing the name from the Collins Casino to the Roman Pools. Fisher's millionaire pals came, and lesser folk followed.

It was just eleven o'clock when Nick arrived, the hour when the powerful and the would-be powerful came to the Roman Pools café to be seen having late breakfast. Nick attempted to get past his anger and that feeling of being fatally stabbed in the back. He had hope. It suddenly seemed to him quite possible that that old and unworthy enemy Buddy McCord had been lying, that he had made up the Caucasian clause just to keep Nick from getting what he wanted.

Half allowing himself to believe that, Nick warily approached the Roman

Pools café. It had blue-and-white-striped awnings, blue-and-white-striped waiters, and blue and white café tables with blue-and-white-striped umbrellas shielding diners from the sun. Though named for Rome, it was intended to look Venetian, Venice a place thought to be the ne plus ultra of world resorts. Nick had driven by the café any number of times but had never felt a desire to go in. By eleven in the morning, the hour to be at the café for breakfast, Nick was usually looking forward to lunch.

Nick bypassed the cordon keeping the unwanted unknowns lined up until the back tables were empty. He stood between a pair of huge spreading Japanese fishtail palms, behind which was the headwaiter's podium. Nick knew from his assiduous reading of the Miami newspapers that Fisher held court every morning from eleven to one at the first table on the left. But the palm trees blocked his view.

He started to move around them when the headwaiter stopped him. He took in Nick's suit, his slicked-back hair, his Woolworth lashes, and said, "It's about time you got here. Follow me." Nick hesitated. Just below his fury and his disappointment and his need to talk to Carl Fisher had been the uncertainty of whether or not Carl Fisher would talk to him. He followed, hoping he would miraculously be led to Carl Fisher. Instead the headwaiter took him to the Greek temple of a ballroom on the far side of the cabanas. Artfully broken plaster columns and nude plaster gods and goddesses lined the walls of the circular room. Under a roof that slid open at night to reveal Miami Beach's velvet sky, Jane Fisher sat cross-legged on the marble floor, an unlikely goddess: Venus in a bathing costume.

Nick recognized her only because she was not wearing the long black stockings regarded necessary by other women when they wore bathing costumes. He had read, as had half the nation, that Miami's Baptist minister had declared Jane Fisher's bare knees "a living example of the Depravity of Modern Woman." Her husband was capitalizing on the sermon, beginning a much publicized tradition of bare-kneed Miami Beach bathing beauties.

Nick, looking down at the pretty woman with the rouged lips, agreed with the minister. Her long unclad legs seemed unnecessarily provocative. Jane Fisher didn't look up from the pastel chalk marks she was making on the dance floor, reproducing in miniature Carl Fisher's polo field. "The band leader, Mrs. Fisher," said the headwaiter, revealing to Nick whom he was being mistaken for.

"About time too," Jane Fisher said. Nick was left standing in the middle of the chalk polo field, Jane Fisher at his feet, on her knees, talking away. "Carl, damn him, is planning a Polo Ball. The guests must wear polo uniforms. The horses are being made of papier-mâché. Everyone who comes has to play. 'No goddamned voyeurs,' as Carl so delightfully puts it. We're going to serve French champagne in silver-plated prize cups." She stood up, wiping the chalk from her hands. "It's going to be excruciating fun, and you're here so we can decide on the music."

She finally looked at Nick and cocked her head to one side. "Are you the ragtime band leader or the waltz orchestra man?" she asked. "No, of course you're neither. Though you're quite pretty enough to be whatever you want to be." She paused, waiting for him to say something, and when he didn't, she put her hands on her hips and straightened her head. "All right, Lord Brentwood, what do you want?"

She wore a black silk turban with a big fuchsia silk bow, and Nick noticed with something like alarm the high-heeled shoes on her bare feet. She unnerved him. He didn't know how to deal with flirtation. It took him a moment to find his voice. "I am here to see Mr. Fisher," he said, feeling uncomfortable and formal. "I am interested in buying land."

Jane Fisher dropped her hands and straightened her head. "I should have known. You have that land-buying fever in those oh-you-kid eyes. You'd better come with me."

She took his unwilling hand and led him out of the ballroom, around the two pools, and up onto the raised platform that housed the café. Her husband was at a newspaper-strewn table, smoking a Cuban cigar and talking on a white telephone, occasionally taking a drink of a dark liquid from a thin china cup.

Both of the Fishers seemed genuinely unaware that everyone in the café was staring at them, that none of the people relegated to the back tables—craning their necks for a better glimpse—had ever seen a woman in bathing dress without stockings before. Nick got a quick impression that these two were always onstage.

"Carl, put that telephone down. I've caught a fish for you. This fellow wants to buy some land. Sell him some, won't you, and then hire him as my personal masseur." She patted Nick on the cheek. "Until the next time, pretty boy."

"What's your name, kid?" Carl Fisher asked, hanging up the phone, pushing aside the newspapers. He wore a soft gray hat with a floppy brim and eyeglasses with round gold frames. He was twenty pounds overweight and he needed a shave. The liquid in his teacup was one hundred proof Scotch.

"Nick Prince," Nick said, acutely aware of the attention he and Carl Fisher were getting. He wished he could sit down.

"You're the Yid who knocked my number-one salesman on his kaflooty and got blood all over the new Chinese rug Jane handpicked. That numbnut just called to tell me he thought you might be on the way to see me. Okay, now you're seeing me." Fisher, holding the cigar as if it were a sovereign's scepter, took a puff from it, looked up at Nick, recognized his discomfort, and relented. "Sit down. Take a load off. I've been wanting to bust McCord in the head for weeks now. You did me a favor. Though don't think for a goddamned minute I'm not going to send you a bill for cleaning that goddamned rug. You want something to eat, drink?"

Nick was relieved to sit down. "No, thank you. I'll just—"

"What're you doing, kid?" Nick had taken a pen from his pocket.

"Writing down my address so you can send me the bill for cleaning the rug."

Fisher laughed, genuinely amused. "Jesus, you are green. I was kidding. Joke. Can you imagine me sending you a bill for twenty-five bucks?" He put the cigar in the ashtray and spat precisely into a brass spittoon neatly hidden behind him in the shrubbery. Then he looked at Nick. "I've seen you before, haven't I?"

"I like to watch the construction—" Nick began.

"You're the goddamned kid in the white suit and the black Olds who's been following me around. I was beginning to think you liked me. You're not a pansy, are you?"

Nick smiled, letting himself relax a little. "I'm interested in how you work. I was studying your technique."

"Hot damn! Maybe I should open a college." Fisher drained the whiskey from his teacup and a waiter immediately refilled it from a silver teapot. "Give this guy a drink, Herb. He needs one."

"No tea for me," Nick said, and Carl Fisher nearly spurted the liquor out of his mouth as the waiter, ignoring Nick, poured whiskey into the teacup sitting in front of him.

"Hey, don't do that again, kid," Carl Fisher said, mopping his face with the napkin. He stared at Nick and shook his round head in disbelief. "You sure are green, kid. That ain't tea. It's pre-Prohibition Scotch. Drink it. It'll put hair on your privates." The headwaiter came up behind Fisher's chair and whispered something in his ear. "Listen, kid, I got some important people— they think—waiting in line to see me. What do you want from me?"

"I want to buy some of your land."

"Listen, kid, you're a very presentable fellow in your little white suit. For Christ's sake, you look like a million goddamned bucks. Look at me. I'm a slob. But I got a policy, and that is: I don't sell to Yids. Nothing personal, but that's how it is."

Nick tasted the whiskey. It burned his throat. He thought of Buddy McCord. Not the Buddy McCord sitting on the real estate office floor but the Buddy McCord crowing in The Royal Palm dressing casino. It wasn't fair. It just wasn't fair. Nick had found his anger again. "Why not?"

"Flagler, a very great man, built Palm Beach for the idle rich. I'm not so great. I'm building Miami Beach for the working rich. The working, *Christian* rich. A lot of them come from Indianapolis. These guys, they smell Jews, they're going to take the first train to Sarasota."

Nick pushed the teacup away. He felt the sour taste of the whiskey and the disappointment working their way to his stomach. "But you never said you were—"

"I'm not advertising *my* Caucasian clause. Everyone knows the Yids stay below Third Street. Or I thought everyone did. Anyhow, now *you* know." He emptied the teacup again, put his meaty hand up, and signaled the waiter for

337

a refill. "Listen, kid, you want my advice, you buy up all the goddamned property you can get your hands on in South Beach. Build there. The Jews need places to stay, don't they? I might even kick in a few bucks."

Nick stood up so abruptly that Fisher, only half playfully, put his hands up as if to protect himself. "You ain't going to bust my nose too, are you?"

"Thanks for your time, Mr. Fisher."

"When you see the Lummus boys, tell 'em hello for me."

"I'm not going to see the Lummus boys."

The anger faded after a while, leaving him with a bitter, whiskey taste in his mouth and a stomach filled with lead. He sat in the car, his fingers gripping the steering wheel, trying to digest the disappointment. Boy, was I green, he said to himself, shaking his head, embarrassed at how he had started out the morning expecting this perfect day to end with his owning three lots on the ocean in Miami Beach. He shook his head, feeling sorry for himself. But when he felt the tears come, he got out, cranked up the Olds, got in, gave the Duesenberg and the Stutz some unnecessary nudges, and drove up Collins Avenue to Thirtieth Street. He had one last chance.

The Collinses' Miami Beach Improvement Company office was, characteristically, a one-room driftwood building with a sloping front porch. It faced the ocean, sitting in the center of the sand beach, the only structure for miles around. It looked to Nick like a swamp cracker's shack, the sort he had seen on his way to Pensacola, crossing the panhandle. A flock of terns sat at the water's edge, screaming at each other. The mangroves had been torn up, but otherwise, the Collinses' land had not been noticeably improved.

Nick, already feeling defeated, walked across the sand to the office and, surprised to find the door open, strode in. At first he thought no one was there, and then he looked out the window and saw her on the porch. She was sitting in a weathered wicker chair, her feet on an old kitchen stool, eating an orange, reading a book. She had short corn-colored hair and eyes the color of the Atlantic on a stormy day: foamy and green and sometimes blue. She looked, Nick thought, like Mary Pickford but without the curls and that simpering expression. She looked like Mary Pickford grown up and become a woman with long, shapely, white-stockinged legs. She beckoned him to come out and round to the porch.

"No one's here," she said as he stood at the foot of the steps looking up at her. "I mean that I'm here, but none of the business people are here. If you've come to see Teddy, he's gone off to lunch, but he should be back soon." She put down the book and the orange and stood up and offered him her hand. "I'm Mary Goodwin. Who are you?"

He took her hand and found he could smile after all. This girl with blue-green eyes was an antidote to the disillusionments of the day. "My name is Nick Prince."

338

"My Lord, what a perfect name for you. Have a seat." She dragged another unpainted wicker chair from the corner, placing it next to hers. Nick hesitated. "Teddy will be back in a moment, really. Do sit down." She watched him as he came up onto the porch and sat in the wicker chair. "Where do you come from, Mr. Prince? Certainly not from Florida. You might be a Russian hero. All you need is a blood-red commissar's blouse and a Cossack's Persian lamb hat and you'd look as if you had sprung full-blown from the book I'm reading." She handed it to him. *Ten Days That Shook the World.* "It's a firsthand account of the Russian revolution. My Lord, it makes me want to jump on the first boat for Moscow. Russia's such a brave new and genuinely democratic world. All the people there are really equal and free."

"Why don't you?" Nick asked, thoroughly entertained. "Jump on the next boat for Moscow?"

"I'm supposed to be recuperating," she said, tucking her legs up under her, smiling at him.

"From what?" He couldn't imagine anyone looking healthier.

"Pneumonia and pacifism," Mary said earnestly. "My family—actually I'm adopted, but I call them my family anyway—are Quakers and live up in New Jersey near the Collinses. We were all pacifists throughout the Great War. But I was the most pacifistic."

Nick laughed. "I'll bet you were." He had forgotten the disappointments of the morning in those first five minutes. He felt as if he could spend the next month on that shady porch in that big wicker chair, looking at the blond girl, listening to her talk, the waves breaking on the beach and the screeching counterpoint of the terns in the background.

"My Lord, I signed every petition that found its way to Moorestown. I went to Philadelphia to march in parades. I gave the first and only speech of my life, standing on a soapbox in the center of Philadelphia's old city hall." She stood up, and using the porch rail as a podium, pounded it with her fist. "Why," she asked, giving the last lines of that speech, "do we want to send our boys to fight and be killed for no other reason than to carry on a geographical war we couldn't care less about?" Laughing, she sat down again.

"You must have been convincing." Nick thought he had never seen a prettier smile, offscreen or on.

"I got my picture in the paper and the sort of notoriety my family hates. 'Traitor,' one woman actually shouted at me on the street. I put my 'War Is Hell' placard away only when we finally went to war." She clapped her hands together and looked at him with dismay. "I haven't hurt your feelings, have I? You weren't some brave hero, were you, making mincemeat of Kaiser Bill's men? You weren't *in* the war, were you?"

"Only in New Jersey," Nick said, smiling at her.

"The very best place to be," she said, sighing with relief. "Anyway, last winter, after the war, when the President was making his nationwide tour on behalf of the League of Nations and world peace, naturally I went to New

339

York to see him." She put a hand to her neck and touched the pierced penny she wore on a chain as a talisman. "Woodrow Wilson is one of my great heroes. I had to wait for nearly eight hours standing on Fifth Avenue in near-zero weather, but I finally saw him, and he touched my hand, though it was so cold, I'm not certain I felt it. It was worth it, but as usual, my bent luck came into play."

"Bent luck?" Nick asked, because he knew he was meant to.

"When I was a girl," Mary said quickly, "a Gypsy palm reader told me I had bent luck. That night Alfred, my brother, put a penny on the tracks, and after the train went over it, it was bent, and he put a hole in it and gave it to me to wear on a chain, and everyone made a big joke of it, but I still wear it because I'm convinced the palm reader was right."

She held up the penny for him to see, and he leaned over and held it in his hand, acutely aware of her lips, of her smell of oranges and sea air. "Maybe if you threw it away, your luck would change."

"It would only get worse," she said, watching him lean back in the chair, thinking how beautifully put together he was. He made her boyfriend up in New Jersey—Randy Hopkins—look like a butcher's block. "Anyway," she went on, deciding that at the advanced age of twenty she couldn't start believing in love at first sight, "I got to meet Woodrow Wilson. And then I had to pay for it with darned pneumonia. My Lord, it was worth it."

She turned to him with that radiant smile. "Old Doctor Deehl said I had to go some place warm, and the Collinses asked me to visit them in Florida. I've been here ever since." She picked up the orange, offered Nick a segment, which he declined, and lay back in her chair, eating it. "Now, of course, I'm fully recovered."

"Will you be going home soon?" he asked.

"I don't really want to go back to teach in the Quaker school and marry Randy Hopkins, who is a lawyer and very nice but not all that exciting. And my parents are afraid for me to come back now."

"Why is that?" he asked, totally caught up in her conversation. She was so thoroughly American, so unlike anyone he had ever met.

"The Red Scare. Up north, federal agents are arresting everyone whose name was ever associated with anarchy or communism, and of course I was—I am—a member of the world peace movement. Mother wrote that an agent actually came to the house and asked all sorts of questions about me. She wants me to stay here, and the Collinses seem perfectly happy to keep me." She tossed the orange rind over the side of the porch and smiled at him. "Now you know everything about me. Tell me something about you."

"What do you want to know?" he asked, caught off guard.

"I don't know. Anything."

"Well, like you, I'm an orphan."

"Do you know who your real parents were?"

"Sure," Nick replied.

340

"I don't." Mary brought her knees up and put her arms around them and stared out at the sea. "I mean I know my mother was a woman named Fanny Tuttle and her mother was what they call a Miami pioneer. Anyway, my mother died giving birth to me in Nassau. I don't know my father's name, and no one seems to remember, though I have been assured I was not born 'out of wedlock,' as they say. The doctor who attended my mother was a Quaker, and he took me back to Moorestown with him, where the Goodwins adopted me and have been sweeter and better to me than any parents could have been."

"Despite your bent luck."

"Don't you make fun of me, Mr. Prince."

"I wouldn't dream of it, Miss Goodwin."

"What *do* you dream of?" she asked.

"It's a dumb dream and it's pretty much over," Nick said bitterly, suddenly remembering. "I wanted to buy land on the ocean and build a hotel that everyone—Gentile, Jew, Negro—could come to and feel he was wanted."

"That's a beautiful dream," she said, leaning forward. "Why should it be over?"

He got out of the wicker chair and stood at one of the posts that tentatively held up the porch roof. He looked out at the calm ocean. The tide was coming up the beach, turning the white sand a dull mud color. He tried to see his hotel, but all he could see was Buddy McCord telling him he wasn't wanted in Miami and he wasn't wanted on Miami Beach. "It's over," Nick said, "because the only place I can buy land is below Third Street, and the whole point of the hotel is that it shouldn't be built in a ghetto."

"Then buy land from the Collinses. My Lord, they have plenty—"

He turned to stare at her, and for a moment she thought he was going to hit her. "I'm a Jew, Miss Goodwin. The Collinses, like Carl Fisher, could be down to their last nickel and they wouldn't sell land to a Jew."

She jumped out of her chair. "I don't believe that for a single minute, Mr. Prince. The Collinses wouldn't—"

"I'm afraid they would, Mary." Teddy Collins, a tall, fair Collins with a long, attractive face and sad, knowing eyes, had, unnoticed, approached the porch. "It's economics. If we sold a single lot to one Jew, then we would have to sell all of our land to Jews, because no one else would buy. And the Jews do not constitute a large enough market. I am sorry to say that we do have a Caucasian clause in all our deeds."

"What the hell is a Caucasian clause, Teddy?" Mary demanded.

"I know the Miami version by heart," Nick said. "I'll repeat it for you, Miss Goodwin: 'Said property shall not be sold, leased, or rented in any form or manner, by any title, either legal or equitable, to any person or persons other than of the Caucasian race, or to any firm or corporation of which any persons other than of the Caucasian race shall be a part or stockholder.'" He looked down at Teddy Collins, standing casually with one foot on the porch steps. "Up till today I thought Miami Beach was free of it. You've only kept it quieter over here." He walked down the porch steps. He stopped and looked at Teddy Collins and then up at Mary Goodwin, including her in his indictment. "And you people are supposed to be Quakers."

"Look," a shamed Teddy Collins called after Nick, "why don't you go and talk to the Lummus brothers?" But the Olds had already been cranked up, the door slammed. Mary ran down the steps to try to stop him, but he was speeding away.

Teddy Collins had come after her. "Are you all right, Mary?"

"I feel as if I've just been hit by one of your famous Florida hurricanes." She looked up at him with her seafoam-green eyes. "My Lord, Teddy, we *must* do something about that shameful clause."

"I can't do anything about it, Mary. It's a fact of life."

"Well, maybe I can." She put her hand to her neck, reaching for the bent-luck penny. "Or if I can't, I bet you a nickel Mr. Nick Prince can."

Nick drove by the Roman Pools. It was early afternoon, and the café was nearly empty. He thought of driving up across the pavement into it, bringing down the blue-and-white-striped canvas awning, pinning the headwaiter against the wall. He had other childish thoughts as he drove down Collins Avenue to the Lummus brothers' South Beach. He stopped at Rosi's New Miami Beach Café, ordered a root beer, and thought of the time he and Selma had danced the two-step to the horror of the Jewish clientele. "It's not fair," he said aloud, banging the tin-plated table, startling two elderly women gossiping over vanilla ice cream sodas. "None of it's fair."

"You okay, Nick?" Rosi asked, waddling over from the cash register, putting his hand on Nick's shoulder. "You want maybe I should pour something a little stronger into that root beer?"

"I'm okay, John," Nick said, getting up, smiling, flipping a nickel at the café owner.

"You don't look okay," Rosi said, palming the coin.

"I'm great." He felt as if he had aged twenty years since the morning. He felt ancient and wise, the lessons he had learned during that day eating away at him like a bitter medicine. He walked the length of South Beach, smiling at the billboard picturing Bigley's Diving Belles in their skirted, stockinged, flat-shoed innocence. The billboard reminded him of Jane Fisher's high heels and bare knees and her near-parody of corruption. He turned back toward the car. I've had enough of Miami Beach, he thought, for a lifetime.

I'll go in with Irving, he decided. He saw himself in the distorting mirror in front of Hardie's Casino. He felt as if the distortion—the fat, corrupt, wavering image—was the true Nick Prince. The lean, straight Nick Prince had been misplaced somewhere between the Roman Pools and the Collinses' Miami Beach Improvement Company.

He sat in the car, in the heat of the Miami Beach afternoon, and suddenly, without premeditation, surprising himself, he brought his fist down on the steering wheel with all his might. It didn't crack. It didn't move. It was as immobile, as strong, and as solid as the Caucasian clause. He put his forehead against the steering wheel and waited for the tears to come, and when they didn't, he got the car started and headed across the Collinses' wooden bridge. I'll go in with Irving, he said to himself again.

He let himself into the apartment. Ida was standing in the kitchen. She was making spaghetti, tears rolling down her round cheeks. "What is it?" Nick asked.

She couldn't say anything. She only nodded her head in the direction of the living room. He found Irving sitting in his club chair in the shadows of the late afternoon, his Palm Beach jacket over his arm, half-moons of sweat under his Arrow shirt sleeves, his collar undone. Irving, normally a healthy sallow color, was the sickly cream tint of the living room walls.

He looked up and saw Nick and shook his head. "Twenty-two years, Nick, I been here, and did you ever hear me make one complaint? One single complaint? Twenty-two years, every time that bastard jacked up the lease money, I paid without a word. Not a single word. The pipes leaked, I paid to have them fixed. The lights went out, I paid the goddamned electrician. The walls needed painting, I paid. I paid and I paid and I paid. I could have owned this dump a hundred times over, the money I paid. And now that bastard Troxyl says I got to get out. I said, 'Look, Mr. Troxyl, I'll pay you sixty bucks a month.' And you want to know what he said? He said, 'Oh, I'm not interested in money, Mr. Prince,' as if he used five-dollar bills for toilet paper. He wants the store for his son-in-law, that no-good bastard Nablo. Not a penny is he giving me for the name or the goodwill. Not one penny."

"But Irving, he just can't—"

"He can't, huh? Haven't you learned anything? I don't have a leg to stand on, Nick. He's got the law on his side. He'll tell the judge he just learned I was a Jew. After twenty-two years getting a check on the first day of every month signed Irving P. Prince, he'll say he just found out I was a Jew, and Jews, according to the Caucasian clause can't own or rent or lease . . ." He stopped talking. He put his hands on his knees and looked down at the purple and pink flowers blooming on Ida's American Oriental. "What am I going to do, Nick? A man my age, to start over? And where we going to live, Nick?" Irving shook his head. "I used to think, Nick, that coming here to this country, to Florida . . . He pounded the chair with his fist. "Oh, what's the goddamn use what I used to think?"

He sat there with his head down, his paunch sliding over the top of his Palm Beach trousers, pain and bewilderment in his pale eyes. Ida came into the living room, looking sick and worried. She put one plump, rosy hand against her husband's cheek. His sagging shoulders heaved and he began to sob.

Stricken, Ida looked at Nick over Irving's head. She had never seen Irving like this. Nick tried to smile, to reassure her, but the defeats of the day made him feel sour, used, empty. He turned away and went to the windows, looking out at the bay toward Miami Beach. He remembered Selma's warning when he was a boy and got, as she said, above himself: 'Someday you're going to know what it means to swallow crow, Nichlaus Levi Prince. And believe me, child, it's going to hurt.' "Today Irving and I swallowed crow," he said to himself. "It hurts."

He went back to the club chair, to the defeated man and the worried woman, the two people he cared for more than anyone else in the world. "What's going to be, Nick?" Ida whispered over Irving's bowed head. "What's going to be?"

"We're going to go where we're wanted, Ida." He leaned over and kissed her cheek. "Tomorrow Irving and I are going to see the Lummus boys."

CHAPTER FOUR

1922

"YOUR MAIL, MISTER PRINCE." Ida, in a flowered print dress that made her rounder and less fashionable than ever, her thick gray hair elaborately curled, handed him a stack of envelopes. "You got a very nice invitation twice the size of any other invitation I've ever had the privilege to view and a letter from Señor de Córdoba from Havana, Cuba."

"Thank you, Mrs. Prince." Nick looked at Ida beaming at him.

"I didn't open them in case there was something personal. I read the return addresses, however." She reached across the desk and brushed an imaginary speck of lint from his shoulder.

"You're the soul of discretion, Ida. Where's Evelyn?"

"She has a terrible cold. Don't give me that lower lip. She's a lovely girl, and she's had one sick day in the two and a half years she's worked for you, and I don't want you to bite her head off when she comes in tomorrow. *If* she comes in tomorrow. You should have heard her sneeze."

Nick gave up that battle, starting another. "You didn't have to run up those stairs yourself. You could have sent Jerry."

"Jerry is helping Mrs. Lipson move her two tons of luggage out of Three-B and into Four-C, where I hope to God she's finally happy. A complainer from the day she arrived. Besides, what else have I got to do?"

They were on the fifth and top floor—reserved for Nick's office and the Princes' living quarters—of the hotel Nick had bought from Renaldo de Córdoba two years earlier. He had paid four thousand dollars in cash for what was then an ocean-front rooming house, known as the Imperial, on Miami Beach's Third Street and Ocean Drive.

Ida had been worried. "You didn't tell me it's right on the beach. That's the Atlantic Ocean out there, isn't it? What's going to happen, pray tell, when the hurricanes come?"

"This place was built to weather hurricanes," Nick had said with a confidence he hadn't felt. "Don't worry about hurricanes, Ida."

"Where's the kitchen? That's what I'm really worried about."

Ida had taken over. She was, she said, in her element. She had had the rooms painted and deloused, American Orientals laid, mahogany-stained pine chests of drawers and slip-covered club chairs installed. She had hired and fired a progression of cooks and had ended up cooking herself when she wasn't behind the desk being sympathetic to irate guests.

The day Irving went to order a new and tasteful hotel sign, he had had an inspiration: *Hotel Imperial Ida* it read (in pink letters on a blue background) when it was in place. Ida turned pink with pleasure when she saw it. She was pink now. With exertion and pleasure.

Nick wondered what he would have done without her. Or what she would have done without the Imperial Ida. All that nonstop energy had an outlet now. It was Irving he had been worried about. He got up from the desk and stood at the windows looking down at the wide white sand beach. "Is that Irving down there?"

"He's teaching Mrs. Francia Meiselman and Mrs. Stephanie Joseph the ABC's of surf bathing," Ida said, running a suspicious and plump index finger along the edge of the desk.

"Irving doesn't know how to swim."

"He says they won't know and that as long as he's the social director, surf bathing comes under his jurisdiction. When I get a hold of that new maid, I'm going to take a feather duster and glue it to her hand. Is this what's supposed to be called dusting?" She held out her finger for Nick to inspect.

He laughed and picked up the mail again. "What did you do all those years before you became the manager of a Miami Beach hotel?" he asked, riffling through the envelopes.

"I cleaned and I cooked, *tateleh*. Just what I do now. Only now it's on a slightly larger scale. Mrs. Epstein, Two-D, says the water in her toilet is brackish. I asked her how she knew, did she taste it? She said she could smell it. Irving's going to look at it later. In his old age he's a handyman as well as a social director."

"Think he's happy?" Nick asked, looking down at the overcast beach where Irving was making peculiar flapping motions with his meaty hands. "Don't you think he misses the store?" Nick had wanted him to open a haberdashery on South Beach, but Irving had refused. "What do Jews know about fancy dressing?" he had said dismissively.

Ida came behind the desk and put her arm around Nick's shoulders. "Happy? That man's like night and day from the way he used to be. I asked him if he was mad at me. For taking over. He said, 'It's your turn, Ida. You think I wanted to spend the rest of my life putting skinny *goyim* from Detroit into Palm Beach suits made in New York?' Twenty-one years was enough, Nick.

"Look at him down there, flirting with those *altas* having the time of his life." She had worked her way around the desk and stood behind him. Bending over, she kissed him on his forehead. "Not to mention me, Nick. Suddenly Ida from Minski-Pinski is a businesswoman. Which reminds me I have to get down to that kitchen. Mrs. Beatrice Rosenhack, the Chicago doctor's wife, is bringing her two lovely daughters for luncheon, the Blue Plate Special."

"Which is?" Nick asked, looking up at her, wondering what all this information was leading to. He didn't have far to look up. Ida standing, even in her new Minnie Mouse high heels, wasn't that much taller than Nick sitting.

"The seventy-five-cent meatballs and spaghetti, which is what it is every day." She touched his cheek. "How come I can never stop touching you? *Oy*, did anybody ever see anybody as exquisite as you? How many white suits, I'd love to know, do you have? You keep the Washington Avenue tailor in business." She shrugged her round shoulders and clapped her hands together with joy. "Your mother and father should see you now. How they would *kvell*. Look at me, I'm only an adopted mother and I'm *kvelling*. Twenty-four years old and already a rich man."

"Please, Ida, I beg you, don't help me count my blessings. I have a long morning."

She didn't listen. "Respected by the entire Jewish community, not to mention the *goyim*. Lavish hotels—all right, some of them are rooming houses— on the ocean on Miami Beach, catering to the *crème de la crème* of vacationing Jewish families from as far away as Minneapolis—and who knows how many stores and houses and empty lots? Thank God and J. E. Lummus." Lummus's bank had been backing Nick in his real estate ventures from the beginning. Ida kissed him once more and went to the door. "You'll come down to the dining room a little after twelve and I'll show Beaty Rosenhack what a gorgeous son should look like."

"And you'll introduce me to Beaty Rosenhack's two daughters," Nick said, getting the point, understanding why Ida had run up the stairs with his mail instead of sending Jerry.

"And why shouldn't you meet two lovely, smart, intelligent, educated, well-to-do, tasteful girls? Nick, it's time." She looked genuinely distressed, standing in the doorway, anxious to get on with her day but refusing to miss an opportunity to pursue her getting-Nick-married-already campaign. "With you it's all business twenty-five hours a day. You're a lone wolf. It's not natural." Her little round face puckered as if she were going to cry.

"What do you want me to do, Ida?" he asked, smiling up at her.

"You'll come down to the dining salon at a few minutes past noon and I'll introduce you to Cheryl and Gail. You'll be polite. You'll talk. You'll bat those eyelashes around. You'll maybe, if there's a miracle, even smile." She smiled to set an example, her round face open and rosy again. "Who knows what could happen over Ida Prince's spaghetti and meatballs? That Gail Rosenhack has some figure." She sketched an hourglass in the air with her plump hands and rolled her eyes.

"Ida, let me skip lunch. You go ahead and arrange the marriage without me."

"Comedian. Someday when you're all alone without spouse or issue, you'll remember this conversation and you'll rue the day you didn't heed Ida Prince's advice."

"I'll be down at twelve-fifteen sharp."

"And you'll make yourself cordial? If you're not going to make yourself cordial, I don't want you at my luncheon table, spoiling my meal, giving me indigestion."

"I'll make myself cordial."

She shut the door and opened it again. "And you'd better look at that letter from Córdoba. And don't forget that fancy-schmancy invitation."

Nick looked at the envelope with its cancellation marked "Havana, Cuba." The letter wasn't from Renaldo de Córdoba but from his lawyer. Six thousand dollars for the Second Street property was agreeable. The Second Street property was a three-story bungalow, not even on the beach but between Ocean and Collins avenues. Two years ago, Nick thought, he could have gotten it for fifteen hundred dollars. South Beach real estate—Jewish real estate, he thought bitterly—was booming. Carl Fisher had been right. The Jews needed a place to stay.

They came from the northeast on Flagler's railroad and they came, increasingly, from the midwest aboard the *Floridian*, the Illinois Central Railroad's luxury train. When they found they weren't wanted in Miami or in Carl Fisher's Miami Beach, they headed for South Beach, renting rooms and roomettes and pullmanettes and economy suites in Nick's hotels and rooming houses. Some stayed and opened businesses in the buildings Nick owned on Washington Avenue: fruit stands, souvenir stands, and a combination of both; kosher and not-so-kosher restaurants; bakeries; meat-and-poultry markets.

Nick, carrying Córdoba's lawyer's letter, moved to the windows on the west wall of his office and looked down on South Beach. The neighborhood teemed with life. "You can walk up Washington Avenue," Irving liked to say, "and except for the palm trees and the weather, you'd think you were on Delancey Street." Yiddish was the lingua franca. Women in a variety of headgear—feathers, cloches, babushkas—haggled with the merchants over prices, quality, quantity. Men in straw, top, and even fur hats sat in the cafés and gossiped over glasses of sweet dark tea.

Nick avoided South Beach cafés, insisting on having late breakfast every morning uptown at the Roman Pools' blue-and-white-striped café. Eventually the headwaiter, impressed by Nick's persistence and Carl Fisher's casual acknowledgment of the boy, began to give him a table toward the front.

Small victories, Nick thought.

"Why don't you stay down here where you belong?" Ida asked one morning early on, when he had come back from a Roman Pools breakfast. They were standing in the Imperial Ida's lobby, a large pink-stucco-walled space featuring a front desk made of bleached bamboo, a multitude of slip-covered club chairs and sofas, and blue glass smoking lamps and green marbleized tables. Half a dozen America Orientals in all of Ida's favorite colors graced the travertine floors. "I'll give you breakfast. A hard roll, a little lox, a little cream cheese, anything your heart desires."

"He goes uptown for breakfast," Irving explained carefully, shifting the chewed-up stogie from the left side of his mouth to the right, "because he still has that *meshuggeneh* dream of building a hotel uptown for everyone. He still thinks that someday he's going to have a hotel with *shvartzehs* performing the breast stroke in the swimming pool, Yiddles playing pinochle in the cardroom and *goyim* taking tea in the lobby. Look at him turning red, white, and blue. He's ashamed, but it's the truth. You still believe in it, don't you?"

"Why not?" Nick, defiant and embarrassed, had asked.

"I'll give you a million reasons why not, and they all start and end with the Caucasian clause. Give it up, Nick."

He hadn't given it up. From the Imperial's top-floor office he looked down at South Beach, and all he saw were Jews. Jews who had spent their lives emigrating from one place to another, looking for a safe home. Brave, resilient people. Nick wanted to give them a home that was not only safe but free.

Reluctantly he put away his dream, sat down at his desk and read Córdoba's lawyer's letter again. He remembered the day he had gone to Renaldo de Córdoba, two years before, and thought, Boy, was I green. And lucky.

The Lummus boys had sold most of their South Beach property by the time Nick had gotten to them, in 1920. The rooming houses they still owned were small and landlocked. Nick felt he had sacrificed enough. He wasn't going to give up the ocean. "Go see Renaldo de Córdoba," J. E. Lummus had told him. "He's selling out and going back to Cuba. He's got that elephant of a rooming house on Third and the ocean up for sale. That should do you."

"Why?" Nick asked, after Renaldo de Córdoba had shown him through the fifty neat, plain rooms of the Imperial. He was a short, thin, fifty-year-old man with tobacco-colored skin and dark, flat eyes that sometimes looked green but more often gray. They were on the top floor, which he had set up as living quarters and office, an arrangement Nick liked and decided to keep. "Why are you selling?" Nick had asked again, looking down at the beach, where a dog was dozing in the sun, salt from the surf coating its fur like icing on a doughnut.

"Mr. Prince," Renaldo de Córdoba had said, smiling a smile that took up most of his thin face, revealing suspiciously pearly white teeth. "In my family we have a legend that goes back to the sixteenth century. It says that the Córdobas one day will find their home in Florida. This is a coat of arms an uncle of mine had painted fifty years ago." He indicated a papier-mâché shield on which an artist had painted three black doves, a cross, and a full moon. It looked like a prop for a stage set. "The genuine Spanish Córdoba coat-of-arms is quite different. But the Cuban Córdobas believe in this one. From each generation at least one Córdoba is sent to Florida to make his fortune. Not many have been successful. My wife thought of herself as an exile in Florida. She did not want to come, but she is a good woman, and besides," he said, turning his hands up, smiling, "she had no choice."

Señor de Córdoba sat behind his desk, folded his neat hands, and smiled again, this time at himself. "I am one Córdoba who has made his fortune. But the tragedy of my life was that my wife and I never had children." He stood up and went to the door that led to the Córdobas's private apartment. "Just this year, at my late age, we have had a miracle. Inez, bring in the baby."

A well-upholstered Cuban nurse, carrying a child, came in, followed by Mrs. de Córdoba, a tiny, shy woman in her early forties. It hardly seemed possible that the big, alert, laughing baby in the nurse's arms could have come from her. The child reached out for Nick's thumb and held it, looking up at him with the most extraordinary green eyes he had ever seen. They were the color of emeralds.

"Would you like to hold her, Señor?" the nurse asked in Spanish, but the meaning was clear. Nick, who had never held a child in his life, who thought that children were living things to be avoided at any cost, found the baby in his arms. She gurgled and giggled, all the while holding onto his thumb.

"She is in love," Renaldo de Córdoba said, wearing a smile that would have shamed the Cheshire cat.

When Nick handed her back to the nurse, her blanket fell back and he saw that the baby had a halo of flame-red hair. It was hard to believe that Renaldo and Inez de Córdoba—those little dry black olives—were the child's parents.

"We are returning to Havana with our child," Renaldo de Córdoba had said, drawing himself up to his full five feet two inches. "She is going to get a good Spanish education. She is going to be a Cuban Córdoba."

Except, Nick thought, that she was born in Miami. "She's beautiful," he said aloud, meaning it. "What's her name?" he asked, taking a last look at those green eyes.

"Floridita," Inez de Córdoba said softly. Renaldo de Córdoba set his price, and Nick, who was too green, as he put it, to argue, met it. Luckily Renaldo de Córdoba had been too honorable to take advantage of him. Nick would have paid twice as much for the Imperial.

Nick put the Cuban lawyer's thick letter in the top drawer of his desk, making a mental note to take it around to his own lawyer before the end of the day. Idly he picked up the oversized pink envelope Ida had been fascinated with. It was thick and shiny and expensive. It had no return address. Nick got ten similar ones a month. Invitations to participate in real estate combines, in the seeding of new Miami subdivisions. I can be a silent partner in a corporation owning land, he thought. I just can't own it myself.

He walked to the windows facing the beach. The sky was covered with an even skin of blue-gray clouds. Irving and his mermaids had retired, presumably for lunch. It's almost time for me to make my appearance as the potential husband, Nick thought, regretting his promise.

Ida had paraded a great many Cheryls and Gails in front of him in the last two years. I feel like a finicky madam, he thought, with Ida as my procuress. He knew what Cheryl and Gail were going to be like. Not so very different from the working-class Polish Jewish girls he danced with at the Warsaw Ballroom on Saturday nights and sometimes made love to. Better educated, more refined, but with matte skin and dull hair and a lack of spontaneity he found paralyzing. "Jewish girls are always careful," he said to himself. "And now look who's a bigot wallowing in generalizations. Maybe Gail and Cheryl will turn out to be the lights of my life. Who knows?"

It wasn't that Ida's diagnosis was wrong. She sensed his loneliness. But Ida has the wrong prescription for the right illness, he thought, going down the stairs, crossing the pastel lobby, nodding to Jerry, the bellhop, and Donald, the assistant manager. He said hello and smiled at Miss Rachel Fiebach and Mr. and Mrs. Paul Sarno and Mrs. Felicia Feinswog, all of whom were making their way to the dining room for Ida's Blue Plate Special like a school of tame fish at feeding time.

He waited for them to enter and then he looked into the dining salon through the glass doors. Ida and her guests were at the large round table, dead center. She's got enough linen on that table to cover every bed in the hotel, Nick thought, amused. Her plump hand was in the air, her mouth open in mid-speech, when she spotted him and gestured for him to come in. He looked at the backs of Gail's and Cheryl's plume-hatted heads and held up his hand, indicating five minutes.

A self-granted reprieve. He escaped through the French doors that led onto the old boarding-house porch and stood for a moment, staring out at the ocean. A thick mist had begun to come in and he couldn't make out where the waters ended and the horizon began. Unknowingly he let out a sigh.

"*Oy*, what sadness." Nick turned and saw Irving sitting behind him in a rocking chair, holding a saucer with a cup of tea in one hand, a large butter

350

cookie in the other. "Such misery no one should know." He slurped his tea, expertly balancing the cup on the saucer. "You're twenty-four years old, *pisher*, and you're a big success. So you don't own a hotel where *shvartzehs* and Yiddles and *goyim* can dunk together in the swimming pool. You're the most important fellow in South Beach. The Prince of South Beach. What more do you want?" He took a bite of his cookie, chewing it noisily. "Get yourself a girl, Nick. Then you'll have something you can be legitimately unhappy about. You want a bite of this cookie? Delicious."

"Thanks anyway, Irving. I'd better save my appetite for Ida's matrimonial candidates."

He took a last glance at the ocean and turned to go in when Irving stopped him. "*Shmendrick*, look what you're doing to that suit. What have you got crammed in that pocket, your last will and testament?" Obediently Nick removed the pink envelope. He looked down at it and, giving himself one more moment before he had to face Cheryl and Gail, he opened it. "What is it?" Irving wanted to know. "An invitation to the fireman's ball?"

"No," Nick said, suddenly cheerful, handing the card to Irving, preparing to meet his fate at the hands of Cheryl and Gail Rosenhack. "It's an invitation to the opening of Carl Fisher's new hotel, the Flamingo."

"And you got invited, *pisher?*" Irving pursed his lips and nodded, impressed. "You got to wear something swanky. The *Herald* said this is 'the most important social event of the year,' and I'm quoting. White tails, maybe. That is, *if* you're going."

"Oh," Nick said, entering the Imperial Ida, "I'm going."

CHAPTER FIVE

NICK STOPPED HIS NEW CAR, a two-seater Reo, on Collins Avenue, two blocks south of the Flamingo. He could hear the music—a band was playing "For Me and My Gal"—from where he was. The new moon was eclipsed by the light from the Flamingo's eleven-story tower. Nick laughed aloud. He's done it, he thought, recognizing both the envy and the admiration he was feeling. Carl Fisher has done it, darn him. I have to hand it to him. He's done it.

The newspapers, the radio, the cafés had been full of news and gossip about the Flamingo for months. "With his Flamingo Hotel, Carl Fisher is ushering in a new era in Miami Beach flamboyance," a Miami *News* writer declared, "establishing a style for hotel architecture, interior decoration, and public relations that will forever change the island paradise on Biscayne Bay."

A week before, Fisher had taken Nick around the hotel grounds, though not inside it. "You got to wait for the inside until New Year's Eve like everyone else, kiddo. It's all big-secret stuff. Makes the goddamned press crazy with anticipation. Did you ever see anything like this place?"

The tower had one hundred and fifty rooms with both bay and ocean views. Six deluxe bungalows had been built around the tower, overlooking Star Island and Fisher's motorboat speedway. When the motorboats weren't racing, providing sport for Indianapolis millionaires, half a dozen gondolas sailed the canal, piloted by giant Bahamians wearing Pharaohlike headdresses and African tribal earrings.

"See those flamingos?" Fisher had asked, putting one hand on Nick's shoulder, pointing nearsightedly at the distance with the other. Hundreds of scarlet and black birds with long necks and Roman noses were grazing, searching for food. "I personally headed the hunting party that caught those suckers over on Andros Island in the Bahamas. Great, huh?"

"Great," Nick agreed.

"Only one problem," Fisher said. "They'll be dead in a week. Who knew that the goddamned snails they eat can be found only on goddamned Andros Island?" He spat into a spittoon concealed behind a gatepost. "Come look at the gardens. Smell that jasmine. These goddamn Japs know what they're doing, kiddo."

"So do you, Carl," Nick said half grudgingly.

"You ain't seen nothing yet." Forty Guernsey cows, imported from Milwaukee to supply milk for his guests, were housed in a stone barn built for that purpose. "Jane went out and spent a quarter of a million dollars on furniture," Fisher complained proudly, taking Nick past the private docks and boathouse, through the laundry, the men's club, the broker's office, the *salon de beauté*, and the shops, restaurants, and nightclubs that were part of the Flamingo.

"It's bigger than most Florida cities," Nick said when they had finally finished the tour three hours after starting out.

"It is a city, goddamn it," Carl Fisher said, lighting a dollar cigar, offering Nick his flask.

Nick sat in his new car fingering the pink invitation he had never expected Fisher to send him. I'm the Jewish exception to Carl Fisher's Caucasian-clause rule. Carl Fisher often invited Nick to his table for breakfast. Fisher liked an audience, and Nick, half envious, half genuinely admiring, enjoyed hearing about the latest Carl Fisher extravagance. "This pretty Yid and I got one thing in common," Carl Fisher liked to tell his Indianapolis cronies. "We both got goddamned guts. Meet Nick Prince, the real estate king of South Beach."

Carl Fisher liked Nick, but he liked the game too. Carl Fisher was the rich kid with all the toys, displaying them to Nick, the poor Yid with his (nice) nose pressed up against the window.

A revolving spotlight at the top of the Flamingo tower illuminated the interior of the Reo for a moment. In the mirror Nick saw himself as Fisher must see him; the odd Jew out. You can invite him anywhere, but you don't want to sell him a piece of land. He might bring the others with the ugly noses and the not-so-swell clothes in with him.

The light moved on, leaving him in darkness, the mirror blank, as if he weren't there. "My family," he said to himself, "has been in Florida for four hundred years, and I'm still the Wandering Jew, looking for a home, relying on the hospitality of Christian strangers." He thought about skipping the ball. He should, he told himself, go back to South Beach and spend his New Year's Eve in the warmth Ida and Irving provided. But he remembered the shared look of pride on Ida's and Irving's faces as he had walked across the lobby of the Imperial in his tails and white tie. He started the Reo and drove up Collins Avenue toward the Flamingo.

Exotic limousines lined the street, the chauffeurs leaning against them, prepared for a long night. Though he was an hour late, tourists still waited on both sides of the covered walk that led to the Flamingo entrance, hoping to see a face they knew, a movie or a sports star, even a politician. They wanted to go home to Louisville or Boston or Waterloo, Iowa, covered with reflected glory, letting drop, as offhandedly as they could, the names of the celebrities they had seen.

Two middle-aged women speculated loudly on the chances of Nick being Rudolph Valentino. One family was certain he was Bill Tilden the tennis champion. He had a momentary urge to stop and explain to them that he was Nick Prince from South Beach, Irving's and Ida's boy. But he didn't. He walked under the elaborate vine-covered trellis, past the gold-and-black-uniformed guards, and up the black-and-green-marble steps to the tiled grand Flamingo entry arch, neon lit in pink and turquoise.

A Bahamian gotten up as a Nubian slave, an enormous scimitar resting against his shoulder, gold-plated armlets circling his huge biceps, accepted Nick's collapsible top hat and the pink engraved invitation. Another Bahamian Nubian—there seemed to be an army of them, all matched sets of *Arabian Nights* genies—led Nick up a series of ledgelike granite steps, through a rain forest, water dripping down elaborate fountains onto an exotic fern and orchid garden.

In the near distance Nick could hear the band playing "Dardanella," women laughing, crystal clinking. He recognized that expensive hotel aroma

353

made up of dollar cigars, French perfume, buttery rolls, crisp new money. He half suspected Fisher of buying the scent in a bottle.

Nick looked up and saw Jane Fisher in a short silver lamé dress and matching turban, her eyes silver-lined and shadowed, standing at the top of the steps. She stood very still, framed by an elaborate tiled archway, looking down at him. She seemed, Nick thought, the very incarnation of the Depravity of Modern Woman.

"You are so beautiful, Mr. Prince," she said, smiling, "you take a girl's breath away. Welcome to the Flamingo. A wonderful example of the Spanish-Rumanian school of architecture, don't you think? Carl, look who's here."

Carl Fisher, in ill-fitting tails and for once without his floppy hat, emerged from La Grande Promenade—the Flamingo's central corridor—to greet Nick. "He's already," Jane explained, "half in the bag." His white tie was undone and he smelled as if he had taken a bath in whiskey, but the hand he extended to Nick was steady.

"You ever see such a goddamned handsome Yid?" he asked, putting his arms around Nick, holding him close for a moment. "Thanks for coming, kiddo. Screwy, but you're one of the few goddamned guys in Miami Beach, Florida, who might have a glimmer of what this place means. To me, personally. To Miami Beach, in general. Welcome to the Flamingo, Nick."

"Congratulations, Carl," Nick said, smiling down at the man who was both his hero and his nemesis.

"Thanks, kid." They stood looking at each other for a moment until Jane said, "You fellows just going to stand there or you going to tango?"

Carl, ignoring her, said, "You want to get a drink or you want to take the tour first?" His eyes behind his gold-rimmed glasses glittered, and not with alcohol. If he's drunk, Nick thought, he's drunk on success. "You don't drink, so you'd better take the tour first. Hey, Fatima, give this fellow the goddamned tour."

A young woman dressed in Carl Fisher's idea of an Arabian houri—gold-studded bra, silky harem pants, her eyes a mass of smudged kohl staring somewhat blindly over a transparent veil—came forward, head bowed. "Fatima live," she said in her idea of pidgin Arabic, "oh, young master, with the blessed here in paradise. Allow Fatima to introduce you to its delights."

"Don't get stuck with your pants down in any of the goddamned bedrooms up in paradise," Carl said, turning away.

Fatima, one of the bevy of houris leading guests through the Flamingo, escorted Nick up La Grande Promenade and then through the lobbies, dining rooms, breakfast rooms, tearooms, writing rooms, billiard rooms, courtyards, conservatories, suites, apartments, cottages, and the speakeasy that took up one floor of the tower. "Designed," Fatima said, putting one languorous hand out to indicate the painted ceiling, "in the style of the Sistine Chapel in Rome." She took him on escalator, gondola, and elevator rides. She showed him the elephant, Carl, Jr., and the saltwater and freshwater swimming pools, the eighteen- and nine-hole golf courses, the rooftop solarium.

By eleven the tour was over, and Fatima left him at the entrance to the grand ballroom, Le Bijou. "I'm free later," she said, dropping the accent, looking at him wistfully through the kohl and over the veil. "I don't suppose you are."

"I'm not," Nick said, smiling and lying. "Wish I were."

Fatima, disappointed, moved off in the direction of the waterfall, and Nick stepped past two more scimitar-armed Nubians into the choreographed confusion of the Flamingo's Le Bijou. The walls and the ceiling were mirrored, creating an infinity of space, taken up by Carl's five hundred guests and the hordes of waiters and busboys and wine stewards and cigarette girls, all in Arabian garb.

The band played "Indianola" on the half circle of a stage at the far end of the room. It complemented the full circle of a dance floor, around which men in tails and stiff white collars guided women in short glittering dresses. The women affected bee-stung lips, bobbed, mannish hair, foot-long cigarette holders. It's more like a movie set than a movie, Nick thought. It's as if this were a scene rehearsal and no one's taking it too seriously. The real thing is yet to come.

"You're disappointed, kid," Carl Fisher said, coming up behind him, putting his hand on Nick's shoulder. "Don't bother to goddamn deny it. Your eyes are at half mast and your bottom lip's droopy. You expected the Ritz and you got the Flamingo, right or wrong?"

"It's a fake," Nick said.

"What'd you expect for two million bucks—reality? You're the hotel man. Not me. I'm just a goddamned theatrical producer."

"You put on a pretty show, Carl," Nick said, relenting, trying not to be disappointed.

"That's my goal, kiddo." Fisher lit a cigar and grabbed a glass of champagne from a passing waiter, upending the glass. "I hate goddamned bubbly. Hey, Anthony, get me a whiskey." He pointed with his thumb at a woman leaving the dance floor. "You want the real McCoy in ladies? There's one."

Nick followed Carl Fisher's thumb and saw Mary Goodwin. She wore an old-fashioned pale green dress, more a tea gown than an evening gown, its silk fabric clinging to her when she moved. Her corn-colored hair looked like flaxen gold under the ballroom's lights. It fell just to her shoulders and was held back on both sides of her face with jade clips that heightened the oceanic color of her eyes. She wore a pendant around her neck which Nick recognized as her bent penny.

Mary Goodwin was holding onto Teddy Collins's arm, laughing at something he'd said, as she bent over to fix the strap of her high-heeled sandal. A young man with hair parted in the middle, seated at her table, looked up at her with what could only be love. A great many men were looking at her. She seemed luminescent, aglow with health and youth and vitality. She was the only woman in that ballroom with an unfashionable suntan. She made the others, bee-stung and eye-shadowed, seem as pale and as artificial as models in a shop-window display.

"Don't get ideas," Carl Fisher said, slapping him on the back. "She's a goddamned Collins connection. Hoity-toity. The Collinses came to this party, but just. I'm a goddamned business partner, on occasion."

"Carl," Jane Fisher said annoyed, coming between Nick and her husband. "Our ex-governor, the unlovely Catts, is at the bandstand insisting on singing a naughty song. You'd better lure him away with that fatal charm of yours before the band leader walks off. Temperamental, our Signorelli."

Mary Goodwin had fixed her sandal strap, and Teddy Collins and the boy with the center-parted hair were both drawing out her chair when she looked up and saw Nick. She opened her mouth as if to say something, as if she could be heard across that enormous room. Nick smiled at her as the band leader, Signorelli, began to sing with unrelenting innuendo "The Sheik of Araby."

"This dance belongs to me," Jane Fisher said, parodying the first line of the song, taking his hand, leading him onto the dance floor. Automatically he put his arm around the silver lamé waist and began to dance. He wished Jane Fisher wore less perfume and didn't move in quite so close. The fabric of her dress was unpleasant to touch. He watched over her glittery shoulder as Mary got up to dance with the boy with the hair parted in the middle. The boy held her as if she would break.

Jane Fisher followed his gaze. "It's useless," she said, smiling up at him. "She's the sort of girl who has tea with William Jennings Bryan and the sadly arthritic Mrs. Bryan at the Villa Serena. You and I, Mr. Prince, are never going to be invited to the Villa Serena. Or next door to Mr. James Deering's Vizcaya either. You're a Jew and I . . . well, I am who I am."

The band had segued into "April Showers" without giving the dancers a chance to change partners. Nick couldn't stop himself from looking at Mary Goodwin. He remembered that afternoon on the Collinses' real estate office porch. She had been so open and friendly. His regret at shouting at her, at stalking off, was a palpable thing, a lump in his throat. Boy, was I green.

"You're giving a girl an inferiority complex," Jane Fisher said, moving in still closer, her thighs touching his. "Give it up, Tarzan. She just broke her engagement to a lawyer up north, and they say she's going to marry the rich and eligible Little Lord Fauntleroy she's dancing with. Otherwise you might have had one itty-bitty little chance. The rumor is she likes Jews. Irene Sloane says she's making a fool of herself at exclusive Miami luncheon parties, campaigning against the Caucasian clause."

"She is?" Nick asked, stopping dead center on the dance floor, until Jane forced him to resume.

"Don't get your hopes or anything else up, baby face. She's an intellectual.

356

She reads books. She's pretty and she's brainy and she's as American as applesauce. She loathes and despises developers like Carl. I sat across from her one afternoon at a William Jennings Bryan Christian charity picnic. Don't faint now," she said, reading disbelief in his violet eyes. "I was invited, and Carl said I had to go. Chicken Little over there went on for fifteen minutes about Carl. Said he would pave over Biscayne Bay if he was allowed to.

"When she found out who I was, she blushed, but she didn't apologize. She just launched into an attack on the Tamiami Trail. She said that when it crossed the Everglades it would kill all the animals who lived in the swamps and jungles. It was a most instructive afternoon." Jane sighed. "Do you think you could deposit me at my table or the bar or the ladies' room or anywhere convenient? This idiotic song is about to end, and as you gave up dancing with me a good ten minutes ago, I will relieve you of me now. You're pretty, Mr. Prince, but you're about as lively as a month-old Spanish omelet. As a matter of fact, I'll get off right here. I see a man." She let go of his hand and moved away, leaving Nick alone on the dance floor.

He stood there, watching Mary Goodwin standing by her table, trying to keep up her end of the conversation with her recent dancing partner, unable to stop looking at Nick. The band was playing a slow, passé war song, a soldier's lament for his sweetheart. Nick smiled and held out his hands in invitation. Mary Goodwin left the boy with the center-parted hair in mid-sentence and came to him.

"My Lord, I have a million things to say to you, Mr. Prince," she said, standing in front of him, her sea-foam-green eyes staring into his violet ones. "But I'm not going to say them now. I would just like to dance this one dance with you without a lot of talk. Is that all right with you, Mr. Prince?"

"It's all right with me, Miss Goodwin." He took her in his arms and felt as if he had found the last piece to the puzzle he had been working on all of his life. Suddenly his black and white world was exploding in full color. "Nights are long when you're not around," Signorelli crooned into the microphone. Nick Prince's chin brushed the top of Mary Goodwin's fair head. Unconsciously he narrowed the gap between their bodies. He was shocked to find that Mary had met him more than halfway.

When the dance ended, Signorelli announced that there were only ten more minutes to midnight. "Half-nude women, I'm told," Mary Goodwin said, "are going to ascend the silver ladder and descend on a mirrored ball. It's supposed to be a very modern New Year's."

"Would you like to walk in the garden while it's happening?" Nick asked, finding it difficult to let go of her hand.

She turned and looked at the Collinses and their guests, all of whom were trying not to look at Mary and Nick. Teddy Collins started to get up, to come to rescue her. "I can't think of any way I'd rather usher in the New Year." She kept her hand in his as he led her through the labyrinth of lobbies to the botanical gardens.

Each of the trees, bushes, and vines Carl Fisher's Japanese gardeners had planted was lit, a small placard giving its name. Mary went from one to another reading the names aloud. "Australian pine, Arabian jasmine—delicious, isn't it?—Brazilian pepper, Chinese holly, Canary Island date palm, Mexican frame vine—not absolutely certain I like that one—Rangoon creeper. Sounds like a villain in a movie." She sighed. "Soon all of Miami Beach is going to look like this. The Japanese gardeners are busy. In a month or two, if you want to see native plants, you're going to have to go to a horticultural museum.

"My Lord," she went on, "look at these Hong Kong orchid trees. They're like chorus girls, aren't they? Not much integrity but so nice to look at. All that weepy purple. Not too dissimilar from your eyes, Mr. Prince. Though your eyes are deeper and more lovely, if I may say so." She stopped under the most lavish of the orchid trees, its branches dripping over her with blossoms. "I'm talking too much. I always talk too much. Especially when I'm scared."

"Are you scared now?" Nick asked, awed by her energy.

"I have a block of solid ice in my belly."

He moved closer, under the umbrella of orchids. Caged nightingales that Fisher had imported from Europe sang their sweet, mournful song. "Why?"

"Look," she said, not answering, pointing to the sky. A rainbow of fireworks was exploding over them. The hotel band was playing "Auld Lang Syne." "It's the New Year."

He reached for her hand, but she withheld it. "Why not?" he asked, longing to touch her.

"I'm afraid if I give you my hand, Mr. Prince, I'll give you everything." She moved away, out of the orchid shelter. "I have a confession. I've been thinking about you ever since we met. You appear quite regularly in my dreams." She touched the bent penny she wore around her neck. She seemed the only natural thing in that specimen garden. "You've been haunting me, Mr. Prince." She sat down on an elaborately scrolled wrought-iron bench.

He came and sat next to her. "I've been thinking about you too, Miss Goodwin. I've been wanting to apologize to you. I shouldn't have shouted at you."

"Yes, you should have. You woke me up, Mr. Prince, to a problem I didn't know existed." She looked down at his open hand and, after a moment, as if she were taking a great chance, put her hand in his. "Once, in Mr. Fisher's café, I saw you having breakfast, and I wanted to come over, but I thought you were still too angry with me, so I didn't." She smiled at him. "But I've been reading about you. In the *Herald's* real estate column." There was another huge burst of fireworks overhead, forming itself into a rocket-lit facsimile of Abraham Lincoln.

"He's one of Carl Fisher's idols," Nick said, looking up at Lincoln beaming down on the Flamingo tower. He shook his head with that grudging admiration he gave to Fisher's accomplishments. "Carl's made his dream come true."

"And yours?" she asked, not seeing the fireworks or the hotel, only that Arrow-collar profile, the Woolworth doll's lashes, the pouting lower lip.

"I've given it up," Nick said, turning away from the fireworks and the tower, looking into her eyes. "I was as green as a new crab apple. I thought I could fight City Hall *and* Henry Flagler *and* Carl Fisher *and* the Caucasian clause."

She jumped up and held his hand with both of hers. "You can, Mr. Prince."

Nick stood up and looked down at her. He thought he had never seen anyone so beautiful, so young, so alive. "I can't, Miss Goodwin. But I thank you for thinking I can."

"You will. You'll see."

"Mary!" Teddy Collins called, his voice cutting through the night.

Mary Goodwin sighed. "We must go. They're worried."

"That you're being seduced by the Jew dog."

She laughed. "That *I'm* seducing the innocent Mr. Prince."

They walked toward the garden entrance and stopped once more under the orchid tree. Nick reached up and pulled down a blossom for her. "Happy New Year, Miss Goodwin."

She took the flower, and then, impatiently, she reached up and kissed him.

"Mary!"

"Happy New Year, Nick Prince."

She telephoned him at the end of the week. He took the call in his office, shooing an inquisitive Evelyn out of the room. "I thought you were going to call me," she said. "But I decided I wouldn't wait another three years until we saw each other again."

"Look, Miss Goodwin, I think it's probably better that we don't see each other again."

"Better for whom?"

"Your friends and family. You."

"I'm getting selfish in my old age, Nick. I don't care about my friends and family. And if I don't see you again I'm going to die a lonely death. I want you to be my escort at a luncheon party in Miami on Thursday. At Villa Serena. Once my friends and family meet you, their prejudice is going to melt."

"They don't want me at their luncheon party, Mary."

"I do. Mrs. Bryan asked if I would like to bring an escort, and I said I would bring you," she lied. Actually Mrs. Bryan had said Mary could bring an escort, but Mary hadn't told her who he was going to be. "I'll pick you up at noon."

Nick was waiting in front of the hotel for her. All he had to do, Nick thought, was have Mary Goodwin, the archetypal *shikseh*, stroll in and ask for me. Ida and Irving and the Mrs. Rosenhacks, Weiners, and Weissmans would all have their long-promised conniption fits right in the lobby. Ida had sensed that "something was up," but luckily the stove was giving her trouble, and she had had to attend to it.

Mary drove up in an old black Ford and started to get out, but Nick forestalled her, getting into the passenger seat. "You're not going to show me your hotel?" Mary asked, looking up at the Imperial Ida.

"Not a chance," Nick said. "Drive."

"You're ashamed of me," she said, putting the car in gear, making a U-turn she shouldn't have made, driving west toward the County Causeway and the city of Miami.

"They wouldn't understand you, I'm afraid."

"They want you to marry a nice Jewish girl," Mary said, looking worried, fingering the bent penny, driving over Biscayne Bay with one hand.

"She doesn't have to be nice."

"My Lord, you're attractive when you're nervous," she said, glancing at him, taking in his half-closed eyes, his protruding lower lip.

"Please keep your eyes on the road."

"It's not my driving that's unnerving you, Mr. Prince."

"It doesn't help."

"William Jennings Bryan may be a pompous, self-involved, misguided egocentric, but his guests are fine, educated people—"

"Don't sell me," Nick interrupted. "I'm in the car, I'm going along with it. It's my turn to have a bellyful of ice. This is going to be a disaster. I've agreed to come to prove to you that we shouldn't see each other again. It's hopeless. You're a *shikseh*, and I'm a Yid."

Mary took a curve with bravado. "You'll see," she said, ignoring Nick's wide-eyed look of fear, half genuine, "that it doesn't matter at all."

A butler opened the door, and then the host took over. William Jennings Bryan—three-time presidential candidate, the Silver-Tongued Orator, the highly paid salesman for George Merrick's Miami subdivision, Coral Gables—heard Nick's name without taking it in. They stood in the stone entrance hall while Bryan expounded for some time on the solidity of the Villa Serena.

"There you are," Mrs. Bryan said, finding them, kissing Mary on her cheek. "Willie's been going on about our hurricane-proof house, I venture." Mary introduced her to Nick. "It's a pleasure to meet you, Mr. Prince." She looked at him through her pince nez, unconsciously made a little helpless gesture with her arthritic hand, and then looked warningly at her husband. "Are you the Mister Prince doing such a marvelous job in South Beach?" she asked, so clearly hoping he wasn't that Nick nearly laughed.

"I'm afraid I am, Mrs. Bryan."

"How, uhm, marvelous." It was a word she used a great deal. "Come," she

360

said, recovering, even taking his arm, leading him across a large coral-stone anteroom into the living room, which fronted Biscayne Bay. "We're having iced tea, Mr. Prince. You'll find no alcoholic beverages here. We keep the law in this house," she said as if she were dead certain they didn't in Nick's.

Six people holding glasses of iced tea turned to look at Nick as Mrs. Bryan introduced him. A matched pair of dowagers, remnants of the Coconut Grove colony, immediately cornered Mary and began reminiscing about her grandmother, Julia Tuttle, whom they had cut dead on any number of occasions when she was alive. William Jennings Bryan began to lecture a Miami real estate investor about the glories of Coral Gables, while the investor's wife and Mrs. Bryan retired to a window seat to cough delicately, to whisper genteelly, to look everywhere but at Nick.

He found himself with a glass of pale tea in his hand, standing under a larger than life size and somewhat lurid painting of Joan of Arc. Her enormous blue eyes were raised toward heaven, two angels stood on either shoulder, disapproving, holding gold crosses in the air. Finally a navy commander named Woolrich Grant and his brother, Newell, a lawyer, came to talk to him. Newell Grant was Nick's age and the commander a few years older.

From across the room Mary gave Nick an encouraging smile. He felt for a moment as if they had been married, happily, for years, as if they had gotten down all the signals, all the shorthand long-wedded and like-minded couples develop. "What do you think of the New York governor repealing the state's Prohibition-enforcement act?" Newell asked. He was just returning from a visit to the north, and the luncheon party was for him. He and his brother had long, equine noses and large, heavy-browed blue eyes. The question sounded like the first in a test.

"The federal authorities are just going to have to enforce it," his brother said, looking at Nick as if he were evaluating him, clearly not liking that well-fitting Palm Beach suit. "That's all there is to it. We've got to keep those New Yorkers in their place, don't you think, Mr. Prince?"

Nick was saved from answering by the butler's entrance into the room to announce that luncheon was served. "Not too bad, is it?" Mary asked before her host offered her his arm and she went into the dining room with him.

Nick smiled at her reassuringly. William Jennings Bryan, sitting at the head of the long, sparsely dressed dining table, made a ten-minute speech masquerading as grace, in which there were as many references to the glories of Florida land as there were to our Lord, Jesus Christ.

"Everyone's land-hungry, aren't they?" the real estate man, on Mrs. Bryan's right, said as he liberally buttered a soft roll. "Are you in real estate, Mr. Prince?"

"Nick owns a great deal of property in South Beach," Mary Goodwin said.

"South Beach?" Newell Grant looked at Nick, identifying him. He smiled, revealing large uneven teeth that heightened the horselike resemblance. "They say you have to speak Yiddish to get into South Beach." He looked around the table, and everyone save Mary, Mrs. Bryan, and Nick returned the smile.

"I hardly speak it at all," Nick said, watching as a servant served him two thin slices of some whitish meat. "But my parents speak it fluently." He looked up at the silent table. "I'm trying to learn, and as soon as I do, I'll give you a lesson, Grant, and then you can come see for yourself what South Beach is all about."

"That's a promise, is it? Good." Newell Grant examined the food on his plate and forked a tired string bean into his mouth. "The trouble with you Jews is," he said, chewing carefully, "that you're all land-hungry. You want to take over all of South Florida."

"And they'll do it if we don't stop them," the real estate man said. He looked at Mary. "Thank the Lord, Mary, for your grandmother's and Mr. Flagler's foresight. The Jew invasion won't work here. We've got the Caucasian clause."

Nick pushed away the gray plate with the whitish meat and stood up. "Thank you so much for your hospitality, Mrs. Bryan. I'll be leaving now."

Mrs. Bryan removed her pince nez with her arthritic fingers and placed them on the table. "Thank you for coming, Mr. Prince."

Nick walked out of the room. "Those Jews and their suntans," he heard one of the dowagers say as he got his hat from the butler. He walked down the impressive Villa Serena driveway and was nearly at the gate when Mary caught up with him.

She grabbed his arm, but he wouldn't stop. "I'm sorry, Nick. I'm so sorry. Please, stop. Talk to me."

He looked at her through his thick lashes. "What did you hope to accomplish, Mary, taking me to this luncheon? You thought those anti-Semites would see me and fall down on their knees and repent? You thought their provincial little bigotries would evaporate when they got a whiff of my Yiddish charm? Wake up, Cinderella. Anti-Semitism is alive and well in Miami."

"Please, Nick, don't shout," Mary pleaded. "I can't think when people shout at me."

He looked down at her and carefully removed her hand from his arm and started walking down Brickell Avenue, past the millionaires' houses, toward downtown Miami. "I know who I am and what I am," he said without lowering his voice. "A second-class citizen. I can live with it. As long as my nose isn't rubbed into it. Thanks for a great lunch. We can do it again next time I feel in the mood for a little abasement."

She had been half running to keep up with him, down Brickell Avenue, oblivious to the traffic and the attention they were getting. She tripped, nearly fell, and stopped. Despite his anger and his resolve Nick turned and looked back. Her hands were over her eyes. He went back to her and looked at her helplessly. "Stop crying."

"I can't."

"What are you crying about? I'm the victim. You're only the innocent by-stander."

She put her hands down and looked up at him, the tears streaming out of her sea-green eyes, her face wet and anguished. "I love you so much, Nick," she said, holding her arms out to him. "I'm so scared. I'm afraid my bent luck is working again. I found you, and now I'm going to lose you. Oh, Nick, I love you so much."

He put his arms around her and held her close to him, feeling her tears on his cheek. "Stop crying," he whispered. "I'll do anything if you stop crying."

"Do you love me?"

"More than anything in the world."

"Then marry me, Nick."

Nick shook his head disbelievingly. "We're standing on Brickell Avenue, stopping traffic, and you're asking me to marry you? Mary, that luncheon was just a little taste of what you'd get if you ever were crazy enough to marry me. You don't know all the snubs and slights you'd have to put up with. It sounds silly, unimportant. But it's a lifelong barrage. The cashier in the restaurant whispering "kike" under her breath. The Irish cop telling you to 'move it, you sheeny bastard.' The Newell Grants of this world making it sound as if the Jews were in a conspiracy against them. You'd be hurting all the time, Mary, and it would kill me." He kissed her forehead. "You'd be a second-class citizen too, Mary. We'd both hate it."

He started to pull away, but she put her arms around him and wouldn't let him go. "I can't live without you, Nick. And you feel the same about me, don't you? Admit it."

"I do. Stop crying, damn it."

"I can't. Marry me. My Lord, I thrive on injustice. You'll see. I blossom on unfair insults. I'll be a better scapegoat than you. I promise." She sensed him weakening, and she reached up and pulled his head down to hers. "I'll get down on my knees and beg you, right here on Brickell Avenue." Her lips were next to his. "Marry me, Nick Prince."

"You'd have to live in South Beach," he said, resisting those lips. "Your friends will drop you like a hot knish. The Jews won't like you any better either. You'll be neither fish nor fowl—not a Jew; not a Christian. You'll always be aware that you're not wanted, either in South Beach or uptown."

"Anything," she said, burying her face in his neck.

"Give it some time, Mary. We've seen each other only on three separate occasions."

"Time won't help. It will just give them a chance to work on us, Nick. You love me too. I know it. There's no sense denying it."

He held her close. "You're ruining my suit. Stop crying. I'll marry you."

She looked up into his violet eyes. "You have tears in your eyes too, big shot."

"That's because I'm so happy," he said, pressing his lips against hers, giving in to the extraordinary need he had for her.

CHAPTER SIX

1923–1925

IT WAS ONE of those slate-gray Sundays in March when the rain threatens and threatens and finally, when it does come, exceeds all of its dreary promises. The justice of the peace—a handsome, dissolute Hungarian named Szuter—was already halfway up Ocean Avenue, dodging puddles, hoping not to ruin his new brown shoes. Irving had gotten out the big black umbrella he had brought with him to Florida thirty years earlier. Its appearance always signified serious weather. With Ida, he escorted Nick and Mary down the Imperial's slippery steps to the car.

"We look like four chickens squeezed into the same pot," Ida said, her arm through Nick's, tears running down her red cheeks. At the car, while Irving held the umbrella over them, Ida reached up and pulled Nick down and kissed him on the forehead. And then, though she hadn't been "a hundred percent" for this marriage, she kissed Mary on the forehead as well. "Today," Ida said solemnly, as if she had never heard the sentiment before, "I want you should know, I did not lose a son. I gained a daughter."

"You're a remarkable woman, Mrs. Prince," Mary said.

"You're not so bad yourself, Mrs. Prince," Ida returned, managing a half smile. "And call me Ida, darling. Everyone does."

Nick left the shelter of Irving's New York umbrella and ran around and got into the Reo. Irving—who had been the only one to give the marriage immediate and total sanction—held the door open for Mary. "Welcome to the Prince family, Mary."

"Thank you, Irving," she said, putting her fine, tanned hand on his arm, smiling up at him. "Thank you for everything." And then the snazzy little Reo, its windshield wipers not quite up to the tempo of the rain, sped off like a car in a Krazy Kat cartoon. Ida, still standing under the umbrella while the rain, with renewed energy, danced around her, thought of her own wedding thirty-five years before on a rainy day in Warsaw. She began to cry again.

Irving put his arm around her, ineffectually patting her round shoulder. "She's a sweet, lovely, intelligent young woman who's going to make him a wonderful wife and their children a wonderful, wonderful mother, and if I knew what you were crying about, Ida Prince from Minski-Pinski, I'd give you a big red apple."

"I wanted a Jewish girl, Irving. I wanted a big, kosher-style wedding with a band and a strawberry-sherbet swan. I wanted—"

"Next time you get married, Ida, *you* can have a strawberry-sherbet swan. In the meanwhile," Irving said, placing his hand on the center of her back, supporting and guiding her up the slippery stairs, "Nick's got himself a good one."

"They could have at least stayed the first night here," Ida said, negotiating the top step, getting under the shelter of the new purple canopy with its gold-embroidered II initials. "It wouldn't have been so terrible."

"And we could have had tea and cookies with them. Maybe played a little pinochle to pass the time." Irving stuck a stogie in his mouth and, cupping his hands to shield the match, lit it. He took a puff, savored it, and blew a smoke ring into the rain. "He couldn't have found a better person, Ida. Admit it."

"All right, I admit it. She's kind and she's smart and she's a real lady. I never saw such hair in my life. And those eyes. A regular *mensh*." She put her arm in Irving's and looked up at the empty, rain-drenched Ocean Drive. "But I'm going to miss that boy so bad, Irving, I couldn't tell you."

She led the way into the Imperial Ida's pink lobby. Ida made perfunctory, soothing, optimistic (whatever was appropriate) inquiries of her guests.

They had parked themselves in the lobby's slip-covered club chairs and were complaining bitterly about the weather, trapped by the rain. Irving organized a bingo game. Eventually the rain stopped, the guests were free to go outdoors, and Ida and Irving escaped to their top-floor apartment, where they spent the evening eating pastrami sandwiches, drinking Swee-Touch-Nee tea, playing gin rummy, and remembering Nick as a boy.

There had been no formal announcement of Nick and Mary's engagement, but their intentions had been made known, and several well-meaning people—William Jennings Bryan was one—had attempted to have serious conversations with Mary about the inadvisability of "such a connection." She had written and then telephoned her stepparents. Disappointed, they had attempted to remain neutral, deciding in the end not to attend the wedding ceremony. She suspected that they had had some communication from the Collinses. She felt better when a cordial, loving note came from her mother inviting Mary and Nick to New Jersey for their honeymoon.

Nick had other plans. The only person besides Irving Prince who seemed wholeheartedly in favor of the marriage was Carl Fisher. "You've got guts, kiddo," he had said when Nick told him over breakfast at the Roman Pools café. "And she's got class. It's a perfect combination. If I had a goddamned son, I'd want him to marry Mary Goodwin too. What do you want for a wedding present aside from an ocean-front acre? I got an idea. How'd you like to spend your honeymoon in paradise?"

The rain was letting up as Nick drove the Reo past the main entrance to the Flamingo and presented his name at the exclusive Heaven's Gate entry to the hotel grounds. He was waved on to the first of the Flamingo's six deluxe cottages—Paradise. Carl Fisher was just leaving the neighboring cottage—Arcadia—smoking a dollar Havana cigar, looking uncharacteristically reflective.

He brightened up when he saw them. "Another sucker," he said, embracing Nick, kissing Mary on both cheeks. "This is legit, ain't it?" he said, stepping back, looking at the two of them, shaking his head in wonderment at their beauty and happiness. "I mean you have a goddamned license and all that?"

"We've got a license, Carl," Nick said. A porter removed their suitcases from the trunk of the Reo and took them into the Spanish Mediterranean cottage with the red-tiled roof.

"Okay," Fisher said, smiling up at Nick through his gold-rimmed glasses. "Just do me a favor, Nick, and don't go ordering lox and chopped liver and having the rabbi pay afternoon calls. If it gets out I got a Yid in here, I'm up the famous creek without a paddle. And try to keep the shouts of delight down." He paused theatrically. "You got an important neighbor next door."

"You going to tell us who it is?" Nick asked, anxious to get inside but sensing—for the first time—Carl Fisher's loneliness. He squinted. Behind the Flamingo's tower the sun was coming out, making the rain look like diamonds.

"I'll give you two clues: He's a terrible lush and a goddamned lousy poker player."

"Don't tell me," Mary said, "you've got our President, Warren Gamaliel Harding next door?"

"You got it in one. He should be accepting a little girl's bouquet at Royal Palm Park in Miami as we speak. He was supposed to be William Jennings Bryan's houseguest, but after a little bird told him William Jennings Bryan serves iced tea and only iced tea, he decided he'd be more comfortable at the Flamingo."

Nick, curling his toes inside his shoes with impatience, said, "Carl . . ."

"Okay. Okay. I could have Jesus Christ next door and you wouldn't give a goddamn." He looked at Mary and smiled. "I don't blame you, Nick. Next time I get married, I'm going to get one just like her." He slapped Nick good-naturedly on the back and moved off. "You kids have a good time. I told them to lay off the solicitous amenities and leave you alone, but you

366

want anything, just pick up the goddamned phone. This honeymoon's on me."

"Thanks, Carl," Nick called after him, regretting his impatience. "Thanks for everything."

"Least I could do," he said, getting into his Duesenberg, sitting next to the chauffeur, telling him to move on. As Nick held open the ivory-embossed front door of Paradise for Mary, he turned and caught a glimpse of Carl Fisher, smoking his cigar in the passenger seat of his Duesenberg. Nick had heard that Jane was filing for divorce. As a man who had the most important guest in the country staying in his new hotel, Carl Fisher didn't look all that happy.

Mary was standing at the pink stucco fireplace at the far end of the sitting room. The door to the bedroom had been left open, and through it Nick could see a huge ebony bed, covered in mosquito netting. He was suddenly nervous. He looked at Mary in her pale dress and thought she seemed unnaturally self-assured. The cottage was eerily quiet. Each step he took on the green-tiled floor made a loud echo. He didn't know what to do with his hands.

"Want to listen to the Victrola?" he asked, looking at the dark cabinet that housed it, a pile of sleeved records neatly stacked on top.

"I don't think so, Nicky."

He moved closer. "Champagne?" He indicated the jeroboam in the oversized wine cooler which looked to Mary like a great khan's funeral urn.

"Nope." She held out her hand, and he had no choice but to come and take it.

Mary had sensed correctly that Nick wanted his Aryan bride pure on their civic wedding day. With difficulty they had restrained themselves during their engagement. They had danced, and there had been chaste kisses, but bodily contact had been more or less limited to hand-holding. During afternoons sitting on the beach, holding hands, talking, she had discovered that Nick, despite those lowered eyes, that curled lip, and his hard-boiled poise, was far more innocent than she. He had elaborated on his dream, envisioning the world evolving into a time and a place when all races would live together in Floridian Moorish luxury. "A Miami Beach heaven on earth," Mary had said, and he had laughed. That he could laugh at himself surprised her. She had found they shared the same sense of the absurd; that they laughed at the same things.

Standing in that tiled, marbleized, pink-stuccoed Carl Fisher whimsy of a cottage, Mary felt chilled, as if a draft of fear had found its way down the chimney. She reached up to touch the bent penny before she realized it wasn't there. She had put it resolutely away, along with her bent luck, the night before. "We could hold hands for a while," she said, sharing Nick's nervousness, reminded of the innumerable wedding-night jokes she had heard about impotent husbands. "We do that so well."

Nick put his arms around her waist and held her close to him. "I'm not afraid I won't be able to make love to you," he said, putting his lips to her ear. "I'm afraid I won't be gentle enough with you." The Miracle of the Male Organ—so called by the book her stepfather kept in his desk, *The Family Book of Sexual Hygienics*—was making itself felt through the thin materials of Nick's Palm Beach trousers and her linen dress. He put his lips on her neck, and she felt as if an electric current had been applied. Her breasts swelled as he began to undo the buttons down the back of her dress. "I want to kiss you all over," he said.

"Are you a virgin?" she whispered as he undid the dress and her undergarments.

"No," he said, bending down, kissing her breasts, running his hands along the backs of her legs.

"Thank God," Mary said, pulling his sleek head closer to her, wanting him to devour her, "one of us knows what we're doing."

He led her into the hilariously Moorish bedroom. In my state, she thought, I'd follow him into the hotel lobby—as long as he doesn't stop touching me. He pulled away the mosquito netting and drew her down onto the bed. He kept his promise, kissing her with those lips everywhere.

Nick looked down at her as he entered her, so slowly she nearly cried out. She wondered whether this was torture or ecstasy. Ecstasy, she decided with the part of her brain that was still in operation when he was all the way inside her, when he started to move in and out and she could feel places inside her body she had never suspected existed.

"I love you, Mary," Nick said, setting off another explosion within her, one he shared. "God, I love you."

She was incapable of speech. All she could say was "Nick," and she said that several times as the passion waned, leaving a sense of warmth and completeness she had never felt before. "Oh, Nick."

He stayed on top of her, in her, kissing her, and then she felt him swelling again and slowly he made love to her once more. Afterward he fell asleep with his head on her shoulder, like a boy. She touched those dime-store lashes and put her finger against that sulky lower lip. My Lord, I am lucky, she thought, crossing her fingers. She couldn't help herself. She had believed implicitly that life was a matter of balances, that the greater one's luck, the worse the disaster to follow. "But I've put that bent penny away," she said, moving her body closer into the curved hollow Nick's body provided. "I'm through with bent luck."

Later they left the bed and moved into the living room. Mary had bathed and put on the pale silk negligée with which she had begun and ended her trousseau. Nick—in white silk pajamas with blue piping—had started a fire. He opened the champagne and served the caviar. "Does one always eat so much after making love?" Mary asked, piling her third cracker with caviar and chopped onions and bits of egg. "My Lord, I'm going to be as fat as a horse."

"I'll still love you," Nick said, avoiding the egg white, which he said made him gag, searching out the yellow yolk.

She looked down at the aquamarine ring he had given her as a wedding present. The stone was far too big, but its blue-green color matched her eyes. "I've never had a really vulgar piece of jewelry before."

"We could take it back and get you something more refined," Nick said, opening a duck-shaped terrine filled with goose liver pâté.

"Not on your life." She held the stone up to the light. "It suits me." She looked at him in his silk pajamas, standing with his champagne glass, staring into the fire. He could have made his fortune in Hollywood, she thought. And then she said, "Is this what love does to one, Nick?"

Nick put down the glass and sat next to her, kissing her. "What has it done to you?"

"It's paralyzed me. My Lord, I can hardly move except to focus my eyes on you. I cannot stop touching you, Nicky. I feel so . . . full of you. As if you had invaded my mind as well as my body and left me happy but not quite right. Simple." She looked into those violet eyes. "How do you feel, Nick?"

"I don't have the words." He kissed her lips and pulled her close to him. "I feel as if I could never have enough of you."

"Stop," she said, feeling that odd paralysis his nearness induced, taking his hands and holding them. "At least for a minute. I want to give you my present."

"You've already given me your present," he called after her as she went into the bedroom, rummaged through her suitcase, and returned with a large, business sort of envelope.

"Happy wedding day, Nicky." She handed him the envelope and kissed the top of his head, propping herself on the sofa arm as he opened it. Puzzled, Nick stared at the thick official paper for some moments. It was a properly executed deed, complete with Caucasian clause, for three prime, semideveloped acres on the ocean between Fortieth and Forty-Third streets, sold to Mary Goodwin Prince. "I'm a Caucasian," she said as he looked up at her, taking a moment to understand. "Marriage couldn't change that. They couldn't refuse to sell to me." She fell over the sofa, landing in his lap. "Now you can have your uptown hotel."

"I don't want an uptown hotel," Nick said, tossing the deed onto the floor, turning her around, kissing her, and slipping his hands under the negligée. "I have what I want."

"I've cashed in the final chip today," Nick told Mary when he had found her, sitting on the beach in front of their house. The tide was coming in, huge waves slamming the beach, nearly drowning out the sea gulls' screams. Nick and Mary Prince had spent the first year of their wedded life together in the sort of happiness she had only read about and Nick had witnessed only in the movies. They had left Carl Fisher's cottage for the rambling, comfortable wooden house Nick had bought on the corner of Fourth and the ocean. They could see the Imperial Ida, towering over her neighbors, from their second-floor bedroom, a block away. Mary found their proximity comforting—as if Ida and Irving were constantly watching over them.

Mary smiled up at him, happily oblivious to the noise of the surf. Her blond head lay against a towel-covered sand pile. Her knees were up, a copy of Dreiser's *An American Tragedy* propped on them. She wore green-lensed sunglasses low on her nose. It was a cool, sunny December day, and Irving, who had spent the morning with her, had insisted on wrapping her in an old green car blanket. "I feel like a beached whale," she said, grabbing Nick's hand, pulling him down beside her.

"Any pain?" he asked, kissing her cheek.

"A few little kicks, just to let me know who's boss." She laughed. "My Lord! When I asked you if making love was going to make me fat, I never dreamed it was going to make me *this* fat." She was nine months pregnant.

"You want something to eat?" Nick asked, concerned.

"I'm too lazy to eat. I'm too lazy to do anything but sit here and hold your hand and look at the ocean. You don't suppose I could have the baby right here, do you? It would be such a calm baby. The sound of the waves is like a sedative." She made an effort to sit up, to stop rambling. "What do you mean you cashed in the last chip? Has Shuster bought the Washington Avenue property?"

Over the past year Nick had been selling his South Beach properties. A retired doctor had just bought the last of his holdings. "He has. At top dollar."

"And well he should. Irving told me that the New Silver Crest subdivision out on Coral Way sold out in a quarter of an hour this morning at the rate of seven hundred and fifty thousand dollars a minute. Dr. Shuster is lucky."

"So are we." Dr. Shuster had paid a thousand times what Nick had originally paid for his buildings. "We're out of the boom, Mary."

"Maybe now the binder boys will stop bothering you," she said, laughing.

Nick laughed too. "One followed me home. He had a great piece of property just a few miles south of Miami." He lay down on the sand, resting his head on Mary's shoulder. "It was yet to be 'reclaimed,' which means it was still underwater, but that didn't stop this kid. 'Ten percent down, Mr. Prince. What's ten percent to a fellow like you?' Moxie. Whenever I see those binder boys in their plus fours, spieling about the chance to buy in on the ground floor, I have to laugh. They wait around the railroad station in Miami and get right into the taxies with the tourists."

"Cheap cars and new roads are giving the people of America a chance to get rich on Florida real estate," Mary said, repeating a William Jennings

Bryan aphorism. She felt the book slipping off her knees, Nick's arm going around her shoulders, her eyes closing. She hoped everyone got rich. Even the binder boys. She felt buoyant, as if she were floating above the earth, looking down on all those men in their tin-can cars coming to Florida to buy land and get rich. "We're already rich," she said, and Nick thought she meant the two million dollars they had, spread around several Miami banks.

"Now you can start building the hotel," Mary said, opening one eye, looking up at him for reaction. A pinch of fear salted her happiness. She wasn't at all certain about Nick's multiracial hotel. She didn't want him to be made unhappy.

"I'm going to take my time," he said. "I want to look at architects."

"Good. Do take your time, Nick." She had learned a good deal in the ten months she had been Mrs. Nick Prince. Once they had driven up to Palm Beach in Nick's new family car, a huge Packard, and had been told there were no rooms available at the Breakers, even though it was off-season and there clearly were. The clerk, like everyone else, read the real estate columns and had recognized Nick, the Prince of South Beach.

They had wound up at a hotel in West Palm. They had toured Palm Beach the next day, half amused, half fascinated by the profusion of Addison Mizner's Spanish, Venetian, Moorish, Florentine, and Gothic-type buildings. The Romantic style was spreading all over South Florida, creating suburbs that lured small-time investors.

Nick studied the buildings and Mary laughed at them, but still their excursion had been flawed. The anti-Semitism, which she had been unaware of before Nick Prince blasted her old foundations away, was even more obvious to her in Miami Beach. To celebrate Ida's birthday Mary had taken her to Le Forêt, a French restaurant Mary knew well on Twenty-first and Alton Road. Ida had never been there, and this was to be a tête-à-tête, a treat for both women, who were growing increasingly fond of each other.

Ida had worn one of her print dresses and talked as she always did, loudly, peppering her conversation with her favorite Yiddish phrases. The head waiter had taken a curiously long time to show them to their table in the empty dining room and was, if not abrupt, at least distant.

"This isn't exactly what you'd call your nice, warm, family atmosphere," Ida said, slurping her vichyssoise, pronouncing it not nearly as good "as my potato soup, but maybe I shouldn't blow my own horn."

When Mary asked for the bill, the waiter sent the headwaiter, who bowed. "The management," he said, "should like to offer the meal to you, Mrs. Prince, in honor of your recent marriage."

"My Lord, that was odd," Mary said when she and Ida were on the street, walking arm in arm toward the shops on Lincoln Road. "I could have sworn they didn't want us there, and then they picked up the check."

"What do goyim know about how to run a restaurant?" Ida asked, having already taken Mary in as an honorary Jew, steering her to the shady side of the street. "In your delicate condition, darling, we don't want sunstroke."

"Ida," Mary said, laughing, "I'm only two months pregnant."

"Nevertheless."

Two days later Mary received a note on Le Forêt stationery. "Dear Mrs. Prince," it read, "your custom is always welcome at our dining establishment. But in the future, we would appreciate it if you entertained your non-Caucasian guests elsewhere."

She kept that note a secret but sent a check to cover the luncheon. "I'm not in the habit," she wrote, "of accepting bribes disguised as wedding presents." She dated her new awareness from the moment she received that note. She finally realized she was no longer Mary Goodwin, welcome everywhere. Now she was Mary Prince, and her husband and her new family were "non-Caucasians," potentially business-ruining clients.

She looked up at Nick. He was drawing with his finger in the sand. His hotel. "Let's go inside," he said. "Ida's bringing dinner over here tonight." Mary held her hands out and Nick got both of them and started to get her up when she stopped him. She put her hand to her stomach.

"The little bastard's getting to be a great kicker," she said, and then she felt an unexpected wetness between her legs. She saw the puddle on the sand before she realized what it was. The next contraction told her. "Nick," Mary said, taking his hands, making an effort, getting up slowly, leaning on his arm. "You'd better get me to the hospital or the baby's really going to be born right here. I'm in labor."

She didn't make it past the first-floor bedroom. Maxwell Maurice Prince was born three hours later, brought into the world by Dr. Lawrence Seigel, Mrs. Ida Prince attending.

"*Oy vey,*" Ida shouted from the bedroom out to the porch, where Nick and Irving were pacing.

"Is Mary all right?" Nick asked, clumsy for the first time in his life, tripping over a rocking chair in his anxiety to get to the draped window.

"I'm fine, Nicky," Mary managed to say. "Just fine."

"The child?" Nick whispered into the window.

"Healthy like a horse," Ida said. "A great big strapping boy. I never saw such easy labor."

"Then what's all the *oy veying* about?" Irving asked.

"He's a blond with a button for a nose. I'm telling you, Irving, this brand-new baby of ours looks like a regular *shaygetz.*"

Early next morning, while Ida was whirling in and out of the kitchen giving the nurse superfluous orders, and Irving was sitting on the porch with his stogie, looking in the bedroom window at a pale Mary and a pink baby—both sleeping—Nick was on the telephone.

"You've got to come, Selma."

"Child, I can't just—"

"You promised."

"A hundred years ago."

"Selma, you said—"

"Child, I have a job with your Uncle Milton. I have six grandchildren of my own and two great-grandchildren. I am no spring chicken. What you want with me?"

"I talked to Milton, and he's buying the ticket for you. You should arrive in Miami tomorrow night around six, and I'll be there with the car to pick you up. You and the baby can have the big upstairs bedroom facing the ocean. We've decided to call him Maxwell Maurice Prince." He hesitated, listening to the sounds of the cross-Florida telephone system. "He needs you, Selma. Selma, I need you. Mary needs you. If you're not on that train, I'm going to have to come up there and get you. Say yes, Selma."

"Yes," she said. "Yes. I'm going to take these poor old bones and put them on that train, and if the Klan gets me and strings me up, I'm going to hold you personally responsible." Her voice softened. "What's he look like, child?"

"Nothing on this earth," Nick said, unable to keep the pride out of his voice. "An angel."

Selma laughed. "When you were a baby you looked just like a little devil. All that black hair and those peculiar purple eyes and that nasty lower lip. But you always got what you wanted, child—you know that, don't you?"

"I'll see you tomorrow night at the station, Selma."

"Child," Selma said, laughing in sudden anticipation, "I can hardly wait."

CHAPTER SEVEN

Spring and Summer 1926

MARY HEARD Nick's car pull into the driveway and felt her body relax, as it always did when he came home. She shifted her position on the wicker chaise longue, but nothing dislodged Little Lou, as Selma called her. It was the first day of June, and Louisianne, exactly two months old, already evinced a personality not dissimilar from her father's. God knows, Mary thought, looking down at the greedy lips sucking at her breast, she looks like him. She had black hair and a pouty lower lip and eyelashes that, Ida said, gave the Fuller Brush man a run for his money. Daddy's girl.

"How's my monster?" Nick, coming round the house, shouted. He didn't see Mary on the porch and headed for the spot down the beach where Selma sat in a chair, under an umbrella, directing Max in the construction of a sand pie. He picked Max up and kissed him. The sight of Max throwing his arms around Nick's neck brought tears to Mary's eyes. "My Lord, I'm getting soft," she told herself, crossing her fingers. The thought of that bent penny sitting in the bottom drawer of her jewelry box tried to force its way into her consciousness, but she wouldn't let it. "Please, God, or whoever is up there," Mary prayed, "don't let anything change. I'm so happy." If I could only, Mary thought, freeze time. She fought it, but she had a feeling that her bent luck was about to change its course. She was too happy.

"Child," Selma said, startled, looking up to see Nick toss Max in the air, "don't you be calling that boy a monster. And stop wiggling him around like that. He's going to bring up his food. Put him right down. Go have your lunch. And you," she said, taking Max's sturdy hand, ruffling his white-blond boy's hair, "get back to work." Max smiled at Selma, and she shook her big, long head. "Child, did you ever in your life see a smile like that? You could make a snowman melt, baby boy."

Nick turned toward the house and saw Mary on the porch, disengaging Louisianne from her breast, closing her blouse. If he looked like an Arrow-collar advertisement, Mary was a model for Motherhood and Milk. He ran across the sand and up the steps and kissed her and a sublimely content Louisianne. The floorboards creaked as he moved. For that matter, in a good wind the entire house swayed. He had offered to move from South Beach to one of the new subdivisions—Coral Gables or Silver Lakes—but Mary had resisted the idea. She had grown to like the South Beach neighborhood, the feeling that South Beach—unlike the subdivisions—had been around longer than a day. And she liked the funny slapdash house, the beach at her door, and Ida and Irving down the block. She liked knowing Selma and her children were in either of three places: the beach, upstairs, or being oohed over by the Imperial Ida guests.

An old friend had written just after Louisianne was born asking Mary to write a piece for his leftist journal on the socialist movement in Florida. She wrote back that all the socialists in Florida could meet in a telephone booth and there would still be room for more. Except for her father-in-law, there were no socialists in Florida. But the truth was that she wasn't interested in doing anything other than what she was doing. All thought of world revolution and peace on a grand scale had left her, except in occasional conversations with Irving. "I've found my true vocation," she told Ida. She pantomimed answering a telephone. "Good morning. Wife and Mother."

And Nick was happy, no longer a landlord, spending his days in a careful, exhaustive study of hotel architecture. He was in the interviewing stage now, meeting with the flocks of architects who were migrating from all over the world to South Florida, searching for fame in the land boom, dreaming of designing entire towns from the ground up.

374

If they spoke of Spanish cathedrals, had framed photographs of pyramids on their walls and imaginatively colored plaster busts of King Tut on their desks, Nick immediately lost interest. He did not intend to have his hotel designed in the new Egyptian mode (Tut's tomb had recently been discovered) or in the by-now traditional Mizner Mediterranean. He wanted a new, fresh style.

"I think I've found my architects, Mary!" he said, taking the fragile bundle that was Louisianne from Mary and holding her carefully in his arms. "I think I've really found my architects."

Mary saw that he could hardly contain his excitement, and so she tried to generate some of her own. "That's wonderful, Max. What's it going to be? Cleopatra's summer house or a Portuguese palace on the Rhine?"

He sat down on the edge of the chaise longue, rocking Louisianne in his arms, looking at Mary, his violet eyes ablaze. "I've discovered an entirely new kind of architecture, Mary. It's a German discipline no one's ever heard of, at least in Florida, called Bauhaus, and it's based on pure functionalism. That's what Carl and Ernst are always saying: Form follows function. Isn't that brilliant? Instead of all those derivative, decorative layer cakes, Bauhaus buildings are designed according to their function. Carl and Ernst—"

"Who are Carl and Ernst?" Mary asked, taking his hand, thinking that despite Max's fairness, he and Nick looked amazingly alike when they were excited about something.

"Two brothers who came to Palm Beach from Germany to build a millionaire's house. But when they got here, the millionaire changed his mind and wanted your basic Mediterranean mélange. They refused to go along, naturally. Carl Fisher introduced us. He said, 'You three nuts come out of the same goddamned shell.' He was right."

He gave Louisianne back to Mary and started pacing back and forth across the creaking porch. "It's so very right, Mary. It's so exciting, this Bauhaus style. All clean and spare lines. No falderal. As different from Mizner rococo as black is from white. No nonsense. And the best thing is, the Yosts agree that, philosophically, Bauhaus is exactly right for my concept."

My Lord, she thought, trying not to smile. When architects began talking about philosophy and concept, Mary worried. "Have you seen any of their buildings?"

"That's the problem. I've seen plans and photographs but no actual buildings. There are lots of them in Germany. None here." He sat down again on the foot of the chaise and took her free hand. "But there's a solution."

She didn't like the conviction in his voice or what she knew was coming, but she asked anyway. "What's the solution?"

"I want to go to Germany. I want to meet the Yosts's professors and see the Bauhaus school and the buildings they've designed. If I'm going to build a Bauhaus hotel, I must see some actual Bauhaus buildings, don't you think? The Yosts are going to come with me."

"When do you leave?" she asked, trying not to sound concerned, abandoned, scared.

"July first." He stood up, not hearing the fear in her voice, and started to pace again. "Louisianne will have stopped nursing by then, and Ida and Irving have agreed to live here while we're gone. We'll take the train to New York—"

Mary sat up, alarmed now in a different way. "You're not planning on us both going?"

He stopped talking for a moment and focused on her, his lower lip just beginning to protrude. "You do want to come, don't you?"

There was such disappointment in those violet eyes that she found herself saying, "Yes, of course, Nick. But Max and Louisianne . . ." He sat down once more and took Mary's hand, the aquamarine ring catching and reflecting the sunlight, turning the exact shade of her eyes.

"They'll be happy as baby chicks with Ida, Irving, and Selma clucking over them. I need you to come with me, Mary. We'll be away two months. A few weeks for travel, a few weeks in Germany and . . . two weeks in Paris. Germany will be work. Paris will be our honeymoon."

"Paris without your Yosts?" Mary said, remembering the two summers she had spent in France as a girl with her stepparents, thinking of the pâté sandwiches they sold at the railway stations, the enticing sour smell of the Seine.

"Paris without the Yosts," he agreed.

"And without our babies," Mary whispered, looking down at Louisianne, who had a smile on her tiny red lips, which meant she had gas. But Nick hadn't heard. He was in the living room, sitting on one of the club chairs Ida had lent them, talking on the telephone, arranging their trip. "And Paris without anyone but Nick," Mary said softly into Louisianne's delicate ear, starting to like the idea.

She woke up and reached across the huge down comforter for him, opened her eyes when she couldn't find him and saw, through the open bathroom door, that he was taking another bath in one of César Ritz's huge marble tubs. Nick, who only showered in America, had become a bath person in France. She half closed her eyes, watching him add more bubbly stuff to the water, taking a boy's delight in the way the bath crystals worked. Even in the bathtub he was cinematically handsome, his thick lashes lowered as he watched the bubbles rise. Her body suddenly ached for his, but she wouldn't disturb him. He was too happy.

I'm too happy, Mary thought. It was their last full day in Paris. The next day they were taking the boat train to Le Havre, boarding the *Queen Juliana*, and sailing home. Home, Mary thought. How I long to be home. Or maybe I long to bring home here. She looked out through the floor-to-ceiling leaded-pane windows at the August sun benevolently shining down on the Ritz gardens. We're rich enough. We could stay in this glorious bedroom and never move, ringing up room service night and day for pâté sandwiches and *cornichons*. Irving and Ida could take the next suite and the children and Selma the one after that. My Lord. Bubble baths at the Ritz, she said, laughing at herself, wondering what had become of the revolutionary girl who was going to hop on a boat and fight for true democracy in Russia.

There was a familiar knock on the main door of the suite, and Mary called out to the floor waiter in her schoolgirl French to enter, to leave the breakfast things. "Madame will serve herself," she said, pulling the bedclothes up around her nude body, watching the benign waiter go into the other room, set the chromed trolley next to the Louis XIV table, and then, with lowered, somber eyes and soft tread, walk across the Aubusson carpet and silently let himself out.

In the bathroom Nick was just getting out of the tub, preparing to shave. She had bought him a new shaving kit in one of the Rue de Rivoli shops that remained open in August. The razor was sterling silver, made by Rolls-Royce, and Nick, while pretending to be stunned by her extravagance, was immensely pleased with it, making a morning ritual of stropping the blade and lathering his face.

"Isn't it nice to have nowhere to go and nothing to do?" Nick called out as he ran the hot water.

"Don't talk to me," she said, stretching luxuriously in the bed. "I'm asleep."

"No you're not. You've been making assignations with the floor waiter, and it's not even nine o'clock."

She sat up, propping the peach-satin pillows behind her. "What shall we do today?" she asked.

"Make love," he suggested.

"And after that?"

"Have lunch at the Crillon."

"No," Mary said decisively. "No more hotels. Not on our last day. We'll have lunch at Chez Anna's, and then we'll poke around the Left Bank."

"Why did you ask," Nick asked, laughing, "if you already knew?"

"Stop talking to me. I'm still sleeping."

"I'll join you in a moment and we can sleep together."

"The chocolate and the croissants will get cold."

"We'll order more."

No more hotels, she thought, waiting for him with the same sort of eagerness she had felt on their wedding day. She added another pillow to those behind her back and saw the framed Bauhaus design one of the Yosts's myriad companions had given Nick. "And," she said aloud. "no more Yosts." She winced as she thought of that endless trek through Germany, from Potsdam to Weimar to Stuttgart to Berlin, led by those blond, invariably serious Yosts. Their endless conversations in monotone went on in railroad stations and in taxi cabs, in constructivist factories and in *Werkbund* schools and exhibitions, on street corners looking up at incomprehensibly rectangular, linear structures.

"This is not a school of architecture," Mary, exhausted and bored, said to Nick at the end of their first week, in a functional hotel bedroom in Dessau where the toilet didn't work. "This is a way of life."

She hated being in Germany. It was so poor and gray and in such a mess—women were pushing wheelbarrows filled with worthless German money to buy a loaf of bread. She began to think of Nick's hotel as poor and gray and doomed to be a mess. He was having a difficult time choosing the name. For a while he and the Yosts were calling it the Hotel Universal, but one day, over lunch in the basement cafeteria of the Dessau Bauhaus, Mary—who had vowed to keep out of it—stepped in. She pushed her tubular chair away from the boxlike table, having finished with the tubular sausage on her plate.

"The Universal sounds like some sort of washing machine," she said. "And since the building is going to look like some sort of a washing machine—"

"So what would you call it, Frau Prince?" Carl, the elder and more deadly Yost asked, the first voluntary question he had put to her since the journey had begun.

A fellow in steel-rimmed glasses at the next table was reading the German edition of the *International Worker*, and Mary, reminded of Irving, said, "I would call it the Hotel International."

"That's a very sound name," Carl Yost—scrupulously fair—said, surprising her. "What do you think, Ernst?"

Ernst too said it was a very sound name. Nick, believing that Mary was taking more of an interest, feeling guilty that she had been so much left out, pronounced it perfect, and so the hotel became the International. Not that the journey was over then. At endless meetings with the more important members of the Bauhaus movement—a Bauhaus hotel in Florida would certainly extend their sphere and importance—the International's plans gradually took shape, the Yosts scribbling designs in their little lined notebooks.

Mary watched them as if they were in a film in which only one character held her interest—Nick Prince, the handsome leading man. Privately she wondered who was going to come to a hotel in Miami Beach—the resort dedicated to the Goddess of Excess—that boasted inch-thin mattresses, metal toilets that swung out of walls, and a two-thousand-square-foot gray tiled lobby with three leather and chrome chairs at one end and a view of a triangular swimming pool at the other, in which, presumably, Jews, Anglo-Saxons, and Negroes would be cavorting.

In Berlin the Yosts invited the Princes to stay with them and their parents in a suburb called Wedding. "It will be an opportunity to witness the tragedy of the German working class," Carl Yost said enticingly.

Mary declined the opportunity, insisting on a luxury hotel featuring a dining room with padded chairs and a menu that offered something other than *wurst*. The Kaiserhof was on the Unter den Linden, its rooms filled with the silk and satin swags, the Biedermeier desks and elaborate radiator covers that seriously insulted the Yosts. "'House and furnishings must be meaningfully related to one another,'" Carl Yost said, clicking his teeth together in disapproval, on his one visit to their suite.

"Sez who?" Mary asked.

He looked at her as if he hadn't realized she could speak. "Gropius, Frau Prince, of course."

On their last morning in Germany, while Nick and the Yosts were visiting a factory that turned out folding armchairs, Mary stood sipping coffee on the small, elaborate, barely functional (And I like it that way, she thought) iron balcony overlooking the Unter den Linden.

The avenue, with its beautiful trees and gray solid government buildings, had been closed for some sort of parade. She watched the marchers coming from the Brandenburg Gate, growing in size and strength and noise as they neared the hotel. The army of angry men passed below her, shouting slogans filled with what Mary, who didn't understand German, felt to be a terrible hate. They wore a variety of shabby, outdated uniforms—as did many men in Germany in 1925—but most of them were in brown shirts. They seemed so ugly, so relentless in their hate, Mary found herself stepping back into the room, shutting the glass doors. She had recognized one word in their tirade: *Juden.*

She didn't mention the parade to Nick, but the following afternoon, when the train crossed the border between Germany and France, she felt unaccountably relieved.

Nick surprised her. He kept a promise he had made and never mentioned the International while they were in Paris. She decided that he had been more sensitive to her needs than she had supposed and she said so. Then he surprised her again. Nick genuinely liked Paris. It was August and the good restaurants were closed and the streets were filled with Americans, but it didn't seem to matter. "The only real way to enjoy Paris," Mrs. Price-Burnes, a British dowager of uncertain age who lived in Paris, weighed two hundred and fifty pounds and was proud of it, said, "is when the Parisians are in Nice."

They had, perforce, shared a table with Mrs. Price-Burnes at a Left Bank café, La Reine Blanche. She had ordered three *croque monsieurs* and ate them with gusto while she regaled them with her philosophy of vacationing in France.

"Never listen to what the French have to say. They always lie. But Paris, my dears, always tells the truth. What she says may be not pretty. It may not even be digestible. But it's always right on the money. Your dear Henry James said there is something right in old monuments that have been wrong for centuries. That is Paris. And some say, me."

She appointed herself their official guide. Each afternoon at two, when it became cool enough, her enormous new Daimler would pull up in front of the Ritz and her chauffeur, who she said was once an Italian general, would ring for them.

She took them to the Louvre, where she lectured them on various objects of art. "I'm having a marvelous time," she said as she ushered them into the dim room where the Mona Lisa was displayed behind thick glass. "And I hope you are as well. Prepare yourselves, however, for a letdown." She pointed to the Mona Lisa, hanging on a silk-covered wall, protected by two guards and a silk rope connecting a pair of faded red-velvet stanchions. "Disappointing, isn't she? Her father made Leonardo paint in the bodice, but I'm not certain a naked bosom would help. It's that smile. More constipated than enigmatic, don't you think? Now you, Mr. Prince, have an enigmatic smile." She turned to Mary. "You are very, very fortunate, my dear. Such a beautiful, beautiful man, and the gravy is that he doesn't seem to know it."

The night before she was to leave for her Cannes villa Mrs. Price-Burnes gave them a dinner party at her Rue St. Honoré house, to which she invited all "the bad American children in Paris." "They drink too much," Nick whispered to Mary as they sat on thick Moroccan pillows on Mrs. Price-Burnes parqueted main salon floor to watch Sergei Eisenstein's film *Potemkin*.

"What did you think of the film?" Mary asked as they walked home, having turned down Mrs. Price-Burnes's offer of her car and the invitation of some hilarious compatriots to sample absinthe in Montmartre.

"I loved it," Nick said, surprising her. It had had French title cards, but the film had communicated its message without words.

"I did too."

They had stopped to look down into the Seine. It was murky. A pair of elderly women sat on its banks fishing, passing a bottle of wine between them. The smell of fish and water and humanity seemed to lie over Paris, an integral part of the humid night. Mary had never felt, she thought, so in tune with Nick before. She was afraid to move. To talk. Afraid to break the magic.

Nick moved first, turning to her, smiling. "I can't wait to get home, can you? I want to kiss and hug those babies, and I want to eat some of Ida's meatballs, and then I want to take the Yosts to see the site one more time, and then I want to build my hotel." He kissed her. "We're so lucky, aren't we?"

She shuddered, and he held her. She wished the word "luck" would be stricken from the dictionary. She never wanted to hear it again. "We are very lucky," she said defiantly, throwing down the gauntlet to whatever bent god watched over them. Our love is too strong, she thought. It will protect us.

Now, on that last day in Paris, Nick came out of the bathroom, all shaved and perfumed from his bubble bath, and stood looking down at her. "Our last day," he said, peeling the bedclothes away, looking down at her body, bending over, kissing her breasts, running his hands up the length of her

380

legs. "Let's spend it in bed," he said, as he lay down next to her. "Let's make the Miracle of the Male Organ last as long as we can."

"Tomorrow," Mary whispered, not quite believing it, letting her hands run down his back, "we go home."

"I am home," Nick said. "Wherever you are, Mary, I'm home."

CHAPTER EIGHT

September 1926

MARY RESUMED LIFE IN THE HOUSE on South Beach, within shouting distance of the Imperial Ida. "It rained every single day while you were gone," Ida told her. "But we had fun anyway, didn't we, Selma?"

"Lots of fun," Selma said in that deadpan way of hers that made them all laugh. During Nick and Mary's absence Max, Louisianne, and Selma had become important members of the Imperial Ida household. Throughout those last dog days of summer, right on into September, they continued to go to the Imperial Ida early in the morning, not returning until bedtime.

Mary had even less to do now that Selma had taken over the children, the housekeeping, and—when Ida let her—the cooking. Nick spent nearly every waking hour with Carl and Ernst Yost, either up in their West Palm Beach office or at the land site. Mary found herself not minding. I am without ambition, she told herself, sitting on the Imperial Ida's porch, listening to Irving slurp his after-breakfast cup of Swee-Touch-Nee tea, watching the surf sweep the beach. Selma sat a little way down the beach under a huge umbrella, holding Louisianne in one long arm, throwing a multicolored beach ball to Max with her free hand.

The Brock Sisters were singing a song called "Lazy" on the Victrola at the neighboring rooming house, harmonizing about sitting in the sun with no work to be done. That's the way I feel, Mary thought. She said goodbye to Irving, hugged Max and Louisianne, asked Selma to bring them home in time for dinner, and returned to her ramshackle house. She got onto the chaise on the porch, allowing herself to drift, indulging herself in a way she hadn't done since her bout with pneumonia.

I've always been a woman of action, she thought, closing her eyes against the sun bouncing off the beach and the water. At least I like to think I've always been a woman of action. She reached over to the stack of books she had bought and was reading when she found the energy. *Gatsby* was on top, *The Sun Also Rises* just below it. She had read them both twice. I wanted to write, she thought regretfully, knowing that now she never would. She leafed through Hemingway's novel. His Paris was very different from the one we saw, she decided. We probably should have gone to Montmartre for absinthe.

She put the book down, wondering if this laziness, this sitting under the sun with no work to be done was symptomatic of some illness. But she knew in her heart that it wasn't. What I'm doing, she said, is savoring every moment, holding on as long as I can.

Early on a Thursday in the middle of the month Nick woke her up to say goodbye. The plans were ready. He was driving up to West Palm and would probably spend the night at the Yosts's. "We're having dinner with a banker who might be interested in financing us," Nick said, getting into his white jacket, smiling at her, not a hair out of place at six in the morning. "Carl and Ernst have convinced me to save my money for decoration and to try to get a bank to front the money for building." He looked in an oval blue-tinted mirror to see if his yellow piqué tie needed straightening, and of course it didn't. "Tomorrow morning we're supposed to have breakfast with a contractor the Yosts like. I should be home for supper."

He bent over and put his nose in her neck, liking the smell of her, sleepy and musky and warm. "You could come with me," he said, sitting on the bed, not wanting to leave her. "We could make a little holiday of it . . ."

"We've had enough of a holiday, and the next one we take, the Yosts will not be invited." She put her arms around him and held him close. He smelled of French shaving soap and American energy. She wanted to ask him not to leave. She wanted him to take off that Palm Beach suit and get into the bed and spend the day holding her.

"You don't mind staying alone?" he asked, looking at her sea-foam-green eyes, reading her mind.

She hugged him one last time and sat up, determinedly matter-of-fact. "Not a bit. My Lord, I have Selma and the children and Fanny and Ida, all at my beck and call. You worry about me too much, Nicky. Now go have a scintillating time with the Yosts."

He kissed her again and went to the door. "I love you, Mary Goodwin Prince," he said, smiling at her. She closed her eyes, making certain she had the mental photograph of him firmly developed in her mind: his pouty lower lip, the violet eyes, his rotogravure good looks.

"I love you too, Nick." She listened and heard the car door slam, the motor start. He was taking the Reo. She had an irresistible urge to go after him, to call him back, to tell him she'd changed her mind. She saw herself sitting next to him during the long drive north, holding his hand, studying his pro-

382

file. Quickly she got out of bed and ran to the window, tying her robe. "Nick," she shouted, but it was too late.

The following afternoon he called. He was still in West Palm, going over the plans with the contractor who had skipped a day on his other job just to meet with Nick. He was as excited as Nick and the Yosts by the prospect of building a Bauhaus hotel on Miami Beach. Nick wouldn't be home until very late.

Mary called Ida and said she could keep Max and Louisianne and Selma for dinner after all. "They're going to have *some* dinner," Ida complained. "Right this minute, as we speak, they're sitting next to me in the kitchen, ruining their appetites, *noshing* on butter cookies. Irving is having a nervous breakdown, turning the place upside down looking for his *yarmulke* and his prayer book. 'Since when are you such a Jew?' I asked him, but he's not answering. Rosh Hashanah is still three days away and he's making me *meshugge*. Maybe he knows something I don't know? Mary, darling, you pop over here and have supper with us."

Mary said she might, just to get Ida off the subject. There was an odd chill in the air, and she stayed in the house, lying on the couch, rereading *Gatsby*, half listening to a WQAM program of dance music. "Bye-Bye Blackbird" came on, evoking that New Year's Eve ball at the Flamingo. She thought of the way her breasts had swelled, betraying her, when Nick had danced with her that first night. A century ago, she decided. It happened a century ago.

A spokesman with a voice like the trumpet of doom interrupted the song to read a communiqué from the national offices of the Weather Bureau. The hurricane that had been threatening Cuba for days had traveled northwest and was passing into the Gulf. There was a wave of static and she missed the last part of the announcement. She dismissed it, wondering why they had thought it important enough to interrupt "Bye-Bye Blackbird" with news of a storm that had already passed.

She roused herself to go out onto the porch. The skies had turned a silvery gray. There was a peculiar light, as if a giant neon bulb were burning above the clouds. The beach was deserted. Max's beach ball had rolled off the porch, and the winds played with it, sending it from one end of the beach to the other, always just out of reach of the surf.

Irving startled her, suddenly coming round the house, puffing on his stogie, his hands ruining the pockets of his suit trousers. "Ida wants you to come right over to the Imperial. This minute. There's going to be some storm. Flooding. Terrible weather," he said, shifting his cigar from one side of his mouth to the other.

"I like weather," Mary said, watching the winds lose the ball to the surf.

"You can like weather from the safety of the Imperial Ida. You come stay with us."

"If it gets really bad, I will," she said, reluctant to leave her home.

"Promise?"

"I promise."

Irving, rather doubtfully, went back to the hotel to report. Mary turned back to the beach, looking for the ball, expecting the surf to have returned it. But it was gone, and she felt an odd sense of loss. The telephone rang. It was, as she knew it would be, Ida.

"Listen, miss. No one likes weather unless the sun is out and the songbirds are singing. Who in their right mind likes wind and rain? You come right over here the minute it gets bad, do you hear me?"

"Ida, darling," Mary said, laughing, "I could hear you without the telephone."

"And I'm keeping Selma and those two poor kids right here all night." She waited for Mary to object, and when she didn't, went on. "Irving says the radio says the storm passed, but I don't trust that radio. If it gets bad, you come right over here, do you hear me?"

Mary reassured Ida that she could hear her and that she would come to the Imperial if the storm acted up. She made herself a sandwich from an Ida meat loaf and took it and a cup of tea back to the couch and *Gatsby*. She wondered how it would feel to be Daisy, to be married to a rich man and in love with a gangster. Movie stuff, she decided, thinking Nick would make a wonderful Jay Gatsby.

At ten o'clock, when the voice of doom announced that the winds had risen to thirty-five miles an hour, Mary went out and maneuvered the Packard so that its back would be to the wind. She hoped Nick had enough sense not to try to drive the lightweight Reo. She had a little trouble getting back into the house, having to use considerable strength to pull the door open against the wind. When she finally got into the house, she realized some seawater had come in with her. She looked out on the beach. There was no moon, and she couldn't tell where the sand ended and the turf began. For no reason she could think of, she bolted the door.

By eleven o'clock the carpet was under a foot of seawater and the radio had shorted. I hated that announcer's voice anyway, she thought. She was on the couch, her knees up, *Gatsby* propped against them. She was, she knew, enjoying herself. The weather reminded her of the New Jersey coastal storms of her youth. She thought of the children and decided not to worry about them. They were safe on the top floor of the Imperial, cosseted by Ida, Irving, and Selma. They would have been frightened and miserable here. She continued to read. A few moments before midnight she noticed the water was now nearly two feet deep. "I'd better give in," she said to herself, "and go over to the Imperial."

Holding her skirt high with one hand, her shoes with the other, she waded toward the door, feeling the cold water around her knees, thinking the American Oriental Ida had lent them would never be the same. It felt all mushy under her bare feet. Just before she reached the door the overhead lights went out. Not that that wasn't expected with the winds and the rain, but still it was scary.

384

Her eyes adjusted after a moment and she found the door and tried to unbolt it. The lock was jammed. The wind sounded as if it were blowing at a thousand miles per hour. She pulled on the door, telling herself this was no time to panic. And then she heard a loud wrenching sound overhead. It was as if a cork had popped out of a giant champagne bottle. Mary looked up and screamed. The roof had blown off the house.

"I will not panic," she said over and over again, unable to hear herself think in the din created by the screaming winds. She found the lock and turned it with a strength she didn't know she had. The door jamb cracked first and then gave, and the door itself flew inward, torn from its hinges, nearly knocking Mary over. She lost her shoes in the effort to keep her balance, and in the next moment she was up to her waist in the seawater and assorted debris that came pouring in through the open door.

Something wrapped itself around her leg, paralyzing her. She couldn't reach down to see what it was, to unwrap it. "Please, God," she, that confirmed agnostic, said, "let it be seaweed." It seemed to be working its way up her leg. "Please, God."

Whatever it was let go. A flash of lightning revealed the dining room table floating by, and she managed to get on top of it. "I am not going to panic," she said aloud. "Max and Louisianne are safe up there on that top floor and Nick is safe in West Palm Beach. And I am safe. The storm will move on and the waters will go down. My life will resume."

But she watched with sickening fear as the waters rose and with them the dining room table. When she looked up, she realized that the table had floated up to the naked roof beams. She caught hold of one as the table rose up and then went down, floating away on the crest of a new, terrifyingly huge wave.

She worked her way slowly, hand over hand, into the corner where the beams and the rafters met and held on for six hours. She said the prayers she had learned as a girl in Quaker school. She told herself stories. She sang every song she had ever heard, half the time making up the words. And all the time, as the winds screamed and the huge waves washed over her, she vowed she wouldn't give in. I'm going to hold on. I want Nick to hold me in his arms again. I want to see my babies once more. Just once more, God, that's all I ask, thinking how absurd she was, clutching a rafter, negotiating with God in the middle of a storm.

At six in the morning the screaming winds stopped as suddenly as if a radio had been turned off. Miraculously the sun came out, and Mary half slid, half climbed down from the corner where she had spent the night. Her hands were bleeding and every bruised muscle in her body ached. "But I held on," she said, wading through the brackish water that covered the living room floor, stepping out directly onto mudlike sand because the porch was gone.

She stood for a moment looking at the house. It was as if some huge animal had died in the desert and all that was left was its skeleton, vultures

385

having gotten everything else. It was obscene, an affront to life.

Resolutely she turned away toward the Imperial Ida, which looked as nonchalant, as casually debonair, its sign at a rakish angle, as if nothing had happened. I must get to them, she thought. They must be crazy with worry. She made her way out onto the street and saw that Nick's Packard was in its usual place, seemingly unharmed. "That's lucky too," she said, feeling somehow buoyant and more positive than she had since they'd returned from Europe.

I had to pay for my happiness, she thought, and, my Lord, I have. Surviving the hurricane is a turning point. I've rounded the last bent curve. I'm certain of it. Suddenly there were so many things she wanted to do. To write. To help Nick. To take her children back from Selma and Ida. "I want," she said, "to start living again."

A group of people stood across from the house, knee-deep in debris, looking surreal in the odd, silvery light, in the perfectly still air, staring at the empty place where the souvenir shop had stood only hours before.

"Terrible, isn't it?" old Mrs. Yagoda said to Mary, and Mary agreed it was terrible. The landscape looked like a war zone, but she couldn't help feeling happy.

"The kids?" Mrs. Yagoda asked. "That husband?

"Fine."

"Ida and Irving?"

"They're all fine."

"You're lucky," Mrs. Yagoda said with a sigh, leaving, going up the littered walk to her hotel.

Mary walked half a block and looked up to see Ida, Irving, Selma, and the children searching for her through the broken glass windows of the Imperial's top floor. She wondered why they didn't look relieved when they saw her. She wanted to shout at them to smile, to wipe those grim looks off their pale faces. I survived.

Ida didn't seem to care. She was shouting, screaming something Mary couldn't make out. She was telling Mary to hurry. "Run," Ida shouted. Mary saw Selma take the children away and Irving put his hands over his eyes. "Run," Ida kept shouting. "Run. For God's sake, Mary, run!" It took her a moment to understand. She never could hear when people shouted at her. And she couldn't run in her bare feet with all that glass in the street. And why should she run? The hurricane had passed. "My Lord, I'm safe—I survived." She wanted to say that to Ida. Ida had stopped shouting. Ida, her round mouth open, was staring up at the sky behind Mary as if she were seeing the millennium. Mary turned and looked up as well. She tried to scream but couldn't. A great wall of seawater was descending on her.

So I did have bent luck, after all, Mary thought as the calm eye of the hurricane passed over her and, saying Nick's name over the screaming winds of the far side of the hurricane, she was drowned by the waters they brought with them.

It took him sixteen hours to drive from West Palm to Miami Beach. In the beginning, each time he had been forced to stop by a washed-out bridge, a road that had simply disappeared, he had tried the telephones. But the lines were obviously down, so he finally gave up and concentrated on getting himself home.

Makeshift ferries got him across the lowlands. All of the new lowland developments were underwater, and Nick thought of the ruined investors all over the country who were waking up to the news that morning. He thought of the people who had lost their houses and their dreams in that one single storm. He remembered, as he forced the Reo through a two-foot lake that had—the day before—been a new highway, Ida asking him if the rooming house he was buying was safe from hurricanes. He had assured her that it was.

All through that endless, anxious trip, as he saw the devastation of South Florida, he realized that the Florida real estate dream was over; the boom had bust. Who would lend money to build a housing development when that housing development could be reduced to dust in six hours by a storm nothing could control? People stood by the side of the road, when there was a road, staring unbelievingly at the piles of rubble that had been their retirement homes, their dream houses, the repositories of their life earnings and hopes. Nick wanted to pray for his family, but he didn't. He was afraid to pray. Afraid that if he let his mind think of what might have happened, it would turn out to be true.

He finally reached Miami, forced to drive around the schooners washed up from the bay. He had seen so much devastation, but those schooners and the overturned cars, the casual dispersal of the roofs of houses and buildings, especially horrified him. People wandered about crying out for family members, sifting through the rubbage to see what could be salvaged. Twice Nick saw bands of looters on the prowl.

A policeman told him all the causeways to Miami had been washed out, but one of the old Flagler ferries was running, bringing first aid to the Beach. Abandoning the Reo, he managed to talk his way onto one. He went to the top deck and saw the destruction of Fisher's man-made islands. The wooden houses that still stood looked as if they had never been painted. The wind had stripped the palm trees of everything, including their bark. They looked embarrassed in the cool air, like proper ladies caught without their clothes on.

The waters were gray and rough. He closed his eyes, letting Mary come into his mind. He was so close. He could imagine her waiting for him, holding open her arms for him as he ran up the steps of the house. He wanted to tell her about the devastation he had seen, the paralysis of the survivors who had come to Florida to make their fortunes and were left now with nothing.

He knew in his heart that she and the children were fine. He could see her discounting the storm when it began but allowing Ida to convince her to bring Selma and the children to the Imperial. He saw them eating spaghetti and meatballs in the dining room, Ida whirling around them, Irving blowing smoke rings for Max, Selma holding Louisianne on her lap, cooing to her, Mary smiling, basking in the warmth of this family she had become attached to.

He jumped off the ferry before it had properly docked and ran across Fifth Street, looking at the skeleton of his house but not seeing it, certain he would find everyone at the Imperial. Usually the pink lobby was filled with people at this hour, but it was September, he reminded himself; off season. The two elderly women sitting in the club chairs just inside the entrance stopped talking when they saw him.

"They're upstairs, Mr. Prince," a white-faced Jerry said. "I'd ring, but we got no electricity." The lobby looked dim, as if it were in mourning, all of Ida's pink and blue glass smoking lamps unlit. He took the stairs two at a time, wondering where this energy came from, wondering why Jerry, normally the most garrulous of fellows, had been so restrained.

The doors to Irving and Ida's apartment were open. He went into the wide hall and thought the place was oddly silent, hearing his footsteps echo on the Cuban tile floor. He felt the wind and the salty air before he saw the broken windows.

"Anyone home?" he called, going through the living room and then into the huge kitchen, where he found all of them seated around the mahogany-stained pine table Ida had brought from the apartment over Irving's New York Gentleman's Haberdashery. It was nearly as he had imagined it. Louisianne, with that black hair and those red lips, was sitting contentedly on Selma's lap, playing with bright wooden blocks. Max was trying to stick his finger through Irving's smoke rings.

Ida saw him first. "Nick," she whispered. Her round eyes were as pink as the lobby walls. She seemed diminished, thinner, as if some sudden illness had robbed her of half her weight and all her vitality. "Nick," she said again, the tears spilling over as she opened her comforting arms to him, and he went to her and bent down, resting his head on her shoulder.

He didn't want to move his head. He wanted to stay in Ida's warm arms forever. He didn't want to know. He felt Irving's hand on his shoulder, and he stood up and looked down into that man's pale, teary eyes. "She's dead, Nicky," Irving said as Ida lifted her apron to her eyes to wipe her tears.

"No she's not," Nick said. "She's lost. She'll turn up. You'll see. I'm going to go look for her. She's probably wondering where we are—" He stopped and looked at Selma, who was crying too. He bent down and kissed Louisianne, who was more interested in her painted blocks, and then Max, who returned his hug.

He stood up and looked at them. "You can all stop crying," Nick said. "I'm going to find her. Ida, Selma, stop! She's okay. I'm going to find her. We'll be back in fifteen minutes."

He stood there, not moving, staring at them until Irving put Max on Selma's other knee and stood up and took Nick's arm. "Come on," he said, leading him into the dark living room. Nick stood at the broken windows in the living room, looking out at what was left of the beach, holding the glass of schnapps Irving had poured for him. He could hear Ida weeping in the kitchen. "I want to see her, Irving."

"You can't, Nicky. They buried everyone this afternoon. They were afraid of plague or cholera or some damn thing. I'm sorry, Nicky. Not that it does much good, but I'm so sorry." He put something in Nick's hand. Nick looked down and saw the aquamarine ring and, without thinking, slipped it on his little finger and began to rub it as if it were a magic talisman, as if he could make Mary appear.

He slumped down in one of Ida's ubiquitous club chairs and put his hands over his face. Irving, smelling of stogie cigars and Lilac Vegetal, sat on the chair arm and embraced him. The only sound in the world seemed to be that of Ida crying in the next room. After a while Irving, tears running down his sad, jowly face, left Nick alone in the dark, closing the door after him, unable to stand the sight of his son's grief.

EPILOGUE

1945

THE 1926 HURRICANE took with it Florida's land boom and Nick Prince's dream of building a multiracial Bauhaus hotel on Miami Beach.

For the first year after Mary's death he busied himself helping Miami Beach recover. He offered low-interest loans to businessmen who would accept a Jew's money—there were a surprising number—and the sort of advice that had helped him build his own fortune. He established a South Beach Credit Union, a South Beach Businessman's Association, and, with Ida, a South Beach Public Kitchen, where one paid what one could afford for spaghetti and meatballs. He was, more than ever, known as the Prince of South Beach.

The 1929 crash was the final nail in the land-boom coffin. Miami Beach suffered through the resulting depression, hotel after hotel going under. The newspapers that had helped to make Miami Beach the most glamorous resort in America now helped to bring about its momentary defeat. It became no longer a place to envy, only one to pity. Nick's money had been more or less divided between the banks that went bankrupt and those that remained afloat. He managed to salvage half his fortune and considered himself lucky. A million dollars in cash was a good deal of money in 1930.

After studying the situation for a year he invested in three new uptown Miami Beach hotels—the Floridian, the Fleetwood, and the Wofford—with the understanding that the management would open their doors to both Jews and Gentiles. Whenever Nick invested in a hotel, he wrote into the contract what he called his Semitic clause. Hotel management continued, however, to hold the line against blacks.

"There's a war on in Miami Beach," read the pamphlet slipped under Nick's Washington Avenue office door. "And the kikes are winning it." Each time a German cruise ship put into Miami, another anti-Semitic tract found its way under Miami's doors. The tracts were right. The anti-Semites were losing the war, Jewish tourists increasingly checking into the formerly restricted Collins Avenue hotels, which welcomed the business.

"What the hell's wrong with goddamn Atlantic City?" Carl Fisher asked. "People go there, don't they?" Nick continued to meet him every morning for breakfast at the Roney Plaza's outdoor café, which stood on the site of the old Roman Pools. He was broke and alcoholic, dying at sixty-five, alone and uncomplaining. The last time he met Nick for breakfast he said, "I had a good run, kiddo. I can't kick."

The Imperial Ida flourished during the Depression under the direction of Ida and Irving Prince. In the beginning, after Mary died, Nick had found it easier to live there, to give up responsibility for the children, for nearly everything, to Ida.

But in 1931, when she was five, Louisianne contracted infantile paralysis. The doctors Nick took her to in New York said she needed a swimming pool, a specially equipped gym, and a trained therapist if she were going to walk again. "She's going to walk again," Nick said. He bought a fifteen-room Mediterranean-style house on the Indian River, the first Jew in that formerly restricted neighborhood, and installed Selma, Max and Louisanne—along with a cook and a maid—in it.

He spent ten thousand dollars on a forty-foot-long indoor swimming pool so Louisianne could exercise in all weathers. He converted the solarium into a gymnasium for her, importing the equipment and the therapist—a large, almost frighteningly dedicated blond woman of fifty—from Sweden. He wanted Ida and Irving to sell the hotel—he had transferred ownership to them—and move in. "She'd die," Irving said, "without a hundred and fifty people to look after every day." Finally Nick had to hire a chauffeur to ferry everyone back and forth every day, to make certain the children, as Ida put it, "got enough to eat" by having dinner in the Imperial's dining room.

He spent considerable time with Max and Louisianne, quite often in the gym. He and Max became as expert on the trampoline and the parallel bars as the therapist, Anneke. True to Nick's prediction, Louisianne began to walk. She had to wear a thick, ugly metal brace, but she could walk. The doctors said she would have to wear that brace for life, but Nick said she would discard it, and later she did. Louisianne's illness had given him a reason to live. He savored every moment with her and Max; he had studied and learned the difficult, heartbreaking lesson of lost time.

As the Depression came to an end he began to receive increasingly attractive offers for Mary's beach-front land, the site of the hotel he wasn't going to build. "It's not mine to sell," he told the real estate developers truthfully. Mary had left her ocean-front acreage to her children, who were legally, according to the laws of the courts, Caucasians, born of a Caucasian mother. Nick had been named as the sole trustee in perpetuity.

Irving died in 1941, in the pink Imperial Ida lobby, in Ida's arms, of a massive heart attack. Ida spent the war making bandages, offering free rooms to Jewish soldiers, their wives, children, and parents, cursing the Nazis, mourning Irving. Nick spent the war directing the conversion of all the major resort hotels in South Florida to housing, training, and indoctrination centers. Later, as the war came to an end, he helped turn them into hospitals and convalescent homes and places of deployment.

When he was eighteen, in the fall of 1943, Max, drafted into the army, was accepted as an Army Air Force candidate and flew with the British RAF, helping to drive the Axis forces out of Africa. Wounded in early 1945, he was sent to England to convalesce and was honorably discharged as a captain in the early fall of that year.

The Imperial Ida's dining room was closed for the afternoon, a huge banner over the front porch reading in pink letters *Welcome Home, Max.* The band, Ziggy Goldstein and his Society Four, was playing "The Miami Beach Rumba" so loudly, Nick had trouble hearing anyone speak. He looked lovingly at Max, whose innocent blond face was turning pink from champagne cocktails. Max, seeing his father's gaze, extricated himself from Ida and the long lineup of eligible young Jewish women she wanted him to meet and attempted to make his way to where his father was sitting.

But he had trouble getting across the room. People were beginning to leave, and they all had to shake his hand, to touch this living talisman who had come through the war seemingly without a physical or emotional scratch. They hadn't seen the long, jagged scar that ran down his back or heard his shouts of surprise and pain caused by the shrapnel the surgeons hadn't been able to remove.

Nick felt as if he'd been holding his breath since Max had left and only

391

now could breathe easily again. He saw old Mrs. Yagoda take hold of Max, so he turned his attention to Louisianne, who—in Ida's estimation—was far more beautiful than she should have been. She was standing at the pink-leather-upholstered bar listening to a young man with broad shoulders whisper anxiously in her ear. Her smooth black hair just touching the shoulders of her beautifully cut white suit, she looked characteristically nonchalant. Nick knew she wasn't. She had told him that morning, sitting on the edge of her bed in her room in the house on the Indian River, painting her toenails Real Ritz Red, redolent of illegal French perfume, that she didn't know what to do about Rodney.

"Do you love him?" Nick had asked, not wanting her to say yes. Not because he had anything against Rodney, who was educated, beautifully mannered, and had a lot of money. He was even the first doctor in his real-estate-rich Miami pioneer family.

Rodney's all right, Nick thought. I'm the one who's not. I don't want her to leave. She was twenty-one and had spent her war working with Anneke in Miami's St. Francis Hospital helping to rehabilitate the seriously wounded. Nick knew she was a wonderfully imaginative, sensitive woman, ready for marriage, but he didn't want to lose her to Rodney's exclusive, clubby world. Or to any world.

She looked up and saw his concern. "I love him, Daddy."

"Then what are you waiting for?" Nick asked with more impatience than he meant to show.

"I'm afraid of all that money. Rodney says if that's the problem, he'll give it away, and of course I don't want that either. I want to be able to go on with my work, and Rodney says that's fine, we can go on having lunch together every day in the hospital cafeteria."

"Rodney is a saint."

Louisianne ignored the sarcasm. She put the last stroke of varnish on her exquisite little toe and, standing up, sensed her father's fear. She put her arms around his neck and kissed his chin. "Of course I'm going to marry him. I love him so much I can't see straight. I'm just fooling around, like I used to do when I was a girl and you gave me a present and I took as long as I could unwrapping it.

"You'll be happy, Daddy. We'll all live together in that great big house of his out in Cutler Ridge and play Monopoly every night." Barefoot, she limped over to the taffeta-skirted dressing table and looked in the round mirror. At fifteen she had been able to give up the brace. The disease had left her with a short left leg, but when she wore her custom-made high-heeled shoes, the limp was scarcely noticeable.

Nick stood behind her, watching her in the mirror as she finished dressing. "So I'm to live with you, am I?" he asked, shaking his head. "Poor old Dad, let out of the attic on his birthday and July Fourth."

"It's time someone took care of you." She turned to him and smiled. "You're going to make the most distinguished grandpa. And not yet fifty."

392

"You're not . . .?"

"Oh, Daddy, don't you think I'd tell you if I were?" She put her arm in his and led him out of her room. They were halfway down the staircase when Louisianne said mysteriously, "And Daddy, today, after the party, when Max talks to you, I want you to remember he's speaking for both of us."

Alarmed, attempting not to show it, Nick said, "What's he going to talk to me about?"

"It's his idea, and I'm not going to say another word. Daddy, do you think we have enough gas to take the Cadillac?"

As Ziggy Goldstein gave his boys a break, Nick watched Louisianne across the Imperial's dining room. She was tightening a gold earring, looking rue-fully up at Rodney, giving her approval to whatever plan Rodney had pro-posed. Then she walked across the dance floor with that nearly but not quite unnoticeable limp that always made Nick want to go to her, to shield her from the pity it produced. Rodney, with his money and his goodness, would protect her.

Louisianne easily detached her brother from Mrs. Yagoda, kissed him carefully so he wouldn't get lipstick on his cheek, hugged Ida, blew a kiss to her father, and, Rodney in tow, disappeared.

Ziggy Goldstein and his band were back, playing an old song, "You Made Me Love You." Max had been trapped again by Ida, who was introducing him to one of her "lovely Jewish girls." Nick saw Selma, wearing the blue hat Ida had insisted upon, standing off to the side, alone. She hadn't wanted to wear the hat. "It's a daytime affair, isn't it?" Ida had asked. "In the daytime ladies wear hats." She had gone over to Washington Avenue and spent twenty bucks on a hat for her Selma.

On an impulse Nick went to Selma and took her hand. "Let's dance."

"Child, I can't dance. Not with these feet and those people out there."

"You can do the Pensacola darktown strutters' shimmy and shock the be-jesus out of them." Selma laughed and gave him her hand. He led her out onto the dance floor as Ziggy Goldstein began to sing the words of that ro-mantic song, bringing back—for both of them—that day thirty-three years before when he had danced her around Rosi's New Miami Beach Café. "I sure do love you, child," Selma said as Ida got everyone else off the dance floor and they all stood around it watching. Selma moved her big feet in time to the music, hating the blue hat that didn't fit, feeling the tears in her little yellow eyes, thinking of the lost years.

When the song finally ended, everyone clapped, and Selma said, "Thank you, child."

"For what?" he asked.

"For making me part of your family. For sharing everything. I been moan-ing and bitching about going home to Pensacola for years now, but I got a confession. I wouldn't have left if you'd of let me. I'm like some old darky slave, child. I belong to you."

"And I belong to you, Selma," he said as Ziggy and his boys went into

"Drinking Rum and Coca Cola," and Max, escaping from his admirers, came and made Selma dance with him.

"I'm too old for all this carrying on, child," Selma said, smiling, moving those hips to the beat, getting "hep." Over her shoulder Max pointed to the beach and Nick nodded, understanding as always.

As apprehensive as a schoolboy about to face his principal, Nick left the dining room, crossed the pink lobby, and let himself out onto the porch. It was one of those silvery Miami Beach winter afternoons, the sun beginning to set, the wide beach deserted. The sea was a pale green, looking as if it were lit from below.

Nick took a deep breath, glad to be free of the humid, smoky haze that hovered over Ida's dining room. He inspected Irving's rocking chairs, thinking they needed recaning and fresh paint. He looked up at the peeling porch ceiling that needed work as well. Everything did. Now that the war was over, they could get to work. He knew that with scheduled airplanes and air conditioning, Miami Beach was going to enter a new kind of prosperity. All it took, he thought, was a world war. Half a dozen hotelmen had already talked to him about investing in some new projects, all huge and fanciful and maybe just possible. He was going to study the situation, and when he felt he knew about it, he would make a decision.

He half closed his violet eyes, staring out at the beach, thinking suddenly of Carl and Ernst Yost, smiling, remembering Mary's description of them as the lesser two of the seven dwarfs. He dozed a bit and woke, sensing the party was over. The music had stopped, and he could hear Ida and Selma arguing in the same way Ida used to argue with Irving, directing the elderly bellhops and desk clerks in the careful removal of the banquet tables. Despite her dance-floor confession, he could hear Selma making noises about going home to Pensacola. She wouldn't leave now. Ida needed her more than ever.

He stretched, reaching his fingers up as if he could touch the sky. Nick Prince, not quite fifty years old, wondered where the past two decades had gone. He touched the ring he always wore on his small finger and allowed himself the luxury of thinking of Mary. She'd be so proud, he thought, of our children. He could hear in his mind that direct voice, that old-fashioned expression, "My Lord." "My Lord, they're good-looking. And nice. Nick, they're so nice."

Then, in reality, he heard the porch door slam and turned to see Max. He had his mother's hair, now cropped far too close, his mother's sea-foam-blue-green eyes and that same direct approach to almost everything, another champion of the underdog.

"You sleeping, Dad?" He sat on the porch balustrade facing Nick.

"Dozing. Party over?"

Max nodded, smiling, his affection overcoming the strangeness they both felt in this still new reunion. He had been so young when he went away, and

394

he seemed so confident, so adult, now. He even smells different, Nick thought. When he left he still smelled like a boy, dirty and sweaty and sweet. He's a man now, smelling of tobacco and after-shave. I feel like the child, Nick decided. He looked past Max, out at the milky green ocean. He wasn't at all certain he wanted to hear what Max had to say.

Max lit a Lucky Strike, the smoke drifting off on the salty breeze. "Dad," he began, but Nick interrupted him.

"If you're going to tell me that you want to leave, that you want to go away to New York or some other place, do me a favor, Max, and don't tell me now. I want you to be with me for a while. We can talk about what you want to do later. Give me some time with you. Hang around the house for a couple of months. We can go fishing."

"You hate to fish," Max reminded him.

"I'll learn to like it," Nick said. "Just stay for a while."

Max looked perplexed and suddenly, gratifyingly, much younger. "I'm not going any place, Dad. I'm going to live at home while I go to the university and maybe, after that, architecture school. You know I saw a lot of houses in Africa—not even houses, more like elaborate huts—made of mud and straw and every other darn thing, and I think they could be adapted to this climate. I have an idea for low-cost vacation housing for people who can't afford fancy hotels—" He stopped and smiled Mary's rueful smile, the one she wore when she found herself talking too much.

Nick thought of that day on the Collinses' real estate office porch when Mary had told him her life story in fifteen minutes and he had repaid her by shouting at her and stalking off. He had reached the point in his twenty years of mourning when he no longer regretted her death. Now he found himself celebrating her life.

"Dad," Max said, putting out his cigarette, field-stripping it out of habit in the approved military manner, leaning forward in that easy, confidential way he had, as if he were telling you a secret he knew you could keep, "I want to talk to you about the land mother left Louisianne and me."

"You could get a good price for it now," Nick said, surprised, not wanting to talk about the ocean-front property. He didn't want to be reminded of his old, naïve dreams. The memory still hurt. "But you probably should hold onto it. You don't need money now. I'll give you all the money you could possibly use and—"

"We don't want to sell it, Dad." Nick looked up at this blond, green-eyed, strange and familiar man, his son, wondering how anyone could radiate such pure and genuine goodness. He was so much like Mary. "Dad," Max said, breaking into his reverie, "Lou and I talked about this before I went to Africa, and if I didn't come back she was going to make the suggestion, but since I *am* back, she says—"

"You're just like your mother was when it comes to getting to the point," Nick said, smiling. "What's the suggestion?"

395

Max took a breath and said, "We want to give the property to the city of Miami. We want to make it a public park with a swimming pool and changing rooms. We want to dedicate it to you and to Mother. We want to call it the Nick and Mary Prince Park, and we decided we'd do it only if you agreed to put your name on it and if the city agrees that it's to be a totally nonsegregated beach. You know, Dad, there're so few public beaches, and there're going to be fewer and fewer, and I've talked to the mayor and he thought that it was a great idea and there's no reason . . ."

Max went on in that Mary-esque way of his, spilling out all his thoughts and feelings. Nick listened, touching his ring while he looked out at the place where the silver-blue sky met the green sea. It was the exact color of Mary's eyes. He stood up and put his arm casually around his son's shoulder, half closing his dime-store lashes so Max wouldn't see the tears. "It's a wonderful idea, Max."

They stayed on the porch, Nick back in Irving's old rocker, comforted by the salt breeze, gazing out on the beach while Max rambled on, describing the beach and the plantings—"We're going to insist they use all native plants, sea grape and buttonwood and Spanish bayonet"—and the pastel colors of the dressing rooms. When Max finally had no more to say and Nick had twice agreed to everything, Max excused himself to telephone an anxiously awaiting Louisianne at Rodney's club. "Dad's with us," he told her.

So Mary had made it possible after all, Nick thought. He could see the park in his mind, all of them—Irving, Ida, Selma, Max, Louisianne, and, yes, Rodney, and certainly himself—swimming in the municipal pool. He heard Ida calling him. "What're you sitting all by yourself in the dark for, darling? Come in. We're going to have another celebration." Max had told her.

Ida came out and kissed him on his forehead, testing for fever, displaying that affection that he had relied on throughout his life. "Would you please come in already? I don't like you sitting out here all by your lonesome."

"I'm coming in already," he said, patting her plump little hand reassuringly. He stood up and smiled at that place where the sun was disappearing at the far edge of the ocean. He used his beautifully pressed linen handkerchief to blot the tears on his handsome face. He opened the screen door—that would need fixing as well—and turned again to glimpse that last ray of sunshine. "And I wasn't," he said to himself and to Mary, "sitting out here all by my lonesome."

The
Doves

BOOK FIVE

CHAPTER ONE

1947

FLORIDA DE CÓRDOBA, hands clasped protectively in front of her ripe breasts, surveyed with satisfaction the purchases she had made in Miami. Marita, her housekeeper, had arranged them on the enormous old ebony bed as if they were merchandise on display in an expensive shop.

"Do you want to say good night to Victor, Señora?" Marita, a tiny, worried-looking woman with hollow cheeks, asked in her barely audible voice. She was standing on tiptoe, looking over Florida's elegant shoulder, viewing the pastel silk blouses, the gold bracelet in its upholstered box, and a sheer negligée with as much enthusiasm as her mistress.

"I thought he was sleeping," Florida said, touching a white wool dress she had her doubts about, wondering how long it would be before her breasts returned to their normal shape, hating the peasant gourds they had become, feeling weighed down by them. She looked in the mirrored wall at the far end of the room, lit by newly installed indirect lighting. The lighting, wonderfully expensive, was a concept she had imported to Havana after seeing it in a retired United Fruit Company executive's Bal Harbour house. The resulting light and the pink-tinted mirror—another borrowed Yankee detail—reflected her brilliant red hair and green eyes, making her look nearly like her old, prepregnancy self. Seven months and two weeks pregnant, Florida thought. Oh, Mamacita, one month and two more weeks and it will be over.

"Victor *is* sleeping, Señora," Marita said, appraising out of the corners of her little black eyes the new and shocking bathing suits the señora had treated herself to. Bikinis! "He tried to stay awake, but he couldn't, poor thing," Marita said, smiling to herself. "Such a beautiful boy."

"If Victor is sleeping," Florida said, trying not to be acerbic—Marita cried at the drop of a hat—"then there's no reason to see him now, is there?"

She had been home for little more than an hour. Home—La Casa de los Córdobas—was a huge white-columned Spanish colonial house of stucco and wood. Situated on the site where, reputedly, the first Córdoba structure in Havana had once stood, La Casa had been meticulously designed and built

399

in 1815 by the last of the Florida Spanish governors on his return to Cuba.

Subsequent Córdobas had installed modern plumbing, garages, garden houses, and idiosyncratic follies as the expensive suburban Vedado section was being built up around its ten acres. But essentially La Casa remained what it had been intended to be: a monument to the Córdobas, past and present. For a time, just after the Second World War, one of the more enterprising tour guides had noisily bussed American sightseers up the hill and around La Casa's walled estate. "The first Córdoba came to Havana in the early sixteenth century," the guide would say, speaking into his bullhorn in remarkably good English. "She was a Spanish exile, a woman with red hair and green eyes, and she established the most famous of Latin America's houses of ill fame on this very spot. It is said that the great De Soto himself . . ." One telephone call had put an end to that.

Florida half missed the tour bus, the gawking strangers, the history lesson booming into the breakfast room while she drank her morning cocoa. The first and last time Armando—who was usually out of the house by six—had heard it, he looked as if he had been electrocuted. Armando de Córdoba believed himself to be the modern protector of the Córdoba name.

Florida, who had grown up on the perimeter of the Córdoba family circle, liked La Casa because it was old and beautiful and her friends envied her having it. But there was something about the formal pine- and tile-floored house that eluded her. It seemed to eat up servants and guests and furniture. It has a life of its own, Florida thought. No matter how many Yankee innovations she added, La Casa never seemed to be affected by her. Not unlike Armando, she thought, picking up the rainbow-colored bikini bra, shaking her head, not wanting to think about La Casa or Armando. "It's going to be months before I can wear it at the club," she said. "By that time everyone will have seen them."

"Did you bring Victor his gun?" Marita asked tentatively. "He said you promised and he was so excited—"

"Yes, Marita," Florida said patiently. "I bought him the largest wooden pistol I could find. 'Miami Beach, Florida,' is written on the handle. It's bigger than he is." She loved Victor, but there was something about him, even at five, that intimidated her. I wasn't ready for him, she thought. But I'm ready for this one. She put her hands protectively on her expanded stomach and smiled. I'm ready for her right now. "Oh, Mamacita, please let it be a girl," she prayed.

Florida had been an only and lonely child, her mother dying when she was not quite three years old. The two surviving photographs of Inez de Córdoba were faded, the woman's face indistinct. When Florida called on her Mamacita to witness some incredible happening or on the Blessed Mother to help her through some crisis, it wasn't the vanishing face of those snapshots she had in mind. Rather it was that of the gray and white composite-stone statue of the Virgin, her arms outspread, her face a study in compassion, that stood just inside the main entrance to Havana's cathedral.

400

Her father, Renaldo, an odd little tobacco-colored man, had died a year after she married Armando. He had always been old in her memory, melting into the background of the dark and somewhat spooky house they had occupied a mile or so away from La Casa. But when she was twelve and had begun to board at the convent, she found she missed his solicitude, his creaky kindness, and looked forward to those holiday dinners she had shared with him in the long, narrow dining room of their house. Still, she had felt somehow deprived. She had wanted a big, strong, decisive father, and Renaldo was a grandfatherly little poppy, pleased with himself, his daughter, his life. Sitting at the opposite end of the tiled dining table at those lonely but somehow comforting holiday dinners, Florida compared her lot to that of her schoolmates and their huge, uproarious families. She had tried to feel sorry for herself, but she couldn't. There was too much love and approbation emanating from the far end of the table. He was so proud of her.

He didn't seem to mind that she—and of course he—were looked upon by the other Córdobas as misfits. Florida's attention-getting red hair and iridescent green eyes were features everyone thought had been bred out of the Córdobas long ago. And Renaldo, with his Yankee accent and effort to appear pure Cuban by displaying that stage-prop coat of arms on his dining room wall, was considered ridiculous. Florida and her father were invited to the larger Córdoba family celebrations, omitted from the intimate and more desirable ones.

Florida had been a painfully young eighteen when Armando launched his heavy-handed courtship. He was ten years older than she was, wonderfully handsome, with black hair, gray eyes, and the famous Córdoba smile. He seemed so very strong, so very certain of what he wanted. So unlike Renaldo. As the eldest son of the reigning Córdoba branch he had inherited La Casa as well as the bulk of the Córdoba fortune. He had recently returned with a medical degree from France and was in the process of reestablishing his father's lifelong charity work, the Córdoba Institute of Nephrology, a clinic dedicated to the study and treatment of kidney disease. All he needed was a wife. Florida, suddenly appearing at a staid Easter family breakfast, brought by some cousin or other, animated and demure, as beautiful as a movie star and yet undisputedly a Córdoba, seemed cast for the role. Immediately she was the only contender.

"Has a miracle ever happened to you, Poppy?" Florida asked when, drunk with no sleep and happiness, she had told her father of Armando's proposal. The future seemed infinite with possibilities. She was going to be Armando de Córdoba's wife. It never occurred to her that she shouldn't marry him.

Her father smiled at her with his ancient lizard's eyes, usually so dry but for once moist with tears. "The Córdobas are famous for having miracles befall them. You are my miracle, Florida. When a miracle happens to you, you must travel with it, Florida, as far as it goes. Don't ask questions. Just hold onto your miracle as long as you can." The marriage, a glorious event, took

401

place three months later, and Florida wasn't to think of personal miracles for another twenty years.

Armando made the mistake of expecting she would be forever grateful. In the beginning she was. He had thoughtfully if unimaginatively introduced her to lovemaking. He provided her with a housekeeper, Marita, a cook, Elena, a chauffeur, Dario, several maids, and a ready-formed circle of club friends who had kept a certain distance before. She took up their interests— shopping, travel, gossip—because there didn't seem to be anything else to occupy herself with. Almost from the beginning she was bored. If Armando thought he had made a mistake, if he was disappointed that his young wife did not metamorphose into the form he had expected her to, he never said so. He was waiting for their sons.

She was still very young when, four years after their marriage, Victor was born. She was unprepared for the demands the voracious baby made upon her. Victor Rolando Ramón de Córdoba, inheritor of the famed Córdoba name, fortune, and smile, had a cupid's face with seductive, heart-shaped lips few women could resist. He looked like a miniature Armando but an Armando come to life with a mischievous, unquenchable energy. How the matrons at the club oohed over him! Victor ignored them all. From the day he was born he had loved his mother with an intensity that made her friends laugh, irritated Armando, and frightened Florida. She felt Victor would have locked her in a room if he could, saving her just for himself.

Now, five years later, Florida looked in the mirror, put both hands on her stomach and said aloud, "Be a girl. Be a pretty, nice, easy girl. Blessed Mother," she demanded, "give me a girl." Laughing at herself, she picked up the snake-shaped gold bracelet by its tail, as if it were poisonous, and asked Marita to clasp it on her wrist. Then she held her arm up and twisted it so that the sinuous pink gold caught and reflected the light.

"Beautiful, Señora," Marita whispered as Armando came into the bed-room and looked down at the bed with a grimace of distaste. He had taken Florida to Miami because he had promised her during their courtship when he was anxious to marry, that they would visit Florida twice a year. He was a man of honor, and Florida was a woman who expected promises to be kept.

"Are we going to sleep on your 'Yankee merchandise,' " he asked, saying the last two words in English, undoing his tie. It was a long, narrow tie, dead black. All of his ties were long, narrow, and black. His ties, Florida thought, hold as many surprises as Armando.

Armando pointed to the wide, painted window louvers to indicate to Marita he wanted them shut. He had a heavy-lidded, handsome face, with a nose that would have been haughty on a man of lesser stature. His voice was a monotone, rarely showing emotion. His thick black hair was slicked back, making his odd eyes seem especially lugubrious. When stung by real or im-agined insults, he had a surprisingly sharp, wounding way with words. His

402

greatest concern, aside from being all that a Córdoba should be, was his institute.

"You'd better have Juana put it all away, Marita," Florida said, turning away from Armando, reaching for the cigarette case she had received as a present in Miami Beach. Armando intercepted her, pocketing the case.

"I thought we had agreed you wouldn't smoke until after the baby was born," he said. Undoing the collar of his shirt, he left her standing by the bed while he went into his dressing room, and Marita and the maid, Juana, gathered up the Miami purchases.

"I'd like my case back now, Armando," Florida said, following him into his gray, windowless dressing room. "I won't smoke," she said, hearing that fine edge in her voice as if it might break. She looked up at him with her emerald-green eyes turning dark and angry and held out her hand. "I want my case back, Armando. I'm not a child. I won't smoke. I wasn't going to smoke. I just want to hold my case. Give it to me."

He looked at her and gave in, reaching into his jacket pocket and handing her the black-lacquered, gold-bordered cigarette case. "Try not to get hysterical," he said, turning away, continuing to undress. "It wouldn't be good for the child."

He joined her in the huge old ebony bed a few moments later, kissing her good night quickly, without meaning. "I'm glad we're home," he said, conciliatorily.

Florida held her wrist up over her head, the gold bracelet glistening in the dim, indirect light. "I should have bought the necklace as well," she said, not wanting a conciliation. "It's not the things you buy that you regret. It's the things you resist you're sorry about."

"Is that going to be your most profound thought for 1947?" He sighed, turning away from her. "If you're not careful, Florida, you're going to wind up like those women at the Olivas' cocktail party, knowing the price of everything and exactly the place to get it."

"You're angry," Florida said, undoing the bracelet, laying it on the yellow marble-topped bedside table, "because Deliciosa Oliva gave me that cigarette case. You think I compromised myself by accepting it." She laughed. "You have such high ideals, Armando."

He raised the heavy lids of his eyes—white in the dim light—and looked at her angrily. "You're always asking me how I feel, Florida. I am going to tell you. I feel compromised each time you make me take you to Miami. I loathe and despise Miami Beach and the Olivas. They represent all that's materialistic and empty in the corrupt United States culture. Cubans, like the Olivas, who play at being Yankees are especially revolting to me. You're naïve if you think that in socializing with such people some of their characteristics won't rub off. And you're even more naïve if you think that I would ever consider living in Miami Beach or anywhere but here, in Cuba. Our family has been here for five centuries."

"Oh, not again," Florida said, turning away.

He caught her wrist and held it. "Yes, again, Florida. Listen to me: I have no intention of giving up my heritage. Havana is the city where I was born and Cuba is my country. The subject is closed, forever. Now, good night. We're both tired, and you need your sleep." He closed his eyes, and in that aggravating way of his, was immediately asleep.

Florida was wide awake. She reached over, opened the beautiful case, and extracted one of the gold-tipped Egyptian cigarettes that Deliciosa Oliva had also supplied. She put it between her lips, but she didn't light it. She felt the baby move about, and putting the cigarette aside, trying to get comfortable, thought about the Olivas' party. It was the sort of party that could never have been given in Havana, and if by some miracle it had, Armando wouldn't have let her attend.

Perhaps it was because they were in Miami and not Havana, but still Florida wondered at the nerve the Olivas had had in inviting the Córdobas—whom they had never formally met—to their cocktail party. Bebe Oliva had started life obscurely in Havana's port and was now worth, it was said, more than the annual Cuban budget. He had once been a great friend of Batista's, but had escaped, according to rumor, that gentleman's armed wrath by several hours. He was not allowed back in Cuba.

Not that he seemed to mind. He and his wife, Deliciosa, and their servants and guards inhabited a mansion that had formerly belonged to a famous American gangster—a huge fortress of a house with a red tile roof—on Star Island, just off Miami Beach. The party was being given in honor of the nominal president of Cuba, Carlos Río Jocarrás, whom everyone called Río. Río's attendance gave the party legitimacy, and Armando, bored by the shopping and the beach and the black and white lobby of the Sans Souci Hotel, where he seemed to spend most of his time waiting for Florida, agreed to attend.

The party had been, at least at first, predictably awkward. The Olivas had attempted to mix Cuban social classes, working on the hopeful assumption that any Cubans who had money and were in Miami Beach had a common interest. They might have a common interest, Florida thought, looking at the small divisions gathered together around the huge oval room, but no one's crossing class lines to talk about it.

Armando had been very nearly rude to everyone save Río, whose politics he deplored but whose genealogy was beyond reproach. "I'm medical," Armando liked to say, "not political." He acknowledged his host, got himself a rum and Coke, and stood in a corner with Río for most of the party, criticizing this vulgar Yankee style of life.

Deliciosa Oliva, who had wrapped her plump body in a bright pink satin Schiaparelli dress, tied it with a huge black ribbon, and then put on more jewelry than anyone would have thought possible, introduced herself to Florida. "When I want to describe for my new friends in Miami the most aristocratic, the most beautiful woman in Havana, I always talk about you, Señora Córdoba. You are exquisite, Señora. Exquisite even now."

"How very kind you are, Señora . . ." Florida pretended to grope for the name, and then gave it up. "If you will pardon me, I must just say a word to Christine. I have not seen her in ages." She had worn a boxy white suit that hid her pregnancy and a new oversized hat that encircled her flame-red hair like a white straw halo. The manicurist at the Sans Souci had talked her into a new, silvery white varnish and had applied coat after coat so that her nails had taken on a luminous life of their own. She had worn no jewels except for a pair of emerald earrings that mirrored her eyes. She had moved around the bulk of Deliciosa Oliva and made her way to the window, where Rio's sister was standing, drinking straight gin, popping tiny black caviar canapés into her mouth.

"If I didn't know you were seven months gone," Christine said, wolfing down the last of the canapés, "I'd never have guessed. You look irritatingly marvelous, Florida. Aglitter, like the Hope diamond. Whereas our hostess," Christine said, her small mouth full, not bothering to lower her voice, "shines dully, like a dime-store gem." Several people next to them, over-hearing Christine's remark, had laughed. Florida laughed along with them but made the mistake of looking at Deliciosa Oliva.

Deliciosa, having overheard—it would have been difficult not to—put on her public smile. But it was an embarrassed, humiliated smile, and Florida felt, despite the new straw hat and the emerald earrings, ugly. She had waited a few moments, excused herself, and deliberately sought out Deliciosa Oliva in the corner, where she had taken shelter with General Speedy Morales's dear but deaf mother.

"You have such a lovely house, Señora Oliva," Florida had said, moved by the tears in Deliciosa's mournful eyes.

"I don't suppose you'd like to see it?" the fat woman, who couldn't have been much older than Florida, said hesitantly.

"I should love to," Florida said gently.

They had excused themselves to Señora Morales, and Deliciosa had led Florida through a series of labyrinthine corridors and palatial rooms, up and down circular stairways, in and out of sumptuous bathrooms, all the while relating the story of her life. She had been a cashier in her father's restaurant in Havana's poor, old section. "Bebe rescued me," she said, and for a moment Florida was jealous of the fat, overdressed woman. There had been so much love in her voice.

"I miss Havana terribly," Deliciosa had said, taking Florida through her upstairs sitting room, as large as a hotel lobby and decorated in an appropriate style. Everything was white. "Especially the music. There used to be a band that played in our street every afternoon. But I don't miss being poor." She stopped and smiled that shy smile of hers. "We get the Havana papers. Everyone from Havana comes to us. I hear about you occasionally." She sat down in an overstuffed white love seat and took a gold-tipped cigarette from a black and gold case.

"Such a beautiful case," Florida said, longing for a cigarette, touching the smooth black lacquer.

"Please keep it, Señora Córdoba. A present from me."

"I couldn't, Señora Oliva," Florida had said, appalled. "I couldn't."

"I would love to do something for you, Señora Córdoba. You are being so kind to me. Tell me, what can I do for you?"

"You could give me one puff of that cigarette." Florida took a long drag, inhaling slowly, letting the delicious smoke fill her lungs, and then exhaled slowly. She hadn't smoked. She had merely taken a puff. "And you could start calling me Florida."

"If you'll call me Deliciosa," the fat woman said, trying a smile. Her black hair, gathered into a thick, shining bun, was pulled so tightly back from her face that Florida wondered how she managed to blink her eyes.

"Done. Just one more puff."

While Florida finished the cigarette Deliciosa talked. "I saw you once before, Florida," she said, loving the sound of the name on her tongue. "It was five years ago at a wartime charity ball for the Mercedes Hospital. Bebe had taken the largest table—he always takes the largest table—and you and your husband were supposed to sit next to us, but you came only for a moment, going from one place to another, stopping in for just one dance. You wore a silver dress with big shoulders and a funny, chic neckline, and you had a huge white orchid in your hair.

"I couldn't think of anything else but you—the way you moved, the casual way you put your purse on the table, your silver sandals—for weeks after. You were born with all the luck, Señora. I was born with just a tiny, tiny piece of it."

"That's not true, Deliciosa. If you didn't give silly cocktail parties for snobbish Cubans, you'd be a perfectly happy woman."

"And you are not, Florida?" Deliciosa asked, taking Florida's hand.

Florida let her slender, elegant hand with the white-enameled nails lie in Deliciosa's fat, delicious little hand and felt an unexpected need to confide in her. "If you want to know, I feel trapped all the time. As if I'm in prison. You don't suppose you could smoke another one of those wonderful cigarettes, could you?" Deliciosa lit one and passed it to Florida. "I have a fantasy I never tell anyone about, Deliciosa. I leave my son, my husband, my home, and all the Córdobas behind. I go to Miami, change my name, dye my hair, take a small apartment, get a job, cook my own dinners, go to the movies when I want to. I'm anonymous. No one knows me. I'm free."

"What kind of job?" Deliciosa wanted to know, caught up in the fantasy.

"I don't know. It wouldn't have to be a spectacular job. In a dress shop, perhaps. I couldn't be a secretary or a hairdresser. I have no skills."

"I could teach you to take cash," Deliciosa said, laughing. "I was very good at it." She sighed. "Maybe we should both run away, Florida."

406

"I couldn't do much running in my condition," Florida said, putting out the gold-tipped cigarette in an ashtray carved out of a bleached elephant's foot.

"You're feeling blue only because you're near your time. All women do," Deliciosa Oliva said comfortingly, reassuringly, as a servant came into the room.

"Señora Córdoba? Your husband is looking for you. He says it's time to go."

"Oh, Mamacita." Florida put on the shoes that she had slipped off and stood up. "I haven't had such a talk in years, Deliciosa. Or perhaps ever. Will you visit me when you come to Havana?"

"I won't be coming to Havana for a long time," the fat woman in the couture dress said, shaking her head, tears again in those sad eyes. "But next time you come to Miami, anytime, you must stay with us. We have more rooms and servants than any hotel. Promise, Florida."

"I shall try. In the meanwhile let's write to each other."

"I will," Deliciosa said. "I will write. I haven't had a girl friend—not a real one—in years."

The two women suddenly, spontaneously embraced. Deliciosa in her shocking-pink dress looked like a mammoth petit four, while Florida, in that white halo of a hat, looked like an angel seven months pregnant. "You are a very generous woman, Señora Córdoba. Very generous."

"And you are a very dignified woman, Señora Oliva. Very dignified. I think we're going to be great friends."

"Imagine," Deliciosa Oliva said.

When they had returned to their hotel suite Florida put her hand in her jacket pocket and found the cigarette case that Deliciosa had put there. She told herself she'd have to send it back, but in the end she didn't. She found comfort in touching it. In the morning, just before she left, she sent Deliciosa Oliva the largest white orchid the hotel florist could provide.

Florida lay in her bed in La Casa thinking of Deliciosa while the baby kicked and moved around. She wished that it was born, that she was free to go to the club the next day, to gossip with Christine and Laura and Tina, to show off the bikini. She felt a sharp pain, as if she were being stabbed. Alarmed, she turned to waken Armando, but the pain was already gone.

She looked at her husband. He had kicked off the light blanket. In sleep he seemed much younger than his years, more like Victor than ever. He is good, she thought, feeling a sudden surge of affection for him. He took me to Miami when he desperately didn't want to go. I'm going to change after the baby is born. I'm going to be nicer to him. More appreciative of the things he does for me. She leaned over and kissed his cheek. Poor thing. All he wants to do is work with his kidney patients and have a well-run house, good children, an occasional swim at the club. All I do is complain.

Another spasm of pain made her cry out. "Blessed Virgin," she said, getting out of bed, standing on the tile floor, looking at the luminous dial that read three o'clock. Aspirin, she decided, going to the lavender bathroom she had had installed exclusively for her own use. She was reaching for the bottle when she felt water streaming down her legs and saw that it was forming a puddle on the lavender tiles. It's too soon, she thought, frightened. The baby's going to be born dead or deformed. I'm only seven months and two weeks gone. "Blessed Virgin," she cried out, holding onto the sink for support, "help me."

Armando came to her, his eyes dull with sleep. "False contractions," he said, putting his arm around her.

"My water broke, Armando." She shouted again with pain. "I'm contracting, Armando." She looked down and saw the blood staining her nightdress and screamed. "Oh, help me, Mamacita. Help me." He picked her up in his arms and carried her down the stairs, Marita following, Juana behind her.

Victor stood on the balcony overlooking the entry hall, sleep in his eyes, his pajama trousers falling down. Suddenly he came awake and shouted, staring down at Florida's bloody nightgown as Armando maneuvered her out the front door. "Poppy's killing her," he screamed, and Marita ran back up the stairs to comfort him, to explain.

Dario, the butler-chauffeur, had the huge prewar Cadillac at the door and helped Armando lay Florida on the backseat. She screamed all the way to the hospital while Armando knelt beside her, in his pajamas, holding her hand, looking at her with his white-streaked gray eyes. "Scream," he told her. "It is all right, Floridita. Scream."

The next ten hours were a haze of harsh emergency-room lights and then the softer lights of a private room, the matter-of-fact voices of the doctors, and always Armando's narrow hand and the pain. "I feel," she told him when there was a respite at eight in the morning, "as if my body is being ripped in two. Am I going to die, Armando? Tell me. I want to know if I am going to die."

He took the cloth from the nurse and wiped her brow. He was wearing a black tie and a gray suit. Someone had brought him clothes. "No, Floridita, you are not going to die. You are having a difficult labor. The baby is coming feet first."

"The airplane," she said, taking the cloth, biting on it. "The baby got all jumbled on the plane." And then she screamed again, her nails digging into his arm, drawing blood. "Blessed Virgin," she whispered to herself, dredging up in her mind that gray stone figure with the outstretched arms. "Mamacita. I don't care if I die now. Let my baby live, I beg of you."

And then she opened her eyes and saw the young, handsome obstetrician, Dr. Galvez, give a nod, and then the nurse came toward her with the mask to make her unconscious. They were going to do a Caesarean section. "No," she said, forcing herself to come awake. "No. I haven't gone through this pain for nothing. I'm going to go through with the rest of it. I don't want to die under a sedative. I want to see my baby." She was shouting. "I want to see my baby," she said again, controlling herself, not wanting the doctors to think she was hysterical. "Please, Dr. Galvez," she said in a calm voice. "Please don't cut me open."

Galvez looked at Armando and the nurse, made a gesture, and the mask and the sedative were withdrawn. The baby tried to be born for the next four hours, and finally Armando, who hadn't let go of her hand during that time, bent over and said, "Galvez is going to have to operate, Floridita. To save your life."

"Is my baby going to live?" she asked, but he looked down at her and shook his head.

She cried out and then stopped, suddenly feeling as if there were a bird trapped inside her, flapping its wings, trying to get out. And then she felt as if the bird were attacking her, and she let go of everything.

"Push," Dr. Galvez said.

With a last effort she pushed, screaming in release.

"The legs are coming," the nurse said, and Floridita felt that slippery mass, that flapping bird, leaving her body slowly, with infinite pain, and finally it was gone.

"My baby," she said. "Blessed Mother, let it live." There was a terrible long silence in the room and then, discordant and nearly comic, a slap against a bare bottom and a sudden cry and then a longer one.

"The baby's alive," Armando said to her, but she heard the disappointment in his voice.

"Is it all right?" she asked as the nurses began to clean her up, as she felt the blessed relief of that cessation of pain.

"It's all right," Armando said, taking off his surgical mask, looking more fatigued than he ever had before. "But it's a girl."

"Thank you, Blessed Virgin," Florida said, closing her eyes. "Thank you."

"She's perfect," the nurse said later when she brought the baby to her. "And she looks just like you. Red hair and great big green eyes. So beautiful, Señora."

"It is amazing," Armando said, coming into the pretty hospital room, looking freshly barbered, nicely groomed. "Two Córdoba redheads in two generations. My great-grandmother—" he began, but Florida cut him off.

"Armando," she whispered, her throat raw from the screaming, taking the baby in her arms, "please don't give us the family genealogy. Not now." She kissed the pale, tiny face, holding her close, cooing to her, taking in the tiny nose and the flame-red hair and the two brilliant pinpoints of green. The baby looked up at her and, opening her perfect little mouth, began to make a pitiful noise.

"She wants to feed," the nurse said, taking the baby so that Florida could open her gown.

"That's not necessary," Armando said. "Marita has a wetnurse waiting downstairs—"

"I've decided I'm going to feed her myself, Armando," Florida said, taking her baby back, putting her to her breast.

"But you said that you weren't going to ruin your breasts, that you—"

"I've changed my mind, Armando." She closed her eyes at the sweet ecstasy she felt, her milk running, her baby drinking. "I want to feed this baby myself."

"Very well." He bent over her and kissed her and then, after a moment, the baby. "As long as you're both all right, I'm going to go down to the institute. Nurse Lopez called with half a dozen emergencies. Marita's seeing to Victor."

Florida looked up at him. "Thank you, Armando."

He smiled at her, his mind already at the institute. "I'll come back this evening to see how you're getting along. I'll bring Victor. He wants to make absolutely certain I didn't kill you." He stepped out of the door and then looked back. "We'd better decide on a name."

"I've already decided," Florida said, thinking of her father's papier-mâché coat of arms. "Her name is La Paloma, The Dove."

CHAPTER TWO

1952

"MOMMY," VICTOR SHOUTED, slamming out of the Cadillac, leaving his sister behind with Marita and Dario, taking the broad, shallow steps two at a time and slinging his school books on the ancient deal table, where he had been told dozens of times not to put them. "Mommy, there's a Ramiro van coming up the back drive. Mommy, what's Ramiro's van coming up the drive for?"

"Victor," Florida said, coming down the main staircase into the hall, "stop that shouting." The hall, three stories high, thirty feet wide, ran the length of the main house. With its marble floors and mahogany staircase, it made, as Victor had discovered years before, a perfect echo chamber.

Florida had just concluded a long, sad, sweet conversation with Deliciosa Oliva. Deliciosa's homesickness for Havana was so palpable, it seemed to seep across the telephone lines like a spilled cup of Cuban coffee. She had decided it was easier to telephone than to write, and she did so every Monday afternoon at precisely two-thirty.

Deliciosa had "adopted" Paloma sight unseen, sending her presents from Miami's most expensive shops, begging for a visit. "If I could have a child, I would ask the Blessed Virgin for a girl just like Paloma," she liked to say.

"Mommy," Victor said, reaching up, wrapping his tough little arms around Florida's neck, kissing and hugging her with an ardor that everyone had predicted would fade but that was now, if anything, more intense. She returned the kiss, thinking how much he looked like a small edition of Armando.

Victor even had Armando's white-streaked gray eyes, an aberration in any family but most certainly among the Córdobas, where the only options were supposed to be black or green. They evoked those zombie fantasies fashionable among her convent school classmates in her youth: tales about the unseeing, cold eyes of the undead. But Victor's grip on her was very much of this world, and she had to use some strength to get out of it. It would be nice, she thought, if Armando displayed—out of bed—some of Victor's affection and Victor some of Armando's daytime reserve. It would have been nice, she thought, if Victor had inherited his father's height as well as his looks.

Victor had had his tenth-birthday party that past Sunday. Fifteen boys from his academy class and from the club's prejunior swimming team had been invited for games and cake and ice cream. When they had lined up to pin the tail on the donkey in the low-ceilinged, trellised summer house, it had been so obvious that Victor was the shortest, Armando had made an excuse to leave, to return to the main house.

"Is there something we can do?" she had asked Armando that night, knowing how disappointed he was. Córdobas were meant to be tall.

"There's nothing to do." Armando had spoken in that doctorish, prescriptive voice of his that made her feel as if she were being forced to swallow some bitter, unnecessary medicine. "He's a perfectly healthy boy. Height is an inherited trait, passed on from one generation to another. Sometimes it skips a generation. Sometimes there's a recessive gene. It might change." He gave that characteristic, exasperated, inner-directed Armando sigh, as if the weight of the world were on his broad shoulders. "Florida, I would appreciate it if we didn't discuss it again. There's nothing I can do about it. And all you can do is pray to your Blessed Mother."

He had left unsaid the fact that Florida's father, the tobacco-colored Renaldo, had been exactly five feet five inches tall, that there would never be an opportunity to have another, taller son. Florida could not, after Paloma's difficult birth, have another child.

"How was the swimming?" Florida asked Victor, putting her arm on his sturdy shoulder, if only to make him stand still for a moment, waiting for Paloma to make her dreamy, poky way up the front steps. It was true that

Victor was too short for his age, but he had developed an easy, infectious charm that more than made up for it. He could, with his Córdoba smile and his way with words, talk himself out of most anything. Everyone, even his victims, liked Victor. Only his father resisted him, and Victor, recognizing Armando's disappointment, met it head on with antagonism.

"I did a double flip and the coach says I'm the best swimmer for my age on the club team and pretty soon I can start entering competitions. Mommy, what's Ramiro's van doing coming up the back drive?"

"Ramiro's van is making a delivery," Florida said, half kneeling, giving Paloma a kiss and a smile. She was five years old and could have been no one but Florida's daughter, red hair ablaze, green eyes glowing. "Did you have a nice time at the club today, Paloma?"

"You should see *her* swim," Marita said. The tiny woman, hands aflutter, emerged from the rear of the house, having accompanied Dario to the garage. It had been instilled in her when she was a child never to enter an employer's home through the main entrance. "One of these days she's going to be as good as Victor, aren't you Paloma?"

Paloma looked up and smiled, and Florida felt her heart expand. "Victor is the best swimmer in the club," Paloma said. "I'll never be as good as Victor." She was fragile and lovely and self-effacing. If Victor was too much like his father, Paloma was nothing—except for the physical resemblance—like her mother. Whereas Florida jumped in, feet first, Paloma tested the temperature with her exquisite little pink toe and then, slowly, inched her way in. Paloma's favorite pastime, aside from swimming, was drawing, and at five years old she could make a creditable crayon sketch of her mother. Paloma could sit for hours, by herself, working in her sketchbook.

"What's Ramiro delivering, Mommy?" Victor wanted to know, again interrupting his mother's thoughts. "Another birthday present for me?"

"No. It's a present from me for all of us." Her father had left Florida some money, which she had, contrary to Cuban custom and Armando's wishes, kept for herself in her own bank account. It had been her father's idea to keep that money separate, and now she was glad she had. Armando would never have given permission for this newest purchase. He disliked anything that was new, anything that smacked of U.S. gadgetry. Florida tried to remain aloof, but she was excited as Victor. She gave in. "Let's go see."

The four of them—Florida, Victor, Marita holding Paloma's hand—ran across the black-and-white-marbled hall floor and out onto the rear balcony overlooking the gardens and the service driveway. Señor Ramiro, a fat, perpetually worried man mopping his forehead with a red handkerchief, was directing the uncrating of a huge box in which sat a smaller box with a seven-inch-square glass screen.

"It's a window," Paloma said, confused.

"It's a television, stupid," Victor said. "A Dumont TV."

"Don't call your sister stupid," Florida told him, letting go of his hand. "You apologize this minute."

412

"I apologize, Paloma." He leaned over and kissed her fair cheek. If he could love anyone other than his mother, it would be Paloma. "Do you forgive me?"

"I forgive you," Paloma said solemnly. She'd forgive him, Florida thought, exasperated, for setting her on fire.

"Where's she go, Señora?" Ramiro asked, looking up.

"Upstairs, Señor Ramiro. In my sitting room." She couldn't help asking, "Will we be able to watch it today?"

"Yes, Señora, you can watch it today," Ramiro said wearily.

Huffing and puffing with real and theatrical effort, the three men carried the heavy cabinet up the stairs and into the long, pale room overlooking the summer house, while a fourth climbed up onto the tiled roof and affixed the antenna.

Señor Ramiro bent down, fiddled with some knobs, and holding his sweaty hands out like a conjurer, said, as if he were personally responsible, "TV from the United States of America." He stepped aside as Bob Smith, several children, and the show's puppet sang the theme song. "It's Howdy Doody Time," Señor Ramiro sang along in heavily accented English, having grown addicted to it, watching Howdy each afternoon in his showroom.

"Mamacita," Florida said, clasping her hands in front of her breasts, sitting down on the sofa. "It works."

"It's magic, Señora." Marita crossed herself. "Magic."

Victor didn't say anything. He sat next to his mother, one hand on her knee, his mouth open, mesmerized.

"It is a window, Mommy," Paloma insisted.

"A window on Florida," Señor Ramiro said, and, making certain his men had gathered up their tools, left.

Armando found them in his wife's sitting room an hour later, not saying a word, simply staring at the Yankee newscast they were watching. "Traffic is light," the announcer said, "except for an accident on Biscayne Boulevard—"

"Florida, what is this?" Armando wanted to know, drowning out the announcer, startling all of them and making Marita jump.

"It's a television set," she said, turning.

"I am aware of that," Armando said somberly. "Where did it come from and how soon can it go back?"

"Oh, no, Poppy," Victor said. "It's wonderful. It's—"

"Be quiet, Victor," he said sharply. "And turn that off. I'm talking to your mother."

"Marita," Florida said, reaching over to the television set and switching it off. "Take the children downstairs and give them their supper. Tell Elena Señor Córdoba and I will be dining in a half hour."

"But, Mommy," Victor said, "I want to watch—"

"Do as you're told," Armando said. Victor took one last look at his mother, her arms crossed as if she were protecting herself, sitting on the thin

413

arm of the white sofa, looking up at his angry father. With a flutter of her hands, she urged him to go.

"I bought it with my money, Armando," Florida said when they were alone, reaching for her black and gold cigarette case, lighting one of the gold-tipped cigarettes Deliciosa continued to supply her with. "It will help the children learn English."

"So that they can share in your preoccupation with everything Yankee. So that they can run with you in the Cuban National Inferiority Sweepstakes. So that their values, their way of life, everything they have is compared—and found wanting—to what is displayed on that box. You don't have to tell me this is a Deliciosa Oliva idea, Florida." He reached for the white telephone. "I'll call Ramiro. It's going back."

Florida put her hand on the phone switch, holding it down. "It's not going back, Armando. I paid for it with my money. This is my sitting room. It is my television."

"This is my house, Florida, lest you forget. And you are my wife." He looked at her with those spit-colored eyes, and she believed that at that moment, if he could have done it, if he hadn't been brought up to be such a Cuban aristocrat, he would have hit her.

Florida looked away, at the cabinet, but she didn't give up. "You once promised me you would take me to Miami twice a year. It was the only condition I made before our marriage. We have not been to Miami in five years. Not since Paloma was born."

"There were emergencies, situations—"

"Please, Armando," she cut in. "You didn't want to go to Miami and you didn't want to honor your promise and so you found a way out. I know how your mind works, Armando. You believe that I haven't kept my part of the bargain. I gave you a son who doesn't measure up and a daughter who doesn't count—girls don't, do they?—and I can't give you any more children, so you have released yourself from your promise." She took her hand off the phone and stood up. She had been holding too much in for far too long.

"It's wonderful to be a Cuban man, isn't it?" she said, meeting his eyes. "A Córdoba, given entrée to every club. It's quite another thing to be a Cuban woman. Even a Córdoba. Oh, stop looking at me in that reproachful way, Armando. I plead guilty. I haven't lived up to your expectations." She studied the long ash growing on her cigarette. "But it's only fair for you to know that you haven't lived up to my expectations either." She put the cigarette in an ashtray, reached over and turned on the Dumont. For a long moment there was no sound in the room but static, and then sound and picture appeared. "You may consider this television as my way of going to Miami, Armando. And, please, don't you say another word about it. Or else I shall go to Miami, Armando. And I won't come back."

She turned away from him to watch a Miami announcer named Tiny Haykin nearsightedly read the six o'clock headlines from a prompter out of

414

sight of the camera . . . "Last night, in Hollywood, *An American in Paris* won the Oscar for Best Picture. Here on home turf there's report of a dawn panty raid on the University of Miami's women's dormitory. Stay tuned for details . . ."

She heard the door shut behind her and turned to the replica of the statue of the Blessed Virgin, the original of which stood in Havana's cathedral. Armando hated it, calling it a poorly executed piece of peasant idolatry. With hands trembling she touched the statue. "It wasn't easy, Mamacita," she said, "but I did it. I stood up to him. I found the strength." What she didn't admit to the statue was what she wouldn't admit to herself. Armando always backed down if faced with enough determination. Despite the Córdoba inheritance, he wasn't a brave man, her Armando.

A week later Señor Ramiro's white van reappeared at La Casa's delivery gate. When Armando came home late and went, as was his habit, to the library, which he used as a study, he came out a moment later. Florida, Victor, and Paloma stood in the black and white marble central hall, smiling and nervous.

"Aren't you going to try it?" Florida asked.

"Who . . . ?"

"You hate the TV so much, Poppy," Victor said, "and your old radio was so old, we decided to give you a new one."

"You do like it, don't you, Poppy?" Paloma, worried, asked. "Mommy says it's the very best—"

"I do like it," Armando said. "Thank you." Formally he bent down and kissed Paloma. Victor put his face up for his kiss, but his father held out his hand. "You're too old to be kissed by a man, Victor," he said, and Florida saw with an aching heart Victor's face crumple at the rejection. "From now on, like men, we shake hands." Then he turned to Florida and kissed her on both cheeks as if he were Batista rewarding a loyal colonel. Then they all trooped into the cool high-ceilinged, book-lined library and stood around the oversized desk—a replica, it was said, of one that had belonged to that first red-headed Córdoba woman.

"What's the occasion?" Armando asked, opening the radio, putting—in that precise way of his—the booklet of instructions flat on the desk.

"To show our appreciation and our love for you," Florida said. She wondered how he would have reacted if she had answered: "This is a bribe, Armando, to salve your wounded self-respect, to make up for the Dumont in the upstairs sitting room, to allow our lives to resume."

He accepted her spoken answer, and after carefully thumbing through the booklet, began to fiddle with the short wave and the long wave and all the other bands of the leather-upholstered Zenith, demonstrating its versatility. Florida soon lost interest, but Victor was enthralled by the Zenith's wires and antennae and map of the world embossed on the leather cover.

"Mommy wanted to buy you a Grundig, but Señor Ramiro said the German sets were too hard to get and he had the Zenith in stock—"

"It's fine, Victor," Armando said. "I would rather have the Zenith."

Later Armando made love to Florida for the first time since the Dumont had come into the house. Afterward she lay in the enormous old ebony bed looking at the indirect lighting, at Armando's sleeping body reflected in the pink-tinted mirror, wondering why she felt so empty. Like a man, she thought, who has just bought the favors of a prostitute he didn't particularly want.

A nightly tradition sprang up. Armando would listen to the news in the library on his Zenith radio. The rest of the family, including Marita, would watch it on the Dumont in Florida's sitting room.

"They say that Río is no longer president," Florida said over dinner some months after the Dumont's arrival.

"How did you hear?" Armando asked, his fork stopping in mid-air, indicating displeasure. She had entered a conversational arena—politics—that Cuban women were supposed to keep out of, especially when guests were present, as they were now. "The governor called this afternoon to tell me, but there was no mention of it on the news."

"The Miami television station," Florida replied. "They always have Cuban news before Radio Havana does."

The long dining room seemed especially still. Its walls were lined with watered green silk and its marble floor was covered with a huge plum-colored Chinese carpet. Juana served the beef from an enormous silver platter while Dario poured wine with his usual elegant, thin-wristed flourish. Dario should be holding that platter, Florida thought inconsequentially. It weighs half a ton. She knew better than to bring it up then or ever. Dario serving the beef would be considered heretical by everyone concerned.

She turned her attention to her guests: Armando's younger brother, Roberto, and his pretty, obedient wife, Consuela. They lived on their cattle ranch with their six children in the south, infrequently coming to Havana to shop and to see Consuela's mother. Consuela had been at convent school with Florida, but she had been too shy to be friendly with the outgoing, vivid girl her brother-in-law had married.

This being a family occasion, Victor and Paloma had been allowed to stay up for the dinner and were seated together at the long table, under the Córdoba coat of arms Florida had insisted on displaying. She had grown up with it hanging on the wall of her father's narrow dining room and found comfort in the three black doves and the large white cross.

Until Florida made her political announcement, and Armando had shown his annoyance at it, Victor had been talking away at his uncle, Roberto, who paid him a great deal of attention and had brought him, as a belated birthday present, a pair of Mexican silver cap pistols in black leather holsters.

416

"Is it true?" Florida asked, persisting, slicing into her beef. "Poor Río." Armando and Roberto, both ex-army officers, looked at her with tight lips. She wondered what made her do these things, what devil caused her to bring up this subject that she knew would only upset Armando. "Mamacita," she asked silently, "why can't I be good and quiet like Consuela?"

"It's true," Armando said after a moment.

"What will happen to Río?"

"Nothing. Batista decided to take on the titles of chief of state and premier. He's had the power all along."

"Río's sister, Christine, is going to be upset." Bored with the subject and with the meat, Florida put her fork down and smiled at Consuela. "And have you heard what the pope has proclaimed?"

"Florida is a fount of information since she got her television set," Armando said dryly.

"What did the pope proclaim, Florida?" Consuela, an extremely devout woman, spoke for the first time.

"That the Virgin Mary after her death was assumed into the heavens bodily as well as spiritually." Florida indicated to Dario and Juana that the table was to be cleared. "Isn't that beautiful?"

Armando, who had given up the Church when he was fifteen, laughed. "Can you imagine?" he asked. "What next?"

"You mustn't be sacrilegious, Poppy," Victor said. "Father Dominic says—"

"I don't give a damn what that blind fool has to say." Armando threw his napkin down on the table and glared at Florida. "I've told you hundreds of times I don't want you filling the children's heads with the mythological garbage and stinking Yankee values of your religion."

"When I grow up," Victor said, coming to his mother's protection, "I'm going to be a Yankee."

Armando reached across the table and slapped Victor's face. The sound of the slap—a flat, final noise—resounded in the dining room. Paloma reached up and traced the red outline of Armando's hand on her brother's cheek. Victor held her hand for a moment, then stood up. "May I be excused, Poppy?" he said with an adult's dignity, the Mexican silver guns riding low on his waist.

"No," Armando barked, "you may not. Sit down until this meal is finished."

Victor looked at his mother in an appeal. "Sit down, darling," she said apologetically, her heart aching for him. "Please."

No one attempted small talk. Somehow Victor got through the dinner, sniffling just once, willing himself not to cry. Paloma offered him her dessert—a rich rum cake Elena excelled at—but he shook his head, afraid if he spoke he would cry. He couldn't look at anyone—certainly not at his uncle, Roberto—so he kept his eyes on the intricate lace tablecloth that so resembled Aunt Consuela's dress. Finally, when the dessert dishes had been taken away and Armando had finished his coffee, he looked at Victor. "You are excused. Tomorrow morning I expect a formal apology. I want you to take that holster off and return those guns to your uncle. You don't deserve them. For a month there will be no television and no swimming at the club."

"But, Armando," Florida said, "he has to practice—"

"My word, Florida, is final. Remember, you are the woman in this house—not the man."

Victor undid the holster. Eyes down, summoning all his strength to keep the tears back, he handed it to Roberto and then, forcing himself not to run, walked out of the dining room. Florida looked at that perfect Córdoba wife, Consuela. Pale with embarrassment, staring down at her hands in her lap and then up at Armando, she said finally, "I will try to remember my role, Armando. In the meanwhile I too wish to be excused." She stood up, her green eyes sparking with fury. "I am going to put Paloma to bed. And then I am going to see to Victor. And then, Armando, I am going to pray." She touched Consuela, who had pulled her white wool stole around her as if she had had a sudden chill. "I am so sorry to have put *you* through this." She took Paloma's hand and, ignoring Armando, left the dining room.

Later, kneeling in her sitting room in front of the stone carving of the Virgin Mary, Florida closed her eyes and prayed. "I don't know what to do, Blessed Mother. Please advise me." She knew she should try to be a good Cuban wife, obedient and self-effacing. There was no doubt that what had happened tonight was her fault. She had wanted to show Consuela what an independent woman she was, and all she had done was create more distance between her son and his father, between her husband and herself.

She knew now that Victor's height had little to do with Armando's lack of love for his son. Victor was too much like his father, and that frightened Armando. Any possibility that he might not be in total control frightened Armando.

If she were a Protestant, she would divorce him and go live in the United States. She would take Victor and Paloma and find a new sort of life. But divorce was not a word that even existed within her Church. She had no choice but to stay with Armando and make the best of her situation.

"Please, Blessed Mother," she prayed, "give me the wisdom and the strength to change." She needed the Virgin's assistance to be more like Consuela, meek and kind, able to turn the other cheek. She prayed for guidance to help Armando and her children, guidance to help herself.

Hours later she walked quietly into the darkened bedroom, sensing Armando was awake. For once he had forgotten to tell Marita to close the louvers. Florida could see through the green-painted slats the outline of the fine old coconut palms silhouetted against the moonlit sky. She heard him sigh, signaling to her that he was awake.

She sat down on the edge of the old bed, took his hand, and held it. "I apologize, Armando. From the bottom of my heart. It was all my fault. I provoked you. I will make every effort not to do that again. I shall try to be the wife you want me to be, Armando. Will you forgive me?"

He sat up and looked at her in the dim indirect Yankee lighting. "Roberto says I am too hot-tempered. That it was my fault. That I am lucky to have you. That you are a true Córdoba woman. That I don't know how to treat you." He kissed her lips. "He's right of course. I will try not to be such a tyrant in the future, Florida. I will try to be more patient with Victor. Roberto left the guns for him, and he can have them after he apologizes." He kissed her again, with more urgency. "I will forgive you if you can forgive me. I don't understand anything about you, Florida." His long, gentle surgeon's hands went around her waist, pulling her to him. "Not one thing. You are a total mystery to me. But I need you. It's difficult for me to say, but after all this time I want you as much as I did on that first day of our life together. I love you, Floridita. You are my life."

"I love you, Armando," she said, wondering, even as he made needy, anxious love to her, whether that was indeed true. As she gave herself to him she realized that love didn't matter; according to the Church, according to Cuban custom, she had no choice.

CHAPTER THREE

1954

"I WANT THE TOP DOWN, Mommy. I want the top down."

"Everyone will look at us," Paloma objected. She and Marita were in the rear, shoulders back, heads up, their spines barely touching the seat, looking like disapproving aunts up from the country. Neither of them trusted the new smell of the slippery leather upholstery or, more especially, Florida behind the wheel. Florida disregarded them, switching on the ignition. The engine, coming to life, gave a satisfactory roar. Marita jumped.

"We *want* everyone to look at us," Victor said. "That's the point, Paloma." Victor was twelve years old and still the shortest boy in his class. His lack of height didn't appear to bother him. The only time he wasn't flashing that Córdoba smile, it seemed, was when he was with his father.

"You mustn't be such an old lady, Paloma," her mother said, pushing a switch on the futuristic dashboard. The four of them watched the canvas top rear up like a mortally stricken jungle animal, waver in the air, and then neatly collapse into the pocket behind the rear seat. Marita closed her eyes, crossed herself, and reached for Paloma's hand.

Florida, ignoring the waves of disapproval emanating from the backseat, put the car into drive and sped through the tall cast-iron gates, out of La Casa's main entrance, thrilled at the power the car had. It was a new Buick, gunmetal blue, with a tan convertible top and tan leather interior. It boasted wire wheels, thick, fat whitewall tires, and a chrome grill that looked as if it could eat a man alive. Dario had spent the morning giving it its first coat of protective polish. The hood reflected the palm trees and mansions that lined the Via de la Rosa.

"Why isn't Dario driving, Mommy?" Paloma called out. She was seven years old, and in her experience only women in Yankee films and television programs drove automobiles. Often they were laughed at for doing so. Beaver's mother had dented the new family Pontiac only the week before, and there had been much soul-searching before Beaver's dad found out and gave his weekly lecture.

"Because this is Mommy's car." Victor was so proud, he couldn't stand it—everyone *was* looking at them. "And Mommy's learned to drive." He turned to look at his mother, her flame-red hair flying loosely in the wind, her green eyes on the road ahead, expertly coping with the powerful car and the Saturday morning traffic.

They had to stop on the Paseo de Coronado in front of the Villa Riviera. The occupants of the cars around them stared at Florida, trying to decide if she was a cabaret performer or the mistress of someone important. Victor watched his mother put on her oversized dark sunglasses. The glasses and her white dress heightened her glamour. She looked like a film star but not one he could name. Florida had her own celebrity.

"Faster, Mommy," he said, putting his left hand on the back of her seat. "I can't be late for dive practice."

"I don't want to go fast, Mommy," Paloma said, holding onto Marita's hand.

"We're not going fast, Paloma," Florida said, unable to resist gunning the car, leaving the gawkers behind. "Victor has plenty of time."

With her free hand Paloma smoothed her gray skirt then let her hand rest on its embroidered black poodle. Florida had brought it back with her from Miami, a present from Deliciosa. It was Paloma's favorite possession. "When I grow up," Paloma said to herself, touching the poodle with its pink rhinestone eye, "I want to be just like Annette." Each Saturday afternoon the Dumont and the upstairs sitting room were reserved for Paloma and her two best friends, Tia and Ramona. They wore sweaters and skirts and watched *Teen Bandstand*, imitating the lindy.

"And when I grow up," Victor said, turning in his seat, making pistols of

420

his fingers, aiming at a passing car, "I'm going to be Broderick Crawford. *Arriba las manos!* Put up your hands!" Victor was a devotee of *Highway Patrol*, dubbed into Spanish and broadcast each Thursday night on Havana television. *"Arriba las manos,"* he said again, perfectly imitating the Spanish actor who dubbed in Crawford's dialogue. His corrupt angel's red lips curled in a terrible smile when he said it, and he said it constantly. It had become one of his trademarks along with his side-of-the-mouth gangster delivery, his cocky, choreographed Cagney strut.

Victor's charm was his most potent weapon. Even in the small, fierce world of his boys' school he won over teachers, older boys, bullies. He won over everyone save Armando. We are such different parents, Florida thought, driving past the guarded gates that led to the Miramar's clubhouse. I cry when they cry and then go out wanting to murder whoever hurt them. Armando assumes it's their fault to begin with.

"Mommy," Paloma asked anxiously, "are you always going to drive?"

"Whenever we use my car," Florida said, pulling up under the club's elaborate canopy and handing the keys to the attendant, who tried and failed not to show surprise.

Victor was already out of the car, racing toward the cabanas to change into his swim suit. "Poky Señorita Paloma," Florida said, reaching for her daughter's hand, holding it for a moment, looking into those familiar green eyes. "I like to drive, Paloma. It makes me feel less helpless."

"But none of the other mothers drive," Paloma said anxiously. "Poppies are supposed to drive."

"That's only true here, Paloma."

Paloma stopped for a moment on the palm-lined flagstone walkway, looking down at her black and white saddle shoes—another present from Deliciosa—holding her mother's hand. "Dario's not going to have to leave, is he, Mommy?" she asked in a thin voice.

"No," Florida said, kissing her daughter, holding her, realizing that the possible loss of Dario was what had been bothering her from the beginning. She was the sort of child who was always bringing home half-dead birds and kittens, who cried when she saw the blindered horses pulling the tourist carriages downtown, around El Capitolio. She was the sort of child who invariably took up impossible causes. "Dario is not going to have to leave, darling."

Holding hands, Marita trailing behind them, they walked through the flagstone-floored clubhouse, smiling at employees and club members, recognized and recognizable. At home. Leaving the clubhouse, they walked around the huge rectangular swimming pool and up a series of steps to the cabana Armando had been renting since their marriage. It was a low, small, pink stucco building in a row of similar structures with a floor of terra cotta tile, a white-tiled bathroom, and a turquoise-and-white-striped canvas awning. There was a small hot plate on which Marita heated up coffee and

421

occasionally soup, an important Sears, Roebuck half-sized refrigerator, a wicker sofa bed for afternoon naps, a white telephone, a shallow closet with a louvered door, and several rattan chairs and occasional tables.

The exclusive Miramar Club, Florida thought idly, changing into her bikini, *de rigueur* for the upper-class women in their thirties who spent their days tanning in front of their cabanas. Deliciosa, in their Monday telephone calls, always oohed and aahed when the club was mentioned.

"I loathe the club," Florida told her. "I swim in the pool, I eat and drink at the table set up in front of the cabana, and I'm sometimes so bored I play canasta with Catherine and Tina de Mars and cousin Flavia de Córdoba. We are all so bitchy and depressed we can hardly stand the sight of one another. Armando and I celebrate New Year's and sometimes Christmas day at the club. The children, when not at school, are at the club. Our husbands always know where to find us. If we're not at home, we're at the club. Don't waste your envy, Deliciosa. It's only another jail."

Paloma, accompanied as always by her Marita, had gone off to look for Tia and Ramona at the smaller, round pool, on the far side of the tennis courts. Florida tipped the boy who had opened the canvas umbrella and was turning over the mattress on the chaise longue, wrapping it in a thick white terrycloth towel. She asked him to bring her a Coke from the bar, though she knew there was one in the cabana's refrigerator. Somehow bar Cokes tasted better. She lay on the chaise under the umbrella sipping from the tall frosted glass, staring at the familiar scene. Waiters, in club livery—white Eisenhower jackets with blue piping, black trousers—outnumbered the members two to one. They moved about constantly and intently as if they were dancers performing some complicated modern ballet.

She and Paloma had been much interested in a news broadcast that showed children taking over for a day the duties of the mayor's office in a small Florida town. Perhaps, she thought, we should take over, just for a day, the duties of the club servants. They could loll in the sun while we brought them bar Cokes and turkey sandwiches, don't spare the Russian dressing. They could experience the boredom of an idyll—

"Darling," Christine Machado said, interrupting her fantasy, using her index finger to pull her sunglasses down to the edge of her nose. The frames, swooping and swirling like a quattrocento mask, were pavéed rhinestones. "I hear you have the most marvelous new auto." She had sprawled on the adjoining chaise, her carefully dyed blond hair wrapped in a turban, her somewhat ripe body looking like a figure eight in her black bathing suit. She smelled of Coppertone and Chanel No. 5. "We're all trying to guess who gave it to you." She removed the sunglasses and turned over, expertly undoing her bra straps with one hand, exposing her fleshy back to the midafternoon sun.

"We haven't seen much of you lately," Christine continued but was cut off by Victor, shouting from the edge of the high diving board. "Mommy," he called, and everyone around the pool looked up. "Watch this."

422

He was too short, they had told him at school, for baseball, that Cuban preoccupation. But he made up for it with his swimming. At twelve he was already a member of the formidable Miramar swim team, competing against other clubs in Havana, Kingston, San Juan, and Miami.

He stood poised at the edge of the high board, his white-gray eyes half closed, putting all of his concentration into what he was going to do next. There was a long silent second, and Victor sprang up into the air, held for a moment, defying gravity, then allowed himself to come down without a wasted movement. The dive had been so beautifully and daringly executed, the people sunning themselves around the Miramar pool clapped.

"He's like one of those flying blue fish one observes at sea," Christine said. "Victor's so young to be so beautiful."

"Paloma's not nearly as fast," Florida said, not liking the look in Christine's eye, taking refuge in mother talk. "But she has wonderful form. She's just made the team as well."

"Are you going to allow her to go with them when they compete out of Cuba?" Christine asked, rejecting Florida's proffered black lacquer case, lighting Florida's cigarette and then fishing a Camel out of her own case.

"When she's old enough."

Christine looked at her and smiled. She was wearing large, round gold earrings that caught the sun and reflected in miniature the scene in front of them. She was, Florida thought, a person who took delight in diminishing the pleasure of others. "And are you old enough to strike out on your own, Florida, darling? We haven't seen very much of you lately. I might as well tell you, there's talk. Those three weeks in Miami sans Armando. That wonderfully vulgar new auto and this extraordinary new driving skill. All these developments presage some cataclysm. One suspects you've become an independent woman at last." She used her thumb and her forefinger to removed a shred of tobacco from her long, dark tongue.

"Independent like you, Christine?"

"Darling, I was independent with a parking-lot attendant two nights after my honeymoon. I shan't forget him. That child made superman look like a castrato." She took a drag and laughed. "Only trouble was, I found out I was sharing him with Jimmy. I suppose that's what made me marry Jimmy in the first place. We have such similar tastes." Jimmy was Jaime Machado, whose grandfather had been Cuba's first dictator. His wife turned on her side and looked appraisingly at Florida. "You've always been such a good little faithful woman. We've all been waiting for you to break out of your cage. Tell me. Who is he?"

"Telling you, Christine, would be like breaking out of one trap and into another." Florida stood up and went to her cabana, grabbing her wraparound skirt and her blouse.

"Where are you going, darling?"

"For a breath of clean air. Please tell Marita I'll pick her and the children up at five."

"Did your husband buy you the Buick?" Christine asked before Florida could get away. "We all assumed it was someone else. I hope it's not Jimmy. He's had his eye on you for years. But don't get too excited. Jimmy's not all that discriminating. Anyway, we all took a vote and decided Armando didn't have the time to go out and buy you a car. He's so busy with that rather alarming nurse of his."

Florida drove out to the beach at Cojimar, parking under the ancient sea grape trees, their branches low with fruit. Elena hasn't made sea grape jelly in years, she thought, putting on the dark sunglasses, looking across the white sand and out across the mild ocean toward where she thought Florida should be. It was an out-of-the-way beach, and even on a Saturday morning there was only one couple there. The man was stretched out on a red-and-yellow-striped towel, his hands behind his head. The woman's dark head rested on his chest. A portable radio, antenna up, was tuned in to a Miami station. Perry Como was singing a song about a man in love with a mannequin in a department store window. The couple, the scene, even the ocean looked rehearsed.

Florida inhaled, letting the warm, comforting, salty air fill her body. She put her hands on the leather-upholstered steering wheel, liking its sturdy, luxurious feel. I've escaped, if only for a moment. She thought of Christine, another caged animal, trying to find some sort of relief in that fetid sexuality of hers.

She lit one of Deliciosa's gold-tipped cigarettes and put her head back against the rich, soft leather seat. Deliciosa is always going on about how lucky she is to have me for a friend. I'm the lucky one, Florida thought, picturing that pink and rosy and newly ash blond friend of hers, missing her more than Deliciosa would ever know.

"We could both get divorces," Deliciosa had said. "They're so easy here. All you do is get on a plane for Reno. With the money I'd get from Bebe we could open a shop, a very snob shop, up in Palm Beach on Worth Avenue . . ."

Divorce was a Yankee option, Florida had said. "You're a Yankee," Deliciosa, caught up in her fantasy, told her. "You were born here, Florida."

But she was Cuban and her children were Cuban, and divorce was not a Cuban option. "I wouldn't have known what to do without Deliciosa," Florida said to herself, thinking of her last birthday, that day of betrayal.

Her birthday came on the fifth of September, which had been a sultry, still Monday. The nervous Sunday-night-television weatherman had talked of a hurricane, but the stylish morning weather girl reported it had gone, blessedly, out to sea. She had planned to attend late morning Mass and spend the afternoon at the club with the children. An ordinary birthday, her thirty-fourth.

424

Armando had asked if she wanted to go to a nightclub—Xavier Cugat and Abbe Lane were at the Tropicana—but she had declined, saying she wanted a simple dinner at home. Elena was going to make her favorite meal: ropa vieja, to be followed by an orange birthday cake.

Armando had returned that Sunday night from a week-long medical conference in Barbados. It was exhausting, he said. He had even been too tired to make love, odd after a week's absence. They had been getting on better lately. She had been feeling not unhappily resigned. At thirty-four Florida knew exactly what the rest of her life was going to be like. Consuela had been spending more time in Havana—her mother was ill—and the sisters-in-law had taken to attending morning Mass together. Consuela lit candles and prayed and talked to her confessor about her minute transgressions. Florida knelt in front of the gray stone statue of the Blessed Mother and found consolation. It's only a life sentence, she told herself. After this there's an eternity to be at peace.

Consuela had called that birthday morning to say she couldn't attend early Mass. The heart specialist Armando had recommended had suddenly had a free appointment and Consuela was taking her mother to him. Armando had left for the institute early, the children had begun their second week of the new school year, and the servants were in the kitchen listening to another installment of their favorite soap opera on Armando's old radio.

Florida decided she wouldn't go to Mass. She would spend the morning in bed. She stretched idly, finishing the coffee Marita had hurriedly brought her before running off to the kitchen and the radio. Perhaps she would treat herself to a telephone call to Deliciosa. Armando complained about long-distance telephone calls, and she had spoken to Deliciosa only two days before, but still, it was her birthday.

She was reaching for the telephone when it rang. "Deliciosa," Florida said into the phone, laughing, certain who it was.

"I am sorry, Señora Córdoba," an unfamiliar voice said. "This is Señorita Muñez. Nancy Muñez. I don't suppose you remember me, Señora Córdoba."

"I'm sorry, I don't," Florida said, cradling the white phone on her shoulder, searching for her cigarette case on the crowded bedside table. The woman's voice was educated and classless, but there was an attitude, a subservient way of hesitating before she addressed Florida. Florida conjectured, as she lit the gold-tipped cigarette, that she was someone's secretary, calling for a charitable donation.

"I used to be your husband's receptionist, Señora Córdoba."

"I'm sorry. I so rarely go to the institute . . ."

"He let me go a year ago, Señora Córdoba. I took a job as a receptionist with Doctor Felix Guitano. Then—"

"Señorita, uhm, Muñez, I have a full morning," Florida lied, impatient with the woman. "If you could tell me what this call is in reference to . . ."

There was a long hesitation and then the woman said, "Your husband used to have relations with me two or three times a week, Señora Córdoba. Usually during the afternoon. He'd call me into the examining room and put me on the table and make love to me. It didn't mean very much to him. It was a release for him. Most times he didn't even take off his clothes. I was a convenience." She paused, waiting for some response. When none came, she went on. "Yet it meant a great deal to me, Señora Córdoba. I loved him. I did whatever he asked me to. But he hired a new receptionist and got me the job with Dr. Guitano right after Eva Lopaz came to work for him. She's his chief nurse, Señora Córdoba."

Florida put out the cigarette and said into the shameful silence, "I don't want to hear any more, Señorita." She had already lost the woman's name. "I'm going to hang up—"

"No, wait," the woman said desperately. "Dr. Guitano took me to the conference in Barbados. Your husband was with Eva Lopaz. They had adjoining rooms at the hotel. They never attended any of the seminars, Señora Córdoba. Dr. Guitano says Eva Lopaz plays your husband, Señora Córdoba, like Liberace plays his piano. Eva Lopaz, Señora Córdoba—"

Florida replaced the phone and lit another cigarette. She thought she should cry. "Women always cry when they find their husbands have been sleeping with other women, don't they?" she asked herself, feeling remarkably dry-eyed.

Perhaps it was a lie, revenge on the part of a discarded employee? But she thought of the increasing amounts of time Armando was spending away from La Casa, of Christine Machado's innuendos, of Armando's heavy and insistent sexuality. Suddenly, needing proof, Florida got out of bed and went to his dressing room, opening the basket in which he put his soiled clothes. Juana had not collected them yet. She fished out a new shirt, one he had bought in Barbados. It was made from some silky material, yellow with green stripes and so unlike him as to be an indictment in itself. Like a television wife, she had expected to find lipstick on the collar, but the collar was clean. Florida crumpled up the shirt and, just before dropping it back into the laundry basket, put it to her nose. It smelled of Armando and of Jungle Gardenia.

She had met Eva Lopaz once, quickly, when she had delivered to his office some document Armando had left at home. She remembered Nurse Lopaz as being milk-colored and young and very much in control. Someone—was it Armando?—had said she was a left-wing intellectual, a socialist. A fragment of a conversation came back to her. They had been at a party at the club and Armando had been talking to a doctor he thought superficial. "Eva Lopaz," he had said, "understands better than anyone I've ever met the need for social reform in this country."

She tried, but she couldn't bring nurse Lopaz's features to mind. All she could remember of her was that insistent perfume she wore, Jungle Gardenia. She reminded me, Florida thought, putting out her fifth cigarette of the morning, of a French chocolate bar. Thin and milky. Expensive for a cheap treat.

426

She looked out through the open slats of the louvers at the yellow day and left the bedroom for her sitting room. She stared at the statue of the Holy Mother for some moments and then got down on her knees and tried to pray. For once prayer and her Mamacita failed her. "I live my life in a doorless, cardboard house," she told herself. "I should have the strength to break out, but I don't." She got up off her knees, rang for Marita and Dario, gave them instructions, and then put through a call to Deliciosa. It was uncharacteristically short and to the point.

She spent the rest of the day smoking, waiting for the children to come home from the club. She explained she would be away for a short while, steeling herself against the tears in Victor's gray-white eyes, the confusion in Paloma's green ones. She gave Marita instructions and a telephone number. The children were to call her every day when they arrived home from school. Otherwise she could be reached only for emergencies. "Señor Córdoba is not to have the number, Marita."

"But if he asks me, Señora, what am I to do?"

"You had best give it to him, Marita," Florida said, embracing her, realizing that Marita would have no choice, that she couldn't resist Armando. "But only if he asks."

Two hours later she was in Miami's irritating, confusing airport, being embraced and kissed by the new ash-blond Deliciosa, one of the Oliva servants trailing behind them as they went to the space reserved for Deliciosa's car. Not unpredictably, it was an enormous white Eldorado convertible. What was unexpected, however, was that Deliciosa put the servant in the rear and took the driver's seat. "I'll put the top up if you want to cry," Deliciosa had said, wiping the tears from her own eyes. "That bastard."

"I'm not going to cry, Deliciosa," Florida said. But later, in Deliciosa's sitting room, Deliciosa's arms around her, of course she did.

Armando arrived on Saturday morning, looking gray and serious and irritated. He had a cold, and the tip of his large aristocratic nose was red, his deep voice husky. The flight hadn't done him any good. Deliciosa, after providing him with a cup of tea, had left them alone in her sitting room. Florida had sat on a pale brocade sofa, smoking. Armando had stood at the window pretending to look at Biscayne Bay, holding a handkerchief to his nose.

He began with an attack. "I could hardly believe you took refuge with the Olivas, Florida. He's a gangster and she's—"

"The Olivas, my very dear friends, are not the issue, Armando." She wouldn't defend herself in any way; she wasn't the one on trial.

"Eva Lopaz is nothing to me," he had said, giving in, turning to look at her, putting the handkerchief in his pocket.

"You're not denying—"

"No," he had said impatiently, walking away from the windows. "Stop this nonsense and come home with me, Florida." He stood over her, looking down at her with those concrete-colored eyes, red-rimmed from his cold. He had reached for her hand, but she turned away, stood up, and moved around him.

She found an ashtray. He tried, awkwardly, to light her cigarette, but by the time he had struck a match, she had lit it with a table lighter. She propped herself up against the blond wood desk from which Deliciosa made her telephone calls. She folded her arms. "Señorita Lopaz has already found other employment," he said. "I've engaged a new nurse."

"That, apparently, hasn't stopped you before."

"Please, Florida. Señora Henriques is a married woman of fifty-five." He sneezed helplessly and fumbled for his handkerchief. Outside, a sad September drizzle had begun, making the day worse. Florida felt hopeless, unhappy. Sorry for him and for herself.

"Florida, come home with me, now," he said, coming as close as he could to pleading. "The children—"

"The children!" The anger came back, surprising her. "As if you ever gave any thought to the children. You want your wife back in place so you can continue your game, playing socialist with Eva Lopaz."

"I told you, she's already—"

"All right, Armando," she said, feeling played out, the leading lady on the closing night of a bad play. She looked at the cup of tea he was sipping and wished she had one herself. I want to go to bed, she thought, and be ill and waited on. "I will return to Havana. But not for another two weeks. You can say I am on vacation. I plan to take a number of vacations in Miami Beach in the future." She had avoided meeting his eyes, but she did so now. "There will, of course, be no more Eva Lopaz. That is agreed?"

"It is agreed," he said, putting the teacup down. "I've told you—"

"You've told me a great many things in the past, Armando." She put out her cigarette—it was obviously aggravating his sinuses—walked to the door and opened it. "You have been invited for lunch, but I assume you don't want to eat with the Olivas. I shall see you on the first of October, Armando. I should get over my hurt by then and we can resume our lives." She stood in the doorway looking up at him, thinking she wasn't afraid of him any longer. I am, she thought, resigned to him. "There will be some changes, but most of them won't affect you."

He started to kiss her but sneezed instead, pulling out a new handkerchief—his pockets were stuffed with them—just in time. Florida supposed she might have imagined it, but she was nearly certain she caught a whiff of Jungle Gardenia from that handkerchief.

"I'd better not kiss you, Floridita," he said, trying to smile, his eyes watery, his head filled with his cold.

"No, you'd better not kiss me, Armando."

"I'll make it up to you," he said, touching her shoulder with his fine spatulate surgeon's fingers. "Things will be the same again, I promise you, Floridita."

428

"I don't want things to be the same again, Armando." She watched him walk across the wide, skylight-lit landing and down the circular stairs and felt a wave of something like compassion for him. He's as much a prisoner as I am, Florida thought. He just doesn't know it.

Florida spent the mornings of the next two weeks taking driving lessons from the instructor at the Miami Beach Quadruple-A Driving School who had taught Deliciosa. Every afternoon she and Deliciosa lunched and shopped and laughed and fantasized about the shop they would open if only Florida could convince Armando to move to Miami Beach.

"You could stay here," Deliciosa said on that last morning as they sat in the white Eldorado at the airport saying goodbye.

"I would if I thought for a moment I could live without Paloma and Victor. Someday perhaps," Florida said, squeezing Deliciosa's hand, kissing that fat cheek, not wanting to get out of that upholstered shoebox of a car, holding on for just another moment to the warmth and comfort and love her friend gave her. "Someday," she said, forcing herself to move.

Armando had taken the time to come with Dario and the cavernous Cadillac to meet her at the airport. He had recovered from his cold, and she let him kiss her. He smelled of bay rum and medicine, but she wasn't reassured. She felt a perverse comfort as they neared Havana—Armando was to be let off at the institute—like that of a recidivist being returned to a familiar cell. Everything would be the same. Armando would make love to her that night. She would find solace in the morning at early Mass, drink bar Cokes in the afternoon at the club, and watch the United States in the evening on the Dumont. Armando might or might not discontinue making love to nurse Lopaz on his examining room table. She suspected that Eva Lopaz was still around, that she was more than a convenient biological receptacle for Armando. He was an armchair socialist. Eva Lopaz, Florida guessed, was an active comrade.

It didn't matter. None of it mattered. She felt as empty, as barren, as useless as the club swimming pool during its annual recementing. As Dario brought the Cadillac to a stop for a street light in front of the Hotel Nacional, she looked across the boulevard at the huge glass General Motors showroom. Next to it was a billboard with Batista's picture and the slogan: *Muchas problemas. La solución? Batista presidente.* In the showroom the Buick, turning slowly on a revolving platform, looked as if it were a rocket about to fly off into the sky.

Armando, giving her hand a squeeze, kissing her affectionately on the cheek, got out in front of the ancient stone Córdoba Institute of Nephrology. "I am glad you are back, Floridita," he said, and though she knew he meant it, she found herself unable to care. She told Dario to take her to the General Motors showroom. If I can't have freedom, Florida decided, thinking of

429

women in Miami Beach driving their own cars, leading their own lives, I want at least the illusion of it.

"I want to buy that Buick," she told the salesman, who didn't quite know how to deal with her.

"For your husband?" he asked.

"For myself."

CHAPTER FOUR

1958–1959

THE MIRAMAR CLUB DINING ROOM'S mirrored ceiling never failed to distract Florida. Whenever she dined there she had a compulsion to look up and see who was reflected in those six-foot lengths of gold-flecked mirror. As always, there were the Eisenhower-jacketed waiters and busboys, the well-cared-for women and the custom-suited men, and the Miramar band playing soft music as accompaniment to the conversation. And I'm dead center, Florida thought, looking up at her face framed by flaming red hair, electrified by her questioning green eyes. Mamacita, what am I doing in the middle of all this?

"What are you looking at?" Armando asked, for something to say. They were waiting for Paloma and Victor. Paloma had been given a special Christmas-afternoon treat, allowed to go to the movies with her friends and, of course, Marita. Florida had let Victor borrow the Buick, and he and his "gang of hoodlums"—Armando's phrase—had gone off on some pursuit she resolutely didn't want to know about. "What are you looking at, Floridita?" Armando asked again, placing his spatulate fingers on the back of her chair.

"Us. A brilliant and handsome surgeon, of impeccable lineage, in his prime. And his thirty-eight-year-old wife, clinging gently to him as they weather the sea of life."

Armando shook his head and smiled. He never knew how to respond to Florida's ironies and had learned not to try. Florida took a last glance upward and lowered her head, not liking what she had seen. She was wearing a silk dress she had bought in Miami Beach the year before at Deliciosa's urging ("Darling, it is *you*") and had never worn. Marita had remembered it, unearthing it from who knew where, saying it was the perfect dress for the season. It didn't suit her, and it wasn't a Christmas red at all, but Florida had put it on to please Marita.

Following tradition, she and Paloma had taken Marita, Juana, and Elena to morning Mass at the cathedral that morning. Florida and Paloma had prayed to the Blessed Virgin while the servants, intimidated, cautiously lit candles. Paloma had sat perfectly still in the smoky, incense-filled place, following the Mass with as much intensity as if it were her favorite television program.

"They're late," Armando said, looking at his wristwatch, taking an unwanted sip from his Cuba libre.

"It's Christmas day. The films probably began late." She looked at that handsome face and realized Armando was disturbed about something. She put her hand on his, and he attempted a smile. "What's wrong, Armando?"

He finished the Cuba libre and uncharacteristically signaled the waiter to bring another. "What could be wrong?" he asked, looking at her with those other-worldly eyes. Then he gave in just a little. "I'm worried about the political situation. The rebels. Batista would shoot me for saying it, but they have a lot of support in the country and some not bad ideas."

"Really, Armando," Florida said impatiently. "The rebels have as much chance of toppling the government as all the other rebels have had over the years. The Miami newscasters don't even mention the rebels." The rebels and their cause were hazy and undefined in her mind. There was some insurgency going on in the south or in the mountains, she couldn't remember which. "I thought you were medical, not political," she said, trying the old expression, worried about this new introspection he had developed over the past months.

But Armando remained stiff and proper and distant. He's frightened about something, Florida thought. She couldn't get herself to believe that this new mood of his was being caused by a handful of students firing rifles in the air in some distant province. She felt a sudden fear, thinking of his recent annual medical examination, wondering if he was holding something back.

She was going to ask when he gave the first genuine smile of the evening. Paloma, in a new poodle skirt (courtesy of Deliciosa) supported by half a dozen stiff petticoats, was making her way across the crowded dining room, turning once to wave at Marita, who stood at the door.

"Poppy," she said before she even reached the table, "there was a huge balloon, and they all went up and away in it, flying round the world, and Cantinflas. . . ." She and Tia and Ramona had seen *Around the World in Eighty Days*. She asked for a Coke and gave them a nonstop and detailed summation of the plot.

Armando listened attentively to his daughter, touching her flame-red hair, looking into her impossibly green eyes. She was nearly as tall as her brother, gawky and shy and graceful and bold all at the same time. It was clear she would grow into her beauty in the next year or two. When she was very young Armando had ignored her, but as she had grown up, learned to be a

431

fine swimmer, brought home glowing reports from her convent teachers, and become better and better to look at, he had found himself loving her. "She is a real Córdoba," he liked to say, as if Victor were an impostor.

When he had asked her what she wanted for Christmas, Paloma had shocked him by saying she wanted to be taken to the Tropicana. "Poppy," she had said seriously as if she had had a chance, "chorus girls descend on trapezes from palm trees. I saw them on television. They're so beautiful. I would love to see them, Poppy. I would love to hear the music and look at all the people dancing—"

"Paloma, eleven-year-old girls do not go to the Tropicana." He had given her a gold circle pin instead, one she had been longing for, the kind Yankee college girls wore. And on Christmas Eve day he took her, all by herself, without Florida or Victor—certainly without Victor—to Harry's American Bar for lunch. It had been filled with Yankees, men in dark suits and women wearing large picture hats. It had been nearly as good as the Tropicana, and now this last, unexpected treat had topped everything.

"I should like to be a balloonist when I grow up," Paloma said, folding her neat hands, looking up at her image in the mirrored ceiling and then at her father.

"I thought you were going to be the girl on the television who tells everyone the weather," Florida said, smoothing her daughter's hair.

"That too. Poppy, do you think I could see that film again? Just once more? It was so wonderful. And next time I should like to go without Marita. I have no privacy, Poppy. None. I might as well be living in a glass bowl."

"Where else would a goldfish live?" Armando asked, touching that hair again, not at all certain he wanted her to grow up.

Paloma was aware, through Victor's hints, of other Havanas, dark and mysterious and half alluring, half repugnant. She was driven to the school each morning by Dario in the old Cadillac, picked up by Florida in the Buick each afternoon. The only time she ever felt private and free was when she was in the club pool swimming. She outswam every other girl on the team and many of the boys.

Paloma stopped talking only when Victor appeared magically at the table, like the devil in the school play. Paloma almost looked for his cloud of smoke. She loved her mother with certain reservations ("Why does she have to drive a car? Why can't she be like other mothers?") and her father unconditionally, but she idolized Victor.

He smiled that cocky smile, as if he had just stolen a million dollars and was going back for more. He looked so much like a smaller version of his father, he might have posed for a period schoolboy photograph of Armando. "Where have you been?" Armando asked, getting that stern look on his face Paloma feared. She didn't know what the trouble was between her father and her brother, but it was always there, solid, like a wall without windows. "And fix your tie. You're not some little Miami Beach gangster, much as you'd like to be one. You're a Córdoba. Try to act like one."

432

Victor tightened his tie, his muscles straining against the dark suit jacket as he did so. He was sixteen and far too short, but he never mentioned his height, and neither did anyone else. He was enormously popular, the first in his crowd of wild, upper-class boys to smoke a cigar, to drink hard liquor, to drive a car, to have a woman. He kissed his mother and then Paloma, making too much of it, as if he were an actor in a silent movie and needed grand gestures to communicate. He sat between Paloma and Florida, smelling a little of beer, displacing the happiness that had been at the table.

"Aren't you going to say hello to your father?" Florida asked.

"He didn't say hello to me, did he?" Victor asked, smiling. "Okay," he said in English. "Let's take it from the top." He stood up abruptly, getting the attention of everyone at the nearby tables. With that choreographed Jimmy Cagney strut, he walked back to the entrance, winked at the maître d'hôtel, and then casually sauntered back to their table. "Hello, Mother," he said. "Paloma." Then, turning to Armando, executing a little bow, he said, "Hello, Poppy. Merry Christmas, Poppy."

Florida was afraid Armando was going to explode, but the waiter came to take their orders, Paloma again launched into the story of the film at the Alcazar, and Victor talked—to Florida—about an upcoming swim meet in San Juan. Armando even made an effort, asking Victor questions about the meet. In this way they managed to get through Christmas dinner.

During that week between Christmas and New Year's the rebels began to be taken more seriously. On Saturday, at the club, Christine Machado said she had a cousin who had been at medical school with the leader.

"Are they bad guys?" Paloma asked, sitting next to her mother under the umbrella. It was a warm Cuban December Saturday, and the Miramar Club was crowded.

"They're dumb guys, Paloma," Christine said, undoing her bikini bra, lying flat on her chaise longue. "That doctor is never going to be able to practice again. Not medicine, at any rate. Or much of anything else if Fulgencio Batista gets his hands on him."

"In Current Events," Paloma said to Christine's Bain de Soleiled back, "Mother Ursula read in El Diario that the rebels had 'suffered a violent beating.'"

"Is that the sort of thing they're reading in convent school nowadays? About violent beatings?" Christine asked, mystifying Paloma, as she often did. "You'd better look into this Mother Ursula, Florida. You don't want the child corrupted."

Two days after Christmas, Consuela, Roberto, their five children, and half a dozen servants came in from their ranch to stay at Consuela's mother's enormous old house on Havana's East Side. "I asked Roberto what the rebels are rebelling against," Consuela said, confused and frightened, covering her fair head with white lace as she and Florida entered the old cathedral for early morning Mass. "He said, 'Everything.'"

"Miami television says that Batista's troops have the situation well in hand," Florida said, turning to the Blessed Virgin's outstretched gray composite arms, thinking that she had to stop using newscaster language. She was beginning to feel that nothing was "well in hand." She didn't tell Consuela, who seemed genuinely upset, that Miami television received its news from Batista's Minister of Public Information.

A new radio station, Radio Rebelde, was broadcasting illegally, at odd times of the day, and it gave a different view of the situation. The rebels, the untrained announcer said, were decimating Batista's men.

"Roberto wants to emigrate to San Juan," Consuela admitted after Mass as Dario drove them through an oddly still and, given the season, unfestive Havana. "He wants us all to settle there."

"Do you want to settle there?" Florida asked.

"I want to settle somewhere," Consuela said, her voice breaking, her words echoing around the rear of the Cadillac. "I want to be safe, Florida."

Florida kissed her and asked Dario to walk with her up the high steps of her mother's house and wait until she was inside. She was glad now that she hadn't taken her car. She had been about to back the Buick out of the garage that morning when Armando had come out of the house, intercepting her. "I'd rather you wouldn't drive yourself to church this morning, Florida," he had said.

"Why not?" she had asked. "I drive to church every morning."

"I'd just rather you didn't. I've been hearing things. A woman alone in a car like that. . . . Humor me, Florida. I'll take the Buick down to the institute. Let Dario drive you this morning."

"But surely Havana is secure," she had said, certain he knew more than he was telling her. "Isn't it?"

"All I know," he'd said, stepping out of the way as Dario backed the Cadillac out of the garage, using his handkerchief to wipe away a thin line of sweat along his forehead, "is that Batista is scared and the rebels have a genuine chance."

She believed him. Nor had she asked where he had gotten his information. There had been a familiar musky scent coming from Armando's handkerchief. But for some reason Armando's handkerchief hinting of Jungle Gardenia had seemed less than cataclysmic. Eva Lopaz's name had been mentioned in *El Diario* and on both the official and unofficial radio stations. She was, it was said, one of the more influential rebels. That she was in Havana, getting her perfume on Armando's handkerchief, made the rebellion suddenly seem both real and close.

I don't care about Eva Lopaz, Florida thought, surprised at her lack of jealousy and even curiosity. There are, she decided as Dario returned from escorting Consuela to hold the door for her, genuinely serious concerns to worry about.

*   *   *

They had been going to celebrate the New Year at La Casa with Consuela and Roberto and their children. But early on New Year's Eve day, when she had gone to pick up Consuela to take her to Mass, she had found Consuela's mother, complaining constantly, being helped into the first of three taxis, their motors running, in front of her shuttered house. The children were in the second, and Consuela and a great deal of luggage were in the last.

"We've been waiting for you," Consuela said, taking Florida's hands in hers. "Roberto's insisting we leave. He's at the institute saying goodbye to Armando, and then he's to meet us at the airport. He's managed to sell the ranch and everything in it. He says we'll be safe in San Juan." Florida could feel her sister-in-law's hands shaking. "I must go, Florida. We will call you when we get there. You will come and visit. I'll be all alone in a strange place. I don't know, Florida. May the Blessed Virgin watch over you."

Florida had never heard her so garrulous. It was true Consuela's hands were shaking and her eyes were red, but she seemed excited and hopeful. Mamacita, Florida thought, watching the taxis leave for the airport, Consuela waving a bit of lace at her through the back window, she *wants* to go.

After church she returned to La Casa and told Elena there would only be four for New Year's Eve dinner. "Señora," Elena wanted to know, having planned on Roberto and Consuela and their five children, "what am I going to do with all this food?"

Christine Machado called to say that the club's New Year's Eve dinner was, for the first time anyone could remember, undersubscribed. She asked if Florida and Armando wanted to join her and Jimmy at the Copa. "We have a table reserved," she said, as if that were a particular triumph, but Florida declined.

"No one wants to go out tonight," Christine said. "What is the matter with everyone? It's New Year's Eve!"

Deliciosa called immediately after, concerned. There had been an editorial in the Miami *Herald* about the rebels. "Why don't you all come here until this thing blows over?" Deliciosa asked. "You could have the cottage—"

"How I would love to come to you until 'this thing blows over,' Deliciosa." In her mind she had a vision of Deliciosa pampering her, making a fuss over Paloma, the three of them driving up and down Collins Avenue in her Eldorado convertible, laughing. But that, of course, wasn't going to happen. She wished Deliciosa the happiest New Year ever and promised to come to her if "this thing" got really bad. She lit a gold-tipped cigarette and smoked it carefully before she went to talk to Victor.

He had had his own plans for the evening, plans that included borrowing the Buick. Florida had to tell him that Armando insisted he remain home, at La Casa, for the entire evening. "We'll celebrate together tonight," she said. "It will be better."

"Better for whom and better than what?" Victor asked, but he sensed Florida's concern and stopped arguing.

435

It was a strange, silent New Year's Eve. Usually, even in that exclusive neighborhood, firecrackers would have been heard exploding all night. But not this night. Paloma sat under the Córdoba coat of arms thinking that despite the electricity in the air, her mother and father were more in tune with each other, more compatible than she could remember. They were caring for each other in little ways, passing foods, smiling, acting in a new and exclusive manner, almost as if no one else at the table existed.

For the first time since Paloma was a little girl they were having a traditional Córdoba New Year's Eve menu: roast pig, black beans and yellow rice, plantains, baked Alaska, champagne. The skin of the roast pig was rich and crisp and made a satisfactory cracking noise when Paloma ate it. She was allowed a glass of champagne, her first. She immediately liked its dry effervescence and tried to sip it slowly to make it last.

There wasn't much conversation during the dinner, but what little there was was cordial. That terrible silent war Victor and her father continually waged seemed, if not over, at least in abeyance for the night. Swimming was their one guaranteed neutral conversational zone. Victor talked about the upcoming swim meet in San Juan, and Armando said, "Maybe we'll all come and cheer you on and visit Roberto and Consuela at the same time. Would you like that, Florida?"

In a gesture rare outside their private moments she reached across the lace-covered table and put her hand on his. "I would like that very much, Armando. A family vacation."

The dishes were cleared a few minutes before midnight, candles were lit, and the old teardrop-shaped crystal chandelier, which had been electrified years before, was switched off. The huge dining room, with its watered-green-silk walls, seemed especially cavernous, the candles throwing shadows up onto the arched and beamed ceiling, the black doves looking as if they might fly off their papier-mâché base.

"Marita," Florida said, "will you call the others in?"

Elena and Juana, looking worried, slipped into the dining room, standing at the far end of the table.

"Where's Dario?" Armando asked.

Elena and Juana looked at Marita, passing out the grapes. "I have looked everywhere, Señor," Marita said. "Dario's room is empty. His clothes are gone. I think, Señor, that Dario has left us."

"It can't be helped," Armando said, putting his fine hands together. "I'll deal with it in the morning. It's nearly midnight." Marita took her place with Elena and Juana as the chimes of the old clock in the hall struck midnight, echoing throughout La Casa, bringing in the New Year.

Silently, in the old Cuban custom, they began to eat the twelve grapes—one for each month—set before them, washing them down with sweet country cider. When they had finished, Armando stood up and, raising his glass of cider in a toast, said, "May our New Year be as sweet and as full as these grapes," and Juana burst into tears.

436

Paloma wasn't surprised. Juana burst into tears frequently. But she was surprised at the tears in Marita's plaintive brown eyes as well as in her mother's. And quite suddenly Paloma felt teary-eyed herself but for no reason she could think of.

They remained in the candlelight for some moments, holding onto that little space of bittersweet calm, and then a single firecracker burst somewhere, and Florida asked Marita to turn on the lights. Paloma was just getting out of her chair when Armando surprised her by saying, "No. Let's all sit for a moment. Juana, would you bring the portable radio from my study into the dining room? I think there is news that we should all hear."

No one said a word while Juana brought the Zenith into the dining room and set it up on the old mahogany sideboard.

"Victor," Armando said, "would you turn the radio on?"

Victor opened the cover with its embossed map of the world and switched it on, tuning in to the government station. "Radio Havana," an announcer said, "is presenting for your New Year's Eve listening pleasure a program of traditional Cuban folk songs." Impatiently Victor turned the dial until they heard the trademark static of the underground station, Radio Rebelde. "Cuba, the rebel forces were victorious today," a hoarse voice was shouting with conviction. "Cuba, we are crushing Batista's men in Santa Clara as if they are cockroaches. Cuba, listen to me. We are winning the revolution. Cuba, prepare for us. Cuba—"

Armando rose, crossed the room, and switched off the Zenith. He turned to stare at Florida as if he had asked a question and was waiting for an answer. Paloma was frightened in a way she didn't recognize. They were all so still and oddly out of focus, as if they were in a school newspaper photograph. They were looking at Florida, waiting for her to say what to do next.

The telephone in the study rang, galvanizing Armando. He left the dining room quickly. They could hear his fine English shoes tapping across the entry hall's marble floor, the heavy study door opening, the telephone stop ringing as he answered it.

He returned a few moments later looking pale. "Who was it, Poppy?" Victor asked, but Armando didn't answer. He stood looking down at the dining room table, both fine hands on the back of his chair, as if he were suddenly old and weak and ill, needing support.

"Victor," Florida said, with what appeared to be total confidence, becoming Mommy once more, "it's time you were in bed. And Paloma, it's long past bedtime for you. Marita, will you see to Paloma? Elena and Juana, why don't you all go to bed as well? You can clean up tomorrow. Good night, everyone. And happy New Year."

With perfect poise she kissed Victor and then Paloma, holding her for a moment. "Happy New Year, my dove," Florida said, her control nearly coming undone. "Happy New Year."

"Who was on the telephone, Armando?" Florida asked after the others had left the dining room. She sat down in her chair, folded her arms across her chest, and felt as if the night had been going on for years and there was no end of it in sight. Elena and Juana, despite her suggestion, could be heard on the other side of the baize door, in the butler's pantry, putting food away.

"Nurse Lopaz." He continued to stand behind his chair, staring at nothing.

"What did Eva Lopaz want?" She spoke in English, not wanting Juana or Elena to overhear in the event the news was catastrophic. For one moment she almost laughed aloud, thinking this was a domestic scene that would never appear on *I Love Lucy:* Lucy coaxing Desi into telling her what his mistress found so important a few moments into the New Year of 1959 that she called him on his home telephone.

"*Se fue,*" Armando answered. Then, remembering he was not to upset the servants, he said it in English. "He left. Batista has gone. He's going to get asylum in the Dominican Republic." He stared at her disbelievingly. "He's deserted his men and Cuba. The government has fallen. Roberto was right. Castro has won. It was so quick. So quick." He pulled out the chair and nearly fell into it. She went to him, putting her arms around him.

"Perhaps we should go," Florida said quietly, thinking of Consuela and Roberto. "So many people we know have gone." She sat on the arm of his chair, her hand on his shoulder. "I know you're not political, Armando, but Dr. Castro may not know that. We are Córdobas, passive if not enthusiastic supporters of Batista. We could go to Miami. The Olivas would take us in, help us get started. There's no reason why you couldn't get a license and practice there. We could have a new life, Armando, a new—"

He pushed her hand away and stood up. "We're not leaving, Florida. What do Eva and her sitting-room communists know? This is just another revolution, just like all the revolutions that came before. Nothing is going to change. In a month or two it will be business as usual. The only difference will be that Fidel Castro will be taking the bribes, not Fulgencio Batista." He opened the door to the entry hall. "We are Córdobas and we are Cubans, Florida. We belong here, in La Casa, in Havana." She knew he was talking to himself, talking away his fear. "You mustn't forget that. Come. We'll go to sleep now. Tomorrow is the new year."

"It's already the new year, Armando," Florida said, following him up the stairs.

CHAPTER FIVE

1960

DESPITE A HOVERING FLY, Florida de Córdoba sat perfectly still, waiting for her son. She seemed to exist in a state of constant anticipation, able to think of only one thing at a time, and then she would think about it obsessively.

Half of her neighbors' radios were broadcasting sound revolutionary advice, while the others were playing out the end of an old-fashioned soap opera, the sort Marita, Juana, and Elena used to listen to in La Casa's kitchen. The early morning aroma of cats and garbage and faulty plumbing wafted into the apartment, but the distinctive odors of Havana's West Side no longer had the ability to make her nauseated.

Neither the radios nor the smells were potent enough to distract her from her thoughts. A pity, she decided. Distractions were important. Sitting on the pitted windowsill, Florida de Córdoba—waiting as patiently as she could for her son, Victor—had a mildly startling revelation: she didn't miss La Casa or the club or even the Buick. What she missed, she realized, were the expensive distractions, the little luxuries that had helped her put off thinking about the unthinkable.

She stood at the narrow window of the cramped two-room apartment they had been assigned some nine months before, looking down at the street for Victor, replaying in her mind the last hours of their life at La Casa.

"It is closer to the institute, Dr. Córdoba," the government representative had said with absolute insincerity. He reeked of old sweat and new garlic and was wearing a blue suit that looked as if it had been made of recycled wool. Armando was giving him a tour of La Casa. The little official had a trick of clicking his tongue against his teeth, presumably in dismay at La Casa's lavish and wasted space. He seemed especially appalled by the size and number of bathrooms. "One of the embassies," he said to the fat woman in uniform who followed him, taking notes. "Albania or perhaps even East Germany, though it's not in a very convenient location, is it?"

They had been given two days to move. "You're lucky," the little government representative had said, his querulous voice echoing around the walls of La Casa's entry hall, "that you're being allowed to stay in Havana."

"Oh, we're very lucky," Florida had said. "We're so very—"

"Florida." Armando—chalk white—had stopped her.

It was then that Florida had gone upstairs to her sitting room, switched on the Dumont—Lucy and Ethel and Fred were in the process of taking over Desi's nightclub—and deliberately, slowly, smoked the last gold cigarette, holding the empty lacquered case in her hands.

Afterward she had given up smoking, United States cigarettes being difficult to find and expensive when they could be found. El Toro, the Cuban brand, with its ropy black tobacco, stained her fingers and scorched her throat. What I miss most, I suppose, Florida decided, sitting on the window-sill in that West Side apartment, is Marita.

Florida closed her eyes and envisioned Marita, with her hollow cheeks and that irritating little fringe of black hair and those plaintive, poignant, sunken brown eyes, and she remembered her refusal (for twenty years) to enter La Casa through the front door. When Marita learned that Dario had left them to join the Revolutionary Army, that he was a sergeant now and had made no attempt to contact her, his friend for so many years, Marita had cried. But when the government bus had come to "repatriate" her, to take her back to the village she hadn't been near in two decades, everyone's cheeks were wet except Marita's. "I don't cry," she said, shaking Florida's hand, standing very straight, "in front of my employers."

"We're not your employers anymore," Florida had said, embracing her anyway, everyone on the bus looking on silently. "Now we're your friends."

Marita had held herself together even after a weeping Paloma had been untangled from her neck. But when the tiny woman walked up the steps of the bus, Florida saw that her shoulders were shaking, that the hand clutching the leatherette handle of her grip was white. When the bus pulled away, Marita hadn't allowed herself to look at them. Instead she waved her free hand—she wouldn't let go of her grip, not with these people—in a regal and final gesture of farewell.

Well, Florida decided, continuing the game she often indulged in, if I can't have Marita back, I'll take my telephone conversations with Deliciosa. And after that I'll take a drive to the beach at Cojimar in the Buick, with the top down. An hour with Consuela in the back of the old Cadillac. The six o'clock news from Miami with Tiny Haykin on the screen, Paloma and Victor at my side. Or just one half hour by myself.

Mamacita, she thought, letting herself hear and smell the humanity around her, it's difficult to be by oneself in postrevolutionary Havana. Or maybe—which is more likely—it's always difficult to be alone when one is poor. Being alone, she decided, is the great luxury.

The cathedral had been closed, and her gray stone replica of the Blessed Virgin had been smashed. But Florida had discovered that she didn't need either the church or the statue in order to pray. They can't, she thought, take

440

prayer away from me. Or perhaps they can. Maybe they have some miraculous new Russian machine, a chromium-plated drill that bores into the heart and kills that part of the soul that makes praying possible.

She turned back to the room. It seemed devoid of color. Before the revolution her life, as frustrating as it had been, was at least filmed in Technicolor. Now it was all filtered through a drab sepia, like the B movies Hollywood used to send to Cuba in her youth. *Curse of the Zombies,* she thought, visualizing Castro's army marching up the Paseo de Colón, the women with their cropped hair, the old street bands pathetically trying their hands at martial music.

Paloma lay on the mattress Armando had brought home from the institute. She had wrapped the sheets Florida had smuggled out of La Casa around her and was holding a pillow in the way she once had held her stuffed panda. Her eyes were closed, but Florida knew she was nearly awake, waiting for the last moment until she had to face the day, holding onto blessed sleep.

"Who could blame her?" Florida asked herself, wondering what calamity in this new world might have befallen Victor. "Blessed Virgin, why didn't we leave when we could? Why didn't we go when everyone else did? Why aren't we in Miami or San Juan, waiting out Fidelito's regime?"

She thought of all their missed opportunities. Armando, finding strength in his weakness, had refused to go. He was a Córdoba, and Córdobas had been in Havana for nearly five hundred years. He was a doctor and had a duty to his patients. He was the only man left in Havana who understood how to operate the city's five dialysis machines. Without me, Florida, he had said too many times, hundreds of kidney patients would die.

In the beginning, it was true, he had spent eighteen hours a day at the newly named People of Cuba Institute of Nephrology operating the machines, attempting to teach others how to do so. But he was too impatient and uncommunicative to be an effective teacher, and none of the young rural nurses assigned to him seemed the least bit capable of learning.

Finally Eva Lopaz had gotten the Czechoslovaks to send a specialist, a teacher who miraculously spoke Spanish, and Armando was able to get some relief. Still, he spent more time at the institute then at home. He was trying, he told Florida, to get them reassigned to the former caretaker's top-floor apartment in the institute. "Wonderful view of the harbor," he said, his gray-white eyes avoiding hers, refusing to accept responsibility for their lives.

Florida hadn't trusted herself to answer him. She again had that feeling of being an animal sprung from one trap only to find herself in a smaller, more deadly one. She prayed so much that it worried her. I'm going to become some sort of religious fanatic, she thought, scourging myself in the streets. She felt shrunken, diminished.

On the other hand, Victor, being Victor, had become inflated, slightly larger, if not taller, than before. One day after his seventeenth birthday he had been inducted into the Revolutionary Army and sent to the mountains for training. He had reappeared in Havana six weeks later wearing spit-polished boots and a tightly tailored uniform, assigned to the newly named Karl Marx Barracks, not three blocks from his family's new home.

Florida had seen him only twice since his return from training. Both occasions had been filled with the taut restraint with which he and his father treated each other. But this morning a friend of Victor's whose mother lived in the building had come to say that Victor had a free hour and would be stopping by.

Finally there was a hesitant knock on the thin door. Florida went to it and let him in, hugging him, not liking the feeling of his starched uniform, cautioning him to whisper lest he disturb his sister. Relieved that Armando wasn't at home, he sat on an unsteady café chair holding his mother's hand and looking at Paloma sleeping fitfully on the makeshift bed. He seemed, in that claustrophobic all-purpose room, suddenly unsure.

"Is it terrible?" Florida asked, kissing his forehead, now not so certain that of all of them Victor would survive in Castro's Cuba.

"It's pretty terrible, Mommy," Victor admitted, looking up at her. Then he laughed. "No private bathrooms. No walls in the bathrooms. We all have to wash and everything in the same place." He stood up, only a little taller than she was. "I got over it," he said, smiling at her. "I get over everything."

Sadly Florida saw that Victor was no longer a boy. That old Victor toughness was still intact, but barely. He had received a new, devastating piece of knowledge in Castro's boot camp: he was as vulnerable as everyone else to physical and emotional force. He wasn't shattered like Paloma; she could see that. But he wasn't entirely whole either.

"Would you leave if you could?" she whispered, looking into those gray-white eyes.

"What? And give up a glorious career in the new Cuban army? Why, in twenty years or so, Mommy, I might even make sergeant." He sat very straight—a Córdoba right down to those highly polished boots—and smiled his corrupt cupid's smile. "I'd leave in a second, Mommy. But not without you and Paloma."

They looked at each other for a long moment, and then he stood up, moving about the room with his old cockiness, touching things, avoiding looking at Paloma, half in and half out of her dark dreams. "Besides," he whispered, coming back to Florida, "I've had a stroke of luck. I'm to be one of the new Cuban sports stars. No more baseball. It's a corrupt Yankee preoccupation. The new, socialist Cuba is to be an island nation of swimmers. Señor Cuesto, my old Miramar coach, is now—thank God—the official Revolutionary Swimming Adviser. Cuban swim teams are going to go out and compete against weak capitalist swim teams and make the world safe for communism. I placed third in the men's tryouts." He showed her the new patch on his left shoulder indicating he was assigned to the official Revolutionary Army Swim Corps.

442

"Remind him of Paloma," Florida said, catching Victor's hand, looking so desperate she frightened him. "Remind your old coach of what a fine swimmer your sister is, Victor. You will do that, won't you? If she can swim, she has a chance."

"I'll remind him, Mommy," he said, looking at his sister, who was just coming out of her fitful sleep. Paloma, he knew, without having to be told, was not taking the revolution well. She looks, Victor thought as he went to embrace her, like a little old lady who has never had enough to eat.

Paloma had been like a robot since Marita had been sent away and they had been forced to leave La Casa. She didn't cry, but she didn't laugh either. She had gone to the new school she had been assigned to—the old convent school had of course been closed—uncomplainingly, only half understanding what her new schoolmates and her new teachers said to her.

Florida suspected her life at the school was torture, and when Paloma arrived home with a cut lip, she had gone to see the head of the school. "She'll have to adjust," that woman had said. "This is a new Cuba, and there is no room for the effete." The director was nervous, trying not to be intimidated by this holdover from the ancien régime and failing. "And she does, after all, stand out. That mock-meek manner. That red hair and those green eyes. Those dainty airs, as if she's always smelling something unpleasant. The children call her The Little Princess Who Can't. She begs for trouble." The woman, sitting behind a folding table that she was using as a desk, ran her hands through her coarse hair and shook her head. "Why didn't you people leave when you could have?" She took pity on Florida when she saw her face. "Perhaps, Señora Córdoba, you should dye her hair."

"And paint her eyes black?" Florida asked and instantly regretted it, seeing the woman's pity evaporate. She seemed less able to cope with this new Cuba than with the old one. Paloma had, on her own, cut her hair in the new, cropped revolutionary style. She nearly always wore a kerchief on her head and kept her eyes downcast. She had of course lost weight and had begun to slouch. She tried, as well as she could, to fade into the background.

Not knowing whom to pity more—his mother or his sister—Victor left the apartment, promising to ask his coach to give Paloma a tryout. He agreed with his mother. It was Paloma's only chance.

"I can't go, Mommy," Paloma whispered desperately. "I can't. I haven't been swimming in months. I don't have a bathing suit. They'll only laugh at me. At my hair and my eyes and the way I stand. I can't go, and please, please," she begged, her voice rising, "don't make me. Mommy," she said, piteously, reaching for Florida, "I'm scared. My stomach is all in knots. I have terrible cramps. Mommy, please . . ."

Victor had kept his word, reminding his coach of Paloma's swimming ability, and soon after his visit word had come from the school. Paloma was to take the following Monday off. She was to appear at the Rosa Luxemburg

Community Gymnasium and Pool—formerly the Miramar Club—to try out for the Revolutionary Women's Swim Team.

Florida moved away from her hysterical daughter, afraid she might give in and keep her home. "You've got to stop being scared, Paloma. You can't miss this opportunity. It's your chance to get away from that school. You've got to get over your fear, Paloma," she said, trying not to shout. "You've got to snap out of it."

"I can't snap out of it, Mommy," Paloma shouted back. "I can't. I'm scared all the time."

"Of what?" Florida asked, losing her patience, afraid of her own fear. She forced herself to keep her distance. There had been enough embracing. This was not, she knew, a time for that sort of comfort. "Paloma," she said, lowering her voice, trying to be reasonable, "you've got to get over your fear. You must if you're going to live. Remember who you are. Paloma de Córdoba. The Córdobas haven't survived," she said, finding herself using Armando's argument, "for five hundred years by being cowards. We've held on through the Indians, the Spanish, and the Americanos. We'll survive Fidel Castro as well. As long as we're strong. As long as we don't give in.

"I made a mistake in letting you cut your hair, letting you hide yourself. You must be proud of the color of your hair, the greenness of your eyes." Finally, because she couldn't help herself, she went to Paloma, sitting on that lumpy mattress, and put her arms around her. "It's no good trying to fade into the crowd. You never will. You're a Córdoba, a hidalgo's daughter and the best swimmer your age Cuba has. You remember that. It will help—I promise."

Paloma took a deep breath and, with a great effort, stopped crying. She looked up at her mother. Florida's hair needed attention, and her face, without makeup, seemed permanently creased with worry. Her fingernails, once so glossy, were unpainted, cut short in the way Marita used to keep hers. Paloma wondered where the woman in the dark sunglasses driving the convertible had gone. She suddenly realized that this revolution was as difficult for her mother as it was for her. She sat up and took Florida's hand. "I'll try, Mommy," she said. "I'm going to learn to be just like you, Mommy. Brave and unafraid."

"Oh," Florida said, kissing her, "I'm afraid. I'm just trying not to let my fear stop me."

It was raining, and Florida hadn't been able to keep Paloma from tying the old silk scarf around her head. She had worn it when they had left La Casa and every day since. They sat silently, holding hands, through the two interminable bus rides it took them to get to the Miramar. At the newly installed entrance turnstile one of the ubiquitous gray soldiers checked Paloma's name off on a list, gestured her in, but refused to let Florida follow.

"Only those engaged in the tryouts, Señora," he said, shaking his little head.

444

"Mommy," Paloma said, coming back to the gate, her face crumbling. "I can't go without you. My cramps . . ."

"Oh, yes you can," Florida said with certainty and reached over the turnstile and pulled the scarf off Paloma's head. "You stand up straight, and hold that head high, and remember who you are. You can do anything," Florida said. "You're a Córdoba." And then half a dozen girls arrived and she had to get out of the way, and the next thing she knew, Paloma had gone.

She waited outside until a small German car appeared and the Miramar's old swimming coach, Señor Cuesto, got himself out of it. He was green and wrinkled, like an ancient turtle, "My daughter is in the tryouts," Florida said, touching his arm. "I'll be very quiet. She won't even know I'm there. I would so much like to watch and—"

"Of course, Señora Córdoba. You'll be my guest." He took her in with him and then lost her as he was surrounded by half a dozen assistants wanting direction. Florida walked through the empty clubhouse, looking in at the old dining salon, half amused, half shocked to see that the mirror had been removed from the ceiling. For a moment she thought she heard crystal tinkling, women laughing, the sound of the Miramar's band playing their standard rumba, "Quizás, Quizás, Quizás." She shook her head, the ghosts disappeared, and she closed the doors, wondering what on earth they could have wanted the ceiling mirror for.

She wandered out by the pool, where girls were beginning to line up, and then over to the pink concrete house that had once been the Córdoba's cabana. The striped canvas awning was gone. Whoever was living in it had put a garish bedspread—Fidel's face woven into the purple chenille—across the glass doors for privacy.

Whereas the pink cabana had been a charming folly when the Córdobas had it, it now looked mean and dispirited with that display of pragmatic patriotism. Florida sat down on a rotting chaise longue, hands clasped together in front of her. The chaise reminded her of Christine Machado and her rhinestoned sunglasses. She wondered on what beach, in what part of the world, Christine could be found, working on her suntan. It was an overcast day with a cold edge to the humidity, the sort of day on which Paloma didn't like to swim. Nervously, Florida watched the girls come out of the locker room. "Holy Mother," she prayed, feeling her pulse race, placing her arms across her chest, "please let her be all right. Let her be chosen. That's all I ask."

Señor Cuesto's assistants were lining the girls up, separating them into six squealing, giggling lines. Most of them had never been in a competition, and a few of them—those who had lived by rivers or the ocean—had never swum in a pool before. They don't know enough to be nervous, Florida thought, and then she saw Paloma.

They had issued her a sad green bathing suit, much too large, ballooning at the bottom, sagging at the waist. She stood very straight, her hair hidden under a yellowed white bathing cap, her white skin luminous in the gray

445

light, aloof from the gigglers around her, perfectly still, like some automaton waiting to be switched on. "Please, Holy Mother," Florida prayed. "Let her do it. Not for me. But for her. Mother of my God, please save her."

Señor Cuesto emerged from the old clubhouse, a gray leather jacket on his shoulders making him look like the Frog Prince gotten up as an impresario. He stared at the girls, recruited from every part of Cuba, shook his head, and blew the whistle that hung around his neck. There was, impressively, immediate silence.

He stood at the edge of the coping, which needed painting, explaining in his gravelly voice what he wanted each girl to do. Then he asked an assistant, a stocky young mulatto woman, who had the requisite short hair but had dyed it an alarming red, to demonstrate. Each girl was to dive and then perform the Australian crawl, the breast stroke, the back stroke, and the butterfly. "Any questions?" he boomed into that sudden and serious silence. None of the girls dared have any questions.

The first group went in, and none was chosen. One skinny little black girl from the second group who seemed faster than sound got a nod of approval from Señor Cuesto. He remained stone-faced throughout the attempts of the third, fourth, and fifth groups. After what seemed like hours, Paloma's line moved forward. The tall, gangly girl in front of her suddenly put her hands to her stomach and threw up in the ill-kept shrubbery. Shamed, she ran off to the locker room. And then it was Paloma's turn.

She paused at the edge of the pool, looking back, seeing Florida. "Mommy," she said, her hands holding her stomach as if she too were going to throw up.

"Next," one of the assistants said, bored with these nauseated and scared and ill-prepared girls. "Next."

"You swim," Florida shouted, standing up and pointing her finger at Paloma. "You do it."

Paloma turned back to the pool. She made a curious gesture, as if she were shaking off bothersome insects, and then she dove into the familiar water. Suddenly a new group of girls was ushered out of the locker rooms and maneuvered into position, blocking Florida's view. By the time she had pushed her way through them, Paloma was getting out of the pool and had completed, for better or worse, her tryout.

Florida couldn't stop herself. She approached the old Miramar Club coach with a diffidence that would have been unheard of a year before. "Did she make the team, Señor Cuesto?"

"She's not on any pills, is she?" Señor Cuesto asked. "Drugs? Antihistamines? She was always a decent swimmer, but today . . ."

"No. No pills. Maybe she was too nervous. She said she was ill, but I made her swim anyway. Perhaps she could try again some other day. It's so important that she make the team, Señor Cuesto. She needs something to—"

"She made the team, Señora Córdoba," he said, smiling at her, wondering what had happened to the startlingly beautiful Florida de Córdoba to turn

446

her into this nervous mother of a woman. "She outswam every other girl. Be at peace, Señora Córdoba. There's no doubt your daughter made the team."

Florida found Paloma wrapped in a frayed towel that said *Miramar* in blue letters, shivering in front of the dressing rooms, waiting for her turn to change out of the green bathing suit. "I had to win, Mommy," she said, laughing her old laugh, teeth chattering. "I was so frightened of what you would do to me if I didn't."

Florida put her arms around her, wet towel or not, and kissed her over and over again. "I knew you would. You're a Córdoba."

That night Paloma dreamed she was being stabbed to death by Señor Cuesto dressed as a Cuban rebel. She woke to find the purloined linen La Casa sheets stained with blood. She began to scream, and she couldn't stop. It took Florida half the night to comfort her, to explain menstruation. "Forgive me, Paloma," Florida said, holding her. "I didn't believe the cramps were real."

In postrevolutionary Cuba there was no Kotex. For days Paloma had to wear rags torn from the linen sheets. But she was happier. She had been transferred to a special school for Cuban athletes. The curriculum allowed her to practice in the Miramar pool three hours a day, five days a week. It was, ironically, one of the more exclusive of the new Cuban schools: only the best athletes were allowed to attend it.

CHAPTER SIX

PALOMA WAS JUST BECOMING her old self, Florida thought bitterly some months later as she sat on the pitted windowsill in the West Side apartment. And now this. She swallowed the last of the thin brown coffee. In this new Cuba there would always be the threat of another directive; some Chekhovian official in some office would be moving them here or there for the greater good of the Cuban people. None of us will ever be safe here, she thought, reading the smudged yellow government letter once more before she put it away and awakened Paloma.

The directive informed the Córdobas that their daughter would be allowed to swim in the winter competition in Jamaica. But when she returned from the competition, in two weeks' time, on December fifteenth, she and her mother were to report to the office of the Central Committee for Redeployment. They were being sent to Camagüey to help with the critically late sugar-cane harvest.

Dr. Córdoba was being transferred to Puerto Esperanza, on the north coast, where a doctor was desperately needed. Señora Córdoba would join him at the end of the harvest. Señorita Córdoba would then be returned to Havana, her school, and her swim team.

Florida, for the first time in months, dressed carefully. "I'm going to see Poppy," she answered when Paloma wanted to know why she was wearing makeup and her last good pair of high-heeled shoes. She walked Paloma to the school bus stop, kissed her goodbye, and then, making certain the yellow directive was still in her purse, she turned and made her way to the Institute of Nephrology.

"We must leave," she told Armando. "We must leave now. Before Paloma and I are in the fields picking sugar cane and you're treating dysentery in Puerto Esperanza."

"It will only be for a short time," Armando said, lighting one of those skinny black cigars, his white-streaked gray eyes trying to find something in his office, twice as large as his apartment, to settle on. "Please, Florida, sit down. You're hysterical."

"I've never been less hysterical." That was true. Everything seemed so clear to her. She hadn't really come to see Armando, but still she felt she had to talk to him, to give him the benefit of every doubt. She knew what his answer to the directive would be. I could have foretold his replies, she thought.

"Florida," he repeated, "will you please sit down?"

She couldn't sit down. She had too much energy. She moved about the room nervously, stopping at the windows, looking through the wooden slats of the blinds at the street below. The office smelled of antiseptic and cigar smoke, and not unexpectedly, Jungle Gardenia. Armando made love to her once a week now, on Sunday afternoons, when Paloma was at practice. Out of a Cuban sense of conjugal duty, Florida thought. She wondered as she walked across the carpeted floor of his office, touching books, examining a blond wood humidor, if he still made love to all of his nurses as well as to Eva Lopaz. She realized she didn't much care.

"Where are you going?" he asked as she picked up her purse and made for the door. "Things will get better. Eva says a year at the most and we'll be back in Havana." He finally looked at her. He had tried—not always successfully—not to mention Eva in her presence. "Eva's been very good to us, Florida," he said apologetically. "They might have put us in jail. Instead we got that apartment, I kept my position—"

"Yes," Florida said, "you managed to keep your position, Armando." Then she left, closing the ribbed glass door after her.

*　*　*

Florida found Eva Lopaz at the end of one of the institute's green, windowless, and seemingly endless corridors. "Señora Córdoba," she said by way of greeting, at ease, old friends unexpectedly meeting each other in a familiar place.

"I came hoping to find you," Florida said evenly, and Eva Lopaz smiled at her as if they were coconspirators. And perhaps we are, Florida decided. The younger woman was, if not beautiful, at least spectacularly self-possessed in a clean tan uniformlike dress. Her black hair was cut short—revolution-approved. It glowed with health, as did the whites of her eyes, her milky skin, her entire being. She looked as if she were up to dealing with anything that might come her way. Florida, her flame-red hair in an elaborate pre-Castro chignon, wearing a silvery dress she had managed to hold onto, felt hopelessly elegant and passée, a model in an old issue of French *Vogue*.

"I understand we have a great deal to thank you for," Florida began, more to fill in the silence than to show appreciation, but Eva Lopaz cut her off.

"I was born in the same block of apartments where you're now living, Señora Córdoba," she said, leaning against the wall, settling in as if she were prepared for a long chat. "I believed in the revolution from the time I was ten years old. Your husband represents everything I despise. Arrogance and ignorance and that machismo that took five hundred years to breed. He's nearly an extinct species." She laughed, showing teeth so perfect, no reputable dentist would claim them. "I used to think I would get over him. I would use him, sexually, the way he used me, and then I would be through with him. Certainly I thought that after the revolution I would be through with him."

She opened the leather satchel she carried in place of a purse and removed a box of Parliaments, offering one to Florida, who refused it. She held the satchel under one capable arm while she lit the filter-tipped cigarette with the Zippo lighter, exhaling the smoke through her short, strong nose. "Do you hate me, Señora Córdoba?" Eva Lopaz asked conversationally, looking with her ordinary brown eyes into Florida's extraordinary green ones.

"Not at all," Florida said truthfully. "I suppose I did once, hundreds of years ago, when I first found out. But certainly not now. Now all I am concerned about is my children's safety, not Armando's fidelity."

Eva Lopaz smiled. "I once saw him helping you into the back of a huge Yankee car, late at night, in front of the Tropicana. You were both so easy with each other, with yourselves. You had no idea how much glamour and mystery and money you radiated. You were two perfect monsters. I would have done anything to trade places with you. Then."

"And now you pity me, Señorita Lopaz."

"No. I'm sorry to admit I still envy you, Señora Córdoba. I've got your husband where I want him, but I'm smart enough to know I'll never have what you have. You know so perfectly well just who and what you are. Even now you hold your head high. You smell like an aristocrat, Señora Córdoba. No matter how much Jungle Gardenia I douse myself with, I still reek of the streets." She dropped the Parliament to the floor and ground it out with the toe of her brown leather shoe.

"The unpleasant truth is that now in Cuba the street fighters are in command. But you're the sort of woman who will always have resources. And great strength, or you wouldn't be standing in this corridor about to ask your husband's mistress for help. It can't be easy. No, I don't pity you, Señora Córdoba. I save my pity for lesser women."

"The revolution has brought divorce to Cuba," Florida said, not certain she wanted this woman's admiration, trying and failing to hold onto her thin dislike, hearing her voice echo in the corridor. "Would you like me to set him free?"

Eva Lopaz laughed. It was a good, genuine laugh, uncalculated, infectious. "So that I could marry him? No, marriage to Armando de Córdoba does not exactly fit in with my political plans, Señora. If I were a man I would set him up in a little apartment off the Paseo de Corazón and keep him as my mistress. Someday, perhaps, I'll be cured of him, but in the meanwhile.... She touched her hair, as vibrant and alive as some expensive fur and seemed almost vulnerable. "No, Señora Córdoba," she went on, dispelling the moment, "you and I, I am certain, agree on the next move." She put her square hand on Florida's arm. "It's time for your own revolution, Señora Córdoba. It's time for your children to leave."

Florida retreated from the hand but not from the woman. "How?" she asked and Eva Lopaz told her.

CHAPTER SEVEN

PALOMA AND VICTOR HAD BEEN GIVEN a detailed list of what they could take (one bathing suit, two sets of underwear, ten Cuban dollars) when the Cuban swim teams traveled to Kingston for the winter competitions. The other team members brought their clothes in paper sacks and looked with amusement and some envy at Paloma's old crocodile case. But they were just a little intimidated by Victor in his tightly tailored uniform and his spit-shined boots.

450

Señor Cuesto had given Paloma permission for her mother to accompany her on the bus to the airport. Victor and Paloma stood on the street waiting for her. They had both said their goodbyes—distant in Victor's case, teary in Paloma's—to Armando.

"I'm not going to go through with this unless Mommy comes," Paloma said, looking at an uncharacteristically ill-at-ease Victor. "I'm not, Victor." She had put on needed weight and had acquired a new, tentative assurance. "Promise me, Victor, she will come."

"She's coming," Victor said, putting his hand on his sister's arm, looking directly at her, attempting to give his words an assurance he didn't feel. "Maybe not for a week or two, but she's coming."

Florida emerged from the apartment house just as the bus came, wearing Paloma's old disguise, that faded silk kerchief, over her hair. She had decided this was one moment not to stand out in the crowd. She tried to be businesslike, finding two seats in the rear of the bus for herself and Paloma. Victor sat at the front, talking to the youth leaders, working his charm, making them laugh with stories of boot-camp training. Florida held Paloma's hand tightly as the bus made its way out of Havana and along the airport road, passing the shuttered elaborate buildings that had so recently served as brothels for visiting Yankees.

Florida didn't see them. She felt exhausted with fear. "I can't cry," she told herself. "I can't even talk, in case someone overhears. We've said our goodbyes in the apartment. We'll be together eventually. I've got to be unemotional."

"You're coming soon, aren't you, Mommy?" Paloma whispered just over the noise of the old diesel engine.

"Soon as I can," Florida whispered back into her ear, holding her hand. "Deliciosa will take care of you till I get there. She's so much fun," Florida said, willing herself not to cry. "She's going to spoil you badly, I know. You'll be a good girl, won't you, Paloma?"

"I'll be very good, Mommy. I'll be waiting for you."

"Mamacita," Florida said to herself as the bus stopped in front of the Air Havana terminal, "if I get through this, I can get through anything." The bus driver said he'd wait, but only for a moment. Predictably, the guards wouldn't let her into the lounge without a pass. It was probably as well. Victor kissed her for a long moment. Then he stepped back and gave her that Córdoba smile, all teeth and good cheer. But she could see from the way his eyes had turned nearly white—just like his father's—how worried he was. "You'll take care of her, won't you, Victor? You must promise me you'll take care of your sister," she whispered, clutching his arm.

"I promise, Mommy," he said, disengaging himself. "Hurry now."

She took Paloma in her arms and held that dear face to hers and thought her heart would now finally break with the effort not to cry, not to show emotion. She had to remember to act her part. Her daughter was leaving for only three days' time. She would be back by Monday. It wouldn't do to break down and wail as if she were losing her forever. "My dove," Florida whispered, "I love you so much. You mustn't ever forget that you are a Córdoba, my darling."

"Mommy," Victor said, warningly.

"Go now," Florida said, opening her arms, freeing Paloma as if she were indeed a bird, a dove set free. "Courage, my darling. Courage."

With frightening gusto they sang the new Cuban revolutionary songs on the old, shaky Pan American clipper, the lyrics filled with threats to their enemies and cheers for the proletariat. When the youth leader, a tall, thin, relentlessly cheery woman named Carla, saw that Paloma didn't know the words, she rummaged around in her paper sack, found a mimeographed sheet containing the lyrics, and with what was meant to be a reassuring smile, handed them to Paloma.

"Sing, damn you," Victor said out of the side of his mouth, and Paloma, the yellow paper trembling in her hands, tentatively joined in. "And smile." She couldn't manage that. Each time she thought of her mother she felt a terrible longing, a loneliness that nearly made her cry out.

Victor, his white teeth flashing, had already charmed Carla, convincing her of his sincere dedication to the revolution. "I'm a true soldier of Fidelito," he said, as if he was offering her a naughty but not unwelcome suggestion. By the end of the flight he was standing on his duffel bag, one arm draped around the male youth leader's shoulder, the other casually holding Carla by the waist, singing praise after praise to the new republic at the top of his voice.

The clipper came to a bumpy landing, one tire at a time, the team members clapped, and Paloma, relieved to be able to stop pretending to sing, left the new revolutionary lyrics under her seat. Victor managed to get in front of her as they disembarked. "You okay?" he asked in English, flashing her a worried glance.

"Great," she answered. "You don't have to worry about me, Victor."

"I know," he said, taking the crocodile bag from her, leading the way across Kingston's airport, decorated for Christmas, hoping she wasn't going to get lost—as she often did—in that haze of hers, as if she were trapped in one of the pink cotton candies they used to eat at baseball games. "Be an actress," he said as the youth leaders waves them toward customs. "Pretend."

"I know, Victor," she said, her voice breaking a little.

"Just a few hours more," he told her.

She took his arm, and that helped. She had been afraid they were going to be separated, afraid of losing him. "I'm going to be all right," she told him on the bus that was taking them to a downtown hostel. I have no choice, she thought to herself.

452

They were served a meal of white rice and black beans on orange Formica tables placed around a plastic silver Christmas tree in the hostel's dining hall. After a dessert of thin vanilla ice cream, the tables were stacked, a portable record player was produced, and some of the older team members began to dance. The male youth leader, Miguel, a thin distance swimmer with a long torso, asked Paloma if she would like to dance.

She wanted to say no, but she caught sight of Victor, holding Carla close to him. Victor nodded his head at her, and she said, "Yes. That would be nice." Over Miguel's narrow shoulder she saw Victor hold Carla close to him and pointedly look at Miguel, dancing half a foot away from her. "I'm an actress in a movie," Paloma told herself. "A beautiful actress. Marilyn Monroe." She closed her eyes and moved closer to Miguel, whose face turned a dark red with embarrassment and pleasure. He smelled of Ivory soap, and she wondered as he pressed himself against her, if he bought it on the black market or had found an old cache.

During her third dance with Miguel, as he awkwardly told her the story of his life while rubbing himself against her, she decided he wasn't the sort who bought on the black market. By ten o'clock, when a new and severe Carla got on one of the tables and started shouting orders at them—"No one is to leave the building under any circumstances"—Paloma felt in control—if not of the situation, at least of Miguel.

She managed to be the first girl in the dormitory and, following Victor's orders, chose the bed closest to the door. Carla, who had won the second shift of guard duty in the toss, came in to make certain all the girls were in bed and bade a special good-night to Paloma. "You got a real cute brother," she said, taking the cot next to Paloma's. "Short but cute. What a personality."

Paloma lay in bed, intensely aware of Carla's presence, her eyes closed, wondering where her newfound bravery had disappeared to. "Courage," Mommy had said. "Remember who you are." "I am a Córdoba," she told herself. "I can and will do what I have to do."

Armando had given her a watch for Christmas. In that last moment with him, in the little apartment, he had held her to him and apologized for the watch. "If it were gold or silver, they might take it from you." They had decided it would be suspicious if both Armando and Florida came to the airport, so he had kissed her goodbye and had shaken Victor's hand and, relieved, had gone to the institute just as if it were another ordinary day in the new Cuba. He had been against this plan, but in the face of both Florida's and Eva's determination to bring it off he backed down.

Poor Poppy, Paloma thought, looking at the luminous dial of the steel watch, thinking this had been the longest day of her life. And it's not over yet. "Courage," she said to herself exactly one hour after the lights had gone out, not reassured by Carla's tossing about in nervous sleep in the next cot. Paloma had worn, as per instructions, a thin T-shirt and light cotton trousers under her pajamas. She was leaving behind, per instructions, the crocodile case. But she couldn't find her shoes.

"Where you going?" Carla asked, awakened by Paloma's futile gropings under the cot.

"To urinate," Paloma said, using the word they had been taught in convent school. The nuns of the Sacred Order of the Holy Mother had not believed in euphemisms.

"Urinate!" Carla said, lying back down on the cot, shaking her head, laughing to herself. "Well, you'd better hurry up and 'urinate.' You need a good night's sleep. You're swimming tomorrow."

Paloma gave up the search for her shoes and stepped into the neon-lit hallway that connected the two dormitories. Miguel was on guard duty, sitting on a gray metal folding chair, rocking it back and forth on its rear legs. He turned dark red when he saw her. He began to stand up and then sat down again. Finally he stood up, his tongue moistening his lips. "Hi," he said, moving toward her, and suddenly, away from the other swimmers, he seemed dangerous. "You come to see me?" He had backed her against a wall.

"Courage," Mommy had said. "Act," Victor had told her. She stooped down and got out from under his arms. "I have to use the bathroom," she told him, placing her hand on his face, stroking it. "Then I'll come to see you."

"Don't be long," he said, and Paloma realized he wasn't a nice boy after all.

"I'll try not to." She faked a pain, and he looked concerned. "The dinner didn't agree with me."

"Do you want a doctor?" he asked, retreating a few steps.

"No, I'll be all right. . . ." She let the end of the sentence fade as she rushed through the swinging door into the women's room, thinking that now she genuinely had to urinate, but she didn't stop.

Paloma shed her pajamas and stepped through the window, looking out, allowing herself to breathe. Victor, in blue jeans and a work shirt, was where he was supposed to be, waiting on the fire escape Eva Lopaz had promised would be there.

She started to tell him about Miguel, but he put his hand to his lips and led her down the fire escape. The iron steps cut into her bare feet, but she didn't dare complain. A black man was waiting for them in a blue Volkswagon camper at the back of the hostel's parking lot. None of them spoke as the van worked its way through Kingston to the airport road. Paloma wondered how long they had until Miguel became nervous and got Carla to go into the ladies' room to find she was gone.

She was suddenly not Marilyn Monroe. She was Paloma de Córdoba, twelve years old, her courage gone. She gripped Victor's hand. "I don't want to go," she said in a small voice, as if the driver couldn't hear. "They'll kill Mommy and Poppy, Victor. I want to swim in the meet tomorrow, Victor, and then I want to go home." The tears had come, and she couldn't stop them.

He put his arm around her. "If we go back now, Paloma, they'll kill Mommy and Poppy and us. We can't go back. We don't have a home in Cuba. We have no choice, Paloma. Would I go if I thought Mommy wasn't coming?" he asked her, looking at her in the light from an oncoming car. "Would I, Paloma?"

"No," she said, giving up, resting her head against his shoulder, not opening her eyes until they had reached the airport.

He led her into the terminal to the all-night souvenir shop, where he bought, with his nearly worthless ten Cuban dollars, a pair of Day-Glo orange flip-flops for her bare feet. "Everything's going to be all right, Paloma." He handed her his handkerchief. It had belonged to Armando and had a large embroidered A on it. "We're going to Florida," he said, as if she hadn't heard it all before. "It's all arranged. Mommy's friend Deliciosa is going to meet us at the airport. She's very rich and very nice, and she's going to take care of us until Mommy and Poppy can get away." He kissed her cheek. "Be an actress, Paloma. Pretend you're a beautiful dove flying to Florida. Courage, Paloma."

She stopped crying and, stumbling in the flip-flops, followed Victor up the steps to the late-night BOAC flight to Miami.

CHAPTER SEVEN

1961

CERTAINLY, FLORIDA KNEW, they were in danger. It was a time when men and women disappeared so completely—entire lives, histories, families wiped out—it seemed they had never existed at all.

During the days following the children's "defection"—which is what it was called—she could sense Armando figuratively holding his breath, waiting. But Eva Lopaz had argued successfully before those in power that in postrevolutionary Cuba parents could not be responsible for their children's politics. Besides, Puerto Esperanza, that dim little fishing village, desperately needed a doctor, and Armando Córdoba was the most loyal Cuban doctor she knew. He was quite ready to officially repudiate his children—on the steps of the capital, if necessary. "He'll prove himself," she said, "in Puerto Esperanza."

In the end Eva Lopaz even arranged it so that Florida did not have to go to the interior to pick sugar cane. She was to be Armando's receptionist-nurse in Puerto Esperanza. They were to live in the back of the surgery, a three-room clapboard cottage.

"Do you mind so very much?" Armando had asked, not wanting an answer, during the long bus ride to Puerto Esperanza. Florida knew what he was feeling: betrayed, debased, furious. "I should never have let them go," he said to her with a terrible and a final disdain soon after word came that his services were no longer needed at the institute. "I should never have listened to you." He blamed her for this final loss of position, this banal exile. "We're to go by bus," he had told her, as if that were the last insult.

Now, sitting on the rear bench of that Sunday-morning bus, reminiscent of the one that had taken Marita away, he was polite, distant, staring out the dusty window stuck halfway open, removing himself from her and the peasants who had filled the bus, returning to their homes after visiting relatives and the new black market in Havana.

Florida was nauseated from the diesel fumes, from the bus that seemed to lurch sideways rather than forward, propelling itself clumsily across roads in need of repair. The fat woman sitting next to her sang an interminable love song to the two startlingly white chickens squashed in the cage she held on her dimpled, little-girl knees. She hadn't had the requisite government pass to travel, but even in postrevolutionary Cuba an old woman with chickens was going to get on a bus, pass or no pass. Her other possessions lay wrapped in a piece of muslin, dyed red, at her feet.

We're down to one suitcase, Florida thought, amused. It was pigskin, bought in Europe when Armando was a student. Now cracked and stained, it still looked misplaced among the cardboard valises strapped on the roof of the bus. Armando looked similarly misplaced, so tall and aloof, so very aristocratic. He smoked his thin twisted cigar savagely, as if it could somehow alleviate his mortification. "It won't be for long," he said, more to himself than to Florida. "Believe me."

"A fitting finale to a glorious career as a Havana socialite," Florida said, attempting to lighten the moment and failing. She found herself, despite the fumes and the pungent smell of the fat woman, looking forward to exile in Puerto Esperanza. Armando was obsessed with returning to Havana, to the People of Cuba Institute. He assumed, without thinking about it, that Florida missed La Casa and the Miramar and her Buick. That she shared his feelings about the bus and the peasants and the dim future in Puerto Esperanza. That she was properly, thoroughly repentant for her role in their fall.

She was amused when he talked about the old icons—La Casa, the club, her Buick—when he promised to get her back her pearls. "The only possessions I want returned to me," she told him as they left the bus in Puerto Esperanza's square, "are my children."

456

Armando retrieved their suitcase as a party official detached himself from the small crowd of villagers who stood under the market's sun-faded green awning, staring at the new doctor and his wife. The village people thoroughly approved of him immediately, arrogance being one of the qualifications of a fine doctor. Florida was a mystery, red hair and emerald-green eyes and that crossed-arms poise as rare to them as fine wine and delicate jewels. The official, nervously using a rayon handkerchief to clean the thick lenses of his metal-rimmed glasses, came up to claim them, to lead them to the surgery. Florida stood for a moment on the narrow main street, watching the bus leave in a cloud of black diesel smoke and brown dust.

If Armando's obsession was with Havana, hers was with Paloma and, increasingly, Victor. I'm yearning for them, she thought, chiding herself for acting like some mother dog aching for her lost puppies. They're fine, she reminded herself twenty times a day. But she couldn't stop herself from dwelling on them, from needing them in a basic, biological way she didn't begin to understand. She had broken down once, bursting into tears some weeks after they had arrived in Puerto Esperanza. It was in the middle of the surgery, and everyone had stopped talking to stare. She had had to go back into the bedroom and sit on the narrow bed and fold her arms across her chest and wipe away the tears and force herself not to feel helpless. "Mamacita," she had prayed, kneeling on the painted wood floor, "don't let me lose hope. It is the one thing I have left."

Armando had sent an assistant for her, and, resolutely, she had stood up, feeling a hundred years old, and returned to her work.

Throughout the long, difficult days, as she ran back and forth across the surgery, she tried to imagine them in Deliciosa's house. Paloma would be going to school. A convent school, she supposed. Deliciosa would see to her uniform, her party clothes. Victor would have gotten some sort of a job. There would be no more school for him. She shivered in the heat of the day. She had a presentiment of Victor working for Bebe Oliva in one of his unexplained businesses, but she forced that thought out of her mind. "Oh, please, Blessed Mother, let them be safe and happy," she said to herself a dozen times a day. But her most constant prayer was to be with them, to stroke Paloma's hair, to touch Victor's hand. She felt as if a powerful force —some supernatural magnet—was drawing her to them and to Florida. "In a month," she told herself. "Two months at best." Eva Lopaz had promised.

She preferred waiting in Puerto Esperanza to waiting in Havana. Here the diversions helped. She and Armando had spent their first night cleaning the surgery and the next night cleaning their room. He had bullied the government official into giving him all the fumigating chemicals in Puerto Esperanza. Armando was nothing if not sanitary. "Even if we're here only a week," he had said, dousing everything with antiseptic, "I'm not going to practice in this filth."

At first she had pulled her hair back, but it was hot and it still got in the way, and finally she gave in and cropped it, wearing Paloma's old scarf over it when she went to the market. I don't like being stared at now either, she thought, remembering Paloma in those first weeks of her new school. She wore an old pair of Victor's blue jeans and a white nurse's tunic. She avoided looking at herself in mirrors.

"It's only a month or so before we get away," she said repeatedly, waiting for Armando to agree. When he didn't, she said, "Puerto Esperanza. Port of Hope."

The tiny Puerto Esperanza colonial church had somehow managed to continue its existence, and she slipped into its coolness at odd moments, finding consolation at the feet of a garish statue of the Virgin. But she discovered she had little time for formal prayer. They worked sixteen-hour days, Armando treating everything from measles to diseases he shook his head over, saying they were textbook cases. He was a competent doctor, remembering his early training, dealing with the patients who lined up each morning outside the surgery door with that Córdoba abruptness they found reassuring. But he took no great interest or pleasure in his work. When they had first arrived Florida had had a momentary fantasy in which they established a new, rewarding life. Armando the Country Doctor; she the Helpful Wife and Nurse. The children returned: Victor went to the university, Paloma excelled in the village school.

"We're criminals," Armando told her, exploding the daydream, "serving time."

"What was the crime?" she asked, but she couldn't get him to answer. He had stopped making love to her before they left Havana. In his mind he wasn't the criminal. She was. He was the innocent victim. She supposed, lying next to him each night, that the end of their sex life was a relief to both of them, the cessation of what had become a dry conjugal act between strangers. It's as if I've never known this man, she thought, this husband of mine. He was isolated in dreams of a return to Havana, to position. She was lost in fantasies of escape: to Paloma, to Victor, to Florida. "Mamacita," she cried, kneeling on the bedroom floor, feeling alone and abandoned even by the Virgin Mother, "I want my children. I need them."

During the days Florida made appointments, calmed pregnant girls, sterilized needles, bandaged injured farmers. Armando treated serious diseases in the room he called mockingly his inner sanctum. They were so worn out at the end of each day, they would fall into bed immediately after dinner.

For Florida it was a welcome exhaustion, but Armando lay uncharacteristically awake, plotting his return to Havana. Once each day he went to the post office to use the public telephone, calling Eva, begging her to get him out of Puerto Esperanza. Three times in that first month of 1961 Armando managed to get to Havana. "Business," he said and Florida wasn't certain he was far wrong.

458

"Easter," Armando promised one night after a Havana trip. "By Easter we'll be back in Havana. We're going to get the apartment on the top of the institute. The Czech doesn't know what he's doing. He's so damned arrogant. We just have to be patient."

"I thought we were leaving Cuba soon anyway," she said, suddenly alarmed. "I thought we were—"

"We can't leave now," Armando said, turning away, avoiding her eyes.

"Eva Lopaz promised," Florida said, running her hand through her ruined hair.

"That was before the Yankees cut off diplomatic relations."

"So what? Everyone has cut off diplomatic relations."

"Try to understand. We're in a state of war, Florida," Armando said in his reasonable voice. "It would be worth Eva's head for her to try to help us get out now." He seemed more confident suddenly, and it frightened her.

"But Paloma and Victor . . ." She felt as if she were drowning and he was on dry land, unable or unwilling to put out his hand to save her.

"They'll return eventually," he said, lighting a cigar, turning away so he wouldn't have to see the contempt—and the despair—in his wife's eyes.

Armando was on yet another trip to Havana when, at four o'clock in the morning on a dull, hot January Monday, a government vehicle pulled up alongside the surgery, creating a little dust storm in the moonlight.

"You don't have a fan?" Eva Lopaz asked, wiping the dust from her face with her square hand. She had entered the back room without knocking, as if she and Florida were old friends and didn't have to deal with hellos, with explanations. She looked as youthful, as capable as ever. "It's stifling in here."

"The fan broke on the second night," Florida said, not moving from the rattan chair in which she had been sitting, reading a two-day-old Havana newspaper that told on each of its seven thin pages of the glories of the revolution. "Armando says it's on requisition." She looked up at the crisp, young, new Cuban woman. "Perhaps you can help, Eva?" she said, deliberately using her first name.

"Oh, I can help, Florida," said Eva, sitting down on the bed. "I'm certain I can help." She lit a Parliament and blew smoke up at the naked light bulb. "Could we turn off the light? It's blinding." Without waiting for an answer she pulled the string, leaving them in semidarkness. The Cuban half-moon could just be seen through the high window. Florida watched the smoke from Eva Lopaz's cigarette rise and disappear. "I came to tell you that Armando's staying in Havana for good," Eva said, as if she were his employer, his proprietor.

"His patients . . ." Florida said, thankful for the dark, not wanting the other woman to see her cropped hair, the nurse's rayon tunic.

"He'll return for a day or two to initiate the new doctor."

"The new doctor?"

Eva leaned forward on the bed, her elbows on her knees, the cigarette held between her perfect teeth. She looked like a bad boy about to tell a secret. "Listen, Florida. Armando has managed to get his 'position'—as he likes to call it—back at the institute. The truth is we genuinely need him. The Czech was hopeless. I'm to bring you with me tonight."

"To Havana?"

"Where else?" Eva Lopaz took a long drag on her cigarette. "We need doctors, and we can use the Córdoba name and image. Image is very important. This is a public-relations revolution. We know that, and now Armando does too. He's quite willing to play whatever role we assign him. Our Armando is going to be a great success in the new Cuba."

"And will I succeed in the new Cuba, Eva?" Eva laughed and Florida, despite the fear that had come over her, smiled. "You have a very fine laugh, Eva Lopaz."

"You *could* be his wife," Eva Lopaz said, ignoring the compliment, thinking the problem out. "You'll be bored, but you *could* still be his wife. Spend the next thirty or forty years attending party functions, maybe taking to drink or to men. You're the sort who just might take to men, because they would certainly take to you. Sexual intrigue provides a certain excitement, but somehow I don't see you engaging in it. Drink, I suppose."

She became silent. The cicadas were making their rhythmic buzzing noise in the adjoining fields. Florida felt afraid, but her fear wasn't, she thought, the paralyzing, betraying kind. She watched the smoke from Eva's cigarette wind its way to the one window in the room and then out into the half-moon night. Eva, in that luminous moonlight, looked like a statue. For no reason at all Florida found herself thinking—for the first time in years—of the conversation she and her father had had after Armando's proposal. She saw Renaldo clearly, tobacco-colored and pleased with himself, sitting under the papier-mâché coat of arms. We were talking about miracles, she remembered. He said I was a child of miracles. That when miracles come my way I must accept them, travel with them as far as they might go.

She forced herself back to the present, to that boxlike cell of a room, filled with the smell of Eva's cigarette, reminiscent of the incense that had once burned in Havana's cathedral. She looked at Eva Lopaz, who seemed for just an instant to resemble not merely a statue but that shattered composite gray statue of the Blessed Virgin that had stood in the stone entry of the cathedral.

Eva stood up, trying to read her watch in the dim light as she ground out the Parliament on the wooden floor. She was so obviously not a Blessed Virgin that Florida laughed. "There's a plane with four other people leaving in twenty minutes. They're supposed to be escaping from Cuba, but they're really Fidelito's men going to infiltrate the anti-Castro forces. Big dramatic stuff. Anyway, there's no doubt that the plane will get through. You'll be in Miami in two hours." She started toward the door. "Come on."

460

"Why?" Florida asked, standing up, prepared to follow. "Why are you doing this for me? Armando?"

Eva Lopaz laughed again. "Armando? I have Armando, for better or for worse, with or without you, Florida. I'm doing this because, though it kills me to say it, I admire you. Even now you are the kind of woman I should like to be. Beautiful and smart and honest in a way I couldn't begin to try for. Not me, Eva Lopaz." She turned away and looked up through the window at the half-moon. "I've spent my life committing purposeful acts, always with the idea of getting me somewhere. Well, now I'm somewhere. I can afford one spontaneous, grand gesture, if only to show I'm capable of it. I've been a communist and an atheist since I was a little girl. But before that I was a Cuban and a Catholic." She turned and looked into Florida's eyes. "This is my one and probably last Catholic moment, Florida. Come. Before I repent and it's too late." She held out her capable hand.

"My things," Florida said, looking around the empty room, thinking that Armando had taken their one suitcase. "I must find something to take them in." Then she met Eva Lopaz's amused glance and found herself smiling again. "Of course. There's nothing to take. Everything I want is already there." She picked up Paloma's old silk scarf, tied it around her cropped hair, made certain the lacquered and much battered cigarette case was in her jeans' pocket, and finally, as if she were making an old-fashioned agreement, put her hand in Eva Lopaz's. Eva Lopaz kicked open the screen door and led her out of that cell of a room, allowing the door to slam after them with finality.

"Armando," Florida said as an afterthought as she stepped up into Eva's military vehicle. "He wouldn't come?"

Eva switched on the ignition, expertly backing the jeep out onto the road. "He wasn't given the option," she said, driving toward the beach. She took out the pack of Parliaments and lit one. "I didn't want to put him in a moral dilemma." She exhaled, smiling. "All he would have done would be to stop you."

"You'll explain?"

"I'll say goodbye for you, Florida," Eva Lopaz agreed, driving onto the beach, to the water's edge. A small white amphibious plane looking like a wading bird, its motors running, waited in the shallows. Eva Lopaz put her arms around Florida and touched her cool cheek with her own. "Armando's the Córdoba who is fated to remain in Cuba. You're the Córdoba who's destined for Florida. You were born there. You were named for her. Go and live there with your children. Go and have a new and good life, Florida. You deserve one."

The two women—Old and New Cuba—stared at each other for a moment, tears in their eyes. "If I had decided to stay in Cuba," Florida asked, "would you have been my friend?"

"You're the sister I would have chosen." Eva Lopaz turned away. "Now

461

go." Florida climbed out of the military vehicle, took off her shoes, and re-fastened Paloma's old silk kerchief over her hair. Clouds had momentarily obscured the low half-moon, but the Cuban stars were shining with an extra brightness. Florida rolled up the jeans legs and stepped into the warm water as the pilot jumped out to help her board the plane.

The other passengers were hidden in shadows. The pilot motioned her to the copilot's seat. "Balance," he whispered, and then, before she was quite strapped in, the plane began to taxi across the smooth water of Puerto Esperanza's little bay, suddenly propelling them up in the air as if they had been shot from a circus cannon.

Florida looked down. Though the moon had emerged from its cloud cover, the miraculous Eva Lopaz and her military vehicle had disappeared from the beach. Without her, Florida felt an old, irrational fear take over, like a selfish friend she didn't much like but knew all too well moving in for the weekend. She tried to keep it at bay, but it kept snapping at the edges of her mind, a determined gossip intent on sharing dangerous and suspect information.

Perhaps, she found herself thinking, I am, after all, being disposed of. Perhaps this is the way they get rid of the people they're not comfortable with. How easy it would be for the pilot to reach across her, open the door, and push her out into the ocean. What a relief that would be for Armando's sense of manhood, for Eva Lopaz's career. Florida de Córdoba wasn't killed or imprisoned; she simply disappeared.

I'm hysterical, she decided, crossing her arms, folding them around her in that characteristic gesture of protection. She looked at the angry pilot's profile and realized that his anger came from genuine fear. Even if Eva's story was true, the plane, after all, stood a chance of being shot down by Castro's anxious coastal army. Not every soldier would have been let in on the secret of the flight.

Her fear let up as the sun, blood-red, began to rise and the white plane flew over the first bits of land, the rocky little Marquesas. It was replaced by the anticipation of seeing and holding her children—her Paloma and her Victor. She felt nearly secure when she picked out the old clapboard houses and martello towers of Key West. As the white plane flew over the keys, she could see below her the turquoise and purple water, the bridges connecting the coral-rock islands lying between the Gulf and the Atlantic like stepping stones for giants.

And then, quite suddenly, as the sun turned white against the cloudless, seamless blue sky, she saw the pink hotels of Miami Beach lining the Atlantic coastline, the surf beating against the white beaches Carl Fisher had built. "I was born there," she said to herself, thinking of her father and his Córdoba pride in having, as he had once put it, conquered Miami Beach.

The plane dipped and turned to the west, flying across Biscayne Bay, filled with causeways and international ships. And on its shore the sprawl of Miami, about to achieve its role as the financial and cultural capital of the

Caribbean basin and South America. And beyond Julia Tuttle's city was the whole of the long, huge, green and blue peninsula, wonderfully alive, growing faster than it had in any other moment of its long history, jutting out into the water like a finger pointing the way to the future.

She dropped her hands and leaned forward, her heart swelling with relief, with the knowledge that she would soon be with her children. And with something more. I am fulfilling my Córdoba legacy, she thought. I am returning to the place where I was meant to be. Ignoring the tears in her remarkable emerald-colored eyes, she tore the silk kerchief from her head, revealing her startling red hair. As the plane began to descend she felt as if she had been suddenly liberated from its steel confines, as if she had grown wings and was, by herself, flying through the clear blue air.

"I'm home, Mamacita," she said aloud, startling the relieved pilot, as the light plane touched land. She didn't bother to wipe the tears away. "Another dove is home."